Shannon backed out of the cave into the wan sunlight and assembled his men. Rolling gusts of wind thrashed the boughs of the small forest.

"Got a storm coming, so let's move," Shannon barked. "The 'vette comes overhead in fifteen minutes. O'Toole, get the ground station operational and set up the nav beacon for a check. They can get a fix on us. Tatum, make camp in the cave. We were lucky enough to find it, so let's use it. It's dry, and it's big enough. That's the good news. The bad news is something else lives there, and as far as I can tell, it has claws and eats meat, so keep the weapons ready. Actually, that's good news. It means there's food."

"Yeah," Tatum said. "Just a question of who does the eating."

And look for these other Del Rey Discoveries . . .
Because something new is always worth the risk!

GENELLAN: Planetfall

Scott G. Gier

A Del Rey® Book
BALLANTINE BOOKS • NEW YORK

A Del Rey® Book
Published by Ballantine Books

Copyright © 1995 by Scott G. Gier

Library of Congress Catalog Card Number: 95-68291

ISBN 0-345-39509-3

Manufactured in the United States of America

First Edition: August 1995

10 9 8 7 6 5 4 3 2

For Jean Maxwell

SECTION ONE

A NEW WORLD

ONE

BATTLE

We're dead, Buccari admitted. A bead of sweat broke loose from the saturated rim of the copilot's skullcap and floated into her field of vision. She moved to keep the mercurial droplet from colliding with her lashless eyes. Humidity controls in her battle suit activated, and she swallowed to adjust for the pressure change.

"Reloading forward kinetics," she reported, breaking the oppressive silence. She glanced up. The command pilot of *Harrier One* stared dumbly at the holographic tactical display.

"Skipper, you copy?" Buccari demanded, switching to flight deck intercom and cutting out the rest of the crew.

The pilot's head slowly lifted, his gold visor catching and scattering the brilliant rays of Rex-Kaliph, the system star.

"Yeah, Lieutenant, I copy," he mumbled.

Buccari's anxiety clicked up another notch. She pivoted in her acceleration tethers to look at Hudson hunkering at his station.

"Nash, status on the fleet?" she demanded.

"Nothing new, Sharl," the second officer replied nervously. "But main engine power's fading, and engineering doesn't answer."

Buccari's scan jerked to her own power screen, confirming the bad news. "Crap!" she uttered, frantically trying to override.

Hudson gulped. "Already tried emergency override."

"Commander, main engines are shutting down," she shouted. "Computer's rejecting command overrides. We got nothing but thrusters."

Buccari pushed back from the instruments. Her scan moved to the tactical display—the blip representing the remaining

3

alien interceptor moved outbound, a belligerent icon deliberately maneuvering for its next attack. She exhaled and looked up to see the corvette pilot still frozen in position.

"Commander Quinn!" she shouted. The pilot, reluctantly alert, turned in her direction. She saw her own helmeted image reflecting into diminutive infinity in his visor.

"Mister Hudson," Quinn said. "We've got ten minutes before that bug's in firing range. Go back to engineering and find out what's happening."

Hudson acknowledged, released his quick disconnects, and pushed across the flight deck into the bore of the amidships passageway. The pressure iris sucked shut behind him.

Buccari looked into space at star-shot blackness. There had been visual contact—brilliant, lancing streaks of argent. Aliens! They had found aliens. Had they ever. They had jumped into a frigging bug nest! A whole goddamn star system filled with aliens. Kicking Legion butt.

Harrier One had destroyed two of the alien ships; she had even seen one explode through the digital optics of the corvette's laser cannon shortly before their powerful directed-energy weapon had been disabled by a hammering near miss.

A flashing radiation warning light on the overhead environmental console captured her attention.

"Radiation damage, Sharl?" Quinn asked.

"Background radiation," Buccari said. "Not weapons detonation—too constant. Probably solar flares from Rex-Kaliph. Sunspots. She's a hot one." Starshine poured through the view screens, casting deep shadows and illuminating the crew-worn flight deck in stark shades of gray.

"Looks bad for *Greenland*," Quinn said darkly. "She got hit bad."

"I'd be worrying about this ship, Commander," Buccari snapped.

"Yeah," Quinn grunted. "You're right. We're out of options . . ."

Buccari closed her eyes as the pilot flipped on the command circuit.

"Attention, all hands," Quinn announced. "This—this is the end of the line. Abandon ship. I repeat: abandon ship. EPL and lifeboats. Two-minute muster."

Buccari gasped as if she had been punched in the stomach. It made no sense; the EPL and lifeboats were defenseless—helpless.

"Kinetics show full reload," Buccari persisted. "Arming complete."

"Move, Lieutenant. You're EPL pilot," Quinn ordered. "I'll finish."

Buccari disconnected her tethers, but her efforts to leave were stymied by the considerable mass of the chief engineer emerging from the access hatch. Warrant Officer Rhodes pushed across the congested deck and strapped into the second officer's station. Hudson reappeared, helmet and wide shoulders wedged in the hatchway.

"Got the laser cannon hooked up to main power!" Rhodes shouted.

Quinn jerked in his station. "What the—the cannon? But main power is gone! What've you guys been doing? Why isn't anyone on line?"

Rhodes held up his hands. The pilot's transmission overrode all communications; Rhodes could not respond until Quinn's questions ceased.

"Goldberg cleared and spooled the fusion ionizers—" Rhodes began.

"But the reactor temps!" Buccari interrupted on suit radio.

"Mains are hot," Rhodes said. "I rerouted power across the aux bus. That killed our comm circuits and kicked over the power manager. Primary bus is friggin' creamed, but we got a shot at syncing in five minutes. Auto-controls are disabled. Fire control will have to be manual."

Quinn spun back to his command console and flipped the weapons switch on the intercom. "Gunner, you on the line?"

The response from weapons control, two decks below, was immediate. "Affirmative, Skipper," responded the gravelly voice of Chief Wilson. "I sent Schmidt and Tookmanian to the lifeboats. What's go—"

"Stay put, Gunner. We got another card to play. You'll be getting a green light on the cannon panel. Update your solution on the bogey and get ready to toast his butt. You copy?"

"Huh . . . roger that, sir," Wilson growled. "No kidding? Bogey's squealing garbage all over the place, but I'm still tracking him solid. Down-Doppler. Estimate no more than seven or eight minutes before we reengage. I don't know what Virgil's telling you, Skipper, but my panel says we're two weeks away from a hot cannon."

Buccari looked at Rhodes. The engineer threw back a thumbs-up with one hand and an "okay" signal with the other.

"Faith, Gunner," Quinn said. "Control sequence is manual, and power's being transferred on the aux bus. Stand by."

Buccari, floating above her station, stole a look at tactical. The alien irrepressibly passed the apogee of its turn. Screeching adversary warnings steadied out.

"Back to your seat, Sharl. Fire control stations," Quinn ordered.

She grimly complied, calling up weapons status as she strapped in.

"Engineering's talking," Rhodes said, punching intercom buttons. "Goldberg patched the circuit. I'm going back to main control." The engineer clambered across the flight deck, hitting both pilots with sundry parts of his body.

"Mr. Hudson, you've got the EPL," Quinn ordered abruptly. "Take charge of the evacuation. Get the marines and nonrequired crew away from the corvette."

"Sir?" Hudson blurted. "I'm not apple qual'ed. I—"

"You heard the skipper," Buccari said. "You've just been qualified."

"But—" Hudson protested.

"Now, Ensign!" Quinn snapped. "Move!"

Hudson stuttered a response, released his tethers, and sailed from the flight deck. Buccari shifted her attention to the chatter on the fire-control circuit. Rhodes and Wilson were discussing preparations for manually firing the energy weapon.

"Okay, gentlemen," she interjected, overriding their transmissions. "Full manual. Pick up the checklist at presync."

"Rog', Lieutenant," Wilson responded. "Ready for checks."

"Power's too low for capacitance alignment, Lieutenant," Rhodes reported. "Need twenty seconds. We're only going to get one shot out of this mess. After we discharge, it'll take a half hour to regenerate. Maybe a lot longer."

"Standing by, Virgil. Let's go over prearm, Gunner," Buccari commanded. She struggled to suppress her rising anxiety. *Was there enough time?*

As she orchestrated checklists, Buccari stole glances at Quinn, concerned that he would slip back into his stupor of self-pity. Perhaps it no longer mattered: their crippled ship was hurtling helplessly through space, all aces played. During the hectic engagement the pilot had used the ship's decreasing power and diminished weapons to full advantage. His last blast of acceleration had been a desperate, spasmodic action, sapping the last gasp from the main engines, but it had propelled the corvette through a pattern of explosions and slicing energy beams, past the approaching enemy. Up to that point he had fought hard and well, with no hint of surrender, but then had come the panicked messages—distress calls—from *T.L.S. Greenland*, the corvette's mothership. The horrible implication of *Greenland*'s desperate pleas for help had melted the metal in Quinn's spine: his wife was a senior science officer on the battered mothership.

"Skipper," Buccari barked, "roll ninety for weapons release."

Without replying, Quinn disengaged the autostabilizing computer, hit the maneuvering alarm, and fired portside maneuvering rockets. The ponderous corvette rolled crazily. Quinn stopped the rotational wobble with deft squirts of opposite power.

"Nash! Evacuation status," Buccari yelled into her throat mike.

Hudson's reply was instantaneous. "Apple needs another minute. Request you hold maneuvers until I get the bay doors open. Lee and the injured are in lifeboat one, ready to go. Number two lifeboat is not being used. Still some confusion about who's staying and who's leaving, but that won't stop us from jettisoning on your command."

An anxious voice—Dawson, the ship's communications technician—broke in. "Skipper!" she transmitted. "Flash override incoming."

"Dawson, everyone to lifeboats," Buccari shouted over the circuit.

"Commander!" Dawson persisted, her voice uncharacteristically agitated. "We've got a clear language burst transmission from a panic buoy. The task force has jumped, sir. The fleet's gone!"

The ship was silent, the crew rendered speechless—no, breathless! The motherships had departed, gone into the massive distances, back over the measureless hurdle of time. Rescue was light-years away now. It would take months—years—for rescue ships to complete a hyperlight cycle. Interminable seconds of silence dragged by.

Buccari slammed a fist on the comm switch and shouted over the general circuit. "Dawson, get your butt in a boat. Rhodes, sync count. *We got a bogey inbound!*"

Quinn stirred. His hands moved automatically, a robot obeying his program. The enemy ship steadily accelerated, gnawing at the corvette's unwavering vector.

"Hudson! You reading me?" Quinn said firmly.

"Yes, sir. EPL and lifeboat one ready to go. What's the plan, sir?" came back the disembodied voice. Hudson had moved quickly.

"I was hoping you had a good idea," Quinn replied. "Right now I want you clear. Establish an outbound vector and hold it. Normal transponder codes. Keep the lifeboat in contact. If you don't hear from me in two hours, head on back to Earth by yourself. Shouldn't take you more than three or four thousand years. If the bugs pick you up first, remember your manners."

Buccari exhaled through a tight smile and checked tactical. The symbol for a planetary body had been showing up for several hours—R-K Three, the third planet from the system's star.

"R-K Three's coming up in sector two," she said. "Might be reachable."

Quinn nodded. "Hudson, get a downlink from the computer. Check tactical. Sector two. Planet in range. Head for it. Good luck, Ensign. Cleared to launch."

Buccari switched the comm master back to the weapons circuit, clipping Hudson's response. "Status, Gunner!" she demanded.

"Main control's predicting three-sigma," Wilson answered. "Mains are spooling. Power forty-five percent and climbing. Should have enough power to fire in four minutes, and we'll finish syncing optics any second. Rhodes's going batshit with shortcuts."

"Okay, Sharl," Quinn said, bringing all of them onto primary circuit. "Let's take care of business. How many decoys left?"

Buccari checked the weapons console. "Three."

"Start laying decoys at sixteen hundred. How many kinetics?"

"Twenty-three heavies and a couple hundred dinks," she responded. She brought her eyes up and scanned the infinite blackness, not seeing—nothing to see. Her attention was drawn back to the evacuation. System panels indicated that launch bays had depressurized. A distant, sharp *thunk* followed by a high-frequency rumble vibrated the ship's metal fabric. Status lights changed, indicating that the bay doors had resealed. A lifeboat and the EPL—the Endoatmospheric Planetary Lander—had launched. The greater part of the corvette crew was away, thrown into the black void.

Chief Wilson broke in. "Fire control has active track. We're warbling the signal and he's jamming, but we have sporadic lock. Power weak but steady. My board is green. Beta three point two and dropping. Passing manual control to the flight deck."

"This is Buccari," she replied in sterile tones. "I have fire control. Arming sequence now."

Quinn flipped back a red switch cover on his overhead. Buccari gave a thumbs-up, and Quinn armed the energy weapon. Amber lights appeared on her weapons panel; a soft bell tone sounded in the background. She flipped switches; amber lights turned green, and the tone took a higher pitch. Quinn disabled the alarm while Buccari stared at the firing presentation on her ordnance console. Range reticles moved inexorably closer; the enemy ship was established on its track, only seconds from long-distance weapons range. A tail chase: she had too much time—time to think about what to do and time to worry.

"Firing range?" she asked.

"Hold until four hundred. We'll have him for lunch," Quinn replied.

Buccari looked up. The enemy had shown far greater range than that.

Proximity alarms sounded. Weapons circuits became hot. Gunner Wilson narrated a stream of weapon status and contact information. Buccari interjected terse preparatory commands while Quinn maneuvered the corvette, optimizing weapon release angles. His maneuvers were ragged; the battle-damaged thrusters were out of alignment, and power inputs were intentionally asymmetrical in a desperate attempt to slew the ship from its ballistic trajectory.

Wilson: "Bogey at ten thousand, sector six. Overtaking velocity point eight. Engagement radius in thirty. Optical scan in tight oscillation."

Buccari: "Roger that. Holding fire, all switches green."

Wilson: "Bogey at six thousand, sector six. Trajectory is veering high and starboard. Now sector five. Scanning."

Buccari: "Stand by to deploy decoys."

Wilson: "Three thousand, sector five. Bogey is maneuvering. Intermittent optical lock."

Buccari: "Roger optical. Firing decoys."

Quinn manhandled the maneuvering jets, causing the corvette to buffet and accelerate laterally. Despite the jerking excursions, Buccari's movements were measured and precise.

Wilson: "Bogey at sixteen hundred, sector five. Bearing constant. Optical lock is firm. He's firing at the decoys."

Buccari: "Roger lock."

She pressed a switch on her weapons board. A salvo of kinetic energy missiles, sounding like popcorn popping, streaked their unholy fires across the flight deck's viewing screen. Quinn rolled the corvette ninety degrees to port and fired a new set of maneuvering thrusters, unmasking additional weapons ports. Buccari pickled another set of kinetic energy missiles.

Wilson: "Bogey at twelve hundred. He blew our decoys away, and he's got us locked in!"

Screaming radar lock-on warnings reverberated through the corvette. The enemy was preparing to fire, the high-pitched *whoop*ing alarm sickeningly familiar. There was no way to evade the impending explosions—not without exhausting their only means of fighting back. Their single option was to stand and fight, the laser cannon their final punch.

"Here go a pattern of dinks and the last of the heavies," Buccari announced, her fingers playing the weapons panel. Distinct *thump*s vibrated through the ship, followed by a chorus of softer popping sounds. Quinn rotated the vessel, slewing it around and uncovering the arcing streaks of destruction as they vanished into interstellar distance. Buccari scanned tactical. The approaching target converged with datum. The range selector activated, automatically resetting the scale and moving the enemy ship back to the rim of the display.

Wilson: "Thousand clicks. Maneuvering away from our missiles. No deception, but heavy jamming. Jump shifting through it with full systems lock-on. Hard lock."

Buccari verified weapons configuration and optics alignment. She scanned tactical. Targeting reticles were perfectly aligned. The next salvo from the alien would blast them to eternity. She clenched the firing grip, moving the trigger guard aside.

"Okay, Gunner. Roger lock," she replied, surprised at her own calmness. "Program firing the load. Standby cannon. Confirm power status." She punched another button, and salvos of missiles sprayed outward at the oncoming destruction.

Wilson responded immediately. "Power up. Board's steady. All systems check. Ready to fire!"

Buccari reverified lock-on and then glanced into the blackness of space. The corvette's missiles were painfully visible—blasts of hot-white fire streaking to starboard, punching into the vacuum in regular intervals, each meteor a shining sliver of steel and depleted uranium.

Why hasn't the bug fired? she wondered. Suddenly her eyes caught an impossibly faint and distant glimmering. She concentrated her focus on a point at infinity and detected the unmistakable bloom of a colossal explosion, reduced to a pinpoint of light by the immense intervening distances.

Wilson: "Six hundred, and—sir! Bogey's fading out! Enemy tracking and fire-control radars have gone down, too. He's . . . gone. Completely off the screen! Something . . . the kinetics must have taken him out!"

Buccari turned to tactical. Warning detects flashed, but the cursors had all returned home and nowhere was there a threat blip. Warning detects were extinguished as she watched.

"Something's wrong," she said, releasing her grip from the cannon trigger. "The bogey decoyed our ordnance. I show no weapons tracks as confirmed hits."

She reset the laser scanners. Nothing! She lifted her head and looked out the viewscreens, and then she turned toward Quinn, gloved hand resting atop her helmet.

"It's gone . . . destroyed," she announced incredulously.

The manic tones of the threat-warning Klaxon stuttered to silence, the only sound the susurrant rush of oxygen through the respirators of their battle armor.

"Let's get the lifeboat," Quinn whispered. He hit the maneuvering alarm.

TWO

LIFEBOAT

The lifeboat oscillated, gently wobbling as pinhead jets fired to stabilize it. Jettisoned from the overwhelming mass of the corvette, it was powerless to do anything but float in space on the impulse vector provided at ejection.

Leslie Lee quelled her incipient panic and took note of the injured marine's elevated temperature and rapid pulse rate. The other lifeboat occupants were strapped in racks protruding from the sides of the cylindrical vessel. Six of the eight stations were occupied. Lee unstrapped and floated through the restricted tubular core. Rennault was unconscious, his arm broken; Lee suspected the spacer marine had suffered internal injuries. She enriched his oxygen and fed a plasma solution through the IV port on his pressure suit. The other injured man—Fenstermacher, the boatswain's mate—was coming around. In addition to broken bones, he had thrown up in his space suit.

The men had been caught off station and were injured early in the engagement. Rennault had failed to strap in and had been hurled around the cabin by the first few frantic course changes. He would have been pounded to death and could have inflicted significant damage on equipment and other personnel if the wiry Fenstermacher had not bravely risked a similar fate by partially unstrapping and tackling Rennault in midflight. Fenstermacher had tethered them both down, securely enough to keep from flying about but not securely enough to escape the thrashing inflicted by the pounding g-loads.

Fenstermacher struggled to lift his head; his inertia reels were locked. Lee released the locks, and the injured man turned to face her, peering unsteadily from behind a smeared visor.

"Smells sweet in there, eh?" Lee chided as she used a pen-light to check pupil dilation, pushing the injured man's head down on the bunk. His eyes seemed normal, but it was difficult to see through the contaminated visor. She leaned over to check his left arm, which was immobilized by an inflatable pressure cast. Lee dimly sensed pressure on the front of her suit. Fenstermacher moaned with a peculiar, melancholy tone. Startled by his groans and mistaking them for a signal of pain, Lee backed off sufficiently to see Fenstermacher's right hand wandering suggestively across her chest. The suit provided no hint of anatomic topography and its coarse stiffness barely transmitted the sensation of contact, but Fenstermacher persistently continued his motion, groaning lasciviously. She looked down at his hand and tiredly pushed it away, smiling wistfully at the presumptions of the living.

"Fool," she said quietly, thickly, near tears.

"Ah, don't worry, Les," Fenstermacher said, breaking lifeboat regulations by speaking, his voice feeble. "We'll make it. Someone will pick us up."

"Yeah, Leslie," said another voice—Dawson's. Lee looked over to station three to see the communication technician's helmet lift from the harness. "For once in his life, Fensterprick is right."

"Why, thank you, gruesome," Fenstermacher said hoarsely. "I take back what I said about you being stupid and ugly. You're just ugly."

"He ain't worth getting angry over," Dawson retorted, "but I sure hope he's in pain. Leslie, either knock him out or make him scream."

"The fleet's gone," another voice darkly grumbled—Tookmanian, one of the weapons technicians. "We are forsaken. Only He will save us now."

"Not now, Tooks," admonished Schmidt, the other weapons rating.

"Praise the Lord," echoed another voice—Gordon, the youngest of the spacer marines.

"Thanks, but I'll put my faith in Commander Quinn and Lieutenant Buccari," Dawson replied. "If anyone can get us out of this, they can."

"The lieutenant sure took a bite out of your tall, skinny tail," Fenstermacher sniped.

"She was doing her job, and I was doing mine, pukebrains,"

Dawson said cheerfully. "Buccari knows what she's doing. She can yell at me any time she wants."

"Okay, you guys," Lee said. "We got rules. Can the chatter." The petty officer sighed helplessly and looked around the cramped interior of the austere cylinder. She floated to her station, noting that the solar cell wings had deployed. The lifeboat was close to a star; electrical power would not be a problem; the lights would be on when they suffocated. She swallowed hard and endeavored to concentrate, but anxiety swept over her. Aliens! The fleet was gone, and the corvette was in trouble. She was frightened.

An indicator flashed. An aural alarm buzzed. Lee reconnected her helmet lead and heard Ensign Hudson trying to raise her.

"Life one is up," she reported, failing to keep her voice calm.

"Roger, one. The bug ship was flashed!" Hudson replied excitedly. "We made it . . . for now, anyway. I'm coming to get you. You having problems?"

"No, sir. Everything's okay. I was checking on the injured." Lee strapped in as she spoke, relieving her tension with activity. Noting that her passengers were reasonably calm and breathing normally, she punched a digital switch several times, thinning down the oxygen being metered to her charges; any oxygen saved now might mean another few minutes of existence.

"How're they doing? I hear Fenstermacher's a hero," Hudson said.

"Yeah, but a real dumb one. And he puked in his pajamas to boot." She realized that radio communications were being fed to every station in the lifeboat. She turned around and looked back at Fenstermacher. His good arm hung out into the center aisle with its thumb up.

"Stop moving. You know the regs!" she commanded. "Fenstermacher, arm back by your side or I'll knock you out!" Fenstermacher's arm retreated, but not before his erect thumb was replaced by his middle digit. She switched off communications to the cabin.

Hudson continued to transmit: "You'll hear contact on your hull in less than a minute. I'm going to secure you with the grapple."

"Mr. Hudson, the fleet jumped. What're we going to do?" Lee asked.

"First things first, Lee. Let's get you rigged and docked, and then we'll take the next step," Hudson said. "If it's any consolation, I'm scared silly, too. Hang on."

"Yes, sir," she replied, gaining reassurance that her lifeboat would soon be taken in tow, relieving her of being alone and easing the burden of powerless responsibility. Suppressing thought, she concentrated on the many checklist items left to do.

"Established in hyperlight, sir. Admiral . . . did you copy? Stable jump," reported Captain Wells, the flag operations officer. "Sir, are you all right?"

Fleet Admiral Runacres floated at the perimeter barrier of the flag bridge. Even in the null gravity of the operations core he appeared to lean heavily on the railing, clenched hands and thick legs spread wide, the weight of concern bowing his helmet low. *T.L.S. Eire*'s bridge watch, in battle dress, moved professionally "below," but anxious glances flashed in his direction. Runacres slowly unbent his neck and scanned the displays. Red emergency signals continued to flash on annunciator panels, defining the ill-fated mothership's status.

"Admiral, we need to shore up *Greenland*'s grid sector," Wells said. "She's gone, Admiral. We caught her in the grid, but she's dead. No signals, no links. They've recovered some lifeboats."

"I see that, Franklin," Runacres said, pushing over to the tactical consoles. The flag duty officers—a tactical watch officer and an assistant—were strapped into a horseshoe-shaped station at the lowest point of the flag bridge. Runacres looked down at the constantly updating status panels.

"*Baffin* or *Novaya* report in yet?" Runacres asked.

"No, sir," the tactical officer reported. Several ships had broken radio discipline during the melee and were continuing to do so in the safety of hyperspace. *Baffin* and *Novaya*, in the rear guard, had not been involved in the action, their captains wisely refraining from adding to the communications tumult. *Greenland*, in the van, had been the only mothership to take hits.

Aliens! He had found an alien race. But at what cost? Runacres straightened, removed the helmet from his slick-shaven head, and rubbed red-rimmed, watery blue eyes with gloved fists, shaking the fatigue and uncertainty from his ruddy countenance. He pushed off from tactical and floated past the stepped-up bridge stations, between the elaborate consoles manned by his somber flag operations officer and that of the corvette group leader, to his own command station.

"Terminate general quarters," Runacres commanded, pulling himself into his tethers.

"Aye, aye, Admiral," Wells said. The burly ops officer removed his helmet and touched a series of keys on his console. He mounted a delicate earpiece on his sweat-shiny shaven head and began issuing orders on the network.

Runacres signaled the tactical officer. "Updated damage report."

"Aye, aye, Admiral," she replied, vigorously keying her console.

Commander Ito floated into position behind the admiral. Runacres lifted his hand without looking up, and the aide placed a squeeze tube in the admiral's palm. Runacres squirted the cool, sweet contents down his throat and waited for the energy rush.

"Damage report, Admiral," the tactical officer said.

"Go," Runacres said.

"*Greenland* destroyed. Catastrophic hull penetration, thermal runaway on reactor drives. Twenty-two survivors reported in lifeboats. Retrieval under way."

"Oh, God," Runacres groaned. Twenty-two survivors out of a crew of four hundred. But he had found an alien race. Another race of killers?

"Preliminary indications *Tasmania* sustained damage from a near-maximum-range energy beam—our own," the tactical officer continued. "Friendly fire stripped away positioning and communication gear but caused no structural problems. *Tierra del Fuego* reports moderate damage from acceleration stress and light radiation exposures."

"*Tasmania*'s corvettes were recovered prior to jumping," the group leader added. "*Peregrine One*, Jake Carmichael's ship, took out three alien interceptors. One TDF corvette, *Osprey Two*, is missing. Skipper of *Osprey One* confirms that *Two* was destroyed in action before the fleet jumped. *Osprey One* and *Two* are both credited with single kills."

Runacres grunted.

"Four of *Greenland*'s corvettes were recovered," the group leader continued. "*Harrier One*, Jack Quinn's 'vette, last reported engaged with alien units, is missing, presumed left behind. Quinn was covering the flight's return to grid." His report complete, the group leader sat nervously silent. Runacres stared at a point far beyond the bulkhead of his spaceship.

"All other ships are operating normally, with all hands accounted for," Wells said, breaking the depressing silence. "Hyperlight grid is stable, but *Greenland*'s grid sector is being patched at long range by *Britannia* and *Kyushu*."

Runacres digested the information, a dizzy sensation making it hard to concentrate. *Aliens.* And two corvettes and a mothership—over four hundred spacers, the cream of the fleet—destroyed or left behind, marooned in time and space. There was nothing to be done. His command, the Tellurian Legion Main Fleet, was withdrawing, committed to returning to Sol system. The emergency recall was automatic, the jump coordinates preset. Now they had to hold the grid up long enough to make the twenty-parsec HLA transit—four standard months.

Greenland's grid sector was Runacres's first concern. If the links degraded catastrophically, the grid matrix would unload, dumping the fleet light-years from Sol. If that happened, it would take many more months, perhaps years, to get home.

"Franklin," Runacres ordered. "*Eire* to assume grid duty."

Wells quickly raised the flagship's skipper. "Captain Merriwether, maneuver to sector one at best speed. Relieve *Greenland* on station."

Runacres studied the *Eire*'s amphitheater bridge two decks below. He watched and listened as Merriwether directed her bridge team and noted with satisfaction the efficiency and teamwork ingrained in her crew.

"On the way, Frank," Merriwether responded, her drawl deep and resonant. "It's Shaula all over again, isn't it, Admiral?"

"Perhaps, Sarah," Runacres answered quietly, looking down at her upturned helmet. "And perhaps not. We survived this time. No one survived Shaula system."

"The fleet wasn't armed twenty-five years ago, Admiral," Merriwether said. "Being able to shoot back made the difference."

"Progress," Runacres grumbled.

THREE

ORBIT

Buccari felt the smile on her face, the exultation of survival painfully stretching the lagging muscles of her cheeks. Her attention returned to the reality of their predicament: the alien ships might have been destroyed, but the task force had retreated into hyperlight, stranding them in a strange and hostile system. Her smile relaxed. The muscles in the back of her jaw tightened.

"Skipper, recommend we safe the pulse laser," Buccari said.

Quinn stirred, switching off the arm master. "Do you have contact with Hudson?"

"Yes, sir. They're still up on docking radar. Give me a second and I'll get you a vector," Buccari said, deselecting firing circuits.

"Engineering! Status on main engines?" Quinn demanded.

Rhodes's booming voice answered. "Sixty-eight percent usable power, but the system is haywired to beat the devil, and the governors may not respond. Cannon coming down. Main engines ready in three minutes."

Buccari established a laser link with the EPL and began receiving telemetry. As she identified the lifeboat beacon, she noticed a proximity alert on the navigation display.

"Commander," Buccari interrupted urgently.

"Yes, Sharl," Quinn answered.

"Sir, Hudson has grappled the lifeboat. On this vector he'll bring the lander alongside in fifteen minutes. But we have another problem!"

"What now?" Quinn asked as he punched in the rendezvous headings.

"The planet . . . R-K Three. At this course and speed we're

heading into first-order gravitational field effect, maybe even a reentry."

Buccari reset the range indicator on tactical; a blinking planet symbol glowed ominously in sector two, and the course indicator pointed to an intersection on the orbital plane. Quinn hit the maneuvering alarm and fired a bank of thrusters, shifting the ship's attitude. The planet pitched slowly into view, fully illuminated except for a thin crescent of darkness. The pilot maneuvered until the planet was dead ahead.

"Look at that!" Buccari gasped. It was close, already starting to fill the viewscreen—and beautiful. Swirls of brown, green, blue, and white marbled the brilliant body. Blue and white! Water and clouds! she thought, her hopes rising.

"Set parameters for a standard reconnaissance orbit," Quinn ordered. "Any mass data? Any electromagnetic traffic?"

"Sensors are pretty chewed up. Computer's only processing spectral data," she replied. "No output yet. No indications of electromagnetic emissions. Nothing. Electronically, it's uninhabited."

"My wife said—" Quinn choked on his own words. "How're we doing on the mains?" he asked.

Buccari sighed and checked her engine instruments. "Restart check complete," she said. "Auxiliary backups functional. Generators are fluctuating outside spec, but Rhodes hasn't tried cross-connecting. He's doing that now." Buccari pivoted in her tethers and stretched to her full limit to flip a switch on the overhead power console. She began the system checks required to set up orbit.

"Roger, restart," Quinn answered wistfully.

Lifeboat pickup went without incident. With the crew members returned to their duty stations, final preparations for orbit began.

"Survey systems are still hammered, but the computer has synthesized a preliminary mass analysis," Hudson said, back at his station.

Buccari interrogated her primary monitor and examined the computer data. The planet designated Rex-Kaliph Three was smaller than Earth, at .91 g on the surface. Precise flight-path calculations indicated that the corvette was not on a collision course; without additional course or speed changes, it would pass the planet on a severely divergent trajectory, receiving a gravity sling into an elliptical solar orbit. A fiery collision with the planet would have been preferable—preferable to being catapulted deep into space without fuel or food.

"Any signs of intelligence?" Quinn asked.

"No, sir," Hudson said. "We've picked up some random coherent signals, but nothing like you'd expect from a technical civilization, certainly not like what we're detecting from the second planet. We'll know more after we make a survey orbit. Only the telescopes and cameras are up, but engineering is working on the sensors—among other things."

"Mains are on line and ready for retrograde burn," Buccari announced. "Trajectory for orbit is good. We won't need more than five minutes of burn at two plus gees. Fuel is ten point four—some margin for error."

"Three minutes to orbit retro, Commander," Hudson reported.

Quinn did not acknowledge. Buccari looked up to find the pilot staring out at the planet, its image reflecting from his helmet visor.

"Beautiful!" Quinn whispered sadly.

Buccari gazed at the brilliant cloud-covered body and nodded. It had been a long time. It looked like Earth. She returned to her checklists.

"One minute to burn. Orbital checklist complete," Buccari reported. She labored on her power console. "Engineering, power readouts are fluctuating. You sure we have a good cross-connect?"

Rhodes retorted with a string of expletives, indicating that he was satisfied with the state of affairs at his end of the ship. Buccari leaned forward, intent on her instruments.

"What's wrong, Sharl? You're worried," Quinn said.

She looked up from the power console. "Nothing I can put my finger on, Commander. Interlocks are off, and there are a dozen primary deficiencies. The whole system is messed up from battle damage, but Virgil's as good as they come. If anyone can jury-rig the plumbing, he can. We don't have many alternatives."

"No good alternatives, but we sure got plenty of rotten ones," Quinn replied. "Okay, I've got the controls. Mister Hudson, everybody to acceleration stations. Pass word for retro. Deceleration load two point two gees." Quinn sounded the maneuvering alarm and pivoted the ship, redirecting the massive main engine nozzles along the retro vector. Lapsed time advanced inexorably.

"Five ... four ... three ..." Buccari's clear voice sounded over the ship's general address system. She verified axial alignment and confirmed that the maneuvering thrusters were armed and functioning. "Two ... one ... zero."

"Throttle at thirty percent," Quinn reaffirmed as he cleared the safety interlock. He depressed the ignition button.

Nothing happened.

Quinn released the button, cycled the interlock, and pushed again. Nothing.

"Engineering! We have a problem," he announced. "What about it?"

Rhodes's voice came back after a short pause. He did not sound confident. "Give us a minute, Skipper. Got a few ideas."

Buccari updated the retro-burn profile. Every minute meant a tighter orbit window and more power required to establish trajectory. More power for orbit would mean less fuel available for getting the crew and their survival equipment down to the planet.

"Nash, give me fuel versus time. Work out a worst case," she ordered.

"I have the trade-offs, Sharl," Hudson replied. "Assuming we get engines to full power, we have nine hours to make worst-case orbit, only we wouldn't have any lander fuel left— we'd be stranded in orbit. The window to get everyone down with fifty kilos of equipment is ninety minutes. After about six hours we'll have to start leaving people behind. Depends on how low our orbit is."

Quinn's helmet pivoted upward as if in prayer. "Run the numbers again," he ordered.

"I already did, sir—three times," Hudson's voice was confident if subdued. "That assumes everyone rides down on the apple. We buy some slack with an injection run. We've got six penetration modules and at least six qualified marines."

Quinn switched off the autostabilizers to conserve fuel. "Rhodes! How're you doing? Give me an estimate!" he demanded.

Buccari was about to repeat the command when Mendoza, Rhodes's senior propulsion technician, came up on the circuit, gasping for breath.

"Commander Quinn, we got it figured out, er ... it's—"

Silence. The circuit went dead, and the ship went absolutely dark, the stark glare of the approaching planet their only light. Buccari keyed her intercom. Silence. She flipped open the control cover on her forearm and activated her suit transceiver. Members of the crew were coming up on the suit radios, saturating the frequency. Hudson took charge of the situation, directing the confusion. No one was in contact with engineering, the mass of the ship blocking transmissions to that most rearward station.

"I'm heading back," Buccari said, releasing her fittings and clearing her visor. As she floated into the tubular longitudinal accessway, the emergency battle lighting flickered strongly on. A red glow bathed the length of the forty-meter tunnel, and Buccari's vision adjusted to the monochromatic pall. Rhodes's bulk emerged from the distant afterhatch.

"Give me . . . one hour to rerun cross-connects," the big man blurted on the radio circuit, his voice an octave higher than normal, his breathing labored, "and to . . . reinforce the secondary circuits. Energy paths overloaded. The power manager locked up, and . . . I had to run a bypass to override. We lost the load. Goldberg . . . is rebooting the power manager."

They met halfway. Rhodes's anguished face, ashen even in the red battle light, ran with perspiration. A bypass on the power manager was a major operation done by a station crew over a period of hours, even days. Rhodes, with only two technicians, had just done one in less than ten minutes. Buccari refused to think of the shortcuts the engineer had employed or their consequences.

Quinn's voice came up over the radio: "We have no choice, Virgil. You take too long and we'll all have nothing but time on our hands."

"Yes, sir, Commander," Rhodes replied. "I understand—"

"Commander," Buccari interrupted. "I'm going back. I'll run the power manager while Mr. Rhodes finishes cross-connects. I think I know why the connect didn't hold."

"Sure, Sharl," Quinn replied. "I'll just take a nap."

Ignoring the sarcasm, she turned to the engineer and smiled. "We got work to do, Virgil."

"Roger, Lieutenant," Rhodes gulped, trying unsuccessfully to return the smile. He flipped his big body and floated aft, propelling himself by hand rungs interspersed down the bore. Buccari followed.

Compared to the gray drabness of the flight deck, the expansive engineering compartment, even under emergency lighting, was gaudily illuminated, with banks of instrumentation lining all surfaces except the aft bulkhead, where an air lock led to the cavernous main engine hold. Next to the lock an observation bay looked out over a labyrinth of reactors, pipes, radiator fins, and turbines. The engineering technicians were engrossed in their tasks. They had discarded their battle suits, stripping down to buff-colored jumpsuits, their shiny-bald heads glistening with perspiration. Buccari removed helmet and gloves, leaving the apparel drifting in a catch net near the hatch.

"Mendoza, force the auto-repair diagnostic on the transmission paths," Rhodes ordered. "Goldberg, I want you to finish the reboot!"

"I've got the power manager, Goldberg," Buccari said, sliding next to the petty officer and hooking her boot around a security tether. "Mr. Rhodes wants you on main memory." The propulsion technician, absorbed in her efforts, looked up with irritation.

"I'll get it! I'm almost there, Lieutenant—" Goldberg started.

"Goldberg!" Rhodes boomed. "Main memory! Reset and reboot—now!"

Goldberg abruptly pushed away from the console, propelling her thin body across the compartment. Spinning and jackknifing adroitly, she gracefully cushioned her vigorous impact next to the main computer control console and was quickly at work.

Buccari analyzed power manager status and was soon consumed by the task of reprogramming the computer. Minutes passed in a controlled frenzy. As she worked, her mind drifted back to the nearly disastrous engagement with the alien spacecraft. With startling awareness she realized the limitless scope of their luck: they were still waiting for the same power sequence that fired the laser cannon. The cannon would not have fired, just as the main engines had not. They should have been annihilated by the alien ship. *How had they escaped?*

Buccari finished her programming and checked the time display on the bulkhead. Precious minutes marched into history. Her eyes would not leave the blinking diodes that marked the time, her entire being focused on the inevitable dwindling of opportunity, the irrefutable and immutable narrowing of existence that the passage of time represented. The essence of life was palpable; her pulse pounded in her ears.

Rhodes's hour was up!

"Okay, Lieutenant," Rhodes said, interrupting her trance. "Cross-connects are firm, but I need ten more minutes to stabilize ion pressures and temps."

"Roger," Buccari replied. "Power manager is resetting. You're only going to get a conditional reset. There's not enough time to get a full null, but it'll be good enough. Good luck, Virgil." She redonned helmet and gloves and slipped into the darkened connecting tube, anxious to once again look out on the shining planet.

It was brilliant. She opened the flight deck hatch to a white flood of natural light and had to squint to see the instruments. She flashed Hudson a thin smile and then hit a button on her wrist controls, causing her gold visor filter to click instantly into place.

"Well?" Quinn demanded. "What's it look like?"

As if in answer, the ship's lighting flickered to normal. Buccari glanced down at her power console as the primary circuit indicators switched to green, clearing most of the error messages on her screen.

"Rhodes needs ten minutes to complete cross-connect, but it looks functional," she reported, locking into her seat. "I wouldn't want to use the power paths again. Main buses are fried, and the alternates are just hanging together. We tested for load. They'll hold. We got at least one shot."

Quinn grunted and busied himself with preorbital checks. Buccari joined the litany of preparation; challenges were answered with responses of unequivocal certainty. The ship was a wreck; systems were out of specification or inoperable, but the checklist moved onward and around those obstacles, measuring their impact and weighing the risks and alternatives.

"Preorbital checks complete," Buccari reported. She saved the checklist deviations to the log file and cleared the checklist screen. She punched a button on the communications panel. "Flight deck to engineering. Your turn, Mr. Rhodes. Status?"

Goldberg responded. "Power manager shows a conditional reset, just like you said. You sure we can't get it to full function by a reload simulation? Mr. Rhodes and me think we can do it in five minutes."

"Go with what you have, Goldberg," Buccari almost shouted. "The power manager may not hold together for that long, and we have a date with a planet in a few minutes."

"Mr. Rhodes says—"

"Ready for ignition, *now*! No more questions."

The circuit went silent. "Aye, sir," Goldberg said at last.

Hudson shook his fingers as if they were on fire. Buccari ignored him.

Quinn came up on the command channel: "Ignition in ninety seconds. Let's slow this bucket down. You ready, Mr. Rhodes?"

"Retro in ninety," the engineer answered. "Engineering is ready."

Quinn hit the maneuvering alarm and broadcast over the general circuit: "All hands to stand by for ... five gees. Five gees for five minutes. Commencing retro sequence now."

Buccari monitored fuel readings and rechecked burn times. Five gees for five minutes would get everyone's attention. She switched the injection profile over to her primary monitor. Klaxons sounded, and a controlled cacophony of chatter emitted from her headset, each station reporting its status. The ship's crew members settled into known procedures, conditions for which they had trained and retrained, the urgency of their struggle dispelling the shock and surprise of postcombat and the helplessness of being in deep space without power.

Buccari's voice droned professionally as she verbalized checklist items rolling down her console display. Quinn's replies were equally sterile. The prominent digital clock was once again counting the seconds to their destiny, the gaudy red flickering a mechanical symbol of the tension rebuilding under the dispassionate routine of the checklist. Buccari rechecked the craft's alignment to the retro-axis for the twentieth time; crosshairs were centered on the thrust vector. A slight oscillation was apparent, but it was within vector limits.

"Orbital checks complete. Twenty seconds to retro," Buccari announced over the general circuit. "All stations prepare for final count."

Quinn locked the throttle at sixty percent, flipped back the ignition switch cover, depressed the interlock, and positioned his hand over the ignition. Buccari's hands curled around the acceleration grips on her armrests, fingertips playing lightly over the controls. She finished the countdown: "Five ... four ... three ... two ... one ... ignition, now."

Quinn depressed the button. After an agonizing delay a surge of pure power pressed her into her seat. Never had five gees felt so good! She sensed the familiar gee-induced vibration inside her eyeballs. Peripheral vision tunneled inward. The red diodes of the ignition timer counted positive seconds into the burn ... 009 ... 010 ... 011. Buccari forced her lungs to exhale a load of air.

"Igni-shun plus fifteen sec-con's. F-fuel flow p-peaking,"

Hudson grunted. An eternity passed, and then Hudson's voice again: "Plus thir-thirty secon's."

Buccari scanned the master display. Warning lights illuminated, some steady, some flickering. The power plant was functioning—outside of limits, but it was holding steady across the board.

"H-how's it look, Sharl?" Quinn grunted into the intercom.

"R-real ug-ugly." Buccari contracted her abdomen, forcing her diaphragm to expel her words. "Sh-shunt's working and the mains are holding, b-but w-we got over four minutes to shake, rattle, and roll."

An ominous *thump-thump-THUMP* vibrated loudly through the frame of the ship. Buccari wrenched her head sideways to look at Quinn, who did likewise toward her. They were powerless to take action. The mains might not take the stress of powering up again. Unless they rode out this deceleration, they would be doomed to death in deep space. If the mains blew, all their problems and their hopes would be over. Both pilots worked their heads forward, returning their view to the engine instruments, to wait.

Four minutes later the timed retrofire terminated. Weightlessness returned, and the Legion corvette *Harrier One* was in orbit.

FOUR

DEBRIEFING

"Excuse me, Admiral," Commander Ito reported, "it's time." The flag aide poked his head through the chromed hatch of the admiral's habitation ring stateroom.

"Right behind you, Sam," the admiral replied. "What's the latest?" Runacres, with Merriwether and Wells at his heels, sauntered through the half gravity of *Eire*'s habitation ring, following the flag aide.

"Of the twenty-two survivors," Ito updated them as they entered the briefing compartment, "four irretrievably died of trauma before being picked up; two others were resuscitated but are in critical condition and no longer capable of meaningful existence. They will be allowed to terminate. Ten others are seriously injured but should recover, two as unregenerative amputees. They'll all be spending time in radtox."

Runacres shook his head wearily. The group leader and other senior members of his staff were already seated, while junior staff members sat at stations outside the sensor perimeter. On the bulkheads in front and to each side of the admiral were segmented vid-images being transmitted from the other ships. Most attendees were quietly seated, although the normal movement of latecomers and kibitzers gave the screens a kaleidoscopic character. Movement ceased as the admiral took his seat between Merriwether and Wells.

Commander Ito, his somber image filling the speaker's vid, commenced the briefing, running down the agenda and designating speakers. Runacres looked at the secondary screens, identifying faces in the electronically connected assemblage but pondering on those no longer in attendance.

The center screen moved into a close-up on the first speaker, a woman, gender obvious even though she was smoothly hairless. She spoke in a firm contralto. A medical dressing masked one of her crystal blue eyes and obscured her fine features. Runacres recognized Lieutenant Commander Cassiopeia Quinn, Jack Quinn's wife.

"*Greenland*'s survey computers had datalink with *Harrier One*'s survey system," she reported. "Instruments show that *Harrier One* was functioning when the fleet jumped—the crew was still alive." A single tear broke loose and rolled halfway down her cheek before it was intercepted by a quick knuckle.

Runacres averted his eyes; a lump grew in his throat—and anger. He should have been notified about this in advance of the briefing. There was nothing he could do about her husband and his crew. The silence was mercifully cut by the resumption of Quinn's narrative.

"And," she continued, her voice firm, "those same instruments indicate that R-K Three is alpha-zed."

Runacres hit his command button and glared at the conference screen. "Excuse me, Commander—Cassy, isn't it?" he interrupted. "First permit me to offer my condolences for the loss of your husband and of so many of your valiant shipmates. Second, allow me to thank you for your courage in making this presentation so soon after your ordeal. I hope your injuries are not serious."

"Thank you, Admiral," Quinn replied, chin up and voice steady. "My injuries will heal; the loss of my husband will not. But . . . there may be hope . . . yet."

Runacres considered the beleaguered female's situation. Her husband was marooned in an alien system, and there was only one reason the fleet would ever return to that system: a habitable planet.

"Alpha-zed, eh?" the admiral replied. "Have you new evidence?"

"Yes, sir, I think I do," Quinn replied, "and I apologize for letting my emotions get the better of me. Permit me to resume, sir."

"Please do," he said.

"Humans have been exploring the stars for two centuries," Quinn said, addressing the conference. "And other than Shaula, our exobiologists have not discovered any life-forms more intelligent than the aborigines of Arcturus Four."

"And all we discovered at Shaula," Merriwether whispered into Runacres's ear, "were the dead crews and destroyed ships of the Hakito Fleet. The *intelligent* life was long gone by the time we got there. We've finally found the bastards."

Runacres allowed his memory to dominate his concentration. Twenty-five years earlier he and Merriwether had been corvette officers on the belated rescue mission sent to Shaula system. The Hakito Fleet, HLA units of the Asian Cooperation, was a year overdue, and the AC leaders had requested the Tellurian Legion to investigate. After obtaining all the necessary assurances and guarantees, the Legion had agreed to the AC request, dispatching two HLA cells to distant Shaula. The frustrated rescuers had found only burned and ransacked hulks—and drifting lifeboats—in gruesome orbit about the star's single barren planet. Some of the lifeboats were filled with desiccated remains, but many were inexplicably empty—leaving over three hundred crew members unaccounted for. It was humankind's first and only contact with a technologically advanced life-form, and it was the reason Legion exploratory units were equipped with missiles and energy weapons.

"Of the two hundred twelve stars discovered with planets in viable orbit," Quinn went on, "only sixteen have had planets capable of supporting life. Of these, only four have had planets marginally accommodating to human existence—one category alpha-three, one alpha-four, and two alpha-fives. The colonies established on these intemperate outposts are not self-supporting, and none has developed a perpetuating birth-rate. All are prohibitively expensive to maintain."

"The two fives are being discontinued," Merriwether interjected.

"We know this," Runacres growled. "What has this to do with—"

"Bear with me, Admiral," Quinn replied. "Rex-Kaliph is a hot and active star, warmer and larger than Sol. It supplies energy to not one . . . not just one, but to two—"

"Preposterous!" a staff exobiologist exclaimed. "Mass ratios and Copernicus's law—"

"Quiet!" Runacres snapped. "Yes, Commander?"

"Rex-Kaliph," Quinn continued, her eyes closed, "provides sufficient energy for two life-supporting planets, one massive and warm and another Earth-sized and Earth-like, if marginally cooler." She paused. The vid screens were dead still, dead quiet. What she proposed was incredible.

"Amazing," Wells said. "Two life-capable planets in one system."

"Two life-capable planets," Quinn said, "but only one alpha-zed."

"And a highly developed race of beings not inclined to share their planets with us," Merriwether said. "Perhaps the Killers of Shaula."

"But now we're getting to my point, Admiral," Quinn said. "Rex-Kaliph Two, the *second* planet from the sun, is the system's primary planet. That's the home of your highly developed race, and that's the planet being so belligerently defended. It's at best an alpha-five biosphere, probably more like an alpha-six. Prior to the attack, survey teams detected electromagnetic activity characteristic of an intelligent and highly technical civilization emanating from R-K Two. That planet is much larger than Earth and quite dense, maybe three times more massive. Gravity on the surface of R-K Two is almost one and a half times that of Earth, and its atmosphere is extremely dense. The spectral lines are busy—lots of oxygen, nitrogen, methane, and gaseous carbon compounds. Surface temperatures are uniformly warm, and the weather appears to be slow-moving and hot. It has a natural condition that exceeds

Earth's worst pollution fears and is not considered permanently habitable."

"Tell that to the aliens," Merriwether drawled. "Must be what makes them so cranky."

"What's your point, Commander?" Runacres asked.

"Sir, we did a broad-channel scan on the third planet," Quinn said. "Everything—atmospheric parameters, temperature ranges, mass specifics, spectral composition—is totally within a very low alpha category. Yet strange to say, there is little to indicate that it is inhabited."

"Your point," Runacres demanded. "What difference does that make?"

"Yes," Wells agreed. "The inhabitants seem quite possessive."

"Yes, but the planets have vastly different, almost incompatible biospheres, Admiral," Quinn said. "My point—my hope—is that R-K Three is as unattractive to the aliens as our colonies are to us. Perhaps, just perhaps, they will negotiate with us."

"*Negotiate?*" Merriwether harrumphed. "These are likely the same monsters that massacred our people at Shaula. They've started their negotiations from a rather extreme position, wouldn't you say? What makes you think they'll cooperate? And excuse me, Commander, but we have seen other planets that satisfy most, if not all, alpha requirements, and none has been a Garden of Eden. Your new planet may not be worth losing more people and ships over, and that may be part of the *negotiations* ultimately required!"

"What do we do now that we've found the monsters?" Wells asked.

"We don't know that we have found them," Runacres replied. "Who says this is the same race? Perhaps the universe is inherently unfriendly—but we've interrupted Commander Quinn. Please continue, er . . . Cassy."

"Admiral, because of the nature of their technologies, I feel certain the inhabitants of R-K Two are *not* the Shaula killers," Quinn persevered. "And R-K Three satisfies the habitability parameters within the most narrow range of any known planet ever surveyed. What's more, we obtained short-range optical and spectral imaging from *Harrier One*."

"Imagery! How? From the middle of a battle?" Wells asked.

"Yes, sir," Quinn replied softly. She hit the advance, and a grainy, highly magnified image of a wispy turquoise sphere contrasting against the velvety backdrop of space shone from the wall screen. Despite the low digital resolution, the opalescent planet looked like Earth.

Quinn broke the silence. "Don't ask me how, but the fleet datalink captured telemetry from *Harrier One*'s survey cameras. The signals were intermittent and barely synced but adequate to confirm broad-channel scans, narrowing the data even further. This planet—R-K Three—is a winner!" She looked about the silent room, a gleam of hope in her eyes.

"Maybe a bit cool," she added.

Runacres knew what Quinn was thinking, and Merriwether verbalized it. "*Harrier One* may have made that planet," she said softly but clearly enough for the microphones to pick up. "We could have people alive in that system. We have to go back."

Runacres sat quietly. Only the Legion Assembly could make that decision.

The orbiting corvette flashed in the red light of the setting sun, completing its second full day in orbit. Two moons moved silently in the ebony heavens, the larger satellite a scimitar of brilliant silver, the smaller moon tiny, lumpy, golden.

"A search radar, Skipper," Hudson said. "Someone's watching us."

Buccari watched the commander clear his console. He had been replaying the communication tapes of the battle. Buccari felt his despair.

"Surprising it took this long," Quinn sighed. "At least they aren't shooting . . . yet."

"Have you a fix on the transmitter, Nash?" Buccari asked.

"Yeah," Hudson replied. "Mapping isn't complete, but the source is located here." He designated the coordinates on their screens. "We'll be out of range in five minutes. Funny. No acquisition signals, no targeting lobes, no interrogations. It's as if they're indifferent."

"They may have other targeting methods," Buccari said. "Optical—"

"No matter. It's time to start moving," Quinn said, as if coming awake. "We didn't come this far to get blown out of orbit. Run the fuel numbers, Sharl."

"The good news is we're in low orbit," Buccari said, scanning her digital clipboard. "We have fuel for an injection run and at least seven round trips carrying standard loads, assuming we have a stable landing site. Any problems or delays and we easily double the consumption. And of course, any serious problems and the lander doesn't get back up to the ship. Makes the rest of the calculations somewhat academic."

"Don't be so damned optimistic," Quinn said.

Buccari smiled, taking the command pilot's rudeness as a good sign.

"I've been working on EPL manifests," she said. "On the first landing I recommend we take down a generator and an auxiliary fuel tank."

"Crew first, equipment second," Quinn said.

"But Commander," she argued, "after we inject the marines, we'll have fuel for seven or even eight landings. We only need four runs to get the crew and their equipment down. If we have fuel problems on the planet, the whole program is over. Anyone left onboard is stranded."

Quinn hit his palm with a fist. "That's my point," he responded too loudly, strain showing in his face. "We load the lander with crew until we get everyone down. We'll review priorities after the first trip. For now do it my way."

Buccari withheld comment. She glanced through the flight deck viewscreen at the ethereal limb of the planet. The corvette was well past the terminator. Her thoughts darkened with the planet below; night engulfed their only hope. No lights twinkled, no cities sparkled—no lights at all. Buccari scanned the unplumbable depths. And then her eyes detected a soft amber glow—a luminescence above the orbital plane, rotating into view on the horizon.

"Nash! I have a visual on lights! What's on the instruments?"

"Volcanoes, Sharl," Hudson stated quietly. "Showing moderate to heavy seismic activity. We could be in for some interesting shore leave."

"Off the deck, Sharl," Quinn ordered abruptly. "This is my watch."

"Aye, Commander," she replied dryly, separating from the station and pushing through the pressure iris. She took the first junction and descended onto the mess deck, stopping at her locker to stow helmet and battle suit. Helmet off, she could once again feel and hear the ambient drone of the circulation systems, the vibrations and whispers of the ship's power systems. The confined and recirculated odors of life in space, stale and antiseptic, assaulted her sensibilities.

The mess deck was congested with the off watch. Sleep

cells were vacant, everyone more nervous than tired. As usual, spacer marines floated around the game tables, although the magnetic dice were still. The hulking, forest-green-clad men watched her, their demeanor uncharacteristically subdued. It had been two days since the emergency sortie, and the rugged warriors, particularly the darker ones, displayed resurgent stubble on their normally hairless bodies, an inevitable result of forgoing twice-daily depilatories and skin scrubs. The air in the corvette was pungent, especially in the vicinity of the marines.

"What's the deal, Lieutenant?" Tatum asked, orienting his lanky body to Buccari's vertical and assuming a respectful, if loose, position of attention. "MacArthur says we're going to inject." Mess deck conversation stopped.

"That's the plan, Corporal," Buccari replied.

"Injection!" exclaimed Gordon, thin-framed and youthful. "Hope Mac tags me."

"Don't be so anxious to die, Boot," admonished O'Toole, a high-browed private. "But don't worry; there's only six fun plugs. You ride down with the rest of the women . . . er, excuse me, Lieutenant. I didn't—"

"No problem, Private." Buccari yawned.

"Sir, what's it like—the planet?" asked Chastain, huge—a giant—his cow eyes wide with innocent alarm. "Can you breathe the air? What are we going to do, huh, sir?"

"Got no choice, pea brain," said Petit, heavy-bearded, barrel-chested, and lantern-jawed. "What else we going to do—hold our breath?"

The giant hung his head, embarrassed.

"Easy, Petit," Tatum warned. "Let Jocko ask his questions."

"Good. It looks real good," Buccari replied. "We got a breathable atmosphere. We know that much. Survey systems are still in bad shape. We should have a reasonable planet profile in a few hours, but Private Petit is right—we don't have much of a choice." She was tired, hungry, and thirsty. Too excited to sleep, she could not ignore her stomach. She pushed by the marines and aimed her body for the galley.

"Where's Corporal Mac?" she asked as she grabbed a squeeze container and drew off some soup. It was hot, deliciously warming her hands.

"Lander bay, Lieutenant," Tatum replied. "Him and the sergeant major are helping Jones configure penetrators." As he spoke, the afterhatch yawned open and Lander Boatswain

Jones, Corporal MacArthur, and a senior enlisted marine floated onto the mess decks.

"Lieutenant, checking good!" the boatswain roared. "Heard the skinny from Ensign Hudson. You whupped up on those bugs. Burned three of them! Flamed butt!"

"Not sure whose butt got flamed, Boats," Buccari replied. "Let's worry about getting everyone down, shall we. Everything ready?"

"You bet, sir. Checking good, with you steering and me flapping," Jones crowed. "Been telling Sarge here how good you are. These boot chewers don't believe you're a legend."

"Throttle back," Buccari said, smiling weakly, "and stop spewing."

"She's Superwoman, er ... excuse me, Lieutenant," Jones persisted. "Lieutenant Buccari and me've won the fleet EPL competitions three years running. No one's ever won it more than twice, 'cept us."

"Don't believe it," Buccari smirked, "especially the part about him being the reason why. I could have done it with Fenstermacher."

"Aw, Lieutenant! Hurt me sorely ..." Jones groaned.

"Lieutenant," MacArthur said, "everyone knows you're the best pilot in the fleet." The lithe, square-shouldered marine stared squarely into her eyes, his own pewter-gray eyes alert and clear. Buccari looked at the deck.

"Mac thinks you're pretty, too, Lieutenant," Chastain said. The marines hooted and banged their bootheels together.

"Why, Corporal!" Buccari declared, pivoting sharply to confront the squad leader. "Thank you. I bet you say that about all the officers."

"Eh ..." MacArthur stammered, blushing as he pushed the hood from his wide forehead. "Hardly, sir—er ... I mean, you're welcome, sir. No disrespect intended." He shot Chastain a withering glare, his fine features revealing determination more than anger.

"You can't be denying your fame, Lieutenant," interrupted the sergeant major, a chesty, square-jawed, broken-veined space veteran. "Sergeant Major Shannon, sir."

"My pleasure, Sergeant Major," she said, turning to meet the newcomer. "I've seen you around the mothership. Sorry we didn't get to meet earlier, but we've been busy." She put out her hand. Shannon enveloped it.

"I would agree, sir," Shannon said. "Very busy."

"You were evidently caught on board by accident?" she asked.

"Yes, sir," the sergeant said. "I was inspecting MacArthur's squad when GQ sounded. Just my luck."

"I hope your luck gets better, Sergeant Major," Buccari said.

FIVE

ON THE GROUND

Buccari moved into the lander bay and found Boatswain Jones, slickly burly in his silver pressure suit, floating at the EPL hatch.

"All strapped in. All injection units checking good," he told her.

"Let's hustle," Buccari said, "before they get claustrophobic."

She made final adjustments to her pressure suit and then dove into the open lander hatch. With practiced agility, she moved forward in the craft, pulling herself into the single pilot station. Positioned in the acceleration seat, she donned her helmet, connected harness and comm fittings, and commenced preflight checkout of the Endoatmospheric Planetary Lander—the apple.

"Compute! Systems status—initiate," she barked. "Pilot Buccari."

Ladder lights on the power console sequenced, and the EPL's control computer replied with a machine-generated voice: "Pilot Buccari. Control authorizations check. Pilot has command."

"Launch sequence," she ordered, adjusting to the snug cockpit.

"All systems checking good, sir," Jones reported from his station.

"Boats, with you onboard I'd be surprised if they didn't," Buccari acknowledged.

They ran through prestart and start checklists. The lander was in good order, and the injection systems displayed green lights. Buccari felt anxious for the marines stuffed into their penetrator casings—human artillery shells.

"Stand by to jettison EPL!" Buccari announced over the radio.

"Apple cleared to launch," Hudson responded. "Report clear. Rendezvous will be launch plus ninety-three. One orbit. Control set to button four. You copy?"

"Roger, launch plus ninety-three; button four. EPL retros in two minutes. Counting down." Buccari settled into the pilot's seat, anticipating the launch of the lander from the corvette, which was itself launched from a larger ship—a spawn from a spawn, each with diminishing purposes, powers, and ranges. But this was her vessel. She was pilot.

To starboard the bay doors yawned smoothly open. An overwhelming blackness crept through the widening aperture. Buccari cut the lights in the cockpit, cursing herself for waiting too long to start night vision adaptation. Red light bathed the cockpit, and a constellation of reflections fell back at her from the umbrella of the canopy. She palmed down the intensity. The white brilliance of genuine stars blossomed.

Vibration hummed through metal; the lander moved outboard to starboard, pushed by a spidery gantry crane, until it was clear of the confined EPL bay. Ahead were the first signs of sunrise, a perfect red-gold arc starkly defining the limb of the ebony planet, silhouetting it against the utter blackness of space. Buccari released the attachment fitting, fired a micropulse on the port maneuvering rockets to initiate a separation rate, and reported "Clear" back to Hudson. At precisely the correct moment she rolled the lander on its back and commenced retrofire, falling toward the dark predawn. The corvette, glinting in the rising sun, retreated on its orbital trajectory and disappeared into black infinity. The flowering sun-star, Rex-Kaliph, climbed rapidly over the limb of the planet—a harsh, glaring blossom of light.

During the helpless waiting and hard chopping turbulence of reentry Buccari considered her drop target. The granite-topped plateau chosen for the landing site was located in the interior of the largest of the planet's four continents. Curving around the plateau was a major river, providing excellent navigational references. A spectacular chain of mountains to the west was a concern; radar returns indicated peaks in excess of eight thousand meters—geological giants. The mountains were ominous, but radar returns also showed the expansive plateau to be hard and flat—an ideal landing site. Hudson had discovered the plateau and unromantically christened it "Landing Site Alpha." Everyone else called it Hudson's Plateau.

Turbulence dampened sharply, and Buccari noticed the EPL's external skin temperatures stabilizing. Reentry was almost complete.

"Flight profile," she demanded. The computer echoed her words, and an abstract presentation of the digital flight envelope, complete with altitude, heading, and attitude readouts, unfolded on the navigation display. The computer began aurally reporting the amount of air density buildup as a function of temperature and pressure altitude.

"Suspend," she ordered. Audio cues abruptly halted. Within minutes the aerodynamic flight symbol fluttered on and held steady, the atmosphere finally biting hard enough to make the lander an airplane.

"Reentry complete, Boats," she said. "Apple's flying." She disabled the autopilot.

"Aye, checking good," the boatswain replied. "Everyone's breathing."

After a wide turn to lose altitude Buccari initiated a course correction, lining the EPL up with the run-in trajectory, moving the sun dead astern. Inverted, she looked through the top of the canopy and made out physical features of the planet. Hudson's Plateau was somewhere dead ahead, invisible, still shrouded in sun-shattered haze. Satisfied with course and position, she rolled upright. The planet moved beneath her, the cloud deck thinning.

"All right, marines!" she broadcast on the intercom, her audience six human projectiles bound tightly into torpedolike shrouds. "Approaching zone. Ejection as briefed. Green light. Counting down . . . four . . . three . . . two . . . one. Bingo!"

The EPL shuddered. In less than a second six penetrators ripple-fired from the tail. Jones came up on the intercom: "Penetrators cleared. Ejection port closed. Nav track good. Fuel pressures in the green. Gun barrels hot. Checking good, sir."

Buccari returned the lander to computer control.

"Okay, Boats. Ignition in five seconds. Checking good,

checking good." Buccari flattened against her seat and awaited
the massive kick of the EPL's engines.

The penetrators streaked into the atmosphere, glowing
brighter and whiter, spreading linearly, each canister containing
a living soul with little to do but impotently count the eternal
seconds. Below, unseen, the dawn's slanted light revealed a
wide expanse of verdant prairie, softly mottled. The river, jade-
colored in the morning sun and steeped in wispy fog, meandered with little purpose but with certain power. To the west
snow-blanketed mountains, radiantly pink, reflected the morning sun, but the senses of the men in the streaking cones were
aware only of their own mortal being—of pulse and respiration
and sweat.

Shannon sometimes considered the lateral acceleration to be
the worst part of the trip—as if he were going to lose his
lunch. It lasted fifteen eternal seconds, the penetrators accelerating in the opposite trajectory of the hypermach lander, decelerating relative to the ground. He smelled the bitter residue of
rocket fuel left behind after the spent motor had separated from
the canister.

He was free-falling feetfirst in a pressurized titanium abla-
tive coffin. Waiting. Waiting in endless anticipation for separation retrofire, which was truly the worst part of the trip. He
checked disconnects for the third time, adjusted his helmet yet
again, and listened to the rasp of his breathing through the
forced-flow oxygen mask. Temperature increased rapidly. After
another eternity he looked at his altimeter, still off the thirty-
kilometer scale. He went through the checks again.

The altimeter finally registered. Shannon waited, ear canals
working to keep up with the compression schedule. He yawned
and moved his jaw, ears and sinuses popping again and again.
Long minutes rattled by. The altimeter unwound with increasing speed; the retros would be firing soon. He straightened his
spine and positioned his head squarely over his neck, shoulders
rolled back. One last look at the altimeter. He closed his eyes
tight!

Whooom! His whole being jarred as if some giant had taken
a club and swung it straight up at his feet. His knees buckled,
but the active retro-harness supported his back and torso; his
spine ached at the base of his neck; his brain felt fuzzy, almost
unconscious. The next one would be stronger. Fifteen seconds
after the first jolt—*Whooom!*—another charge fired from the

base of the cone, an explosive blast directed straight down at the planet, a cannon shot trying to propel his shell back into space. And ten seconds later, yet another. *Whooom!*

Shannon shook the fog from his stunned brain. His rate of descent was in the safety range. He reached down and pulled the separation release, trying to beat the automatic sequence, but the onboard processor was faster. He heard and felt the shrill rattle of his drogue shoot deploying overhead, and he prepared himself for another jolt, a very welcome one—the jolt of his parafoil filling with air.

As usual the benevolent and satisfying *ka-thump* flushed away Shannon's anxieties. With the parafoil deployed and sta-bilized, the bottom two-thirds of his penetrator slipped smooth-ly from his body, the reentry canister plummeting groundward. Dangling against the variegated backdrop of the planet below, Shannon could see his size-twelve boots encased in impact webbing, still attached to the control section around his belt. He cleared the webbing and stowed it. Scanning the target area, he picked up the loop of the river and adjusted his drift. On course, target in sight. Reaching up, Shannon slipped the quick-release fittings on the penetrator's aerodynamic top sec-tion; the shell structure oscillated in the slipstream. With the last fitting uncoupled, it slid smoothly along a tubular back-pack railing until it was secured between his shoulders like the shell of a turtle.

Shannon checked his men. Something was wrong with number five—Private Chastain. Five was drifting noticeably downwind, falling out of the bearing line. At worst Chastain was already dead, suffocated or traumatically exposed by a pressure failure. At best he was simply unconscious, knocked out by bad positioning or a faulty harness during the retro-blasts.

Shannon keyed the transmit button on his control belt with a series of quick double pulses followed by a single pulse cor-responding to his own position in the drop. After a short pause he was rewarded with a short double click—Petit—another short pause, and then three mike clicks—O'Toole—followed quickly by four—Tatum. A long, empty pause ensued—finally, six clicks in three quick pairs. Six was the squad leader, MacArthur. Number five, Chastain, was not in the game.

Shannon keyed his UHF: "Six, stick with five. Proceed to Alpha. Standard procedures. Copy?"

"Six copies," MacArthur's voice came back matter-of-factly.

Shannon swung around to reestablish contact with the landing site. A turbulent layer of clouds boiled up from behind the mountains to the west and south. Ragged pinnacles, their snow-covered granite tops easily reaching past his altitude, Shannon moved his gaze downward and observed the sinuous loop of the river delineating his target. He shook out his control shrouds and deployed his high-lift, high-drag secondary. Lieutenant Buccari had put them right on target—not bad for a Mach-twenty pass. Shannon estimated less than thirty minutes to touchdown. He checked his altimeter and, breaking regs, loosened his oxygen mask to sniff the rarefied atmosphere. A hint of sulfur? It was cold—colder than he had expected.

Shannon reviewed the preflight briefing. Hudson's Plateau was immense—fifty kilometers from the cliffs at the river's edge to the first line of jagged mountains. And high—over two thousand meters above sea level and over a thousand meters above the river valley. The great river encircled most of the plateau, and the mountains to the south and west encompassed the rest. As Shannon glided over the precipice marking the edge of the plateau, he detected banks of steam spewing from the cliffs. Fingers and spirals of vapor broke loose and sailed briefly in the wind before dissipating. Lakes dotted the granite plain, and a dragon's spine of rocky karsts tailed down from the awesome mountains. Ensign Hudson had described a central lake with three islands that was to mark their primary landing site on the plateau, and there it was, nestled against the spine.

The last five hundred meters of a drop were the most interesting. Topography that had been one-dimensional at five thousand meters pushed upward into view. Valleys and mountains, hills and cliffs, rifts and shadows reached out, providing perspective and depth. The pale granite of the high plateau rose to meet him. Shannon located his quick-release fittings one last time and tightened his helmet strap. Flat rocks streaked with crimson and gold lichen skimmed beneath his feet. He yanked on his risers, killing forward velocity and stalling the leading edge of his foil. He took four chopping steps and stopped—a stranger on a new world.

It was very cold.

MacArthur watched Chastain float away from the line of bearing. He locked down his turtle shell and shucked off his harness webbing. Chastain was drifting to the south and losing ground to the east. They were in for a hike. The other parafoils disappeared against the dark backdrop of the mountains.

As Chastain's foil spiraled mindlessly downward, MacArthur's scrutiny went to the innocent-appearing terrain. Treeless, rolling plains stretched northward, meeting the horizon in an indistinct haze. To the south the river curved toward them, its main watercourse spreading in interwoven braids across sand and gravel bars, the sun glinting dully from the many channels of the sinuous waterway. It was as if four or five rivers had collided together, converging and diverging around shoals and islands, unable to agree within which bank to flow.

Beyond the river to the south the ground climbed into ragged foothills and beyond that to distant, hoary mountains. Huge clouds roiled around the shoulders and heads of the massive peaks, and a thick layer of altocumulus poured through valleys rife with blue-green glaciers.

The rolling prairie land below, mottled brown and green, took on definition. The wind gathered strength and veered from the north. They were being blown closer to the river, but there was ample room; a spreading valley lay between them and the larger river. Two symmetrical peaks venting steam and smoke marked the head of the valley.

At seven hundred meters MacArthur looked down for another check. Something was peculiar—the brown and green pattern of the land slowly shifted; *the ground itself was moving*. He stared harder and, doubting his vision, saw animals in countless numbers. A vast herd of grazing animals covered the visible plain! Several herds, and probably herds of different animals. The masses directly below were a deep reddish-brown. Off to both sides and randomly in the distance he could see smaller groups, lighter-colored—golden, almost yellow in tint.

MacArthur verified the drift rate. With some maneuvering he could avoid falling into the herd; its ranks thinned toward the head of the valley, and the wind was bearing him away. Chastain, heavier and unguided, was falling into their midst. He should stay near Chastain, but Chastain could already be dead. Why get caught in a stampede?

But perhaps Chastain was only unconscious and needed first aid. Perhaps Chastain would suffocate in his oxygen mask. Maybe Chastain's parafoil would catch the strong surface wind and drag him around the countryside; it was windy enough to threaten both men with that prospect. MacArthur grabbed his assault rifle from its attachment point on his turtle pack, checked the magazine, and prepared for landing.

The descent, the illusion of holding gravity at bay, had lasted almost an hour, but the inevitable reality of the looming surface became evident. The animals took individual shapes, round-shouldered, big-headed, and short-horned with shaggy coats and thick legs—not unlike Earth buffalo. MacArthur watched Chastain's deadweight landing, practically on the backs of the large beasts. As when a helicopter landed in a wheat field or a rock was thrown into a still pond, the animals, sensing Chastain's arrival, recoiled in a pattern of expanding ripples, and the area around Chastain's point of impact cleared rapidly. Chunks of turf and dirt flew into the air, propelled by the bucking and kicking creatures. The nearer animals surged against their neighbors, and soon a circular area within three hundred meters of the fallen man's flapping parafoil was clear of the large beasts.

Chastain's inert form collapsed bonelessly onto the ground, face first and helmet bouncing. His parafoil dumped its load and collapsed, only to flutter erect with fitful gusts of air, tugging Chastain's large body across the dung-spotted terrain in slow jerks. MacArthur, still high in the air, maneuvered downwind, turned into the wind, and landed squarely in the middle of Chastain's luffing foil. Grabbing his own shrouds, MacArthur spilled air and released his quick disconnects. He noticed absently that the ground was soft, boglike, but dry and springy. Tundra! It was tundra or taiga plains, like the far north of Canada. Memory invoked the hiking and hunting experiences of his youth. It required effort to walk.

After bundling both foils and securing them with shroud lines, MacArthur struggled to clear Chastain from his rig. He lifted the marine's brawny shoulders from the dung-strewn ground—and dropped him! Slugs! Black, amorphous creatures as big as his thumb exploded from the heap of greenish-black dung on which Chastain had come to rest. A host of squirming vermin slithered from the disturbed manure. Most of the wiggling slugs burrowed industriously into the porous undergrowth, but dozens flowed over the prostrate marine. Fighting his repugnance and checking the ground under his own boots, MacArthur gingerly rolled the injured man over, pulled him onto some reasonably clear ground, and flicked off the slimy worms with his gloved hand. The dropping slugs disappeared immediately into the tundra.

Chastain was breathing but unconscious, nothing obviously broken. MacArthur disconnected him from his harness, allowing the massive pack to fall away. He rolled the big man over on the soft ground, slid open his visor, and released his oxygen mask. Chastain shuddered; his eyes flashed open. He was wall-eyed with panic; his mouth gaped, and he inhaled, only to exhale violently, throwing hands over his mouth and nose, jerking his head spasmodically back and forth.

"Can't breathe!" Chastain retched, exhaling words from empty lungs. "Can't bre—" Chastain's groping hands found his mask; he pulled it over his face, wild eyes narrowing to slits. He attempted to sit up, but a stab of pain shot through his body—he stiffened and fell supine, holding his mask to his face with both hands desperately, like a drowning man with a life preserver.

MacArthur reached to remove his own mask. No sooner had he broken the face seal than he was stricken with an acrid pungency, an odor beyond description and magnitude. Tears welled, and sharp pain penetrated nostrils and sinuses. He fell to a knee, trying to expel the painful sensation from his nose and lungs. Then he slammed his breathing apparatus back to his face and dared to breathe. Nausea surged through him. Fighting panic, he sucked in a lungful of oxygen.

MacArthur's breathing passages slowly cleared, but a sour, metallic taste clung to his palate. He looked at Chastain; both men were frightened. Their only communication alternative besides sign language was the radio. MacArthur broke regs and activated his transmitter.

"Air's no good. Big trouble, Jocko," MacArthur gasped, looking around, checking the slowly moving herd. The buffalo had calmed and were grazing on the spongy, dung-spotted turf. A few had moved closer, although none approached closer than two hundred meters. The motley red-brown beasts were massive, as tall at the shoulder as a man, with fur-shrouded fat humps similar to those of prehistoric mastodons or musk oxen. Mature animals carried a stubby but sharply hooked rack of black horn.

MacArthur stood erect and looked down at Chastain. The big man was pale and wide-eyed, still suffering from his dose of atmosphere. "Where you hurt, Jocko?" MacArthur asked.

Chastain closed his eyes, his breathing rapid. His hand activated his transmitter. "My back. Multiple retro—hit like a ton of bricks. Musta blacked out. What we going to do, Mac?"

MacArthur, still dizzy, tried to think. Their breathing systems would supply oxygen for two to four hours at the most, probably closer to two, considering the stress.

"Let's move. Can you walk?" he asked, fearing the worst.

"Don't know," Chastain responded. He tentatively rolled onto his knees. Between the two of them they were able to hoist Chastain erect, but only barely. Hunchbacked, listing heavily to his right side, Chastain staggered down the decline, struggling to lift his feet from the indentations caused by his ponderous weight.

MacArthur shouldered his pack and gathered the fluttering parafoils. An idea came to him. He removed his pack and attached it to Chastain's, arranging the turtle packs in tandem. He secured both parafoils to the assembled mass and gingerly redeployed the foils in the freshening wind. To the skittish dismay of the buffalo, the parafoils billowed open and jolted their load over the uneven terrain. Using harness webbing for a lanyard, MacArthur followed the wind-powered sled, breaking into a trot to keep pace. He quickly caught up with his crippled cohort.

"How you doing, Jocko?" MacArthur asked over the UHF as he pulled abreast, holding the jerking cargo back against the strong winds.

"Not sure I can, Mac," Chastain gasped, his sweaty face ashen.

"Yes, you can, Jocko. If I lose sight of you, I'll wait."

Chastain nodded, and MacArthur pulled ahead. Despite his words, MacArthur was worried. How could they escape what they could not see?

The terrain transformed as they descended. Crystalline escarpments spotted with livid lichen protruded from the taiga, the footing firmed, and the ground lost its sponginess. As MacArthur topped a small rise, he spotted a line of scraggly yellow-trunked trees. Beyond the trees the valley expanded and descended steeply into the haze. MacArthur knew the valley ended at the great river, but he also knew the lower they descended, the higher they eventually would have to climb.

"You'll see some trees in the distance, to the right. I'm heading for them. We'll check out the air when we get there. Keep it in gear, marine!" MacArthur exhorted Chastain over the radio, trying to reassure himself as well as to keep Chastain moving.

MacArthur clattered ahead, moving at a jerky lope, the hard

shells of the turtle packs careening off the rocks. The wind abated, no longer carrying the urgent power evident on the higher terrain. MacArthur had to pull the equipment through swales and over gentle ridges. After an hour, sweat-soaked and exhausted, he gained the wind-bent trees he had seen from the top of the valley and sat heavily on one of the many quartz-veined boulders jumbling the area. He rested head and arms on trembling knees; a gnarled and twisted tree, its trunk rough and mustard-colored, its spiky needles green-gray, provided an oasis of cold shade.

It felt exquisite to rest, but survival fears held sway. Insulated by his helmet, MacArthur could hear only the pounding of his heart and the rasping of his lungs. He lifted his head and checked the thin stand of trees. Five paces distant a clear spring bubbled from a flower-shrouded seep, forming an energetic rivulet that meandered out of sight over granite steps. The sight of the water triggered a desperate thirst.

MacArthur fatalistically inhaled a full breath of oxygen and fingered the fitting on his mask. Loosening his helmet, he let the mask drop from his face. An insistent current of chilly air caressed his sweaty cheeks. He pulled off his helmet. His hearing was assaulted by the persistent symphony of nature, and a brittle breeze swept over his exposed neck and brow. Still holding his breath, he shivered.

Positioning his mask near his face, MacArthur partially exhaled and then cautiously sniffed the air. It smelled horrible: an offending stench of incredible magnitude—terrible odors, a bitter conglomeration of offal, carrion, sewage, and burning chemicals so persistent and penetrating that all senses were assailed and dulled. His body begged to collapse into some minimal essence, to sleep, to escape. His head ached. His eyes watered, but somehow he knew that it was not fatal. He could breathe; his lungs could process the atmosphere. He could breathe without the involuntary spasmodic rejection experienced in the landing zone. It was horrible, but it was air, and the prospect of running out of oxygen lost its urgency, if not its fear.

He looked down at the clear spring at his feet. Water, yes. It had to be. What did it matter that the air was breathable, if the water was undrinkable? Without water they would die, too. They were marooned.

Casting helmet and mask aside, MacArthur fell to his knees. He sniffed at the pulsing fluid, but smelled only the horrid air.

He sipped at the water, trying merely to sample it, but thirst trampled caution, and he drank noisily of the sweet liquid.

SIX

CLIFF DWELLERS

The gods of the sky were angry, and Brappa bore witness to their displeasure. Brappa and the other sentries had seen fliers descending from the heavens. They had not been drunk on thickweed. There had been thunder in the morning skies and star bursts to the east. Not lightning but bright blossoms of red and yellow—in a sky devoid of clouds! After the brilliant lights came more terrible noises, more thunder! So loud, his ears still rang. And from out of the bright fires and noise came the four fliers, high overhead in the cold, liftless morning skies, flying toward the lakes.

Brappa, son-of-Braan, lead sentry of the morning watch, danced nimbly down the precipitous granite face. The golden glow of dawn overflowed into the river valley, illuminating and melting the thin crust of frost decorating the upper rim. He chased the sunrise down the chasm's walls, jumping lightly into the air every few steps, spreading diaphanous membranes and gliding softly to his next landing, there to run three or four landbound steps and jump and glide again. His leaps covered many spans. If he had wanted to, he could have soared the entire descent, but he needed time to think.

Brappa passed a vent and relished the sulfurous wetness, the vaporous plume quickly dissipating in the cold air. His descent brought him into an ever-increasing field of spewing mists and steam vapors, the air redolent of minerals and humidity. He neared the lacework of terraces that defined his colony's homes. The river, visible through wisps of steam, moved powerfully, its might channeled within the cliff-sided chasm, slate-gray in the early light, the sun not yet able to mottle its turbulent surface with familiar splotches of pale green and white.

Brappa, son-of-Braan, landed softly on the moist granite terrace before the assembly portal. Sheltered above by a ragged cornice of glistening quartz-veined rock, the shelf was the largest terrace on the cliff, ten spans deep at its widest point and running for more than seventy along the sheer face. A low, randomly crenellated wall bordered its precipitous edge. Between the crenellations grew an abundance of brilliantly flowering plants giving off a heady conglomeration of aromas. Beyond the wall steam poured upward from the river chasm, showering the plants in a persistent mist through which sunlight dappled and danced in beaded rainbows.

Penetrating the cliff face was a peaked arch looming two full spans higher than Brappa's knobby head—the assembly portal, crafted of obsidian and mounted with a massive lintel of contrasting white jade. Skillfully sculpted pink marble boulders stood at the shoulders of the entryway, spreading outward in diminishing sizes. Gurgling water splashed over the boulders, draining into pools. Rock-lined gutters at the base of the cliff face carried the waters away. An ancient foot-worn stairway elegantly hewn in the granite bedrock emerged from the rough terrace and climbed for thirty wide steps evenly into the cavern.

Brappa sedately folded his wings into a complex double overlap and climbed the steps. Dark-mantled and humpbacked, he had bowed legs and a head shaped like a black mattock. Sinewy, hard-muscled forearms, each with three slender digits and a long opposed thumb, hung past his knees. A soft pelt of fine black fur covered his body except for his chest and belly, which were covered with longer cream-colored fur, the markings of a flying cliff dweller—a hunter. Less than half a span in height, but he was still young.

Three similarly shaped but quite taller figures appeared at the threshold of the portal. These creatures' heads and necks were covered with charcoal fur similar to that of the smaller figure, but their body fur was completely cream-colored. They were guilders, their heads large and rounded, whereas the shorter figure's crown revealed a marked protuberance. Over the eons the echo-ranging and soaring abilities of the larger guilders had atrophied, and their bodies had evolved for different needs. Guilders were taller, heavier, more skillful, and in many ways more intelligent. Hunters would say guilders were less brave.

The tallest guilder was ancient and wore a necklace of beaded emeralds and garnets, the badge of the gardener guild. Brappa halted and bowed low, hands flat with palms up, in obeisance to the council member. Brappa had much to say, but the rules required silence.

"Why art thou here, hunter?" the council elder whistled ceremoniously but with a tremor. He, too, had heard the distant thunder.

"I bid thee long life, elder. On orders from Kuudor, captain-of-the-sentry, Excellency, I am the morning watch, bearing tidings of strange happenings," Brappa squeaked and chirped.

"It has been spoken. Follow," the old one commanded glumly as he turned slowly and retraced his steps. The other guilders, apprentices, resumed subservient positions inside the great portal entryway.

Brappa followed the elder into the antechambers. Vaulted arches and delicate columns of wondrous craftsmanship stretched ever higher as they progressed down the widening hallway; intricately carved alabaster and jade mosaics lined smoothly polished alcoves. The domed assembly hall, a cavernous amphitheater over fifty spans square, opened before them, illuminated by myriad guttering spirit lamps flickering their yellowish glow.

Brappa had attended assembly before, and the young hunter was conditioned to the anonymity of the crowd and the hushed babble of the masses. On this morning the great hall was empty. Water gurgled through overhead aqueducts, and the echoes of their shuffling footfalls seemed deafening. Brappa's talons clicked on the sparkling stone inlays of the black marble floors. The brittle silence of the empty hall discomfited him, but as a hunter—even if only a sentry—he displayed courage. With repressed disdain he noticed guild apprentices pushing mops and sponges, laboring to stay ahead of the natural condensation and humidity of their labyrinth. Hunters did not push mops.

Brappa and his escort skirted the grand hall and mounted a divided stairway curving around each side of a marble balcony cantilevered from the stone walls. Atop the stairs the elder signaled for Brappa to wait, languidly waving a bony hand toward the balcony. As the ancient disappeared from sight behind staggered rows of massive columns, Brappa squatted on a varnished wooden perch. He was intrigued by the intricate drainage system running around the periphery of the great hall; most of the channels were not visible from the lower levels. He traced the paths and confluences of the aqueducts and cascades as they drained the upper levels and brought the water out of the rock for use by the commune, both as aqua vitae and as natural art.

Braan, leader-of-hunters, stood in the stone dock as the old one entered the council chambers. The elder took his ordered position, that of a subordinate, at the end of the black marble table. Braan knew the gardener had seen over a hundred winters, yet he was still the youngest of the eleven ancients. There were no hunters on the dweller council, for hunters did not live long enough. Cliff dwellers, hunters and guilders together, had no leader, only the eldest—Koop-the-facilitator. Koop, wearing the green jade of the fisher guild, was exquisitely ancient, his unruly head fur completely turned to radiant white.

"Braan, clan of Soong, leader-of-hunters, speak thou for the sentry?" old Koop twittered.

Braan, snout gruesomely scarred and head fur streaked with white, was not the oldest hunter, yet he was the leader of all hunters, for he was the most able. As leader of the hunters Braan frequently addressed the elders. A leather thong adorned his neck out of respect.

"He is of my blood. His words art mine, Excellency," Braan said.

"What of the news?" Koop asked directly, rudely ignoring convention.

Braan was not offended, for the facilitator was old and meant no harm. "Facilitator, I know only rumors. Truth can best be defined by those who bear witness. I confess impatience. I fetch the sentry." He did not wait for permission but hopped from the dock and darted through the maze of columns.

The leader-of-hunters found the alert sentry on his feet, head bowed respectfully. It had been a full cycle of the large moon since Braan-the-father had left on the salt mission. Brappa-the-son had stood a sentry tour in the interim. Braan solemnly returned his scion's honorable bow and then chucked him under his long chin. The son slowly looked up and displayed multiple rows of tiny razor-sharp teeth in a joyful grin. Braan slapped his son on the back and pushed him firmly into the chambers.

Braan's pride was well served. Brappa, son-of-Braan, took the dock with dignity and poise. The novice delivered his scanty details firmly and was not shaken when the elders, particularly the steam users and stone carvers, asked probing questions. Braan listened silently, for the facts were confusing. His son, the lead morning sentry, had seen flying creatures that were neither hunter nor eagle, nor were they the angry sounding machines of the legendary bear people. A manifestation of the gods? The perplexed elders slumped on their perches and whispered among themselves. Brappa, son-of-Braan, stood silently, waiting.

Unbidden, Braan moved before the council. "Elders, a proposal."

"Proceed, hunter," said Koop-the-facilitator, sorely fatigued.

"It is feared gods have descended upon the land, or perhaps bear people of myth have returned. This must be investigated with a hunter reconnaissance to the lakes. If gods or bear people have descended to the ground, we will find them. If bear people, we will defend ourselves. If gods, then we will show reverence. Long life."

Braan pivoted, chirped for Brappa to follow, and marched from the chambers, talons clicking with impunity.

Braan strode swiftly through the assembly hall and proceeded outside onto the wide terrace, pausing only to shake out his membranes. He marched up a stone ramp onto a crenellation in the flower-bedecked wall and pushed himself gracefully out over the steam-filled abyss. Brappa, but two steps behind, duplicated every move. The hunters, father and son in tight formation, settled into a swooping glide, searching for rising currents of air. Picking up speed, they banked sharply downriver, leaving the wide terrace in the foggy steam.

After echo-ranging their way along the cliff walls and riding the meager morning convection currents, the two fliers emerged from the broken strands of steam. Flapping huge wings with slow, silent beats to break their advance, they landed softly on the terrace of the hunter chief's residence. The enveloping steam was less dense at this higher altitude, and warrens of hunter residences could be seen pockmarking the face of the rocky cliffside. Cooking smells blended with the mineral-rich steam, pleasantly tempting olfactory receptors. The residence was distinguished by a cleverly crafted perimeter wall of black marble and gold inlay—a gift to Braan's legendary great-grandfather Soong from the stone carver guild in appreciation for routing the eagles.

Ki, wife of Braan and mother of Brappa, possessed the acute hearing of all dwellers. She waited on the narrow terrace, holding an infant on her hip. Ecstasy at seeing both son and husband radiated from her countenance. She stood silently until Braan removed the leather thong from around his neck.

The mother commenced the welcome. "Welcome home, honored husband. And welcome, my beloved son," Ki warbled, and bowed, averting eye contact.

Brappa returned the bow. The father remained silent.

"'Tis good to be returned to the warm mists of my mother's home. Sentry duty is cold, but . . . but I do well. I have friends," Brappa replied, also avoiding his mother's eyes. "Please forgive my ill-chosen words, for I meant not to complain."

"I heard no complaint, son-of-mine. It has been twenty days since thou went to duty, and thou art grown even more," she graciously spoke.

"Thank thee, my mother, for so saying. Thou art kind and generous," Brappa responded properly, compliment for compliment.

The infant, Brappa's sister, quiet to this point, lost patience with the formal progress of the reunion. She waved skinny arms, her incipient wings brushing the mother's face. She yelled, her high-pitched voice and nascent echo-ranging system clashing together. Braan, chuckling, relieved his wife of the tiny burden, encompassing the chick with his wings. The infant squealed with the rough handling, happy to have gained her objective. Custom satisfied, son and mother also hugged, Brappa's wings overlapping and enveloping Ki's diminutive form. They were unconcerned about the overt familiarity; the mists of the river valley were thick this morning, and hunters were perversely proud of their affections. And at this elevation they were among only hunter clans.

Nevertheless, they politely moved their embraces and good feelings into the low-ceilinged domicile, a precisely chiseled cave with the surpassing luxury of six chambers, unique in that it did not connect with neighboring caves. It had two other exits—a mixed blessing. Hidden and small, the exits provided ventilation and emergency egress, but they were also avenues for predators. Eagles, growlers, and rockdogs occasionally still evaded sentries, terrorizing the cliff dwellers, particularly the hunters, whose homes honeycombed the higher cliffs. Spirit lamps and the familiar gurgle of rapidly moving water welcomed the family as they stepped inside, and the odor of baking fish and green onion soup combined with other smells of hearth and home.

They ate quickly and noisily. Brappa asked his father about his foray to the northern salt flats, but Braan had little to tell. A routine salt mission: the great herds were migrating, and the smell was worse than the memory of it. They had seen whiterumps, field dragon, and many, many eagles. Growlers had been encountered, but fortunately the hunters had avoided serious conflict. The predators were glutted with the flesh of the buffalo, typical for this time of year. The quota demands had required a large group of salt bearers. Braan wished for an easier solution to satisfying the dwellers' increasing appetite for salt. The expeditions were too big, too vulnerable.

Braan indicated he was through, and the family ceased eating. He looked at his son.

"Report to the sentry captain and secure permission for three capable sentries to accompany warriors on a reconnaissance mission. I request thee be included, although it is Kuudor's choice. Present the sentry captain with my respects and inform him the expedition will depart on the afternoon thermals. Go," Braan commanded.

Brappa acknowledged, his excitement poorly suppressed. Stopping only to give his mother a fleeting glance, the sentry darted through the home, jumped on the low terrace wall, and leapt into the mists, wings popping loudly as he heaved air downward.

Ki slowly followed her last living son to the terrace and watched him depart, as wives and mothers of hunters had watched their fathers, husbands, and sons generation upon generation. Ki had already lost two sons, stout and brave—and so young. Too young.

"He is ready," Ki spoke sadly. She turned to stare into her husband's eyes, as she did only when they were alone. "Take care of my son."

It was a plea and a command. Braan moved close to his wife and held her face in his hands, rubbing her forehead against his, softly transmitting and receiving sonic bursts. Ki stepped backward, trying to smile, large eyes welling with moisture. Her husband had only just returned from one dangerous mission and was about to embark on another, taking with him her remaining male-child. Hunters lived short lives of endless struggle. Her husband was the leader of all hunters. Duty was his touchstone, and death his faithful companion.

"And please take care of yourself, glorious husband." She bowed.

Braan gracefully returned the bow. The hunter stood erect and silently padded into one of the smaller chambers. Opening the hidebound wooden chest that he had closed tightly just days before, Braan extracted his leather armor, iron knife, and shortbow and quiver. He somberly donned the equipment and, pausing only to squeeze his wife's hands, departed over the edge, wings whipcracking steamy air. Echoes died quickly in the mist.

The moaning had stopped—soft, gently expulsive sounds like a distant, plaintive foghorn. Rounding the windswept lakeshore, Shannon felt as if they were being watched. He was profoundly relieved to make the shelter of the yellow-barked trees.

"Found . . . a cave, Sarge," Petit gasped. The marine lay in a heap behind a scraggly log, barrel chest heaving for air. Shannon dropped to a knee behind the fallen sprucelike tree and tried to control his own breathing. He could discern little about the cave; the small opening was elevated, and the shaft—if it was a shaft—dipped sharply away. A rocky overhang shadowed the entrance area. Tatum, fifty meters ahead, leaned heavily against large rocks beneath the cave. Shannon looked down the hill and traced their path across the plateau.

After leaving the higher ground of their landing, the terrain near the lake had deteriorated into spongy tundra. Game trails provided paths but also tended to meander and disappear into the reed-choked water. Magnificent white blossoms grew in abundance, their vines intertwining with lake reeds and tundra vegetation. The flowers sprouted from bulbous nodules in the vines. Shannon made a mental note to investigate them as a food possibility. But those thoughts were dispelled by the desultory moaning that came from all around them yet came from nowhere.

His concentration was taxed. Carrying thirty kilos of equipment made every trudging footstep an epic effort, and the adrenaline rush generated by the penetrator insertion had given way to total fatigue. After rounding the lake the ground began climbing.

Full planetary gravity pulled on every muscle and every tendon. Shannon's heart fluttered, his eyelids sagged, and stinging perspiration blurred his vision. His ears rang, and blood pounded in his head. He shook the fog from his brain.

The main stand of yellow-barked spruce was behind them, down the gentle hill toward the lake. Only a few stunted trees remained between them and the rocky escarpment that held the cave. The ground was firm and matted with a fine weave of low vegetation. Early-season berries, blue, black, and bright red, sparsely dotted the hillside.

O'Toole landed heavily at Petit's side. He peeked over the log and then looked down at Petit.

"You okay?" O'Toole panted. "You look ugly. Uglier than usual."

Petit raised his head and then laid it back down, unable to respond.

"Drink some pig juice, Petit," Shannon ordered.

Petit rolled his muscular body on its side, his pack thudding onto the ground. After a swig of precious field stimulant, his eyes cleared and his color returned. "Yeah," he gasped weakly. "I'll live. Gawd, I'm out of shape for this cross-country stuff."

"Gravity," O'Toole wheezed.

"It's less than Earth," Shannon snarled.

"Been a long time since any of us been back on Earth, Sarge," O'Toole huffed.

"Quit whining. Get together, Petit," Shannon snapped. "Cover me."

Shannon forced himself erect, knees protesting. He stalked across the clearing and climbed the rocks until he was even with Tatum. The dark cave lay just beyond. Tatum twisted to face him; perspiration dripped from his nose. Rocky terrain blocked the chilly wind.

"What've we got, Sandy?" The rising elevation permitted Shannon to look over the tops of the trees, out over the lake, to the rising plateau rim where they had landed. Faint, filtered sunlight danced off the rippled lake. A penetrating gust of wind whirled around the protecting rock, whipping up dust. The trees rustled softly.

"Not sure, Sarge," Tatum replied. "Thought I saw something. Just a movement." He had a glove off and was chewing on his thumb. He spit out a shred of nail.

"Think it was making the noise?" Shannon asked. Tatum shook his head.

Shannon nodded and walked between the boulders, climbing the cascade of lesser stones toward the cave. Leaving the lee of the boulders, he felt the coolness of the air on his sweat-soaked body. The ground transitioned from loose rock and ta-lus into slab rock and hard pack. He searched for signs of habitation, for any sign of life. The cave was going to be their home. He reached down to his calf scabbard, extracted his short-bladed survival knife, and fitted it to the muzzle of his assault rifle. Bayonet in front of him, Shannon covered the dis-tance to the cave opening.

It was empty. High enough for a man to stand erect at the threshold, the cave widened and increased in height for about ten paces and then converged sharply to a low rock wall. A dark gloom filled the cave, but there was sufficient light to reveal the absence of occupants. A dusky odor hinted at large animals, and tracks patterned the gritty floor; fist-sized drifts of black, matted fur were scattered in the recesses, and crushed and splintered bones gave an indication that this was the home of a meat eater. Paw prints in the sand were doglike, bearing ominous signs of long claws—the first sign of animal life, competitive and visceral, the tracks of a carnivore.

Shannon backed out into the wan sunlight and assembled his men. The sun-star peeked from its shroud of high stratus and was quickly masked by swollen cumulus barreling overhead. Rolling gusts of wind thrashed the boughs of the small forest.

"Got a storm coming, so let's move," he barked. "The 'vette comes overhead in fifteen minutes. O'Toole, get the ground station operational and set up the nav beacon for a check. They can get a fix on us. Tatum, make camp in the cave. We were lucky enough to find it, so let's use it. It's dry, and it's big enough. That's the good news. The bad news is something else lives there, and as far as I can tell, it has claws and eats meat, so keep the weapons ready. Actually, that's good news. It means there's food."

"Yeah," Tatum said. "Just a question of who does the eat-ing."

Braan and three warriors soared silently over the casements of the redoubt. They presented themselves with imposing dig-nity to the young watch adjutant, who reciprocated with equal carriage, alertly sending for the sentry captain. Young sentries stared in unabashed awe at the fierce presence of armed veter-ans. The adjutant, seeing disarray on the sentry common, correctly ordered the piper to sound "Assembly." The screeching call catalyzed the buzzing and chirping groups. The milling crowd became a formation of sentries wearing freshly tanned leather armor and carrying shortbows and pikes. In contrast, Braan and his seasoned companions wore thick, sweat-darkened battle hides and carried iron knives in addition to their thick attack bows.

Braan's comrades were famous warriors. Braan had wisely gone to old Botto, clan of Botto, and requested assistance. The venerable Botto, once leader-of-hunters but now too old to journey down the cliffs, was held in great esteem for past deeds and good manners. Botto would have suffered an insult if his clan had been excluded, and he directed his two eldest sons, Bott'a and Tinn'a, to be Braan's lieutenants. The third stalwart was Craag, clan of Veera, the clan of Braan's wife. The tall, grizzled Craag was second only to Braan in the hunter hierarchy.

Kuudor, clan of Vixxo, captain-of-the-sentry, an old campaigner and mentor, marched in their direction. Kuudor's gait revealed a severe limp, and his left shoulder was scarred and barren of fur. The crippled veteran halted smartly, front and center of the assembled sentries, adjutant at his side. Braan and his company approached. The blooded warriors exchanged formal greetings, their eyes sparkling with memories of shared danger.

Braan spoke first, as was fitting: "Kuudor, captain-of-the-sentry, three sentries are requested in service of the elders. We foray to the northwest, to the vicinity of Three-Island Lake, to conduct reconnaissance. To return before the large moon is new."

"Braan, leader-of-hunters," Kuudor responded. "This mission feels of grave import or such proven warriors would not be commissioned. It is an honor to assign sentries to this endeavor, and three worthy novices have been chosen." Kuudor turned to his adjutant and gave orders.

Brappa, clan of Braan, was first called; Sherrip, clan of Vixxo, Kuudor's grandson, capable and strong—one of the best fliers—was next called; and the adjutant, Kibba, clan of Kiit—clever and a leader of his peers—trilled his own name last. All marched forward proudly.

The strongest and bravest were going forth. Kuudor turned to his remaining charges and gave a short, impassioned exhortation. A new adjutant directed the gathering in singing the death song—a series of mournful, haunting wails—and as the somber notes faded in the rising wind, the adjutant thrust his pike skyward, commanding a round of lusty hurrahs. The cheers of the formation resounding in their ears, the patrol formed up, warrior and sentries shoulder to shoulder. Braan, at the formation's head, screamed a command and marched to the precipice. The others followed, unfurling membranes in time-honored syncopation, hopping from the cliff's sheer edge and launching on the urgent winds, tremendous wings cracking like thunder as they sought out the impatient breezes. Burdened with leather and iron, the seven cliff dwellers sailed into the void—and sharply upward. Upward they spiraled, the strong northwest wind blowing them out over the river chasm. But no farther! Braan countered the wind by slipping and skidding against it, trading vertical lift to maintain his position over the ground. Upward the hunters soared until they were but motes in the blue sky, soaring on the rising air currents, landbound creatures no more.

SEVEN

FIRST LANDING

The EPL rumbled and vibrated in the turmoil of atmospheric reentry. Plasma gases danced across the windscreen.

"How're the passengers, Boats?" Buccari shouted into her mask.

"Checking good, Lieutenant," Jones replied. "Fenstermacher and Dawson are keeping everyone real loose—real garbage mouths they are. Dawson's just tearing Fenstermacher apart. And Leslie Lee can hold her own, too."

"Fenstermacher brings out the best in everyone," Buccari said, perspiring in the glowing reentry heat. The massive deceleration of the reentry over, she felt changes in airspeed as the thermal warping of the airframe steadily diminished. The pres-

sure of the gases flowing through her suit umbilical eased; she
worked her jaws and yawned.

"Reentry complete," she reported. "Compute . . . command:
auto-disconnect." The flight computer disengaged the controls,
and Buccari gently pulled the lander through sweeping rever-
sals. Her feather touch moved the nose of the lander to starboard, and the tracking bug on the course indicator drifted
slowly back onto the programmed course. She approached the
"descent funnel," the signal from Shannon's ground navigation
beacon strong and steady. Reluctantly, Buccari reactivated the
autopilot and leaned back.

Decelerating against gathering pressure, unpowered, its engines held quiescent, the lander bucked in the hypermach turbulence. Thickly sleek and delta-winged, the silver EPL, a
fuel-laden glider, screamed into a wide, slicing turn, dragging
a double explosion across the new land.

"Mach two point five, altitude on schedule," Jones said. "In
the groove. Engines hot and feathering, fuel pressure in the
green. Checking good, Lieutenant, checking good."

Buccari double clicked the intercom button. She watched the
landscape roll by as she searched ahead for topographic cues.
On the head-up display the "roadway" in the sky showed as
two straight converging lines. They were on final. The autopilot held altitude while airspeed decayed rapidly. The EPL
dropped to transsonic as the glide slope indicator eased resolutely to center scale. Established on glide slope, the altitude
readout resumed its steady decrease. Buccari peered ahead. In
the distance the bend in the river marked Hudson's Plateau.
Mountains loomed ominously beyond. She was heading
straight into a range of vertical granite, but it mattered not; if
she chose to abort, she could accelerate straight up—emergency procedure number one: return to orbit.

"Landing checks complete, Lieutenant," Jones reported.

"Checking good, Boats," Buccari acknowledged, flattening
out in her seat and cinching her harness. The edge of the plateau passed beneath them. Buccari detected steam rising from
the river, and the radar altimeter beeped at the sudden decrease
in altitude. Airspeed decayed rapidly, but glide slope remained
in the funnel. Terrain features sharpened; a lake passed down
the left side. The landing configurator initiated; wingtip fences
snapped erect. A growling noise vibrated through the craft, signaling movement of the massive articulating flaps as they
crawled out and down from the trailing edges of the delta

wings. The lander flared, its nose elevating steadily, blocking her view of the mountainous horizon. She went to the gauges.

Touchdown was imminent. Airspeed fell away; the nose of the craft rotated smoothly toward the vertical—and past! Well past! With alarming intensity, the guttural bass of the main engines exploded into activity, and Buccari was firmly pressed into her acceleration chair. She felt more than heard the engine gimbal motors grinding through their pivots. Beneath her feet the pulsing of the hover blasters joined the cacophony, and the nose of the ship slowly fell back toward the horizon. Huge snowy mountains loomed to each side, but suddenly all view was blocked by rising dust and debris. As abruptly as they had started, the main engines wound down with a plaintive whine. The hover blasters screamed for a second longer, and the lander shivered to a jolting halt. The apple was on the ground.

Predawn had revealed starlit skies. Peach-colored alpenglow illuminated the great peaks, giving a hint of the sun's impending presence. Brappa came awake and uncoiled from Craag's warmth. Craag also stirred to activity. Brappa was stiff, but he felt excited, strong. He was also hungry, and the fragrance of burning wood stimulated his metabolism. The watch mates hopped into the clearing to a welcome sight: Kibba had prepared a tiny smokeless fire with twigs kept dry from the night's rains, and Kiit was slicing fish fillets into thin strips for cooking. The ravenous hunters queued up and, using sharpened sticks, held the fish in the flames long enough to be civilized— which was not very long.

Craag finished eating. Brappa spit out fish bones and stood to follow; it was time to relieve the watch. The clear morning air was shattered by massive, stuttering explosions! Brappa clasped hands over his ear openings, but it was too late; detonations swept their campsite. Dazed, ears aching, Brappa looked anxiously at the other hunters. Even Braan and Craag were wide-eyed and frozen. The two warriors shook off the effects of the horrible noises and became alert and resolved. Inspired, Brappa felt his own courage grow warm and strong within.

He was the first to hear the passage of the alien ship. Brappa whistled a sharp warning. The unpowered craft made an audible noise, hissing loudly through the air. It was immense, silver, and cold-looking; it caught the bright sun, reflecting the red rays painfully into the hunters' eyes. The sentry, mouth gaping, watched the awesome flying object as it flew from sight. Moments later the air shuddered with distant rumbling vibrations.

Braan faced the hunters. "Our mission reaps fruit, but we have not yet learned of its taste. Expedite your preparations. The thermals come early today."

Shannon's marines sprinted toward the lander and assumed their assigned defensive positions. Shannon warily scanned the rim of the plateau, his senses heightened. The lander's arrival had announced their presence within a wide radius.

"Sergeant Shannon, Buccari here," Buccari's voice came up on the UHF.

"Yes, sir. Welcome to our new home, and a mighty pretty landing, I might add. Bit noisy, though," Shannon responded.

"I had nothing to do with it, Sergeant. Autopilot does all the work," Buccari said. "I have six new inhabitants and equipment to off-load. I plan to rendezvous with the 'vette on the next orbit."

"Piece of cake, Lieutenant. As soon as we can touch you. You're pretty hot, er . . . the ship, I mean, is hot . . . er, as soon as we can touch you, uh . . . the ship. Sorry, sir. We'll get—" He stopped, bemused and enchanted by the laughter coming over the radio.

"Relax, Sarge," the pilot finally replied. "I copy."

"You aren't powering down, Lieutenant?" Shannon asked after several minutes. The lander's skin temperature was stabilizing rapidly in the cool, breezy air.

"I'm running tertiaries at idle so I can keep a generator on line. I need to keep the fuel pressures up—takes too much fuel and time to reignite otherwise, and too many things can go wrong doing a cold start," she answered. "I'm pretty comfortable right here. This gravity isn't bad if you can stay on your back. I might just take a snooze."

"You saw what?" MacArthur asked, dropping the gathered wood.

"A bear!" the big man exclaimed. Purple stains colored his lips and tongue.

Sonic booms echoed in the valley. Both men jerked at the noise and stared at the sky, searching for the lander. Only the twin plumes of thin smoke from the volcanoes on each side of the valley marred the deep blue heavens.

"What the hell you been eating?" MacArthur sighed, bringing his eyes back to the surface of the planet. "Geez, Jocko, it could be poisonous."

"Berries," Chastain replied, dropping his eyes and wiping his mouth with the back of his hand. "They're all over the place. I picked a bunch for you, too. They're real good."

"Yeah, well, let's see how good you feel in a couple of hours," he said, falling to his knees next to the small fire. "A bear, eh?"

"Looked like a bear," Chastain said. "Up there, on the ridge."

MacArthur looked up. The ridge climbed in the distance, winding back and forth to the summit of the westernmost volcano. Smoke and steam rose from the top, shredding into the stiff breeze that also held at bay the stink of the buffalo herds.

"On its hind legs, next to that humpy rock pile," Chastain said. "It was twice as tall as the rocks. It disappeared over the ridge." He stood, hunched over. "It was reddish-brown-colored, sorta."

"How's your back?" MacArthur asked, still looking up at the mountain.

"Hurts bad when I move wrong, but it ain't as bad as yesterday. I could try and carry my pack." Chastain's face twitched in discomfort.

"We'll wait one more day," MacArthur said, staring uphill.

"I got the fire going, like you told me to."

"Huh, Jocko? Oh, good," MacArthur replied, turning from the mountain. "Let's cook up some field rations to go with those berries. As soon as I eat some real food I'm going to climb that mountain."

"Can I go with you, Mac? I don't want to stay ... by myself."

"No, Jocko. We got a big hike in front of us, and I want you ready."

An hour later MacArthur neared the ridge where Chastain had seen the animal. The location was above the tree line and devoid of vegetation and was cut with ravines, affording abundant places of concealment. MacArthur climbed until he reached the distinctive pile of boulders marking the position. He halted and looked back at the camp. Chastain, no larger than half a fingernail held at arm's length, waved enthusiastically. MacArthur waved in return and somberly considered what Chastain had said about the size of the animal. Twice the size of the rock pile? The rocks came up past MacArthur's shoulders. He threw Chastain a final wave and resumed hiking.

After three hours of climbing, the ridge faded into a shoulder of the mountain and talus, and scrabble gave way to rocky slabs and short vertical ascents. MacArthur traversed the northern face of the mountain, endeavoring to get a clear view of the plateau. To the north the rolling plains, alive with herd animals, stretched into the haze. MacArthur was hypnotized by the splashes of mixed golds and browns. The herds moved slowly around and through each other—countless animals, their ranks stretching to the limits of vision, their scent only a memory.

MacArthur came upon old lava flows and steaming vents. Despite his exertions and the unaccustomed gravity, he felt comfortable; the sun was slow in chasing the shade from the north face of the mountain, but humid steam vents smelling strongly of minerals and sulfur provided welcome warmth. MacArthur worked his way around the side of the mountain, across a surface of unrelieved igneous rock and congealed lava flows, sterile and bleak, until the distant plateau came into view. He checked his chronometer—fifteen minutes to go. Two hundred meters from the summit the terrain changed dramatically: a small crater dominated the landscape, the truncated tip of what once had been the mountain's summit, its sides steeply banked with hardened lava flows. Thin streams of smoke and steam drifted up from its depths. Clammy, sulfurous currents caused him to blink, but fresh winds flushed the summit, making it only a nuisance.

MacArthur settled in position. At five seconds to the hour he turned on his radio, listened briefly, and broadcast: "Alpha Site, Alpha Site, Insertion Six. Alpha Site, Alpha Site, this is Six. Do you copy?"

Everyone else was at the landing site. O'Toole reclined next to the radio, having little to do but listen to static. The transmission jerked him to attention. It was weak, almost indecipherable. It was MacArthur.

"Roger Six, this is Alpha. You are weak and broken. How do you read, Mac? Over."

"Loud an . . . ear, Alpha. I rea . . . five by fi . . ." MacArthur's reply was cracked and whispery.

"Roger, Six. You are unreadable. Hold while I get Shannon

on line. Break. Insertion One, Alpha Site. Insertion One, this is Alpha. I got MacArthur," O'Toole broadcast.

"Roger, Alpha. One here. I hear you loud and clear, but you're all I hear," Shannon replied. "MacArthur's batteries must be low, or he's just too far away. Ask him how Chastain is."

O'Toole played with the squelch and turned up the volume. "Okay, Six," he said. "Give me your report, but talk slow. You are very weak. How is Chastain?"

The reply was unreadable. O'Toole could decipher nothing. Shannon jumped into the confusion and told O'Toole to ask only questions with yes or no answers and to have MacArthur answer with discrete transmission pulses: one for yes, two for no. With frustrating effort O'Toole was able to comprehend a portion of MacArthur's report—Chastain's injuries were minor, they had seen animal life, and they were not in danger—but little else.

"Enough," Shannon transmitted. "Terminate the connection. All we're doing is wearing down his batteries and giving the bugs a signal to localize. Order him to proceed to Alpha and to communicate, if able, at standard times."

O'Toole complied. He could no longer hear MacArthur.

MacArthur stood and stared across the distance, the magnitude of their challenge apparent. The elevation of Hudson's Plateau was much higher than his current position, and there was still the river to cross, a serious hike. Heading straight for the plateau would require skirting the plains herds and their overwhelming musk, and, once arrived at the base of the plateau, they would have to ford the river. Then, once across the river, they would have to make a direct ascent on vertical cliffs. Perplexed, he looked to the south and saw the rising hills beyond the river.

Something passed between him and the sun. MacArthur squinted into the brightness but saw nothing. He thought to remove his helmet, to widen his field of vision, but as he lifted his hand to the fitting, a fierce blow struck the back of his head. He tumbled down the steep lava slope, his head slamming to a jarring halt. Dazed, he shook his head to clear his vision and looked around, trying to find his assailant. The shadow again! MacArthur looked up.

A Gargantuan bird with an astonishing wingspan dove from the sky, monstrous talons swinging menacingly. Instinctively,

MacArthur pulled in his feet and, a split second before the gigantic bird tore into his chest, leapt to the side, receiving a painful glancing blow to his left shoulder. Talons gored flesh and knocked him sprawling in the brittle cinders. Stunned, MacArthur rolled onto his knees and drew his pistol. The giant raptor wheeled for the kill. Huge! Black-bodied, with white and tan pinions, its reptilian yellow eyes fixed in a predatory stare. MacArthur squatted and clasped the service automatic in both hands. With cool urgency he elevated the weapon's sights and aimed at the feathered breast filling the skies. Three rounds exploded from the pistol, each slug pounding into the big bird. It fell from the skies like a feathered stone.

From the bottom of a black well his thoughts returned—and his pain—and panic! He could not see. He could breathe only with difficulty. Something heavy and warm pressed his body into the rocks. A breeze caressed his hand—the hand holding the pistol. He dropped the weapon, pulled his hands and legs beneath him, and pushed to his knees; the weight on his back grudgingly lifted, and blinding sunlight struck bleary eyes. Dizzy and bedraggled, MacArthur squirmed from beneath the feathery carcass, retrieving the pistol as he struggled clear.

He crawled away, scanning the skies, pistol cocked upward. Blood flowed down his shoulder. Cuts and abrasions stung palms, elbows, and knees. His head reeled, and sparks danced before his eyes. He put a hand to his helmet—the headgear was cracked, shattered through the crown. A cold breeze seeped around his sweaty head. MacArthur pulled the helmet off and cast it aside. Worthless now, it had saved his life. His body ached; he trembled. Chilly air and the first stages of shock took over. Still on his knees, he darted nervous, ducking glances between the skies overhead and the mass of feathers lying on the ground.

Clambering to his feet, MacArthur warily examined the creature–like an eagle, but huge! He gingerly poked at the crested head with the barrel of his pistol. It was dead, its yellow eyes staring but not seeing. Tentatively, MacArthur grabbed hold of a wing and lugged it out to its full extent. It was three times as long as a man was tall. He moved around the carcass and repeated the process with the other wing. Wingtip to wingtip the span measured fifteen paces across! The gaudy orange beak, fiercely hooked, was as long as his leg! He stood erect over his fallen foe, amazed at the power and substance of the attacker but also feeling an atavistic flush of victory. He shook himself and returned the pistol to its holster. Drawing his survival knife from its ankle scabbard, he hacked off chunks of the eagle's proud breast and carried them away in his shattered helmet. Tonight they would have something besides berries to eat with their field rations.

EIGHT

SECOND LANDING

"Welcome to Hudson's Plateau." O'Toole grinned, standing on the cave terrace. Petit and Gordon carried the injured Rennault on a stretcher; Lee and Fenstermacher supported each other, while Goldberg and Dawson plodded in the rear. O'Toole scurried down to help with the litter.

"Hot damn, solid ground!" Fenstermacher blubbered, a grin creasing his exhaustion.

"Nancy spotted a flight of birds way up in the sky," Goldberg said.

"Oh, yeah? Sarge wants to report all animal sightings," O'Toole said. "Say, did you hear the noises? The groaning sounds?"

"You mean the flowers?" Dawson asked.

"Huh?" O'Toole replied.

"The big white flowers," Lee joined in. "We checked them out. The flower grows out of a bladder that holds air until the sun warms it up enough to force out the air. Must be a pollination mechanism. We already gave them a name."

"Fartflower," Fenstermacher deadpanned.

"You little jerk." Dawson laughed. "Leslie has a better name."

"Looks like we'll be naming a lot of plants," Lee said quietly.

"So what's its name—" O'Toole started to ask, and then he

remembered Shannon's instructions. "Oh, Sarge wants tents set up in the clearing. The cave's too small for everyone. Sarge wants us to double up. He says we got to post sentry right away. Petit, you and Gordon get your helmets on and post the watch. Show Gordon the rotation."

Petit and Gordon stood to put their gear in order. As Petit walked close to Goldberg, he gently bumped into her, catching her arm.

"It's going to be cold in these tents," he said with a grotesque smile. "If any of you ladies was interested in sharing my sleeping bag, it would be my pleasure to double up."

Dawson, too tired to speak, threw a rock at the marine.

"Knock it off, Petit!" O'Toole snarled. "You know the damn rules."

"Moaning glories," Lee said wistfully, breaking the uneasy silence. "We're going to call them moaning glories."

After sunset Braan spiraled down to the big island. The rest of the hunters descended in pairs at cautious intervals. Silently they glided from the ridge top, hidden by darkness, neither moon yet visible in the night sky. At the base of the island's rocky spire Craag and Tinn'a carefully rolled back small boulders, revealing a tight cave. Cliff dwellers had been to this island many times. Caches had been excavated, their entrances carefully camouflaged, to be used by fishing parties. Braan assigned watches, and the hunters settled into their duties.

Morning arrived still and cold, a patina of frost glazing the rocks. The lake was invisible, shrouded in a blanket of fog, the islands jutting eerily into the clear air above. Fish rippled the water, but Braan insisted on maximum stealth, forbidding fishing. They would eat roots and grubs.

With alarming abruptness sounds from across the water broke the muted silence—clanking sounds, metal striking metal, groans and protestations, loud yawns, and a steady gabble of voices. A fire flickered orange in the gray shroud of dawn. The hunters, even those scheduled to sleep, took covert positions on the high ground to witness the gods. What clamorous gods!

The first golden rays of sunshine illuminated the peaks of the snow-mantled mountains. A breeze stirred. Kibba whistled softly and pointed. On the lakeshore, less than a bowshot away, stood three strange beings, their long legs hidden in lingering mists. Two were extremely tall; the third was smaller but still easily the height of a guilder. They had white, round heads covered with caps the color of yellow rock flowers. The large ones wore forest-green garb, while the shorter one wore a sand-colored covering. The short one bent, scooped a small container in the water, and lifted it to eye level. One of the big ones pointed, and all three walked down the beach, the smaller one struggling to keep pace with the long strides of the other two.

The creatures rounded a bend in the shoreline and approached the rocky tumble from which fell a small waterfall. One of the green-clad giants clambered up the boulders and moved along its face until it straddled the descending streamlet. It bent and put a hand in the water and then stood erect, shaking its head vigorously. It returned to the beach, and after several minutes the strange beings turned and headed away from the waterfall, returning along the shoreline to their camp.

Braan threw his body from the island peak and swooped low over the foggy lake, occasionally flapping his membranes. The visitors did not look back. Braan heaved air downward, struggling up to the sheltered waterfall. He perched next to the small cascade and watched it tumble noisily into the lake below. A profusion of wildflowers clung to the crevices and crannies, and gnarled fir trees stubbornly hugged the rocks; higher up, two twisted and weather-whitened tree trunks leaned over the brook. At that moment the sun broached the rim of the plateau and cast the pure light of morning over the scene, but Braan barely noticed. Breathing heavily, he sought a vestige of the alien presence. He could smell them—a curious, sour scent. He sniffed the air for other reasons—another scent, the stale spoor of rockdogs, assaulted his awareness. Danger was near.

Braan warily continued along the rocky elevation, away from the lake. He ascended a rock-tumbled ridge and prowled a shallow canyon cradling another babbling stream. A breeze rustled the isolated clumps of grass and wafted the sweet smell of abundant wildflowers. The exertions of the climb and the sun's bright rays warmed his blood, dulling his attention. Without warning, one of the strange creatures walked from behind a boulder. It was looking at the ground and picking rockberries. It sensed Braan's presence and turned to face the hunter. It was tall, nearly twice Braan's height, and covered in sand-colored material—not skin or fur. It had grotesquely long legs and hands with five fingers—strong-looking hands. The tall, flat-faced being's wide, big-lipped mouth was stained with

rockberry juice. It had monstrous, ungainly protrusions of skin
and cartilage coming from its round head, and it had blue eyes!
Blue as the sky. The strange creature's pale eyes stared out at
him, startled at first, revealing a fleeting fear. The fear dissipated, leaving only curiosity.

The representatives of the different races stood—confused
but instinctively unafraid—as if a sudden move would cause
the tableau to disintegrate. Braan stirred first. Suppressing the
urge to take flight, the hunter scrambled uphill. The long-legs
watched him climb, taking a few halting steps after him—to
prolong the encounter, not in pursuit.

"Damn," Dawson muttered.

The sun was sliding high, the moaning glory chorus dying
out. But the midnight-blue berries growing sparsely on the tortured, ground-hugging shrub were exquisite. Big, juicy—and
real. Like grapes. She tried not to eat too many, but they were
so good. She picked rapidly, spitting seeds. It was time to head
back. O'Toole had said he would watch the radio while she
was out but not to take more than an hour; he needed to get
the beacon ready. Dawson had set out for the little stream and
followed its course up into the flower-bedecked defile. She
was retracing her steps and was absorbed in picking berries
when she looked up and saw the creature. A giant bat?

Taloned feet caught her attention, as did the spindly digits of
its hands. Unbelievably, the little animal carried a bow and
wore a leather garment. Dawson stared down at its long, narrow face, large black eyes unflinchingly locked onto her own.
She sensed intelligence and tried to say something, but her
voice failed. Dawson exhaled—she had been holding her
breath. The creature warily turned and waddled uphill, moving
quickly over the rocks. Dawson swallowed, breathed deeply,
and reluctantly headed down the hill. O'Toole would be angry.

Braan circled to maintain contact with the tall newcomer.
The long-legs moved unsteadily downhill, carrying its container of rockberries. Berries—it was not a meat eater. Braan
was attracted to subtle movement on the hillside. Rockdogs—
two of them—skulked along the shadows of a line of boulders
above and ahead of the long-legs. Stalking.

Rockdogs were cunning and dangerous, one of the most
dangerous of adversaries. Braan looked around. There were always more than two to a pack. The rank and musty dog scent

was strong, the animals directly upwind. Braan nervously scanned the downwind rocks, looking for dogs still hidden. The hunter loosened his wings and pulled an arrow from his quiver, ready for fighting or fleeing. He climbed, watching the parallel paths of the animals below but also watching for surprises from above. The waiting rockdogs held their positions, shiny pelts blending into rocky shadows. Two more rockdogs crept into view! Events were out of Braan's control. If the long-legs were gods, they were about to be tested by the appetites of nature.

The long-legs walked awkwardly and obliviously down the rocky hillside, using its hands to stabilize its clumsy leaps and bounds. It was only paces from ambush and looking at the ground, completely unaware of the impending danger. Braan noticed movement farther downhill.

Dawson stumbled and stopped to catch her breath and admire the view. The fog had blown clear. Sunlight reflected from the golden lake, and the rim of the plateau stretched starkly across the near horizon, delineating the immeasurable distance to the unresolvable prairies beyond. She reached into the bucket and grabbed another handful of berries. Thirsty, she knelt by the sparkling stream and drank deeply of its icy water. The sun warmed the red lichen-streaked rocks, many of them faceted with quartz and pyrite crystals.

Getting to her feet, she looked down the hill. The cave entrance was out of sight, but she saw marines milling about, preparing for the hike to the lander site. She wanted to see the landing, but someone had to watch the radio. She stretched and stared into the blue skies, thinking about the peculiar animal. Perhaps her eyes had played tricks on her. She took a step forward and froze—thirty paces downhill Tatum was crouching behind a rock, his assault rifle aimed at her.

"Sandy, don't shoot! It's me—Nancy!" she shouted.

"Not aiming at you," Tatum replied in a throaty whisper. "Freeze."

Dawson looked up and saw two black animals above Tatum.

"Behind you," she whispered, slowing raising her hand.

Tatum turned his head. The closest dog lifted a grizzled muzzle and snarled, baring ferocious canines; its chewed and notched ears were laid back on its head, and a magnificent mane of silvered hackles rose across its back. It sprang. Tatum swung his assault rifle, discharging it on full automatic. The

leaping rockdog died before it fell to the ground, a volley of
explosive slugs shredding its raven chest. Rifle blasts exploded
the silence of the still morning, sending waves of echoes
bouncing through the valley and across the lake. The dog pack
scattered like leaves before the wind, frightened by the detonations of man.

Braan's eardrums throbbed. Flames had belched from the
stick held by the green-clothed long-legs. The rockdog had
been slapped down in midair, and the vicious jackhammer con-
cussions had caused Braan actual pain. Braan was dizzy. Gods!
The power of gods! Magic power—the power to kill! Frozen
with awe, Braan watched the long-legs. The green-clothed one,
the long-legs with the magic stick, even taller yet, put an arm
around the obviously frightened sand-colored one. The green
one scanned the rocks—a hunter. The sand-colored long-legs
was not a hunter, much less a god. The sand-colored one
pointed uphill. The long-legs-that-killed peered in that direction and, without looking down, leaned over and grabbed the
carcass by its scruff. Together they dragged it down the hill,
leaving a trail of blood. Meat eaters, after all.

"Would you look at that!" Fenstermacher shouted.
Dawson, holding her berry pail, followed Tatum as he
lugged the trophy across the clearing. Tatum lifted the ebony
carcass above his shoulders and dropped it in a splatter of gore
and dust.
"Fresh meat," he shouted. The humans approached cau-
tiously. The beast, even in death, was fearsome; fangs and
claws sprouted from bloody black fur.
"Who knows how to skin it?" Gordon asked.
"Skin it? Why?" Dawson said. "Can we eat it?"
"I'll butcher it," Shannon announced from the cave terrace.
"But it will be tougher than anything you have ever eaten."
"I bet it lived in the cave," Tatum said, squatting and exam-
ining the animal's claws.
"Yeah," Shannon snapped. "While I'm gutting that SOB, I
want you marines to get your butts in gear and get the nav
beacon out to the landing site. Tatum, get 'em going!"
"You bet, Sarge," Tatum said, standing erect. "It jumped
us."
"Used up enough f—frigging ammo," Shannon snarled.
"There was three more of 'em, but this is the only one I

shot," Tatum replied. "Dawson saw something else, too. Tell 'em, Nance."

Shannon bounded from the terrace to the tenting area. He unsheathed a jagged-edged survival knife and strode up to Dawson. He bent his head slightly and stood nose to nose with the tall lady.

"What the hell you doing walking off by yourself like that? I told everyone to stay with the group at all times. I don't care if you have to take a crap. You do it with company, and that company will have a loaded weapon with them. You *hear me*?"

Dawson tried to return the sergeant's stare, but Shannon's demeanor was too fierce, too belligerent; she could not maintain eye contact. His dark eyes were red-rimmed and sunken, surrounded with black shadows, his face and head covered with week-old stubble, thick and grizzled. Dawson unconsciously ran her hand down the nape of her neck, feeling her own incipient crop of red hair. Averting her eyes, she meekly replied, "I hear you, Sergeant."

Shannon mercifully redirected his glare and squatted next to the carcass. He commenced to stab and tear at the animal's belly.

"So what else'd you see?" he asked softly. Before she could respond, Shannon looked up at the marines still standing around, curiously awaiting Dawson's story. "Am I going crazy, or did I not tell you leadbutts to get your asses in gear? Get moving, *now!*"

Everyone jumped. Petit and O'Toole grabbed the beacon, slinging rifles over their shoulders, and double-timed toward the lake. Tatum and Gordon followed. Mendoza, uncomfortably carrying a rifle, and Fenstermacher, with a holstered pistol, moved off to take sentry positions above the cave. Leslie Lee stood on the cave terrace, watching and listening. Dawson looked up at the medic and then back down at Shannon's broad back.

"So what'd you see?" Shannon asked as he yanked out the entrails with a liquid, ripping sound. Dawson stared, fascinated by the gore. Feeling her stomach wamble, she swallowed; dizziness threatened to overcome her. Shannon's hands and wrists were crimson with blood, his jumpsuit sleeves rolled up to his meaty tattooed biceps as he tore the pelt from the back of the bloody carcass, using the knife to lever it free, leaving behind pink marbled flesh.

Dawson opened her mouth, but no words came forth. Tasting hot, acrid berries, she turned her head, put her hand over her mouth, and ran to the edge of the clearing.

As Braan worked his way back to the lake, he observed the green-garbed long-legs making their way along the northern edge of the lake. Braan reached the high rocks above the lake, unlimbered his wings, and leapt out over the sparkling green water. The hunter glided most of the way to the island and then let himself settle onto the clear surface. The waters were warm. Braan landed softly and folded his wings, catching enough air to maintain buoyancy, and, with only his eyes and nostrils exposed, paddled to the island. Craag awaited.

The explosive reports had frightened the hunters. They feared for their leader's well-being, but their fears had been assuaged on seeing Braan traversing the cliff face. The commotion in the aliens' camp had also attracted their attention, and they watched the strange beings depart for the high plateau. The hunters listened in awe as Braan related his adventure.

"The long-legs are powerful," Braan said.

"Why were you not harmed, Braan-our-leader?" Bott'a asked, a bold question.

"The sand-colored one had not a magic stick, and I made no move to attack. The rockdogs attacked," Braan replied. The long-legs had not desired to harm him; Braan realized that the long-legs did not perceive him to be a threat even though he was clearly armed. A good portent.

The silent hunters pondered the events. Braan suddenly deduced why the strangers were returning to the plateau rim. The thunderous craft would return. The aliens were being delivered to the plateau by that silver ship. Every explosion heralded the arrival of more long-legs.

"Today there will be great noises, as yesterday and the day before. The flying object will return. More long-legs will be among us," Braan announced. The hunters marveled at their leader's prediction.

The second landing was not routine. Penetration and approach were normal and transition was routine, but touchdown was rough. The lander wavered severely, skidding and tottering. Buccari felt lateral forces tilting the nose of the lander. With lightning reactions she disengaged the autopilot and jammed in a hard control input, offsetting the unprogrammed yaw. She was lucky, catching the excursion in time. A split second later and the lander would have toppled from its skids and exploded with a full load of fuel, killing crew, passengers, and all marines in the vicinity. The corvette crew stranded in orbit would also have died, only more slowly.

As she waited for the lander's skin temperature to stabilize, Buccari checked her instruments and command programs. With tertiaries still turning, she and Jones ran a diagnostic on the control systems but could find no indication of what had caused the unruly control inputs. When the skin temperatures fell within limits, the marines and passengers moved the bulky cargo clear of the lander and staged it for transportation back to camp. Quinn had surprised Buccari by insisting that the planet survey package be transported to the planet. Buccari had not argued; they would need the medical supplies, the seeds, the raft, and the tools.

Reluctantly, Buccari shut the lander down. She checked her chronometer; the corvette would be overhead in fifty minutes. She took off her helmet, unstrapped from her station, rolled out of her seat, and climbed clumsily down the steeply slanted center passage to the aft cargo door. Gravity felt as welcome as a headache. Buccari stepped heavily onto the surface of the planet and recoiled at the bright sunlight. She was uncomfortable—a hatched fledgling, raw and exposed. Buccari took a deep breath of natural atmosphere into her lungs, so different from the insipid air of space. She could taste moistness. A sweet, humid scent flooded her sinuses. She sniffled.

Buccari scanned the exhaust-blasted rock at the base of the lander, her vision unaccustomed to focusing at a distance and reluctant to range outside of a narrow realm. Forcing herself to squint outward, she saw yellow and white blossoms clinging in profusion to the granite slabs of the plateau. Obsessed with the thought of touching real flowers, she trudged from the blackened rock to the nearest cluster of blossoms, knelt stiffly beside them, and delicately immersed her face in the shallow garden. The odor was euphoric. The quartz-shot rock beneath her was warm and smooth; her discomfort melted into the receptive granite.

An impatient buzzing caused her to sit upright as a tiny black and yellow bee retreated from her newly claimed flower patch. A clutch of saffron butterflies flitted nervously about, moving unsteadily against a gentle headwind. She laughed aloud and fell on her side, head on an elbow, to watch the off-loading of cargo, but then she noticed Shannon rounding the lander, headed in her direction. Reluctantly and with dismaying effort, she pushed to her feet and met him halfway.

"Nice planet, Sergeant," Buccari said.

"Thank you, Lieutenant, but I had very little to do with it," Shannon said. "Big autopilot in the sky, you know?"

"Touché, Sergeant." She walked in step with him toward the lander. "Well, something's wrong. Had a secondary control input at engine cutoff. I was lucky to catch it and even luckier not to overcorrect."

"What's your plan, Lieutenant?"

"Don't think there's an option. Unless Jones can find something mechanically wrong and fix it, we'll be going for orbit as she stands." Buccari blinked at the horizon, still finding it difficult to look to a distance. "We'll fly it out manually. Fuel's no problem."

They walked up to the lander as Jones was shutting the access hatch. Jones pulled his helmet off and disconnected his suit power umbilical.

"Nothing, Lieutenant," Jones announced. He smiled at Shannon and nodded a greeting. "Gyros check out, and the thruster servos check good. No leaks. I'll keep looking, but all the obvious things pass muster. You sure it was the port side that fired? Playback shows nothing."

"No, Boats, I'm not sure. It happened too quick to check instruments. I just jammed power. Maybe I dreamed it. It happened so fast," she said.

"Nah, we was definitely slewing. You saved the ship, Lieutenant."

Buccari smiled and flexed her biceps. She turned to Shannon. "Let's prepare a sitrep for Commander Quinn."

Hudson read Buccari's message over the general circuit. References to the possibility of intelligent life captured Quinn's attention, but only momentarily. Quinn's focus—the focus of everyone on the corvette—was the status of the EPL. The lander was their bridge to existence, their ladder to life. The corvette was starting to feel like a coffin.

Rhodes and Wilson, at their respective watch stations, were playing chess on one of the corvette's computers. Quinn brought up the three-dimensional representation of their game on his own monitor. It was nearing endgame. Rhodes, playing black, was vulnerable to white's rook and pawn attack. It looked like mate in less than five moves. Quinn changed screens and ran a systems status check, sardonically chuckling at the ruinous state of his ship. His thoughts wandered involuntarily back to the motherships and to his wife. With conscious effort, he swept away the depressing thoughts and returned to the chess game.

"Sir, I downlinked the diagnostics and EPL maintenance data. Anything else?" Hudson asked, sitting at his watch station on the flight deck.

Quinn sat silently. Buccari and Jones were the best apple crew in the fleet. It was up to them to get the lander back to the corvette. There was nothing more he could do.

"Tell her good luck," Quinn replied, staring through the viewscreen. He shook off his dread and returned to the instruments.

"Fifteen down safe and six to go ... counting Buccari and Jones," Hudson chattered over the intercom. "This planet looks more like home every day. Not paradise—whatever that is—but fresh air and water and life. Flatulent flowers, big bats with bows, and fifty-kilo carnivores."

"Anything is better than slow death in a tin can," a voice—Rhodes's—responded over the intercom. Quinn brought the chess game back up. Rhodes made a defensive move.

"Ah, Virgil, my friend," Wilson said over the intercom. "We don't know what we'll find down there, now, do we? It may well turn out in a few days we'll wish we had the privilege of dying in space, surrounded by things we understand."

"Horsebleep, Gunner!" Rhodes responded. "You're dead for sure in this bucket. It's only a matter of weeks before it falls out of orbit, and we'll be dying of thirst long before that. I don't care what you say. You're like the rest of us; if you can delay pain and death, you will."

The intercom went silent. Hudson finally reported back: message to Buccari received and understood. Quinn acknowledged and returned to monitor the chess game. Rhodes's defensive situation was getting worse. Wilson's rook relentlessly menaced the black king, leaving Rhodes's position untenable. Yet Rhodes refused to concede, desperately seeking a counter that would take the pressure from his king and shift the weight of the attack to his opponent.

"Same-day rule!" Wilson needled. "You still there, Virgil?" Rhodes grunted an obscenity over the circuit. Wilson continued. "No, I reckon survival instinct says it's better to get off this burned-out pile of metal and live for as long as we can. I feel it, too. I want to get down. But just wait—it's warm here. I don't want to die in the cold."

"You're wearing your helmet too tight," Rhodes's disembodied voice answered. "You're going to live fifty more years, Gunner, and we'll find you a regular tropical island down there. It's a whole new world. No people . . . except us. Here's my move."

"You know, Virgil," Wilson said quietly. "Chess is a lot like life. You start off with lots of power, but it ain't developed—you can't use it. You have to try things. Some things work; some don't. If you use your pieces well, you get to play longer, but there's no getting around it—sooner or later you start to lose your pieces, your fuel, your power. And after a while you're down to the endgame, making do with only the last few pieces, kinda like getting the most out of an old dog or an old horse—or an old beat-up corvette." Wilson made a seemingly distant and unrelated move.

Rhodes advanced a piece. "Okay, Gunner. Enough bullshit. Your move."

Quinn watched as Wilson moved the white bishop with tantalizing slowness across the board, attacking the black king. "Time to start another game, Virgil. Checkmate."

NINE

DECISIONS

Buccari strapped into the cockpit. All systems were responding, but there was no hint of what had caused the lander to misbehave. She read through the ignition and takeoff checklists. She was nervous. She had performed full-manual takeoffs, but only from Earth. Earth, even with its encompassing strife and poverty, had abundant recovery fields, and the penalty for failing to make orbit was simply coasting to a runway, refueling, and trying again or, worst case, having someone do it for you. This was her first cold-iron restart from the surface of an alien planet. She would get only one chance to do it right. Fuel was critical, and anything short of complete success would mean leaving four men stranded on the corvette for the rest of their very short lives.

She peered out. The skies were a glorious mixture of coral and orange with violet and gray-scalloped clouds spaced evenly overhead, a splendid reward for the coming of night. A solitary erect figure stood in the distance, fading into the dusk—Shannon. The other marines were not visible, but she knew they were there, deployed as guards around the EPL. Guards against what?

She was anxious to return to the planet. She had seen flowers and smelled natural air. The corvette was dying, and life in space was a poor substitute for living under the warm sun of a virgin planet. But then she put her hands on the controls and felt the narcotic thrill of latent speed and power. The heavy, trigger-laden control stick transmitted an electric sensation, a stimulation resonating deep within her. The massive throttle accepted her strong grip and promised explosive acceleration beyond dimension. She donned her helmet and secured the fittings; the hiss of air brought back her professional world like a light switch illuminating a dark room.

"Okay, Boats. Ready for ignition. Checking good."

"Checking good, Lieutenant," Jones responded. "Temperatures and pressures in the green. Starting injector sequence."

Jones read off the checklist, and Buccari responded with the countdown. At time zero Jones initiated the ignition sequence; fuel pressures climbed into actuator ranges, and the tertiaries ignited, providing power and superheat. At ignition plus three seconds, main igniters commenced detonating in stages; a low-level static rasped in Buccari's helmet speakers. The hover blasters screamed their high-pitched screech, and the secondaries fired from the tail. The EPL slowly lifted from the exhaust-battered rocks. The annunciator panel indicated that the landing skids and stabilizer nozzles were stowed. The main engines gimbaled to line up with the lander's arcing center of gravity as the nose of the craft searched for vertical. Buccari's firm hands rode the controls, balancing the craft on a column of fire. At ignition plus six the lander's main engines exploded with a monstrous kick of power, crushing Buccari into her seat. She grasped the high-gee "catapult" handles adjacent to throttle and sidestick, acceleration forces clawing at the muscles of her forearms and neck. Fighting the leaden inertia of her body and the dullness of her mind caused by the compression of her brain, she forced herself to concentrate on the lancing flight of the lander. Vision tunneled before her, and peripheral vision was eradicated; her eyeballs rattled in her skull.

Seconds seemed like hours, but they were mere seconds. The acceleration schedule altered dramatically, and she adjusted g-loading, dropping it consistent with dynamic pressure optimizations. Buccari flexed her arms and shoulders against the cramping strain.

"Nice job, Lieutenant," Jones said. "Never wavered from profile. Escape velocity in fifteen. Temperatures stable. Checking good."

"Roger, Boats," she exhaled. "Checking good." She smiled, proud of herself. Full-manual takeoffs from planetary gravity were done only in an emergency. Things could go very wrong very fast. She peered into the deep purple of the thinning atmosphere.

The hunters breathlessly watched the phosphorescent fireball scream into the pastel heavens, a white-hot exhaust trailing an immense tongue of orange flame. As the silver-tipped explosion neared the high wispy clouds, the roaring missile brush-stroked brilliant shades of red and yellow instantaneously across their dark undersides. The glowing rapier leapt from the planet's shadow and into direct sunlight, trailing a glorious and starkly white plume. Braan rubbed his eyes, trying to wipe out the fiery ghost images. Gradually they faded, allowing his night vision to adapt to the descending dusk. Braan hopped from the rocks. Hunters not on watch followed, congregating in the rocky clearing adjacent to their cave entrance. They sat dumbly.

"Even if not gods, they are frightening beyond comprehension." Craag spoke first.

"Gods would be less frightening," Bott'a said.

"They are not gods," Braan added softly. "I have been near to them. They are frightened ... perhaps more frightened than we."

"Then they are dangerous, for the frightened eagle crushes its own egg," Craag said.

Silence returned to the little clearing. Bott'a jumped lightly to his feet and motioned to Kibba. The watch mates wordlessly departed through the bushes. It was their turn to collect food, and fishing was too good to sit around talking. Brappa followed. Craag remained.

"Thy plan, Braan-our-leader?" Craag asked directly.

Braan was not offended. Craag had proved his loyalty many times over. By waiting for the others to depart he had rendered due respect. Braan looked the warrior in the eye, something done only in challenge or in affection, and smiled to indicate the latter.

"A difficult situation," Braan said. "We must inform the council."

"Should we not leave watchers?" Craag asked. "I volunteer."

"Yes. We will learn by watching the long-legs." Braan grew apprehensive. "My son will expect to stay with thee," he said.

"If thou desire, I will insist on one more experienced."

Braan almost smiled. "Thou hast forgotten the pride of youth, my friend. It would not do to coddle my son."

"Perhaps the long-legs will go away," Craag said hopefully.

"No," Braan whistled. "Our futures are tangled."

Buccari, still wearing her EPL pressure suit, floated onto the flight deck and strapped in. She was exhausted. The responsibility of flying the lander to and from the planet, the inability to make a mistake, had taken its toll. Quinn and Hudson watched her without speaking.

"What's your guess, Sharl?" Quinn finally asked.

"No idea, Commander." She yawned.

"Maintenance diagnostics are going to take time," Hudson said.

"Without mothership systems it'll take at least two days," Buccari said. "We'll run a simulation. Jones is loading the programs, but I think Nash or Virgil should supervise. Jones's out of gas."

"Virgil, er ... Mr. Rhodes just called in," Hudson interjected. "He's already relieved Jones. He knows EPL maintenance as well as anyone."

"You were right, Commander ... about getting the crew down first. We may not have many flights left in the old apple," Buccari admitted.

"There may be nothing wrong with the lander," Quinn replied, "and any decision would have had risk. Be thankful that most of the crew are safe. Without them on board we have enough air and water to take a couple of days to find out what's wrong, and you can use the rest."

Buccari floated numbly in her tethers, grateful for having been overridden.

"Nash, let Sergeant Shannon know about the delay," Quinn said.

The smell of roasted rockdog hung heavy in the still darkness. The winds had calmed. The smoke from the dying campfire disappeared into star-blasted skies. The humans were quiet, sitting back or lying down with bellies full of tough meat. In the flickering light Shannon and O'Toole labored with a crude smoking oven. Raw meat would spoil quickly; cooked, it would last longer.

Shannon straightened and tried to loosen the kinks in his tired muscles. Satisfied that O'Toole understood what to do, the sergeant walked into the darkness to use the latrine ditch. He detected a faint glow on the horizon. A tiny limb of the planet's smaller moon broke into view and palpably climbed the black sky, pulling its irregular mass after it.

His bladder relieved, Shannon sat down on the trunk of a downed tree and stared into the distance, stiff and tired, mesmerized by the moonrise. Fatigue displaced his vigilance. He was anxious for the commander to take the burden of responsibility. Shannon was trained to lead but not to be the leader. His career had been dedicated to faithfully executing the tactical orders of superior officers. This was not a tactical situation—it was a survival situation, and there was more than just marines to worry about.

A twig snapped. Instantly alert, Shannon abandoned his stupor on the fallen log and moved toward the noise, pulling his knife. Soft rustlings emanated from the shadows, sporadic and barely discernible. The marine crept obliquely toward the desultory sounds, trying to flank the noisemakers and manufacture a silhouette against the faint glow of the fire. His own blade glinted in the guttering light. Slowly he pinched inward, sliding from tree to tree, staring into darkness.

There! Movement. He retreated behind a rough-barked trunk, stealthily lowering into a crouch. Twisting to keep his weight balanced, aching knees protesting, he rounded the tree and peered into the black shadows. His peripheral vision revealed indistinct forms, four-legged and long-necked. Small beasts, less than waist high to a man.

Movement and sharp noises erupted from Shannon's flank, startling the animals. In the blink of an eye they bounded from sight, their delicate leaps hardly stirring the fir needles.

"Sarge!" A stage whisper—Tatum's voice. "Sarge, is that you?" Tatum's gangling form materialized from the darkness, assault rifle pointing ahead threateningly.

"Yeah, it's me, Sandy. Put down your rifle before you ruin my day." Shannon sheathed his knife and stood erect, feeling dull pain in his bones. Another figure materialized—the tall form of Nancy Dawson. *Women!* Shannon cursed to himself.

"Evening, Petty Officer Dawson," he said.

"Good evening, Sergeant Major," she said, a spark in her voice. "Just thought we'd come out and give you some company."

"Thank you. Appreciate it."

"See something, Sarge?" Tatum asked. "Or did we, er . . . interrupt you?"

"No, Tatum. You didn't frigging interrupt me," Shannon said, grateful it was too dark to see the look on Dawson's face. "Saw some small animals, kinda like deer."

Shannon plowed through the thicket in the direction of the campfire. Tatum and Dawson followed, catching the whiplash of the branches.

"You should be more careful, Sarge," Dawson admonished. "Could have been something big and dangerous, and you out here all by yourself—with just your knife!"

Shannon was tired, but he held his temper. She was right. He should not have wandered into the darkness alone. He admired Dawson's boldness, but he wished she would not lay it on too heavily. Tatum would spread it around enough as it was.

"Made your point, Dawson. You're right. But don't think I'm going to take back that chewing out I gave you. I did that for your own good and to make a point for everyone else."

They walked into the circle of firelight but were still out of earshot of the rest of the crew.

"Fair enough, Sarge," Dawson said quietly, clear eyes glowing orange in the flickering light. "But I didn't come after you to get even. I asked Sandy to go looking because I was worried—worried about you." She smiled, a warm smile for him alone, and then walked quickly away.

Shannon stood, abashed, unable to cope with the direct sentiment. He glanced at Tatum still standing at his side, sporting a silly smirk. Shannon did not have to speak; the look on his face was as eloquent as it was fierce. The smirk vanished, and the corporal wisely double-timed back to his tent.

MacArthur cringed as he sniffed the air, the fetid stink of the buffalo herds alarmingly pungent in the stillness of morning. He turned to his partner. Chastain settled under his load like a strong-hearted beast of burden. As much as possible had been removed from MacArthur's pack, whatever they could do without having been wrapped and buried. Yet his lightened pack still rode heavily. His shoulder was weak, the laceration not healed, and it was painful, but MacArthur could no longer endure the waiting. The lander flights had stopped. Something was wrong.

They hiked down the valley toward the great river. Spongy taiga disappeared as they traversed sections of weathered lava rock pocked with steaming sulfur vents, reminders of the smoking mountains on their flanks. The yellow-barked fir trees increased in number and size as the spring led them downward, flowing through cauldrons of bubbling mud before joining a crystalline artesian upwelling, and onward, growing into a small stream as tributaries added to its happy gurgle. They observed two breathtaking geyser eruptions and heard the distant roaring exhausts of numerous others.

Dainty birds with red and yellow plumage serenaded their passage, and the hoofprints of small deer were seen, although the animals remained hidden in ample cover. The brush thickened as they progressed; runs of alder and willowlike bushes impeded movement along the running water, and berry brambles lined the stream banks, their incredibly thorny branches covered with bright red fruit. Blueberries, initially thick underfoot, disappeared as they descended.

MacArthur saw the paw print in the soft ground next to the stream.

"Jocko!" he gasped. "Look at this! Here's your bear!"

It was a forepaw with a span three times that of a human hand. Predatory claw marks impaled the muddy soil.

"Christ, it's huge!" MacArthur said, stepping back. He looked around warily for more tracks or their source.

"Told you!" Chastain blurted. "What do we do if we see one?"

"Don't shoot . . . unless you have to." MacArthur stepped out, senses heightened.

Chastain's round face brightened. "My papa useta tell me about David Crockett. You ever hear of David Crockett, Mac?" They plowed through bushes, the stream noisy to their left.

"Yeah, I heard of Davy Crockett," MacArthur said. "Wore a coonskin cap." Several seconds went by; Chastain seemed to be thinking. MacArthur forged ahead, fighting the bushes. He moved away from the stream.

"My papa says David Crockett used to hunt bear by smiling at them."

"What, Jocko? Smiling? You kidding me?"

"Yeah—I mean, no," Chastain continued. "David Crockett would see a bear coming, and he would just stand there and smile. The bear would get confused and stop . . . or something. I don't remember what happened next. But my papa says it's a true story. David Crockett use to hunt bears by smiling at 'em."

MacArthur chuckled. They broke through blue-flowered thickets and moved onto an outcropping of lichen-covered rock where the stream joined a similar-sized tributary. The terrain descended sharply, filling the watercourse with splashing white water. In the distance they glimpsed the river valley. Beyond the valley MacArthur saw foothills reaching into hazy ridges, and beyond the ridges were magnificent white-shrouded peaks partially obscured by a mantle of low clouds. The sun-star exhibited a golden halo of ice crystals, a portent of change.

The land gradually flattened, the adolescent river running smoothly with occasional deep stretches. In the shadows swam dark-backed fish, and the fish invited the attention of bears. MacArthur rounded a bend of large boulders and found himself a dozen paces from the broad back of an ursine monster. The bear stared into the water, massive forepaw poised to strike. MacArthur froze. He eased a forearm straight up, fingers spread, and slowly turned his head, moving a finger to his lips. The marine retraced his steps, waving behind his back for Chastain to retreat. Walking backward, MacArthur did not see the loose rock on the river's edge. The crumbling shelf gave way, and MacArthur, with a loud splash and an involuntary half-choked yell, slid into the rushing water. The flailing marine scrambled onto the rock bank and clumsily regained his feet. Chastain moved forward.

The giant beast wheeled and was on them, great flanks and

shoulders convulsing, shaking away clouds of dust and flies. Growling belligerently, it reared to its majestic height, menacingly glaring down at them with beady golden eyes. It was bigger than even the largest Earth bear; its ears were floppier, more pointed, and its wet black nose and wolfish snout were longer, but the differences were overwhelmed by the similarities. It stank of fish and wet fur; its coat, ragged and mangy, was the color of bright rust, with a dusky mane draping back and shoulders. Powerful muscles rippled under its hide, and massive forepaws with cutlass claws waved in the air. The bear sniffed the breeze, opening and shutting its mouth to gather and taste the strange scents, drooling and displaying dreadful yellowed fangs. It remained ominously quiet, perplexed by the sight of humans. MacArthur, dripping wet, was afraid to move. His rifle was slung over his pack, and his pistol was buttoned into its holster. He dared to glance sideways, to see if Chastain was ready. Chastain stood with rifle in hand, but it was aimed at the ground. Disbelieving, MacArthur could only stare at his companion. Chastain stood confidently erect, cherubic features broken by an idiot's grin. MacArthur's eyes rolled skyward. His trembling hand crept toward his holster.

The vignette held for eternal seconds. Slowly, very slowly, MacArthur worked his pistol free and got ready to repulse an attack, while Chastain just stood—smiling. The bear fell back on its haunches and closed its mouth. MacArthur looked at Chastain and back to the bear, trepidation abating. Unable to resist, MacArthur's mouth formed a toothy grin. More time crept by. The bear dropped to its front paws, slowly turned, and lumbered out of sight behind the rocks.

MacArthur released his breath and forced the muscles of his mouth to relax, wiping a frozen grin away with a sweaty palm. Inhaling a week's supply of air, he holstered his pistol, jerked his rifle from his pack, and signaled for Chastain to return the way they had come. Keeping as quiet as they knew how, the marines made a wide detour before turning back in the direction of the river.

Half an hour later Chastain broke the silence. "Hey, Mac, what's a coonskin hat?"

TEN

THIRD LANDING

"Take the generator!" Buccari shouted. "That's crazy!" She and Quinn had retired to the mess decks, joining Rhodes and leaving Hudson on the flight deck. Gunner Wilson was on watch in the communications center.

"We need a power source," Quinn said patiently. "Nearly everyone's down and safe. Now's an acceptable time to take risks. With fuel from the lander we can keep the generator running for years. We can recharge our electrical equipment. We can generate heat. We can keep some level of civilized behavior. It'll be a long time before we're rescued, and Shannon says it's cold down there."

"Commander, I understand," Buccari debated. "That's what I wanted in the first place, but ... you were right. The lander is unreliable. I say we load everyone in the lander and get down on the planet while we can. It's too risky to try two runs."

"The lander has gone through a full diagnostic, and we fixed everything that was possibly broken. Right, Virgil?"

"We found all sorts of discrepancies. Full maintenance checks always do," the engineer declared. "We switched out the blaster control. All systems look good."

"All systems look good," Quinn cajoled, his tone revealing his impatience. "Enough discussion. Two more flights, Lieutenant."

"Yes, sir," Buccari said, struggling to sound supportive. "The sooner we try it out, the sooner we'll know what we're up against." She noticed Quinn's fatigue. His eyes had dark circles, his features were haggard and worn, and his head and chin stubble were grizzled and scruffy.

"Two more flights," Quinn repeated with less of an edge to

his voice. "Virgil and I will keep this hulk alive for a few more orbits. You and Jones take Chief Wilson and Mr. Hudson down with the generator. I have a feeling we will be in for a long, cold winter."

She had to admit it; the generator made sense.

MacArthur and Chastain broke through the last line of brambles. Their burgeoning little watercourse spilled out of its defile and was soon lost in a wide, shallow gravel-rattling flow. Large bars and shoals built up by previous floods and currents were strung at irregular intervals across and along the valley bottom. Many of the buildups had reverted to solid land, overgrown with trees and underbrush. Smooth stones and fine gravel crunched beneath their boots.

"Don't you want to make camp?" Chastain asked.

MacArthur checked the skies. The overcast was darker. Winds had shifted from the south. The weather was changing—had changed! His shoulder pain was dulled by the long day's efforts.

"Let's keep moving," MacArthur said. "Looks like rain, and I don't want this river rising any higher. I figure no more than four or five kilometers to high ground." He crunched across gravel. The first finger of the river was wide but barely ankle-deep.

"This won't be hard to cross," Chastain said. "It's a bunch of shallow rivers."

"Yeah," MacArthur grunted, looking into the distance. A fine mist hung in the air, and a low rumbling intruded into his awareness. The next channel was deeper and more powerful but only paces across. They lifted their packs overhead and forded the opaque green-gray torrent. Chilled by icy waters, the marines trudged onward, crossing more and more fingers of river. In midvalley they heard a double sonic boom.

"They're still there," Chastain said, looking upward. MacArthur said nothing, staring futilely into the clouds. The noise signified the presence of other humans and paradoxically made the marine feel even lonelier. He moved out with renewed vigor.

Shannon stood on the high plateau and stared into the overcast. Lee, with her medical equipment, stood at his side. The double sonic boom had echoed overhead ten minutes earlier— the lander should be on final. There it was—a black pinpoint against gray clouds, growing larger. He passed the alert over helmet radio. He had to get the cargo off fast; the weather was deteriorating.

The lander had definition; he made out the cruciform shape of wings and tail hanging in the air, rock-steady on glide slope; magically, it grew larger. Closer, it appeared to settle and accelerate slowly to the right, his offset from the landing point generating enough parallax to provide perspective. The EPL commenced landing transition, slowly raising nose attitude and bleeding off airspeed. Huge flaps were deployed, and the craft approached in a silent, graceful swoop. The nose of the craft suddenly jerked sideways. The lander oscillated back and forth, a cobra with its hood fully deployed. Something was wrong!

Buccari was ready. She felt the renegade inputs. They had come earlier this time, before main engine firing. She had two options: abort the landing—hit full igniters and blast back into orbit—or ride it in, hoping the retro programs would work correctly while she overrode the controls. Training and logic said to wave off and return to the corvette. Intuition told her the lander was only going to behave worse the next time. In a fraction of a second she chose to fly the landing and get those on board safely down.

The controls kicked in her hands; the autopilot had not disengaged. She fought for control, using both hands on the stick.

"Boats!" she roared. "Kill the control master! Disengage *now!*"

Jones moved in a blur, hitting the master control switch, overcoming ingrained conditioning. The retros would have to be manually fired!

Buccari felt the flight controls relax. She moved her left hand to the power quadrant and engaged retro-igniters. Monitoring the main fuel feeds, she hit the ignition with quick pulses. The main engines rumbled into life. She checked the engine gimbal angle indicator; it had set correctly during the transition. Buccari fired hard on the hover blasters and felt the nose surge backward. She eased up on the blasters and applied more power to the mains. The craft oscillated into the correct attitude for landing, but it was burning fuel at a horrendous rate! She moved to deploy the landing skids and noticed that Jones had already done so. With nothing left to do but pray, she tweaked power down. The lander settled to ground with an ugly, scraping bounce. She urgently secured the fuel flow to the mains and blasters, afraid to see how much fuel was left. Forcing herself, she stared at the gauges. Tears welled in her eyes. The fuel levels were so low! But she knew what she had to do. The decision was easy.

"Boats, get this thing unloaded and made ready," she shouted.

"But Lieutenant—" Jones started to speak.

"Get moving, Boats!"

"But Lieutenant, no way this bucket's going to make it to orb—"

"Jones," she hissed. "That's an order."

"Aye . . . aye, Lieutenant," Jones replied softly.

"Lieutenant, Shannon here," Shannon's voice came up on the radio. Buccari looked outside and saw the sergeant. Lee and another helmet-masked marine stood nearby. Tatum, judging from his height.

"Yes, Sergeant, and don't say anything about the landing!" she replied, trying to calm rampaging emotions.

"Aye, sir. It looks like you still have a problem."

"A big one, Sergeant." Buccari leaned back, sensing the nagging pressure of gravity against her back. "I've got to rendezvous with the 'vette as soon as possible. I can't shut down, and I'm below critical fuel." It was a confession.

"I'm no pilot, Lieutenant," Shannon transmitted, "but I know when things are out of control. Are you sure you—"

"You're right, Sergeant," Buccari cut in. "I'm the pilot. Listen up. Notify Commander Quinn as soon as the 'vette comes over the hill. Tell him to start looking for me on the acquisition radar. I'll be needing help. I'll make contact as soon as I clear the atmosphere, but he may have to start maneuvering before I can talk to him."

"Aye, aye, Lieutenant," Shannon said. "Understand. He gets you on radar and meets you halfway. He can boost to orbit after he gets you."

"Yessir, Superwom—I mean Lieutenant!" Jones shouted. "We can—"

"Not we, Boats," Buccari replied. "You're grounded. I'm going solo. Leaving your big body behind will help the fuel curve."

"No, Lieutenant! I—" Jones wailed.

"Stow it, Boats!" Buccari cut him off. "Watch the skin

temps. Off-load that generator and get this piece of junk ready to go!"

"Aye, aye, Lieutenant," Jones mumbled, continuing to curse softly as he released his mike switch.

Takeoff was easy. The lightly loaded lander punched through the lowering overcast and reached escape velocity with minimum acceleration. Bursting through the thick cloud deck, Buccari confronted the glaring explosion of a setting sun. Ignoring the Olympian scenery, Buccari set the fuel consumption parameters to a bare minimum and accelerated out of the atmosphere in good shape. The rendezvous coordinates, given available fuel, indicated a critically narrow flight profile, but it was still theoretically possible to coast up to the corvette's orbit—with absolutely no fuel remaining. The crew of the corvette would have some work to do to bring her aboard.

Within minutes of attaining orbital velocities her engines were starved.

The EPL was an unpowered satellite in extremely low orbit—too low! She verified that her identification beacon was emitting. Fifteen minutes later her IFF system was interrogated. The corvette had located her.

She came up: "*Harrier One*, lander's up. Come in, *Harrier One*."

Quinn's relieved voice responded. "Okay, Sharl, we got you. You're low and ahead of the 'vette. Real low! Can you elevate?"

Buccari was elated to hear his voice. "Sorry, Commander. I'm dry as dirt. You'll have to come get me. Sorry for the inconvenience."

"Sit tight, Sharl. We'll catch you in about an hour."

The orbiting ships slipped into the darkness of the planet's shadow. Buccari realized she had less than two hours of air remaining.

On board *Harrier One* Quinn choked back the lump in his throat. No one had ever executed a manual landing to a one-gee planet with a fuel balance sufficient for returning to orbit. Buccari had performed a miracle—well, almost. The corvette still had to retrieve the EPL. Buccari would go down in pilot history . . . if they were ever rescued.

"Main engines ready to answer," Rhodes said. "I sure wish we could get to her with the maneuvering jets."

"Me, too, Virgil, but that would take about two weeks. She might get a little impatient." Quinn started the main engine ignition checklist carefully. Neither man had confidence in the wounded power plant.

Quinn keyed the microphone. "Sharl, Quinn here. We have to fire the mains. You know what that means. We don't need much, but it's hard to tell what will happen. I thought you should know, in case you see us screaming by."

"Rog', Commander, I'll throw out a net," came Buccari's stolid reply.

The two men proceeded deliberately through the checklist, rechecking and verifying. Quinn monitored the engine instruments, trying to interpret the myriad danger signals the engine instruments were throwing back at him. His professional tools were a mess, but his objective was clear. They were doomed to die in their respective orbiting coffins unless they could unite and combine assets. The corvette could not enter the atmosphere; it was a large space vehicle with no aerodynamic controls. It had fuel, but its engines were crippled. The EPL, their planetary lander, was adrift in orbit, capable of penetrating the atmosphere and landing on the planet but trapped in orbit without the fuel required to initiate a deorbit burn, much less enough fuel to land safely.

"Mighty low orbit, Commander," Rhodes interrupted the checklist.

Quinn looked up from his console. They were in a decaying orbit.

"Yeah . . . low," Quinn said. "So we pick up the apple and boost back to orbit, where we load it with a full bag of fuel and head for the deck, to live happily ever after. If that song breaks down, we'll have to come up with a new verse."

"I'm ready to start singing," Rhodes replied tensely.

Quinn took a deep breath and commenced the ignition checklist. It was only a two-second burn with one percent power—a pat on a baby's ass.

". . . three . . . two . . . one . . . zero." Quinn hit the ignition switch. The engines fired and held for two seconds and then extinguished as programmed. Both men screamed in delight.

Quinn hit the transmit button. "We're coming, darling!" he shouted.

After a pause Buccari responded, her voice theatrically stiff: "Excuse me, Commander, but were you addressing yourself to me?"

* * *

The soft rumbling had grown steadily over the past kilometer, sometimes eclipsed by the gravelly cacophony of the individual streams but never completely lost. It was a distinct noise—a vibration, a loud, crashing background ambience. MacArthur crested a gravel bar to gain a vantage point. He peered into the misty gloaming and saw the river. The primary channel spread before him, perhaps three hundred meters across, moving smoothly with obvious power. Upstream and downstream MacArthur saw white water—cascades of turbulence bounding over and around large boulders—the source of the ambient roar that had been haunting them.

It was their last hurdle; the bank opposite rose steeply, and the foothills beyond were tantalizingly close. The men moved across the bar, curious to approach their challenge. MacArthur stopped at the edge, his confidence slipping. The river churned and roiled, moving swiftly to their left. Downstream, surging white waves seasoned with crystalline humps of green-black water crashed and rattled over a spectacularly rugged section of rocks.

"Let's walk downstream. If we cross here and don't make it, it'll be a rough ride." MacArthur had to repeat himself because of the noise.

They hiked over slippery rocks, past angry sections of chewed-up water crashing around jagged pinnacles. The noise was deafening, and the air was thick with mist. MacArthur's apprehension grew. He began to doubt their ability to make it across at all, much less before nightfall. They confronted a barricade of debris, an accumulation of bleached-out limbs and logs impeding their progress, but as they worked through it, MacArthur registered an idea. Wood! They would make a raft of driftwood. It would be ungainly, but if they could find a calm stretch of river, they could make it. It would not have to be a big raft, just enough to take their weight.

"Jocko, start collecting wood," he ordered. Grimacing, he slid straps from his aching shoulders and deposited his load on the rocks. Feeling suddenly and deceptively springy-legged with the lightening of his load, he stretched his back and shoulders. They were reasonably high above the water. If he could not find a likely spot to cross the river, they would camp there for the night.

"Try to find some large pieces. Couple of meters long. Enough for a raft. I'll check out the river," he went on.

Chastain shucked his big pack onto the rocks with a crunching thud.

Gloomy dusk was surrendering to impatient night. MacArthur scanned the river downstream, searching for telltale spumes of luminescence indicating rocks and rapids. The crescendo of the rapids abated; he could hear the torrent at his feet. The river flowed more gently, still with good speed but without the urgency associated with turbulence. He walked farther; the loudness receded. The river melded into darkness, but the low cliffs of the far bank gave him a dim perspective of distance. He slowed his pace. The river could be crossed with a raft. He stopped and stared one last time into the darkness—the decision had been made.

As he peered into the murk, clouds to the south pulsated with flickering blue light and a low rolling cannonade of thunder echoed up the river valley. He turned and headed back, leg-weary, stumbling over loose river rock.

Council chambers echoed with clicking talons. The hunters were ushered before the elders; that was unusual at this late hour—the elders fatigued easily. But the explosions from the sky, louder even than thunder, had reached the cliff dwellers' deepest fears. It had started again! The elders were frightened. The hunters lined up before the council, and Braan moved into the dock. For once he waited to be addressed, as was proper.

"I bid brave warriors welcome. Braan, leader-of-hunters, of clan Soong, please speak," Koop-the-facilitator said politely.

"Long life, Excellency; I am humbled," Braan said with unusual ceremony.

A cool breath of air fluttered through the chamber, causing spirit lamps to gutter and dim. The storm rolling up the river valley was a severe one—brilliant threads of lightning had guided the hunters' flight down the cliff face. Raindrops had pattered on them as they had approached the portal of the grand assembly hall. An angry night.

"Braan and his hunters have returned," the facilitator said, his expression intense, "and the mysterious thunder plagues us still. What news of its source?"

"Visitors . . . powerful visitors, O elder," the somber Braan said. "Loud noises from their flying machine. Each time it soars, noise rends the air and more strangers are come."

"Bear people?" the facilitator asked.

"Not bear people," Braan replied. The hunter leader proceeded with his detailed report, exceeding the limits of dweller knowledge. Braan was interrupted with astonished exclamations. Braan begged to proceed, endeavoring to answer the parts with the whole, but there were mysteries here for which he had no answers.

"They are not gods. They are tall and strong and have clear eyes, but they fear injury and death," Braan stated, hearkening to the rockdog incident. "Yet they kill like gods—from a distance, using sticks that spout loud noise and flame. Weapons we cannot match."

" 'Tis the stick that kills, not the being?" a steam user asked.

"The long-legs kill with the stick," Braan affirmed.

"Have they wings?" a fisher asked. "Did not initial reports attribute to them the power of flight?"

"No wings. With the exception of the silver machine, they cannot fly or soar. Or at least were not seen doing so. They walk slowly and clumsily wherever they go."

"Thy recommendation, Braan, leader-of-hunters?" Koop asked.

Braan pondered and said nothing. This was not rude, for a direct question was an invitation to consider deeply. The facilitator sat back, content that he had asked an important question.

Braan's answer, when it came, was not unexpected. "Our knowledge is insufficient to make a choice. Our alternatives are to kill them or to become their allies. Both alternatives offer serious consequences. Killing them could only be done at dear price, for they have powerful weapons. Yet kill them we can, for they are few and we are many."

Braan paused and looked about the chamber. The elders each fixed him with a stare of undiluted fear. Braan worried for the future.

"Becoming allies is likewise a dangerous path," he continued, "because it can be done only if the long-legs so desire. By offering ourselves to their compassion, we lose the advantage. If they prove treacherous, the cost in dweller lives would ultimately be far greater."

"Should we not attack immediately, before more long-legs arrive?" Bott'a-the-hunter asked impetuously—and rudely. The elders stirred.

"The young warrior's question is appropriate," Braan said quickly. "Certainly, to attack swiftly would increase the likelihood of victory. But it would also eliminate all other options. We would become enemies—a difficult condition to alter."

"Thy recommendation?" the facilitator persisted.

"Their numbers are not yet a cause for concern. It will take many landings of their flying craft to threaten us. If they are to be our allies, we must test them," Braan said.

"Test? And how?" Koop asked.

"I know not . . . yet. Continued surveillance will reveal our path. Hunters will maintain a sentry until the snows come. Perhaps the cruelty of winter will resolve the matter."

The council members talked briefly among themselves. Koop stood erect. "Braan, leader-of-hunters, thy plans are our plans. Perhaps the long-legs will define their own fate—and ours—regardless of our wishes. We meet next in one cycle of the small moon."

Braan bowed in good form and led his party through the grand assembly hall and out into the blustery night. Pouring rain and thrashing breezes eliminated all thought of soaring; Braan walked to the lift. He looked forward to seeing his wife and family, but he remembered Brappa, still in the field. The warrior Craag would take care of his last son.

The night grew old. Rain fell hard, blown sideways by gusting squalls, and white lightning danced in the clouds, shooting salvos of strobing illumination. MacArthur, wiping rainwater from his eyes, stood back from their handiwork and waited for a blast of lightning to highlight their creation. Chastain knelt and used a stout stick to crank tight the bindings on the last of the cross-supports. He deftly secured the knot and tied off the excess line.

"That'll hold," Chastain said proudly, sitting back on his knees.

Continuous lightning flashes, striking closer each time, splashed his features with white-blue brilliance. A ragged, air-boiling bolt struck the riverbank only a stone's throw away; thunder exploded in their faces, loud beyond comprehension. Their ears rang, and electricity hummed in the air, tingling fingers and toes. Ozone stung their nostrils.

"Holy smokes!" Chastain shouted.

"Yeah, I'll second that!" MacArthur laughed nervously. "Too close. Let's move behind that gravel bar and set up shelter. Wait it out." Another blue-hot streak of lightning flashed to the treetops on the hills beyond the river. A shock wave blew against their cold, wet faces.

Hours crept by. Winds abated and the lightning flickered to the west and north, but the rain fell harder—a deluge. MacArthur checked the raft. The river was rising. The rain-swollen river crept inexorably beneath their makeshift craft.

"Time to go," MacArthur shouted. Unbelievably, Chastain had rolled over on the wet rocks and fallen fast asleep. MacArthur envied his companion's stalwart nature. He debated waiting for morning, but the rising river was answering his worst fears. No telling how much water would be coming down the channel in the next few hours, but MacArthur had a hunch it would be significant.

Chastain rousted out and dragged both packs to the raft, diligently securing the equipment. MacArthur tried to help, but his body responded poorly. His head and shoulder throbbed. He removed his glove and slipped a hand beneath his coat and his clothes, exploring clammy bare skin. The shoulder felt wet, but then, his clothes had been soaked through for hours. He pulled his hand out. His fingers were sticky and slippery at the same time, and even though it was dark, he knew the hand was covered with blood.

"You all right, Mac?" Chastain asked.

"Let's go," MacArthur replied, reaching for a corner of the raft. Chastain copied his action, moving the raft only slightly before the river buoyed its weight. The current was strong. The men walked into the water and were quickly in to their waists, the forceful river tugging urgently on their unwieldy craft and weary bodies. The icy water jolted MacArthur into alertness; survival instincts pumped adrenaline into his battered system yet again.

"Push off," he ordered, gasping. "We'll pole it across."

Rain pouring from black skies drilled the wooden raft and its hapless crew. Darkness was total. The marines pushed into the impatient current, jumping sidesaddle onto their tiny craft. The raft tottered dramatically, Chastain's greater bulk overballasting it to one side. The burdened logs spun slowly in the rain-gushing murk.

MacArthur gripped his pole firmly, shoulder protesting. He extended the branch to its limit, searching for the gravel of the bottom, and felt nothing. The jiggling current tried to bend it from his hands.

"Too deep. Can't touch bottom," he said. Chastain groaned. MacArthur, dizzy from black nothingness, took a deep breath.

"Let's swim," he said, sliding into the water. Treading black water and clinging to the raft, he could tell from the craft's severe slant that Chastain was still onboard.

"C-Come on, Jocko. Can't ... by myself." MacArthur spewed frigid water.

"I can't swim, Mac."

"Yeah, sure, Jocko. L-Lets go," MacArthur responded.

"No, Mac! They cheated me through the tests. I played football."

MacArthur dropped his forehead against the weathered wood. He floated alongside for a few seconds, thinking, shivering. Rain hissed.

"J-Jocko. You can get in the water and paddle or you can stay up there. M-maybe we'll drift gently ashore. Or maybe we'll run out of deep river and find ourselves running this pile of sticks through a set of rapids like the big ones behind us." MacArthur stopped to catch his breath and spit out water.

"You know what will happen if we hit rapids?" he sputtered. As he uttered those words, his ears detected a faint noise—a rumble. Rapids! Rapids were coming!

"Get your ass in the river!" MacArthur screamed. "You hear that?"

MacArthur's side of the raft slapped into the water as Chastain's bulk slid off opposite. The big man thrashed his legs and flailed his free arm wildly; the raft turned in a circle.

"Slow down!" MacArthur shouted, but Chastain could not hear; white-water noise drowned his words. MacArthur sensed the current accelerating. The surface of the river dipped sharply, as if the torrent were running over a shallow, irregular bottom—over big rocks!

"Hang on, Jocko!" MacArthur yelled. His foggy brain tried to think, but the roar of broken water dominated his senses. The river narrowed, the constricted waters piling current upon current, forming a tortured pattern of choppy waves. The raft pitched and bucked in the troubled waters. A ghostly phosphorescence surged from the darkness. The raft was sucked toward the wet glow and was jerked downward behind it, the reflected upwash spinning the raft and ejecting it onward.

They were on smooth waters again, gently revolving, the crashing noises slowly subsiding behind them. MacArthur took a deep breath and held his face up into the relentless rain. The drops felt warm compared to the chill of the river. He shivered.

"We made it! We made it, didn't we?" Chastain exulted.

"Yeah," MacArthur replied, not wanting to tell him they had navigated a small set of rapids. He tried to match Chastain's stroke, the raft still spinning in the current.

"Keep the river coming from the same direction and don't burn yourself out," he admonished, his lower jaw trembling with cold.

They paddled diligently, the effort warming their bodies against the bone-chilling waters. Both shores were invisible, the darkness complete, the lightning long past. Heavy raindrops splattered around them, a whispering curtain of water. MacArthur wondered how far downriver they had been carried and how many hours of hiking would be added to their trek. They talked little, the chattering of teeth making conversation untenable. A low rumble flirted on the edge of their senses, cutting in and out of the rain hiss and the splashing of their arms.

"Shh! H-Hold it!" MacArthur gasped. He strained, trying to detect a noise he did not want to hear. There it was, clearer now—a deep-throated blend, far off. He uttered an expletive.

"Harder, Jocko," MacArthur shouted. They pulled vigorously, backstroking; the ungainly raft plowed across the hardening current.

"I hear it, Mac," Chastain gulped. "A big one, ain't it?"

"Oh, yeah," MacArthur said.

They paddled desperately, splashing and gasping for air, but the noise encompassed them, dominating all other sounds. The river flowed firmly and smoothly, the current a living thing, a flexing muscle. The noise increased to a full-fledged bellowing din, rivaling the sound of a rocket engine at full power. The pain in MacArthur's shoulder was eclipsed by panic.

The river fell from under them. Raft and crew soared into a black void. MacArthur screamed at the top of his lungs and separated from the raft. It was a short drop, but in the blackness it lasted an eternity. A maelstrom rose to meet them, and in it they were swallowed, jerking end over end, helpless, for eternal seconds. And as suddenly as they had been swallowed, they were ejected, flushed to the surface of the turbulence. MacArthur felt yielding contact; it was not a rock. A bullstrong fist grabbed him by the back of his coat and hauled him bodily to the raft. Half-drowned, spewing water, MacArthur grabbed onto smooth wood with both hands and pulled his chest onboard. He felt Chastain's great arm across his back, trying to hold him against the bucking forces. Water washed over them. They struck hard against rocks, jolting and careening in circles, spinning into the wake of foaming granite islands, and all the while violently bouncing and plunging. Plunging and bouncing, the raft spun and galloped, more under the water than atop it.

The raft was no longer rigid; the bindings had loosened. A massive rock loomed from the darkness. The hapless craft struck solidly and held fast to the sheer upstream face of the monolith, pinched mightily by the overwhelming weight of an iron current. Magnificent water pressure crushed them, pinning them helplessly to the raft, which was itself held in tight bond to the rock. MacArthur felt the raft flexing and warping, its bindings working looser. With gut-wrenching speed the lines unraveled, and the greater portion of the raft, including their packs, explosively separated and was carried away down the left side of the rock. Chastain's iron-strong fingers dug desperately into MacArthur's arm as the remaining small piece of raft broke loose to the right of the rock, returning the sodden marines into the crashing cascade. Within seconds their meager raft was reduced to a single small log. Both men, clinging helplessly to each other, grasped the splintered wood, the focus of their entire being.

ELEVEN

LAST LANDING

"Commander, this sorry excuse for an orbit ain't going to last," Rhodes reported from engineering. Holding his breath, Quinn dared to exercise the main engines one more time, all but stopping the closure rate. The power plant, vibrating insanely, threatened to explode. Orbital decay alarms brayed continuously.

"Hang on, Virgil," Quinn responded, nursing the thrusters. "She's in grappling range in ten minutes. The maneuvering jets can do the rest."

The EPL was no longer a point of light in the distance; it had shape and color. Red, white, and blue strobe lights flashed with irritating brilliance. Quinn eased the forward vector with axial thrust, diminishing the rate of closure. He turned off the corvette's strobes, and the lander pilot answered, extinguishing her own.

"Coming up on you, Sharl," Quinn announced over the radio.

"Roger, Commander. Best approach I've ever seen," she answered.

Quinn played the vernier thrusters delicately, setting the approach vector. The lander drifted down his starboard side.

"Piece of cake," Quinn mumbled. With visual reference no longer available, he concentrated on the docking display. Despite excursions caused by orbital drag, he brought the corvette to a halt relative to the lander and moved the huge ship within range of the gantry. After some touchy jostlings, the lander was secured in its bay and the hangar doors were sealed.

"Too easy," Quinn transmitted. "Initiate boost when she's clear."

"Roger that," Rhodes responded from the lander bay. "Should be quick; the bay has repressurized. Okay, the hatch is opening. On my way."

Quinn acknowledged and returned to setting up the next boost. In less than a minute Buccari glided onto the flight deck. Her features were drawn and fatigued, but she favored him with a supernova smile, green eyes glinting in the white light of sunrise.

"Thanks for picking me up. Sorry about the short orbit," she said.

"Welcome back. Let's just say we appreciate your effort," Quinn replied. "And besides, we didn't have anything else to do."

She floated to her station, replaced her helmet, and plugged her umbilicals into the console. "Where are you?"

Quinn brought her up to speed, and she was immediately absorbed in the flight deck situation. Orbital decay was past critical. The air temperature in the corvette had risen uncomfortably, and Quinn was constantly maneuvering the wallowing craft.

"Phew, I thought it looked bad before!" Buccari said, checking the instruments. "This power plant is really chewed up. Virgil, whatever did you do to these engines?"

"Begging the lieutenant's pardon, but we used 'em to come get you," Rhodes's voice came back over the intercom.

"Well, I guess they look fine, then," Buccari replied.

Quinn laughed. He was excited for good reason. They were going to pull it off. A short boost to a safe orbit, refuel the lander, and they could all safely return to the planet.

"Okay, stand by for boost. Twenty seconds at two gees," he ordered.

"Ready here," Buccari said.

"Engineering, aye," Rhodes reported.

"Two lousy gees, baby. You can do it," Quinn exhorted aloud as he rechecked the throttle settings. "Counting down . . . three . . . two . . . one and ignition now!"

The engines exploded into life—

—and stopped! Fuel pumps and compression turbines normally masked by engine tumult wound down with plaintive screams. A resounding thump resonated through the ship, more metallic banging, and then—silence! Warning lights glared and flickered obscenely.

Buccari and Quinn turned to each other.

"Rhodes, start pumping fuel into the apple!" Quinn shouted.

Buccari was unstrapped before Quinn started talking. She propelled herself into the hatchway and through the crew area to the lander bay, retracing her path of only minutes before. Rhodes came through on her heels and took over refueling. Buccari jackknifed into the lander and started preflight checks, feeling as if she had spent her entire life in the confined cockpit. The corvette danced, pitching and yawing with increasing amplitudes.

"We're losing it!" Quinn shouted over the intercom. "How long?"

Buccari noted the fuel gauges registering a minuscule amount; they were making progress. She did a mental calculation and checked their position relative to the desired landing site.

"We have three considerations," she responded. "One is just getting out of orbit without burning up or running out of oxygen. Two is having enough fuel to do a soft landing—apples aren't famous for belly landings. And three, landing near our people—it's a big planet. We could land and never see the crew again."

"I got the picture! How much time?" Quinn shouted.

"At least ten minutes to get fuel for a controlled deorbit. I don't know where we'll crash, but at least we'll leave orbit without running out of air. It'll take at least twenty minutes to get enough fuel for a controlled landing. Could be over an ocean," Buccari replied calmly. "It will take almost forty minutes to get the fuel we need, land where we want to, and expect to walk away, and that depends on when and where we leave orbit. Anything after that's gravy. Virgil, do you agree?"

"Roger, Lieutenant. Close enough for me," Rhodes replied.

Quinn fought the monster, not surprised by Buccari's summary. Falling out of orbit was the least of his concerns—he fought the jerking and flailing ship. Forty minutes raced slowly by. Quinn made up his mind.

"Enough fuel," he commanded. He struggled to stay ahead of the excursions. "Get your butts in the lander. Sharl, deploy the apple when Rhodes gets inside. I'm staying. You can't launch the lander without someone stabilizing the corvette."

No response was forthcoming. Precious moments elapsed.

"Rhodes, Buccari, you copy? I want both of you in that lander *now*!"

Still nothing. Quinn caught a movement behind him. He turned to see Buccari and Rhodes floating on the flight deck, arms crossed on their chests. Buccari pointed to her helmet in the vicinity of her ears and gave a thumbs-down. Rhodes did the same.

"There's no time for this," Quinn groaned.

"Nice try, Commander, but we're not leaving without you," Buccari said. "Stop feeling sorry for yourself . . . sir."

"Buccari, dammit! I gave you an order!" Quinn was angry and thankful at the same time, a tough combination to deal with. "None of us is going to get out of here if I don't hold the ship steady. The gantry won't take the inertia changes. Even you can't get a lander out of this ship!"

Buccari watched Quinn wrestle the controls, the realization of the commander's words sinking in. "No! There has to be a way for all of us to make it," she moaned.

Rhodes had remained silent. "I got an idea," he said.

Quinn and Buccari turned to look at him expectantly.

"The skipper holds the 'vette down until we clear, and then he comes out the EVA hatch in his battle suit. We take him on board through the apple's main hatch. It's been done before."

"Sounds good!" Quinn barked. "Get going. I want you clear in five minutes. Go!" He returned his attention to the buffeting corvette.

Buccari and Rhodes flew back to finish the fueling disconnects. Buccari went straight to the EPL cockpit.

"Opening bay doors," Rhodes reported.

The big doors crept open, fluttering as they spread. Buccari felt queasy. Door interlocks signaled green, and she ordered Rhodes to activate the gantry. Mooring locks released with their familiar clacking sound, and the lander floated free—for an instant. It banged back on its moorings, making a sickening hollow-metal noise. The EPL had become a loose cannon! The mooring points fell away; the lander separated, elevating within the confines of its womb, straining the gantry attachments. Seconds later the lander slammed back down on its moorings.

"Goose the gantry! Get it off the locks before we bottom out again!" she yelled. She watched the doors wave and felt the lander move vertically. She knew that the vertical forces were seriously deflecting the fragile gantry crane. The lander drifted inexorably outward, clearing the mooring locks with a glancing, grating contact. "Not too bad," she muttered. The lander was made tough. While still inside the door overhang she pulled the gantry release, opting to drive the lander out with maneuvering thrusters. She accelerated clear of the corvette, timing the vertical oscillations of the door almost perfectly—almost! One of the EPL's vertical fins clipped the descending upper bay door with a resounding clang.

"Oops," Buccari mumbled into the intercom.

The EPL broke from the stark blackness of the corvette's solar lee and into the brightness of the sun-star. From four hundred meters away the massive corvette appeared stable, but stabilizers were firing constantly. Spikes of blue flame erupted from the thruster ports.

"Commander, we're waiting for you to clear," she broadcast.

"Hate to leave . . . a real picnic," Quinn gasped. "Five minutes."

Buccari marked the time. The nose of the corvette pitched

slowly downward. A rolling motion commenced soon afterward, both motions accelerating perceptibly.

"Lieutenant," Rhodes spoke up from his operator's station. "I'd like to open the main hatch. Cockpit is isolated, and seals are good."

"Roger, cleared to open the main hatch," she responded, concentrating on the EVA port of the tumbling corvette. Vertigo plagued her; she shook her head again and again. She did not want to miss Quinn's exit. The spinning ship would send him on a tangential vector, the direction unpredictable. She piloted the lander between the sun-star and the corvette to get maximum contrast on Quinn's space suit. Another two minutes dragged by. The tumbling increased in magnitude. Another two minutes. She tried to contact the commander on radio, in vain. He was shielded from her transmissions until he emerged from the corvette.

There he was—floating free, tumbling, an unbelievably tiny speck against the expansive bulk of the corvette, which was itself spinning against the infinite backdrop of the black void. She blinked, straining to verify that it was not just a vertigo-induced spot in her vision.

"I'm out, Sharl. Do you have me? I don't see you," he said, a hint of panic in his deep voice. His ballistic trajectory changed abruptly. He had strapped on a maneuvering unit.

"Tallyho, Commander. Coming out of the sun." Buccari pointed the EPL in his direction.

"Contact. Hold your vector, Sharl. Two minutes out," Quinn transmitted, controlling the rendezvous.

"Roger, holding." She brought herself back to the job at hand. "Okay, Virg, let's set up an orbital boost. Get some altitude so we can think about our next step."

"Aye, aye, Lieutenant," Rhodes responded. "Everything looks good. I'm showing thirty percent fuel. We should be able to set down real soft."

"Rog', concur. I figure we boost eight clicks. We can afford it."

"You're the captain," Rhodes responded.

The checklist was almost complete when Rhodes interjected: "Skipper's coming aboard."

Buccari glanced over her shoulder. Quinn glided to the open hatch, his maneuvering jets firing like sparkling diamonds. He retrofired against his forward vector, halting smartly at the mouth of the gaping hatch, hooked a foot on the hatch rim, and pulled himself into the rectangular opening. She returned to her checklist.

"I'm up," Quinn said tersely.

"Commander, we're elevating. Fuel's good, and we could use the time to think this one out," Buccari replied, not asking permission. He was cargo. "What's your state?"

"Six hours of air," the commander replied.

"Six hours, aye. Plenty of time," Buccari reflected. "Virgil, let Shannon know we're coming in for breakfast. Commander, I want you to remember this on my next evaluation."

"Sharl, if I didn't think you'd spit in my eye, I'd give you a big kiss."

"Tsk, Commander! You're much too old. Money and promotions will do."

Rhodes interrupted. "I fixed the engines."

"Some fix!" Buccari replied. "Work something out with the skipper on your own."

Quinn muttered something incoherent and obviously off-color.

"First things first," Buccari said. "Stand by for acceleration. Buckled in back there?" Quinn replied in the affirmative. Buccari continued: "Two gees for fifteen seconds. Ignition . . . four . . . three . . . two . . . one firing now."

The primaries jolted into life. The small ship jumped, but Buccari's elation was brief. EXHAUST OVERTEMP warning lights glared ominously. She aborted.

"Nothing's going right!" Rhodes said over the intercom. "Systems check coming up."

His news was not welcome. "Gimbals trashed on one and two," he reported then. "One hundred percent asymmetrical! You couldn't use the engines for a landing retro if you wanted to. With those overtemps, even the reentry retro's gonna be pretty stimulating."

They sat silently. The planet rolled by overhead, filling the viewscreen. Buccari watched the terminator approach and pass, the darkness of night a relief from the brilliance of the cloud- and sea-reflected sun.

"Sarge! They're in the lander. Lieutenant Buccari made it!" O'Toole shouted.

Shannon crawled from his sleeping bag into cold dampness. Dawson bolted by him, pulling on a hooded jacket. She pushed O'Toole out of the radio operator's seat, pulling the hard copy from his hands. A hooded lantern provided illumination, and a tarpaulin hung across the cramped alcove, preventing its glow from escaping into the nerve-dulling downpour. The lightning had stopped.

Shannon staggered into the dim circle of light, a thermal blanket draped over his broad shoulders. The low-hung lantern accentuated his haggard features, his grizzled growth nearly all white. O'Toole handed him the message.

```
TO:      HUDSON/SHANNON
FM:      RHODES

DTG:     011659 0233 ST

LOW UNSTABLE ORBIT FORCED ABANDONMENT OF HARRIER ONE.
QUINN, BUCCARI, AND RHODES ON BOARD EPL.

ORBIT TRAJECTORIES DICTATE REENTER NEXT ORBIT. EPL DAM-
AGED. UNABLE TO USE MAIN ENGINES. EXHAUST NOZZLES NO
LONGER GIMBAL.

SET UP BEACON IMMEDIATELY. BUCCARI DIRECTS BEACON TO BE
ESTABLISHED AT EXTREME NORTHWEST END OF LAKE, WITH ONE
ONE ZERO DEGREE (110/2) TRUE RADIAL LINED UP WITH MAXIMUM
DIMENSION OF LAKE AND CLEAR OF ISLANDS. GLIDE SLOPE FIVE
DEG. WILL ATTEMPT WATER LANDING. ESTIMATE TOUCHDOWN AT
0410 ST.

RESPOND IN REAL TIME BEFORE 0330 ST IF UNABLE TO COMPLY.

ACKNOWLEDGE.

RHODES
AR
```

Adrenaline coursed into Shannon's veins. *A water landing? In the dark?*

"O'Toole, roust 'em out! All hands. I want the beacon up within the hour. New location. Break out the raft from the survey package. Get Tatum up here. Move!"

Dawson pounded out an acknowledgment draft on the radio console. "Anything special you want to add, Sarge? I'm ready to reply."

Hudson joined them in the circle of light. "You have flares in the planet survey package, don't you, Sergeant?" the ensign asked calmly.

Shannon understood immediately. "Tell 'em we'll run a flare line down the east side of the lake. And give them a weather report," he said, walking to the entrance. "Ceiling three hundred meters, maybe lower. Visibility practically zero. Raining. Winds calm. That'll cheer 'em up."

"Roger," she replied, and typed rapidly. "Anything else?"

"Just tell 'em we'll be waiting," he said.

"Roger that," Dawson replied. She hit the transmit button, shooting the burst message to the heavens. Shannon moved back to his sleeping bag and pulled on his rancid clothes. He shivered.

"Retroburn in ten minutes," Buccari announced.

"I want you out before touchdown," Quinn insisted for the third time, his voice rising in volume, as if the sealed hatch between him and the cockpit needed to be shouted through. The lander had ejection seats, but only for the pilot and the systems operator.

"Sir, shut up!" Buccari snapped. "All due respect, of course," she added, teeth clenched. "Rhodes will initiate ejection—on my command or sooner if necessary. I plan to ride it to touchdown. That's the plan."

Tension remained heavy. Buccari forced her thoughts onto other problems.

"You sure this little ejection seat will get me out?" Rhodes asked.

Buccari snorted. "It'll be close. Don't worry about the seat, but you'll have to suck in your gut to get through the hatch. I'd be more worried about the parachute."

Rhodes forced a laugh. "Speaking of hatches, I've worked through the overrides. I can open the hatches as soon as we slow to approach airspeed. She'll sink like a rock."

"She'll sink like a hot rock regardless, assuming she stays in one piece," Buccari added. "What do you think, Commander? Open all hatches?"

"All hatches," came back the sulky reply.

Buccari detected fear in the commander's tone. He was powerless, and in being powerless, he was scared. Buccari was also scared. Quinn had no chance unless she set the lander down on the lake. An unpowered, night-instrument approach through a black overcast—thick and solid—a bad bet! She had only one shot. There would be no wave-offs.

"Beacon's up and all tests check, Sarge," Tatum panted. Rain poured in rivulets from the brim of his soggy cloth cap, sluicing down to join the cascades from his poncho. Shannon peered into the darkness. In the distance a flashlight flickered, emitting a feeble beam, revealing little. Everyone was in position, ranging down the northeastern shore of the lake, ready to light off the survival flares. Shannon racked his brain. How was she going to pull it off?

"Good job, Sandy," he said. Tatum had packed the assembled beacon at double time over the sloppy terrain. "Nice night for a swim."

"Beautiful. Just friggin' beautiful," Tatum huffed.

Shannon took the flashlight from Tatum and held it to his watch. "Twenty minutes, I reckon. Let's make sure O'Toole and Jones have finished preparing the raft." He gave the flashlight back.

"Phoowee, she's running hot!" Rhodes screamed over the intercom.

"But she's running!" Buccari screamed back. The lander was pointed backward in orbit, engines firing against the orbital vector. Rhodes had disabled the worst of the nozzles, but damage to others had created havoc with temperatures and fuel flows. "Ten more seconds and we're golden!"

Seconds crawled by. Buccari retarded the throttle, and the EPL's engines quieted, along with the nerves of its occupants. She made an adjustment to the lander's attitude, pitching the nose around with a maneuvering jet until reentry attitude was set. The glow of plasma around the forward viewscreen cast a pulsing amber light on her drawn features. Buffeting rocked the craft. They were dumb, blind, and helpless, the intense heat and turbulence of the reentry masking all communications. The flight controls were useless until the atmosphere grew thick enough to respond. They were totally committed.

Lee lugged her drenched medical satchel. It was not designed for hiking in the rain; nor was she. Gravity punished her back and legs; her breathing was heavy, and she alternated between perspiring and shivering. She collapsed on the heavy bag, wiping water from her eyes. The poncho was too large, and the hood flopped over her face. Whenever she moved, she needed to push the hood back in order to see. Sitting on the equipment to rest, she pulled the hood over her head, failing to first empty the reservoir of accumulated rainwater. It ran cold and wet down her neck, racking her short frame with shivers.

She turned to search for Fenstermacher. Despite his bad arm, the boatswain had stubbornly helped her lug the equipment from the cave. She heard him slogging toward her, his form appearing in the murky downpour. She shined the flashlight beam on the ground, watching raindrops slap the surface of the lake.

"Anything new?" she asked.

Fenstermacher, carrying two flares, splashed up and sat heavily on the bag, making contact with his skinny hips against her round ones. She moved to make room, and he slid over, again making contact along their thighs. She had run out of room, so she just sat there, not minding. It was warmer, and she actually liked Fenstermacher. Strangely, everyone liked Fenstermacher.

"Nothing," he answered, short of breath. "They must be inbound. O'Toole will help with your first-aid kit. I'm not much good with this broken arm."

"Nonsense; you helped getting it here. You should have stayed in the cave with Rennault. You have a long way to go before you're back to normal. Not that you were ever normal."

Fenstermacher remained silent, uncharacteristically letting the jab pass.

"Hope they make it," he gulped in despair, putting his chin in his hands. Lee looked at him for a few seconds and then put her arm around his narrow shoulders. Both of them returned their stares to the small circle of light of the flashlight beam.

The bearing indicator on the head-up display moved from the stops and settled. The lander had drifted north. Buccari reset her approach track, and the bearing indicator adjusted. Distance readouts commenced. The landing window was good, but there was no margin for error. The EPL was flying. She wiggled the sidestick gently.

The large moon, in its first quarter, cast faint light on the cloud deck. The small moon was full but contributed less illumination than did the dense constellations of stars. Dark mountain peaks rose above the silver clouds, giving reference to her velocity. Marching away, far in the distance, rising above the mountains, lines of towering cumulonimbus flickered magically.

She verified that fuel had been dumped. Precious fuel—worthless because of the damaged nozzles. Only enough fuel to ignite the hover blasters remained, and she retrimmed for a no-fuel approach. Her scan narrowed. She debated whether to keep the autopilot engaged. The computer could fly the approach better than she could—if it worked. The autopilot had only shown problems on final. No, she could no longer trust the systems; too many things had gone wrong. She swallowed, half to clear the building pressure in her ears and half to push her doubts back into her being, and then she switched off the auto-controls.

Trailing double thunder, the glinting lander descended for the cloud deck. Buccari banked smoothly, airspeed dropping in the turn. She steadied on a truncated base leg and watched the timer count the seconds. Airspeed and altitude bled off rapidly, and the first tendrils of cloud obscured her forward vision with ghostly wisps of cotton. The lander skimmed deeper into the silky vapors. Her view of the stars flickered and was gone.

Shannon's head jerked at the sonic booms. Rain fell in his eyes and across his face. He returned his vision to the ground, wiping the water from his eyes.

"Five minutes! Turn on flashlights—white beams," he shouted into his helmet radio. The marines had traded their cloth hats for helmets. "Acknowledge!"

The marines responded. Everyone was ready, but for what? If Buccari missed the lake to the right, she would kill his people. If she got lucky and landed in the water, then what?

Shannon reached down and touched the inflated raft. Shannon could swim well, but he had a deep-seated fear of the water. He did not look forward to pushing out onto the black, rain-spattered lake. He checked his watch; it was time to ignite the flares.

"Light 'em off!" he commanded over UHF. In the distance a bright red flare erupted into life, followed by another and yet another, until a necklace of red sparklers pierced the drizzle, illuminating and defining the shoreline. He reached into the raft, took out the search lantern, and turned it on, pointing it into the skies.

* * *

The lander rolled onto final and dropped subsonic, the black fuzziness of clouds still obscuring forward vision. Raindrops vaporized against the viewscreen. Buccari concentrated on the head-up, noting her radar altimeter coming on line. She would be dragging it in; there was no excess airspeed. A good thing—she did not want to force the EPL down on the lake, but did she have enough energy to make it?

She checked distance to the beacon, made an alignment adjustment, pushed her nose down for airspeed, and armed air brakes and spoilers in the unlikely event she stayed fast. The glide slope indicator moved steadily to center. In quick succession she activated wingtip fences and leading-edge slats, dropped the first increment of flaps, and armed hover blasters. She was ready. Only flaps and blasters to go. Rhodes's voice droned steadily as he read off radar altitude and distance to the beacon for Quinn's benefit. Buccari concentrated on holding the lineup and glide slope. Airspeed was good. She dropped the next increment of flaps. At thirty-four kilometers from the beacon the radar altimeter abruptly decreased by a thousand meters—the plateau's edge.

Ten kilometers to go. On glide slope and on course. Attitude trimmed a bit fast, the nose not quite high enough, but that was the side on which to err—plenty of time to correct it. She tapped the rudder and eased stick pressure to port, and the lander corrected an incipient drift. Five kilometers. She added flaps, and the nose ballooned slightly. Buccari compensated, holding the slope. Three kilometers. *Where were the bottom of the clouds?* She checked altitude, pushed the nose down, and added the last increment of flaps.

Red flares! She saw flares strung in a ragged line to the right of her nose. Airspeed approached stall. The radar altimeter said ten meters. She eased the nose back and held the wings level, using only the rudders. Impact was seconds away! She forced herself to hold attitude—no jerky movements. With startling immediacy the tail of the lander met the water, and simultaneously—more luck than timing—Buccari fired the hover blasters, offsetting the impact and keeping the nose from slapping forward. She yelled at Rhodes to eject.

And found herself screaming hysterically into the wet night, a living projectile being rocketed violently out of the crashing craft below. Before she could comprehend the fact, she was swinging into the water, a deadweight at the end of a pendulum, her canopy having opened just enough to retard the impact. The reality of freezing water snapped disjointed thoughts into focus. She surfaced clear of the chute and fumbled for the disconnects, but they had been pulled high on her shoulders by the yanking deployment. Frantically treading water, she located the fittings and disengaged her harness from the enveloping shrouds. Panic struck as she felt snaking nylon wrapping around her ankles. Fighting to stay calm, she submerged and worked to separate herself from the tangle. Excruciatingly slowly, one by one, the clinging lines fell away. She surfaced and weakly frog-kicked onto her back.

The impenetrable blackness of her surroundings defied consciousness, her helmet shutting out all sounds except for the beating of her heart and the explosions of her labored breathing. With difficulty she removed the headgear, letting in the splashing of the lake—and the cold water. She spit out a throatful, and then, as if in a dream, she heard yells carrying across the chop. A bright beam passed over her.

The EPL, a crazed dragon descending from the clouded heavens spouting evil flames, mushed into the lake, throwing before it a tremendous crest of water. A crashing emerald-green wave surrealistically illuminated by blazing hover blasters surged upward. The lander disappeared, but the fiery blasters continued to burn submerged, lighting up the roiled lake around the sinking craft like a huge Chinese lantern. After eternally long seconds the blasters extinguished, their fuel exhausted.

Buccari had hit the mark, not a hundred meters from where the raft was waiting. As Tatum pulled on the oars, Shannon kept his eyes on the ejection seats exploding from the cockpit, their trajectories diverging, one forward and one aft of the impact point. Shannon ordered Tatum to steer for the closest, fifty meters away. He directed the powerful search lantern, holding his balance against the colossal waves surging from the steaming and bubbling crash site.

The first wall of water was powerful and steep, nearly capsizing the raft. Shannon was thrown against the giving sides of the raft and saved himself from going overboard by grasping the lifeline along the gunnel. He recovered and moved back into position to search the thrashing lake, struggling to stay upright on the bucking and twisting raft. He saw something—the powerful spotlight reflected from a white, gaping face—Buccari! Shannon removed his helmet and peeled off his poncho and boots, yelling directions to Tatum. With powerful strokes Tatum brought the raft within range, and Shannon dove into the frigid water. He surfaced beside the struggling pilot.

"Nice landing, Lieutenant," Shannon sputtered. He grabbed her by the torso harness and pulled her to the raft.

"Kiss my ass," she choked.

"That's ... an order I can live with ... sir," Shannon replied, spitting water. He grabbed the lifeline for leverage and pushed Buccari up by her rear as Tatum pulled her by the arms into the raft, dumping her unceremoniously into the water-washed bilge. Shannon hauled himself over the stern and pointed in the direction of the other ejection. As Tatum rowed, he reported back to the beach on his helmet radio. A rain-muted cheer drifted across the troubled water.

The lake's surface remained tortured from waves rebounding between the shores. Shannon yelled loudly and held the search lantern over his head, directing the downpour-shrouded beam in slow, sweeping circles over the rain-drilled waters. Buccari, shivering, crawled, slipping and sliding, to the bow. Nothing could be heard other than the noise of Tatum's oars, the water slapping the raft's bow, and the hissing sound of raindrops striking the lake. Flares burned dimly on the lakeshore. Tatum stopped stroking, lending his eyes to the search.

Shannon wailed the names of the two men: "Rhodes! Commander Quinn!"

They listened—to the sounds of water.

Buccari pointed and called out, "Over there! I see something!"

Tatum bent to the oars and propelled the raft on the designated heading, pulling alongside a shape in the water—a parachute! They leaned over the side, reaching and clawing for handfuls of sodden canopy, and pulled together, dragging the fabric through the raft and off the other side, searching for the shrouds. The shroud lines came to hand and were in turn pulled relentlessly inward. The thin, biting cords seemed of interminable length, but they could feel the bulk at the other end and hauled with greater desperation. Rhodes's body came to the surface sideways, shrouds tangled around legs and torso and around his neck. Tatum and Shannon flopped the heavy limp form into the raft, where it lay without movement.

Buccari lost her balance and slipped, landing with her face next to Rhodes's helmet. Shannon heard her gasp. He knelt and pulled the helmet release. The helmet came off with a sucking sound. Rhodes's fully open eyes stared vacantly—the look of the dead—lips deep purple, his skin faintly blue. Suffocated.

Buccari drew a breath, put her lips over the unconscious man's mouth, and blew firmly into his lungs while pinching his nostrils. Shannon knelt down and pushed rhythmically on Rhodes's chest with his powerful fists, which was difficult to do in the yielding bottom of the raft.

"Let's get back to shore. Maybe Lee can do something. We got another one to look for," Shannon said. Buccari did not respond, frantically continuing her resuscitation efforts. Shannon leaned back on his knees and watched. He signaled impatiently, and Tatum grabbed the oars and rowed. The flares on the beach were dying one by one.

Shannon pushed Buccari aside and took a turn trying to breathe life back into the man. Buccari sat back, exhausted, on the verge of shock. The raft stubbed the shore, and a dozen hands hauled it out. Shannon gave instructions to get Rhodes out of the raft, while Jones and Hudson helped Buccari, her legs wobbly with shock and cold. She took three steps and collapsed.

"Get her back to the cave!" Shannon commanded, and Jones, sobbing in his joy, picked her up bodily and started moving.

"Bullshit!" the lieutenant mumbled, regaining awareness. She struggled until Jones set her down. Her legs buckled. Jones held her erect by her shoulders.

"Shannon, get that . . . raft back on the lake!" she ordered. "Commander Quinn is out there! I'm not leaving until . . . we find . . ." She fainted.

"Wrap her in blankets and take her to the cave!" Lee snapped as she pounded on Rhodes's chest, swearing through gritted teeth.

With Buccari unconscious and wrapped in blankets and a poncho, Jones and several others headed off at a trot. Shannon and Tatum pushed the raft back out on the lake. They were moving from shore when Fenstermacher's howl brought everyone to a halt. Fenstermacher pointed into the darkness of the rain-beaten lake, where something was surfacing. All flashlights swung to bear on the dripping shape, the steady rain attenuating the light beams. Chest deep in the water, it was man-shaped but larger; two massive arms moved weakly at its sides. It stumbled, unable to support its own weight. It fell and then tried to stand, its arms waving, beckoning.

"It's Commander Quinn! He's in an EVA suit!" Hudson shouted.

Rescuers ran splashing to the commander's wallowing form. Water streamed from the space suit as it was hauled up the rocky beach. Shannon shouldered his way into the crowd as the commander's suit seal let go with an audible hiss. Quinn's tired face peered out into the flashlights, ghostly pale and soaking from his own perspiration.

"You okay, Commander?" Shannon asked, stepping into the jerky ring of beams.

"Felt better, Sergeant," Quinn gasped. "What ... Buccari and Rhodes?"

"Lieutenant Buccari's all right, Commander," Shannon replied. "She's been taken back to the cave. Lee is working on Mr. Rhodes down the shore."

"Doesn't look good for Virgil, Commander," Wilson said, his voice catching. "He got tangled in his shroud lines."

"Lee says he had a stroke, Commander. He bought it," Hudson added somberly.

Quinn sat there and nodded his head slowly.

"Check and mate," he said softly, a eulogy.

SECTION TWO

SOCIETIES

TWELVE

SECOND PLANET FROM THE STAR—KON

"Can you be sure?" the blue-robed giant thundered as he reared onto elephantine hinds, straining against the iron chains of gravity. Jook the First, Emperor-General of the Northern Hegemony, was famous for his prodigious strength, infamous for his intoleration, and notorious for his ruthless disregard for life.

"Begging forgiveness, Supreme Leader, I cannot," Scientist Director Moth whimpered. The astronomer's anxiety glands burped yet again, audibly this time. Moth could smell his own fear-scent rising in clouds. He stared at the floor, his broad-nosed, pebbly-skinned image reflected in polished onyx, his muddy brown eyes wide with terror under painfully rigid brow tufts. Why had he been so rash?

"Could it have been but a clever ruse?" Jook asked, dropping back into his hydrostasis throne. The ruler's ponderous form moved leadenly, searching for comfort on the midnight-blue pneumo-pillows. "Their communication signals could have been made deceptively simple for the very purpose of making us curious."

"Yes, Exalted One," Moth replied, trying desperately to anticipate correct answers. Surely his career, if not his life, was in the balance. "Communication signals were of remedial simplicity. I tendered the hypothesis of peaceful contact because of the nature of the intercepts. Simple patterns and numerics, music, geometric formulas would all be typical of such an attempt, Exalted One." Moth displayed his most obsequious posture and awaited his fate, a trembling mountain of misery alone at the center of the imperial court.

117

"General Gorruk, your opinion," the Supreme Leader barked at a stern visage sitting on a lower level of the black marble throne. Gorruk, commander of the imperial armies, clad in belted khaki with red trim, lifted his gigantic body erect. Gorruk, easily three times the mass of a human being, was even larger than the Supreme Leader. On his epaulets sparkled the silver starbursts of the Planetary Defense Command. Moth was amazed at the time the barrel-chested, slab-faced general took to formulate his response. Such blatant hubris.

"I think," General Gorruk rumbled, luxuriant black brow tufts stiffening and vibrating with concentration, "that this is a waste of the emperor's time. It is transparent. The invaders were closing on our planet to attack, as they did during the reign of Ollant. Trickery."

Gorruk stood over Moth; the prone scientist sensed the general's pulsating body heat and smelled his irritation. Moth clinched shut his eyes and pressed his forehead to the floor.

"Why?" Gorruk queried. "Why does this worthless heap of intellectual offal pretend to your precious attention? The Supreme Leader has greater concerns. Our race is saved from another invasion, the enemy routed, chased from our system—again! Planetary Defense Command, with overwhelming assistance from the Northern Hegemony's strategic rockets, vanquished the intruders. What more news can this worm provide? You, Supreme Leader, taking advice from a petty bureaucrat, a so-called scientist. A sniveling coward. Smell him! Why is he even here?"

"Because I directed him to appear, General!" Jook growled darkly.

"Yes." Gorruk sneered. "Only remember your solemn vows to—"

"General Gorruk!" Jook roared, bolting upright. "Remind me not of the Vows of Protection! We shall never be surprised again!"

"You! Scientist!" Gorruk shouted, adroitly changing the point of attack. Gorruk, a behemoth among behemoths, always attacked.

"Yes, great General," Moth said tremulously.

"How?" Gorruk asked, hot poison in his voice. "How is it that our enemies fly to our solar system at will and we are unable to leave? They have come again, penetrated our planetary system, from somewhere, somewhere out in the deep universe.

They bridge the distances. Why is that? What physics do they have that we do not?"

Moth remained silent, too frightened to speak.

"Speak, you worm!" General Gorruk screamed at the prostrate figure.

Moth raised his face. "I beg mercy, General. I am but an astronomer. It is not for me to speak about things I know not."

"General Gorruk!" Jook commanded. "Return to your court station. You are aggravatingly correct. We will never again permit alien battle forces to attack first. But that is not the issue." The ruler glared down at his general officer. Gorruk stood tall, immobile, resolute.

"Kneel, Gorruk!" Jook bellowed, veins bulging across temples and thick neck, brow tufts fanning apart. "These are my chambers. Down, Gorruk. *Now!*" A harbinger of doom, the sour odor of imperial anger wafted across the court. The palace guard shifted nervously. Hulking forms, blasters ready, moved inward from shadowed alcoves.

Gorruk, in slow motion, momentarily leaned his bulk onto callused hands and padded forearms in subservience, his own anger-scent commingling dangerously with that of the emperor. Rising from the bow and remaining naturally on all fours, he marched back to his position.

Air circulators hummed into high-volume mode.

"With utmost respect, Great Leader," interjected another court official, a slighter figure robed in brilliant black-trimmed white. It was the delicate, golden-skinned noblekone Et Kalass, Minister of Internal Affairs, standing easily to his hinds. "I must agree with our courageous commanding general," he said, his voice soothing and calm. "The aliens, regardless of intent, have been repulsed. Let us focus on the all too familiar problems of government."

The minister signaled with a languid wave. Moth felt a slight tug on his cloak and then a sharper one. The scientist turned to see an attendant of the chamber motioning for him to follow, which he gladly did, crawling on all fours as even the exalted general had finally done. Clear of the chambers, the blue-liveried attendant turned and addressed Moth with condescension. "Minister Et Kalass is interested. You will be contacted on the morrow."

Moth watched the attendant lumber away, his gravity-distended belly dusting the floor. The scientist was awestruck to be in the imperial palace, but he was even more anxious to return to his normal milieu. A crawling lackey provided an escort down the crystal hall and through the low-domed, thickly columned rotunda, where a pantheon of prior emperor-generals, many removed from power in small pieces, stared down with malevolent glares from gilded frames. A bronze of Jook stood atop a low pedestal in the center of the sunburst-emblazoned chamber floor.

They passed security positions, weaving through magnetic field detectors, chemical sniffers, and ultrasonic inspection cages where heavily armed guards monitored information consoles. Once through the rotunda, his escort departed, and Moth continued on all fours through the heavily buttressed entryway and down the parade ramp. He crossed Imperial Square, circumventing the gardens, and trundled out the intensely guarded front gate, joining the murmuring crowds of crawling kones moving thickly along the cracked sidewalks of the wide avenue. Work shifts were changing, and the faces of the milling workers and laborers—trods—ranged from sullen to stoic. Moth was relieved to be out of the tense environment even if it meant having to mingle with mobs of tight-jawed proles.

It was an unusual day, cloudless, the air clearer than usual. Even the smooth hills rimming the capital to the south and west were visible—if just barely—adding a vertical dimension to the squat skyline of the capital. An adobe-colored ocean to the northeast disappeared into thick smog, revealing no horizons. Overhead a haze ring encircled the low midday sun, the sky a peaceful cream color with tints of yellow and rust. Victory Tower, five times higher than any other municipal structure, jutted dimly into the sky, a vague stiletto pointing at the bright bull's-eye of the sun.

Very pretty, Moth thought, ambling along at an uneasy canter, jostled frequently by the passing multitudes. He made a direct path to the transit tube and stood in line at the identification gates. It took only fifteen minutes to get onto the boarding platforms—over half the gates were working. It took twice that long to catch a car; the first two trains to pass had been appropriated by the Public Safety Militia and did not stop, their long cars whisking through the station, helmets and weapons discernible in the blurring movement.

An hour later he debarked at an outpost where the stationmaster recognized him and called for transportation. Minutes later Director Moth trotted through the main entrance of the

Imperial Astronomical Institute and was once again an important kone.

"I hope it went well, Director," said Scientist Dowornobb, his prodigious and brilliant young assistant, an astrophysicist as well as an accomplished astronomer. Together they crawled toward the administrative offices, passing the commodious operations center. Director Moth noted with satisfaction the programmers gawking as he went by. Some of the females were so brazen as to lift their eyes. He would have to crack down on such behavior, but for now he enjoyed the rare fame associated with being called before the Supreme Leader—and living to tell about it.

"Quite well," Moth replied arrogantly. "Have you finished the trajectory mapping? I am told we may have to provide additional information as soon as tomorrow." The director crawled into his suite of offices, going to the terminal to read his mail.

"The mapping is finished, Director, but the results are indeterminate," Dowornobb answered, recoiling in mock anticipation of his master's anger.

"Indeterminate? Indeterminate!" Moth shouted, glaring at the clowning assistant. "Why indeterminate? Pay attention. Say something!"

"Yes, Director," Dowornobb raised downcast eyes and irreverently looked skyward. "The largest alien ships just, eh . . . disappeared simultaneously. Gone. Magic. Indeterminate. Poof! There is no evidence that any were destroyed or even damaged, though our interceptors engaged within lethal range. They just vanished—the large contacts, that is." Dowornobb moved to a terminal. Dowornobb was a genius. His lack of manners and decorum was usually overlooked.

"We were able to track a contact after the disappearance of the primary units." Absorbed in his data, Dowornobb dropped all deference to Director Moth. "The aliens left one functioning ship behind. This corresponds to the military debriefs." He stared at a report, all but ignoring the director.

"And?" Moth asked impatiently. *"And?"*

"Huh . . . oh." Dowornobb looked up. "All engagements but one have outcomes."

"And?" Moth struggled to contain himself. His theories came from Dowornobb's analysis. Moth was dependent on his assistant, particularly now that the emperor was interested.

"Some of our ships never came back." Dowornobb stated.

"I know that! Many were never intended to return. They were ordered to intercept quickly, beyond operational ranges at peak intercept speeds. We knew some would run out of fuel. They blew themselves up rather than be captured." Moth was not supposed to reveal that.

"Oh!" Dowornobb said in quiet shock. "That explains much . . ."

"Yes, kone! On with it!" Moth insisted.

"Well," the assistant continued. "Our ships all sent back successful reports, claiming to have eliminated the enemy. But trajectory analysis does not bear that out. One alien ship, I am certain, was still moving after our interceptors were recalled or destroyed. Er, perhaps *destroyed* is not the correct term."

"What? Are you sure? Where did it go?" Moth blurted in a most undignified manner. "It has been days. They will ask why it has taken so long for us to report this."

Dowornobb smiled his irritating little smile. "Well, there really is no good excuse, of course, but you could explain it by telling our illustrious leaders that the ancient data processors they make us use are just too slow. Our telemetry links are serialized, and the trajectory data file is quite large. Now, if we had the hardware those Public Safety vultures have to keep track of the dissidents, we could—"

"Stop, Scientist Dowornobb!" Moth exclaimed, panic in his voice. He looked about with darting glances. "I will not tolerate seditious talk. You have demonstrated your technical competence, but please do not test my loyalty."

"Genellan," Dowornobb said matter-of-factly.

"What? Genellan?" Moth queried.

"It went into orbit around Genellan," Dowornobb replied soberly. "A very low orbit, barely resolvable. It has disappeared since."

THIRTEEN

THE TEST

Brappa paddled languorously underwater, fishing patiently. The food chain was well served in the warm waters near the spring, where he stalked a cluster of fat fish swimming near the sandy bottom. Expelling air, the hunter struck with blurring speed. Tooth-lined jaws seized an unsuspecting member of the school.

The hunter smoothly surfaced, fish in his teeth.

Brappa simultaneously glimpsed the raft and heard Craag's warning whistle. The raft of the long-legs was between him and the island. Brappa slipped silently beneath the surface, the fish preventing him from taking a deep breath. Submerged, he kicked frantically for the rocky mainland and the protection of its boulders. He waded ashore and peeked across the lake in time to see the raft slide onto the beach.

Inconvenient, but at least it was a change. The weather had kept the long-legs in their cave. With the cessation of rain during the night and the arrival of bright morning skies swept clear by strong north winds, the morning had been busy. Descending from their camp in noisy groups, the long-legs had washed themselves at the shore, splashing and paddling. They were raucous and incautious beasts. And now they were out on the lake on a raft.

Brappa moved bravely up on the shore among the rocks to eat the fish; the hunter's fear had lost its edge. His appetite, on the other hand, was quite sharp.

"The water's much warmer!" Goldberg exclaimed, cupping her hand in the lake. "The hot spring must be coming from the island."

123

Tatum pulled easily as Goldberg dragged her fingers in the lake.

"Sandy, row us over to the island," Dawson directed.

Tatum complied with strong, full strokes. Goldberg sat in the stern and flirted with the lanky marine, watching his powerful shoulders and arms move the unwieldy craft. Tatum smiled at her and winked. Goldberg turned her head. When the raft lurched onto the sandy beach, Dawson jumped into the water. She grunted and huffed, hauling on the steel ring in the raft's nose.

"Wait a second, Nance," Tatum said. "You ain't hauling this boat with me sitting in it."

"The water's so warm," Dawson shouted. "Pepper, you have to feel it!"

Goldberg moved from the stern, leaning against Tatum as she slid slowly around him. She jumped to the beach, splashing water with a conspiratorial squeal. Tatum hauled the raft up on the beach. The women removed their boots and thermal leggings, rolled up their jumpsuits, and waded into the water. Both were soon falling and splashing, their jumpsuits drenched. Tatum briefly watched their antics but then started looking around.

"Sandy! Come on," Goldberg called out. "You need a bath. You stink!"

Tatum walked to the shore, hands on narrow hips.

"My clothes are finally dry. I ain't getting them wet, and you ain't prepared to see me without," he lectured. "Sarge said I wasn't to let you ladies get scared."

They hooted, and Dawson splashed water. Tatum moved out of range.

"Hold it down. I'm going to look this island over." He disappeared into the bushes.

Brappa watched and listened. The long-legs with the sand-colored clothing were playing in the water. They did not look dangerous. The tall, wide-shouldered one with the green covering looked powerful—a giant. His strides were large and quick, and he was alert. Brappa became concerned for Craag, but the giant eventually reappeared, looking over his shoulder.

Brappa heard a rumbling sound. Deep within the ground, a fault slipped and a clutch of tremors jolted the ground. The rigid plateau jiggled; shock waves rippled the granite as a quake rolled across the land, moving rock laterally and displacing lake water. The disturbed, pulsing fluid bunched at the margin of the lake, gathered energy, and rebounded from the southern shore, accelerating and amplifying as it approached the channels between the islands at the northern end. The lake erupted with tall, choppy waves that swept across islands and northern beaches, propelling the long-legs' raft onto the island, over the tops of small thickets, striking the base of the granite hillock.

Brappa was less fortunate. Quakes were common, and the hunter knew what was happening but could do nothing about it. Waves struck Brappa full force, casting his small body violently onto the rocks, knocking him unconscious and breaking his forearm. The waters receded noisily from the stony shore, and within minutes the lake stood calm, stirred only by the breeze.

"Wow! Tidal wave!" Fenstermacher yelled.

Buccari heard the boatswain's mate shouting as she ran down the hill. Fenstermacher and Gordon stumbled about the wet fir needles, collecting their fishing gear. A nearby patch of moaning glories began hooting with increased frequency, as if shaking off the wetness of the lake's surge.

"You guys okay?" Buccari asked.

"Yeah," Fenstermacher said. "No problem. It was kinda fun."

Shannon was right behind her. "Where's Tatum?" he shouted. "Where's the raft?"

A hailing came from across the lake. Tatum, Dawson, and Goldberg stood on the beach, the partially deflated raft just visible high on the rocks.

"There!" Buccari shouted, pointing toward the island.

"Everyone all right, Sergeant?" Quinn asked, joining the cluster.

"What're they doing over there?" Buccari asked.

"Tatum asked to use the raft to check out the hot springs, Lieutenant. I said it was okay," Shannon replied. "O'Toole, Gordon! Swim over to the island and help Tatum salvage the raft."

O'Toole and Gordon stripped to their long underwear and waded in. Dawson and Goldberg were already swimming back. Presently the women, heavy in sodden jumpsuits, slogged from the lake and excitedly described the hot springs. Buccari watched the raft recovery and half listened to their narrative. The growing crowd buzzed with excitement. To add to the enticement, the raft was dragged out of the lake at their feet, and Tatum and his helpers all enthusiastically proclaimed how hot the water was out by the island. Everyone was about to break ranks and go swimming.

"Sarge," Tatum said, "we should check out the island."

"What did you see, Sandy?" Shannon asked, holding up his hand.

"Nothing I could put my finger on," Tatum answered. "It just looks like it's been used. Might be some paths, and I thought I heard some, eh . . . whistling."

"Whistling?" Quinn repeated dully.

"Okay, Sandy," Shannon snapped. "Scout the island. Take three men and check it out. Float weapons over on a pack shell." He turned from Tatum and looked around at the assembled group. "No swimming until the raft is repaired," he ordered bluntly. The crowd grumbled its disappointment. Shannon's face reddened.

"Shut up and listen to me! This ain't no goddamn son-of-a-bitching beach resort," he shouted. "There will be no—I repeat—*no* daylight swimming. Assuming the island's clear, we'll organize swim parties, but only when the sun is down." Shannon glanced at Quinn but continued.

"All swim parties will have an armed sentry on watch. I'll say this again, and I want everyone to remember—we're strangers here. We don't know what's out there. We were shot down by hostile fire, and we're in their territory. We will stay hidden. Does everybody understand?"

Quinn nodded. "Well said, Sergeant. Let's get back to our watches. Now that we have found the hot springs, we'll figure out a way to use it. Break it up."

The group dutifully made its way along the shore back to camp. Buccari drifted away, listening to the flowers moan, feeling apart from the chain of command. Hudson joined her.

"That was quite an earthquake," Buccari said.

"You mean an R-K Three quake," Hudson replied.

"Yeah," Buccari said. "That's what I meant to say. An R-K Three quake. Real poetic!" She walked to the water's edge while Hudson wandered down the shoreline.

"Look, a dead fish!" Hudson shouted, jumping onto the rocks where the sandy beach ended. "The wave must've washed it ashore. If it's fresh, we can take it back for food."

Hudson worked his way over the rocks to the fish and gingerly picked it up by the tail, hoisting it to eye level. "Hey, look!" he said suddenly. He hopped across the rocks and bent down, his new crop of blond hair flashing in the bright morning sun.

"Jeepers! Sharl, come look!" he whispered. "First-class ugly!" Hudson drew his pistol.

Alarmed, Buccari stepped across the rocks to where Hudson was stooping. Something slumped deep in the rocky puddles. A leather membrane had unfurled and lay partially spread, and a leg equipped with ominous talons pointed into the air. Dark red blood oozed from where its ear should have been. Its mouth lay agape, and a gleaming line of serrated teeth glinted whitely in the bright sun. It was obscenely ugly. Buccari stared in disgust. Suddenly the animal's torso moved. The lung cavity slowly expanded and contracted—it breathed.

"It's alive!" she shouted, taking a stumbling step backward. The animal remained unconscious. Buccari looked at Hudson, wondering what they should do. She moved closer, knelt down, and tentatively touched the extended membrane.

"It's covered with fur—soft fur," she said, examining it carefully. "Look at those talons! Maybe we should shoot it and put it out of its misery. Wing looks broken. Huh! That's . . . not just a wing. It's an arm and a hand! This must be like the big bat Dawson saw."

"What'll we do, Sharl?" Hudson asked, tentatively touching the wing.

"Don't know," she answered. "I don't know how bad it's hurt. If we just leave it, it may come to enough to crawl away and die in pain. Let's take it back to the cave and see if Lee can do anything." She jumped down and gently lifted the animal's head.

"How do you propose we do that?" Hudson asked.

"Take off your butt bag," she directed.

"What?"

She smiled sweetly. "That's an order, Ensign."

"Pulling rank. What if I didn't have on any underwear?" he asked, shedding his flight suit.

"You think I care? Hurry!"

Hudson did as he was told.

"B-r-r-r! It's chilly," Hudson said, looking undignified in green space thermals and boots.

Buccari spread the flight suit on the sand, and they gingerly

lifted the limp animal from the rocky puddles. The creature
was surprisingly light for its size. Grasping the ropy sinews of
its legs and arms, they positioned the animal's limbs within the
suit and zipped it up. Buccari wrapped the arms and legs
tightly, forming a straitjacket.

"That should hold it," she said. "If it starts thrashing, set it
down. Watch out for the mouth."

Braan circled over the island, observing the events unfolding
on the ground. He watched helplessly as the long-legs carried
away the limp form. Craag's "all clear" lifted into the air, and
the hunters recklessly descended. Craag stoically related the
tragic events to Braan. Upon completion of his report, the warrior demanded to be blamed for Brappa's capture, demonstrating abject sorrow to his leader. The sentries were embarrassed
for the esteemed hunter.

"Craag, son-of-Veera," Braan said, the loss of his son
weighing heavily on his soul. "Craag, my comrade in battle
and life, despair not. The quake put the sentry Brappa down.
It was not in thy power to control. The rocks trembled; the
gods exhaled. To accept blame for such power is conceit, my
brave and faithful stalwart. Thou were but doing thy duty. That
is all a leader can expect."

The sentries nodded approval, but Craag's despair was immense.

"Yep, same beast," Dawson said. "Only the one I saw was
carrying a bow and wearing leather."

"Sure, Dawson!" Fenstermacher needled. "An Indian with a
little bow and arrow. We'll call him Tonto."

"Get off my back, midget," Dawson replied, "before I pop
you."

"You haven't popped anything since you were twelve!"
Fenstermacher replied, wisely moving out of arm's reach.

"Enough!" Buccari snapped. "Sarge, move 'em out of here."

"Okay, you heard the lieutenant," Shannon said, physically
pushing people from the cave. "Everybody back to the tents.
We'll open the zoo later. Lee needs space to work."

"Can you do anything, Leslie?" Buccari asked.

"I don't know, sir. It all depends on how wild, ah . . . Tonto
gets if and when he comes to," Lee said as she gingerly moved
the leathery skin from around the lipless mouth, revealing
razor-sharp teeth. "This little bugger could do some damage."

"Can't you sedate it, tie the mouth shut, and feed it intravenously?" Hudson asked.

"It's dangerous giving drugs to animals," Lee answered. "It could die before we knew what happened. The only thing I can do for sure is set the bone and keep it immobile. Maybe try an analgesic, but even that's risky. Let's tie Tonto up and keep those wings from flailing. We'll keep his mouth free so he can eat. Everyone be careful."

Braan and Craag moved silently through the woods below the cave, their night vision sharply adapted, although night vision was almost unnecessary. The long-legs made it easy; a large campfire burned in the center of the tents, casting its yellow light broadly. The alien beings had finished cooking and eating, but the flames were kept high.

Stalking through the thickets of the small forest, Braan heard curious noises. They moved cautiously toward the disturbance, listening. A rhythmic rustling of the leaves and branches accompanied by quiet moans and heavy breathing greeted their advance through the underbrush. The hunters halted and looked at each other in the dim firelight. The noises increased in intensity, and the moaning became insistent. The cliff dwellers were amazed that the long-legs around the campfire, less than fifty spans away, paid no attention to the mysterious noises. Intrigued, the hunters moved closer, arrows nocked in bows. The noises increased to even higher levels of intensity. The hunters moved still closer, cautiously. Braan detected movement through the shadows and pointed. They peered through the boughs, and it dawned on them. Craag squeaked a stifled giggle—dwellers enjoyed similar pleasures. Braan moved stealthily away from the insistent noises, while Craag lingered for several moments. They would have much to report.

Buccari stared at Tonto. Tonto stared back, blinking frequently, immense eyes the darkest brown, almost black, with catlike pupils. Eyelids serviced the eyeball from top and bottom, giving the eyes a sinister quality. Fenstermacher had just finished changing the blanket beneath the animal after the creature had fouled it.

"He was trying to tell us," Buccari said, putting her face close to the animal's. "That's why he was looking so panicky and squirming around. We should untie him. Next time he acts like that we should take him outside. Look at those eyes!"

"Don't get too close, Lieutenant," Lee cautioned from her sleeping bag.

"Hush, Les, and go to sleep," Fenstermacher said. "I'm on watch."

"That makes me feel better," Lee responded flatly, turning her back.

Buccari was fascinated with the creature. She insisted on helping care for it, feeling responsible for bringing it to camp. She was pleased when it began drinking and eating small amounts of fish. Everyone was amazed at how docile it was. Lee suggested that the head injury had rendered it senseless and unaware, no longer capable of survival in the wild, but Buccari was certain the creature realized it was being helped.

Buccari reached down and touched the callused fingertips at the end of the beast's good arm. The spidery fingers immediately closed on her extended finger, but not tightly. She left it there momentarily and then pulled gently away. She wrapped her hand around the animal's closed fist and pressed softly. The animal watched her intently, blinking, seemingly content with the unspoken reassurance.

Suddenly the creature's head jerked to the side. It struggled against its bindings.

"What's wrong, fellow?" Buccari asked, recoiling in alarm.

Tonto squeaked loudly, a broken high-pitched trill. His mouth and throat worked vigorously but emitted only intermittent chirps. Fenstermacher joined Buccari at the animal's bedside, staring down at their agitated patient. Lee threw off her sleeping bag and came over. Dawson looked up from the radio but stayed where she was.

The sentry had been the only obstacle. Craag had distracted it by rolling rocks down the incline, and Braan had easily moved past the perplexed guard, silently hopping along the large boulders before the cave mouth. Braan looked at the camp spread beneath him; he was in full view of the long-legs, darkness his only shield. Braan whistled softly. Brappa responded loudly.

"Hush!" Braan answered. "I hear. Art thou well? Art thou in danger?"

"I am injured, my father," Brappa replied. "I was foolishly injured."

"The nature of thine injuries? Can thou escape?"

"My arm is broken. I cannot fly. Also, I am bound."

"Art thou in danger?"

"I think not, my father. The long-legs seem interested in my well-being. They have made efforts to fix my arm, and I am encouraged. They feed me, and the pain lessens."

The activity was attracting attention. The long-legs below stirred, and shouts went up to the sentries on both sides of the cave.

"Thy news is good, my son. I am encouraged. Make no effort to escape unless thou perceive danger. We will make a plan," Braan said. "Be of stout heart. Our sentry post is moved to the middle island."

Harsh beams of light played against the cliff face. Killing sticks were visible.

"I understand. Please go now, my father!" Brappa pleaded.

The sentry moved closer to Braan's position. The hunter furtively shrilled the signal to take flight, and Craag, higher on the rock face, leapt into the night, attracting the attention of the searchers. Braan launched from his lower position next to the cave, exploding the air with his wings, pushing his body over the long-legs' camp and struggling mightily to gain altitude. Light beams jerked into the blackness, following the noise, and the white rays found Braan as he flailed desperately for clear air. Screams of long-legs increased, and killing sticks were raised.

Buccari's voice rose above the crowd, "*Hold your fire!* I'll shoot anyone that fires a weapon. Hold your fire." She stood silhouetted at the mouth of the cave, pistol in the air. Shannon towered at her side. Flashlight beams held the airborne beast captive in midflight, its wings beating slowly and evenly, ratcheting it higher into starlit skies. Finally it made the limit of the man-made light, wings set, gliding into the night. The spacers, sober after Buccari's threatening order, burst into excited discussions. Their injured guest had had visitors of its own kind.

"There were four of them!" Petit shouted from his sentry post.

"How the hell did four of them get that close? They were

practically inside the cave! You awake, Petit?" Shannon exco-
riated the sentry.

"They must have flown in, Sarge," he replied weakly.

"Flown in, my ass!" Shannon continued. "I'll talk to you
later."

Shannon stared with disgust into the night skies. Buccari left
him on the cave terrace and walked back to the side of the injured animal. Tonto rested quietly on his back, large eyes fully
open in the dimness, glinting softly, reflecting light from the
lamp across the cave.

"So you had visitors, eh, little buddy?" Buccari said, unty-
ing the bindings. "Tell 'em to stick around next time. We could
use the company."

FOURTEEN

GOVERNMENT SERVICE

The Public Safety truck skidded to a halt inside the front
gate of the Imperial Astronomical Institute; a squad of militia
troopers spewed forth, securing the gate. Scientist Dowornobb
was with Director Moth when they received word that all gates
had been similarly impounded.

"They are going to take me away!" Moth whined. "Charged
with incompetence and seditious behavior. They will shut
down the institute."

"Surely, Director," Dowornobb said, "our work is too important."

Yet Dowornobb's fear also expanded. The director had been
permissive with the freethinking scientists, largely at Dowornobb's instigation. Perhaps Director Moth was correct; repres-
sive disasters had happened at other institutions. Not knowing
what else to do, Dowornobb watched the soldiers being deployed throughout the grounds. He could smell the director's
fear—and his own.

A second motorcade rumbled through the institute's main gate. An escorted convoy of Internal Affairs vehicles moved expeditiously into the courtyard of the main compound, and a contingent of officials and their bodyguards were disgorged. Dowornobb stared in disbelief as Et Kalass, the Minister of Internal Affairs, garbed in luminous black and white, moved from an armored car. The slight noblekone stood on his hind legs and transported himself thus through the main doors. Dowornobb and Moth hastened to the lifts. Grim-faced militia guards intercepted them en route and provided a silent escort to the main reference room, where the minister and his party awaited.

"Honored, my lord," Director Moth fawned, bowing prone before the minister. Dowornobb attempted to slink against the wall, but a guard muscled him to room center.

Et Kalass ignored them, studying instead an expansive mural depicting a rendering of the night sky as seen from above the planet's milky atmosphere. Minutes dragged by in silence.

The minister broke the spell. "Quite nice. Determine who commissioned it. I would have a similar production in my home." An aide acknowledged the command. The minister turned to face the scientists, and Dowornobb could hear and smell Director Moth's fear glands exploding into action. His own immediately followed.

"Be at ease, scientists," Et Kalass commanded. "There is no need of apprehension. Relax! Control your temperatures." He reclined on a reading couch. A young, powerfully built noblekone dressed in militia garb and standing on his hind legs leaned presumptuously against the back of the minister's couch.

"Please sit," the minister commanded. Lounges were brought forward. "May I introduce you to Et Avian, my nephew," he went on, indicating the noblekone, "and to Chief Scientist Samamkook, my science adviser." Et Kalass bowed graciously to the ancient commoner standing on all fours immediately to his right.

Moth and Dowornobb politely leaned onto their hands. Samamkook reciprocated, and pleasantries were exchanged. Dowornobb was honored to meet the great astronomer whose published works in their field constituted the final authority. The minister allowed social niceties to run their full course, which Dowornobb determined to be most peculiar if they were being arrested. And why bring along the venerable scientist?

"I come on behalf of the Supreme Leader ... and of the royal families," the minister said, going immediately to the point. "Your report on the nature of the signals intercepted during the invasion piques our interest. It is quite easy to conclude that we repulsed a nonaggressive force. That in itself does not concern us overmuch. The horrible events marking the end of the Rule of Ollant will not be repeated. We have acted in the best interests of our race. Nevertheless, we want to know what happened, and you of the Imperial Astronomical Institute have a unique perspective. There are rumors you have uncovered additional intelligence of interest." Et Kalass gave Dowornobb a pointed look.

"Yes, my lord," Director Moth nervously volunteered. "We have completed an exhaustive analysis of all radar trajectory information recorded during the engagements—massive data accumulations. We started the first iterations several days ago, and the results have only just today become, eh ... publishable. Scientist Dowornobb has finished the compilation and will have his final report ready by, er ... soon."

Dowornobb looked nervously to Samamkook, who stared impassively at the wall.

"Scientist Dowornobb," Et Kalass commanded. "Please summarize your report. I am told you have interesting conclusions. I could never read through scientific journals. Some reference to Genellan, I believe."

Dowornobb glanced nervously at Moth and proceeded to give a detailed synopsis of his findings. He was allowed to finish without questions.

"A compelling set of deductions," Samamkook said. "According to your theory, the alien vessels entered our system, loudly announcing their presence with electromagnetic emissions on all frequencies. These signals were overtures—attempts to establish communications." Dowornobb nodded his agreement.

"We reacted quickly," the old scientist continued, "too quickly to realize the nature of the visitors. Or perhaps we did not fall into their trap—a possibility that cannot be discounted. Though I am inclined to do just that, given subsequent events. We attacked! The aliens barely defended themselves, choosing to retreat, somehow to, uh ... disappear, leaving behind a few smaller vessels. These unfortunate vessels were destroyed during the engagements, except for a mysterious ship that managed to elude our interceptors. That single visitor may have found refuge." Samamkook held his wide jaw in a massive hand.

"Genellan is no place for higher orders of civilization!" Moth said. "They may have gone into orbit, but to what purpose? The planet is bitterly cold and noxious—hopeless!" He sat back and looked about.

"Hopeless for us, Director," Samamkook said. "Yet life abounds on that cruel planet. Assuming they had the means to leave orbit—a large assumption—then it is no less likely they could endure."

Dowornobb could not imagine living on Genellan. He had seen the queer fur-covered animals brought back for the zoos, but the conditions on the surface seemed so adverse. The miserable landscapes and weather were beyond even his fertile imagination. The sulfurous atmosphere—

". . . nobb. Scientist Dowornobb!" The minister was calling his name.

"Ah, yes, m-m-my lord," Dowornobb said, recovering.

"You have made progress on their language?" Et Kalass returned to stare at the star mural.

"Well, m-my l-l-lord," the young scientist replied, "their language is not yet revealed. I have run the signals through language programs, but it has not given us much to work on. It has provided symbology that might be useful—pictographs and signs. We could establish some communication, somewhat like children talking."

"Excellent. We can help you improve on that." The minister exchanged a meaningful glance with the young noblekone and then stood and walked out, his entourage following. Moth and Dowornobb assumed positions of respectful farewell and were soon alone.

The door to Dowornobb's apartment crashed open in the early hours of the morning. The kone, reluctantly awake, sat up in his bed.

"Who's there?"

A dark form shifted silently in the entryway to his bedroom. Other hulking shadows followed, filling the short corridor leading to his small sitting room.

"Who's there?" Dowornobb pleaded, now fully awake. Fear swelled within his great breast. He prayed for the intruders to be robbers or thugs—criminals. For if they were not outlaws, then that could only mean they were government agents.

FIFTEEN

MERCY

"Shannon sure was tight-jawed," Petit said as they cleared the tundra of the central plateau. The granite slabs and rocky scrabble of the higher elevation made for easier hiking. "I thought sure he was going to ream me for letting those critters get close to the cave. He didn't say nothing about it."

"Good thing, too," Tatum said. "The mood Sarge was in, once he started chewing tail, he wouldn't have never stopped."

"So, what's up his butt?" Petit asked.

"Quinn didn't want to send out a search party," Tatum replied. "I don't think the commander wants anyone to move out of sight of camp."

"Why?" Petit asked. "He afraid we'll get lost like Mac and Jocko?"

"Who knows? Maybe," Tatum said, looking around; no cover was afforded by the flat, featureless terrain.

"Wouldn't none of us be on patrol if the lieutenant hadn't waded in," Jones added. "Heard 'em talking. Lieutenant Buccari wouldn't take no for an answer."

"She said we should also be looking for a better place to settle. She says winter on the plateau is going to be miserable," Tatum said.

"She's something else, ain't she?" Jones replied. "Best damn officer in the whole damn fleet."

"So why's Shannon so jacked?" Petit persisted. "He got his patrol."

"Yeah," Tatum said, "but he wanted to go himself. He's worried about MacArthur—and Chastain. And he needs a break from old mother Quinn."

The patrol headed east, arriving at the plateau's edge early in the afternoon. Tatum was uncomfortable. A noxious sulfur

136

odor bit at their sinuses, and the raw height of the plateau was intimidating. The brink was not sharp but curved gently away from his feet, rapidly gaining in pitch with each advancing step. The rolling plains far to the east, hazy in the distance, were part of some other world. Their world was flat, and it ended abruptly only paces away. Petit and Jones stayed clear. Tatum edged backward to join them.

With no apparent way down, Tatum hiked along the meandering brink of the precipice, hoping a navigable cleft or rift would show itself, enabling them to descend and backtrack along their original parafoil flight path. They found nothing.

Sentries sounded the alarm. Strange beings were reported on the salt trail. Kuudor sent for Braan, and the leader of hunters quickly arrived, Craag at his side. The hunters studied the long-legs struggling up the steep, narrow path traversing the cliff face. One had his arm around the neck of the other, being half carried along.

"The smaller one is damaged," Kuudor observed.

"The larger one is deeply fatigued, but thou art right, captain-of-the-sentry; the smaller long-legs is near death," Craag agreed, impressed with the efforts of the big creature.

"They are not gods," Braan said aloud.

"But they are compassionate," Craag added.

"Also unlike the gods." Old Kuudor spoke with sacrilegious candor.

"We are in their debt," Braan said.

"Thy son is not free, leader-of-hunters," Kuudor said. "Be wary of paying debts not owed."

The sun was high in the cobalt sky and gaining intensity. The cliff face doubled the sun's intensity, reflecting it on the struggling long-legs and blocking the cool northwest wind.

"Almost there, Mac," Chastain huffed. "Keep moving; we can make it."

The trail narrowed and climbed vertically; the river chasm yawned to their right. Flowers, purple and yellow, grew in abundance, and thick-stemmed thistles with white spiked blossoms lined the dusty path, providing psychological relief from the precipitous drop. It was hot. Chastain plodded up the trail, hoping for a switchback to take them from the perilous cliff face.

"You okay, Mac?" Chastain sucked air. "Say something, Mac. What're we going to do when we get to the top? Mac!"

MacArthur gasped. Chastain was thankful for the gasps, signals that MacArthur was still alive. Doggedly, the big marine trudged the endless slope, his swollen tongue filling his throat and mouth. They desperately needed water—the irony of the large river that had nearly drowned them flowing so abundantly a thousand meters below. And in the near distance ahead, pulling Chastain forward—teasing him—a waterfall plunged from the cliff top, its white sheet of water atomizing into angel hair mists.

"Almost there, Mac. Almost . . . there. The path is . . . flattening . . . out," Chastain wheezed dizzily. The big marine fainted.

Braan and Craag glided above the fallen long-legs. The creatures, lying like death in the dust, stank, a bitter smell, the malodor of putrescence mingled with animal scent. The cliff dwellers landed above the path and analyzed the still forms. Nothing moved. Braan whistled, and a dozen hunters appeared over the edge, cautiously approaching the still forms. They carried bowls, vials, and an animal skin litter. They obeyed Braan's instructions issued from his position above the activity. Craag hopped down to assist, using his wings as a parachute.

The smaller long-legs was rolled onto the litter and carried away. Its body was deteriorating rapidly, maybe too rapidly. Its life was in the hands of the gardeners. The other was immense. Braan marveled at the creature's physique, a rival to the mythical bear people. It was dehydrated, but that could be remedied. Other sentries deposited bowls of water and vials of honey next to the fallen giant and departed quickly. Braan and Craag moved in concert beside the stricken alien, each dumping a bowl of water on its head. The giant stirred, and the hunters silently pushed from the cliff face, swooping out of sight.

Chastain's ragged, thirsty dreams splashed wetly to an end. He awoke blurry-eyed, with a terrific headache. Water! He licked at the liquid running from his hat. He snatched the hat from his head and squeezed salty moisture into his mouth.

Where had it come from? MacArthur? No, Mac was hurt! Where was Mac? Chastain panicked, thinking MacArthur had gone over the edge. His brain clearing, he noticed that the thistles had not been trampled. He also noticed the bowls, two empty and two brimming with clear liquid. And vials. He sat in the dust, perplexed, shading his eyes. He yelled MacArthur's name, his voice croaking as it escaped his dry throat. He looked at the small bowls of tempting liquid and touched one. His thirst took charge, and he unsteadily and greedily brought the laden bowl to his lips and drank deeply—too deeply—choking on the life-giving fluid. Coughing and hacking, he stopped to clear his lungs and then drained the bowl. He looked at the plain crockery, no more than a cup in his huge hands, curiously turning it over and around, looking for a clue. Nothing.

He picked up the other vessel and drank more cautiously but still deeply. He sniffed the water as he drained the dregs. Done. He was embarrassed and guilty for having drank both bowls. Confused, he looked down at the vials and picked one up. It had a stopper made of soft, pulpy wood. He pulled the cork from the vial and sniffed its contents. He could not figure the smell. He tipped the vial, and a clear amber fluid oozed thickly onto his finger. He touched the dollop to his tongue. Sweetness! Liquid energy! Chastain held the vial over his throat and let the wonderful viscous substance run into his mouth, licking and sucking at the container. He looked at the second vial, sorely tempted, but placed it in the zippered pocket of his jumpsuit. Evidence.

Recharged, he stood and yelled MacArthur's name, a full-throated bellow echoing across the face of the cliff. Again he yelled, less loudly, and a third time, but to himself, softly. He looked up the trail; he looked down the trail, taking indecisive steps. Silence. He sat heavily and looked around, wringing his hands. The sun cooking his sweaty head stirred him to action. Chastain put on his hat and rose to his feet, stooping to pick up an empty bowl. He hiked to the top of the cliffs and found, prominently positioned atop a flat rock, another vial of honey. Chastain consumed it without guilt; he did not require two vials of proof.

He was on the plateau. Racking his sun-dulled and food-starved memory, he recalled his injection briefing. Still uncertain, he headed over the rolling terrain of the plateau, sadly glancing over his shoulder, hoping to see his friend.

The unconscious one was carried under the streaming waterfall and down the bore. At the tunnel's end the rough-hewn chamber turned sharply and opened abruptly on a terrace lodged in a deep vertical fissure. A pentagonal platform supported by a network of pulleys and blocks filled the lateral space within the fissure—an elevator.

The hunters bundled the limp creature onto the platform, and the elevator dropped smoothly to the next level, where a soft-wheeled cart was waiting to receive the burden. An elder wearing the emeralds and garnets of the gardener guild supervised the loading. Apprentices relieved the hunters and wheeled the cart away. The curious sentries chirped excitedly and jumped from the terrace into the void, their wings unfurling and grabbing the strong updrafts.

The cart trundled down a smooth-surfaced slanting corridor lit by flickering spirit lamps. A runnel of water gurgled down a bermed gutter against one polished wall. The corridor ended in a high-ceilinged cavern partially open to the sky. Two other caves converged on the opening, revealing a panorama of blue sky and river valley, and another lift platform cantilevered out over the abyss. Support cables for the lift, made from chains, angled back sharply, running through a hole cut high in the rock wall. Mechanical noises and the hissing of steam emanated from a chiseled window halfway up the stone wall. Guilders were visible; a steam user commanded the mouth of the opening, monitoring the movements below. The cart rolled out into sunlight, and the gardener waved his hand at the lift supervisor. The platform dropped smoothly.

The elevator passed intermediate landing points before it stopped at a cabling terminus, the river still far below. The cart was pushed from the platform and navigated through a level, if sinuous, corridor, a tunnel in which curious cliff dwellers stood to watch the procession. Another lift station received them, and the process was repeated, continuing the ride down the face of the cliff. When they debarked, the steam was thick and warm and the unseen river rumbled nearby.

SIXTEEN

REUNITED

Buccari awoke in the dark hours and could not go back to sleep. She slipped from her sleeping bag, grabbed boots and clothes, and crawled from the tent she shared with Lee. The wet chill of early morning seeped through her thermal underwear and made her shiver. She squatted next to the campfire embers and kindled a handful of tinder. Wood chips sputtered and ignited, flowering into warm tongues of flame. She added two logs. The banked ashes provided a foundation of heat, and flames soon curled about the logs. She stood over the flourishing pyre and pivoted, warming herself in stages. With her back to the fire she looked into moonless skies, at the glory of the morning constellations, stars sparkling and dancing, great slashes of crystalline points of light so dense as to make the black velvet skies appear to be textured with sharp shards of broken diamonds. Young stars, they seemed newly minted.

Adequately warmed, she sat down on a log, back to the fire. As she laced her boots, something caught her attention—the flap on Shannon's tent was slowly folding back. An arm protruded and then a back; an entire person cleared the tent entrance and stood erect, looking about surreptitiously—Dawson. The tall petty officer pulled her hood over her head and cinched it tight as she walked. Her path took her by the campfire. Buccari turned to the fire, but Dawson had noticed her. The communications technician walked up without hesitation.

"Morning, Lieutenant," she whispered, and sat down, leaning close to the flames, her countenance tired but peculiarly fulfilled.

"Good morning, Dawson," Buccari replied, uncertain whether to be angry or indifferent—or envious.

* * *

Morning broke cold and still; a thin crust of frost covered their exposed camp. Tatum rolled out of his bag, expecting to see the plateau's edge and the eastern horizon beyond. Instead, a thin wall of foggy vapors, slow streamers of misty steam, rose delicately into the sky—a curtain of steam held together in the cool, stable air, curling in laminar wisps high over their heads, there to magically dissipate. Petit stood morning watch, his burly form silhouetted against the steamy white veil. Through the curtain a heavily filtered, eerie orange sun broke from the horizon, its cold rays attacking the curtain of mist. Tatum turned to see Jones straggle from his sleeping bag.

"Gawd!" Jones said, ogling the veiled sunrise. "Like a fairy tale."

"Fairy tale!" Petit turned to face the other two. "Too damn cold for a fairy tale. Get that fire going and cook some breakfast."

"Make it quick," Tatum said. "Shannon wants us back by sunset tomorrow, and I want to cover as much of the rim as we can. There's got to be a way down."

As they ate the sun's warmth forced the steam away from the cliffs and down the vertical walls. By the time the spacers started walking, only an occasional wisp crept over the edge. Tatum was relieved to be moving; standing next to the cliff edge induced a vertigo, a dizziness of altitude and insecurity.

Late in the morning Tatum noticed the soaring creatures, minute specks of black against an infinitely deep backdrop of blue. The marines were tending to the west of south, the curve of the plateau rounding away from their intended track. Higher ground lay ahead.

"Not going to see much on this patrol," Tatum said, checking the sun.

"Beats sitting around the camp twiddling our thumbs," Jones said. "I'm going to volunteer for more of these Boy Scout trips."

Tatum laughed. "Wait till it rains or you can't find food or water."

"I can take it," Jones said. "I should've been a marine. I'm tough."

"You'd never pass the physical, Boats," Tatum kidded.

"What the—what's that supposed to mean?" Jones replied.

"You can tie your shoelaces and technical stuff like that. Too many brains," Tatum answered as he scanned the far distant plains with binoculars.

"Didn't notice you have any problem with your laces," Jones said.

"Never untie 'em. Sarge ties 'em for me. That's why he's a sarge. Took him near twenty years to learn."

Petit heehawed like a jackass.

They hiked on, rarely silent, frequently raucous.

"A river!" Petit shouted, pointing ahead. "It runs over the edge!"

The men advanced on the small stream, climbing a modest elevation. The terrain had changed; the land bordering the cliffs was broken with abrupt rises and outcroppings jutting from the flat rock. The plateau rim descended, and tundra grasses resumed in desultory patches. The stream, swollen with recent rain, gurgled over the cliff and launched into wind-whipped spray.

The bank was steep, the waters deep and fast. Tatum swung his vision upstream, searching for a convenient ford. He followed the river into the distance and saw movement. He put the field glasses to his eyes.

"Something—someone's foraging out there. Along the river! Way out!" Tatum said, alerting his comrades. He handed the glasses to Petit.

Petit lowered the glasses. Tatum asked, "Is that who I think it is?"

"Chastain," Petit answered. "He's limping, but I recognize his walk."

They took off at double time, but it took over an hour to get within shouting range of the wandering marine. Tatum debated firing off a round, but Chastain was heading toward the main camp. It would be a waste of a bullet. Eventually Chastain responded to their hails, turning and crouching in alarm. His fear turned to recognition, and he ran toward them, stumbling and falling to his knees.

"Where's MacArthur?" Tatum shouted.

Chastain, displaying a painfully radiant sunburn, staggered to his feet, mouth and hands stained purple from berry juice.

"Don't know," he mumbled, shoulders slumped. "I lost him."

"What d' ya mean, you lost him?" Petit snapped. "You big—"

"Shut up, Petit!" Tatum shouted. "Jocko, you're back with us. You're okay. But where's Mac? Where did you see him last?"

Chastain, tears streaming down his cheeks, babbled apologetically, making confused references to big rivers and bears and beautiful valleys. They listened, Tatum asking questions whenever Chastain's explanation became too cryptic. The day was fading into afternoon. If they searched for MacArthur, they would be overdue, and that would get Shannon highly exercised. Chastain needed food and medical attention. Frustrated, Tatum scanned the skies and saw more of the winging creatures. The large birds were soaring westward.

MacArthur awoke, blindfolded. His head was immobile, and he could not move his extremities. He felt naked yet warm and comfortable. His last memories were of a profound and desperate need for water and of excruciating pain in his infected shoulder. He was no longer thirsty, and his shoulder no longer pained him. Panic lurked, but he felt too relaxed. A mild odor permeated the air—sulfurous. His stomach growled.

"Hello," he whispered hoarsely. "Anyone there?"

He heard movement, quiet and unobtrusive, a presence.

"I know you're there," he croaked, his throat thick. He listened. Hours went by. He slept. He awoke and listened and fell asleep again, certain that he was being drugged.

He awoke again. There was movement in the room. MacArthur waited and listened, his hearing grown acute in the stillness. A noise impinged on his awareness, a whistling fading in and out of frequencies higher than he was capable of following. Out of boredom MacArthur whistled a few notes. The noises stopped with alarming abruptness. He tried whistling more notes. Nothing. He whistled "shave and a haircut—two bits," the familiar "long-short-short-long-long" pause "short-short" singsong. He whistled the ditty several times. At least he had precipitated a reaction. Even if it was silence.

Suddenly high-pitched noises answered—a soft trilling, almost too highly pitched to perceive rhythm: "shave and a haircut—two bits." Someone was there! They had answered. He whistled again. They reciprocated in a lower pitch. He heard them communicating. They sounded excited. They whistled the ditty; he returned it. More noises with arrhythmic gaps. Much of the communication was beyond his hearing range, few of their sounds below a soprano's highest notes. He whistled only the first part, the first five notes, and stopped. Nothing. He repeated himself and waited. And again. And then the two short notes came back from his unknown hosts. He did it again, and they quickly answered. He waited. Something whistled the first five notes and stopped. He supplied the ending. They did it again. He whistled his part and then started to laugh. It was ludicrous. He lay on his back, buck-naked, whistling a mindless ditty. And someone or something was answering him. His laughter was hearty, uncontrolled; tears rolled from his eyes. Something touched his face. He tried to flinch away, but his head was tightly bound. His tears were gently wiped away.

"Elder, may I ask the status of the injured long-legs?" Muube asked.

"A most resilient creature," Koop-the-facilitator replied. "A serious infection and malnourishment, but it responds well."

"Very good. What happens now?" the herb master asked.

"The council is considering options, Master Muube," Koop said. "Though I am told the leader-of-hunters wishes to release it."

The ancients waddled past mist-drenched planters. The orchids were of all shapes, sizes, and colors, rigorously organized.

"Impressive, herb master," Koop said, moving from blossom to blossom like the honeybees buzzing about their heads.

"I am grateful, elder," Muube replied. "A bountiful year for our medicines."

"Were it so for all our resources," bemoaned Koop, stopping before a colossal yellow and black orchid, staring reverently at the variegated blossom.

"Beautiful!" the elder whispered reverently.

The guilder ambled down the endless line of planters, steam welling up the cliff face, sunshine sparkling through spectral mists, the buzzing of honeybees melding with the muted roar of the river far below.

Braan, with the relief sentries, returned to the lake, landing on the second island. The watch captain briefed Braan. The long-legs' watercraft had been repaired. Twice daily, just before sunrise and just after sunset, the ungainly craft made the round trip, escorting splashing long-legs as they swam to the hot springs. The green-clothed ones spent large amounts of time exploring, and the raft had approached their new position on two occasions.

"The long-legs will soon explore this island," the watch captain said. "Perhaps it is time to move to a safer location."

"Safer? We can move only so many times," Braan responded, "before we are forced to move from even our homes."

"What now, leader-of-hunters?" the off-going watch captain asked.

"Return to clan and cliff. Await thy next duty, warrior. But caution, a patrol of long-legs comes," Braan warned. "Avoid them. Thou art relieved."

The weary off-going watch departed on favorable winds. Braan, satisfied that the watch was in place, soared over the lake on a fresh updraft. Rising through a caravan of puffy clouds, he glided along the ridges. Wary of rockdogs and mindful of the long-leg sentries, Braan landed and established an austere camp. And waited.

The sun set, evening dusk grew thick, and the campfire cast a flickering glow among the tents. The returning long-legs patrol walked up the hill. A sentry shouted, and the camp emptied into the tent area, surrounding the returned Giant-one. Sentries moved from their posts, closer to the welcoming din. Taking advantage of the distraction, Braan pushed from the high rock and silently glided to the cave terrace. His luck held—the cave was empty of tall ones. Brappa lay unattended, torso and wings wrapped with soft cloth, but he was not bound to his crib. Braan moved close and softly alerted his son to his presence. Brappa acknowledged and listened carefully to his beloved father.

MacArthur awoke on the hard granite of the high plateau, the morning sun already tall in the eastern sky. He shivered. Shaking dullness from his brain, he stiffly gained his feet. It was a crazy dream. His shoulder? It ached, but he remembered how much worse the pain had been. He peeled back his clothes and looked in amazement at his bare shoulder. The wound was closed, and the ugly gray and yellow streaks running down his arm were gone. He owed his arm, if not his life, to someone. But to whom? To what?

And Chastain? Where the dickens was Chastain?

He took inventory. His clothes were clean and dry, but his knife and pistol were gone. He crouched and checked his surroundings. Nothing moved. He searched for clues—tracks or broken ground—but saw only inscrutable granite. With one last look around he stumbled off at a trot, feeling peculiarly fit. After a hundred paces the reality of inactivity overcame him, and he slowed his pace. He was on the plateau; the landing site could be no more than a day's march.

He was exhausted and famished when he finally arrived at the landmark lake with the islands. The sun was an hour set, and clouds, pushed along by a cold wind, obscured the stars and moons. The lithe marine yawned and blinked watery eyes. Through the bleariness he detected a glow against the hills, a hint of light. A campfire? The marine shook off the chill and stepped toward the beacon.

As he rounded the perimeter of the lake, the soft spray of campfire light disappeared. A ridge of rugged karsts rose before him, and the smell of spruce grew stronger—and burning wood. MacArthur stalked the hillside. He detected a sentry leaning against a tree and recognized Mendoza, the propulsion technician. His relief was overwhelming; trembling, he wiped tears from his eyes. But a feeling of perverse pleasure displaced his joy. MacArthur stole silently by the unaware sentry.

The camp was settled in for the night. A meager fire burned in the tent circle, near which sat Ensign Hudson and Chief Wilson. Gunner Wilson was telling space stories. MacArthur crawled close and listened to the ridiculous old saws, enjoying Hudson's affected gullibility. O'Toole walked down from the rocks, and MacArthur retraced O'Toole's steps to the cave. O'Toole threw a log on the campfire and joined in with a yarn of his own. MacArthur lay in the needles and listened for a languid minute, enjoying the embrace of the quiet evening. But his stomach growled. Hunger rampant, he rose to his feet and walked calmly into the dim circle of light, hat low over his eyes. Sitting down on the far side of the fire, he held his elbows high and put his hands on his face, stretching and yawning. The warmth of the fire was delicious.

"Gunner—" MacArthur spoke softly. "You're so full of crap. That young officer is never going to respect you, you keep lying to him like that."

The storytellers looked up. Wilson opened his mouth to retort, and recognition froze his tongue. All eyes simultaneously opened fully wide.

"Sheee-it," Wilson sniveled, recovering. "What a pure asshole, MacArthur. Well, I'm the only one's glad to see you, but only because you owe me money."

Hudson and O'Toole shouted at the top of their lungs, emptying the tents and the cave. The campfire was overwhelmed with the crew of *Harrier One*. Chastain burst from a tent, dragging it with him. Staring in tousled disbelief, he grabbed MacArthur in a bear hug and lifted him into the air.

"How long you been back, Jocko?" the smaller man shouted above the din, feeling a twinge of pain in his shoulder but too happy to complain.

"Over a week!" the big man answered. "We sent patrols out looking for you, Mac, but they came back empty. I told Sergeant Shannon I was heading out tomorrow to look for you myself. This is home, Mac. I told them about the valley, Mac, but this here's a good camp. We got a cave and beds and hot water and—"

MacArthur laughed despite the pain in his shoulder and begged to be put down. "If it's so great, get me some food!" he shouted.

Shannon sprinted down from the cave with Quinn, Buccari, and the rest of the cave occupants close behind. They arrived as Wilson was rescuing MacArthur from Chastain's embrace.

"Not dead or injured," Wilson said. "Maybe brain-dead. You okay?"

"Just sick to my stomach 'cause of your ugly face," MacArthur said.

Shannon muscled his way through the crowd, Quinn on his heels.

"Corporal," Quinn shouted. "Are you all right? Private Chastain said you had a badly infected shoulder. He thought you were dead."

"Where the hell you been, Mac?" Shannon blurted.

MacArthur looked at his shoulder. "Thought I was dead, too," he said.

Quinn turned to the crowd and shouted. "Everybody back to bed or to their post—right now! MacArthur'll be here in the morning. Break it up. Lee, take a look at his shoulder." The crowd fell away, but not before they had all hugged the corporal or at least slapped him on the back.

MacArthur climbed to the cave, following Lee to her sick bay. Shannon followed, firing questions, but Quinn interceded and suggested that questions wait until morning. Shannon and Quinn stayed on the terrace and conferred in low but obviously heated tones. Rennault, injuries on the mend, walked by MacArthur on his way to his sleeping bag. They exchanged greetings. That was when MacArthur noticed the other patient.

"What in the—what's that?" he asked, peering into the shadows. Lee had set Tonto off by himself. Fenstermacher walked up to the animal, smiling stupidly.

"Leslie had my baby," Fenstermacher yawned.

"Joke's getting old, Winfried!" Lee said with great suffering. "It's an animal we found next to the lake after the earthquake. We had a tidal wave. It washed onto the rocks and broke its arm. Did you feel the earthquake, Mac?"

MacArthur walked slowly over to the creature's bed.

"Yeah," he said, studying the beast. It blatantly returned his stare, blinking rhythmically.

"Why didn't you let it go?" MacArthur asked, looking down at Lee.

"It's an animal. It's got a broken arm. It would have rebroken the bone and probably died," she answered. "It's done real well, and it can leave if it wants to. It stays here, almost as if it knows we're helping it. We named him Tonto."

MacArthur returned his attention to the ugly animal and gave it a wink. The animal stared back impassively. MacArthur scratched his sunburned nose and walked over to where Lee had laid out a sleeping bag for him. A night's sleep sounded inviting, maybe more so than food. Lee followed him, brandishing a flashlight. MacArthur looked up to see the animal intently observing. Fenstermacher grumbled something, and the creature shifted its gaze.

"Winfried!" MacArthur suddenly said, watching the animal. "Nah, Fenstermacher; your name ain't really Winfried, is it?"

Lee said, "Oops," and started peeling back MacArthur's jumpsuit.

Fenstermacher sat up in his sleeping bag and glared.

"Thanks, Les," he grumbled. "Yeah. Winfried. So what?" he challenged.

"Nice name," MacArthur replied. The animal followed the conversation. "Goes with Fenstermacher." Fenstermacher snarled a superb string of expletives and rolled over, his back to the others.

"Looks good. You look real ..." Lee said, strong hands working the muscles around the wound.

"She says that to everyone," Fenstermacher mumbled from the corner.

Lee was quiet, looking at his shoulder from several angles.

"Sutures!" Lee said loudly and abruptly. "What happened to

you?" she asked. "Who took care of you? These sutures are professional."

MacArthur looked at his shoulder. Their curiosity piqued by Lee's outburst, Quinn and Shannon also walked over.

"Don't know," he said. "One minute Chastain's carrying me, and the next I wake up blindfolded in a warm place. Couple of days later—who knows?—I wake up again. My pistol and knife are gone, but I'm alive and my infected shoulder is almost healed." MacArthur stopped and looked from face to face.

"That's the story," he continued. "That's all there is. Chastain should have told you about everything else. I nearly got us killed in the river. Oh—and the valley! The valley! After we got swept down the river we found a valley with a big lake full of fish and ducks and big otters. We saw little deer and bears and something that looked like an elk . . ."

Quinn picked up a bowl.

"We were going to wait until tomorrow to show you these," he said soberly. "Someone gave water and honey, real honey, to Chastain the day he lost you. Lee, give him the vial."

Lee handed MacArthur a glazed ceramic tube.

"Taste it!" Quinn ordered.

"Honey? I've heard of honey, I think. What is it?" MacArthur asked.

"A food made by bugs—real bugs—honeybees," Lee said. "There used to be a lot of them on Earth. Still have bees, I guess, but no honeybees."

"There're still some left," Quinn said. "A luxury of the rich."

MacArthur pulled out the stopper and tentatively tipped the container over. A viscous drop fell on his finger. He touched it to his mouth and immediately knew he wanted more. His saliva glands welled warmly around his tongue. Quinn took the vial and handed him a chipped bowl.

"Is any of this familiar?" Quinn asked.

MacArthur felt a wave of fatigue wash over him.

"Sorry, Commander," MacArthur replied. "Nothing. I don't recall being fed or drinking anything. They kept me blindfolded and, uh . . . drugged, I think. I slept a lot—almost the whole time. I remember whistling."

"Whistling!" Shannon exclaimed.

"Yeah," MacArthur returned. He sat erect, his memories holding fatigue at bay. "Funny thing. After I lay there for a long time, I thought I could hear them talking, only their talking was real high-pitched, like whistling, only higher even. I, ah . . . started whistling at them. They whistled back."

"Whistling!" Quinn said, looking at Shannon and Lee. "Whistling! Seems we've heard some whistling around here, too."

MacArthur looked at the animal. It stared back. Quinn related the events of the night they were visited by Tonto's friends and of the whistling sounds thought to be communication.

MacArthur listened to the story and pondered it. Then he stood and walked over to the animal. The ugly beast stared up fearlessly. MacArthur licked his lips and softly whistled the first five notes of the singsong ditty: "shave and a haircut." The animal registered the sounds with a start, its expression clearly revealing that it was analyzing them. MacArthur whistled the same five notes again. Fenstermacher moved, standing as if to provide the answer. MacArthur waved him back down. The animal watched the movements and gestures, glancing briefly at Fenstermacher. It returned its unwavering attention to the man standing over him, and MacArthur whistled the ditty again and waited. He was about to do it again, when the animal opened its mouth just enough to show a fine line of teeth. It shrilled sharply—two short notes.

"Two bits!" Fenstermacher shouted.

SEVENTEEN

RETURNING THE FAVOR

MacArthur awoke and could not remember. He looked about the cave and saw Fenstermacher sitting next to the little fire. A murky grayness filtered into the cave.

"Fensterma—Winfried! What time is it?" he groaned,

forcing open sleep-crusted eyes. He remembered the animal and turned to look at it. It was staring at him.

Fenstermacher glanced out at the foggy morning. "About a half hour to sunrise, gruntface. It's hard to tell, it's so foggy out," he replied.

MacArthur stretched. "Then I haven't been asleep very long."

Fenstermacher laughed. "You lost a whole day, jarbrains. You've been asleep through all three watches."

MacArthur shook soreness from his good shoulder; he must have lain on it the whole night. He coughed, trying to wet his cotton-dry mouth.

"I believe you," he mumbled as he rolled out of his bag, stiffly putting his legs beneath him. His body ached with the accumulation of abuse.

"Quinn and Shannon want to see you. I'm supposed to go get 'em," Fenstermacher said. MacArthur heard footsteps and turned to see Lieutenant Buccari materialize from the mists.

"Well . . . go get them," Buccari ordered. Fenstermacher smiled and flipped an exaggerated salute as he trotted into the fog.

"Good morning, Corporal," Buccari said. "You've had a good sleep."

She walked to the animal and held out a finger. The beast reached out and eagerly clasped it, emitting a delighted squeak. Buccari smiled, and her green eyes sparkled gayly. Her lovely face was framed by a feathering of auburn hair. MacArthur was enchanted.

"Eh, good morning, Lieutenant. Don't be too hard on Fenstermacher. He just wanted to give me a chance to, eh . . . take care of, uh . . . nature's call." MacArthur self-consciously pulled on his jumpsuit and sat down to pull on his boots.

"Damn, of course! I'm sorry," she said, blushing. "I'll watch Tonto."

"Er, ah . . . Tonto seems to know who you are, sir," he said. "He likes you." MacArthur caught her eyes with his and smiled happily. She remained outwardly impassive, but her eyes brightened.

"I brought him in," she said, staring him squarely in the face. "Go take care of whatever you need to do. I'll let Commander Quinn know."

"Yes, sir. And thank you," he said. MacArthur passed the returning Fenstermacher and received directions to the latrine.

Fenstermacher told him about the hot springs and highly rec-
ommended that he take a dip.

"You stink bad" was the way Fenstermacher put it.
MacArthur laughed heartily and slapped the boatswain's mate's
hat from his head, sailing it off into the rocks. MacArthur
stumbled stiffly down the hill, leaving Fenstermacher swearing
with his usual surpassing skill.

They approached the cliff edge. Buccari marched at a hard
pace behind MacArthur, frequently making eye contact with
the injured creature carried papoose-style on the corporal's
broad back. Quinn and Shannon came after her. Tatum
watched the rear.

Tonto occasionally stared into the air. Buccari looked up and
was not surprised to see soaring black specks.

"Sarge," MacArthur said, stopping, the cliff only paces
away. "This is where I woke up. Maybe we should make camp
and see what happens."

"Why don't we just put the bug down and back away?"
Shannon asked.

"Tonto might run off," MacArthur said. "That won't prove
anything."

"What are we trying to prove?" Shannon asked.

"Good question, Sergeant," Quinn replied. "I guess we'd
like them to understand what we're doing—that we're returning a favor."

The commander walked toward the edge of the cliff, remaining comfortably removed from the lip. He looked along
the precipice and then back into the skies.

"I agree with Corporal MacArthur. Let's make camp,"
Quinn said.

Buccari shucked off her heavy pack, went up to MacArthur,
and unstrapped the injured creature. Its body was passively
limp. It intently watched the skies.

"Why don't I take Tonto away from the group and sit with
him," she said. "Maybe something will happen if they see him
walking around."

She carried the animal on her hip toward the edge of the
cliff and sat down on warm granite. Carefully unwinding the
cloth swaddling, Buccari released the creature's wings and legs
and stood him erect. She held him by a light leash. Tonto stood
calmly, staring into her eyes or glancing past her into the skies.
Buccari was absorbed with clearing the animal's bindings and

dressings. Occasionally she lifted her gaze, but she mainly focused on the creature in front of her. The others busied themselves setting up camp.

Tonto stood erect, taller than Buccari in her sitting position. She leaned back and watched the creature hop about, never putting tension on his leash. He whistled and clicked and stretched his good arm, extending the membrane and allowing it to flutter in the wind, all the while keeping the broken arm close to his body. Buccari was intrigued with the mechanics of the wing. A bony appendage emanating from the animal's forearm extended the wingspan past the wrist and hand for almost a meter. At full extension the wrist and hand acted like an overcenter lock, holding the wing rigid on the downbeat. When the wing was stowed, the arm rotated and the appendage folded back on the forearm, arranging the excess webbing around the creature's lower back in a smooth fold. She watched the creature as it gracefully stowed the good wing.

Buccari also marveled at the animal's fine fur. She reached out to the silky pelt. The animal watched her hand stroke its fur and, after several strokes, leaned against the pressure, its eyes closing to slits. Suddenly the creature's pliable muscles hardened into iron; its eyes opened wide and stared directly over her shoulder, toward the cliff. Buccari looked up to see Quinn, MacArthur, and Tatum frozen in action poses. Shannon had a pistol in hand, and Tatum had grabbed a rifle. Buccari rolled to her knees and slowly turned her head.

Two hopelessly ugly animals, generously scarred, stood between her and the precipice. Like the humans behind her, they were postured dynamically, eyes slitted to combative intensity. The newcomers wore thick leather chest and groin protectors, and one carried a pike that was half again as long as the creature was tall. Involuntarily Buccari cleared her throat. The fierce creatures' eyes darted to her, registered no threat, and snapped back to the men. She moved onto unsteady legs and found herself to be a head taller than the newcomers. She reached down and disengaged the clip holding Tonto's harness and leash. With a slight shake of her hand the harness came loose. She stood up and pushed the injured creature toward the newcomers.

Tonto grabbed her finger.

Buccari looked down at the clinging animal and tried to smile. She gently broke loose, took three steps backward, and waited. Tonto hopped over to his comrades, while the creature

with the pike waddled forward and placed the weapon at
Buccari's feet. Uncertain what to do, she turned and looked at
the men. She sighed with relief as Tatum and Shannon put
their weapons on the ground. MacArthur, finger to his lips,
walked over to Tatum and pulled Tatum's knife from its calf
scabbard. He moved past Buccari and laid the knife at the feet
of the foremost animal. MacArthur stepped next to Buccari
and picked up the pike at her feet. The animal bent easily and
picked up the knife. And then it bowed elegantly. MacArthur
bowed in return. Standing erect, MacArthur startled everybody,
including the beasts, by cheerfully whistling the seven-note
ditty. As if rehearsed, Tonto, standing close to his fellows,
whistled the same notes in return but stopped short of the last
two. MacArthur firmly whistled the two final short notes.

Tension palpably lessened, but movements were still
guarded and nerves were taut. The newcomers grabbed their
injured comrade and hopped to the cliff's edge. Without looking back, they pushed off and dropped from sight. Piercing
screams shattered the silence.

EIGHTEEN

GORRUK

"They deserved to die," Gorruk snapped, his huge body
trembling, his brow tufts oscillating like tuning forks.

"You are hopeless," Jook rumbled. "Why do you act so?
You represent my regime. Executing an entire regional government was stupid!" They lounged in Jook's private chambers,
drinking *kotta* wine and smoking precious *wahocca* cigars. The
imperial entourage had been dismissed.

"Regional bureaucrats!" Gorruk roared, surprised and growing angry. He expected commendation for his decisiveness.
"They would not obey procurement orders. My armies must be
fed."

"Yes, yes, it is critical that your forces be provided for—their moment draws near—but even useless bureaucrats have a purpose," Jook replied. "Now, to replace them: utter chaos. Tax revenues will disappear."

Gorruk glared sulkily at the Supreme Leader. Politics and government were too much for his direct mentality. He struggled, resisting mightily the urge to throw the emperor-general's own past back in his face. General Jook's history—the scourge of the unification wars—was replete with mayhem and terror.

"You cannot threaten death whenever someone disagrees with you," the ruler preached. "I have learned this the hard way. Too much fear can be counterproductive. You create only martyrs."

"Yes, Jook," Gorruk replied. "But—"

"You will address me in the *proper manner!*" Jook bellowed. Both giants, staggered by drink, lurched to their hinds; the yellow scent of their mutual anger exploded into the air. Subtly concealed doors burst open, and a dozen armed members of the palace guard burst into the chamber, powerful snub-blasters aimed to kill. Air circulators kicked in.

Gorruk, exceedingly clever, was also extraordinarily courageous. Standing erect, he deigned not to look at the guards.

"You will address me in the proper manner," Jook said smoothly, an imperious smile creeping over the wide expanse of his grainy features.

"Yes, Exalted One," Gorruk said at last, smiling only with his mouth.

Jook laughed with a ground-shaking rumble. He dismissed the guards with an impatient jerk of his beaker, splashing wine on the floor.

"Oh, too well do I understand you," he sneered, nodding his monstrous head. "Yes, it is difficult being the general, but, my comrade, it is far more difficult being the emperor-general."

"I must defer," the surly general snarled without sincerity.

Jook poured another great vessel of wine. "Tell me, General Gorruk, what is your opinion on this matter of the aliens?"

Gorruk's intellect struggled to rein in his furor. With effort he suppressed his bile and focused on the new subject, little improving his temperament.

"The aliens . . . my leader?" he snorted. "Routed into space for another four hundred years, perhaps forever. History taught us well."

"Hmm, I wonder," Jook replied. "What have we really learned?"

"Your Excellency?"

"Who knows what really happened four hundred years ago?" Jook asked.

"We were attacked from space," Gorruk said, "and the decadent governments of the nobility were destroyed. The generals defended the planet."

"And ruled with wisdom and perfection ever since. You have read too much official history, General," Jook said, growing introspective. "Our planet was attacked, but by whom, by what? The generals did not defend the planet—the attackers just went away. They just went away."

"But the Rule of Generals was established all the same," Gorruk said. "The noble houses lost their hold on power, and—"

"And our planet has never been the same," Jook interrupted. "The global trade networks and economic exchange agreements that were natural extensions of the noble houses were never reimplemented. The hemispheres became separated by more than just the equatorial deserts."

"But we have solved our problems," Gorruk said, amazed at Jook's revisionism. "Our populations no longer overwhelm our resources. We have not suffered famine in over two hundred years, and crime is all but eliminated."

"So true," Jook agreed. "Famine has been superseded. It is a poor government that allows its soldiers to die of starvation."

"Our armies have united the entire northern hemisphere," Gorruk said. "Given the right conditions, we will reunite the planet. We will make possible a global prosperity and security that never before existed, even under the nobility."

"So says the history written by our militant ancestors," Jook said. "I am told the nobility read from different volumes."

"Bah," Gorruk said. "Their version of history is irrelevant."

"And yet our noble friends are not so helpless. They have assumed positions of responsibility and power in all the technologies and sciences and even the military. And they have regained power in five southern hemisphere countries. Perhaps they are trying to rewrite history, eh, General?"

"Perhaps. And perhaps after we have conquered those renegade southern nations we should clean the vermin out of all houses."

"Hmm, it has been considered," Jook mused. "But no one

has figured out how to make the economy run without our friends. The global economy has never been as robust as it was before the Rule of Generals. Even without kingdoms to rule, the nobility control the purses of the world."

"Our world has changed, Your Excellency," Gorruk responded. "Do not forget, during the Reign of Ollant the nobility directly controlled both the northern and southern prosperity spheres—a significant advantage."

"True. The southern tribes are spiteful and noncooperative. The deserts have given them false security for too long."

"We shall fix that!" Gorruk exclaimed. "My armies will be ready."

"Yes," Jook said, "but in the meantime we should not overlook other opportunities. Let us return to this matter of the aliens. Our Minister of Internal Affairs believes the second invasion was different—"

"Yes, we were prepared," Gorruk interrupted. "We intercepted and destroyed the alien invaders before they came close enough to attack."

"But who were they, General? How come they to fly between the stars? Were they the same race that attacked our planet four hundred years ago? Who knows? But we should pay heed to Et Kalass's activities. Our noble friends have even gone to the expense of funding an expedition to Genellan."

"I have heard of the alien mystery ship!" Gorruk said. "A waste of time and money. Even if true—which I doubt—any alien shipwrecked on that ice planet is long dead. We can ill afford to expend energy sniffing about for alien bones. We have a war to plan and execute."

"Where is your curiosity, General?" Jook asked.

"I am a soldier . . . not a scientist," Gorruk answered.

"Nevertheless, General," Jook said, "Kalass is up to something. I desire you to watch our good minister's actions. Let us not discount Genellan too readily. Perhaps, just perhaps, there is something there. It would be wise to have an agent on the scene. You can do something, can you not?"

"I always send the best," Gorruk snarled.

NINETEEN

EXPLORATION

"Everyone's talking about your argument, Sharl," Hudson said, plopping down next to her on the lake beach. "You went thermal."

"Damned difficult to have a confidential discussion," she replied.

"Sorry I butted in, but we heard you yelling and thought you were in trouble. You were about as confidential as a collision alarm."

"Sound carries up in those rocks," she said.

"Particularly swear words," Hudson mumbled.

"I got pretty cranked up, eh?" She laughed. "Well, I'm not sorry."

"The commander looked angry. Very angry."

"He'll get over it," she said, the smile fading from her face. "I had to get him to stop moping about his wife. To start making decisions. And if he wasn't going to start exploring for a better place to settle, then I sure as shit was. MacArthur says there's a valley down the river that has everything we need, and MacArthur knows what he's talking about. This plateau is going to be frozen hell in less than three months."

"Everyone's with you, Sharl. They know you're right," Hudson said, "but nuking the commander sure made them nervous. Thought Shannon was going to wet his skivvies when you ordered both of them on patrol."

She chuckled and lay backward, stretching out in the firm sand. A fleet of woolly clouds passed in review, highlighting the dark clarity of the stark blueness. Two stars twinkled dimly at the zenith. Unseen, a jumping fish made a noise like a hollow barrel being thumped. A flock of tiny gray birds, common now with the maturing summer, flitted low over the shore, swerving to avoid the earthlings. A flower moaned somewhere.

"I wonder if it will make any difference?" she said presently.

"What? Shannon wetting his—?" Hudson turned to face her.

"This planet's longer day and year. Will we live longer, too?"

"Why should that make any difference?" Hudson answered, bending over to pick up another rock.

"Why not?" Buccari mused. "Our bodies might adjust to the daily and annual cycles. Our bodies may choose to live the same number of days or maybe the same number of winters. That could mean we might live ten or twenty percent longer in absolute time."

"Nice dream, but I don't think so," Hudson replied, walking to the water's edge. "The body won't know the difference."

"I'm not so sure. It may take a few generations to make a difference. If nothing else, we're sleeping the same six to eight hours every day, so we get an extra two point two three hours of waking time. The percentage of time we sleep has gone down."

Hudson contemplated her logic. He walked to the water's edge.

"You might have a point, Sharl," he concluded. "But I bet we have to pay it back somehow. You don't get something for nothing."

"Even the months are longer," Buccari remarked, "assuming you use the big moon as the reference. It takes thirty-two days between full moons."

"Actually, the little moon might be more convenient." Hudson threw the rock far out into the lake. "Takes fourteen days to cycle. We double the period and have a twenty-eight-day moon month just like on Earth. Whatever, it's sure nice to have long summer days."

"Let's see how we feel after spending a winter here," she replied. "A winter like we've never seen. We need to get off this plateau."

The patrol halted at the rise next to the cliff edge. MacArthur wiped the perspiration from his forehead and looked up to see dozens of cliff dwellers soaring across the cloudless sky. Two cliff creatures glided much lower than the others. He slipped off his pack, unzipped a side pocket, and pulled out a small notebook.

"Now what do we do?" Petit asked.

"We leave this," MacArthur said. "Gotta find the mailbox."

"Hand me the book, Corporal," Quinn ordered.

"Yes, sir," MacArthur said as he handed it over. He watched the commander carefully. The skipper had been moody since leaving the camp. "Lieutenant Buccari and Mr. Hudson did a really good job, sir."

"Looks like a comic book," Petit said, looking over Quinn's shoulder.

"From the mouth of an expert." MacArthur laughed.

"What's that supposed to mean?" Petit asked with a snarl.

"Just a joke," MacArthur said, smiling.

"Why ain't I laugh—"

"Cut it out, both of you," Shannon ordered, walking back from the edge of the plateau. Shannon's moodiness since leaving camp had been no less apparent than the commander's.

"That's about what it is—a comic book," Quinn replied, breaking the tension. "Lieutenant Buccari doesn't think we'll ever be able to speak their language, or they ours, so she prepared this notebook of icons and cartoons as a first step in communications."

"It looks like they aren't accepting deliveries," Shannon remarked.

"Lieutenant Buccari said we should put up a cairn of rocks, seal the book in a utility pouch, and leave it," MacArthur said. "What do you think, Commander?"

"Do it," Quinn replied, handing the book back. "Let's get going. I'm anxious to see this valley you and Chastain keep talking about."

Their task completed, the patrol moved along the jumbled cliffside, stopping to fill their canteens in the river.

"Trail starts over here," MacArthur said, looking out over the dizzy traverse. The river crashed over the precipice behind them.

They descended the narrow ledge, hugging the cliff wall for the rest of the day. As the day ended, the trail flattened and mercifully turned away from the river gorge, providing a place to make camp for the night. In the twilight MacArthur looked out across the plains to the twin volcanoes in the distance, which were still far below his elevation.

Morning came quickly and was pleasantly warmer than the

frosty plateau mornings, promising a hot day. After a long morning of dusty downhill hiking, the patrol came to a thinly forested tree line, where the trail switched back to the north-west, descending sharply to the river. MacArthur noticed a narrow valley on the opposite bank. Below them the powerful watercourse jogged sharply to the north, necking down to a turbulent constriction.

"Chastain and I intercepted the trail up higher," he said, relaxing in the sparse shade of some firs. "I haven't seen any of this."

"Options?" Quinn asked, looking down the steep trail.

"The valley is three days from here, downstream," MacArthur said. "If we stay high, it's downhill all the way. If we go down this trail to the river, we'll have some serious climbing later on."

"What do you think, Sergeant?" Quinn asked. "Do we follow this path and see if it tells us anything, or do we head for MacArthur's valley?"

"We should check out the neighborhood," Shannon said.

Quinn pointed downhill, and MacArthur pushed off without further discussion. As he made his way down the steep path, the corporal glanced into the blue skies and saw two motes circling high overhead.

"We're being watched," he said, pointing out the fliers.

"Maybe they got Lieutenant Buccari's book," Shannon suggested.

"You think they can read?" Petit asked. "They're stupid animals."

"You can read, can't you?" MacArthur chuckled. "Sort of?"

"Bite my—" Petit snarled.

"I told you to cut it out," Shannon snapped. "Especially you, Mac."

"Sorry, Petit," MacArthur apologized. "But someone patched me up, and if it ain't those ugly buggers, then something else lives up there."

Petit grumbled an acknowledgment.

"Let's move," Quinn ordered, moving ahead to take the lead.

The rocky trail fell precipitously as it reached toward the river, switching back and forth across the face of the gorge. MacArthur saw the bridge long before the patrol reached it. Shrouded in mist, the bridge spanned the river at its darkest and narrowest point, reaching almost two hundred meters in length. At its lowest point the bridge was fifty meters above the frothing white torrent. Upstream, at a level higher than the bridge, the river crashed over tall cataracts, throwing thick mist into the air, obscuring the view and making conversation impossible. Downstream, swirling waters careened between the gorge walls, swinging to the north and out of sight.

The immensity of the plateau was even more spectacular from this lowest of vantage points. Rock walls mounted vertically, their imperceptible slant exaggerating a sense of infinity with incredible perspectives. The sun, just past its zenith, was already setting behind towering cliffs, and river mists fractured the rays of light, sending improbable rainbows across the chasm.

MacArthur again detected two cliff dwellers gliding through the mists, heading for wet rocks above the bridgehead on the opposite side.

"Suspension . . . chain link . . . !" Quinn shouted over the river's roar.

MacArthur examined the fist-sized links and followed the converging and diverging catenaries of the support cables as they swooped down from the cliffs on either side of the river. Parallel chains came out of the bedrock at his feet, forming a narrow bridge bed. Treads slick with river moisture were firmly attached at half-pace intervals, presenting more open space than floor. The view of the water far below through the bottom of the bridge was unnerving.

MacArthur checked the chain cables for corrosion but could find only traces of oxidation. Some of the mist-chilled and dripping links appeared to be newer than their neighbors. The workmanship was rough and unpolished, but the individual links were well forged and continuous. He placed a foot on the first tread and tentatively tested his weight. The bridge was solid. MacArthur walked across, gingerly avoiding a misstep into the tread gaps. The others followed one at a time. The river below served notice of its power, not that MacArthur needed reminding.

Once across, there was nothing to do but to follow the trail. It tracked upstream along the steep cliffside of the opposite bank for a hundred paces and then climbed sharply to a point where the rock wall of cliff plunged sharply to meet it. Reaching the bottom of the V, they found themselves in the narrow valley observed from the heights of the opposite bank. The trail leveled and meandered upward, traversing the valley's steeply sloping sides, making for a distant point at the head of the valley. Small stands of yellow-barked fir sprinkled the vale, but for the most part the rock-strewn valley was devoid of vegetation.

They walked through the afternoon, stopping next to a rock-bottomed brook that defined the fall line. The trail leveled, and intermittent patches of taiga prairie grew larger and more continuous. Behind them the plateau was undiminished—a ziggurat hanging high over their heads. Craning his neck, MacArthur turned to scan the massif, subconsciously taking a step rearward. Upstream, the face of the plateau curved gracefully away until it presented its profile, revealing the irregularity of its surface. Terraces, overhangs, promontories, and craggy pinnacles ranged along the silhouetted granite.

Flows of steam emanated from the river, climbing in snaky streamers from the base of the cliff or from the river. The thick tendrils ascended on humid air currents and merged with other wisps and vapors appearing to vent from the cliffs themselves. As the afternoon breezes died and the temperature dropped, the veils of steam visibly thickened and grew more persistent, approaching and occasionally ascending past the crest of the cliffs—thin black wisps against the yellow gold of the evening sky. The shadowed cliff face turned gray and flowed upward.

MacArthur forced his gaze from the steam-faced colossus. The rivulet they had been following had diminished to a trickling, flower-shrouded seep spring. MacArthur stood erect and sniffed. "You smell it?"

"Smell what?" Petit asked. "All I can smell are my own armpits."

"Animals, millions of them," MacArthur replied. "Musk oxen or buffalo or something. When we get to the top, you'll see them, and man, will you ever smell them."

"Commander," Shannon said, biting at the air like a big dog. "We should make camp for the night as soon as we get to the top. I don't see much benefit in hiking out on the plains. We're totally exposed. No campfires tonight."

"You call the shots out here, Sergeant," Quinn answered.

Daylight retreated. The insidious pressures of the spreading openness nagged at the men, their discomfiture exacerbated by the looming presence of the plateau at their backs. They finally walked on the spreading prairie, and as they walked, the smell took on a metallic palpability, a foreboding essence. The patrol topped a tundra-covered hillock, and the distant herd of musk-buffalo came dimly into view. The humans studied the serenely grazing animals.

"Phew!" Petit moaned. "We ain't going to camp in the middle of this shit stink are we?"

"Stow it, Petit," Shannon said.

"I gotta agree with Petit on this one, Sarge," MacArthur said. "Why don't we head back to the spring and make camp. The smell wasn't too bad back there. Shouldn't take us more than a half hour. Tomorrow we go back and pick up the trail to the valley."

"Sounds good to me," Quinn agreed. "What do you think, Sarge?"

"I just want to get off this open ground," Shannon said. He took one last look at the musk-buffalo, turned about, and started walking toward the river; the others followed. The horizon line formed by the plateau was high above them, a starkly black silhouette against the last deep red tints of twilight. A thick flight of first-magnitude stars already sparkled overhead. Darkness descended, and the rolling hills of the taiga plains lost their definition in the dusk.

"What's that?" Shannon gasped. "Look! Up there! And there—"

"Yeah!" Petit whispered. "I see 'em. Lights, all over the cliff."

The men stood like statues, staring at the solid blackness rising before them. Faint lights, subdued glows, flickered intermittently along the face of the cliff. The yellow-tinted emanations faded and returned, screened by the currents of steam wafting vertically. Faint, almost imperceptible lights were sprinkled across the face of the plateau, lending it a magical, ephemeral quality. The face of the plateau ceased to be rock and instead became a galaxy of stars embedded with shifting constellations.

"That's worth the walk," Quinn whispered.

Braan listened to the long-legs' exclamations and understood their awe. The lights of the cliff had been a source of strength and a beacon of safety for countless hunters returning from the limitless plains.

"What are you thinking?" Craag asked.

"They have seen our homes," Braan said. "We have little left to hide."

* * *

"Goldberg's pregnant," Lee said quietly, matter-of-factly.

"She's what?" Buccari asked a little too loudly.

"Pregnant, sir." Lee spoke softly.

Buccari looked at Lee with wonderment, as if the medic had two heads. "But—how?" she blurted, immediately feeling as stupid as her question.

"Cruise implants don't last forever, sir," Lee sighed patiently, "especially in full planetary gravity. Goldberg was due for overhaul last month. Mine's due in six months, Dawson in about three. If memory serves, yours is due in less than a year. With this much gravity, who knows?"

"Damn!" Buccari whispered. "Who's the father?"

Lee glanced into the bright blue skies and rolled her large almond eyes back into her head. The cool breeze teased her growth of shiny black hair.

"Might be easier to say who isn't," she replied, raising well-formed eyebrows. "We'll have to wait for family resemblances to tell us, or a DNA test if we ever get back to civilization. She thinks Tatum."

"Good grief!" Buccari almost spit. "Commander Quinn will be pissed . . . when and if his damn patrol ever returns." She looked up and scanned the rim of the plateau. His patrol was three days overdue.

"Well, I wouldn't be too hard on her," Lee said meekly.

"What? I'd think you'd be the angriest," Buccari responded. "Or at least the most worried. You're the one that has to deliver the baby. Or can you . . ."

"An abortion?" Lee pondered, as if she had not even thought of that option. "Too risky. I wouldn't know what to do. Too risky."

"What will Commander Quinn say?"

"Doesn't matter. Goldberg's still pregnant. I'm not worried," Lee said. "Goldberg's young and healthy. She does the work, not the doctor."

"It'll be delivered in winter, for goodness' sakes! Who knows how bad the winter will be? What a time to be having a baby! How thoughtless."

"We should probably thank her," Lee persisted, her meekness fading.

"Thank her?" Buccari half shouted.

Lee nodded. Buccari turned and noticed Rennault walking toward them.

"That's what Nancy says," Lee whispered. She stopped talking as the marine came within hearing. Rennault nodded as he walked by.

"Dawson knows?" Buccari asked as soon as Rennault was out of earshot.

"That's how I found out," Lee said firmly. "Yes, sir, we should thank her. Nancy says that Pepper's, ahem . . . activities have taken, uh . . . a lot of pressure off the rest of us. From the rest of the females."

"That's not supposed to be a joke, is it?" Buccari asked. "You're serious! I'll say she's taken a lot of pressure."

It was not funny, but she started laughing. The mental images generated by Lee's statement overcame her sense of propriety, and the laughter built on itself. Lee also started to giggle. Their laughter was interrupted by a commotion from the sentry station above the cave.

"The patrol!" O'Toole shouted. "Across the lake. They look whipped."

Buccari ordered Tatum, O'Toole, and Chastain to come with her: perhaps someone was hurt. She set out at a trot but soon slowed to an even hiking rhythm. As she neared the patrol, she could tell that the men were no worse than exhausted.

"Are we glad to see you," Quinn mumbled. He was sapped. Fatigue had insinuated itself into every level of his being; his eyelids drooped, and his mouth moved disjointedly.

"Welcome home," Buccari said. "Tatum, take Commander Quinn's pack. Everyone grab a pack. These boys need some help."

She went up to MacArthur and started to undo his pack straps. The marine laughed as he shucked off his pack and swung it onto her shoulders. His hand brushed her neck as he moved a shock of her short hair so it would not get pinched by the wide straps. Standing sideways to MacArthur, Buccari pulled in the hip belt to the limit, then did likewise with the sweaty shoulder straps. Chatter abruptly ceased, and the men all tried unsuccessfully not to stare; she realized that her movements had accentuated her femininity—the smallness of her waist, the flaring of her hips, and the swell of her breasts. Suddenly and uncharacteristically she grew hot and red-faced with embarrassment. She turned her back on the men and stepped out toward camp.

She had been gawked at before, but MacArthur's laughter seemed very personal and his touch had ignited a subtle chemistry. Now was not the time to tell the commander about Goldberg's pregnancy. Buccari hearkened back to Lee's words and why they should not be too hard on Goldberg, and suddenly she understood the insidious pressures to which Goldberg had succumbed. Their lives were uncertain, and physical attachments were islands of hope. Danger was near, apparent to the consciousness, but deeper, from deep in the racial memories of the subconscious, another awareness was surfacing: the species was threatened; lust was both an escape and a solution.

"Commander Quinn, the message!" MacArthur said, breaking the silence. Buccari paused.

"Oh," Quinn mumbled. "Almost forgot. We got a letter in the mail. It was on the same cairn where Corporal MacArthur left your icon book. It's written in similar form, so I guess it's for you." He walked over to his pack, unzipped a pocket, and pulled out a swatch of folded material. He carefully unfolded it and handed it to Buccari. The material was of heavy stock, a stiff cloth or linen. A stick figure of a man, identical to the icon she had used, was precisely drawn. Beneath the icon the letters "M-A-N" were printed with a draftsman's skill, just as she had presented the icon in her book. Next to the pictograph for a man were drawn two other figures, stick figures stylistically representing another race. One was much shorter than a man, an acute inverted isosceles triangle for the head, short-legged, and arms extended with membrane wings opened, obviously a representation of a being like Tonto. The other was taller although still shorter than the man, winged but less apparently different from a human. Beneath the winged icons were markings, evidently letters in the alien language signifying the creatures' names.

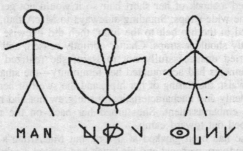

Buccari stared, fascinated. Her drawings, done with pen and straightedge, seemed awkward and hurried in comparison to the precision of the drawings held in her hand.

"There's two different types!" she whispered.

"Male and female?" MacArthur ventured.

"Wonderful!" she said. "This is history! The first contact with high-order extraterrestrial intelligence!"

"The third contact," Quinn yawned. "The massacre at Shaula was the first; the second was our fleet getting blown back into hyperlight. This is the third."

"The first peaceful contact, then," she corrected, her excitement unabated.

"But that's not all," Quinn said. The commander's energy seemed to increase as his memory replayed the events of their patrol. "At night the plateau . . . the cliff face is covered with lights. Amazing! And there's a bridge over the river. And MacArthur's valley is an ideal place to build our settlement when the time is right to move." He was babbling in his fatigue.

Buccari looked up at the commander, thinking he was delirious, but she noted all four of the patrol members nodding their heads in affirmation, a far-off look in their eyes.

TWENTY

THIRD PLANET FROM THE STAR—GENELLAN

"We land at Goldmine Station, on the continent of Imperia," Et Avian said. His demeanor had transformed with his departure from Kon, and he wore simple working clothes devoid of badge. Only the golden complexion reminded Dowornobb of the noblekone's untouchable rank. "Goldmine is the only permanent facility on Genellan. Gold is no longer mined, of course; only rare metals."

"Are there no other inhabited sites?" Dowornobb asked.

"There is one, opened only during the summer—a small science station," Et Avian continued, "on Corlia, the other major continent, eh . . . here. It is called Ocean Station." The noblekone pointed at the chart on the computer terminal. "For the study of planetary science. The other scientific sites were shut down centuries ago. The cost to run them was exorbitant. I worked as an engineer at the last industrial site, an offshore pelagic platinum extraction facility."

He shook his considerable bulk. Et Avian was large for a noblekone. "I was hoping never to be that cold again," he lamented.

Dowornobb was surprised that a noblekone would consent to travel to the frozen planet, much less work there. Prisoners had been sent to die on cruel Genellan in the ancient days, when the ore and fur trades had been profitable. Population pressures on Kon had been eased by the massacre of the Invasion and subsequently held under control by rigid breeding laws. As a consequence the planet was self-supporting. Mining the ores and minerals of Genellan had become uneconomical. Other industries, such as fur trapping, had also atrophied.

Dowornobb, once he realized that he was going to Genellan, had researched the third planet. Kones, under the auspices of the Imperial Northern Hegemony, maintained a scientific presence on Genellan. It was underfunded and begrudgingly maintained—just enough to protect the imperial property claim from poaching by other, less powerful nations of Kon. Not that any other nation was interested in that or capable of doing it.

Three enjoyable months had elapsed since Dowornobb's impressment. The young scientist ate well, which was important; he no longer had to put up with Director Moth's harangues; and he was able to use the high-performance computers of the Public Safety data network to link with his orbiting telescopes.

Dowornobb looked around the ship cabin. He was one of four specialists on Et Avian's science team charged with searching out the nature of the aliens. Scientist H'Aare, the renowned physicist, and Scientist Mirrtis, a metallurgist, were assigned to learn what they could of the technologies and propulsion systems that allowed the aliens to bridge the stars. Scientist Kateos was a linguist and a female, which made things difficult. Common females were forbidden to speak publicly. Librarians, medical doctors, and linguists acting as translators were the only notable exceptions; research, medicine, language, and translating had become, by tradition, exclusively female occupations. Other than those specific duties, females were expected to listen and obey. Dowornobb condoned breaches of that convention, but only with females he knew well and only when he was certain no one would be punished. Et Avian insisted that gender difference be ignored, as it was among the nobility, which was fine with Dowornobb but not with the others, particularly the four militia soldiers assigned to protect the team—hard cases all. The transit to Genellan had passed slowly, and the female had been predictably ignored.

Their trip had commenced with a gut-crunching blastoff from Kon to a Planetary Defense orbiting station. After a two-day layover, a constant-acceleration shuttle rocket had boosted them on a direct flight to the third planet. Fortunately, Genellan was in the optimal position for direct intercept. After depositing their landing module in orbit, the shuttle picked up fuel and a return cargo on the back side of the planet and, using the gravity of Genellan for an energy sling, was already whipping back on its return to Kon.

Reentry to Genellan was nominal. Their module settled onto the station platform, and turbulent deceleration was replaced by stillness and the planet's comfortably low gravity. Lander systems whined down; pressurization systems surged and pulsed, causing Dowornobb's sinus passages to flutter. A loud *thunk* signaled the attachment of the umbilical tower, and soon the warmth of the station's environment flowed into the passenger spaces. Dowornobb luxuriated in the satisfying lungfuls of full-pressure air. A crewman signaled to debark.

As the team crawled down a telescoping access trunk Dowornobb gawked through a window. Immense distances! Uncomfortable distances! His eyes struggled to focus on far-away images. The air was so clear. The fables were true. Dowornobb felt as if he had magnifying glasses over his eyes. He could see forever.

"The air is invisible!" he said to no one in particular.

"Because there is almost no air there," Et Avian said.

The newcomers clung to the ports, staring at the magnificent landscape. The colors were so starkly defined: a vivid cobalt sky spotted with luminescent clouds. Verdant grasses swept to ivory-tipped mountains on one side and to the scintillating oceans on the other. Translucent domes arched over their heads, refracting the solar radiance and generating prism images that shifted slowly with the sun, and more rapidly with the position of the viewer.

"Oh, it is so very, very beautiful!" Mistress Kateos gushed. The female immediately realized her error and dropped her head in abject subservience.

Everyone turned and stared. There was no excuse for such gross behavior. Mirrtis turned pale and coughed. Even Dowornobb was appalled. H'Aare, standing next to the hapless linguist, crawled quickly away.

"We will have time for sight-seeing later. Let us move on," Et Avian ordered. Luckily, the soldiers were already down the ramp and had not heard the outburst. The noblekone went to the female, picked up one of her bags, and headed down the ramp. Dowornobb watched the unexpected act of forgiveness and impulsively went over and picked up her other bag. He smiled sympathetically at the cowering female and walked off, pretentiously still on his hinds, just as the noblekone had done. Adding the extra burden of Mistress Kateos's bag to his own luggage required the full use of his forearms, and it was more convenient to remain erect. It felt natural in the light gravity. Dowornobb self-consciously looked backward and noticed that the others had fallen back from habit, crawling down the ramp on all fours, their bags carried over their backs or suspended from hooks and pouches at their midsections.

"Solar flares," insisted the managing director of Goldmine. "Solar flares blinded our network during the period. A tenuous object was reported, but we attributed it to solar flares."

Dowornobb looked at Et Avian and received a look in return communicating the noblekone's opinion of the managing director: a total incompetent.

"Let us move forward," Et Avian continued. "Do you have any data that suggest a landing or an impact with the ground?"

"Or," Dowornobb interrupted, "can you provide orbital parameters?" He turned to Et Avian. "I can do a simulation and run a distribution pattern of the most probable impact areas. The orbit would also define areas the aliens would have viewed as likely landing areas." Et Avian cast him a quick glance, at once a reprimand and a thoughtful stare.

"Aliens?" the director asked. "Are you saying aliens landed on Genellan?"

"Of course not!" the noblekone replied. "Scientist Dowornobb uses his own vocabulary. The object of our search is a suspected probe launched by southern mineral poachers. We have been tasked to determine the nature of that probe. Scientist Dowornobb's selection of words runs to the dramatic. Ha-ha-ha."

The director laughed politely. Dowornobb attempted to appear contrite, which he was. He had forgotten the noblekone's instructions. Dowornobb looked around the room, and his eyes were caught by Mistress Kateos. She stared audaciously at him, and he returned the stare, unable to help himself. She slowly averted her eyes, but she had looked into his soul.

The orbital simulation took only a week. A tremendous swath of debris had been deposited across the lake-studded terrain of western Corlia. Dowornobb ran the results to Et Avian, who was impatient for action. Summer had only one full month remaining. The weather would quickly become unpredictable after that time, except in one dimension: it would get cruelly colder.

Et Avian received permission for a suborbital launch to Ocean Station, the science facility on Corlia. He transmitted search coordinates and ordered fuel-staging to commence immediately.

The science station was located on the delta of a major river that met the northern shore of a fertile and nearly landlocked equatorial sea, the most temperate area on the planet. On rare occasions in the summer courageous kones even dared to touch bare toes to the frigid ocean waters.

Their suborbital module landed on a wide steel platform without a closed debarkation tower. The travelers were issued rugged suits with pressurized helmets. Fuel tanks carried on their backs were bulky, but the gentle gravity made them manageable. Once attired, the science team clambered down a ladder to a portable platform. From there they descended to the surface of the planet. Suited scientists escorted them to a waiting tracked vehicle.

After a short, bumpy ride the truck ramp opened to grass and sunshine. A smallish scientist awaited—without a helmet—his complexion swarthy, his posture erect. He smiled largely at Et Avian and even dared to shake the noblekone's hand. The visitors were escorted through a sturdy air lock, at which time they removed their helmets and talked excitedly.

Mistress Kateos remained quietly apart, but Dowornobb, fervent with adventure, flashed her a spontaneous smile. She glowed enchantingly with embarrassment.

"Take care of your breathing units," the bareheaded scientist said, his demeanor ebullient and infectious. "We have few spares, and I guarantee you will be uncomfortable without one.

"Welcome to Ocean Station," he continued. "My name is Et Silmarn. I am chief scientist here. It is a pleasure to have visitors. Particularly old friends." He nodded fraternally to Et Avian and picked up a breathing unit.

So the scientist was also a noblekone. But his complexion was so dark, not the soft gold of the high families. The other scientists assigned to the base displayed the same swarthy coloring.

"Et Avian has briefed me," Et Silmarn continued, "on *our* mission. I will be accompanying you to the lakes as one of your pilots. We leave at first light.

"There is insufficient room inside the station for everyone to eat and sleep, so you will be camping out. The sooner you acclimate, the better. Before you go outside . . . I mentioned the breathing units. You can breathe the air—what there is of it. A caution: even though the atmosphere is thin, there are high levels of poisonous gases that can make you sick or even kill you, particularly in the seismically active areas or near the great northern herds.

"But it is not the toxic gases that will cause you the greatest risk; it is the absence of air pressure. The low gravity that some of you are obviously enjoying"—he glanced at Dowornobb who still stood upon his hinds—"results in a low-pressure atmosphere, less than half of what you are used to. There are mountains here of sufficient height to cause your blood to boil."

He glanced about. "That, of course, would be quite high, but it is theoretically possible. The point is: wear your breathing unit and take care of it. You cannot run out of air, but you can exhaust the fuel for your compressor. A fuel load should last a person in reasonable shape over a week. However, none of you is in decent shape, including even your mission leader," he added good-naturedly.

"We will be heading outside. After you put your helmets on, I want you to find the regulation controls on the right side. These buttons and dials will control the richness, the pressure, and the temperature of the air. You will also find controls for your helmet speaker, head-up display, and headlamp.

"The next point: it is a very cold place. You have been provided an insulated suit with your breathing unit—a Genellan suit. The breathing unit bleeds heated air into the suit's insulation ... the difference between life and death. When we go north, the temperature will drop far below the very coldest spot on Kon. And that is during the day. At night and the farther north we go, the more miserable it will get, and it will get more miserable than your worst nightmare." Et Silmarn scanned his nervous audience.

"Enough bad news. Time for good news. The science and the scenery are why we are here. I want half of you to put on your breathing units. After we have been outside for a few minutes, those without units will put on their units. Once they have successfully donned their units, the others may remove theirs so they may sample the unfiltered and unpressurized air. The lesson: always make sure at least half the group is wearing breathing units. You can share breathing units."

They were herded into the air lock, and its door slid noiselessly shut. H'Aare immediately put on his helmet, as did Mirrtis and two of the sullen soldiers. Dowornobb tried to avoid looking at Mistress Kateos, but his eyes disobeyed. She caught his gaze yet again. Dowornobb felt peculiarly happy and excited to share the adventure of the new planet. He nodded at her, and neither donned a helmet.

The outer door *whooshed* open. The air lock flooded with sunlight and with sound. Dowornobb swallowed hard to equalize pressures as a chilly blast of air made his eyes water, but his discomfort was eclipsed by the unadulterated freshness and clearness of native sounds and smells. The smells! Dowornobb's olfactory glands overloaded with a symphony of fragrance. Such sweetness and body—a cloying sensation surged through his extensive sinus network. He sniffled. Such sights! They were surrounded by verdant forests domed with bright blue skies, and tall on the northern horizon, razor-sharp in the clear air, a jagged line of snowcapped mountains rambled into the distance.

The kones milled onto the tree-dotted sward surrounding the station. Red birds and yellow hopped and fluttered on an emerald lawn, chittering and warbling. A bareheaded scientist scattered seeds and crumbs across the grass, and dozens of other birds converged, dropping from the trees. Mistress

Kateos moved quickly to the activity and stared, enraptured at
the abundance of color and sound. She glanced at Dowornobb
and smiled like a child. Dowornobb could not help himself and
returned the innocent expression. He felt light-headed but was
not certain that it was due to the lack of carbon-oxygen compounds.

Et Silmarn continued his lecture. The newcomers listened, the
distractions of the scenery difficult to overcome. Dowornobb,
disquietingly happy with the attentions of Mistress Kateos, tried
to inhale the whole world, take in the bright colors, and hear the
shifting blend of gentle sounds, but after several minutes another sensation overflowed the others. It started as a tickling between his eyes and quickly became an irrepressible imperative
welling up from the back of his head. To no avail, he tried to
stifle the explosions. One after another, colossal sneezes erupted
from deep within his massive body. Embarrassed, he realized
others were also sneezing.

"A signal to put on your breathing unit," Et Silmarn advised. "Pollen. You will get used to it."

Dowornobb looked at Kateos, her face flushed and wide-
eyed. She returned his glance, eyes laughing. As they put their
helmets on, they took a lasting look at each other, excited with
the delightful experience they had shared.

TWENTY-ONE

EVIDENCE

No one slept well, wearing a helmet. Haggard and weary as
they were in the predawn, all were enchanted by the vast array
of luminous patches and extremely bright individual stars pulsing from moonless morning skies, so different from the muddy
nights of Kon.

Their revelry was brief, the bracing chill of the air all too
real. Headlamps were pointed to the job at hand, and the

explorers-to-be broke down tents and packed up camp gear. The end of summer was nearly upon them.

As the sleepy scientists stumbled and shivered down the dark pathway toward the station, brilliant banks of arc lights rippled on, spreading a stark glare. A pair of aircraft sat on the matting, reflecting the artificial light from their polished, white-painted flanks. Squatting on low-pressure tires, the sturdy craft had stubby fuselages and drooping wings mounted high to facilitate downward surveillance. The aft portion of each fuselage split and tapered into twin booms with a connecting elevator mounted high above the ground. A single large engine nacelle with vectorable ducting was mounted over the wing spars.

"Stow your gear in the aircraft," Et Silmarn ordered. "Abats, we call them."

After a startlingly animated discussion between Et Avian and the corporal of the militia guard, the team was split, with Et Avian, Kateos, Dowornobb, and two soldiers in one of the craft and the rest of the team in the other. Et Silmarn was to pilot Et Avian's plane; Scientist Lollee, another station engineer, was assigned to pilot the other craft.

"Abats?" Dowornobb asked Et Avian. "Is that not a mythical bird of prey?"

The noblekone nodded. "It also is the name we have given to a bird species on this planet. We will talk about real abats later. See, the sun rises."

The sunrise, through layers of clouds, was extravagant; golden rays spiked with orange and coral forged unevenly into the eroding deep blues and purples of the retreating night.

With the glorious sunrise at their back, the loaded aircraft revved engines to high rpm and released brakes. Each sprang forward, rolling from the matting onto a grassy strip before lifting clumsily into the air. The second plane fell into trail position, and both planes banked sharply to the north, toward the mountain passes. Dowornobb sat, glued to the window, watching the jagged, snowcapped peaks drift by, some just off their wingtips.

"I want you to work together," Et Avian said, interrupting Dowornobb from his sight-seeing trance. Mistress Kateos sat to his left. Dowornobb avoided looking at the female, for she was constantly staring at him. He noticed the soldiers listening, their contempt clearly evident.

"Yes, Your Excellency," Dowornobb said.

"This will require you to communicate," Et Avian continued. He looked into each of their helmet-shrouded faces.

"Yes, Your Excellency," Dowornobb repeated.

"Communicating means two-way communications, talking and listening, each in their proper turn," Et Avian said.

The noblekone was certainly driving home his point. Dowornobb wondered how to respond. "Yes, Your Excellency" was the best he could do.

The noblekone glared at Dowornobb. He looked over to the female and then back to Dowornobb. His huge eyes rolled in his great head.

"Mistress Kateos," he said firmly, looking at Dowornobb. "I am sorry. I had hoped we might surmount this situation with our departure from Kon. Konish males seem incapable of breaking our mindless conventions. You must help them. Introduce yourself to Master Dowornobb. Inform him of your needs and skills. We will be flying to the search area for the next two days, and it would be time better spent if you were to develop an understanding of each other's mission."

"Yes, Your Excellency," Kateos said, chin up. "I understand. I will endeavor to make Master Dowornobb appreciate my contribution to the team."

"Very good," Et Avian said. He looked at the soldiers. "I will leave you alone, for I have business with Corporal Longo."

The noblekone moved across the cramped and narrow aisle to engage the lead corporal. Dowornobb knew that Et Avian had wanted all the guards on one plane and the technical team on the other. The lead corporal, Longo by name, had bluntly refused, maintaining that his orders were to watch over everyone; separating the groups would make it impossible for him to carry out his orders. Dowornobb had to agree with the logic, but something was amiss . . .

"I speak eight languages, Master Dowornobb," Kateos said proudly.

Such vanity, Dowornobb thought. "I did not know there were that many different tongues on Kon," he replied awkwardly.

"Oh, there are at least twenty modern languages and ten times as many dialects. The north is more homogeneous, because of its history of totalitarian regimes. After the Great Massacre the rulers of the north consolidated many isolated tribes and suppressed their languages. Some were simply killed off. The southern regions never succumbed to the genocidal tyranny of the north."

Dowornobb looked up anxiously. He himself was inclined to talk obliquely about the inadequacies of government, but he knew where to draw the line, particularly when talking to strangers. The female was talking treason.

"I have been all over the planet working as a translator for the Minister of Internal Affairs. Ironically, as long as I am translating the silly words of some pompous official, my voice is received and welcomed. I am frequently requested by name to act as the official interpreter for opposing leaders." She talked rapidly, as if unburdening herself, a dam broken.

"Oh," Dowornobb ventured nervously.

"I have heard the alien tapes," she blurted conspiratorially. That reached past Dowornobb's discomfiture.

"The tapes from the Astronomical Institute? But most of it is not spoken communication," he replied. "The transmissions are all over the spectrum."

"Oh, I have listened to only the audio range," she said. "His Excellency wants us to work together, so you can explain to me what else is on the tapes."

"Hmm," Dowornobb pondered. "We cannot do much without a datalink."

"No, His Excellency is not expecting that on this trip. Our objective is to examine the wreckage. Master Mirrtis and Master H'Aare are rocket propulsion and technology experts. I am to look for artifacts and documentation which might help to reconcile the language. I am also an accredited archaeologist."

Dowornobb's respect for Kateos was growing, not so much from her words but from her demeanor, the strength of her personality.

"Mistress Kateos," he said. "Your credentials are impressive, but please . . ." He moved closer. "Control your opinions. The Supreme Leader has ears everywhere." He signaled with his eyes.

She gulped, features firming. She peeked at the soldiers.

"Master Dowornobb," she said quietly, squeezing the corners of her mouth. "I am sorry. Of course my opinions deserve not the light of day. It is just that I am so excited with the prospect of working with you."

"You are excited . . . by working with me?" he asked.

"Oh, yes!" Her deep brown eyes stared brazenly through her visor. "You have been most kind. You helped me with my bag, the day we landed, after I blurted out my feelings shamelessly! That took courage. You seem interested in my well-being, unlike the others. I have never been treated thus. You even smiled at me—in a public place! You are most kind."

Dowornobb blushed. Kones did not often give or receive compliments, except empty, formal ones. He was confused. The warm feeling on his face spread to his heart and—alarmingly—to his gland bladder.

"And you are so intelligent," she continued, moving closer. She touched his arm. "Et Avian said you have risen rapidly in your science. You are considered among the most elite astrophysicists and astronomers. He called you a genius."

Dowornobb was becoming infatuated. He had never received such praise. He was aware that the institute published reports under Director Moth's name, occasionally with credit for his research, but he did not know that the authorities recognized his primary role in their authorship. He was immensely gratified.

"And you are so bold!" She would not stop, nor would Dowornobb dream of stopping her. "His Excellency was appreciative of your initiatives in discovering the crash site."

Kateos stopped talking. She stared fully into Dowornobb's face, and her gaze was far more compelling than any words. Dowornobb gave thanks that he was wearing a sealed suit and that everyone was wearing helmets and air filters, for his gland bladder erupted at that moment, the essence of his emotions literally exploding from his body. Dowornobb was in love.

"We are landing for the night," Et Avian announced. They had spent hours covering a multitude of topics and issues. Dowornobb could tell that Et Avian was impressed with his and Mistress Kateos's depth and breadth of knowledge.

"We are descending quite low," Dowornobb indicated, his helmet pressed to the thick window, feeling the vibrations of the powerful engine. The terrain was mountainous, although the peaks were less numerous. Pockets of snow and grimy glaciers clung to the mostly dry and barren slopes, and hazy cloud formations shrouded the lower ranges. The pulsating glow of fiery-red lava peeking through the haze made Dowornobb soberly conclude that the clouds were steam and ash spewing from a chain of volcanoes. Calderas marched across his view, the terrain tortured and broken with faults and ejecta.

"It is most spectacular at night," Et Avian said from the

window seat behind Dowornobb. "At night the landscape is traced with intertwining ribbons of hot red, and the magma ejections are beyond words."

"Must we land so close?" Dowornobb gulped.

"We will not land so close as it seems!" the noblekone laughed. "You may wish we had landed closer, for it is warmer near those infernal rocks."

The landscape changed abruptly from ash-colored lava flows to flowing fields of grass. Knife-edge ridges lifted high into the air, enclosing the grasses and the low-flying airplanes in a steep-sided valley. A scintillating stream ran parallel to their flight path. The aircraft banked sharply into the brisk afternoon wind, and as the abat leveled its wings it seemed to stand still. The pilot applied heavy power, the engine overhead vibrated strongly, and the ground floated up to join the wheels. The abat bounced slightly and rolled to a stop.

It was bright and sunny, the sun still high in the west, yet icy-cold air rushed in when the doors were opened. Though the kones were forewarned, the temperature plunge took their breath away. In near panic, they adjusted the temperature settings higher. Power units consumed fuel faster. The scientists sickly realized that they were going to be outside in these conditions for over a week—a prison sentence! Et Silmarn and Et Avian herded their charges into action. The other pilot, Lollee, industriously drove stakes into the ground to use as tie-downs for the airplanes. The ground trembled and swayed beneath their feet.

"Do not worry about the seismic tremors. It is a permanent condition at this site. The sooner you get your tents up, the sooner you get out of this wind," Et Silmarn shouted, the gale whipping his words away.

Using the airplanes as windbreaks, they anchored three tents securely. Et Avian and the pilots claimed one tent, the four soldiers quickly disappeared in another, and the four scientists occupied the third. The conditions were crowded, but everyone appreciated the additive nature of body heat.

"Beautiful, is it not?" Et Silmarn asked as he came through the thermal lock. The four scientists huddled in their Genellan suits and dolefully watched him. "It is unseasonably moderate," Et Silmarn continued. "The air in the tents is warming quite nicely. Turn off your breathing units. You cannot eat with helmets on. The first thing we are going to do is prepare a meal, so watch carefully and learn. You must know how to cook for yourself."

Et Silmarn organized the cooking equipment, setting up a stove in a vented alcove despite the rolling tremors. The meal was quickly prepared and consumed. The air in the tent warmed, the scientists grew relatively comfortable, and, with hunger quelled, their anxieties diminished. A conspiratorial conversation common to shared adventure erupted spontaneously. Scientist H'Aare allowed himself to converse with Mistress Kateos. Scientist Mirrtis talked with animation, still only to the males; however, he did not object or react with even a hint of revulsion when Mistress Kateos cautiously participated.

"We have a chore: we must refuel our abat," the noblekone announced. "We must do this every day, so the better we get at it, the less time it will take. Listen carefully!" Et Silmarn explained tasks and assigned duties. They listened to the instructions, put on helmets and suits, and followed the pilot into the cold.

Although it had grown cooler, the kones now anticipated the breath-stealing coldness. With only a few well-intentioned shoves and shouts, barrels of fuel were rolled from staging areas and their contents were pumped into wing bladders. Their job done, the scientists piled good-naturedly into their warm tent, feeling a sense of teamwork that previously had been missing. They resumed their conversation, and all four participated as equals.

"You will post guard around the clock," Et Avian ordered, his regal patience wearing thin with Corporal Longo. He removed his helmet to scratch his nose.

"It is too cold, Your Excellency," Longo whined. "We cannot withstand these conditions. We were not told—"

"Your mission is to protect us," the noblekone continued. "What are you going to do, hide in your tents? Who is going to protect you?"

"From what is there to be protected—besides the cold?" Longo asked impudently.

"You have Genellan experience," the exasperated Et Avian said. "Surely you know the dangers. This continent has bears and predator lizards, pack scavengers and abats, catamounts and blackdogs. The cold is the least of your worries."

"P-predator lizards, Your Excellency?" Longo swallowed.

"Yes, predator lizards. What field experience have your men had?"

"We were facility guards at Goldmine Station, my lord, nothing more."

"And—?" Et Avian asked.

"That is all, Your Excellency," the lead corporal replied. "None of us have spent more than a few nights in the field, Your Excellency."

Et Avian stared at Longo. "Post a guard," the noblekone commanded. "I will check on it. Be prepared but do not be afraid. It is unlikely anything will come close to our tents. The animals are wary. If something comes snooping, fire your weapon into the air. That will scare anything that lives on this planet." Et Avian turned, stooped, and crawled from the tent, not bothering to put on his helmet, anger providing sufficient heat to get him to his own tent.

Longo knelt in the center of the tent. The wind fluttered its thick walls.

"Do you think he suspects, Colonel?" one of the black-clad soldiers asked.

"*Corporal*, you idiot!" Longo snarled. The soldier dropped his head.

"Perhaps," Longo replied then. "B'Aane, you have the first watch. Two hours. Lootee will be next, and then Rinnk. What he said is true—they are just animals. Loud noises will scare them."

"Only if you see them," Lootee said.

"Shut up and obey!" Longo snapped.

The scientists of Ocean Station made a fishing trip up the wide river almost weekly. The ocean shore teemed with fish, crustaceans, and sea mammals, but one particular fish, called a speckle fish, was everyone's favorite. It was caught only in the fresh water of the great river. Scientist Kot and Technician Supree had been assigned the duty of taking the motorized skiff upriver to replenish the supply of that fish. It was pleasurable duty, a day off from the monotonous data checking and compiling that characterized their research work. Officially, they were to take meteorological readings and collect biological samples.

With the sun still below the horizon, Kot and Supree loaded the skiff and headed up the slack current of the great river, aided greatly by the first stages of a flood tide. Their destination was far upriver, to a place where the great ribbon of water took its last wide meanders before splitting into the sloughs and marshes of the brackish delta. The long ride in the frigid morning air was punctuated by sunrise—a stately metamorphosis of night into day—and a welcome rise in temperature. The riverbanks came alive with the morning; herds of long-legged gazelles grazed placidly in the frequent clearings, multitudes of river birds screeched at the passing skiff, and aquatic animals splashed in and out of the water, seeking refuge in all directions. They came upon two schools of placid round-backed river monsters. The broad white dorsals rolling gently across their path were the only impediment to their speedy trip north.

The kones finally beached their skiff on a familiar islet; its crescent beach, a favorite place, was swept by the direct rays of the sun through most of the day and was shielded from the northerly breezes by a low bluff. The river ran wide and deep to both sides, providing ample protection from field predators, although a clutch of furry, flat-tailed animals had taken up recent residence.

While Technician Suppree shooed away the varmints, Scientist Kot unloaded the equipment and set up fish traps. Once the nets and traps were set, the kones took fishing poles and cast their lines out into the current. The hard work done, they commenced to relax. With the sun high enough to provide the necessary warmth, they took turns removing suits and helmets for half-hour stretches. The sun-baked sand held the chilly winds at bay, permitting them to soak their great muscular bodies in the marginal warmth. After a half hour the chilled sunbather would don suit and helmet and check the traps and nets for any catch, while the other scientist would undress and bravely recline in the soft sand. Occasionally a pole tip would dip and bend nervously, and the suited kone would lumber over and reel in a wriggling fish. These biological samples were accumulated in a well in the hold of the skiff.

Fishing was good, and the fish tank was filled by early afternoon. With the sun no longer overhead, the afternoon breezes swirled around the bluff protecting the sandy cove. The day was ending, and the pleasantly sun-burnished kones, both fully suited, collected the fishing equipment.

"I will load the nets, Suppree," Kot said. "Start the afternoon readings?"

"Real work!" Supree whined. He grabbed the instrumentation satchel from the boat and walked a hundred paces upriver, disappearing around the low bluff.

The technician immediately reappeared, lumbering through the sand on all fours, yelling unintelligibly. Kot dropped the nets, wondering whether to jump in the boat and start the engine.

Supree stopped and turned about. "Come! Quickly!" he shouted, heading back up the sand. Kot followed at an uncertain trot.

A section of raft remained tied together, grounded on the beach at the foot of the bluff, the long bitter end of a line trailing in the clear current. Two tiny green helmets and a single pack were lashed tightly to the logs. A miniaturized weapon was firmly strapped to the pack. Supree and Kot stared down at the foreign objects, circling the sunken raft, even walking in the icy water.

"A helmet," Kot said, figuring out the latching mechanism and lifting it from the raft. "But it is so small." It rested easily in the palm of his hand.

"A weapon, no doubt," Supree stated, unbinding the rusted rifle from the pack. His thick finger was too wide by half to fit through the trigger guard. "Et Avian will want to see this when he returns from the north."

A week later Dowornobb held the helmet in his hands, fascinated by its miniature size. How could a being with a brain so small travel between the stars? Maybe its brain was not held in its skull. Maybe it had two heads. After all, there were two helmets and only one pack.

"Ironic," Et Avian said, holding the other helmet as if it were a holy relic. "We fly across the continent to examine debris that tells us nothing, while the best clues wash up on our front door."

"No, Your Excellency," H'Aare interjected. His enthusiasm for the search had steadily developed, escalating his personal emotions to almost a fervor. "We learned much from the wreckage."

"And we are better prepared for next year," Mirrtis added with surprising enthusiasm. He had suffered more than most from the harsh elements.

"What His Excellency means is we found no clues to the aliens—no writings, no pictures, no tools," Kateos said, her voice firm. Dowornobb felt a strange pride in the female's assertion.

"Yes, Mistress Kateos," Et Avian added. "We now have a clue to their appearance. But we also know two facts that are even more important: one, they are on Genellan. And two, we can narrow the search to the river valley."

"That remains a large search area," Scientist Lollee said. "We cannot search any more before the cold season. They will probably die in the winter, if they are not dead already. Only dumb brutes can live through a Genellan winter."

Dowornobb glanced at Et Avian, who stared resolutely at the equipment. The Genellan winters, incomprehensibly vicious, were beyond hope. Dowornobb shifted his attention and noticed Corporal Longo standing silently in the corner.

TWENTY-TWO

OUTBOUND

Young Brappa was selected for the autumn salt expedition, a warrior's rite of passage. When Kuudor informed Braan of his son's selection, the hunter leader's paternal instincts filled him with foreboding: many sentries never returned. But Braan quickly dispelled his paternal anxieties. Salt missions were fraught with problems; he would not be distracted by selfish worry. The size of the expedition was Braan's concern. The elders had proclaimed the salt requirement, and the pronouncement tore at Braan's heart—one hundred full bags. Braan sighed and swallowed his protests; there would be many hunter abodes to visit. As their leader, it was his responsibility to notify the warriors of their obligation to volunteer, and since hunters never refused duty, Braan's visits were received with grim respect.

Delicate chimes heralded the eve of the salt mission; young sentries with thin bars of silver dangling about their necks glided along the cliffsides, the clear tinkling sounds too cheerful for the intended purpose. The golden skies of evening darkened to night, and hunter families celebrated with somber thanksgiving. The selected warriors and sentries slept well, secure in their courage and proud of their responsibility.

At dawn all hunters, young and old, dressed for battle and ascended the cliffs, their straggling multitudes clogging the pathways and tunnels of the colony. By midmorning thousands of warriors crowded the cliff rim, a sea of black eyes and leather wings. Pikes and bows prickled above the horde, a field of pointed blades. In the center of the massed hunters, arrayed in precise ranks, a hundred battle-armored sentries stood proudly, graduating sentries awaiting their final test. At their head was ancient Kuudor, captain-of-sentries. Five second-year sentries maintained a ceremonial tattoo, beating granite rocks with tuned metal bars, while all other sentries posted vigilant guard along the cliff rim. At Craag's signal the beaters became still.

As always the winds freshened with the rising sun. Braan stood alone and silent atop the rocky rise overlooking the common. Pivoting with dignity, the leader-of-hunters raised his wings to embrace the four winds. As Braan turned he screamed ancient chants powerfully, beautifully. All hunters felt hot blood rushing through their veins; the fur on their spines bristled with emotional electricity, with anticipation and apprehension. They joined fervently in Braan's harmonics, creating a resonant vibration. The strings of their shortbows vibrated, and dust elevated from the ground—an ecstasy of hope and fear.

The prayer completed, Braan screeched fiercely and thrust his black pike, pointing at Kuudor. The captain-of-sentries marched to the front of his arrayed charges, halted, and ceremoniously whistled the names of fifty sentries, including Brappa, son-of-Braan. The drummers initiated a quick marching beat. The named sentries hopped forward, picked up a dark bag, and fell into a double line formation facing the edge of the cliff, expressions stoic and movements precise. The massed warriors chirped raucously to the marching beat, acknowledging the suppressed fears of the young sentries, reminiscing over their own first times. Braan signaled, and the beaters halted with a flourish. Clicking in unison, the sentries who were not called closed ranks smartly, looking simultaneously relieved and disappointed.

Braan brandished his pike and pointed sternly, this time at Craag-the-warrior. With grave authority Craag sang out more names—the names of sixty warriors. One by one the sixty stepped forward, most grabbing salt bags. The first ten, master warriors, including Tinn'a and Bott'a of clan Botto, shouldered only their weapons. These would be the scouts and guards, and they formed the first rank. The next fifty warriors were experienced but less seasoned. Each would associate himself as an instructor and bodyguard to a novice, responsible for the sentry's survival and training. They formed interleaved ranks with the sentries.

The sentry common roiled with nervous movement and sound. Braan raised his arms dramatically. Silence fell, and the gurgling noises of the nearby stream drifted across the redoubt. Braan screeched lustily, demanding praise for the volunteers. The cliffside was drowned in ritual bedlam. With explosive volume the assembled hunters screeched the death song. All warriors sang for death, a death of honor, a passage to final peace: the hunter's plaintive acknowledgment that life was over, that he had fought to the limits of his strength—that he was ready to die.

The hideous screaming built level on level to pitches and frequencies known only to dumb brutes and cliff dwellers. In the continuing din, Braan raised his pike and the drummers initiated a rhythmic marching tempo with side beats and flourishes. Braan glided from the hilltop and joined Craag at the formation's head. The two hunters marched over the cliff's edge, cracking their wings with explosive power. The formation followed, one rank at a time, to the whistling cheers of the multitude. As the salt mission rose on fresh updrafts, the formation altered, the ranks sliding outward and joining until a large V formed, giving each hunter undisturbed air. The whistles and screams from those left behind increased in intensity and volume. Thousands of hunters followed the salt expedition into the air, leaping out over the river and rising vertically on the convection currents heaving upward against the face of the plateau. A billowing horde of black bodies soared majestically and noisily upward as the wavering V of the salt mission faded to a faint line on the northern horizon.

"Look!" MacArthur shouted. He pointed ahead, toward the plateau's edge. A thin black cloud drifted skyward. Buccari lifted binoculars to her eyes while MacArthur and the other patrol members—O'Toole, Chastain, and Jones—stared at the ascending column.

"Our friends," Buccari said, taking the glasses down and watching the spectacle unaided. "Thousands of them." She handed the glasses to MacArthur. The humans took turns watching the wheeling masses. Gradually the cloud of fliers thinned and spread, dissipating, individual motes gliding down the cliff face.

"What's that all about?" MacArthur asked.

Buccari glanced at the corporal and shrugged.

"Maybe they'll be waiting for your letter, Lieutenant," he persisted.

"It would be nice," Buccari replied tersely. She was impatient to drop off the next batch of pictographs. Nothing had been received from the cliff dwellers since the initial tease. She scanned the skies to the north and west. The weather was changing.

Her patrol was headed for MacArthur's valley, a last foray before the snows of winter. Buccari stifled her frustration. She had wanted the entire crew moved to the valley before winter struck. According to MacArthur, in the valley tundra gave way to topsoil, temperatures were warmer, wildlife was abundant, and the forests were thicker and more diverse.

Yet Quinn had elected to winter on the plateau. Buccari worried about the commander's decision-making abilities, concerned that his emotional distress was infecting his judgment. He spent long hours alone and made decisions only when pressed. On most issues he seemed indifferent or distracted, but for some reason he had taken a strong stance on the issue of not leaving the plateau. Two sturdy A-frame log structures and a solid meat house had been constructed downhill from the cave; a magnificent woodpile for the winter's heating and cooking requirements had been accumulated. And there was the cave. The cave provided an element of permanency and an essence of security. The crew was emotionally attached to the first campsite. Quinn, seconded by Sergeant Shannon, proclaimed that they were prepared for winter.

The arrival of winter was mysteriously uncertain. There was a bite in the wind and the air smelled different, but Buccari had insisted on one last patrol before winter snowed them in, tugging at Quinn's mantle of leadership, cajoling and badgering. Quinn conceded, if only to stop her harping. Buccari organized the patrol and set out immediately. She was going to be prepared for the spring, and learning more about the valley was imperative to those preparations.

"We got some cold weather coming," she said now.

"It's damned cold now," Jones said.

"What's the matter, Boats?" O'Toole asked. "I thought you liked playing marine."

"Yeah, Boats," MacArthur said. "Act like a man. Right, Lieutenant?"

"Yeah, Boats," Buccari said. "Act like a man. Move out, Corporal!"

"Aye, Cap'n," MacArthur replied, stepping out toward the horizon.

Braan glided along, measuring altitude by the pressure in his ears. The thermals were unseasonably strong, and the autumnal southwesterlies pushed the hunters rapidly over the plains. An auspicious start.

Hours passed. Thermals lifted them high, yet Braan's initial well-being was tempered by the changing elements. An innocent parade of puffy cumulus had exploded into a threatening line of towering nimbus. Concentrations of billowing turbulence blossomed upward, fluffy white tops curling ever higher, their bottoms black and heavy with rain—thunderstorms. Braan veered to the west, hoping to slide behind the rain giants. Hours of soaring remained, but flying into the crazed craw of a thunderstorm would not get them to the salt flats. Ominous booming of thunder rattled sensitive nerves in Braan's sonar receptors, and searing blue streaks of lightning arced between the roiling mountains of moisture. The hunters pressed forward, skirting the bruised clouds, but the course ahead grew solid with storm. The hunter leader set a sinuous detour, descending slowly through a dark valley of rumbling behemoths. Braan screamed a command along each wing of the echelon, and Craag, leading half the hunters, descended, falling behind and forming a separate V. Wispy vapors and occasional raindrops sailed through the formation, and high overhead, dark clouds cut off the last bright rays of the sun. The hunters accelerated their descent, fighting increasing turbulence and decreasing visibility.

Sonar pulses of frightened hunters discharged randomly, their locating organs firing off sonic feelers. Braan in the lead, with nothing to guide him except eyes and instincts, remained quiet. Turbulence rocked him insistently. A pelting rain started.

And then hail. Braan screamed: every hunter for himself. A nimbus cell had swallowed them. There was no telling which way the powerful and turbulent drafts would throw them. Braan held his glide straight ahead, increasing his rate of descent, hoping the formation would stay with him. His hopes evaporated. He felt powerful updrafts. The longer the hunters remained in the air, the more scattered they would become. Braan repeatedly screamed the dive command and pulled in his membrane wings, bunching them behind his back. The elevator updraft pressed him but could not hold him; the lead hunter pointed his nose downward and knifed through upwelling winds.

He fell through the bottom of the clouds, black grayness suddenly brightening to the midnight green of rain-soaked plains rising to meet him. Braan flattened his body and allowed his membranes to ease into the rushing slipstream, bleeding off vertical velocity. Halting his descent, he struggled to keep his wet body in the sky, beating the air with powerful strokes. He circled relentlessly downward in driving rain, screaming for a rendezvous. Answering cries came from all around, and as he drifted to the hail-strewn tundra, other hunters hopped and glided to his location, marshaling to his cries. Miraculously, after a half hour of whistling searches, everyone was on the ground, regrouped and without serious injury. Their adventure had started.

The line of thunderstorms passed, harbingers of a fast-moving front. The flint-edged wind shifted to a firm northerly, and temperatures dropped sharply; hailstones crunched underfoot, and bright gashes of cold blue sky sailed rapidly overhead. The hunters would have to march; the cold, wet air would not lift their weight. Warriors formed in two columns ten spans apart. Braan deployed experienced pickets on each flank and ordered Tinn'a to take two warriors forward as an advance guard. Craag dropped back with the remaining experienced warriors; growlers usually attacked from the rear. The vast number of plains carnivores were to the east, where the great herds were beginning their migrations, but straggling buffalo remained in the area, and even small herds had packs of four-legged death stalking them. Braan screeched, and the hunters hopped forward. The hunters' short steps moved the columns doggedly across the wet tundra. Braan proudly watched his son waddle by.

Squalls swept the rolling plains, unloading gray sheets of icy

rain on the hunters' bent backs. A deluge had just passed when
Tinn'a's warning cry drifted to his ears. Braan halted the columns and moved forward. Tinn'a was on the point, crouched
on a low ridge, slightly below the crest. As Braan approached,
a great eagle gliding easily in ground effect lifted above the
low elevation of the ridge. Braan screamed for Tinn'a and his
scouts to retreat, for they were too few to thwart the monstrous
killer. He was not worried about the hunter columns to his
rear; their firepower would discourage a dozen eagles.

Tinn'a's scouts retreated, converging from either flank.
Tinn'a silently unfurled his wings and pushed mightily down
the shallow slope. Braan noted with alarm the quick turn of the
eagle's head as it registered the movement of Tinn'a's wings.
The eagle pounded the air and rose higher. It wheeled and,
with the wind at its back, closed the distance with alarming
speed. Braan had no choice; the hunter leader screamed again,
but this time it was the order to attack. Braan leapt into the air,
deploying his wings thunderously. He pushed forward, laboring
to gain speed and altitude, brandishing his shortsword.

The intrepid scouts responded to Braan's command. Their
wings cracked unfurled, and they bravely rushed to intercept
the eagle, skimming across the damp downs. Tinn'a swung
hard around to join the assault, his wingtip shooting up a
rooster tail of water and hailstones from the sodden ground.
Braan's forward velocity and Tinn'a's momentum to the rear
caused them to pass in opposite flight, separating the warriors
more than good tactics would dictate, but action was joined,
and they could not delay. The hunters screamed the death cry
and closed on their great rival for the skies.

The eagle's glare fixed on Tinn'a. Yet as the hunters narrowed the distance, Braan detected a shift in the predator's attention. Undaunted, Braan bore straight forward, aiming his
sword thrust at the eagle's malevolent yellow eye. The eagle,
disconcerted with the directness of the small creature's assault,
maneuvered, but Braan sharply adjusted and met the eagle
head-on, striking a vicious liquid blow. The collision knocked
the hunter into a tumbling spin and out of control. Braan flared
his wings and cushioned his splashing jolt onto the soft
ground. The indomitable cliff dweller somersaulted and leapt
back into the air, struggling for altitude.

Screaming horribly, its momentum carrying it higher, the en-
raged eagle regained sight of the hapless Tinn'a. Half-blind,
furious with pain, it dove at the trailing hunter, obsessed with

the thought of ripping the small winged creature to pieces. Tinn'a, far below the eagle's altitude, could not attack, but neither could he turn to run. Tinn'a bravely held his glide, and just before the eagle impaled him with grasping talons, the crafty hunter dipped sharply, trying to evade the overwhelming attack. Too late. One of the crazed eagle's talons struck Tinn'a a murderous blow across his back, and he was hurled like a stone to the ground.

The two scouts converged on the eagle and wheeled with it, trying desperately to keep up with the faster and more proficient flier. Braan, thrashing the air to gain altitude, watched the three fliers head back in his direction. Tinn'a's inert form lay on the ground. The huge eagle descended toward the stricken hunter, talons spread wide. Braan, much closer, folded his wings and plummeted, landing heavily beside the immobile Tinn'a. The hunter leader's hands and arms moved with blurring speed. Braan unsheathed his shortbow, drew an arrow, nocked it, and bent his bow to the target. The eagle, sightless in one eye, canted his cruel beak to the side, the better to view his prey as he dove from the sky. Braan loosed the arrow; its iron-tipped shaft sliced the air and dug deeply into the glaring evil orb, finding the great brute's small brain and shutting out the creature's last light. With a tortured screech the eagle feathered its massive wings, halting its dive. It collapsed from the sky, blinded and mortally wounded.

The scouts landed on either side of the shuddering bird, bows pulled taut, ready to shoot. Braan nocked another arrow. The hunters, lungs heaving against rib cages, warily circled the fallen raptor. The eagle trembled in its final death throe and was still.

"Let us—" Braan gasped, "see to our comrade."

Braan hopped over to Tinn'a. The warrior lay in a twisted heap, still alive, his breathing quick and shallow. Braan carefully arranged the injured hunter's limbs, trying in vain to make Tinn'a comfortable. The warrior's back was broken. Tinn'a's eyes fluttered open.

"I was not quick enough, Braan-our-leader," the hunter whispered.

Braan said nothing; his most difficult duty lay upon him. He looked to the skies and began the death song, but with subdued volume and measured pace. His wail spread over the downs with mournful slowness and softness. At the correct time Tinn'a's scouts added their voices, and even Tinn'a, given the

honor of singing his own death, joined in feebly. The hunters
wept without shame. When it was right, Braan knelt on
Tinn'a's chest and carefully, affectionately grabbed hold of the
injured hunter's head and twisted it fast and hard, breaking his
neck and snapping the spinal cord. They dug a shallow grave
and covered it with a cairn of rocks. Tinn'a, clan of Botto,
a warrior in life, was buried holding the eagle's head—a glorious warrior in death.

The smell of cooking meat and the clatter of implements
brought Buccari awake. Reluctantly leaving the warmth of her
sleeping bag, she crawled painfully from the tent. The morning
was frigid; a layer of hoarfrost coated the landscape, and a few
lonely wisps of steam flowed upward past the cliff's edge. Beyond the timid mists the hard line of the eastern horizon promised a new day, the first rays of sunlight spilling over the
unrelenting margin of earth and sky. A single high cloud glowing salmon-pink against the neon-blue sky testified to the impending brilliance of the unrisen sun. MacArthur and Chastain
hunched over a small fire. MacArthur looked up.

"Morning, Lieutenant," he said cheerfully. "Got lucky and
caught a marmot in our trapline. We can save the dried fish for
dinner."

Buccari swallowed hard and exhaled. More greasy meat.

"You okay, Lieutenant?" MacArthur asked with gentle concern.

"I'm fine, Corporal," she replied, correcting her facial signals. "Just a bit stiff."

"You aren't the only one. Had to kick O'Toole out of the
rack this morning to get him up for his watch. He could barely
move. It's that soft camp life."

She looked up to see O'Toole breasting the rise, returning
from the stream. "Where's Bosun Jones?" she asked.

MacArthur pointed to the tent with his thumb just as Jones
groaned loudly, the sound of a large man in agony. The tent
flap moved aside, and Jones's wide face and burly shoulders
emerged into the chilly morning, his head and back covered
with a blanket.

"She-it! It's cold!" Jones shivered, his eyes barely opened.
"Excuse me, Lieutenant," he quickly amended, seeing Buccari.
"I meant to say that it was right pleasant out. Refreshing, even."
He slowly straightened his back and stretched mightily. His liq-

uid brown eyes blinked slowly, and then he took notice of the cooking marmot.

"My, that smells good!" he drooled. "But I hope you got more than just one of them rock rats for us to eat."

"You going to eat the whole thing, Boats?" O'Toole asked as he walked into the camp. "Just like you hog the whole tent. I feel like we're married. You sure you're not Irish?"

Jones smiled. "It was cold. Best time to make friends," he mumbled.

"Speaking of friends, Lieutenant," O'Toole continued. "Your notebook disappeared sometime after I came on watch. I checked it first thing, and it was there, but it wasn't about an hour ago, and there were tracks in the frost. They headed over the cliff."

"Finally," she sighed. "Did they leave anything in return?"

"Not a thing, sir."

By the time the sun rose above the distant eastern horizon, the salt expedition had trekked many spans. The dusky odor of musk-buffalo drifted into their awareness. Scouts sighted a herd to the east. The hunters chewed thickweed and altered their course to stay clear. Predators of all types, rapacious and long inured to the stink, doggedly stalked the great herds, worrying the fringes, attacking and killing the old and the sick. Braan veered west, hoping to avoid the inevitable growlers. They were nearing the salt lakes.

Braan moved forward to join the scouts, the terrain lowering sharply to flat desolation; to the north were the white-tinged lake beds. Herds of musk-buffalo ranged to the east, and constant activity dotted the plains in that direction. Brown dust filtered into crystalline skies, tumbling up from the pounding hooves of the plains animals. A scout signaled, and Braan's attention was jerked forward not by the scout's alarm but by a shrill banshee ululation wafting over the downs—buffalo dragon. Striding into view across the rolling tundra were two of the ferocious long-legged beasts. One monster halted abruptly and whirled to glare menacingly at the hunter columns. Its powerful fluted neck stretched upward, lifting its terrible head above a thick-plated dorsal. Canting its head, the reptile sniffed at the air, spiked tail twitching nervously. As suddenly as it had stopped, the creature pivoted and ran after its mate. Braan sighed with relief.

It was unusual for dragons to be about in daylight. The

splendid animals were efficient killers, but for reasons unknown to Braan, the dragons avoided the hunters, as if they were cognizant of the cliff dwellers' potential for retribution. Braan was thankful for this mystery, for he respected the terrible beasts. He had seen dragons bring down charging musk-buffalo with indescribable power and ferocity.

"Braan-our-leader!" a scout twittered, pointing. "Growlers!"

Upwind, well clear of the hunters and posing no threat, a large pack of growlers moved at a trot, warily following the dragons. Their gray manes and silver pelts were already turning; in two months they would have thick white coats. Instinctively Braan turned in the opposite direction. He saw more growlers coming at that flank. A scout screamed the alarm. There were only six, but they cantered directly at the hunter columns, skinny tails flailing the air like nervous whips.

The downwind scout rose into the air and slanted for the oncoming danger, circling slowly away from the cliff dweller columns. The experienced scout hit the ground awkwardly, only strides from the startled scavengers. The burly beasts leapt abruptly sideways and reared onto their hind legs, baring yellow fangs and efficiently hooked claws. A ferocious rattling, grumbling explosion of their displeasure rent the air, a preternatural harmony of growls and howls.

The wily hunter stumbled and hopped three or four times before flapping noisily into the air. The growlers, tails erect, recovered from their surprise and lunged to the chase. The scout landed frequently, shaking the fatigue from his wings but always jumping into the air just as the growlers pounced, staying tantalizingly out of reach. Braan watched with approval, and the column veered farther west, moving rapidly behind the chase. When the growlers were clear, the exhausted scout worked into the air and glided to the rear of the column, leaving the scavengers directionless and frustrated.

TWENTY-THREE

ENCOUNTERS

The hunter columns marched onto the stark flatness of alkaline lakes, the landscape barren, surreal, without perspective. Life was reduced to two dimensions, existence pulled down to utter flatness, distances obscured by shimmering lines of cold heat rising from silver mirages. The hunter leader ranged ahead of the expedition, using scouts as messengers. The columns of impatient hunters passed old excavation sites that were smooth from wind and rain. Braan knew the advantages of getting salt of the highest purity; every grain of salt carried over the distances was dear. An extra pound of pure salt refined from the harvest would justify the added hours of hiking.

Braan stopped. Through thermal distortions rippling from the surface of the bright white salt could be seen small erect animals. Alert to Braan's presence, they were frozen and poised for action. The wind was from Braan's left and carried no dangerous scents, nothing but the stale, acrid odor of the salt flats. Braan whistled softly to the closest scout, ordering him to fall back to the main body with instructions to form for attack. Braan motioned for the other scouts to spread to the flanks. Warily testing for rising air currents in case retreat became necessary, Braan continued forward. As the distance closed, the bleary air cleared and a familiar scent reached his nose. A tribe of mountain dwellers materialized from the wavering whiteness.

Braan halted a hundred paces short of the encampment, displaying his bow and sword openly but without menace. His scouts held their positions a shortbow shot out on each flank. The mountain dwellers had seen Braan coming and were waiting with pikes and knives at the ready. Only a few carried shortbows. Braan made a quick head count; close to seventy mountain dwellers were spread over the salt digs. Their leader, a furtive creature with a knife held threateningly in his wiry grasp, limped toward Braan, stopping ten paces away. He was a hunter, the same as Braan, only smaller and darker, pitch-colored to Braan's charcoal, and there was no cream-colored patch on the smaller hunter's chest. The little warrior was old, a veteran of many battles, with massive scars waffling his wrinkled countenance. The mountain warrior's peculiar eyes were the color of pale tea.

"We here first, cliff dweller," said the mountain dweller chief.

"No dispute, warrior-from-the-mountains," Braan answered. "Be at peace."

The aged warrior peered across the wavering distances to the cliff dweller scouts and past Braan, trying in vain to discern the magnitude of the cliff dwellers' main body. Braan sensed the mountain dweller's anger and frustration.

"No need for fear, warrior," Braan consoled. "Thou art wise to use all thy hunters to gather salt. The snows of winter will soon be upon the land."

"We done this day," the surly creature said, his dialect difficult to comprehend. The mountain dweller chief glowered at the taller cliff dweller. Some dweller tribes, particularly those of the mountains, raided other tribes, stealing harvested salt rather than expending arduous efforts mining it. Some tribes captured hunters with the salt, forcing their captives to carry the salt back to the raiding tribe's colony, where the prisoners were enslaved or killed.

"An excellent site," Braan said. "The salt here is pure."

The gnarled and gimpy hunter, brandishing his knife, snarled. "Do not attack, tall one," he said. "Go away or we fight. My warriors have much battle. We not run."

Braan allowed his vision to drift over the head of the ravaged leader to scan once again the skulking gaggle of mountain dwellers. They were tired and malnourished. A desperate foe was a bitter adversary.

"Threaten not, warrior-from-the-mountain," Braan replied evenly. "Continue digging and depart in peace. We pose no threat unless thou make one of us by foolish acts." He turned and unfurled his wings. He paused and returned to face the twisted visage of the mountain dweller.

"Thy hunters are hungry. We have killed an eagle. What can be spared of its flesh will be brought to thee as a gesture of goodwill." Braan turned and cracked his wings, catching the air. A weak thermal boosted him, and he used the height to glide toward his expedition. The scouts retreated on foot, covering his movement.

Autumn had touched the riparian underbrush along the great river. Isolated islands of yellow and copper fringed the more prevalent darkness of spruce and fir foliage, providing depth and perspective to the narrow tributary defiles veining into the larger valley. But the autumn glory revealed during the days of hiking along the great river paled in the splendor and fullness of MacArthur's valley. Buccari's patrol arrived in the valley near the first light of day. Breasting the slanted outlet falls above the river, the din of thrashing rapids pounding around them, Buccari stared over the placid lake waters into the deep and magnificent setting. Beams of pure gold from the low morning sun crafted facets of rainbows in the mists, and vivid autumn hues glowed softly, doubled by reflections from the mirrored surface of the lake. In the distance a festival of earth tones gave way to tracts of blue-green mountain forests through which a waterfall fell in multiple cataracts, dashing from the steep-sided foothills at the base of the towering mountains. Nestled high above, a white-frosted blue-green glacier flowed sinuously around white-shrouded peaks and tors, all resplendently reflected in the serene lake.

"Oh, my! It's wonderful!" Buccari exclaimed, her breath taken away by the pureness of the vision, the painful weight of the pack forgotten. "I never want to leave this place."

"I know what you mean," MacArthur said, reaching down with his foot and shattering the crystalline film of ice on a puddle. Visible puffs of warm air spewed from the speakers' mouths, punctuating their wonder.

MacArthur walked past her, and she followed, stumbling, unwilling to divert her gaze from the gaudy landscape. Great flocks of waterfowl exploded from the lake, the noise from their wings rivaling the sounds of the river left behind. The patrol picked its way along the gravelly lakeshore, moving deeper into the valley. Buccari finally brought her gaze back down to her feet and noticed a tall, bushy thatch growing abundantly in the marshy shallows. Birds fluttered around and through the tall grasses, perching frequently to peck at the golden reeds.

"Hold on for a second, Corporal," she ordered. "I want to

look at something." She removed her pack, sat down, and took off her boots.

"Time for a break, anyway," MacArthur said, shedding his pack. "You got blisters?"

"See that bushy-headed grass?" she replied, wading into the frigid ankle-deep water. "Looks like a grain." Buccari inspected the chest-high thatch for seeds and was delighted to find dense rows of ricelike grain. She picked the tiny husk-covered seeds and shelled the chaff, leaving behind pale white germs in the palm of her hand. Her instincts told her that she was looking at food. Buccari hacked off some stalks and carried them to shore. She sat down, and the corporal joined her.

"I've tramped by here a dozen times. Never thought to check for grain," MacArthur said.

"You wouldn't have seen anything until a few weeks ago," Buccari replied. "This is small stuff." She stripped the seed into a cook pot.

"Can I help?" MacArthur asked. He grabbed a stalk and started stripping it. Buccari watched him work, his hands agile and sure, his face a study in concentration.

They made quick work of the stalks. When they were done, they looked at their meager collection. It was food—the makings of bread, the staff of life. Buccari looked up and started to speak but caught MacArthur staring intently at her. She looked away quickly, her demeanor eroding before involuntary emotions.

"You have to take the husks off," she said, fingering through the seeds, separating the lightweight shells from the germ, her voice as husky as the grain. The pressure again. She was feeling the pressure of living in a natural world, a world of animal drives. Her world had been reduced to fundamentals. It no longer mattered that she could fly a spaceship; her computer skills were useless, her military rank irrelevant. She was facing the prospect of learning how to be a woman—a woman in a primitive world. The thought was not consciously formulated, but her instincts shouted the dictate, echoing it through her subconscious being. She felt the pressure.

The mountain dwellers disappeared in the night. Braan knelt and examined their abandoned equipment, the signs of panic written in the remains. He had seen hunters from other tribes only a dozen times in his long life, and each time the meeting had been characterized by extreme fear and distrust. Braan

contemplated the blatant differences between his own cliff
hunters and those of other tribes, the tribes of the mountains,
and was bewildered.

"Where should we dig, Braan-our-leader?" Craag interrupted. His lieutenant had posted the perimeter guard as ordered. Braan quickly studied his capable and intelligent cohort
and was grateful for the cliff dwellers' advantages.

"Concentrate on areas already excavated but do not dig
more than the depth of a field pike. If more area is required,
dig upwind and ensure that the top layer is removed."

"Bott'a has found the excavations to be fouled," Craag said
angrily.

"Fouled?" Braan replied, startled.

"Dung slugs, ashes, excrement. They did not want us to
have the advantage of their work. Perhaps we should have
fought them."

"No, my friend," Braan replied thoughtfully. "We were right
to let them go. Start new excavations. At least we have an understanding of their fears. Let them continue to wonder about
us. In the long run it will be to our advantage."

"Mac, you and Chastain finish scouting the valley," Buccari
ordered. "I'll keep Boats and O'Toole here. We need the
food." She was angry that she could take only a limited
amount of the precious seed back to the plateau. Why hadn't
they moved to the valley? She was also angry because she
would not get to see more of the valley. That would have to
wait until spring. She tried not to show her foul mood.

"Aye, Lieutenant," MacArthur replied. "We'll be back in
three days."

Buccari watched the two men head out along the lakeshore
and disappear around a point of land. She was both relieved
and sorry to see MacArthur disappear—his presence was disconcerting.

She went to work, directing the two remaining men.
O'Toole and Jones hacked great sheaves of lake grass and carried them to an area of cleanly swept flat granite, where the
seeds were stripped. Once a quantity of raw grain was accumulated, it was put in a tent bag and pounded against the rocks
to break down the husks. After threshing, the grain was tossed
into the air over the flat rocks, allowing the wind to blow
through the airborne mixture, catching the lighter chaff and
sweeping it downwind. This beating and tossing process was

repeated until the husks were flushed from the grain. After two
days of laboring in the sun and wind, the three spacers were
burned and sore, but they had accumulated almost thirty kilos
of white grain.

"Ready for the return march, Braan-our-leader," Craag said.
Harsh winds blew straight as a nail, driving stinging salt into
red-rimmed eyes and white-crusted fur.

Braan walked the line of burdened warriors, checking their
physical condition and providing encouragement. Heavy salt
bags strained fragile frames, unnatural loads for airworthy
creatures. He came to his son and slapped him solidly on the
back. Brappa turned and lifted his chest, proud and capable,
saying nothing.

Braan checked his own ponderous bag of salt, shrugging it
against the set of his shoulders. He lifted his sword, pointed to
the south, and started hopping slowly between the columns.
Craag and the rear guard, not carrying salt bags, waited until
the columns moved away. Scouts and pickets, deployed far
ahead and to the sides, turned to their missions.

The salt flats were left behind. The hunters scaled the rising
downs, returning to the rolling tundra. The unwieldy salt bags
rode heavily, and the hunters perspired under their loads despite the chilly bite of the quartering northerly. A gray layer of
clouds scudded overhead, dropping an occasional splatting
drop of rain. The young sentries steeled themselves to their
loads, anticipating the cliffs of home. The experienced warriors, knowing better, blocked their minds to all things.

On the second day growlers attacked, a modest pack, fourteen animals, led by a silver she-beast. The rear guard spotted
them loping over the crest of an adjacent rise and whistled the
alarm. The picket moved to intercept. The columns halted but
did not put down their salt bags. Salt bearers shuffled in position and sniffed nervously. Dropping and retrieving the salt
bags would only tire them. Braan expected the rear guard and
the pickets to turn the pack. He screamed into the wind, and
the columns staggered forward.

The she-beast halted before the crest of the rise and stood
erect on her powerful haunches, raising her eyes above the
near horizon. Hunter whistles and screams floated in the wind.
The growlers dropped low and skulked over the hill, turning
slightly away from the columns.

A hunter picket and two of the rear guard took to the air.

They wheeled together and glided smoothly over the low ridge straight for the stalking growlers. The picket confronted the scavengers first, followed in rapid succession by the guards, swooping low, tantalizingly close. Jaws snapped, tails twitched, and guttural growls lifted into the breeze; the beasts jumped to their hind legs, trying to intercept the darting hunters, but to no avail. The hunters landed beyond the pack and sucked hard to regain their wind, waiting for the growlers to pursue.

The she-beast followed the fliers with cruel eyes. Her pack rumbled nervously as the wily scavenger smelled the wind. She looked to the nearby hunters standing alert on a knoll of tundra and then back to the massed columns in the distance. The she-beast growled deeply and headed downhill toward the more numerous opportunity. Her pack grudgingly followed.

The rejected lures struggled into the air, screaming. Braan heard their urgent alarms, ordered the columns to halt, and moved to face the oncoming fangs. Craag's attack cry pierced the wind as that brave warrior and the balance of the rear guard hauled themselves skyward. Braan screamed the order to drop salt bags. He deployed six warriors to the opposite side of the massed hunters, positions vacated by the defending scouts and guards. It would not do to be surprised.

Braan ordered the left column to face the charge with weapons ready. The right column would be his reserve. He dropped his salt bag and flapped tiredly into the air. The growlers, no more than a long bowshot away, bounded down the slope at the formed hunters, their horrendous howling increasing in volume and intensity as they neared their kill. Craag's hunters dived on the lead beasts, firing their arrows in a glide, a difficult and inaccurate tactic. Craag was buying time—time for the rest of the rear guard and pickets to marshal. The pack reacted to the perils of Craag's missiles, slowing and slinking sideways. A growler fell, an arrow impaling its throat.

The she-beast barked and redirected the pack's charge, but the delay allowed five of Craag's warriors to form a defensive line directly in the growlers' line of attack. Craag and two pickets joined the line as Braan neared the action. The defenders spread apart in a gentle crescent, intending to enfilade the pack with deadly shortbows. The growlers, heavy viselike jaws slavering with foam, yellow eyes rimmed with crimson, closed on the hunters' defensive position. Craag screamed the command to fire. Bowstrings sang, and arrows buzzed into the ranks of the charging predators. Three tumbled to the ground, dead or mortally wounded, but the charge carried through the hunters' position. Craag's warriors scattered into the sky, pivoting into the wind and crawling desperately above the maws of the angry growlers.

The attack lost its weight. The she-beast limped forward with an arrow dangling from her shoulder. She stopped abruptly, snatched the arrow with her jaws, and pulled until it ripped from her hide. The pack moved past her, toward the strong smell of prey, but at a wary lope. She followed, blood running from an open cut on her head where another arrow had plowed its furrow.

Braan was ready. The columns separated, and the column closest to the attack moved in line abreast, steadily up the grade, preparing to fire an overwhelming barrage. Doomed, the dumb beasts advanced, breaking into a gallop, growling and snarling magnificently. At thirty paces Braan signaled, and half the bows in the facing column—those of the novices—fired. Three growlers fell, and two others staggered back, limping. Braan screamed again, and the arrows of veteran warriors sang viciously through the air. Four more growlers dropped in their tracks. The few still capable of running, arrows bristling from their hides like quills, turned in rout. The hunters cheered lustily and then chanted the death song in tribute to the fallen foe.

"Well done, warriors!" Braan shouted. "Retrieve thine arrows. The march continues." He watched in satisfaction as the jubilant hunters scoured the ground for their precious missiles. Craag's guards skillfully butchered the creatures, rolling the skins tightly—trophies that would soon become grievous burdens. Braan said nothing, for once he, too, had proudly brought his first growler skin home, and many others thereafter.

"Hey, it's Corporal Mac and Jocko!" O'Toole exclaimed abruptly, pointing down the shore. He shouted and waved at the returning men. They carried a pole over their shoulders from which hung considerable cargo. Buccari enviously squinted across the distance, guessing at their burden. As much as she had wanted to scout the valley, she knew she had made the correct decision. She stared proudly at the large backpacks filled with seed.

"They killed something," Jones said. O'Toole jogged down the beach and joined MacArthur and Chastain, taking one end of the bough to which a beast had been tied. "It's a little deer.

Look at the antlers!" Lumpy tent bags also hung heavily from the shoulder pole.

"Welcome back!" Buccari said, offering her hand. MacArthur looked down, struck dumb and stupid by the simple gesture. He looked back at her face, smiled largely, and took her hand with a firm grip. Smiling, she pulled away from MacArthur's lingering grasp and took Chastain's big hand. Chastain's grip was gentle, and his smile eclipsed MacArthur's.

"Mac, let me show Lieutenant Buccari the roots you brought her, er . . . the tubers!" Chastain said excitedly. The big man lumbered over and yanked off one of the tent bags.

"Corporal MacArthur, you brought me a present?" Buccari asked with affected girlishness, and everyone laughed. MacArthur looked down at his feet, color rising through his thick beard.

"Go ahead, Jocko," MacArthur said, recovering his composure. "You can show 'em to the lieutenant as easily as I can."

Chastain wasted no time. He walked over to Buccari, hulking above her, and held open the bag. Buccari gingerly reached in and pulled out a russet fist-sized nodule. It looked like a potato. She looked up smiling.

"What's it taste like?" she asked.

"We boiled 'em," Chastain answered. "They taste like sweet potatoes."

"We saw bears dig them up," MacArthur said. "Most had gone to seed."

"We musta eaten fifty of them," Chastain added. "Careful! They'll make you—er, they give you the runs!" He blushed.

"Specially if you eat fifty of them," Buccari said, laughing.

Brappa forced himself forward one step at a time. Bag straps cut deeper with every step, his back ached, and his feet dragged on the yielding tundra. He was not alone in his suffering. The pained breathing of his comrades, a pervasive sobbing, revealed the misery surrounding him. At last they saw the cliffs.

A comfort at first, the clear skies of the third morning revealed the stately cliffs, but the landmark became a tease. Two full days of hiking did not draw them closer. The cliffs hung aloof, tantalizing the weary hunters, filling heads with hopes and dreams. Nor could Brappa purge his mouth of the salty taste or his nostrils of the alkaline smell. Nights were short, and sleep did not cure his fatigue. He awoke faithfully from the same horror—a dry, coughing nightmare of overwhelming sensations and the taste and smell of salt. His thirst expanded daily, his mouth dry as dust. His eyes burned. He did not complain.

"How fare ye, Brappa-my-friend?" asked the warrior Croot'a.

"The journey is long, Croot'a-my-friend. I have learned of myself."

"Then thou art blessed with true knowledge, Brappa-my-friend." They slogged along, the columns stringing out, the vanguard over the horizon. From behind he heard whistles admonishing the salt bearers to keep up. Brappa gritted his teeth and closed the interval.

"There will be water tonight," Croot'a said. "We camp at a spring. That is why the column extends. The warriors look forward to washing away the salt. They pull forward in their eagerness."

Brappa had no energy for eagerness toward any purpose, but thoughts of water involuntarily caused his mouth and throat to fill. He swallowed, and the taste of salt welled within. He waddled faster.

Buccari reached the tumbling cascades marking the end of the valley and its confluence with the great river. The huge river crashed and boiled below, in stark contrast to the placid valley. Her patrol was returning to the plateau. Her dissatisfaction with Quinn's decision to winter on the plateau was a gnawing cancer.

The packs were leaden. Chastain and Jones carried the grain, their camp gear and the venison distributed among the other three. Buccari's pack pulled heavily on her already weary shoulders. It was going to be a long, uphill hike home.

We aren't going home, she thought. We're leaving it!

The weather changed. The wind shifted to the south, the temperature rose slightly, and the dim light of dawn was filtered by a moody overcast. It began to snow, the first flakes drifting lightly to ground. By midmorning the cliff dwellers had left a thin trail, which was rapidly obscured by softly blowing flurries. By noon, the ground was covered and visibility had been eradicated. The columns tightened up. Pickets and guards peered nervously outward; growlers would not be deterred by snowfall.

Brappa slogged along, watching the footfalls of the salt bearer in front of him. Deadened to pain, his body had passed the numbness of total fatigue. Chilly wind cut through his bones; his legs were like stumps. He lifted each foot from the ground and carried it deliberately forward, placing it beneath his falling mass jarringly, praying he would not stumble. Irrationally, he looked up to see if the cliffs were any closer—he had forgotten it was snowing. The snows mercifully masked the taunting cliffs. Brappa began to think that he would die.

"Thou art doing commendably, Brappa-my-friend," panted Croot'a, the young warrior. "Braan, leader-of-hunters, must be proud of his son."

"Thank thee, Croot'a-my-friend," Brappa responded. "Thine encouragement is precious, but please spare thine energy. Waste not effort on my account."

"Thou art obviously doing well, since thou remain verbose and long of wind."

"Croot'a-my-friend, shut up!"

"Very good advice."

"How you doing, Lieutenant?" MacArthur asked, dropping back and falling in step. The forest was thinning out, the roar of the river barely audible in the steep distance. Buccari lifted her head, trying to mask her pain.

"I'm okay, Corporal," she said between deep breaths. She looked at him and smiled, perceiving his deep look of concern. She knew that the steepest, hardest part of the hike still lay ahead. "I'll make it."

"You're a helluva marine, Lieutenant," MacArthur said quietly.

"Thanks . . . I guess." She averted her face, her smile turning into a grimace, but she felt better for his compliment.

"Crap! It's starting to snow!" Jones exclaimed, looking up into a vague sky.

A wind-driven flurry of dry snow dusted the forested hillside, the chilly breeze whispering through evergreen boughs.

"We're in for a good one," MacArthur said evenly. "Keep the pace up. We have to make the cliff trail before the snow gets too deep. It'll be a sumbitch to climb now."

"How much farther?" Buccari asked.

"Don't know," MacArthur replied. "We may be in trouble."

The patrol put their heads down and trudged up the mountainside.

The blizzard descended, and Braan took the lead, kicking through burgeoning snowdrifts, his visible world reduced to a fuzzy white hemisphere extending but a few paces from his uncertain position. The salt bearers stumbled along in Braan's wake, plowing the dry and powdery snow aside. The hunter leader stopped and tried to sense his position, feeling deep within his instincts. The valley head was near, but even Braan was losing confidence.

Braan heard a dim and faraway whistle. His sagging shoulders lifted with hope—the relief column! Braan vigorously returned the signal call and repeated it in the direction of his expedition. Muted screams pierced the storm. Another whistle! Braan oriented himself to the signal and pressed through the blizzard. Shadowy figures of hunters materialized from the whiteness.

"Return in health, Braan, leader-of-hunters," Kuudor whistled. Snow covered his fur-shrouded form. Two sentries, cold and excited, flanked the sentry captain.

"Greetings, Kuudor, captain-of-sentries," Braan chirped. "Thy presence is heartwarming. A difficult expedition but successful. Thy students have been faithful to thy teaching. All performed well, and all return as warriors. Good fortune but for the loss of a faithful warrior. Brave Tinn'a, clan of Botto, has joined his ancestors."

Kuudor's shoulders sagged in relief, but he also mourned the loss of the indomitable Tinn'a. Kuudor turned to a sentry and dispatched him to deliver the news to the elders.

"Sentries stationed to mark the trail await thee," Kuudor said with ritual. "Thy burden is now theirs. Let us proceed."

Kuudor stepped forward, handed Braan a growlerskin cape, and lifted the salt bag from Braan's shoulders, settling it on his own. Braan thankfully relinquished his burden and covered his raw shoulders with the fur. Braan whistled, and the columns surged forward. Another dim whistle sounded ahead, and as the columns arrived at the next sentry's position, that hunter moved into the column, relieved one of its exhausted members of his heavy salt bag, and marched alongside. Onward the salt bearers marched, listening for the sentry beacons ahead, waiting for fresh backs to relieve them of their loads. The bone-weary cliff dwellers gave up their onerous burdens as if being reborn. Many cried, overwhelmed by the succor. And thus they were guided down the narrow and steep valley and across the ice-encrusted bridge. An agonizing uphill journey remained, but their numbers and energy were expanded to the task.

The forest ended abruptly. The patrol was in the open, above the tree line. The clouds lifted momentarily, revealing the precipitous ascent. MacArthur stopped and stared upward.

"Why don't we start climbing?" Buccari asked. "We have to go up."

"We could, I guess," MacArthur replied, turning to face her. "That path cuts along the edge of the cliff, and it switches back over those higher ridges to the left. If we blindly head up, we may find ourselves boxed in on one of those steep cuts, dead-ended."

"So what are you saying?" Buccari asked.

"I'm scared," MacArthur said, looking her in the eyes, ". . . sir."

Buccari turned and looked up, but the clouds gave only a brief respite; the ceiling descended, enshrouding them in foggy flurries.

Hunter scouts detected the long-legs camped on the edge of the salt trail and stalked them from the edge of the blown snow's limits.

"Long-legs command the trail, Braan-our-leader," the scout reported. The hunters stared into the flurries, the wind lifting the plush fur of their capes.

"It is true, Braan-our-leader," Bott'a reported. "They are positioned so that we cannot pass, but they are not vigilant. We could easily overwhelm them."

Other scouts acknowledged Bott'a's assessment. Kuudor also advocated direct action. The storm was in full sway. The footing would only get more treacherous.

"Wait here," Braan commanded.

"The snow is only going to get deeper. Now is the time to move," Buccari insisted.

"Move where, Lieutenant?" MacArthur asked. "Where's the trail?"

Buccari's anger eclipsed her exhaustion; her fatigue overwhelmed her good sense. She stared into the swirling snows, frustration blossoming like a weed.

"MacArthur! Lieutenant!" O'Toole whispered urgently. "Behind you."

Buccari turned to see one of the flying creatures ten paces away, its hands raised with empty palms. Buccari regained her composure and emulated its actions.

"He looks familiar," Buccari remarked quietly. "Look at the scars."

"Yeah, we've seen him before," MacArthur answered, bowing. "When we returned Tonto, he was there. He must be their leader—their captain. Look! He has Tatum's knife."

The creature stepped forward, looking agitated and frightened. Brandishing the man-knife, the animal pointed up the mountain and then to its own chest. It sheathed the knife and flashed the fingers of both hands many times. The creature moved slowly toward them, hands forward, as if to push the humans backward, but it did not come too close. It pivoted its body up the slope and walked in place.

The bewildered humans looked at each other, trying to find meaning in the creature's charade. Buccari approached it and pointed to herself and then to the rest of her patrol and then turned uphill and marched in place, just as the hunter had done. The hunter looked around at the humans and repeated the pushing-back gesture impatiently.

"He wants us to move back, Lieutenant," MacArthur said.

"I concur," Buccari replied. "Let's do it."

The humans collected their gear and moved back into the thin line of fir trees. The creature whistled into the deadening snow; a muted answering whistle sounded and then several more whistles, each farther away, diminishing in the distance. Moments later the first scouts hiked nervously by. After the scouts came the rest of the expedition, slowly, in single file, many bent grotesquely with huge bags on their backs. Dozens of cliff dwellers filed by—scores. They kept coming as the snow fell harder and the temperature dropped steadily. And kept coming.

"Anyone been counting?" Jones asked.

"Somewhere around a hundred fifty," Buccari said.

"Hundred and sixty-two," MacArthur said. "About a third carrying bags."

"They sure look tired," O'Toole said. "Wonder what's in the bags."

"Food, I guess," Buccari said. "Probably stocking up for the winter."

The long file of cliff dwellers ended. The last few, without
bags, walked alertly past and disappeared into the blowing
snow. Three cliff dwellers, including their captain, remained
stationary, dim forms in the falling snow. Buccari picked up
her pack and struggled painfully into the straps. MacArthur
supported its weight.

"Ooph! Thanks," she said, looking at his feet. She raised her
head and ordered, "Let's move! They're waiting for us!" She
turned and trudged up the steep hillside toward the waiting animals. When she had closed half the distance, the cliff dwellers
turned and started climbing.

TWENTY-FOUR

AGGRESSION

Gorruk braced himself as the command vehicle curved in an
abrupt arc around an obstacle, the swaying motion quickly
dampened by autostabilizers.

"Third Army was surprised in the desert by six divisions of
tanks and is heavily engaged, General Gorruk," the helmeted
adjutant shouted. "It has taken heavy losses. Sixth Army will
be in enemy radar range in fifteen minutes and is still undetected."

Gorruk, in battle uniform, acknowledged the information
with a nod. His command vehicle trailed the forward elements
of the Sixth Army's attacking divisions; it rolled smoothly over
the soft desert sands, its tank treads reaching down and pulling
sand from the ground, propelling it backward in a continuous
rooster tail. Gorruk's attention drifted from the situation display on the computer screen in front of him. He allowed his
gaze to return to the panoramic viewscreens of the bus-sized
armored command vehicle. The featureless terrain was broken
by the billowing dust of tanks and armored personnel carriers
strewn solidly across the horizon. Broken-down troop carriers

and supply lorries, overcome by the elements, were passed with irritating frequency, their crews doomed to desiccation.

The equatorial deserts of Kon were continuous, blazing-hot belts of sterility, time-proven natural barriers between northern and southern interests. Conflicts, mostly petty economic squabbles, were frequent, but collision between hemispheres was almost impossible. Prior to the Rule of Generals commerce had leapfrogged the hemispheres, trade routes over the dead lands made possible by mutual support and benefit. Interhemispheric trade had been central to the healthy worldwide economy during the timeless history prior to the invasion, and its absence was inevitably pointed to in explaining the moribund health of the economy since then. Jook the First was convinced that reestablishing commercial links between hemispheres, forcibly or otherwise, would renew the international economy, thus solidifying and amplifying his power.

Gorruk was tasked with developing strategic plans for the assault. After years of frustrating analysis and preparation during which even the indomitable Gorruk refused to acknowledge acceptable odds for success, a rare meteorological event occurred. The sun-star erupted with solar flare activity during the planet Kon's approach to orbital perigee. Gorruk's astronomers and meteorologists predicted that this anomalous thermal radiation pattern would cause a loss of symmetry in the atmosphere's heat balance, resulting in a skewing of weather patterns. The atmospheric equator would tilt slightly for almost a full cycle of their largest moon. Gorruk was informed of this momentous happenstance and, true to his opportunistic nature, ordered great forces into motion. His army would be ready if the forecasts proved accurate.

Gorruk's scientists watched as the planet's immensely stable weather system began to shift ponderously, creating local anomalies that would occur only once or twice in a century. The meteorologists' predictions came true. Portions of the northern hemisphere that were normally inhabitable became torrid. Hot gales swept over crops, reducing the land to bitter dust. Farmers wept and retreated from their homes. Yet on the opposite side of the globe, searing equatorial desert winds abated and a low ceiling of clouds mercifully covered large parts of the sterile zone. Blast furnace temperatures mellowed to merely scorching, and the deserts became tolerable—an opportunity to cross their trackless wastes.

Gorruk, behind monumental stockpiles of logistic supplies

and massive accumulations of weaponry and ammunition, exhorted his generals and men into a religious frenzy. It was time for the grand stroke, risking everything for an opportunity to shift the balance of global conflict. Eight armies of the Hegemony, spearheaded by armored columns and mobile infantry, moved southward into the wastelands. An eight-pronged pincer lunged across the sere and forsaken landscape, an irrepressible force moving inexorably onward.

Gorruk would have preferred to lead the actual assault. It was his passion to personally close with the enemy, wielding his own death-inflicting weapon fiercely in hand, to see the terror that overwhelming strength and indomitable courage could exact from a stricken enemy. Yet he also knew that his job as supreme military commander precluded such tactical pleasures. He had to avoid physical engagement. He could not risk being eliminated, leaving the armies without their decision maker. Generals, regrettably, must lead from the rear.

Coded transmissions confirmed the progress of the advance. His satellites were still working but no doubt would soon be destroyed. Gorruk's eight armies ground forward, closing on southern objectives. What had not been anticipated was the untimely desert deployment of enemy tank divisions in sector nine. That was unfortunate for General Klarrk's Third Army salient—Klarrk was getting cut to pieces, and no reinforcements could be spared—the fortunes of war.

"Good, we are on schedule," Gorruk said. "Have the strategic rocket forces supporting the Sixth verified launch yet?"

"Yes, General," the brigadier answered. "The first coordinated wave of missiles is in the air, and the tactical fighters and bombers are in position to follow the ballistics."

Gorruk looked into the sky. The cloud ceiling was breaking up as predicted. He should be hearing the attacking aircraft any moment.

"With the exception of the Third Army, it goes well, General Gorruk," the brigadier remarked. "The first and fifth salients have reached their objectives and have overrun positions. The enemy is totally unprepared."

"Of course," Gorruk replied.

"Your Excellency," Et Kalass pleaded, his dignity slipping away. "We are making progress. We have photographs and video of the wreckage of one of their spacecraft. "We must—"

Jook sat on his pillows and listened contemptuously. "Too

late, Minister," the Supreme Leader said. "The die is cast, and
irreversible actions are under way. We are at war, and war is
everything." As if in punctuation, a deep rumble shook the
huge palace. One of the enemy's rocket bombs, launched in
desperation, had reached the capital city. Jook did not deign to
look up.

"General Gorruk's valiant forces have established a secure
bridgehead in the southern hemisphere," Jook continued. "The
armies of the Northern Hegemony are victorious today, victorious beyond our wildest expectations. General Gorruk has
spanned the wastelands. Within weeks he will march on their
industrial centers. It is but a matter of time before they capit-
ulate."

"A quarter of a million kones have died," Et Kalass blurted.
"A dear price."

Jook glared down at the minister malevolently. "Not dear by
half, *my lord*!" the Supreme Leader retorted. "It is but small
down payment to the dogs of war. We are at war. What did
you expect? Do you not understand? Gorruk has crossed the
deserts. In force! Imperial armies are triumphant!"

"Gorruk may have crossed our deserts," Et Kalass persisted,
"but the aliens have the power to cross the infinite universe.
We forgo a greater opportunity."

Jook lunged to his feet, mouth open, on the verge of shouting. With great effort he contained his emotions and slowly reclined.

"I have seen your reports," he said calmly. "I share your
views, Minister. Finding the secrets of the alien ships must
take high priority. However, at the moment I must consider the
activities of our generals on a higher plane."

"Yes, Exalted One," Et Kalass replied. "The—"

"I am told it is winter in the area of search operations," Jook
said. "A terribly inclement time on a miserably inclement
planet. What opportunity exists for us there? What would you
have me do? Can it not wait until next year or even the year
after?"

"My science team remains on Genellan, Your Excellency,"
the noblekone pleaded. "Gorruk's shuttle removed the military
personnel but left Et Avian. Our little war broke out, and there
has not been a shuttle since."

"We are at war, Minister. All boosters must be conserved for
purposes that advance the good of our cause. I am told those
on Genellan are in no danger. We will resupply them when it

is necessary." Jook stared down from his elevation. "You are dismissed."

Et Kalass, realizing logic would not penetrate the ruler's adamantine priorities, pivoted on his hinds and walked out. Et Kalass had not been surprised by the commencement of war; however, he had not anticipated Et Avian being stranded, nor had he expected Gorruk's horrific success. Events were out of control. How to mitigate their impact? Global conquest by the northern generals would be a monstrous setback to his plans—to the restoration of the nobility. Perhaps the survival of the nobility was cause to relegate the aliens and their power of interstellar travel to a lower priority. He would have to adjust to the vagaries of political reality. Jook was correct—when at war, war was everything.

SECTION THREE

ESTABLISHING RELATIONS

TWENTY-FIVE

COMMUNICATION

The wind stiffened at dusk, blowing snow sideways. Cliff dwellers packed the cold whiteness around the salt bags, building low-walled enclosures over which they draped animal hides. Chewing spartan dinners, they scurried into the shelters, piling atop more hides and atop each other. Four heavily bundled dwellers remained outside, positioned around the humans.

"Sentries," Buccari said, squinting in the fading light.

"Or guards," MacArthur rebutted. "A matter of semantics."

Buccari stared at MacArthur. "Semantics, eh? I didn't know you were a philosopher, Corporal," she said into her ice-crusted scarf.

"Philosopher? No. Well, maybe, but only when it gets warmer," MacArthur replied, burying a tent stake sideways in the snow. "You know," he remarked without guile, "our little friends are smart. They sleep together and stay warm. Being warm is more important than philosophy." Buccari tented alone.

"Perhaps," she answered, hiding her face behind her scarf.

MacArthur straightened abruptly. She turned to see two cliff dwellers approaching through the falling snow. She remembered the mannerisms displayed during previous contact. MacArthur followed her lead.

Braan bowed in return, pleased by the display of manners. The long-legs stood erect and looked at each other. Braan took the initiative and whistled the special low notes. The hairy-faced one responded in kind, although the short one was obviously the leader. This one uttered grunts and pulled back the flap covering the shelter. It pointed—obscenely extending the first finger—rudely signaling the hunters inside. The hairy-

219

faced one kicked snow from its foot coverings and entered. Braan rudely pointed at Short-one-who-leads and indicated that it should go next. Short-one-who-leads moved in next to the taller one.

Braan directed Craag to enter the enclosure. Craag hopped through the drifts, shook snow from his growler cloak, and courageously moved next to the long-legs. Braan followed, pausing to feel the peculiar fabric of the tent. He left the tent flap open, the last hint of daylight illuminating their council. Panic welled in Braan's belly. Sitting close to a potential enemy was against all instinct. The odor of the long-legs, sour and dank, pervaded the tent's interior, and Braan suddenly missed the sweet breezes of the snowstorm.

"Definitely the same bugs that took Tonto back," MacArthur said. "Look at the scars on the leader's nose."

"Captain!" Buccari said, pointing at the lead hunter, anointing him. The creature recoiled sharply from her pointed finger. She looked at her hand and slowly dropped it. The cliff dweller relaxed.

"Captain doesn't like to be pointed at, does he?" she observed.

"Evidently not," MacArthur replied.

"But he pointed at me when we were outside," Buccari said, perplexed.

"Yeah, but he was uncomfortable," MacArthur replied.

He pointed his finger into the air. The cliff dwellers watched suspiciously. MacArthur moved his hand slowly in their direction. When his finger was pointed at Captain, the creature gently pushed it aside. MacArthur nodded, and both cliff dwellers bobbed their heads up and down. Captain reached out and firmly grabbed MacArthur's hands, extending the marine's fingers in a praying position. The cliff dweller, holding his own hands in the same manner, thrust them toward MacArthur, withdrew them, and then did the same toward Buccari. Pointing the long index finger on his three-fingered hand toward MacArthur, he shook his head and pulled his finger away, using his other hand.

"Interesting!" Buccari said, her hands together. "Pointing with one finger must be impolite."

"Progress," MacArthur said. "A good first step—proper manners."

A dark form in the snowy gloom moved across the tent opening.

"Mac, you there?" Chastain asked loudly.

The cliff dwellers recoiled at the booming voice.

Buccari spoke softly: "Chastain, move away from the tent. We have two of the animals in here." Chastain's shadowy hulk moved silently away.

Buccari, using both hands, pointed to the tent entrance. The creatures bowed vigorously and scrambled through the opening. Buccari and MacArthur followed, the cliff dwellers already invisible in the snowy gloaming. Buccari looked up at MacArthur, feeling the warm spot on her thigh where his knee had touched her. She was excited; they had taken another step toward establishing contact with the strange animals, but her excitement was heightened by physical contact with her own kind.

"Good night, Corporal," she said, trying not to smile at the handsome face. She put her hands together in cliff dweller fashion and put them next to her cheek. Then she stuck out her fist with her thumb extended, jerked it over her shoulder, and said, "Scram!"

"Aye, sir," MacArthur replied, moving away in the darkening snowfall.

"Oh, Mac, er . . . Corporal," Buccari called after him.

"Yeah . . . Lieutenant," he replied, quickly turning.

"Tell everyone how to point. Wouldn't want any incidents." MacArthur pointed as if firing a pistol. "You got it," he said.

She laughed and crawled into her tent, wearing her clothes against the penetrating chill. She climbed into her sleeping bag, sealed the thermal flaps, and zipped the bag over her head. Snow-muted laughter drifted in. Her stomach growled incessantly, but she fell into an exhausted coma of dreamless sleep.

The hikers awoke in the flat light before dawn, camped on the edge of the world. The blizzard of the previous evening had masked the proximity of the cliff face, mere paces from their tents. Cloudless skies arched high above, the air transparently clear. MacArthur studied the terrain. The rock wall of the river valley, covered with snow, appeared vertical with no hint of a trail. Beyond the precipice, past the sinuous gash of the great river, spread the rest of the world in virgin white, waiting for the sun's golden rays to pour over the eastern horizon. Visibility was limitless. Beyond the twin volcanoes, their sullen summits issuing wisps of sulfurous smoke, the plains rolled to infinity, softly white and featureless in their snowy mantle. Far, far away, on the distant northeastern horizon, beyond the curve of the planet, jagged tips of another mountain range bathed in the sharp, golden aura of daylight revealed the coming dawn.

MacArthur stared, mesmerized at the vast scale and depth of his vista. In outer space one could see infinite distances, but the view before him was more powerful. It was dimensionalized by finite objects, objects a human being could understand, objects that had weight and size, with a clearness and granularity far exceeding reasonable expectations. One could see a star, but one could never comprehend one. Intellectually, maybe, but never viscerally.

And his hearing was acute. He detected the twitter and chirping of cliff dwellers, shrill and constant, as they hiked up the trail, their encampment cleanly evacuated. The loud voices and industrious clankings of the humans were amplified, every word, every syllable clear and distinct. The powdery snow squeaked plaintively under the soles of their boots. Heightened senses enhanced his feeling of physical power. He felt powerful—omnipotent. He felt alive.

"Daydreaming, Corporal? Sun's not even up," Buccari said. She slogged through the dry snow to his side, only paces from the brink. He looked down into her face, one rapture replaced by another. She had not put on her ragged scarf, and her complexion glowed with high color. The first spark of the sun peeked over the horizon. It flashed in her green eyes.

"Morning, Lieutenant," he said, turning to watch the sunrise. "It's beautiful." His words exploded in vaporous puffs.

The eastern horizon had been a stark demarcation of land and sky, a hard, bold line of definition. The fiery sun overflowed the boundary, its red-gold splendor suffusing all realms. Feeble rays of warmth touched his exposed face, enforcing his sense of well-being.

"Wonderful!" she replied. They turned to each other, sharing a mutual resonance. MacArthur forced himself to leave the moment.

"Running behind, aren't we?" he chided. "Our friends are moving out."

"You're right," Buccari groaned, stretching her back. "We better hustle. Then again, we don't have to worry about losing them, do we?"

The advance of the departing cliff dwellers was marked by

a gash of tracks up the mountain. Two of them, Captain and his constant companion—Lieutenant Buccari had christened him X.O. for Executive Officer—loitered at the rear of the column. The dwellers lifted a hand and turned to the steep trail. The column stretched far up the ascent until it disappeared around the profile of the cliff, a necklace of black pearls in diminishing perspective.

Braan heard panicked whistles. The hunter leader moved rapidly up the side of the halted column, Craag following close behind. The terrain was nearly vertical, and the traverse was perilous; hunters lay on their sides, leaning against the rocky slope, feet dug securely into the packed snow. Three animals protected each salt bag, moving it several hundred paces at a turn. Braan and Craag stepped over the hunters and their cargoes, the trail too narrow for them to walk around.

"Caught up with 'em!" said MacArthur in the lead. "Take a breather."

Buccari, in the number two position, leaned a shoulder into the snow and loosened the belay.

"Forgot how steep," she said, "and how narrow this trail is."

"The snow might have something to do with that, Lieutenant," said Jones, number three. "You're checking good, sir. I'm just trying to keep up with you."

"Thanks, Boats," Buccari replied. "We should have stuck with EPLs. I'll take a short fuel, bad alignment reentry any day."

"I'd go anywhere as long as you're the pilot," Jones said.

"She's got my vote, too," MacArthur joined in from above.

Buccari grinned at the marine, but he was staring up the trail, his back turned. She looked down at Jones and smiled nervously. Jones smiled, but not comfortably. O'Toole and Chastain stood close together, talking quietly, pointing nonchalantly out over the void.

"Let's move," MacArthur said.

Buccari felt the slack go out of the belay. She had exhaled, moved her weight over the path, and dug a boot into the packed snow for another step forward, when urgent whistling came from above. Snow cascaded down the fall line onto their heads.

"Keep moving!" MacArthur shouted. "Get out from under that snow!"

The whistling heightened in urgency. More and different sounds sliced the still air, screams of panic and desperation. A switchback appeared, and Buccari followed MacArthur on a short climb before traversing in the opposite direction; the path widened slightly. Able to look upslope, she comprehended what was happening: a team of bag bearers had lost control of their precious load. A cliff dweller with a bag strapped to his back lay spread-eagled on the steep slope, his leather-covered talons and fingers sunk desperately into the deep snow. The snow beneath him was moving inexorably downward. Two cliff dwellers not burdened with bags leapt into the air.

"Jocko!" MacArthur yelled down the hill. "Untie and take one of the lines back to where the snow was falling on the path. One of the bats is over the edge with a bag on his back, and his hold is about to let go."

Buccari wondered what good Chastain could possibly do standing beneath a potential avalanche.

"The rest of you come up to this wide spot and give me the other rope," MacArthur shouted, moving ahead and pulling the rest of the group with him. "Jocko! If he's falling, don't try to catch him or he'll take you with him. If he's sliding or barely moving, give it your best shot. Be careful, Jocko! Take off your pack."

Chastain pulled one rope away from his comrades and removed his pack, driving the frame deep into the powdery snow. With rope in hand he retraced the trail and disappeared from sight. MacArthur removed his pack as he waited for the second rope to be cleared from the waists of his fellow climbers. The bag bearer had slipped another body length, and the slope was increasing.

Before Buccari could say anything, MacArthur pulled the rope free and clambered on all fours across the face of the cliff, cutting beneath the trail in a direct route to the falling hunter. He stopped and coiled the rope, placing it over his head and shoulders. MacArthur kicked the edges of his boots into the yielding snow and crabbed across the cliff.

Braan flapped mightily, holding his position over the salt bag. He whistled permission for the salt bearer to release the salt bag, but the plucky hunter stubbornly held on, begging for help. Braan noticed additional movement on the slope and was astonished to see a long-legs. It could not glide to safety. It would fall to certain death. The long-legs was very brave—or crazy.

Braan watched the long-legs take a rope from his shoulder and shake out the coils. With a jerky flick, one end of the rope was tossed to the spread-eagled hunter. It snaked across the salt bearer's forearms. Suddenly Braan had an inkling of what the long-legs wanted. The long-legs took the remaining coil of rope and threw it feebly up the hill, the effort causing him to slide abruptly downhill. Shouts and screams erupted from the long-legs waiting at the switchback. They crawled, panic-stricken, up the trail.

Braan screamed and dove for the bitter end of the rope. The leader of the hunters landed in the snow, grabbed the rope with his talons, and leapt into the air, pulling mightily, struggling to regain the path.

MacArthur felt sick to his stomach. Every move he made caused the snowpack to slide. Digging in his boots did no good; everything was moving. He looked at the bag bearer. It had grabbed the end of the rope and was tying it. *To the bag!* "No! Tie it around your waist!" MacArthur spoke as loudly as he could without exhaling strenuously. Even heavy breathing seemed to move the snow. "Crap," he whined, his face buried in the soft snow. "I killed myself for a lousy lunch bag."

Braan dropped the end of the rope into the waiting hands of cliff dwellers and jumped into the air, flapping over the deteriorating predicament. He made his decision.

"Untie the bag. Give the rope to the long-legs," he commanded.

"Braan-our-leader," the salt bearer whistled as he untied the rope, the movements accelerating his descent. "I have failed." The sliding hunter threw the rope to the long-legs who grabbed it greedily.

"The salt is gone, warrior. Fly now, so thou may redeem thyself with future effort," Braan screamed, struggling to gain altitude.

MacArthur clenched the rope in his gloved hands. He looped it around his right wrist and arm several times to secure it and then reached over to the cliff dweller with his left hand.

He shouted, "Grab hold! Take my hand!" But the animal had slipped out of reach.

The bag bearer looked dumbly at MacArthur, then glanced up at the dweller laboring in the air overhead. The bag bearer shrugged its shoulders and chirped. It started sliding down the precipice, clearing itself from the bag straps.

MacArthur screamed, *"Heads up, Jocko! Stand clear!"*

Cliff dweller and bag slid from sight. MacArthur closed his eyes.

The creatures flapping overhead moved away from the cliff. With shocking abruptness they screamed in unison and soared out over the river valley. The cliff dwellers on the trail also raised their voices in squeaky bedlam. Suddenly MacArthur felt himself moving upward with powerful jerks, and he looked up to see Jones and O'Toole hauling on the line. Jones's strong arms grabbed his coat and pulled him onto the narrow path. The meager trail appeared as wide as a jet runway.

"What happened to Chastain?" MacArthur gasped. "O'Toole, check on Jocko." O'Toole moved cautiously back down the precarious path toward the switchback.

Curious and highly animated cliff dwellers crowded around the gasping human, Captain foremost among them. MacArthur looked up as Captain solemnly bowed. MacArthur, still on his knees, did his best to return the gesture, but his mind was on Chastain. Buccari stood a few paces downhill, looking up at him as if she were looking at a ghost, her face ashen, tears glistening in the bright sun.

"That was the stupidest trick I have ever seen, Corporal!" she shouted, eyes flashing green sparks. "Why didn't you throw the rope over from the trail?"

"I thought it would be quicker . . ." he started. MacArthur felt old emotions, emotions not felt since he was a small child. He put his head down and tried to rationalize an appropriate response. He could not; the lieutenant was correct. He had made a poor move. He looked at her, amazed at the power of her emotions. She was not just chewing him out—she had been scared witless by his peril.

"You're right, Lieutenant," MacArthur said. "I guess I didn't have a plan until I got out there, and the options narrowed too fast." Buccari stood there, shoulders heaving.

"Excuse me, Lieutenant," MacArthur said, breaking the emotion-laden silence. "I got to check on Chastain. Our problem's not over." He slipped and skidded past her down to the switchback in time to see his men leaning into the hill, Chastain carrying the bag. Two dwellers hiked a cautious distance behind. A third hunter, a tiny speck in the distance, tramped up the trail far below.

Seeing Chastain unharmed loosened a surge of warmth through MacArthur's body. The big man was a part of his being; they had shared too much. MacArthur felt the infinite obligation of owing his life to the gentle giant, and Chastain was simple enough not to care. Chastain looked up, and his features erupted in an immense grin. MacArthur felt his own face stretch with happiness. The big man lifted the gray bag over his head—a trophy.

With startling clarity MacArthur understood the passing sequence of emotional transactions. His own fears over Chastain's well-being and the subsequent joy felt at seeing him whole were cathartic. MacArthur realized that Buccari had suffered a similar catharsis and that he was the focal point of her emotions. He was warmed by the thought—and confused. He looked up the trail and saw the lieutenant, hands clasped over her chest. He waved—a subdued wave, a subtle signal. Buccari waved back in kind, quickly and easily.

MacArthur looked back at Chastain. The big man trudged upward, the bag slung over his shoulder.

"Ho, Mac!" he shouted. "This bag's filled with salt!"

"Salt?" MacArthur replied, grabbing Chastain's sleeve. "These guys are risking their lives for salt?" Yet as he spoke, he realized how much they, too, needed salt.

"I heard you yell," Chastain said proudly. "I look up and see the bat sliding down the mountain. He's holding on to the bag with his feet, flapping his wings hard. Stubborn—like you, Mac. But he's coming straight down, and the bag starts bouncing, so he lets go. The bag rolled right into my arms. It was going pretty fast, but I had a wide spot to stand on. But then the little bat flew right by me, screaming so loud, I almost jumped off the trail."

"You did great, Jocko!" MacArthur slapped the big man on the chest. Chastain glowed with pride. "I'd like to hear the bat's version. I'll bet it was falling like a son of a bitch."

Captain and X.O. glided into the snow above the switchback and hopped down, showing no fear. Captain chirped and whistled to the cliff dwellers trailing behind the humans and then moved directly in front of Chastain, bowing deeply. The other animals, catching up with Chastain, also bowed.

"Bow, Jocko," MacArthur ordered gently. "You're a hero, my friend."

"Cut it out, Mac." Chastain smiled self-consciously and bowed awkwardly. He offered the salt bag to the little animal. Captain bowed deeply again. Chastain, confused, returned the bow. MacArthur smiled at Chastain's gracelessness. X.O. stepped forward and accepted the bag. The creatures all bowed yet again.

"Okay." MacArthur laughed. "Everybody bow one more time, real low."

Swirls of first-magnitude stars dotted velvet skies. The last murky hints of dusk revealed a line of salt bearers winding along the brink of the plateau far ahead of the exhausted earthlings. The humans trudged upward, miserably chilled by plummeting temperatures and rising winds. A full moon elevated into the eastern skies, outshining the stars and casting an eerie light over the snowy landscape. The river falling over the cliffs had lost much of its volume and voice, but its cascading spray spread phantasmically in the soft light. Silky sheets of gossamer snow sifted across the crusty whiteness, drifting into patterned dunes of sugar dust. MacArthur worried that the drifting snows would mask the trail. He stumbled faster, pulling the patrol with him.

"What's your plan, Mac?" Buccari panted.

"Not sure, Lieutenant," he huffed, his breath emanating in huge moonlit puffs. "Maybe—we can find where they go over the edge. Maybe they'll invite us for dinner."

"What—a—dreamer," she wheezed.

"Dreams—are all we have," he grunted.

"Philosophy again!" she said, stopping to catch her breath.

"Why—is it so cold when that subject comes up?" he gasped, pushing unmercifully, opening on the others. The dwellers were almost to the stream gorge, surprising MacArthur by staying so close to the plateau's edge. They should be heading away from the cliffs to ford the stream.

They did not cross the stream. As MacArthur approached the point where the stream fell over the cliff, the snow-blown tracks moved sharply downward, toward the brink. For twenty nerve-wracking paces the trail descended and swung to the left, *over* the cliff edge. MacArthur followed the trail, knees quaking from fatigue and from acrophobic terror. Wind tugged at his clothes. The pack dragged on his shoulders.

The trail veered hard left beneath an outcropping of rock. The rocks under his feet were suddenly hard, gritty, and clear of snow. He looked back to see Buccari and the rest of the patrol tentatively pursuing. He turned to the trail and looked ahead. The path, slipping farther beneath the overhang of the cliff, continued to curve until, fifty paces ahead, he could see the stream waters exploding into the river canyon. The trail led under the moving water! Needles of icy spray stung his face, and patches of ice threatened his footing. He plodded forward. Jagged icicles hung like fangs, glinting dully in the moonlight.

Visibility beneath the overhang was nil. Past the roaring mists the trail turned sharply along the cliff. Large boulders reared up on his right hand, reaching and melding with the cliff overhang, forming tunnels and obstructing the moonlit view of the canyon. Captain and X.O., covered with heavy skins, waited in the shadows, blocking the path. Other shadows softly creaked and clanked along the walls. MacArthur halted and bowed. The cliff dwellers before him reciprocated but did not move aside. He waited, eyes adjusting to the gloom.

"What now?" Buccari wheezed, teeth chattering, as she caught up.

"You got me," MacArthur replied. "Why don't you take over."

"Thanks a bunch," she panted, dropping her pack on the ground.

Brittle breezes tumbled through the rocky openings, whipping icy crystals onto their heads and shoulders. Buccari stepped forward and pointed in cliff dweller fashion down the trail. She grabbed her shoulders and shivered, signaling coldness. Captain shook his head gently and pointed to the cruel ground. Buccari turned to MacArthur.

"It's cold, Mac," she said. "Should we just pitch our tents?"

"Yeah, no vacancy," Jones rejoined, teeth rattling with cold.

"Hey, Mac!" O'Toole whispered hoarsely. "Something's coming. Look!"

MacArthur peered down the winding path. A procession of luminous globes rounded a distant curve. Captain retreated toward the lights.

Braan moved quickly to the lights. Eight apprentices carried glowing spirit lamps on staffs. They escorted Kuudor and four heavily bundled elders, including the facilitator. Elders! At the cliff tops!

"Long life and good tidings, facilitator," Braan said.

"Good eventide, Braan, leader-of-hunters," Koop replied, his eyes aglint. "Thy return was heralded. Kuudor's sentries speak of adventures and a full bounty of salt. Great praise."

Braan bowed in gratitude.

"Stories of thine exploits provide the colony with much fodder," the facilitator continued. "Is it true a full salt bag was rescued by a long-legs? At foolish risk to their lives? In our behalf?"

"All true, facilitator," Braan spoke. "The long-legs demonstrate peaceful intent. We have made progress with communications."

"Dost thou not worry in revealing this entrance?" asked another elder, a stone carver. Kuudor, captain-of-sentries, bobbed his head in silent agreement.

"It cannot be helped, elder," Braan responded. "They are curious. It is but a matter of time before they discover this and other entrances."

"Thy recommendation, leader-of-hunters?" the facilitator asked.

"The long-legs have passed all tests. Permit them to enter the barracks for the night. On the morrow we will present them to guilders more capable in the ways of communications."

"So be it," Koop said. The ancient stared into the darkness with uncharacteristic boldness. "It is cold, but I would see the creatures."

"Here they come," Jones said.

The procession marched closer, globes casting diffuse shadows along the ground. Captain appeared from the darkness, whistling sharply. Shedding his cloak, X.O. ran to an opening and jumped into the empty blackness, wings cracking sharply as he disappeared downward. Captain picked up the fur and approached Buccari. A head shorter than the human female, he bowed and handed her the silky pelt. Buccari accepted it, bowing in return. She gratefully wrapped the pungent leathery skin around her back and shoulders, the soft fur deliciously covering her neck and much of her lower face, cutting the wind.

"It's because you whined about being cold," MacArthur whispered.

"Eat your heart out, Corporal," she retorted.

"Hey, these guys are taller," Jones said.

"They're the other ones!" Buccari gasped. The new arrivals

were taller than she was. "The other kind in the drawings. And not females."

The procession stopped several paces away. One of the taller ones, an ancient creature, whistled softly, and the light bearers came nervously forward. Captain walked fearlessly between the humans and grabbed Chastain's hand, improbably pulling the human to the front. The light bearers staggered nervously backward. Chastain shyly looked at his feet.

"Going to eat you first, Jocko," O'Toole whispered. Buccari elbowed the marine.

The creature dropped Chastain's big paw and whistled to the members of the procession, indicating MacArthur and then pointing with two hands to Buccari. The old one whistled intricately in response and bowed directly to her. She nervously bowed back. The ceremony over, the procession shuffled around and walked sedately away.

"Well," Buccari said, "I guess we've been introduced. What now?"

Captain indicated that they should pick up their packs and follow him.

The next morning the dwellers, after waiting for the late-rising strangers to arrive, watched with amazement when the long-legs were escorted into the chamber, the taller ones ducking their heads to avoid striking the uneven ceiling. Their ugly round faces were splotched and burned by sun and wind. They smelled horrible.

The cliff dwellers, including the elders, stood uncertainly at their perches. An awkward silence ensued. Eventually Koop-the-facilitator signaled for all to sit, which everyone did, the cliff dwellers first and then the long-legs. Koop remained standing.

"Braan, leader-of-hunters, thy report?" he whistled.

Braan stood forth and summarized what they had learned about the aliens. The elders asked questions. The long-legs sat and watched.

"There is little we can do," Braan said, "without a means of communication." He turned and faced the steam users, gardeners, fishers, and stone carvers.

Steam user Bool had been assigned the task of interpreting the drawings. He in turn delegated this assignment to his assistant, steam user Toon, a capable intellect in his own right. The drawings were simple, and Toon had compiled a translation scheme and added pictographs he felt would assist in expanding the communications foundation.

"Master Bool," the facilitator said. "Hast thou a recommendation?"

"With permission, facilitator," Bool said. "Steam user Toon has analyzed the pictographs and has expanded them. I offer Toon to work directly with our visitors."

Koop nodded approval, and steam user Toon, clutching his manuscripts, stepped unsteadily toward the sour-smelling giants.

Buccari watched, fascinated, trying to determine what was happening.

"Look. On the tall ones' necks," Jones whispered. "Diamonds! Rubies! And those are emeralds!" He pointed, and MacArthur grabbed his hand.

"Manners!" Buccari hissed. Her interest piqued, she turned and examined the necklaces. The gemstones glowed luminously, their large facets sparkling with rich color.

"Jeez, Boats!" she croaked, craning her neck. "You're right!"

The dwellers were not a little irritated at their gawking. Buccari composed herself as the taller creature approached. His face was oddly formed, wider and flatter than the others, and he was burdened with large bound tablets.

"Whew, he's an ugly bugger," O'Toole whispered. "Looks like a lizard. What's he carrying?"

Included in his burden Buccari recognized the notebooks she and Hudson had used to compose pictographs. The dweller halted at a low table in the middle of the room and deposited the books.

"Everyone sit tight," Buccari ordered as she presumptuously stood, walked over to the table, and sat, gesturing to the cliff dweller to do the same. She slid a book in front of her and studied it.

"Fantastic!" she exclaimed over her shoulder. "Lizard Lips here has taken our pictographs and developed a shorthand system."

The door was open. Buccari smiled at the creature. She pointed with two hands at the manuscript, demonstrating joy at what was before her. She clapped her hands and whistled the ditty. The creature apparently understood, hesitantly clapping its four-fingered hands together. Soon all the dwellers were clapping hands and chirping.

The noises halted when Buccari brusquely reached across the creature and grabbed a writing implement, a stylus with an ink wick squeezed in a fine-tipped clamp. Stylus in hand, she flipped through the manuscript, stopping to copy symbols onto a square of stiff linen. The creature at her side squeaked and chirped as she wrote.

A high overcast painted the calm afternoon winterscape in muted tones. The spindly yellow-barked evergreens contrasted green-black against a blanket of powdery snow. Packed footpaths stitched the campsite, connecting shelters, watch posts, woodpile, meat house, and latrines. Hudson looked up into the heavy underbellies of the clouds rolling ponderously across the white-shrouded mountains. The small canyon above the camp echoed with the hollow *thunk-thunk* of wood chopping. White and yellow splinters of wood fluttered across the radius of hard-packed snow as Tatum swung the long ax. Beppo Schmidt worked on boughs and branches with the hatchet, while Fenstermacher used a hammer and a heavy chisel to split logs.

"Another storm's coming," Hudson sighed, lifting his parka from a tree branch. He had worked up a sweat. An icy chill flowed across the small of his back. "Looks like a big one."

"Where—the—hell—are—they?" Fenstermacher grunted in time with his hammer blows.

As if cued, Mendoza, on watch above the cave, shouted, "The patrol! I see 'em. They're back!"

Hudson jerked his eyes from the storm clouds and turned to scan the vast whiteness of the plateau. The lake with its three islands, hard frozen except for irregular blemishes of black and gray marking the welling hot springs, provided the only relief. She was back. Finally, the patrol was back. Through the trees a cluster of dark forms plodded along, leaving a trail of blue prints that disappeared in a faint melding with the near horizon of the high plateau rim. Hudson exhaled, muttering a silent prayer of gratitude.

Leather-hinged doors to the A-frames groaned open. Shannon came first, followed by the rest of the crew, shouting and cheering. Even Commander Quinn, gray-faced and gaunt, blanket over his shoulders, stepped outside despite Lee's efforts to keep him in the shelter. Shannon ran up to the cave terrace to better see over the treetops.

"Jupiter's balls, Mendoza, you let 'em get close enough," he growled. "Tatum, you, Gordon, and Petit come with me."

"I'm coming, too, Sarge," Hudson said, pulling on his parka. "Dawson, help Lee get Commander Quinn back by the fire. Chief, keep 'em working on the firewood. Okay, let's go."

They took beaten paths down to the lake and onto the pure flatness of its surface, to the near island, using its beaches to get past the largest of the steaming hot spring holes. Beyond the island Hudson plowed through virgin snow, running ahead of the marines. He met the patrol halfway across the lake. They were walking fast, and they were all smiling, looking none the worse for wear.

"Where you guys been?" Hudson blurted. "We've been worried sick."

"And it's nice to see you, too," Buccari replied, green eyes and grinning teeth flashing from her sun-darkened, wind-burnished face. Her backpack was grossly overloaded, and she held her thumbs under the shoulder straps to relieve the pressure.

"Here, let me take your pack," Hudson said, moving behind her and lifting as she released her waist strap. "Ooooph! What's in here, rocks? You didn't carry this all the way from the valley?"

"She sure did," MacArthur said. "The lieutenant's an animal . . . sir!"

"This little lady is Superwoman!" Jones added exuberantly. "Sir!"

"We spent the last two nights with the cliff dwellers, Nash," Buccari blurted as Shannon and the others slogged up. "We've established contact, Nash. Real contact! Wait till you see their drawings. They've created a dictionary of icons. They're truly intelligent creatures—advanced intelligence. We've made solid contact."

"No shit!" Petit said. "Those bat bugs intelligent? You sure?"

"Petit, shut up and take Jonesy's load. Gordon, get O'Toole's," Shannon barked, grabbing MacArthur by the shoulder and spinning him around to get at his pack. Tatum, knees buckling, had already taken Chastain's bloated backpack onto his equally wide shoulders. "Welcome back, Lieutenant. We were worried about you guys."

"Ah, Sarge," MacArthur chortled. "I didn't think you cared."

"Not about your sorry ass." Shannon laughed. "Not with your luck."

"So what did you see, Sharl?" Hudson said. "What—"

"Wait until we get back to camp," Buccari replied. "There's too much to show and tell. How about you guys? How's Pepper?"

"Hyperpregnant," Tatum replied, worried. "Any day."

"Commander Quinn's real sick," Hudson said. "He caught that virus we've all had, but Lee thinks it's changed to pneumonia. He's bad off."

A gust of wind swept the lake. They all put their heads down and started retracing the trail. Individual flakes, large and buoyant, swirled gently downward. The rustling of the trees was the only sound.

TWENTY-SIX

NIGHTMARE

Tatum, rifle slung over his shoulder, clasped the frozen meat in one arm and pulled on the guide rope. He leaned into the gale. Powdery snow whipped up from the ground and fell from the skies. Visibility was zero. A whiteout.

The line around Tatum's waist yanked sharply; its nether end vanished in whiteness. Tatum waited. Yelling was futile; wind blew his words into oblivion, and he did not want to risk frostbite. The belaying line tugged again, urgently. Tatum let the gusts push him back along his own wake, the plowed furrow already blown smooth. Rennault waited at the end of the safety belay. Tatum put his head next to Rennault's mouth.

"Thought . . . saw something!" Rennault shouted.

"What?" Tatum asked.

"Couldn't tell for sure . . . movement . . . low to the ground."

"Why the hell pull me back? Let's get inside." Tatum leaned

back into the freezing wall of wind, pulling on the guide rope leading to shelter.

Rennault shouted, but Tatum kept moving, intent on returning to the warmth. A muffled scream brought him up short. The safety line jerked tight—viciously tight! Throwing the meat down, Tatum swung the assault rifle from his back and crouched low, waiting. The belaying line tugged painfully hard. Irresistibly, it pulled Tatum over onto his back, jerking him from the guide rope. Flailing, Tatum rolled helplessly in the snow, unable to gain purchase, until he found himself in the middle of snarling mayhem. A nightmare! White-pelted phantoms, growling horridly, fought over some undefinable object. Thrusting his legs deeply in the snow, Tatum gained stability and fired at the scuffling creatures, the muzzle blasts flat cracks in the gale. One of the things fell convulsively to the snow. The others disappeared into the blizzard. The line went slack.

Tatum peered into the stupefying whiteness. He saw nothing—nothing but the belaying line fading from sight. He pulled tentatively. Resistance. Something was there! He pulled harder, but it would not budge. He leaned backward, taking the strain with his legs. The weight on the line—Rennault or what was left of him—yielded. Tatum forced his legs to push to the rear, hauling the deadweight along the furrow marking his path to the shelters. Tatum yelled. The gale hammered his words into his mouth. He glanced over his shoulder, frantically peering for the guide rope, blinking wind-driven snow from his freezing eyes.

The belaying line stiffened vibrantly. In desperation the marine fired a shot down the line, his aim high, in case it still mattered. The line jerked angrily and went slack. Tatum resumed his backward march, staring wide-eyed into the vertiginous blizzard. Backward he struggled. An eternity passed before his shoulder ran up against the rope linking the shelters to the meat house. Grasping the line, Tatum slung his rifle over his shoulder and pulled himself hand over hand, helping his back and legs move the invisible anchor of Rennault's body. Slinging the rifle had been a mistake.

It came from the direction of the shelters, a growling white blur of fangs. The marine twisted to bring the rifle to bear, but the burly creature was on him, leaping for his neck and face. He threw his arm up, and the frenzied beast seized it in outsized mandibles, taking ferocious ripping bites above the elbow, driving the marine backward into the snow, growling maniacally the entire time. Yellow eyes, insane with ferocity, glared malevolently into his. Animal spit and human blood splattered against his face as he struggled to extricate the rifle. His weapon was fouled in the ropes. With an effort born of desperation, Tatum cleared the rifle from its tangle and swung the barrel. Holding the tip of the weapon steady with his numb hand, he thrust the muzzle into the growling, pulsating rib cage and fired four rounds. Heat from the barrel flowed through his glove as the creature died, its frenzied jaws still grinding, its throat still rattling.

Tatum could not look at the animal; he could only gape at his arm. His fingers would not move; they still clasped the hot rifle barrel. He set the rifle stock in the snow and prized the fingers loose. Blood pulsed from his wounds, streaming hot down his arm. He felt dizzy. He shook cobwebs from his eyes and tried to think. He removed the sling from his weapon and put his mangled arm through the slack loop and pulled it painfully tight. He pulled even harder, biting his lip, tasting his own blood.

Teeth clenched against a rising tide of agony, Tatum resumed his march. Pulling hard, he closed the distance to the shelters. Several times he felt nibbling jerks on his gruesome trolling bait, but the sensations were dreamlike. Shock set in, reinforced by the numbing intensity of frigid winds. His back hit the solid logs of the A-frame, and he slumped against the icy wood, relieved to have his back protected from the wind. And from attack. He fell unconscious.

Shannon looked up from his cards.

"Where the hell is Tatum? You hear something?" he growled.

The wind howled, a manic ambience that dulled the mind, the eighth day of the storm. The earthlings huddled helplessly in their shelter, a ragged collection of refugees. Some played cards in the smoky light. Others slept. Unreliable daylight leaked through the apex of the peaked roof, where the sheet metal flue penetrated the logs. The wind-battered metal rattled insanely, and snowmelt dripped and hissed down its length. A musty odor eclipsed all sensations, and sneezes punctuated the whistling draughts more frequently than did civilized conversation.

Shannon checked his watch. "Crap! They've been out over

twenty minutes. Chastain, you and Gordon get your gear on! I'm out!" Shannon threw down good cards and stood.

"Crybaby!" Fenstermacher said, dealing. "Marines can't play poker."

Lee giggled, a lonely sound.

Shannon ignored them and grabbed his hat and coat, while Chastain and Gordon retrieved weapons from the stacked arms in the cold corner.

"Problem, Sergeant?" Quinn coughed from the warmest corner. Dark circles surrounded sunken eyes. He had lost too much weight.

"Tatum's overdue, Commander," Shannon replied. "Better find out why."

"Right, huh ... good idea, Sergeant," Quinn replied listlessly.

Goldberg looked up anxiously at Tatum's name, a hand on her grossly distended abdomen.

Walking in a crouch, Shannon stepped over the sitting and reclining humans, moving from the warmer area near the fire to the uncomfortably cold area adjacent to the door. A gutted marmot, dripping blood, hung from the rafters near the door, slowly thawing.

Seeing what was about to happen, the occupants groaned and pulled their sleeping bags higher. Shannon flipped his hood up, zipped his coat over his chin, and pulled on his gloves. Chastain and Gordon helped move the heavy door inward far enough for them to squeeze through. Wind swirled, blasting through the open door, sprinkling the interior with fine crystals. The men used their feet and free hands to move snow, packing a ramp to the elevated surface. Shannon trudged into the drifts and found the guide rope leading downhill. Rising snow had almost covered it.

Shannon followed the rope, breaking his own rule by not belaying to another person. Gordon and Chastain followed in his wake. If Tatum was wasting time in the other shelter, he was going to get a supreme ass chewing for bringing them out in the blizzard. The sergeant plowed around the corner of the cabin and saw the body slumped in the lee, a dusting of snow covering the corporal's face and clothes. Shannon grabbed the marine and shook him violently. He looked into the injured man's face. Tatum's eyes opened, blinked once, and slowly shut.

"Get him inside!" Shannon yelled, lifting Tatum's right arm

over his neck and pulling him toward the sleep shelter. He noticed the safety line trailing away and felt the invisible leaden weight at its end. Growling noises separated from the insane howl of the wind.

Explosions! Rifles firing in full automatic spit bullets past his head. Deafened, Shannon fell facedown in the snow. As he lay, stunned, something heavy struck him bluntly in the back—an animal, a heavy animal! For an instant it stood, and then it pivoted sharply, footpads and claws seeking purchase on the material of his coat, and was gone. Shannon struggled to his knees; he was drowning in the yielding, frigid whiteness. Gordon and Chastain continued sporadic fire. Shannon heaved upright, ears ringing painfully, to find three steaming carcasses within arm's reach, their thick white fur splotched with livid streaks. One shuddering heap rose on powerful forelegs, materializing into a prognathous, saber-toothed horror. Gordon fired a single shot, knocking the yellow-eyed demon's head sharply backward. It was still.

The door to the near shelter sucked inward, and MacArthur scrambled through the drifts, rifle poised threateningly, eyes wild. He was hatless, coatless, and bootless, his hair bedraggled, his bearded face imprinted with the indentations and lines of a makeshift pillow. MacArthur registered Shannon dragging Tatum through the snow. His mouth fell open, but his eyes lingered for only an instant. He scanned the white nothingness of the howling blizzard. A shouting crowd followed MacArthur through the narrow exit, rifle barrels slicing the air.

"Get him inside!" Shannon shouted, taking his knife and cutting through the line around Tatum's waist. He handed the rope to Chastain. "Rennault's on the other end."

"What the hell?" someone shouted—Gordon. "What are they?"

"Nightmares," Shannon gasped. "Goddamn frigging nightmares."

"Bring him over here," a disheveled Buccari ordered from the door of the shelter. She and Dawson hurriedly cleared a space by the fire. "Gordon, get more wood. Boats, get Lee and her first-aid kit—fast!" Shannon laid Tatum on the ground next to the stove and headed for the door. He still felt the claws on his back, and his ears still echoed with neck-chilling growls.

Buccari stared at the bleeding marine. With Dawson's help she stripped off his coat. Arterial bleeding increased as he warmed, a pumping fountain of life. Buccari pinched the pressure point under his arm. Tatum moaned—a good sign.

"Need help?" It was MacArthur, shivering, his sock-covered feet soaking wet.

"Take care of yourself first," Buccari replied. "You look like hell."

"How is he?" MacArthur asked, ignoring her.

"His arm's hamburger, and he's bleeding to death," she said, her stomach fluttering. "We need to get the tourniquet on."

"Let me," MacArthur mumbled. "Hold the pressure." He knelt, opened the loop of the sling, and ran it up Tatum's arm just short of Buccari's hold on the pressure point.

"Okay, Nance, grab his shoulder and squeeze hard," he ordered. "Tighter! I want white knuckles." Satisfied with Dawson's grip, he pushed Buccari's hands away, briefly inspected the muscular arm, and slid the looped sling as high up as he could, snugging it under the armpit. Blood pulsed freely.

"Hold him down," MacArthur said. "Nance, lean on him."

MacArthur stood, holding the free end of the strap, and put a wet foot on Tatum's mangled arm. Grunting, he pulled with all his might. The bleeding dribbled to a stop.

"Cover him up," MacArthur said. "Keep him warm."

"They find Rennault?" Buccari asked. Blood covered her hands.

"Yeah," he replied, shivering. "Most of him. They put him in the meat house." He walked over to his sleeping bag.

The door opened with a snowy blast, and Lee tumbled in. Chastain plodded behind her, carrying the medical kit, and Shannon followed both of them. Lee walked unsteadily to the injured marine and took a long look at the arm, testing the tourniquet.

"Shit!" she said, shaking her head. "Has he been conscious?"

"Barely," Buccari answered, wiping away gore.

"Shit!" Lee shouted, and turned to Chastain. "Put it down." Chastain, pathetically frightened, set the equipment down as if it would explode.

Shannon moved into the circle of light, staring at the bloody mess.

"Jocko! Get Jones!" he snapped. "We'll need the horses."

Buccari felt her stomach leap. She took an unconscious step backward.

"Oh, shit," Lee whispered between clenched teeth. She rum-

maged in the equipment and came out with syringe and vials.
"Hope this stuff is still good. Get a larger fire going and boil
water. Sarge, we'll have to cauterize the wound. See if you can
find a piece of flat metal we can heat to red hot—a big knife
or one of Chief Wilson's frying pans."

Lee pulled a bone saw from her bag and looked at it with
loathing.

"I'll need help," she said. The medic glanced around the circle of people and stopped when she came to Buccari. Buccari
understood why: she was the senior officer—the leader. She
was supposed to take charge, but all she could feel was revulsion and panic.

MacArthur, in dry clothes, shouldered through the ring of
spectators and took the vicious saw. "Ready when you are,
Les."

Half an hour later they started. Tatum regained consciousness, remaining lucid despite the drugs. Lee gave orders while
Chastain, Jones, and Shannon struggled to restrain the injured
man's frantic spasms. Dawson hugged Tatum's head, blocking
his view, while MacArthur, pale-faced and silent, maneuvered
the saw over the tortured limb. Buccari, her resolve shored by
MacArthur's determination and courage, stood close by, holding a frying pan in the roaring fire, perspiration rolling down
her face and neck. She was grimly relieved that Tatum's
screams of agony drowned out the wet, rasping, scraping
noises of the bone saw. The ravaged arm fell away, and Lee
liberally washed the spongy stump with an antiseptic. Buccari,
using rags to insulate the pan, pressed the glowing-hot frying
pan to the pulpy end of the traumatized limb. Tatum, biting on
a rag, screamed twice and mercifully passed out. The sickly
smell of cooking flesh permeated the narrow confines.

The storm stopped two days later. Bright, heatless rays of
morning sun found the chinks and gaps in the rafters of the
shelters, inducing the hapless occupants who were still asleep
to awaken and look once again upon a world with horizons.
The dawn air, dense and transparent, revealed a host of morning stars twinkling thinly overhead, displaying their arrogance,
daring to be visible during the light of day.

Cold! So cold! Faces covered and hands thickly gloved, marines and ship's crew struggled from beneath the blanket of
winter. Of their shelters, only the peaked ridge beams protruded into the new day. The thin forest was reduced to a field

of pygmy trees drifted in virgin powder. The humans standing
next to the shelters looked anxiously across the shrouded lake,
vaporous breath freezing in the air. Snow chirped under their
footfalls, and every whisper, every sound, flew fast and far in
the iron-hard air. In the distance, connected to the camp by a
trail of snowshoe prints, two hikers made slow progress.
Avoiding the smooth craters that identified the hot springs,
they plowed across the shallow bowl of the lake, trudging in
velvet shadows.

"Couldn't stop her, Gunner," Shannon said. "Didn't want to.
We can't just hide in our shelters. Those things aren't going to
go away."

"You could've sent a couple more men," Wilson admonished.

"Those two can move as fast as anyone," Shannon responded. "Sending more men would only have slowed them
down. The nightmares won't be a problem as long as the visibility's good. They've got plenty of ammo."

Ammunition. Shannon thought grimly about the limited supply. He worried as he turned and scanned the softly mounded
terrain. The thick blanket of snow had eradicated the sharp
edges of their rock-tumbled world, and that worked to soothe
his anxieties. His vision slipped outward, over the muted
ridges and foothills to the awesome and lofty granite giants;
the snows could not dampen the sharpness of those spires.
Low rays from the rising sun gave the alpine vista a wash of
colors from soft gold to brilliant alabaster, presenting the hard
lines of precipitous terrain in emphatic relief. Shannon felt a
reverence, a sense of awe.

"What did Commander Quinn say?" Wilson persisted.

"He's out of his head," the sergeant replied. "For dinner, if
you cook up any of those furry devils, don't grab Rennault by
mistake."

"Not funny," Wilson retorted. The men stomped their booted
feet for warmth. Both carried rifles.

"Let's check out the lake," Shannon said. "Maybe we can
still fish."

"How's Tatum?" Wilson asked.

"He doesn't know how to complain," Shannon replied.
"How's Goldberg?"

"Real good," Wilson said. "I thought Tatum going down
would do her in, but it seems to have had the opposite effect.
She's gotten tougher."

"Going to have to be damn tough to bring that baby into this world."

"So's the baby," Wilson sighed.

They struggled through the snow, plowing a trail to the lake.

"Nance is pregnant, too," Shannon volunteered.

Wilson looked at him. "You ever have kids before, Sarge?"

"I never even owned a goddamn dog."

"Think they'll take us in, Lieutenant?" MacArthur gasped.

"Don't plan on giving them a choice," Buccari huffed, adjusting the ride of her pack. The backpacks were loaded heavily with firewood.

It had grown dark, and the long day's hike over loose snow had taken its toll. Buccari trudged in MacArthur's wake, ungainly in her crude snowshoes. It was painfully cold, too cold to talk.

Something moved in the gray distance.

MacArthur stopped and peered into the gloaming. The large moon, a crescent settling behind the mountains, offered little assistance.

"Saw it," she whispered, checking their rear.

"Good," MacArthur replied. "Didn't know how to break the news."

"Stick to the plan?" she asked.

"Yeah. Soon as it gets too dark to see, we'll build a fire."

"Pretty dark now," Buccari said, unshouldering the carbine.

"Careful with that," MacArthur said. "You're a little too anxious."

"I'm not anxious," she sniffed. "I qualified 'expert' at the academy."

"You ever shoot anything that moves? Or bleeds?" MacArthur asked.

She shook her head.

"Crap, it's cold," he said, turning his head.

The false light revealed only the texture of snow and their own footprints trailing into the distance behind them. Stars, subdued by an icy overcast, twinkled feebly overhead.

"I'll shoot first," MacArthur continued, head still turned to the rear. "This assault rifle will do a lot of damage, and there's no sense in wasting bullets. If you have to shoot, make sure you're aiming at the target. Don't just point—"

"Mac!" Buccari shouted. Yellow-fanged, mustard-eyed nightmares pounded out of the darkness, their growls rising in pitch like an approaching locomotive. MacArthur threw up his arms and ducked sideways. The first beast struck his shoulder and knocked him into the snow, unholy jaws snapping for purchase and finding nothing but backpack and wood. Buccari had no time to think—a second snarling creature was leaping straight for the bare whiteness of MacArthur's face. Her carbine barked, and the nightmare twisted in midtrajectory, landing in a convulsing, screaming pile. Other creatures scattered into the dusk.

She swung her weapon to bear on the violence at her feet. The nightmare, straddling the fallen man, ripped and tore at MacArthur's bedroll. MacArthur's rifle was still slung over his shoulder. The marine, trying to protect his face, struggled to sit. Buccari staggered to find a safe line of fire. With explosive abruptness muzzle flashes lit up the dusk. Three gut-muffled reports from MacArthur's pistol rent the air. The animal jerked violently and slumped to the ground, its whiplike tail slapping a pattern in the snow. And then it was still.

MacArthur shed his pack and crawled, trembling, to a crouch, assault rifle in one hand, a smoking pistol in the other. He pounced on Buccari's nightmare, slamming his rifle butt on its skull. Bloodcurdling growls whimpered to silence.

"You okay?" she panted, wrenching her eyes from the saber-toothed monster at her feet. It was dark. All she could see was his silhouette.

"Yeah. Yeah, just—some scratches. Time to build that fire."

"Sentries report the sound of long-legs' death stick," Craag reported.

Braan nodded thoughtfully. The dwellers stood in the outermost chamber of his residence. Brappa-the-young-warrior, grown taller and backlit by the hearth's golden glow, stood in the tunnel passage leading to the main living area, listening to the news. Soft noises of mother and child came from within.

"What dost thou make of it, my friend?" Braan asked.

"Growlers are about. 'Tis likely a patrol of long-legs makes their way to us, and they have been beset by hungry beasts," Craag answered.

"Can we not help?" Brappa asked impetuously and insubordinately.

Braan excused himself and turned gently to his son.

"Brappa, my offspring! Brappa-the-young-warrior," Braan said. "Dost thou not have enough to think about with thy wedding on the morrow? Spare thy courage for the ultimate test. Leave this trivial matter to old hunters."

"*Eeyah!* Young warrior!" Craag added. "Gliss, thy mistress to be, my young sister, is fair and strong. Growlers are as playthings by comparison. Thou must save thine energy and wiles if thou art to be the master of thy residence. Marriage and mortal combat are as first cousins."

A derisive hoot emanated from the direction of the fire glow, where Ki-the-mother sat by the hearth. It was a time of felicity in the house of Braan and universally for all hunters of the cliff colony. Winter season was for marriage and mating. The ferocity of cold storms kept the tough animals near home. The young hunters, the sentries, still posted at the cliff edges, were ever vigilant for encroaching enemies, but the mature hunters found themselves idle. With the scars and injuries of the summer campaigns behind them, well fed and of welling energies, the experienced warriors directed their attention inward, to their families. It was a time for training, for teaching, for telling, and for touching.

"Apologies, my father and my brother-to-be," returned the chagrined young cliff dweller. "I have intruded where I belong not. I apologize for the directness but not for the essence of my question. The long-legs took care of me in my need. Is there not something we can do to help?"

"A fair question and from the heart, but for now we must wait. It is too cold. We cannot fight in the open under these conditions. Permit us to finish our discussion."

"Sarge! I heard gunshots," Gordon shouted as he came through the door of the dayroom shelter, bringing with him a wave of frigid air.

Shannon glanced up from his meager and greasy dinner and looked over at Chief Wilson. Wilson shook his head, keeping his eyes on his plate.

"How many, Billy?" Shannon asked.

"A couple—maybe three or four," he responded. "Way out. You could barely hear 'em. You know how sound carries in this cold air. Beppo heard 'em, too."

Shannon stared past the sentry's shoulder. There was nothing to do.

"Mac's just taking target practice. Let me know if you hear more."

* * *

"You're bleeding," Buccari said. She kindled a small fire. It flared, its amber flames revealing a ragged gash down the corporal's cheek.

"S'afraid of that." He removed his glove and gingerly touched his bearded face with bare fingertips. He glanced down at the bloodied fingers and grabbed a handful of snow to hold against the wound. "I got more work to do."

The marine checked the wind. The air was still. Using a snowshoe, he dug deeply, throwing snow into a pile next to the widening hole. Satisfied with the depth and breadth of the excavation, MacArthur walked out of the hole and proceeded to stomp on the snow pile and the area around it, adding more snow and packing it hard. Returning to the pit, he carved out a lateral hole—a snow cave—under the area he had compacted. He transferred the burning brands from the small fire to a spot before the cave opening. He laid the packs and their supply of wood at the cave mouth.

Buccari leaned up against the side of the pit, keeping her eyes outward, looking for movement. She glanced at the industrious marine as he melted snow in a cooking pan.

"Don't be watching me, Lieutenant," he said. "Keep your head up for more nightmares! You've got sentry duty, or do you want to cook?"

"Sentry, aye!" She struck an alert pose. The small moon rose in the east, an illusion of brightness. Vague shadows moved at the limits of vision, but she could not discriminate any beasts with certainty. MacArthur left the snow crater briefly to hack apart one of the carcasses. Cooked on skewers over the flames, the charred meat was greasy, tough, and gristly, yet the ravenous hikers consumed goodly portions with relish, sitting as prehistoric humans had sat many light-years away both in time and in distance.

Sated, Buccari melted a pot of snow and drank the water.

"With all due respect, Lieutenant, you'll be peeing all night."

She laughed at the prospect. "Where's the latrine, now that you mention it?"

"Over there." He pointed opposite the fire. "Doesn't make sense to take a walk, does it?"

"No," she said. "Let me clean that scratch before the water cools."

"From latrines to my face," MacArthur said. "What am I supposed to think?"

"At least you're smart enough to make the connection," she said, dipping a rag in the water and throwing on another log.

Buccari knelt in front of MacArthur, wet rag poised. The corporal looked up at her, gray eyes sparkling in the dancing light of the fire. The gash, running from the fat part of his cheek diagonally into his beard, was deep enough to have required stitches in a civilized world. It would make a wide scar. MacArthur winced as she dabbed the cloth around the wound. As she was swabbing the injury, a lock of hair fell repeatedly in front of her eyes. MacArthur reached up and gently jammed the tress under her hat brim. Buccari smiled, feeling embarrassment and other emotions.

"Thanks. Hair sure gets in the way." She stood and looked away.

"Pretty hair," he said shyly. "Keep it out of your eyes. You have the first watch." He pulled the shredded sleeping bag from his pack.

"Use mine," Buccari said, amazed that MacArthur would even think about sleep. "I can wrap yours around me. What do I do while you're sleeping?"

"You ever hear of Jack London?" he asked, exchanging sleeping bags.

"Yes, but—oh, I get it. It's cold. Time to talk philosophy."

"London wrote about wolves . . . and fires," MacArthur said without levity. "That's the philosophy that matters: keep the fire burning. Nightmares will understand fire; best argument I can think of, but be ready to shoot. Use the rifle but have your pistol ready. Give me the carbine." He positioned the sleeping bag and crawled in. "Wake me up in two hours, and then it's your turn to sleep. We'll do two-hour shifts."

She sat down in the mouth of the cave and tensely scanned the darkness surrounding the crater. The opposite side was trampled low, and she had a good view. But behind her, directly over her head, the view was obstructed by the packed mound of snow. The feeling that something was there weighed heavily. She threw another log on the fragile fire and leaned against the shredded sleeping bag and the yielding snow, soaking in the feeble warmth. She checked her watch. Two minutes had crept by. Amazingly, MacArthur was already asleep, his breathing deep and slow. Her own eyelids slipped downward. Shaking fogginess from her brain, she stood slowly, warily turning her head to peek over the snowbank.

Nothing. Nothing but the black night. She turned and looked

past the fire and detected dim sparks of light floating in the air in pairs. The cruel stares of three predatory animals hung suspended in the distance, three neat pairs of eyes glowing red in the firelight.

"Aw, shit!" she whispered. Her cold hands perspired. She threw another precious log on the fire and lifted a burning brand into the air. Sparks sprinkled about her as illumination spread over the gray-shadowed snow. Surrounded! She counted ten beasts and stopped. There were at least thirty, all stealthily moving toward her.

"MacArthur!" she exhaled breathlessly. "Mac!"

She kicked his foot, afraid to take her eyes from the frightening vision on the snow. MacArthur stirred, moaning softly.

"We got company, Mac. I need . . . need your help."

The marine eased from the cave and rose to a crouch. "At your service," he muttered, moving closer. His hip touched hers.

He took the assault rifle, replacing it with the carbine.

"That one's closest," MacArthur croaked, indicating a fierce specter directly across from the fire, its huge undercanines shooting up past the top of its snout. "Let's hope he's the leader. Hold your ears."

MacArthur took quick aim through the flames, exhaled, and fired one round, dropping the animal like a lump of mud. The other monsters evaporated into darkness.

The marine checked his watch. "Kick my foot before you fire at the next one." He took the carbine, handed her the big rifle, and climbed into the cave. He leaned on his elbow and peeked at the fire.

"Go easy on that wood. It has to last." He flopped down and zipped the bag over his head.

"Beppo! I heard another shot," Gordon whispered excitedly. His breath glowed in the faint light of the little moon. Both men listened quietly.

"*Ja*, me, too," Schmidt answered. "You tell Sarge, and I will wake up Mendoza and Chastain for the next watch."

"Another death stick explosion, Braan-our-leader," the sentry said.

"Only one?" Braan asked.

"Only one," the messenger replied.

"A good sign." Braan dismissed the sentry.

* * *

MacArthur breathed heavily in his sleep. An hour had crawled by. Buccari arranged the crumbling logs, causing yellow flames to flare brightly. Close by—behind her—a rumbling growl reverberated over the edge of the snowbank. Adrenaline flushed warmly through Buccari's body, but the back of her head and neck went cold. She pivoted, simultaneously raising the assault rifle to her shoulder. Two fanged horrors crouched, coiled to spring from the high side. Buccari locked the rifle sights into line with the leftmost animal's nose and squeezed the trigger just as the animal lunged. She staggered backward, her booted foot disturbing the fire. The predator jerked back in midleap, a large-caliber bullet ripping its throat, and fell from the air, thudding into the snow at the mouth of their cave. The other nightmare vanished.

The sleeping bag zipper sang like a buzz saw. MacArthur bolted from the cave, firing his pistol and kicking viciously at the twitching carcass as he leapt over it, twisting and turning. Buccari stepped back and allowed the marine to discharge his pent-up fright. He came to a trembling halt, lowered the smoking pistol, and slowly erected himself from the stooping, bunched-muscle crouch into which he had contorted himself. He looked at Buccari and then down at the inert animal. He kicked it again—hard.

"Nice shot," MacArthur said, shaking his head. "Thanks for the warning." He blinked at his watch, having difficulty focusing his eyes.

"Believe me," she laughed, wondering that she could laugh and be petrified at the same time, "if I had had time to kick you, I would have—with pleasure."

"Hmmph." He yawned, looking down at the nightmare. Grunting, he bent over, lifted the limp carcass, and heaved it from the crater. He looked at his watch. "I got an hour. That's enough."

"No!" she insisted. "It's still my watch!"

Without a word he yawned, turned away, and crawled into the cave. "Put more wood on the fire, Lieutenant," he said, pulling the top of the bag around his head and shoulders but leaving it unzipped.

Buccari rubbed her bruised shoulder. She looked at the dead animal and acknowledged an atavistic gratification. She wanted more. If it was kill or be killed, then she was ready to play.

The night was long, but in the dim light of predawn Buccari and MacArthur climbed from the carcass-littered snow crater and continued their slow trek to the cliffs. Not long after sunrise a patrol of hunters made a rendezvous.

Toon offered his respects and requested a moment of Bool's time. The older steam user lifted his snout and aimed it at his underling. Toon's request no doubt concerned the long-legs; that seemed to be the only subject about which Toon cared anymore. While Toon was doing an excellent liaison job—the elders had commended Bool on his choice—many of Toon's important duties had gone wanting, and Bool was personally required to fill the void. His work groups were behind on corrosion inspections and link replacements for the lifts in addition to the never-ending requirement to clear sediment from the accumulator channels.

"Steam user Toon," Bool replied superciliously. "What require thee?"

"To presume on thy time, sir. A matter of the long-legs."

"Short-one-who-leads returned this morning, did she not? Art thy communication efforts progressing in a satisfactory manner?"

"Most superbly satisfactory, master," Toon replied, his tone and choice of words obsequious and supplicating.

Bool's interest was piqued. "State thy business, steam user Toon."

"The long-legs have requested succor. They ask to be taken under our roof," Toon responded directly, taking his cue from Bool's abruptness.

"Impossible!" the older dweller sputtered. "We cannot support twenty long-legs. They are huge! They eat so much, and constantly!"

"Nineteen, master," Toon replied. "One has died. Another is injured."

"Dead!" Bool exclaimed. "Oh, no! May its soul rest. Tragic! Oh, my!"

"Master Bool," Toon said with unusual intensity. "The elders must be informed. I apprise thee before word reaches the elders."

"Thy loyalty is commendable, steam user Toon, and thou art correct. We must inform the elders immediately. I shall request an audience."

* * *

The biting wind was a two-edged sword: it had blown the snow from the plateau, but the temperatures were cruel, the bright sun providing only light without heat. The return hike from the cliffs had been punishing. They trudged on the ice-armored lake below the camp; Buccari feared frostbite in her extremities. She peeked forward into the rasping gusts; her watering eyes detected someone hurrying to meet them.

"Shannon and—Hudson," MacArthur shouted into her ear.

"Hope everything's okay," she screamed. The blurry apparitions gave Buccari a sense of foreboding. They met in the lee of the island, the wind blunted by trees and rocks.

"You're in command, sir. Commander Quinn died last night," Shannon shouted, his face hidden behind a ragged muffler. "Fever took him away. Lee did what she could, but he went fast. Just gave up and died."

Buccari momentarily forgot the cold. Commander Quinn, the senior officer, was dead. The decisions were now truly hers to make. She was responsible; she was speechless. She stared at her feet.

"Tatum's the one we need to worry about, Lieutenant," Shannon yelled against the wind thrashing through the trees. "He's in bad shape—infection's set in, maybe blood poisoning. Lee says it's only a matter of time before gangrene takes over."

"We need to get him to the dweller colony," Buccari said, shaking off her thoughts. "We need to get everyone to the dweller colony. At first light tomorrow we're heading for the cliffs. The cliff dwellers have given us permission to stay there."

"Aye," Shannon said, looking up. "Best news in a long time."

"We'll have the wind at our back on the return," Hudson shouted.

"Don't count on it," Buccari replied. "Look at those clouds. A front's coming. Bad weather and a wind shift. Let's get moving before the storm hits."

Large downy flakes sifted gracefully from an amorphous ceiling. The snows would last for a full moon, maybe longer. Kuudor, captain-of-the-sentry, wearing black otter fur, slogged between posts through the delicate shroud of snow. The guard had been doubled, and he was checking sentry stations for vigilance. The pointillistic forms of two other hunters materialized from the textured curtain of snowflakes—Craag and Braan in white growler skins and nearly invisible.

Braan spoke first, as was fitting. "Tidings, Kuudor, captain-of-the-sentry."

"Hail and well met, Braan-our-leader. Greetings, brave warrior Craag," the sentry commandant returned, using the ancient forms.

"All is in order," Craag said. "Thy sentries are well taught and serious."

The old warrior swelled with pride. "This storm is ominous," Kuudor responded. "It will last many days."

"It does not look good," Braan replied. "Daylight endures but one hour more. After dark the growlers will have their way."

"Perhaps the long-legs are not coming," offered Craag. "To wait would be wise."

"Perhaps," Braan replied. "But I think not. Short-one-who-leads said they would return this day. That creature seems sure-minded."

"I am told Short-one-who-leads is a female of the race," Kuudor said.

"It would be true," Braan stated.

"Strange beings, allowing smaller and weaker females to lead," Craag ventured.

"Perhaps their females are the more intelligent, as with guilders and hunters," Braan responded.

"We would never allow a guilder to lead us into battle!" Kuudor exclaimed. "Guilders have neither the will nor the means to fight, and they lack courage."

"Evidently female long-legs have the necessary attributes," Braan answered. "I doubt not their courage."

"Most curious. You will pardon me, warriors, for I must complete my rounds," Kuudor said. He saluted and stepped away and was immediately swallowed in a white matte curtain of snow.

MacArthur rechecked his compass and refigured his reckoning. A constant worry, the snow masked all directional references. He looked around, his anxiety level rising. Goldberg was done—Mendoza was bodily carrying her. Lee and Fenstermacher tried to help, but it was all they could do to help each other. Shannon had his hands full with Dawson, but at least he was keeping her moving. Tatum was the problem:

too heavy to carry, he fainted with disturbing frequency; it took two men to keep him moving. MacArthur, recalling the delirium and fever of his own infected shoulder, knew how his friend felt. The dwellers would heal Tatum—if only they could get there in time.

"How's Tatum doing?" MacArthur asked. Chastain, carrying an enormous backpack, supported Tatum's lanky weight. Hudson attempted to help, but Tatum's sagging body and the absence of a left arm made it awkward.

"Dunno, Mac," the big man gasped. "He ain't stirring."

"How're you doing, Jocko?" MacArthur asked. "You need a relief?"

"I'm okay," Chastain wheezed, plowing through the yielding whiteness.

"I'll take a break," Hudson gasped.

"Sure thing, Mr. Hudson. I'll tag O'Toole," MacArthur said. He hated to take O'Toole off guard detail; he wanted his best guns on the line. MacArthur walked toward the rear of the refugee column. The column was stringing out dangerously.

Movement to his right—something vague and without definable shape. MacArthur halted and stared into the downy precipitation. He strained to distinguish what his peripheral vision had discerned but could see nothing. He shook his head to clear his tired brain and pulled his face protector away from his eyes, giving him a wider field of vision, but to no avail. His five senses could tell him nothing, yet he was certain something was lurking in the drifts, only paces away. Buccari, walking on snowshoes alongside the column, came up to him.

"I don't like you staring like that," she said. "What'd you see?"

"Something . . . maybe," MacArthur responded. He looked at her. She looked away.

"The last time we made this trip was more fun," he said, smiling behind his scarf. "I only had you to worry about."

"Thanks a bunch," she replied sarcastically, turning to face him.

"Don't get me wrong," he protested. "I worried about you at first, a lot! But after the first night I worried more for the nightmares."

"Flattery!" she said. "I accept your praise, fierce warrior."

"Praise easily given, fair damsel."

MacArthur briefly touched her shoulder as they turned and walked together. They trudged up the column to where

Tookmanian and Schmidt, struggling under their large back-packs, kicked through the snow. Petit and Gordon followed, also heavily burdened, wallowing in the whiteness.

"How much farther?" Buccari asked.

"Can't be far," MacArthur replied. "Maybe a kilometer." He glanced sideways into the falling snow. The nagging feeling would not leave. "We're too spread out," he said. "I want the rear closed up. Let's take over the rear guard from O'Toole. I'm putting O'Toole with Chastain. Tatum's really slowing us down."

A single rifle shot sounded from the head of the column. Burping automatic fire shattered the cottony stillness. MacArthur lunged ahead with Buccari in his wake. Growls reverberated in the air. As he came back even with Tatum, he saw five wraithlike snowy apparitions, their paws throwing up a furious churning of snow, charging the column from the opposite side. Tatum and his attendants blocked his line of fire. MacArthur dove behind the men, plunging into the dry snow, and fired a burst into the black-rimmed maw of the closest beast. Buccari's carbine stuttered over his head. Another nightmare fell. Chastain stumbled, dropping Tatum facedown in the snow. Someone screamed. Hudson drew his pistol as two ferocious animals rammed into him, jaws snapping for flesh. MacArthur rose to a knee and fired a round into the closest beast, knocking it squealing and whimpering. Chastain stepped forward and grabbed the other growler by its thick scruff and heaved it into the air. The agile, twisting beast landed on its feet and withdrew.

The other growlers swerved at the rifle reports but maintained their attack. Snarling animals leapt for Chastain's hamstrings. A burst from Buccari's carbine hit one of the growlers in the shoulder, knocking it down, but the remaining growler struck at Chastain's buttocks and drew blood. Chastain went to his knees. Hudson, on the ground, coldly put his pistol behind the growler's ear and squeezed off two rounds. The growler fell dead.

MacArthur leapt to his feet. Hudson, clothing torn and bloodied, helped Chastain stagger to his feet. As Buccari rolled Tatum's snow-covered form faceup, more rifle fire exploded from the rear of the column.

Explosions of death sticks reverberated along the cliffs. Braan and Craag, bows drawn, rushed into the snow. Kuudor deployed two sections of archers and called up the next watch as reinforcements. With nothing further to do, he drew his bow and marched forward, confident that his sentries would stand their ground.

The reports from the death sticks were louder, the frenetic explosions coming in desultory bursts and random single shots, all muffled by the deadening snowfall. Shouts and screams wafted through the flurries, the long-legs' rumbling voices growing louder and louder. Sentries gave the alert—movement had been seen. The first hulking form appeared, and then several more materialized, heavy bodies sinking into the snow. The first one to stagger by was colossal. It carried the limp form of a fallen comrade. Two others followed closely behind. They were frightened by the cliff dwellers' sudden appearance. One giant shouted, apparently telling his warriors not to point death sticks at the hunters.

"Craag! Guide them!" Braan ordered. "We will help those that follow."

The next group came out of the blizzard—another injured one attended by three heavily burdened long-legs intent on keeping the hurt one moving. There was much shouting and screaming. Confused, the long-legs frequently stumbled and fell into the deep snow. Kuudor bravely approached, grabbing one by the hand. Two of the long-legs, seeing dwellers and sensing that safety was near, left the injured ones and returned toward the gunfire, all the while shouting with low, booming voices. Braan followed them into the unyielding whiteness.

From out of the dusk-darkened snowfall came the largest of the long-legs. He was injured, leaving a trail of blood and staggering ponderously through the powder. He struggled with the limp form of an injured comrade. The two long-legs returning to the fray relieved him of his burden, leaving the giant standing unsteadily, looking lost. Braan was concerned that he might fall, but three more long-legs came out of the flurries; two of them grabbed the big one's arms and pushed him forward, supporting his great weight. The third one took his rifle and turned to face the rear, maintaining a protective guard. Another long-legs advancing from the snows appeared, and they retreated together.

More shots, nearby! Craag was at his side, and Kuudor, bows drawn and ready. And more shots! Brilliant flashes of orange. The cliff dwellers flinched and recoiled at the barking death sticks. Growls! Snarling growlers! The hunters smelled the deadly animals despite the chemical reek of death stick magic. The scent of blood was also strong as snowflakes drifted gently downward, serenely oblivious to the carnage.

"Fall back, Lieutenant! Fall back!" MacArthur shouted. "O'Toole! Boats! Who else is still here? Shout your name and close up!"

No answer. It was just the four of them, formed into a tight huddle, their backs together. They knew that cliff dwellers were close by. They had made it! Almost made it—the four of them still needed to break off the engagement. They could not turn and run.

"Keep moving. O'Toole! Watch our backs and lead the way," MacArthur ordered. "Do you see anything? Any cliff dwellers?"

"Not yet. Which way do we go, Mac?" O'Toole asked helplessly.

MacArthur glanced at his compass, trying to hold it steady. Uncertain, he pointed in the general direction. They could be marching straight off the cliff.

Growlers exploded from the gray blizzard. Buccari's carbine and Jones's pistol barked viciously and were quickly joined by the lower-pitched and angry reports of MacArthur and O'Toole's heavy automatics. Only two of the growlers survived to close the gap, and one of those was dispatched with MacArthur's bayonet. The last growler fell to the ground with three arrows in its throat. The firing stopped. The humans stared at the shaft-studded growler and looked about for the unseen archers.

Fur-shrouded cliff dwellers materialized, bows drawn and arrows nocked. One of them approached and indicated with a sharp gesture that they should follow.

"It's Captain!" MacArthur shouted, recognizing the dweller leader by his manner and gait. "Follow him!"

The hunters turned and ambled over the snow, their broad feet keeping their lightweight bodies from sinking. The humans followed, struggling to keep pace, eyes scanning the snowy gloom.

TWENTY-SEVEN

WAR

It had gotten very late. Runacres was escorted from the inner offices of the west wing to the empty lobby of the deserted assembly forum. Only janitors puttered about, attempting to bring order to the hallowed chambers of that last bastion of democracy on Earth, such as it was. Runacres proceeded to the east entrance alone. He knew the way well. His footfalls on the lacquered floor echoed from the mahogany paneling and high ceilings of the interminable corridors. His pace was measured, neither quick nor slow, but then again, gravity was a nuisance. From habit he enjoyed reviewing the yellowed oils of ancient leaders and war heroes hanging from the walls, along with mildewed draperies and innumerable faded, dusty campaign banners and flags. The glorious past.

He entered the east wing rotunda.

"Guard! Attennn-huttt!" the captain barked. Elite troops of the Alberta Brigade in polished helmets, bayonets, and boots cracked explosively to attention. Runacres pulled on his thick reefer, donned his heavily braided cap, and tossed a spacer salute, flipping a hand from the cap brim, neat and quick, unlike the chest-thumping, fist-in-the-air salute of the Legion Federation Peacekeepers. He laughed at the irony of that appellation as he stomped into the snowy night.

Night reigned over Edmonton, but there was precious little darkness. Arc lights illuminated the capitol mall all the way to the distant Defense Ministry in which he had labored the past several months. Armed patrols in combat fatigues, some leading dogs, crisscrossed the grounds. Other than ground-wire trolleys, there were no powered vehicles within the administration perimeter. Runacres elected to make the short walk to the General Officers' Club, a refreshing prospect after so many

257

hours in closet session and probably quicker. Jupiter, he hated the politics! His planet was dying.

He glanced at his watch; it was two hours after their agreed-on meeting time, but he knew they would be waiting. He walked through the brass and teak lobby of the officers' club and into the secluded apartments reserved for the occasion. Merriwether stood at the window, watching snow fall softly through the harsh glare. The others, clustered on leather sofas and easy chairs near the amber glow of the fireplace, jumped to their feet—all except Quinn, who remained seated, staring at the floor. A magnificent oil of an ancient sail-powered dreadnought heeling to the wind hung above the mantel.

"We're going," Runacres announced stolidly. "The president wants us on that planet. We've been authorized to use all available means."

He looked around the silent room, not knowing what to expect—anything except silence. Quinn suddenly looked up at the ceiling, her eyes glistening in the firelight.

"I'll get the word out, Admiral," Wells replied, putting on his winter cap. "We have a few logistic problems to iron out."

"More than a few, Franklin. Get on it," Runacres said. He turned to face the geologist. "Commander Quinn, your report was the hammer. The president's advisers swallowed the hook. You are to be commended on your efforts. I know how hard you worked for this."

"Thank you, Admiral," Quinn replied, color just starting to flow into her face. "I really believe my—h-how soon, sir?"

"Of course you do, Cassy," Runacres replied softly. "We'll have to see how soon Franklin can crank up the refit. Not sooner than three months, probably more like six. We must be prepared to do battle."

Muzzle blasts from heavy artillery thundered across the land. Pig-snouted cannons erupted, hurling hunks of demon iron screaming through tortured skies, and distant, low-pitched explosions beat an arrhythmic dirge day and night. Black clouds of greasy smoke tumbled skyward from hideously orange tongues of flame raking the brutalized horizon. Joined in mortal combat were the konish armies of north and south. Devastation spread, and word of war flew in the wind. Millions of panicked civilians and thousands of furtive soldiers fled southward, forming endless refugee columns, filled with despair and absent hope.

Gorruk's hordes poured into the cratered and torched salients. They did not appear to be conquerors. Parched and blackened by the sun, the troops of the north were also refugees, fleeing from the unmerciful heat and winds of their forced march across the arid sands. The soldiers stumbled forward relentlessly, knowing too well the searing tribulation behind them; they would rather die attacking the unknown than repeat the ordeal of the deserts. As the dehydrated hordes reached the pitiful tributaries draining the contested lands, they would raise immense cheers and stampede the feeble watercourses, falling and wallowing in muddy ditches like cattle. Their footholds established, the northern armies flowed inexorably southward, supported by massive logistics convoys. Engineers, ruthlessly employing prisoners, struggled to erect rail systems spanning the deserts, striving desperately to complete their slave-driving atrocities before the weather systems returned to normal, causing the deserts to revert to impassable infernos.

The southern tribes had put aside their arguments and rivalries. Gorruk's daring invasion had eclipsed petty trade and boundary squabbles, putting in their stead a full-blown threat to their very existence. They knew that Jook's iron-fisted general did not subscribe to civilized conventions of warfare. To Gorruk, war—by definition—was total war. Torture, genocide, plunder, the torch—all of these and more were weapons in his arsenal of terror. The kones of the south were victims of their own complacency. The equatorial deserts had not been the ultimate barrier, after all. Madmen knew no barriers.

"Rather obvious, is it not?" Et Kalass asked wryly. He stared from his fourth-story penthouse overlooking the regimental parade field. Lovely orange-blossomed *kotta* trees lined the grass-covered fields. The atmosphere was thick with particulates and smog—as usual. The muted sky, clear of clouds yet still murky, was tinted almond, complementing the bright blossoms.

"I am unable to respond, Your Excellency," said his militia commander, General Et Ralfkra. "The satellites were possibly defective—or already sabotaged, built with time bombs installed. There is no proof they were destroyed at our hand."

"Proof is rarely a weapon of justice, certainly not of the ilk served by our friend Gorruk," said the ancient kone lounging in the corner.

"Our wise and worthy Samamkook is correct, of course," Et Kalass agreed. "We may have to relent. How goes Gorruk's latest attack?" He turned his attention from the window, back to the long wall of his office suite, on which strategic maps were arrayed.

"He has broken out to the west, along the Massif of Rouue. Et Barbluis is ready for him at the highlands. They engage at day's end."

"So many to die!" the minister said. "When will we be free of this?"

"With the restoration, m'lord!" the general said a bit too loudly.

"It is dangerous to flatter ourselves," Samamkook said.

"Truth and freedom were in our past," Et Ralfkra said. "So will they be in our future."

"Only if our kings are pure and wise—a difficult challenge for mortal kones, good General. Even those of unblemished nobility," Et Kalass reflected. "And let us not forget: our pretender is himself in grave danger."

Gorruk's attacking advance was met by superior forces occupying developed defensive positions—a recipe for disaster—but Gorruk was not to be denied. It was a disaster, a disaster for both sides, and despite horrendous casualties, casualties no sane military commander could tolerate, Gorruk's forces rolled over the bodies of dead multitudes and climbed the high ground. Marshal Et Barbluis's lines were irresistibly bent and then finally broken by Gorruk's maniacal charges, ammunition depleted on both sides, blasters melted, soldiers reduced to scratching, clawing, stabbing, and clubbing. General Gorruk was prominent on the front lines, exhorting and goading, brave and resolute, constantly exposing himself to enemy fire. At one critical juncture he personally led a charge against an enemy strong point, suffering a superficial wound. He was seen to wipe the blood across his face as he pressed onward, onward toward the objective, screaming the battle cry of his ancient tribe. His men, witnesses to the inspiring charge, carried everything before them and would not be stopped. The southern army retreated, gravely mauled, leaving the field to the bleeding barbarians of Gorruk's decimated armies.

TWENTY-EIGHT

WINTER

"A girl!" Buccari announced, walking into the low rock-walled barracks. "Goldberg's doing fine."

A cheer erupted from the crew, followed by raucous comments and laughter. Cliff dwellers peeked into the barracks area, curious. Buccari, closest to the entryway, used crude sign language to indicate a pregnant belly and a babe in arms. The old female attendants went away chirping, smiles on their ugly faces.

"So ... uh, who does it look like?" Tatum asked.

Everyone laughed and hooted, pounding the tall marine on the back.

"So who does it look like?" he persisted.

"It's not an it, you big dork!" Lee admonished. "It's a she! Her name's Honey. She looks like a little monkey, just like all newborns."

"Fenstermacher, you dog!" Wilson shouted.

"Leave me out of this!" the little man protested. "I'm innocent."

"You mean impotent," O'Toole jibed.

Laughter echoed from the narrow walls—for a change. Cramped quarters and forced indolence had been telling; tempers ran short, and attitudes were sour. Their small world had become a prison.

"Do you think I can see her?" Tatum asked softly.

"Won't hurt to ask," Buccari said. "I'm expecting Lizard soon. I'll write out a request. Anyone else want to go?" It was a silly question; they all raised their hands. "I'll see what we can do." She laughed.

"So what did you see?" Hudson asked.

261

"Corridors, polished floors. Running water. Lots of rock. And elevators! They have elevators," Buccari said.

"They covered our heads," Lee added. "Pepper's room looks like this, only smaller and much warmer. She says they never put her under anesthetic. She had to work hard, and it took hours, but she feels good—and strong."

"Get this!" Buccari exclaimed. "They delivered the baby under water! Goldberg says they put her in a dark room with a stone tub filled with hot water."

"That used to be done on Earth," Lee said.

There were few sanctuaries at Goldmine, the science expedition's retreat for the winter. Dowornobb and Kateos, mature adults, realized they were suited for mating and wished to discuss the delicate matter fully and candidly. They discovered the necessary solitude under the dome housing the station's fruit and vegetable gardens. The agricultural dome did not have elevated pressure, but the temperature was moderated. By the kones' perspective it was uncomfortably cold. Dowornobb could not even imagine what it was like outside.

Frigid winds blew leaves and debris against the dome's surface. It was snowing. The first soft flakes of the season whirled before driving winds, striking and sliding across the translucent surface; ridges of white snow accumulated on the dome's seams. Embedded heating coils in the dome shell kept the ridges wet and narrow, causing melting snow to slide downward across the dome in long streamers of ice. Dowornobb and Kateos sat on a green bench, helmets off, staring dreamily at the strange precipitation and its effects on the dome. They had talked for many minutes yet had said little.

"I am told each snowflake is unique," Kateos sighed.

"Et Silmarn claims the entire ground, as far as the eye can see, will be covered in white by the end of the day," Dowornobb said. He stood, walked to the dome, and tested its temperature. He yanked his bare hand away and returned it to his glove. "Ouch! Quite cold!"

He ambled back to the bench and looked at Kateos. She sat unnaturally quiet and demure. Dowornobb had grown accustomed to her loquaciousness and spontaneity—characteristics she revealed, with interesting exceptions, only to him. The import of their conversation was affecting him in similar ways. He sat, picked up her gloved hand, and gave it a gentle squeeze. She pressed his in return, averting her eyes.

"Our lives have become complicated," he said.

"Yet at the same time more purposeful," she replied softly. "Our lives are more defined." She looked upward and outward, staring resolutely through the falling snowflakes.

"I wish to express my feelings, Mistress Kateos," he said softly.

"You have done so already, and without words, Master Dowornobb." She turned to look deeply into his eyes. If Dowornobb had retained any thoughts of independence or equivocation in the matter—which he did not—that sweet, simple, yet intense glance would have crushed all ambivalence. Dowornobb felt his gay heart and free soul climb through his eyes; he desperately wanted to belong to the female, and in wanting to belong, he needed also to possess.

"It is said that life is long, no matter how few the days, when life is shared," he said after many entranced moments.

"And it is said," Kateos added, continuing the litany, "that true love is a perpetually blooming flower that knows not seasons and can never die."

Dowornobb's passions swelled, and doubts vanished. His love scent lifted. "Mistress Kateos, our lives are uncertain. I am but a common kone, and I cannot promise comfort and wealth—"

"If certainty and wealth were that important to you, then I would rather not continue this conversation," she interrupted most rudely.

"Please, Mistress Kateos," the exasperated male said, struggling to maintain his composure and train of thought. "Your welfare and happiness will be my responsibility. You must permit me to express my concerns even if I am incapable of eloquence."

"Yes, Master Dowornobb," Kateos replied. "Want not eloquence if you speak sincerely."

He stared into her large, lustrous brown eyes and found himself a dazed wanderer, lost in love, not caring where he went but ever so thankful for the chance to take the voyage. Time floated by. The air thickened with his essence.

"Master Dowornobb?" she whispered, bringing him back to the moment.

"Yes?" he said blankly. "Oh, yes!" His objective clearly in front of him, he shored up his resolve yet again and stated his position. "I want you as my mate, forever and without end."

There! It was said—a bit tersely. But she made it so difficult for him to think and talk. She looked down at the ground. No response was forthcoming. Just as he was about to expound further, she spoke.

"I have no choice in the matter. You have selected me, so I am bound to submit and to obey. It is the rule—my life is yours. Of course, I am honored." Her head bent low in submission; a large pellucid tear welled up and clung to her lower lid. She blinked, and it fell to the ground.

"Thank you, Mistress Kateos, for your formal acceptance," Dowornobb said quietly. Now it was easy for him to speak. Her abject posture injected him with the urgent need to relate his feelings. Dowornobb was a scientist and a freethinker. He loathed the orthodoxy of his society, especially if it would interfere with his ability to express his emotions or understand the emotions of another.

"We share a bond, an understanding, a feeling," he stated quietly but with escalating passion, "something deeper and more profound than ancient rules." It was his turn to lecture. "I want to be your companion. I want you to be my companion—for life—forever and always. I want you as my mate not because I have ordered it so and not because I am willing to take social responsibility for your children. I want you to be my mate because, and only because, you wish to be. If that is not the case, you may walk from me and not turn back. I will not invoke the social rules, and I would be disappointed if those were your reasons for submitting to my wish."

She gazed into his face as he lectured, and her demeanor fairly glowed with each word of admonishment. Dowornobb detected her scent exploding in waves.

"I promise you!" she declared effusively, taking Dowornobb aback. "I promise you that my acceptance demonstrates my expression of free will. I am yours forever. I am yours because I want to be. You are my master."

"I am your mate," he said emphatically, their scents blending.

She squeezed his hand, tears flowing freely down her beautiful face. "My mate, this promise is an undying flame. It will always be kindled, and it cannot be extinguished," she said with a liquid fervor that made Dowornobb's emotional bubble nearly burst with boundless ecstasy.

Stemming his exhilaration, Dowornobb stared into her eyes and declared his love. "The promise is the marriage. The marriage is the promise. We are mated. I will file the necessary papers."

"We must keep them isolated," Koop-the-facilitator whistled. "They are boisterous and rude! They are unclean, and they smell bad. We fear they may be evil!" The assembled body of elders and guild representatives listened to the harangues cataloging the questionable behavior of their guests. The cliff dwellers could not countenance the long-legs' voracious appetites, their rambunctiousness, their rudeness.

"With immense respect, my elder," Toon chirped from the visitors' gallery, standing without sanction and unrecognized. "May I speak?"

The facilitator looked down from the assembly podium, irritated with the impudent interruption. The hall was occupied primarily by members of the dweller congress, the duly elected guild and hunter officials.

"Ah, supervisor Toon!" the facilitator acknowledged. "Thy reports art the basis of our findings. What is it thou would say?"

"I humbly address the council," the steam user replied. "My reports have not served thee well, for while thy decision to continue the quarantine may be correct, thy logic for doing so is faulty."

The assemblage murmured at the steam user's blatant affront.

"The crude behavior of the long-legs should not be seen as evil or base," Toon continued hurriedly, desperately holding on to his courage. "The long-legs are different. We should reserve judgment until we have a better understanding. Arrogant and ill mannered, yes, but they are not evil. They desire to be good, but they act as individuals, selfishly and without common purpose."

Murmurs grew louder. Toon raised his voice and continued. "I humbly propose the long-legs be provided with labor, even if it means exposing them to our society. Gainful employment will exhaust their energies in worthwhile endeavor, and it will serve to give them value in our eyes."

The great hall was silent. The council of elders stared down at the lone engineer as if he were an insect. The silence lingered.

"Toon's words have merit," interjected Braan, leader-of-the-hunters. He stood erect, not apologizing for the parliamentary breach.

Koop glared down. Such disruptions reflected ill on his leadership.

"The hunter leader is recognized," the facilitator warbled with poorly concealed resignation.

"Permission to speak is humbly accepted," Braan whistled as he took the speaker's dock, talons clicking obnoxiously.

"Hunters have billeted the long-legs for four cycles of the small moon and have watched the long-legs firsthand—not from rumor or from steam user Toon's reports. The long-legs have good qualities—many good qualities. If they are evil, then we are equally so."

Remonstrative jeers whistled around the assembly hall. Braan turned and belligerently scanned the members, defiantly waiting for the disruption to attenuate. The floor was his.

"It is true they behave offensively," the hunter screeched over the din. "They gesture obscenely. They stare with fixed eye contact! They consume great amounts of precious food, only to convert it to malodorous waste! They seldom wash, and their bodies stink. They are loud. They respect not our customs. They even fight among themselves. All of this is true. Yes, it is true! But that does not provide reason to condemn. It illustrates only that they are different."

A long speech for a hunter. Braan concluded: "Listen to steam user Toon. His counsel is well measured." The hunter returned to his seat.

The hall was silent, and the facilitator recognized Toon.

The spacers waited nervously in the dark, damp cavern. Although they could not see the river, its muted roar required them to raise their voices. Steam was thick and warm around them, yet icicles dripped from the ceiling and along catwalk chain railings. Dim globes stretched out before them, a string of dingy yellow pearls disappearing in the distant curve of the cavern. Sixty meters below and on the other side of the channel another necklace of spirit lamps ran parallel to the first, following the channel course at the cavern's bottom. Dwellers worked in the dim light, splashing, scraping, and pounding in the wet channel bottom. Lurking in shadows behind them, a mysterious guilder stood between lamps, watching them.

"Who's that?" MacArthur asked.

"Lizard's boss," Hudson replied. "That's the guy we have to impress."

"He's not impressing me slinking in the shadows," O'Toole said.

"Stop staring," Shannon said. "It makes them real nervous."

The spacers turned their attention to Buccari and the cliff dweller walking toward them. The beings from different worlds had been scouting the cavern, silently communicating, using sign language and writing.

"We're sediment cleaners," Buccari announced. The taller human males circled the twosome, compelling the dweller to take an involuntary step backward. Buccari reached over, put an arm around the dweller's back, and firmly pulled him into their huddle.

"Mr. Lizard's been explaining the accumulators to me," Buccari said, "and why they need to be cleaned. This cavern is one of four accumulator channels. They have closed and drained it so sediment-cleaning teams can clear away rocks, silt, and other debris that have been deposited since the last cleaning. All four of the channels are behind schedule for cleaning. Last year's flow was one of the heaviest in their history, and it left behind tremendous amounts of sediment and debris. We are to join one of the cleaning teams, and after we learn the job, we train the rest of our crew and form our own team. It's a big job."

"Sounds like forced labor to me," Petit said.

"We're working for food and shelter," Buccari told him. "No one's forcing you to do anything. You can leave anytime you like, Petit."

"Eh, sorry, Lieutenant," he replied. "I didn't mean—"

"Yeah, that's okay," Buccari said. "This place gives me the creeps, too." Liquid scraping noises echoed through the dripping, musty cavern.

"We need the work," MacArthur said. "Let's get going."

"Okay, you know how important this is," Buccari said. "We earn our keep, and we have a chance to prove we're not worthless, which our friend tells me is the case right now. Anything beats sitting around on our fannies all winter."

"What do they accumulate in an accumulator channel, Lieutenant?" Shannon asked.

"Energy! Potential energy to be precise," Buccari replied. "River water is selectively diverted into a channel, depending on the availability of water and energy needs. Each channel has a series of geared waterwheels used to hoist large weights up vertical distances. The cables suspending these weights can be disengaged from the waterwheels and connected to other drive mechanisms. It's a gigantic mechanical storage battery."

"That must be how they drive the elevators," Hudson said. "Did you see the weights and the gearing systems? They must be something."

"Just a peek," Buccari replied. "That's still off limits. Lizard was reluctant to tell me about it. I just kept asking questions until he caved in. So to speak."

MacArthur snorted. "How is it so warm in, uh—a cave this big?"

"Steam," Buccari said. "They collect steam. Water flowing through the channels is diverted into some sort of magma chamber. This produces gobs of steam, which is collected in low-pressure accumulators and released to drive pistons and turbines. A lot of steam backflows into the caverns. Lizard has cautioned me a dozen times on the dangers of steam geysers and scalding water."

"Hot showers, eh? All right!" O'Toole said.

"Yeah, hot! Very, very hot!" Buccari warned.

"Does that mean they have electricity?" Hudson asked.

"No, not that I can tell," Buccari answered. "I couldn't explain the concept to Lizard, either. All the steam energy is dissipated mechanically or used directly as heat."

"What do we use for tools?" Shannon asked.

"Good question. Evidently our tools are waiting for us. Let's go," Buccari said. "We have to climb to the channel bottom. Be careful. Our friend keeps telling me the work is dangerous, so keep your mouths shut and pay attention."

"Aye, aye, sir!" they shouted in unison.

Hundreds of spirit lamps were shrouded with dark blue globes. The hall flickered in yellows and blues. The quiet chittering of the gathered masses abruptly lowered in intensity as two hundred votaries, adult females dressed in orange robes, appeared at the entrances and dispersed into the hall, moving slowly about the central stage, lighting more candles. Bool, sitting in the masters' gallery, watched the scintillating patterns, enchanted as any child.

"Toon's idea has proved to be an excellent one," Koop whispered. The elder had stopped for a subdued chat with the old steam user. Together, the dwellers watched the multiplying points of light.

"Without question, sagacious one," Bool responded. "My doubts have been dispelled. After only two moon cycles of instruction the long-legs are twice as productive as an equal number of dwellers, despite their inexperience. With another moon cycle of experience they will clear sediment at thrice the rate of our best teams. We are designing special tools to take advantage of their leverage and reach."

"Is it only because they are so strong?" the facilitator asked. "I am told they destroy tools because they wield them with such force."

"Perhaps," Bool responded. "And yet Toon tells me they have brought innovation to the task. We have been doing it the same way for so long that we have stopped looking for other ways. It goes well. Sediment clearing is actually on schedule—a miracle."

"Excellent to hear—sssh! The ceremony is starting. I must take my place. Good year and long life." The facilitator moved to his position behind the central podium as high-toned bells rang sharply. The votaries arrayed themselves, and the hall fell silent.

The celebration of the shortest day of the year began with the prolonged, rhythmic pealing of a single bell—a sweet tone. Then the singing began, distant and muted. Rich harmony and expansive breadth of tone emanated from the cliff dwellers, their delicate mechanisms physically resonating in the glory of transsonic music—a deep, nearly sexual stimulation overwhelming all other senses. The procession of choirs commenced. Singing grew in volume and intensity as thousands of females robed in royal blue filed in, stately and erect, moving as slowly as the passage of the stars. Time was not perceived, for the singing was ethereal, and all present prayed it would never end.

Another bell, large and deep-toned, pealed three times, and the elders slipped from their perches. A crooning rose from the choirs, signaling the arrival of the judges and priestesses—females all, robed in black. The regal entourage moved with dignified yet graceful speed to positions around the great hall. Several mounted the stairs to the central stage. Over half were small—hunter females—including the high priestess, for hunters were the best singers.

The high priestess moved to the raised stage center and

faced the multitude, lifting her arms high, wing membranes luminously backlighted in blue, the very image of beauty and purity. Yellow fires danced at her feet, highlighting her prominent features. She slowly lowered her arms, and all present, male and female, adult and child, raised voices in harmonious accord, increasing the volume in a majestic crescendo. The high priestess raised her arms once again, and the female tones surfaced from the powerful male background harmonies; a lush ululation rose in wave upon wave; alternating harmonics of male and female origin, a yin and yang of sound, tumbled around each other, melding into one. The high priestess, feeling the time was right, dropped her arms sharply.

Silence.

The high priestess stared outward and upward, eyes closed, her vision confined to the sonic realm. She uttered sounds musically, quietly. Yet every pure harmonic emanation was clearly heard by each dweller in the hall. She projected—transmitted—her message at a multitude of sonic levels, and the acute receptors of the audience received and resolved her vibrations.

"We are blessed, my people," she trilled. "We are blessed. With children. We are blessed with salt and warmth. We are blessed." She paused. The audience responded with a musical affirmation, an "amen" of surpassing harmony.

"We are blessed, my people," the litany continued. "We are blessed. With food. We are blessed with flowers and families. We are indeed blessed." The audience responded with greater passion.

"The gods abide in our hearts and in our souls. They live in our rocks, in the mountains and cliffs. They live in the waters of lakes and rivers. We are blessed. They look down from the moons, and they illuminate the sun and the stars. Each tree, each blade of grass, each drop of rain, each starry snowflake—they are each and every one a benevolent and compassionate spirit. We are blessed. The gods are everywhere, and they are just. The gods are just and fair. We are blessed. We are so very blessed. Let us sing! Let us sing our thanks for our many blessings. Let us sing."

The voices in the assembly hall were forcefully raised in harmonic unison, a powerful testimony to the rising fervor of the moment. Wave upon wave of multidimensional sound permeated the great hall, rebounding from still stone walls and reinforcing the next wave of song newly sent forth. The younger fledglings in the audience could only tremble before the power of the uplifted voices. Bells sounded in rolling peals, and the harmonious tumult continued unabated. Spirit lamp globes vibrated, and the very rock on which they stood buzzed in sympathetic harmony, warming with the transmission of sonic energy.

Time passed but was not measured, and when it was right, the high priestess raised thin arms. Blue and gold light danced from her wings, and the concord of tones and whistles, of bells and songs, subsided in subliminal thresholds, falling through innumerable levels of frequency and harmony, until only a small portion of the choir was left chanting. And with lingering glory, the last exquisite sounds drifted into exalted silence. The high priestess scanned the audience from her elevated platform. A radiant smile reflected her contentment and inner light.

"We are blessed. We are blessed with the voices of our ancestors," the high priestess said, tears of joy giving her speech liquid qualities. "We are so very blessed." The assembled multitude responded humbly but with great passion.

The deep, heavy bell tolled again, six times, and the high priestess gestured dramatically. Judges strode forward—nine tall guilder females. They arrayed themselves, solemn and imposing, behind nine onyx podiums. They wore the same orange robes as the votaries, but they also wore necklaces of sparkling onyx. The audience was as silent as the very rock, for it was the time of reckoning. Those dwellers who had willfully caused harm would be banished, doomed to die in the freezing wastelands.

"We are blessed," intoned the high priestess, "with justice. Let justice have voice!"

The hall was still, a stillness beyond silence. And the trials began.

"It's cold!" Fenstermacher complained, feeding the ante.

"It's cold every day!" Chief Wilson said, dealing the cards.

"Stop complaining! It's a hell of a lot colder back at the cave," Dawson chided.

"So what's going on, Lieutenant? Why the day off?" Wilson asked. He sat on a deep pile of furs, looking at his poker hand.

Buccari pored over stacks of dweller writings—the dictionary. The collection of writings and drawings had grown large. Hudson and MacArthur were helping her organize the icons and symbols.

"Liz wouldn't say," she replied. "He said we had to stay in our barracks today. Some kind of religious day—a holiday, maybe?"

"There are extra guards down the passageway," Shannon said. "I pass."

"A religious day?" Fenstermacher asked. "What kind of religion do they have?"

"Hard to say," Buccari answered. "Some kind of animism."

"What?" Fenstermacher persisted. "They worship animals?"

"They worship everything," MacArthur answered. "To them every rock, tree, and mountain has a soul. They worship the planet. And they have different sects or life purposes—the tall ones, the workers, actually pray to the rocks, or to the plants, or to the fish, or to the stream, depending on their training. The hunters worship the wild animals."

Buccari looked up. The marine, standing close to her, was suddenly embarrassed and avoided her eyes.

"You're picking this up quickly, Mac," she said thickly. "Keep at it. More of us need to communicate with our new friends. It's like learning how to read." MacArthur blushed and smiled weakly in return.

"Yeah, Mac," Hudson agreed, absorbed in the material before him. "This stuff is ambiguous, and Sharl, er—Lieutenant Buccari never buys my interpretation. Like this, Sharl; check this out."

"What's it in response to?" she asked. Hudson had organized a keying system to match questions with answers.

"It relates to the series of questions on other races and peoples," Hudson replied. "We were trying to determine if they had ever seen other aliens or flying machines."

"Yeah," Buccari said. "And . . ."

"I read this sequence to say they've seen flying machines but not recently—not in four years, and then only rarely before that. They also describe giants or bear people. Here, tell me what you think." He pushed the parchment sheets over to Buccari, and she stared at them. MacArthur moved tentatively closer.

"You're right, Nash," she said after a while. "This indicates that the dwellers saw loud rigid-wing flying objects. Four winters, er—years ago." Buccari stared at the pages, shifting her view. "Their mythology includes stories of large people—giants or bear people—emerging from such flying machines.

The bear people had weapons that made music or sang. Weapons that killed from great distances."

"Giants, eh?" Wilson remarked. The poker game halted in midhand.

"Don't forget," Hudson said, "they think of us as giants, too."

"Not quite the same, Nash," Buccari interrupted. "Lizard uses this term *big* to describe us. The term he uses to describe the mythical beings seems to be more emphatic, a difference of degree. Liz makes it clear that no living dweller has seen one of these mythical bear people, but many dwellers have seen their flying machines."

"How about the singing weapons?" MacArthur asked. "Lasers?"

"Good guess," Shannon said soberly.

Everyone's attention was drawn to the entrance to their living quarters. Chastain and Gordon walked in, shaking snow from their furs.

"We thought we heard something," Chastain said.

"Like what, Jocko?" Buccari asked.

"Music, bells, whistling, or—something. Weird noises. It kinda got under your skin. Kinda pretty, though," he said thoughtfully.

"I miss music," Dawson said absentmindedly. She started humming a long-forgotten tune. After a short period she stopped abruptly and looked around, embarrassed.

"It was pretty, Nancy," Lee said. "Don't stop."

"I'm embarrassed," she replied.

"You mean embarrassing," Fenstermacher chuckled. Dawson's thrown boot missed badly.

Wilson stood up. "I used to sing. I remember some old songs."

"Don't go singing beer-drinking songs," Shannon jibed.

"Yes! Keep it clean, Gunner," Buccari requested.

"He can't even breathe and do that," Fenstermacher needled.

Everyone laughed as Wilson chased Fenstermacher into the cold passageway. Buccari turned back to the dweller writings and pondered the future. It was going to be a long winter. She looked up to see MacArthur staring at her. He grinned bashfully and turned away, his color rising. No one but Buccari noticed.

Dawson and Wilson began harmonizing an ancient carol. Soon all were singing, and it was beautiful.

TWENTY-NINE

SPRING

The alpine lake in MacArthur's valley was expansive, a full day's hike to circumnavigate. At its southern end, on the eastern side, a finger of forest protruded, forming a cove. Wooded islets further protected the mouth of the harbor. MacArthur had seized on the locale early in his valley explorations. Besides sheltered access to the lake, there was an abundance of wood—evergreen and hardwood—and the soil seemed favorable for planting. But the primary attraction was the spring, an irrepressible knuckle of sweet water bubbling from the ground. It flowed energetically across flower-margined stones to the cove's sandy beach.

"Ouch, this water's cold," Goldberg said, squatting next to the gurgling spring, rinsing fish entrails from her hands. Fat lake fish lay beheaded and gutted on the rocks. A hunter perched near-by, watching with obvious interest. Dawson had named him Bluenose.

"Chief Wilson's got a pot of water on the fire," Dawson said, cleaning her knife in the sand. "Let's see if we can clean off some of this smell."

"I feel like I've been gutting fish all my life," Goldberg moaned.

"Cheer up," Dawson said, throwing Bluenose a piece of fish. The hunter deftly caught it in his long jaw and swallowed it whole. "Hudson says today is our anniversary. We've been here one Earth year."

"That's supposed to make me feel better?" Goldberg asked, looking up at the sound of a tree crashing to the ground. Tookmanian and Schmidt were clearing timber up the hill. Downhill, near the cove beach, Lee and Mendoza tilled black, muddy soil only recently uncovered by receding lake waters.

One of the tall dwellers, a gardener, scurried about, hoe in hand and a satchel of seeds about its neck.

"Give me a hand, little momma," Dawson pleaded, collecting her gear, including a pistol. At least one person in every work group was armed; the cove's largest drawback was the number of Gargantuan bears that still considered it their territory. Two grizzled monsters had already paid with their truculent lives; their furs were stretched on tanning frames downwind from the tents.

"Damn, Nancy, are you getting big!" Goldberg exclaimed, helping the awkward Dawson to her feet, both women grunting like teamsters. Dawson's clothes no longer fit, and she was draped with loose furs and hides. Makeshift robes shifted indelicately as she gained her feet. Above a pair of men's space boots rose the twin pillars of her bare white legs, sharply muscled and covered with fine red hair. A tangle of pelts attempted to cover her heavy-boned frame and distended belly. Her freckled, coarse features were sunburned. An explosion of fiery red hair shot from her head.

"A pregnant cave woman!" Goldberg hooted.

"Don't tease, Pepper!" Dawson pleaded. "You ain't no bargain."

"Thank you," Goldberg replied with exaggerated sophistication, posturing a lean body that had been made hard and wiry by unending work.

"Let's haul this bear bait up to the tents," Dawson said, eyeing the opportunistic hunter. "Can't leave it here."

"I stink," Goldberg whined, putting the cleaned fish into a basket.

They walked uphill to the tent circle, where the odors of wood smoke and leather blended flagrantly. Fenstermacher, laboring with strips of precious hide, sat on the ground next to the cook fire. He struggled to stitch two strips together, binding them around a wooden frame.

"Brat's awake," Fenstermacher grumbled, concentrating on his work. "She's making noises. Already makes more sense than her old man, but what ain't smarter than a marine?"

"Thanks for watching her, Winnie," Goldberg said, putting the fish next to the fire and taking a dipper of hot water. After washing the scales and smell from her hands, Goldberg leaned into one of the tents. Honey lay on her back, nestled in furs, playing with her toes. Goldberg leaned over and grabbed the brown infant, saddling it on her hip.

A layer of clouds scudded darkly overhead, threatening more rain. They had already suffered one ferocious storm. Goldberg draped a plush nightmare skin over Honey's back. The baby clung tightly to her mother.

"I can't believe Shannon is letting you use those hides to build a boat," Dawson said. "What a waste."

Fenstermacher squinted in concentration, a length of rawhide in his mouth. He mumbled something obscene.

A monotonous thumping drifted across the clearing; Tookmanian and Schmidt still labored at the forest's edge, their axes arcing in the sharp light. Uphill from the tents, near the gushing spring, sat Chief Wilson, his ample bottom firmly planted on a stump carved into a chair; a dweller ax lay at his feet. Buccari and Shannon stood with him, gesturing with sweeping motions. Tonto, Buccari's ubiquitous companion, perched on a fallen log.

"Hey, Chief," Goldberg shouted, "I'm tired of women's work. All we do is sew and clean fish."

Wilson and Buccari turned. Shannon was already facing the two women, his eyes affectionately on Dawson. Wilson was wet with perspiration.

"Too damn bad, Goldbrick!" Wilson snapped. "I don't know what to say. Here!" He reached down and grabbed the ax, throwing it at Goldberg's feet. Tonto's head jerked upward. "Take my job and chop and haul those logs. I'll be happy to do a little sewing. Yeah! And after I get some sewing done, I'll still have time for my other job. Yeah! Real man's work—cooking!"

"Whoa, Gunner! Easy does it," Buccari interjected. Her auburn ponytail, streaked from the sun, twitched across her shoulders. "Goldberg wasn't trying to make trouble."

"Hrmmph," Wilson snorted. "She never *tries* to."

"You hit Chief Wilson at the wrong time, Pepper," Buccari said. "Be patient. You have a baby to take care of, and Dawson's not in shape to do much of anything. Give it time."

"Sure, Lieutenant," Dawson jumped in. "Gosh, Chief! Didn't know you'd lost your sense of humor or we would've been nice to you, just like we usually are."

"Pick on someone your own size, Dawson!" Wilson snarled.

"That's more like it," Dawson replied. She winked at Shannon, put her arm around Goldberg's back, and gently pushed her up the hill.

"Come on, trouble, let's go see how the guys are doing," Dawson said.

The two ladies continued walking, leaving the tent clearing. Goldberg shifted the baby to her other hip and readjusted her furs as they walked into the forest toward the quarry where most of the men were hewing rocks. Large-boled trees and thick underbrush lined both sides of the climbing path.

"The bitch!" Goldberg spit.

"Pardon me?" Dawson replied. "You can't—"

"Bullshit! Who's she to tell us to be patient!" Goldberg snapped. "She's the boss man. An officer! She has no idea what it's like for us."

"Come on, Pepper! Enough," Dawson replied.

"She's not one of us. She doesn't know what it's like to be treated like a woman! We get all the crap jobs, and she gets to be king shit!"

"Slow down, Goldie. You're not making sense." Dawson grabbed her large belly and inhaled.

"I'd like to see her pregnant. That'd get her off her high horse . . . the bitch."

"Pepper! That's not right!" Dawson stopped. "We're lucky she's strong. You wouldn't want her job, not even for a ticket home. She's got all of us to worry about! And how would you like to try and tell these muscleheads how to act? You think that's easy? She's doing it! And they listen to her. She's the boss!" Dawson belched.

"She outranks everybody. They have to listen," Goldberg rebutted.

"Nonsense! If Buccari showed even the slightest weakness, they'd run over her like dogs. It'd be the law of the jungle, and you know it." Dawson hiccuped.

"But—" Goldberg started to say.

"Nobody got us pregnant but ourselves!" Dawson interrupted, hiccuping again.

"Didn't know you could get pregnant by yourself," Goldberg retorted.

"You know what I mean. The law's on your side. Until you get pregnant. And then the responsibility's all yours. You take the consequences. Right? Give Buccari credit for not getting pregnant. Give her a lot of credit. I bet she's been having a tough time."

"Nobody would have her. It'd be like humping mud . . . frozen mud."

Dawson laughed. "That wouldn't stop these marines. She's smart and she's gorgeous, and you know it. You're just jealous."

Goldberg started crying, and so did Honey.

"Come on, Pepper," Dawson said softly. "I'm sorry, but it's just not fair to pick on Buccari." She pulled Honey away from her mother.

"You're right," Goldberg sobbed. "But I'm tired of being cold and dirty. I'm tired of cleaning fish—of eating fish. Oh, Nancy, we're never going to be rescued."

"Oh, Pepper," Dawson said. "Who knows? But getting down on Buccari isn't going to help matters. She needs our help." She put an arm around Goldberg's shoulders and pulled her close. Goldberg stiffened, but the embrace was irresistible; the fetus kicking in Dawson's womb became a shared sensation, and Goldberg's short arms moved reluctantly around Dawson's tall waist.

Dowornobb and Kateos flew as loading crew for the fuel-staging flights on the fourth and final leg of the last staging flight, each leg a half day of flying, prepositioning barrels of fuel for future search flights. Scientist Lollee was the pilot, and Et Avian the copilot. Their destination was a large, steep-sided plateau that Lollee had been to once before—four years earlier.

"Et Silmarn told us about flying creatures that live in the mountains along the river," Kateos said. "Mountain fliers. Have you seen them?"

Kateos leaned over the backs of Lollee and Et Avian. Dowornobb slept on the floor of the passenger compartment.

"Three times," Lollee answered. "But always from the abat. You find them only in the far north. Very elusive—they soar on the updrafts, reaching remarkable altitudes." He adjusted his trim and reset the autopilot to track the river channel.

"The official reports are from the early days," he continued. "In the early days mountain fliers and other Genellan animals were hunted for their fur. Mountain fliers were found in abundance, but their numbers were greatly reduced during the fur trading. An ugly business."

"Et Silmarn joked about the creatures' intelligence," Kateos said.

"No joke," Lollee replied. "They possess intelligence. Some were found wearing leather garments and carrying weapons. I have seen pictures of the relics. The early science teams spent more time in the northern latitudes looking for rare metals. An organized science expedition has not come this far north in nearly two hundred years."

"Why has there not been more exploration?" Kateos asked. "I should think we would want to find out more about these creatures."

"Our government does not want to expend the resources. It is difficult and expensive to support extended operations this far north—and dangerous. The upper Corlian Valley is a cold, unforgiving place," Lollee responded. "Herds of musk-buffalo abound. Your breathing units will not help for long around the musk-buffalo. Huge bears, too! There are many, many bears in the river valley, not to mention predator lizards, abats, and growlers. You must be wary at all times. And the volcanoes in the Corlian Valley have high sulfurous gas emissions. And it is very, very cold. A most treacherous region."

The river curved in a wide arc to the west, and Lollee banked the craft to follow its course. The sun, setting behind the majestic mountains, shone like spun gold through wispy auroras of blown snow.

Buccari stood on the lodge site, discussing building plans with MacArthur and Shannon. Lizard stood at her shoulder, stylus and parchment in hand. Two guilder stone carvers watched and listened, their tools laid neatly before them. Tonto and X.O. waddled uphill from the cove. With earsplitting suddenness Tonto and X.O. screamed, whipped out their membranes, and pounded into the air. The guilders jumped with alarm and hopped about nervously, clasping bony hands together. MacArthur leapt to his feet, his eyes jerking skyward. Buccari started to speak, but then her ears also detected the sound. It took a second for her brain to process the mechanical signal. *An airplane engine!*

"Airplane!" she shouted. "Get under the trees! Kill the fire!"

The aircraft appeared from behind the valley's northeastern rim, still catching the full light of the sun, starkly white against the deep blue sky. So civilized in appearance, so familiar in design and function—it was difficult not to run into the open, yelling and screaming, difficult not to throw armfuls of wood on the fire, signaling the craft to return, to rescue them from their barbarism. But it was not a rescuer. It was the enemy. The airplane's undeviating course carried it along the river and out of sight to the west. The sound of its engine echoed from the high mountains long after it had disappeared.

The campfire had been small, and Wilson doused it completely with a large pot of water. The valley was covered in shadows; it was unlikely that the plane's occupants had observed the cloud of steam.

The humans recovered from their amazement, dropped their tools, and converged on the camp area. Tonto and X.O. dropped from the sky, and the other dwellers joined them, chattering intently. Within minutes everyone was assembled around the smoldering campfire, looking like frightened children.

"Have they found us?" MacArthur asked.

"They're close," Buccari replied. "It's taken them long enough."

"What do we do, Lieutenant?" Chastain asked for everyone present.

Buccari looked at the worried faces and tried to hide her own fear.

"There's not much we can do," she said, straining her troubled mind for a plan. "No fire—at least tonight. We have plenty of dried fish and biscuits." She stooped and picked up a rock.

"We've talked about this before, and I keep arriving at the same conclusions. Sooner or later we'll confront them." She sat down on a stump. "When that time comes, we must not show hostility or aggression, and—this is the hardest—we must not show fear. We must appear strong and confident yet cooperative."

"What happens if they start shooting?" boomed Tatum.

Buccari looked down at her feet, hiding her face behind a fall of copper-bronze hair. She moved the sun-streaked tresses away with her hand.

"We'll probably die," she said firmly.

The humans stirred nervously. Hudson jumped to his feet.

"We can't run, and we can't hide—for long," he said. "We can try to stay hidden for as long as possible, but once they find us, they'll catch us. We can't fight them."

"Why can't we hide?" MacArthur asked. "This is a big planet. They don't live here."

"Several problems," Buccari responded, looking into the marine's serious face. "They'll narrow down the search area. Then our biggest problem comes into play—we're a group.

Maybe, Mac, you by yourself and possibly the marines as a group could avoid detection and capture indefinitely, although I wouldn't give good odds. The only way to survive the winter is to be prepared, and that means building shelters and raising crops while the sun shines—activities that leave big tracks." She glanced around the clearing, noting the straight lines and clutter of their nascent settlement.

"The rest of us are less adapted to running and fighting," she continued. "Sooner or later we'll leave a trail that brings them to us. When that time arrives, when they show up, we must show strength, strength of character. And then be prepared for the worst."

"It's better to fight," Tatum said. "Can't the rest of you adapt?"

"Look at Goldberg and that little baby! Look at Dawson!" Buccari rebutted his argument. "Try to tell me you can run and fight with that on your hands."

Tatum looked at his feet and said nothing.

"Once you start shooting at the aliens, you become their enemy," Buccari said, pressing the point. "And they will hunt you down."

"But they shot at us in space," Chastain complained.

"It's their system. They make the rules," Buccari answered. "We have a chance of convincing them we mean no harm. That's our best hope. You shoot at them, and I guarantee you'll piss them off, and then we're all dead. Or worse."

"Shouldn't we go looking for them—the aliens?" O'Toole asked. "I'd rather find them before they found us."

"Yeah! We could take them out!" Tatum said, fire in his eyes. His tone surprised Buccari. Tatum, even with one arm, was transforming back into a soldier, a trained performer of mayhem. She looked at the marines and noted similar transformations in all of them: an enemy was near. They were not listening. She looked to Shannon for support.

"O'Toole!" Shannon snapped. "How much ammunition?"

"Sergeant!" Buccari snapped. "Come with me." She pivoted on her heel and marched to the cove beach. Shannon followed.

"Bad move, Sergeant," Buccari said when she was out of earshot of the crew. "You don't know where the plane went or even if it landed."

The waters of the cove were mirror flat. Two gaudy waterbirds navigated across the serene cove opening, creating smooth and persistent wakes. On the far bank of the lake, seen through the opening of the cove inlet, a herd of lake elk watered, at peace and unafraid.

"Sir," Shannon insisted, "there can't be many bugs on this planet. We take out the airplane, we buy time—weeks, maybe months. Perhaps the difference between being rescued and not."

"I understand. I don't agree, but I understand. Why not just lie low?" she asked, trying to stay calm.

"And I understand your point of view, Lieutenant," Shannon said. "Commander Quinn told me I needed to make the decisions for the marines. I would like to exercise that professional discretion, sir. We're not in a Legion spacecraft now. We're fighting for our lives—on the ground. That's my job."

Buccari looked up at the square-jawed marine and realized that his ego and sense of purpose were sitting squarely on his brains. That he would invoke Quinn's name was a clear signal that he was not ready to accept her leadership.

"Sarge," she said. "Only one of us can be in charge of this mess. Go play your games. But remember, if you start a war, my friend, you better head for the hills. Don't come back. I don't care how much we need you."

"Sir, what if we make peaceful contact?" Shannon asked.

"I know you'll try, Sergeant. That's my hope."

Shannon's marines jogged over the rocky terrain, marching along the cliff-sided riparian valley. The angry river crashed and tumbled on their right hand; white-water rapids filled the air with noise and moisture. Shannon looked backward, checking the disposition of his men. A gaggle of hunters waddled far to the rear, struggling to keep up. It was too early for thermals. Eventually they would take to the air and leave him behind. He resumed his fast march.

The white aircraft appeared overhead. The tumult of the cataracts overwhelmed its engine noises, and the alien craft was on them. It jerked abruptly and banked hard on a wing.

"Hold your fire!" Shannon shouted over the crashing water.

"They know where we are," MacArthur yelled at the sergeant's side. The plane angled around for another look, climbing to a higher altitude.

"Hell!" Petit shouted, lowering his rifle. "I could've blown them out of the sky."

"Hold your fire! Don't even aim your weapons!" Shannon bellowed. If they attempted hostile action now, it was unlikely to succeed, and their hostility would be reported back to the alien authorities. Buccari's words haunted him.

"What now?" MacArthur shouted.

"Nothing," Shannon said. "We stay right here until it goes away. I don't want to give them an indication of which way to go. Just stand here and look friendly, like the lieutenant told us to do in the first place." He raised his arm and waved. MacArthur nodded in agreement and held his open hand tentatively in the air.

Lollee flew low so they could see the wildness of the river.

"Look!" he shouted. "Hiding in the rocks! Next to that waterfall—aliens!" The stick-thin green-clothed creatures with white upturned faces were clearly visible, scrambling along the rocks. Some attempted to hide, though two aliens stood conspicuously in the open.

"They are so thin," Et Avian said.

"I see them," Lollee said. "They have weapons." He pulled out binoculars and handed them to Et Avian.

"Interesting they would just stand there," Kateos remarked.

"What else can they do?" Dowornobb replied. "There is no cover, and we know they are of high intelligence—running around like frightened beasts would not make sense. They know they have been seen."

"Careful; they could fire their weapons," Kateos said.

"Instead they are waving!" Et Avian said. "Rock your wings, Lollee!"

The pilot complied, banking his craft quickly back and forth. They flew over the aliens again, their flight path taking them down the river to the mouth of a spreading lake valley. The richness and grandeur of the sunstruck valley registered with Et Avian. He realized that the valley was where the aliens had settled. It was beautiful, the early-morning sun flowing golden across its width and breadth.

"Land there!" Et Avian ordered. "Over there, on the far side of that valley, above the tree line. It is the closest point on this side of the river."

Lollee followed the noblekone's pointing finger, adjusting his course for the eastern slope of the valley.

"Wait, shh!" Hudson whispered. "The airplane! Hear it?"

Buccari listened to the stillness, heart pounding in her chest.

And then her heart stopped: a whining engine growled ever louder.

"It's coming!" she said, sick to her stomach.

Nerve-tugging noises echoed across the lake and reflected between the valley flanks. Louder and louder! There it was, flying low over the lake. It came abreast of the cove inlet and banked sharply. The straight lines and right angles of the stone foundation were like signals from a beacon. The plane climbed and flew two wide observation circuits. The humans, some hiding under trees, a few peeking from the tents, some frozen at their tasks, watched helplessly. Buccari stood in the middle of the clearing. After the second circuit the plane flew to the east, disappearing over the treetops climbing the side of the valley. The faint sound of its engine altered abruptly.

"It landed on the ridge," Fenstermacher said. "The damn thing landed!" He came running up from the lake, joining the others gathered around the cold ashes of the fire pit.

"Gunner," Buccari barked, moving into action. "I'm going to meet them. I want you to collect everyone and move out. Grab as much food as you can carry. Break down the tents and stand ready. If all goes well, I'll come back with our visitors. If you hear gunfire, get moving—fast! Head for the dweller colony. Rendezvous with Shannon."

"Nash—" She turned to Hudson. "Get two pistols. Let's go greet them."

"Me, too. I'm with you, Lieutenant!" Jones insisted.

She looked at the broad-shouldered boatswain. He was balding on top; the hair along the sides of his head had bushed out, and his gray-shot beard was full. He wore baggy elkskin leggings and a parka made from rockdog pelts. He looked every bit the savage.

"Nash, three pistols!" she shouted. Jones smiled largely, and Buccari nervously returned his infectious enthusiasm. A peculiar sadness washed over her, displacing her fear.

Lollee brought out wheel chocks and put them under the big tires. The valley slope was wide and clear, but the grade above the tree line was steep. He had flown a tricky wing-down approach, skidding along the canted terrain.

Et Avian, excited and nervous, walked under the wing, waiting for Lollee to secure the aircraft. The noblekone had decided to make contact. The aliens had not fired their weapons at the low-flying abat, and they had not run away. Et Avian read these as positive signals. And the aliens were constructing a settlement, another indication of peaceful intent or at least an indication of a desire for peace.

"Master Dowornobb and Mistress Kateos, stay with the plane," Et Avian ordered. "We will leave one blaster." He handed his laser unit to Dowornobb. Lollee slipped the other blaster unit into one of his deep chest pockets.

"Let no one approach," Et Avian continued. "We will be back in two hours."

"If you are not?" Kateos asked sternly. Dowornobb rolled his eyes.

"We will be back," the noblekone replied severely, and he laughed. "A good question, Mistress Kateos. Unfortunately, I do not have a better answer."

The pilots turned and moved rapidly down the hillside, starting a traverse toward the aliens and their rectangle of rocks. Lollee took the lead, bending onto his front legs and breaking into an easy rolling gallop; the massive muscles of his flanks and upper arms rippled under his loose-fitting thermal suit. Et Avian ran on two legs and was much less graceful, frequently slipping and stumbling on the grassy slopes. They entered the conifer forest, and the temperature dropped sharply in the shade of the trees. Lollee slowed, allowing the noblekone to close the gap.

"Sometimes it is better to crawl," Et Avian panted, coming even.

"Crawling is a state of mind, Your Excellency," the commoner responded, breathing hard. "If moving fast and staying surefooted is the objective, then it is wise to use all of your limbs. The hill does not respect your lineage."

"Well said, Lollee, and true."

Et Avian leaned over and landed on his hands and forearms, trotting easily. Lollee pushed off with a leap, and the two kones moved down and across the face of the hill, moving fluidly in the light gravity, dodging and weaving between fir trees.

"Spread out but keep me in sight," Buccari ordered, voice low and tense. "Keep the weapons holstered or hidden. When we see them, I'll walk up to them, real friendly. Stay away from me until I tell you different. If things get nasty, shoot in the air to warn our people. Now, spread out."

Hudson went to the left, and Jones moved out to the right.

They ascended above the thick underbrush of the hardwood forest and entered open pine glades, hiking past the trunks of tall, straight trees. Buccari stalked at a deliberate pace, eyes and ears searching for conspicuous sounds or movements. A screaming bird called in the distance. They continued, the rustle of needles underfoot the only noise. After a kilometer, the tall trees gave way to the shorter mustard-barked fir trees. Hudson moved closer.

"We're near the bears, Sharl," he whispered. "One of the dens is just over that rise." They stood on an upslope mounted with a sharp ridge.

"Steer to the right," she replied. "A kilometer to the tree line?"

"If that." Hudson edged away.

Buccari gave hand signals to Jones, shifting him farther to the right. The trio resumed their climb and had not gone ten paces when a ferocious roar from behind the near ridge obliterated the silence. Amid the growls and roars could be heard the sounds of heavy footfalls and grunts, and a peculiar metallic ringing reverberated through the animal din. A scream—a scream unlike any scream ever heard by humans—soared into the skies.

Three mother bears and their cubs had spent the morning tearing apart the rotten tree, flushing out swarms of insects from the crumbling humus. The huge beasts sat on their great posteriors patiently, if incongruously, eating the tiny bugs. Gargantuan pink and purple tongues licked and dipped over the moldy limbs, and massive claw-studded paws rent the deteriorating bark. The cubs, grown impatient with the pastime, had moved across the clearing and cavorted in yellow wildflowers under dappled sunlight.

Lollee, with Et Avian close behind, burst into the clearing between the she-bears and cubs. Lollee froze, big brown eyes opened wide in stark terror. With a fatal hesitation, he reached for his blaster and swung it from his belly pouch. The bears, roaring their deepest displeasure, exploded to their feet with blurring ferocity.

Et Avian, lagging behind, was the closest target. The noblekone was knocked from his feet, dazed and helpless, his helmet slapped away by the vicious impact of an immense claw. Lollee, seeing Et Avian down and about to be mauled, fired the blaster at the attacking bear, cutting it in two, just as a second bear rammed him against the bore of a pine. The third angry mother closed her cavernous jaws over Lollee's haunch, dragging him relentlessly to the ground.

With strength born of fear and love for life, Lollee struggled to his feet, fighting desperately to train the blaster on his brutish adversaries. His gasping efforts were no match for the taller and heavier bears. With renewed fury, the towering beasts overwhelmed the valiant kone, ripping and tearing his body maniacally, crushing his helmet from his head. Lollee screamed horribly as he died.

Buccari topped the ridge and stopped, aghast. Jones and Hudson caught up with her, and all three stared down at the hellish scene before them. Blood flowed freely from the alien held against the tree, covering the combatants and the ground with crimson gore. Great growling bears insanely mauled the alien's body, the dying creature still clutching a weapon in its bloody hands. A second alien lay only paces away.

"The aliens!" Buccari gasped. "They're as big as the bears."

"Let's get out of here, Sharl." Hudson grimaced. "We're not going to stop those monsters, much less the bears, with these peashooters."

"Mr. Hudson's right, Lieutenant," Jones huffed. "The bears'll be after us next."

As the humans watched, the downed alien staggered to its feet and stumbled toward the mayhem, mindless of its own safety. Its courage moved Buccari to action; she sprinted down the slope, her pistol ready, her mind blank, her nerves and muscles reacting to the emergency. Below her one of the bears lifted its gore-spattered snout toward the surviving alien. The great beast turned abruptly, towered fully erect, and roared—a noise primeval and terrible. The horrible growl resounded majestically through the forest, halting the giant alien as if it had been hit with a stout stick. The bear roared again, a foul blast of ferocity, nose curling grotesquely, saliva dripping from its bloody maw. The alien's shoulders sagged, and it turned away, but then it hesitated and turned back to face its death bravely. The bear charged.

Buccari dodged past the ravaged alien, its mangled corpse still being worried viciously by the closest bear. She fired a single shot into the wild beast's head as she ran by, not stopping to see its effect. She trailed behind the monstrous hulk of the attacking bear. With incredible speed and ferocity the charging beast knocked the surviving alien on its back and bit down with knifelike teeth on the alien's shoulder. Buccari heard the brain-numbing crunch of bone. The giant alien, wide-eyed with terror, looked imploringly at her. Buccari ran up to the bear's thrashing and gnashing head, repeatedly firing the pistol point-blank into its meter-wide skull until her pistol magazine emptied. The immense bear rolled its head in slow motion to stare at her, its tongue lolling, and then the animal fell away, heavy. And dead.

The flat cracking of pistol shots sounded behind Buccari. She whirled toward the noise. With tooth-rattling force, a massive paw struck her solidly on her shoulder, knocking her violently across the clearing. Dazed, spitting dirt and bark, she looked up to see the remaining bear staggering after her, its red-rimmed eyes intent with rage, obsessed with killing— killing her. Blood streamed down its skull, soaking its grizzled mane. In two heartbeats Buccari cleared her brain and bunched her feet beneath her body, ready to leap to either side. Her left shoulder was numb. Beyond the approaching bear she saw movement from the alien, and farther away she noticed Hudson struggling with his pistol, trying to reload. Jones was nowhere in sight.

Mere paces away, the bear lurched and whirled with fantastic speed. As the bear spun, she saw Jones clinging to the beast's fur, resolutely stabbing a survival knife into the brute's back. Jones, as strong as he was, was an insect to the ursine monster. He was shaken loose and flung violently clear, landing limply on his head and neck amid the decaying pieces of bark and the swarming bugs. Jones shuddered convulsively and lay still.

With the knife impaled in its back, the great bear pounced on Jones's inert form, snatching his head and neck in cavernous jaws. Looking more like a rag doll than a large human being, Jones was viciously shaken back and forth, his head held firmly in the bear's mouth. Hudson ran up to the animal, aiming his pistol.

"Shoot!" Buccari shouted. *"Shoot!"* she screamed. "Shoot now!"

Hudson jockeyed for position and fired two shots and then another. The insane bear, impervious to Hudson's bullets, worried the limp human. Suddenly a metallic ringing resounded, the air smelled of ozone, and an energy beam blasted the bear squarely in the back, exploding fur and muscle. The monstrous

beast collapsed in a bleeding heap with Jones's lifeless body at
its side.

Buccari and Hudson turned to see the alien, blaster in hand,
standing next to its dead mate. As they watched, wondering if
they would be its next target, the alien collapsed.

THIRTY

CONTACT

Gunshots! Chief Wilson nearly jumped out of his skin.
Goldberg moaned and hugged her baby.

"Move," Wilson ordered. "Grab what you can and get moving. Now!"

"Chief!" Fenstermacher shouted. "Here come the marines!"

MacArthur and Tatum ran into the camp at a full sprint,
shedding their packs. Chastain was behind them, running along
the beach, just coming through the cove opening. The rest of
the marines were not in sight. Chief Wilson, surrounded by a
frightened crew still frantically packing equipment, stood and
met them coming up the hill.

"I heard gunshots!" MacArthur gasped, staggering. "Where's
Buccari?"

"She, Mr. Hudson, and Jones went up to meet them, Mac,"
Wilson said. "She told us to stand tight. If we hear gunfire,
then we're supposed to find you guys and head for the dweller
colony, she said."

"Some plan." MacArthur sucked wind. "Come on, Sandy;
the boss needs some help."

"What should we do, Mac?" Wilson asked.

"What she ordered you to do, Gunner," MacArthur said, his
breath returning. "Get your asses in gear. Sarge will be here
soon, so you can get his opinion. We're going up the hill.
Come on, Sandy."

The marines double-timed up the grade and disappeared into the trees.

"Fenstermacher, get 'em going," Wilson shouted, pushing people into movement. Chastain trundled by, breathing too hard to talk, stopping only to throw off his pack before following MacArthur into the woods.

"What is that popping sound?" Dowornobb asked.

"Light-caliber weapons," Kateos answered, leaping to her hinds. "I have heard such noises from battlefields when I worked as a translator."

"But we do not carry such weapons," Dowornobb said. "Oh, no! The aliens have attacked Et Avian." He hefted the blaster and walked around the aircraft.

"Et Avian! Can you hear me? Report in!" he shouted, keying the transmitter on his helmet radio. "Scientist Lollee! Report in!"

There was no response.

"Should we investigate?" Kateos asked. The noises had stopped.

"I do not have an answer," Dowornobb replied.

"Perhaps their helmet transmitters are out of range. Why did they not take a field radio?"

"A mistake," Dowornobb replied dolefully. "We will wait."

Minutes crept by. Dowornobb decided to venture to the tree line, and Kateos insisted on accompanying him. As Dowornobb crept from the shadow of the airplane's wing, he detected movement. Something moved from the shade into the sunlight. An alien! Two-legged, erect and spindly, tiny head covered with golden hair, it waved at them; it beckoned. Dowornobb looked disbelievingly at Kateos, and she at him. They returned their attention back down the hill.

"It brandishes Lollee's blaster!" Dowornobb shouted. "The aliens have killed Lollee!" He raised his weapon, aiming it at the alien. The alien dropped out of sight in the long grasses. The grasses would do little to attenuate the beam; Dowornobb started to fire.

"Wait! It could have discharged the blaster at us," Kateos whispered, putting a hand on his arm. "It did not. It is trying to communicate."

"A trick!" Dowornobb exclaimed. "How else would they disarm our comrades?"

"Hold," Kateos said. "Wait here and protect me. I will go forward."

"That is inappropriate, my mate. We proceed together." He lowered the weapon.

"As you wish, my mate." Kateos pointed. "Look! The alien shows itself. Do not aim the blaster."

The alien crouched nervously in the bright sunlight, holding the blaster's barrel straight in the air. It wore faded buff-colored garb with streaks of black-edged crimson smeared across the front. With emphatic intent, the alien threw the weapon to the ground and waved its arms in an agitated manner. It pointed downhill and walked backward into the forest shadows, waving its arms. Kateos fell on all fours and loped toward the mysterious creature.

"Something is amiss!" she shouted. "Et Avian needs our help!"

Dowornobb knew it was a trap, but he could not forsake his mate. He bounded after the headstrong female.

Hudson heard thudding footfalls, and his own strides lengthened in fear. He tried not to look backward but could not help himself. One monstrous alien was on his heels. It had fallen into a gentle trot, easily matching his pace. The other giant had stopped to pick up the discarded weapon and was galloping frantically to catch up.

Hudson breathlessly led the aliens down the forested hillside, quickly reaching the clearing, where he found Buccari, sitting in the sun with her back against a tree, dressed only in her thermal underwear. She attended the stricken alien, holding its great head in her lap, the alien's shattered helmet at her side. Buccari had used her jumpsuit as a bandage; the material, black with seeping blood, covered the alien's huge neck and shoulder. Across the clearing, Jones's body lay in the cool shadows, limbs composed and face covered with his fur jacket. Nearby, two cubs fretted and pulled on the carcasses of the destroyed she-bears, whining and mewling.

"You were right, Sharl. They had crewmates—good grief, the smell!" Hudson gasped. "They must've lost control of their bowels!"

Buccari nodded silently, hair falling in her eyes.

"You okay, Sharl?" Hudson asked, glancing over his shoulder.

Buccari looked up, wet tracks running down her grimy face.

She wiped away tears with the back of a hand. "We were a team, Nash. Jones and me," she wept. "Jones was—my—"

"I'm sorry, Sharl, but . . . we got visitors."

Buccari shook the hair from her face and lifted her chin. She sighed heavily, firm resolve returning to her strong features. "Yeah, I guess we have other things to worry about now, don't we?" she said, her voice growing louder. She grimaced in pain.

"Yeah!" Hudson said. "You sure you're okay?"

"Shoulder's killing me," she groaned.

"What do we do now, Sharl?" he asked, turning to face the aliens.

The monsters had stopped at the edge of the clearing and were slowly making their way on all fours. They communicated quietly, a low-pitched, melodious sound with infrequent word breaks. Helmet amplifiers gave their speech a hollow, mechanical tone. The spectacle of injury and death did not seem to deter them as much as did the human presence. They looked nervously at the activity of the cubs and at the sundered carcasses of the dead bears.

"What now?" Kateos asked, edging closer to Et Avian.

Dowornobb lifted onto his hinds and walked over to Lollee's gruesome corpse. He sniffed the dead kone and delicately touched the side of the scientist's mutilated neck, a perfunctory search for a pulse.

"Scientist Lollee has expired," he announced.

He bravely approached Et Avian, wary of the petite alien. He was touched by the alien's obvious compassion for their leader.

"Et Avian is injured grievously," Kateos said. "The wounds are deep, and the bones of his shoulder are crushed. He must receive treatment or he, too, will die."

"What are we to do?" Dowornobb asked helplessly. "Scientist Lollee is dead. There is no pilot other than Et Avian, and he certainly cannot manage the task."

"I know not," the female replied. "Can we fly the abat ourselves?"

"I cannot. Can you?" Dowornobb moaned.

Kateos shook her head. She removed her breathing unit and slipped it over the noblekone's head, securing the pressure fittings around his neck. The long-haired alien made efforts to help, its spindly fingers hardly able to span the helmet's locking lever.

"Let us carry Et Avian to the abat," Kateos said. "We must get him out of the cold."

The compressed air revived Et Avian. He stirred; his eyes bulged open in fear and pain, but then he saw the alien and lay still. He slowly raised his hand toward the alien's white face but shuddered in evident pain, his arm dropping heavily to his side. He turned his head, recognizing Kateos.

"Aliens—saved my life," Et Avian gasped. "One of them died—d-died in our behalf. We—must be—"

He fainted—mercifully unconsciousness.

Brappa gained altitude on the rising currents. He dropped a wing and crabbed to the north, toward Craag's marshaling signal and the rest of the hunter scouting party. He knew not what to make of the furious activity. The flying machine was ominous enough, but the incredible death struggle was frightful beyond words. Short-one-who-leads had again proved to be a brave and fierce warrior. They would have much to report. Brappa wished he understood more about what he had seen. Of one thing only was he certain: the bear people had returned.

MacArthur, lungs burning, topped the spruce-lined ridge and stopped short as Tatum ran up his heels. He recoiled at the carnage spread across the clearing below; the blend of putrescent odors was staggering. He detected a human body—Jones—laid out on the opposite side of the clearing, not far from a trio of cubs whining among the fly-infested carcasses of three adult bears, but it was the monstrous, gory mass of a dead alien that dominated MacArthur's attention. The hulking creature lay slumped at the base of a small tree, its thick space suit shredded, its bowels eviscerated, its fleshy, gross-featured face contorted in death. Chastain, gasping and sucking for air, joined MacArthur and Tatum, breaking their morbid trance. The marines stumbled across the bloody clearing and up the wooded slope opposite, following the trail of blackened needles and leaves—and the horrible smell.

They climbed upward for an eternity. MacArthur's frantic thoughts focused only on Buccari. He burst from the tree line and stopped, relieved and astounded, as Tatum and Chastain staggered to a halt behind him. In the distance, walking through knee-high grass, Buccari, Hudson, and two hulking alien beings struggled under the weight of a third alien. A crisp breeze had risen, but the bitter, cloying stink hung heavily in the air. MacArthur sprinted toward Buccari, forgetting his cramping muscles and burning lungs. He shouted her name.

Buccari snapped around, dark hair swirling in the breeze, glinting copper in the sunlight. "Stop!" she yelled. "Put down your weapons. We need to help them."

They set the injured alien next to the airplane. Buccari and Hudson stepped quickly away from the aircraft. The ponderous aliens stood with their backs to the plane, watching nervously.

"Put down your rifles!" Buccari ordered. "Drop the damn rifles, *now!*"

MacArthur let his piece fall and signaled for the others to drop theirs. Tatum and Chastain carefully placed their rifles on the ground.

"Damn!" MacArthur gasped, stepping away from his weapon. The fetid smell was overwhelming. "They're smelly. And big! What happened?"

He approached Buccari, observing her carefully. The thick fabric of her underwear had been torn away from her pale shoulder, and a bloody contusion glared angrily through the opening. Her left arm hung straight, immobile. MacArthur winced in empathy, feeling her pain and wishing he could transfer it to his own body, sparing her.

"You okay?" he asked, returning a wary eye to the aliens.

"I'll live," she said, her voice barely audible. "I think my shoulder's dislocated. One of those bears took a swipe at me."

"You sure made them pay for it," MacArthur blustered, striving to overcome his own fear. "Don't ever get that mad at me." He peeled off his jacket and draped it over her shoulders, daring to put an arm around her waist. She accepted his embrace.

"Jeezus, Mac! Boats is dead!" she suddenly cried, tears gushing. She clenched her eyes shut and twisted away, holding her face with a grimy, bloodstained hand. MacArthur withdrew his arm and watched as she waged an internal battle to regain her composure.

The aliens stirred; they opened the plane's cargo door and bent to pick up their injured comrade. Buccari, her emotions under control, stepped forward to help, but MacArthur gently pulled her away. He and Hudson each grabbed a tree trunk leg and assisted in hoisting the injured alien into the aircraft's commodious cargo area. The aliens began administering medical aid while the curious humans milled around outside. The cargo door eased shut.

Suddenly the door swung open. One of the aliens, holding Buccari's bloodstained jumpsuit, tentatively stepped from the aircraft. MacArthur stared at the alien. It was huge! Taller even than Chastain or Tatum and easily twice Chastain's bulky weight. Its face could be discerned through the wide helmet visor, a gentle monster's face with fleshy, rounded bovine features. Its skin resembled grainy leather—hairless except for wiry tufts over bulging brown eyes. Its mouth was a lipless gash under a bulbous snout with widely spread nostrils. The alien handed the bloody garment to Buccari and leaned over onto its front legs, putting its face on the ground. Buccari looked at MacArthur in embarrassed confusion and then cautiously tapped the creature on its tremendous shoulder, indicating that it should return to the airplane. With surprising agility, the massive alien hopped aboard the aircraft.

Kateos pulled Et Avian's garments from his wounds and was encouraged. The bleeding had abated, and the noblekone's pulse was steady, albeit weak. She cleansed the wounds with antiseptic, applied a sterile dressing, and covered his prostrate form, trying to keep him warm.

"He is in great pain but seems to be resting now," she said as Dowornobb climbed into the airplane, shutting the cargo door to keep in the warmth. Kateos had taken note of her mate's activities with approval. They owed much to the tiny, long-haired alien.

"More aliens approach!" Dowornobb reported, his fear smell gushing forth. Kateos saw aliens in dark green striding across the field. All carried weapons, and Kateos discerned fear in their features. The little long-haired one walked up to the newcomers and began talking, pointing down the hill. The green-garbed alien with one arm grabbed a weapon and waved it fiercely at the abat.

"Now's our chance!" Tatum shouted, brandishing his rifle. "They're helpless. We got 'em! I say we kill the bugs and push the plane into the trees. They'll never be found." The marines nodded in affirmation.

"At ease, Tatum!" Buccari ordered.

"Put the rifle down, Sandy," Shannon ordered softly, inspecting the aircraft. It was huge, with long, drooping slab wings and massive low-pressure tires—representations of a technological society capable of employing deadly weapons and effective search techniques. "You might be right, Sandy," he said, "and then again, they may have already reported in on the radio. Listen to the lieutenant. There's no harm in checking things out first, and everyone on their toes—these guys have lasers."

"Bullshit, Sergeant!" Buccari barked. The sun reflected angry red highlights from her hair. "We've already gone over this ground!" She snatched Hudson's pistol and walked up to Tatum. Tatum stood his ground.

"Anyone even thinks about hurting these—these bugs is going to have to come through me." Her eyes were furious. Shannon stepped toward the confrontation, but Buccari took another step closer to Tatum. She pounded the pistol butt against the tall marine's chest, pointing the barrel straight up to his chin. Tatum did not move.

"Tatum, think about it!" she cried. "We saved an alien's life. Now we *have* to help them so their leaders will know we mean no harm. It's the clearest, most unambiguous message we can send. We got real lucky, and Bosun Jones's already paid with his life. Jones doesn't need revenge. We both know what Boats would have wanted us to do. Think about it, Tatum! Think! Don't screw it up!"

Tatum retreated a half step and nodded sharply. Shannon eased closer, took the rifle from Tatum's hand, and softly clasped the marine's shoulder. MacArthur gingerly reached in and removed the pistol from Buccari's grasp.

"What transpires?" Dowornobb asked. "How can they stand the cold?"

"The smallest one argues our cause," Kateos replied, donning a spare breathing unit. "But what now? How will we get Et Avian back to Ocean Station? He needs medical assistance. The cold will kill him if his injuries do not."

"They are coming in," Dowornobb said. He shut off the cargo section, sealing in warm air for Et Avian, and opened the smaller crew door forward. He stepped back from the door and watched the aliens climb awkwardly up the forward ladder. They were so delicate, their legs and arms like plant stems, their skulls unbelievably tiny. They chattered rapidly, frequently at the same time. Showing great curiosity, they looked everywhere. They gawked at the flight deck and, using crude sign language, requested permission to go forward. Dowornobb did not know what to do. He nodded.

The aliens moved into the seats. They pointed at instruments, and then the small one, using only one arm, pulled on the flight controls. The taller one, using both arms, was able to move them to full travel. It was impossible for the small one to see over the instrument panel or to reach the foot pedals. The taller one could manage, but his attention was captured by a map case.

"The small one is female," Kateos said knowingly.

"Whew, it's stuffy," Buccari said. "Why don't they open a window?"

"Look! Charts!" Hudson cried. "Take a look! They aren't stopping us."

"You're right. Wha—Wait a minute!" Buccari exclaimed, glancing at the monsters. "Something's wrong. They should be in a hurry to take off. Their friend's seriously hurt. Why aren't they pushing us out of here? Why aren't they starting the engines?"

"Maybe he's not hurt that bad," Hudson said with a shrug.

"He's in bad shape," she said. "I don't care how big and strong he is. He's going to die without some medical treatment. And soon."

She stood and approached the aliens. Grimacing in pain, she used her hands to make takeoff motions. The aliens watched her carefully and talked anxiously. She was not getting through. She pulled the charts from Hudson—satellite composite topography overlaid with a navigation grid and strange markings. One was dog-eared from use, a flight track lined across it. Buccari recognized the scratches and notations, not understanding the words but knowing for certain their purpose: landing points, fuel consumptions, en route times, headings. She traced the flight track to its origin, noting that it followed the river all the way. The chart hypnotized her; she stared with fascination at the depiction of the terrain and the scaled distances.

Buccari tore her concentration from the chart and confronted the smaller giant. She pushed the chart in front of the alien, her finger on the point of origin. She dragged her finger along the flight track on the chart and pointed to the controls. She pointed at each of the aliens, making flight control motions with her hands. The smaller alien looked at Buccari and pointed in the distance, downhill in the approximate direction where the murdered member of their crew still lay, and then the alien pointed to the pilot's seat. After a short hesitation, the alien pointed at the injured alien and immediately thereafter gestured toward the other forward seat.

"They have no pilot," Buccari moaned. "Tatum's going to get what he wants."

Hudson sat silently. Then his face brightened. "We could fly it back. It's an airplane, isn't it?" he asked.

Buccari stared straight ahead. "You're right! Damn straight! *You* can fly it back," she said, turning back to him. "But you'll have to do it alone, Nash. I can't go with you."

"Me? Alone? Without you?"

"Yes! Yes, it's got to be," she insisted. "Nash, they need me here, and my shoulder's screwed up! I'd be worse than useless. I'd be in your way. I can't reach the rudders. I can't even see over the panel. You can fly this truck. We have to get the injured alien to a doctor, and fast!" She moved from the pilot's seat, making room for Hudson.

"Sharl!" he cried. "I need help to figure out the systems."

Buccari patted him on the head as if stroking a spaniel. "You've already figured most of them out, and you're the only pilot here. Once you get this hog into the air, all you have to do is follow the river."

"What about fuel?" Hudson asked. "This thing's going to need refueling."

"I bet that's what these markings indicate here, here, and here," she said, excitedly pointing to the chart. "They have prestaged fuel or airfields, and I bet these two can help. Get in that seat and figure out how to start the engine. I'm going to tell Mac to bring up your gear and some food. I'll be back. Okay?"

Hudson looked down at the chart and then out the front windshield.

"Sharl! This is crazy," he groaned, sliding into the pilot's seat.

"It was your idea," she shouted as she went out the crew door.

Dowornobb followed the alien's uncertain movements. The engine was revved high, vibrations rattling the abat. He watched the alien fumble with the controls, apparently looking for the parking brake. Dowornobb reached down and disengaged the lever. The plane lurched forward. As the craft bounced and jostled down the grassy hill, the skinny alien retarded the throttle, shouted with glee, and slapped Dowornobb on the shoulder. The alien chattered to himself, and Dowornobb answered so as not to seem rude. The alien looked at him strangely, and Kateos giggled.

Their craft shuddered and jolted over the rough terrain. The alien turned the airplane and headed it up the grade, adding power to keep it moving over the soft, steep ground. After opening up enough clear area for a takeoff run, the alien turned the abat and accelerated downhill into a stiff breeze. The plane gained speed and, after a short bouncing run, slipped into the air, wallowing into a climbing turn. The aircraft banked over on a wing, and Dowornobb caught a lingering glimpse of the skinny aliens left behind on the ground, still waving. The alien pilot turned his somber countenance to the serious business of flying the airplane. The river ran under their left wing, and they were on course for Ocean Station. The golden-haired alien stopped talking.

Eventually Hudson established limited communications with the helmeted aliens, primarily as a result of the persistence of the smaller of the two monsters. Its—her—name was Kateos; her voice was deep and resonant, made even more so by the artificial amplification of her helmet speaker. The larger alien answered to "Doorknob." They called him "Huhsawn."

Hudson watched as Doorknob talked on the radio, wondering what the alien was telling his friends. The flight down the river had been awesome and endless. Refuelings had gone without incident, and they had spent an uncomfortable and sleepless night on the ground at their first stop. Now their destination was nearing, and not soon enough; the late-summer sun was sinking below the horizon, and Hudson was exhausted and frightened by the prospect of flying the strange aircraft at night over the surface of an unexplored planet. Fuel was uncomfortably low; his back ached from stretching to see over the instrument panel, and his eyelids felt like sandpaper. The last hour had been the worst, fighting to overcome the fierce bucking and jostling turbulence of the mountain passes. He needed to land and to get some sleep.

The sight of a limitless ocean spreading to the south revived him. Doorknob pointed to the right, away from the river, and Hudson saw the last rays of sunlight reflecting from unnatural structures. A chill fluttered across the back of his neck; his gut tightened—he recognized his own fear. Pumping up his resolve, he banked the plane and pulled power, heading for the bittersweet signs of civilization. Bright sparks of electricity—artificial light, floodlights—beckoned. His physical discomfort evaporated, replaced by dread.

The sun disappeared behind the high northern mountains, but the indigo twilight provided ample illumination as he circled the alien compound. What looked like a rocket booster had been erected near the center of a brightly lighted metal ramp equipped with gantry cranes and rail tracks. A large blocky hangar and two smaller structures squatted at the edge of the matting, and a round two-story building stood by itself in a small cluster of foliage. Aliens ran from the buildings, moving toward the ramp area. As Hudson watched, white lights popped aglow, outlining the perimeter of a runway.

Piece of cake! Hudson thought, pumping up his courage. He extended his flight path away from the buildings and descended. The controls were stiff, but the big plane was rock steady. Hudson dropped an increment of flaps and pulled the power to idle; the aircraft floated onto the grass strip and quickly slowed to taxi speed. A ponderous alien, giving hand signals, galloped from the awaiting cluster of giants. The signals were understandable, particularly the final signal—the signal to kill the engine—a slicing motion with the flat of the hand across the neck. Hudson wondered if his own neck was in danger. He closed the throttle, secured the fuel, and switched off the battery.

It was uncomfortably quiet. The endless vibrations of the long flight no longer rattled his entire being. Hudson turned to Doorknob, and the smiling alien slapped him on the shoulder extremely hard. Hudson attempted a smile, but fear eclipsed all emotions.

Cargo doors opened roughly, and cool, humid air flowed into the cockpit. Hudson smelled the long-forgotten scent of ocean. A crowd of shouting aliens clambered noisily and heavily into the cargo compartment, grabbing at the injured alien and hoisting him onto a stretcher. All stole lingering glances at Hudson, broad noses swelling and twitching behind face masks. Left alone in the aircraft, Hudson slowly rose from his seat and moved to the crew door. Doorknob stood at the foot of the ladder, holding up a massive hand.

THIRTY-ONE

TURNING POINT

Gorruk's hordes climbed the thinly defended gorge and assaulted the high mountain passes, streaming onto the fertile alluvial plain of the valley Kingdom of Penc. Its defenders, in total disarray, fell back into the crescent-shaped valley—a rout. Devious sabotage and fifth column infiltrators had undercut their defenses, and the first assaults had overrun forward positions. The southern troops were pushed aside and hacked apart by northern commandos. With the mountain roads clear of defenses, Gorruk's armored columns motored through the main pass, grinding relentlessly over the rich fields. Phalanxes of hungry, battle-hardened soldiers radiated outward from the narrow mountain trails. Artillery blasted screeching shells overhead while engineers established bridgeheads. The northern armies advanced, pillaging and sacking.

The Supreme Leader called his victorious general home to celebrate the great victory. The imperial capital had turned out to welcome General Gorruk, and a formal audience was held to decorate the military heroes of the campaign. The court of Jook the First was resplendent in banners and battle flags.

"Hah, that old toad Barbluis assumed we would press him from the bloodstained heights of Rouue," Gorruk gloated, addressing the court. "He never dreamed we would attack to the west. And Penc is a worthy prize. My armies will eat like noblekones this winter, thanks to that senile noblefool's complacency." He glared with ill-concealed contempt at Et Kalass.

"A glorious victory, General Gorruk," Jook the First stated. "Your armies have achieved much. A most glorious victory."

"We salute you, General!" Et Kalass exclaimed, his voice clamorous but his facial expression inappropriately somber. The minister signaled theatrically, and a lackey jumped on the

301

podium at Jook's feet and led a rousing cheer. The entire court and the attendant citizens yelled their thunderous acclaim, the hurrahs echoing and reverberating through the polished halls.

Gorruk, lantern jaw held high, basked in glory, yet his thoughts dwelled on the noblekone standing across from him. The cheers subsided, and the decorum of the court returned.

"General Gorruk, what is your next step?" Et Kalass inquired.

Gorruk's intense gaze darkened. "That is a *military secret*, Your Excellency," he replied with vitriolic tones. "Enough questions!" He turned and bowed to Jook. "Your Greatness, permission to depart. My presence is required at the front. For we are still at war."

"And so you must return, General," Jook rumbled. The Supreme Leader had grown larger and more obese, his self-indulgences and depravities legend. Dissipation ravaged his countenance, but stern malignancy and wary cunning still radiated from behind half-shut eyelids.

"To my duty, Supreme One. My armies are engaged," Gorruk replied, hiding his disgust. To think the odious leader had once been the scourge of the north.

Jook nodded, and Gorruk marched from the hall to more and greater cheers.

General Et Ralfkra, the Public Safety Militia commander, walked into Et Kalass's inner office on an announced matter of urgency. The minister anticipated what the general was going to tell him—but he was wrong!

"He was not in the hovercar!" Et Ralfkra said bleakly.

"What!" Et Kalass would have yelled, but his throat constricted, and the sound he made was more of a squeak. The first attempt at assassination was always the best.

"Three sources have reported Gorruk's arrival at field headquarters. He knows of the assassination attempt and is sending agents to investigate."

Et Kalass moved from his desk and sat heavily, chest down on the massive lounge, his mind grinding over the events.

"What is our next step?" Et Ralfkra asked.

"Continue the march." The minister spoke calmly, his courage and resolve returning. "Our positions in this government are too valuable to abandon. Double our personal guards and set up the necessary agents to block Gorruk's inquiry. We will be under siege."

"How will this affect Et Barbluis's plans? What should we tell him?"

"Unchanged. He is to proceed," Et Kalass replied. "We may not have eliminated Gorruk, but I am sure we have distracted him. The distraction may serve our purpose, if to a lesser degree."

"I will send the signal," the militia commander said, but he did not immediately depart. He stood indecisively. Et Kalass noticed the general's agitation and sat erect in the lounge.

"What is it, my friend? You have something else?"

"Minister, the news is sketchy, and I am told his condition is stable—"

"Et Avian! Something has happened to Et Avian?" Et Kalass interrupted, his golden complexion blanching.

"Please, sir! Be at ease and allow me to finish. Et Avian is alive and returning to Kon on the booster you dispatched, but he is badly injured. By a wild animal. His shoulder was broken, and he suffered muscle and tendon damage. The injuries are serious, but he is out of danger."

Et Kalass's panic slowly dissolved. He fell back on the lounge, shaking his head. The pressures were too much. Et Avian must survive; his time had come.

"And more news, Your Excellency," Et Ralfkra reported.

Et Kalass's head snapped up, searching the general's expression.

"Well? Good news or bad? I have had enough bad news, General."

"I do not know, Your Excellency. You must tell me. Et Avian made contact!"

Crescent-shaped, the steep-sided and narrow valley of Penc curled to the south and climbed in stages to the lake passes, so named because of the large artificial lakes. Gorruk's armies advanced steadily toward the serene bodies of water, their going made more difficult by the narrowing and climbing terrain. The retreating southern defenders regrouped, harrying and slowing the advancing columns but paying a dear price.

The four lakes at the high end of the valley had been formed by great dams built millennia earlier, prideful artifacts of ancient konish engineers—beautiful, peaceful reservoirs graced with rustic stone bridges and bordered by ancient cedar groves. A third of the natural valley had been displaced by those engineering wonders, forming a series of deep lakes, each one monumentally higher than the one before—oceans stacked upon oceans. Tunnels and aqueducts hewn through the ridges surrounding the valley carried the clear mountain water to farms and cities throughout the region. Penc was synonymous with rich and abundant agriculture—and with water.

Gorruk paced the floor of his field headquarters, devising the next phase in his aggressive strategy.

"General, our armies have reached the first dam," the aide reported.

"Very well," Gorruk replied, uncharacteristically distracted. It was not the first time someone had tried to assassinate him, but he knew Et Kalass was behind the latest attempt, and that thought infuriated him. Gorruk moved to the master status panel and scanned the real-time displays that continually updated the positions of his forces. His armies were taking the upper hand on all fronts. Gorruk had received word that Et Barbluis was even withdrawing from the plains behind the Rouue Massif. Perhaps his armies could move to the central flatlands unopposed. Nothing would stop his armies then.

A runner entered the command center and handed a dispatch to Gorruk's aide. The aide scanned it quickly and came directly to Gorruk, his face a mask of pale horror. The runner left quickly.

"G-general, we have c-confirmed reports indicating sappers have mined the lake dams," the aide reported, taking a hesitant step backward.

Gorruk's great snout jerked upward. It was unthinkable. Blowing the dams was unfathomable. Unfathomable! Destruction beyond comprehension. The southern generals were not *that* desperate. They did not play by those rules. *Rules?* Stark reality dawned on Gorruk's strategic and intellectual horizon. He turned the idea over in his head and acknowledged the tragic ingenuity. His respect for the old noblekone Et Barbluis rose immensely. He had been suckered.

The first explosions breached the highest edifice, and torrents of water broke onto the lake below it. Coordinated detonations set along the moss-grown span of the lower dam ripped the centuries-old structure apart, and the combined waters of two reservoirs descended majestically on the third dam. It in turn was torn asunder in perfect synchronization by another series of blasts, and the full fury of the unleashed waters descended on the last lake and dam, the largest of all. The doomed stone was crushed by the descending hydrodynamic forces even as the explosives detonated. The explosions were loud, but the banshee scream of the waters eclipsed all sounds. Ripping and gouging with the force of a nuclear explosion, the torrent streamed into the upper valley, crashing and sloshing, carrying everything before it. Soldiers, armored vehicles, barns, trees, herds of farm animals were dashed away in tumbling chaos; the roiling, turbulent onslaught careened down the valley bottom, thundering with a resounding tumult. Et Barbluis observed the spectacle from a safe elevation, his grief monumental. He had destroyed the valley, along with many of his own soldiers still fighting the enemy. His stomachs knotted; he could not breathe. Time stood still—tragedy held constant. War was an obscenity.

The cataclysmic scene unfolded. The routed battalions of the north surged backward, creating a chain reaction of panic. Explosive rumblings from the unfettered cascades converted panic into pure terror. Apocalyptic noises from the valley's head resonated in the air. Birds screamed. A gigantic rolling, churning wall of water poured into the valley from the upper horn, its inertia swirling wide and high against the far slopes of the valley, only to come crashing down onto the valley floor, sweeping across it with ruthless power. The heart-stopping sound of water pushing gravel, magnified on a titanic scale, preceded the arrival of the flood. Gales of yellow dust tumbled into the air from the winds compressed before the deluge.

Frantic armies trapped on the valley floor sprinted helplessly, abandoning weapons in the field. Torrents of living flesh, streams of hysteria, hordes of northern troops frantically crawled along the lower slopes, clawing and digging at the sheer rock, obsessed with escaping the deluge. In vain—the roaring waters avalanched by, sweeping away the living and the dead.

When the slithering waters receded to the scooped-out banks of the River Penc, the green peaceful valley was transformed. The once sparkling, crystalline river ran brown and thick, like melting chocolate, and the pastoral valley had become the surreal landscape of a nightmare; muddy ooze slid from exposed rocks, and the deep humus was no more. The loamy topsoil had been flushed from the bedrock and tossed into the rocky river gorges. Primeval muck, animal carcasses, and the bodies of soldiers were cast among the boulders. Carrion birds arrived in great numbers.

THIRTY-TWO

HUDSON RETURNS

Weeks went by slowly. Foliage on the margins of the lake thickened into the lush, deep greens of early summer. The humans listened nervously for the sound of airplanes—in vain. No aircraft appeared. But Dawson had a baby, a healthy black-haired, blue-eyed boy named Adam. Shannon was its proud father.

"Lieutenant," Shannon said, squinting into the afternoon sun. "After we complete the main lodge, I'm going to build a house for Nancy and the baby, if it's okay with you."

"And for yourself, too?" Buccari replied, watching MacArthur as he supervised the positioning of timbers alongside the rock piles. Cliff dwellers hopped about importantly, providing strident assistance. Her left arm was in a sling. After they had buried Jones and the monstrous alien, MacArthur had relocated her shoulder. Then he had held her tenderly, and she had allowed herself time to cry in his arms.

"And for yourself, too?" she repeated, turning to face Shannon.

Shannon looked at his boots. "And for myself, yes, sir," he replied.

"Certainly, Sergeant," Buccari responded, realizing there was no other workable answer. The integrity of the group was splitting, but not for the worse. Another emotional priority had emerged, a priority that superseded the essence of team or crew. A family had formed.

"We should build one for Tatum and Goldberg, too," Buccari said.

"And Lee and Fenstermacher," Shannon added. "And what about you, sir? With the women out of the lodge, you'll be wanting your own place."

Buccari turned sharply and looked at the heavily bearded marine. It was an honest, concerned face, paternal and frank. His implication was innocent, but Buccari was momentarily nonplussed. Her thoughts went to MacArthur; his nearness reinforced the flood of emotions and physical sensations welling within her mind and body.

"Lee and I can still live together, Sergeant," Buccari replied hurriedly, cutting off her thoughts. "Leslie hasn't mentioned moving out of our tent yet."

"Lee's pregnant, too, Lieutenant."

She stared at Shannon and shook her head in disbelief.

"Nancy says so," Shannon said softly.

She was speechless, but it did not matter; the sound of an airplane engine eclipsed all other thoughts and sounds.

Et Silmarn banked the abat in a gentle curve over the lake. Hudson pointed out the cove, and the massive pilot nervously grunted. The geometry of human construction was more apparent than ever; humans scurried about the clearing like disturbed ants.

Et Silmarn slipped the airplane toward the grassy slopes. Winds were strong and steady. Choppy turbulence rattled the airplane and its occupants about, but the pilot skimmed the treetops and settled gently onto the hill, rolling to a bouncing halt. The kones moved quickly and efficiently, immediately refueling the wing tanks. Four sealed barrels of fuel were rolled across the open grass and placed within the tree line—provisions for future needs. As the kones worked, Hudson walked down the hill toward the human encampment.

"Huhsawn! Huhsawn! Stuh-hop!" Kateos shouted. The linguist had made remarkable progress. She trotted after him, Dowornobb and Et Silmarn close behind. The other scientists, all pilots, remained at the plane.

"Huhsawn! Waytah fo-ah meee, pool-leeze," she pleaded, her helmet-amplified voice deep and resonant but also hinting at nervousness. The titans shook the ground with their footsteps. Hudson smelled their fear.

"Wee go-ah witha yew. Wee see-ah more hewmanns," Kateos rumbled emphatically.

"Huhsawn! Look-ah fo-ah b-bears!" implored Kateos. "B-berry danger!"

Hudson concentrated on the phonetics and put them in context.

"Right! Very dangerous! Follow me," he instructed. He walked over to Dowornobb and pointed to the laser blaster. "Be ready!" he commanded, and pantomimed pointing and shooting the weapon. Dowornobb nodded vigorously, touching the big weapon suspended from a harness on the front of his chest. Hudson turned and headed down the hill at a jog. The kones followed easily, trotting on four legs.

They met a solitary Buccari standing in an open glade of yellow-barked trees. Her jumpsuit was patched and cleaned, but faded stains streaked across large sections of the sun-bleached fabric. Hudson noted her injured arm and wondered why she had come alone, but as he drew closer, he caught glimpses of Shannon's marines in the underbrush. Hudson signaled for the kones to hold their position and closed the remaining distance alone. Buccari surprised him with a one-armed embrace. He returned it with unchecked emotion, trembling in the excitement of being reunited. She backed away and looked up at him, wet-eyed and smiling hugely. Hudson wiped his eyes.

"Ah, I was so worried, Nash. You okay? You look good!"

"I'm good, I'm great!" he blurted. "Your arm. How's your arm?"

"Sore but getting better. I can lift the elbow a little." She peeked around his shoulder at the colossal beings. "So, huh . . . what happened? Are we friends?"

"Too much to tell, Sharl! I don't know where to start. They treated me well, but except for Kateos, they mainly just left me alone. They're suspicious and afraid, but yeah—they're friendly."

He pivoted to face the kones, waving at them to approach. "You should hear Kateos speak Legion, Sharl!" he exclaimed. "Amazing. You can hold a conversation with her. That's her specialty—languages. She's sharp! Real sharp! Dowornobb's not bad, either."

"So she is a female—did you say Doorknob?" Buccari responded.

"Yeah! Dowornobb. I'm not kidding," Hudson said. "That's his name."

"What now?" she asked, checking the sun. "It's getting late."

"Yeah," Hudson answered. "They plan on spending several nights here. Kateos says the most important thing is learning to communicate. She wants to talk. I couldn't get any more than that out of them. There are two more kones back at the plane. They'll come down later."

The mammoth, hulking beings towered above them, nervously watching. Their peculiar pungent odor came and went in waves.

"Damn, I forgot how big they were," Buccari said nervously. She squared her shoulders and bowed, holding her hands at waist level, palms upward—the dwellers' greeting. The kones replied in kind. The one called Dowornobb fumbled with his weapon, slinging it over his shoulder. They stood erect, and Hudson formally introduced them.

"Welcome!" Buccari said slowly.

"Thang-ah yew, Sharl. Wee owe yew b-big thangs! B-big thangs to Sharl!" Kateos stepped forward and extended her hand. Buccari glanced warily at Hudson.

"I taught them to shake hands," he said. "And they wanted to know all about you, but they could never pronounce your last name. You're a hero. They say 'Sharl' real well."

"Yeah," Buccari said, her small hand disappearing in turn into each of the gigantic but surprisingly gentle gloved hands. "Let's go back to camp. We can talk better there."

"Yesss . . . talk-ah," Kateos said. "We talk-ah with Sharl."

Buccari smiled at the kone and turned downhill. She signaled, and Shannon's marines abruptly moved, revealing their positions. Et Silmarn made a transmission over his helmet radio, and the kones, treading alertly on all fours, followed.

"So, how was the flight?" Buccari asked.

"Tiring! It took two days. I never did get that truck trimmed."

"Huhsawn b-ber-ah good-ah . . ." Kateos struggled for the right word. "Pilot-ah . . . ver-ah good-ah pilot-ah."

"She is good!" Buccari complimented. Katoes smiled proudly.

"And getting better fast," Hudson said. "Real fast!"

"How is the injured, er . . . alien?" Buccari asked.

"They call themselves kones," Hudson said, helping her. "He made it back alive and is doing well, or at least he was when he left the planet. There was an orbital lander sitting on their launchpad when I arrived—not a coincidence, it turns out. It had been sent expressly to retrieve Et Avian—that's his name. Guess what, Sharl? He's a member of their nobility. You saved the life of a very important kone. They worked on him at the science station for about a week, gave him a lot of blood. Once he was stabilized, they launched him back to Kon."

"Kon?" Buccari asked. "Is that their name for R-K Two?"

"Right. This planet is called Genellan."

"Genellan! I like that. Much nicer than R-K Three," Buccari said.

"Planet-ah named Genellan," Kateos said, smiling through her visor.

"Why do they wear helmets, Nash?" Buccari asked, smiling back.

"Air's not dense enough for them," Hudson said. "The backpack is a compressor and heating system. To them this place is cold—miserably cold. Even their southern base is considered cold, and Sharl, it's awesome. Looks out over a tropical ocean, and it's beautiful. I walked on sandy beaches that went forever, and I swam in the ocean. It's beautiful, wonderful, the closest to paradise I've ever been."

"Even without human beings for company?" she said.

"Paradise has a price."

At the sound of engines, all the cliff dwellers ran in near panic for shelter. A flight of hunters wheeled high overhead; keen eyes discerned movement in the trees—humans and others—bear people. Braan studied the activity. The leader whistled commands and dove for the trees. Others followed, except for two hunters left aloft to maintain a soaring vigil for as long as the dying thermals would hold them. Braan and his warriors landed on the backside of the wooded peninsula below the long-legs encampment.

"They won't talk about it," Hudson said. "They won't say why they attacked the fleet or what is going to happen now. The bad news is their planet is at war."

"Wee cannah tell-ah wha' haffen when-ah war-ah over," Kateos said.

Buccari was growing accustomed to the paragogic inflections of the prodigious creature; she also detected resignation—sadness—in the female's words. The kones sat around the campfire, relishing the heat but remaining wary and acutely attentive to the movement of the humans. A huge, thick rubbery tent had been erected in the clearing. The kones were to stay for three nights. Their one clear objective, besides bringing Hudson back and learning more of the human language, was to establish a schedule and a plan for future interchanges.

"What-ah message should-ah I bring to my leaders?" Kateos asked.

"Tell them we came to your star in peace," Buccari said. "We mean no harm. We are stranded here. Will your government accept our presence?"

Kateos seemed perplexed by the question. The conversations had been painfully slow, mostly introductions and attempts to define roles. It was clear that Et Silmarn was in charge.

Buccari rephrased the query: "Can we stay on Genellan?"

Katoes turned to Et Silmarn and spoke her melodious tongue. They talked at length, many words for such a short question. Kateos nodded sharply.

"The war-ah on Kon muss' end-ah," she said. "Your quess-chun must-ah wait-ah until war-ah end-ah—"

"How long? How many days until war end?" Hudson asked.

"Cannot-ah tell," the kone answered. "Maybe not-ah end-ah."

"It must end . . . sometime. Do you want us to stay on Genellan?" Buccari asked in frustration. "Do *you* want us to stay here?" She opened her arms to include all of them.

Kateos nodded and translated. Et Silmarn spoke only two words.

"Yesss," Kateos said emphatically. "Wee learn from-ah yew."

"What—" Buccari started to ask, but Kateos interrupted.

"Sharl. It-ah b-ber' cold-ah for-ah kones. B-ber' cold-ah. Sun gone. Can wee stop-ah for-ah now? Start-ah in more-ning? More-ning is right-ah word-ah, Huhsawn?" she asked. Hudson nodded and smiled. "It-ah iss b-ber' hard-ah to talk-ah. That-ah iss why wee come. Wee mus' learn talk-ah." Her great body was shivering.

"Yes, of course. We talk in morning," Buccari replied, standing up. The kones ponderously extended to their full intimidating height and with little ceremony retired to their tent. One of them hunkered at the tent's entrance, a laser in his big hands—a guard. He was clearly frightened—his eyes darted around the surrounding campsite—and cold. He shivered violently but refused to leave the door of the tent for the warmer vicinity of the fire despite Hudson's polite entreaties.

Soon after the kones disappeared, baby Adam began to cry loudly. Dawson exited her tent carrying the bawling infant. The konish guard turned to the noise and watched intently as Dawson sat in front of the fire, joining Shannon. Dawson settled the child under her furs to nurse, and the baby's complaining stopped. The guard poked his head into the konish tent, and within minutes all the kones reappeared. They tentatively crawled to the campfire, staring owlishly at Dawson, firelight reflecting from their helmet visors, the ones in the back rising to their hinds. Buccari stood to confront the gaping kones.

"What is it, Kateos?" she asked. "Do you have a question?"

Kateos sat back on her haunches and held her hands in supplication. "Sharl, yew have . . . new hewmans? Small hewmans? I not-ah know word. Childs?" she asked quietly. "Wee would-ah pleese seee? Pleese!"

Buccari turned to the curious firelit faces of her own people.

"Nance, they want to see Adam," she said. Dawson looked frightened.

"Nancy," Hudson said. "If you don't want to, that's okay."

Dawson stirred and adjusted her furs, bringing the infant out on her lap. Adam was swaddled in rags, remnants of clothes and blankets. The nervous mother wrapped the infant in a thick hide to protect it from the chilly night air. The kones shuffled nervously and whispered loudly. Dawson, holding the newborn in her arms, stood and tentatively approached the first row of kneeling giants. Shannon rose to his feet and moved protectively behind Dawson.

"What's the deal, Lieutenant?" Dawson asked.

"You got me. They must not get to see many babies," Buccari replied. "Stop there, Nancy. Nash, bring them one at a time."

Dawson halted next to the crackling fire. Kateos's great bulk crawled forward. Dawson tilted her shoulders so the light of the fire could illuminate the baby's round, pink face. Firelight danced from Adam's clear blue eyes. His tiny lips, moist from suckling, cast flame-colored highlights. A small fist burst free from the furs and wandered with purpose into the infant's sucking mouth. Kateos stared, unblinking. Tears streamed down her face, falling against her helmet visor. Shannon looked nervously at Dawson, but the kone's emotional reaction had banished the mother's fears.

* * *

"What transpires?" Craag asked brusquely.

"They examine the long-legs whelp," Braan replied. "Most peculiar."

Cliff dwellers, hidden by darkness, had entered the long-legs' campsite and were peering at the spectacle, black eyes scintillating in the firelight.

"The long-legs trust the bear people," Craag said. "Perhaps the legends are wrong and the bear people are not evil."

"Perhaps," Braan replied. "Perhaps it is only cliff dwellers that bear people kill."

"Is it not possible the long-legs will become allies with the bear people—against us?"

Braan rudely said nothing, his right as leader. He endeavored to catch the attention of Brave-crazy-one.

MacArthur knew the cliff dwellers did not like the kones, so when he saw Captain and X.O. out of the corner of his eye, he was surprised. He jumped to his feet and started to shout but instinctively bit back his words. The cliff dwellers signed danger. The kones noticed MacArthur's abrupt movements and watched him alertly. MacArthur looked away from the surreptitious hunters, stretching and yawning, attempting to ease the unsettling effects of his initial actions.

"Well," he said too loudly. "I'm going down to the lake and haul in some shoreline. Lieutenant! Sarge! When you get a minute, I'll be needing your help." Turning quickly, he set off down the gentle slope toward the dark lake, leaving the bemused humans looking at each other. The kones, captivated by the babies—Goldberg had brought Honey out to join Adam in the spotlight—lost interest in the disturbance.

In dim moonlight MacArthur made contact with the hunters approaching the cove beach. Together they walked across the narrow peninsula to the lakeshore. Glittering stars and a haunting sliver of a moon sparkled from the velvet waters, and gentle waves lapped the rocky shore. A night creature hooted mournfully. As MacArthur's eyes adapted, he detected other hunters moving wraithlike through the shadows.

Buccari and Shannon arrived. Under the insignificant light of the new moon Buccari rendered a formal greeting. Captain returned her salutation and presented a parchment—a message from the elders. It was too dark to read; Buccari slipped it under her furs.

"Captain doesn't trust our new friends," she said.

"The kones are the giants, the bear people in dweller mythology," MacArthur said. "The cliff dwellers are afraid of them."

"So am I," Shannon said.

"So should we all be if the dweller legends are true," Buccari said.

"Blasting the fleet into hyperlight wasn't a good start with us, either," Shannon said. "Do—"

A soft whistling caused Captain to turn abruptly. The hunter leader turned back to MacArthur and flashed adroit hand signals in the dim light. The cliff dweller leader had learned MacArthur's sign language with ease and was as much teacher as student.

"Someone is coming. One of ours," MacArthur translated. A rustling noise marked the approach of a two-legged animal—Hudson.

"Did you put our friends to bed?" Buccari asked. "What was that all about?"

"Yeah, they're back in the tent. I'm not certain," Hudson replied.

"They act as if they've never seen children," Shannon said.

"I don't think they have," Hudson answered. "Kateos garbled something about konish children being taken from their mothers as infants, but she wasn't making much sense. They're very emotional. What's going on?"

"Captain delivered a letter," Buccari answered. "Let's find some light and decipher it. I have a feeling that it's a warning to avoid the kones—as if we could."

"The cliff dwellers know something we don't," MacArthur said.

"The kones seem peaceful," Hudson said. "They treated me well."

"All we've met are scientists," Buccari said. "Watch what happens when the political or religious leaders get involved."

"Lieutenant, are these the Killers of Shaula?" Shannon asked.

"It's a big galaxy, Sergeant. It sure smells like it, but who knows?" Buccari said. "Enough for now. Nash, I want you to notify each member of the crew that they are not to discuss cliff dwellers around the kones. Top secret. Let's learn as much as we can and be as nice as we can—but try not to tell them anything. We've got three days of diplomacy ahead of us. Don't blow it."

THIRTY-THREE

A GENELLAN YEAR

Summer advanced; the settlement grew in steady stages but never fast enough for Buccari. Shannon knew he was in trouble before she spoke.

"Where the hell are they?" she snapped, flipping a thick braid of sun-streaked auburn hair over her shoulder. Lizard followed her like a dog, stylus in hand. Two other cliff dwellers—stone carvers—labored on the lodge foundation, setting stones and nervously watching the heated exchange. Whenever kones were present in the valley, the cliff dwellers became invisible, but with the kones gone, the knobby-headed creatures scurried about the settlement with characteristic single-minded purpose.

Shannon looked down at the striking, if stern, visage. "MacArthur thinks he can get close enough to the buffalo to get some of their hides. I gave him permission to take Tatum and Chastain across the river and give it a shot. I take full responsibility, sir."

"Sure, Sarge," she snapped, "you always do, but—dammit, I want this lodge and palisade up as soon as possible. With Hudson and Chief Wilson gone south, we're a bit shorthanded, now, aren't we?"

"Yes, sir. The rest of us will take up the slack, Lieutenant," Shannon continued. "We need the hides, sir. Mac doesn't want to shoot any more lake elk. Tatum says there aren't that many in the valley. Killing off the local herd won't help us in the long run."

"Okay, Sergeant," she exhaled, turning to continue on her rounds, the cliff dweller mimicking her movements. "It's a

good call. I just hope they survive the stink. The musk is awful
strong today."

"They'll do okay, sir," Shannon replied as Buccari marched
away downhill toward the planted fields on the flatter margins
of the cove.

"Whoee, Sarge," O'Toole whistled. "Thought you were
buttburger."

Petit and Gordon, leaning against large rocks just transported
from the quarry, laughed. Shannon's neck grew hot.

"You helmetheads better start putting real muscle on those
rocks instead of just your fat asses," he snapped. "Move! You
heard the lieutenant."

The marines crept over the low ridge and looked down on
endless herds. A rippling herd of gray-striped tundra gazelles
bolted from their scent, and a giant eagle soared low over the
downs, its monstrous wings flapping lazily. The river valley
lay behind them. To the west, billowing ash and steam, were
the twin volcanoes; beyond the volcanoes were the cliffs of the
plateau, and beyond the cliffs were the perpetually snowcapped
mountains, gracing the horizon with their ponderous majesty.
A land of immense vistas—and immense odors.

"Good grief, Mac!" Tatum exclaimed, gagging. "How can
you take this?"

The cinnamon-red and burnt-umber backs of musk-buffalo
formed a placid sea of pelt and muscle. Interspersed at irregular distances were small concentrations of lighter-colored animals, muted straw-yellow and gold. MacArthur looked
skyward and saw Captain and Tonto soaring overhead, the
hunters his nearly constant companions. Returning his scrutiny
to the grazing beasts, he pondered his options. He had to get
closer. No wasted bullets! MacArthur could think of only one
strategy.

"Stay put," he ordered, rising to his feet. "I'm walking until
I get close enough to shoot."

"What!" Tatum exclaimed. "Closer? The smell will kill us."

"I said stay put! I'm going solo. If it gets bad, I'll turn
back."

"I'd say it's bad enough now," Tatum groaned.

"Gotta kill him to stop him," Chastain said. "Careful, Mac!"

MacArthur grinned as he checked the action of his assault
rifle.

"Have to get damn close to hit anything with that," Tatum said.

"Then I better start walking," MacArthur muttered. He would go right at them, slow and steady. The smell was immense. His head throbbed, and his sinuses burned. His nose and eyes started to run, and he worried that his eyesight would be too blurry, but he pressed forward, the musk-buffalo oblivious to his presence. At three hundred meters some animals lifted their massive heads and looked in his direction. Still too far away. The first shot would stampede the herd. There would be no second chance.

The prodigious smell assaulted MacArthur's sanity. He reeled with nausea, constantly shaking fuzziness from behind his eyes. He stopped, dropped to a knee, and threw up until his stomach was empty, and then he retched and gagged for many more minutes. His guts purged, he staggered to his feet and continued his drunken march toward the milling buffalo. He heard soft lowing and bellowing. He forced his vision to focus and noticed the nearest animals moving away slowly, the press of the herd holding them in check. When would they spook? Could he get a shot off? Out of the corner of his eye he detected a motion; Captain and Tonto glided low over the tundra grasses, coming straight for him. The dwellers landed at his feet, skipping and hopping to a halt, chattering and squeaking, flashing hand signs urgently. MacArthur stared stupidly, unable to comprehend. His throat burned. With effort he recalled his mission and began walking but immediately stumbled and fell, leg muscles stiffening and joints locking.

The dwellers waddled close and lay next to him. Captain waved both hands frantically, indicating that MacArthur should stay on the ground. That was unnecessary because MacArthur was physically unable to stand. The trio lay flat, concealed by the yielding soil and short prairie grasses. Something was happening. MacArthur shook fog from his brain and strained his vision outward. He had walked farther than he had intended. The animals had moved, and he had penetrated into the herd. Buffalo grazed placidly on three sides, and some were slowly moving around behind, less than a hundred meters away, closing the gap and coming closer. He gaped inanely at the cliff dwellers and waved a hand feebly in thanks, trying to smile. He dry heaved instead. The cliff dwellers huddled on each side of him, intent on his condition.

MacArthur wanted to sleep; unconsciousness would end his

misery. Captain prodded annoyingly at his elbow, and he dreamily opened his eyes, trying hard to be irritated. MacArthur looked into the hunter's sinister eyes, its scarred snout practically touching his numb nose. The little creature chewed on something, and its breath smelled sweet, all the more remarkable because the odor distinctly penetrated the miasma of buffalo musk. MacArthur's brain labored to process the foggy input, but the noxious effects of the musk were overpowering; he felt his nervous system shutting down. The rifle fell from his hands, his fingers unable to answer the commands from his misfiring brain. MacArthur sprawled and half rolled onto his side. He had withdrawn from his body, and all that he had left was his vision—and his lungs! His breathing, heavy and labored, was the only sound in his universe. All else was silent.

Buffalo drew near. One was but fifty paces away, downwind and coming closer. MacArthur endeavored to stay interested in the beasts. He tried to remember his mission. His mission! What mission? Apathy and fatigue brought sad and restful thoughts, and he felt his last bit of self-will slip into eternity. Coma was near, death not far behind.

Something vigorously shook his head. Vaguely annoyed, MacArthur focused on Captain's ugly face. The dweller's mouth opened, and a bony little claw reached into the tooth-lined maw and pulled out a wad of spinach-green material—a cud, masticated and churned with saliva. MacArthur, still detached from powers of deduction, watched dully as the dweller's hands came into contact with his own senseless mouth. Strong, wiry fingers—warm and leathery—pried open his slack jaws and inserted the lump of dark green on his tongue. Captain brought the human's chin to, closing MacArthur's mouth on the strange substance. MacArthur wanted to sleep. To die.

The same sweet smell he had detected earlier manifested itself as a sensation on his taste buds. A sensation—something felt! Like an explosion expanding outward, nerve endings reawakened to the electrical impulses of consciousness. Muscles twitched with spurious signals, and a section of his brain still capable of command ordered his jaws to grind juices from the green pulp in his mouth. Awake again—the sweet taste and smell rushed through his palate and sinuses and down his throat. The cliff dweller had given him a stimulant of wondrous power; MacArthur felt alert, psychedelically aware. The colors of the world pulsed with intensity. His mission! He remembered his mission with obsessive fervor.

Buffalo grazed about him—more easy targets than he had bullets. MacArthur slowly turned his head to look at the hunters. The dwellers watched him intensely, concern dominating their obscene features. MacArthur opened his mouth, holding the green substance between his teeth, and displayed it to Captain. Both creatures—man and hunter—grinned conspiratorially. The cliff dweller made a shooting motion with his hands. MacArthur recovered the rifle and turned his body slightly, aiming the heavy-sighted weapon at the neck of the nearest buffalo—a large bull—barely thirty meters away. The movement caught the animal's attention; it jerked its head upward, alarmed. MacArthur and his furry comrades froze, the hunters staring with rapt attention at the barrel of the weapon. Both creatures held hands tightly over their ear openings, wincing and flinching with painful anticipation.

MacArthur fired one round. The bull staggered, took several stuttering steps, and crashed heavily onto its side, raising a cloud of dust. The cliff dwellers, stunned by the rifle's report, recovered from the explosion and jumped up and down, whistling and chirping. The buffalo herd reeled against the noise and blindly dashed in full flight—a stampede! MacArthur moved awkwardly to his knees, the muscles of his extremities not responding fully. He worried about getting run down—an imminent possibility since buffalo were galloping randomly in all directions. Two bulls leading a frantic herd bore down on his position. The cliff dwellers pointed—rudely—at the driving animals, nervously hopping from leg to leg and unfurling their wings.

MacArthur sighted down the barrel of the rifle, placing the bouncing forehead of the biggest bull atop the knife-edged sight. The buffalo were close! He squeezed the trigger, and the big rifle kicked violently against his shoulder. The small herd pivoted as one, swerving hard away. MacArthur swore for wasting a bullet and took aim at the same bull. But the animal was wounded, and its pace slowed amid its panicked mates. The stricken animal lumbered to a wobbly halt, staggering lopsidedly away from the herd. It slowly fell to its front knees and collapsed on its side, bellowing in fear and agony as it died.

The dwellers, hands still over their ears, screeched their delight. The rest of the herd bolted away, giving MacArthur only hindquarters at which to shoot. Two bullets, two hides.

Enough. MacArthur chewed vigorously. The substance in his mouth yielded juices like sparks of electricity crackling against his teeth and throat. He felt tightly wound, a coiled steel spring; his senses were acutely raw; he could see forever; the sounds and smells around him were abundant and crisp, each a separate and distinct event. Pungent buffalo musk billowed through the air, almost visible, a brown, dusky odor—not pleasant but no longer putrid. He could smell the tundra grasses, the gunpowder, the cliff dwellers; he could smell his own sharp body odor and the high-grade machine oil used on the rifles. But— But something was wrong! The dwellers were whistling—whistling at him. Too loud; it hurt his ears.

The clouds! The clouds were flowing like wild things overhead! They were changing colors—luminescent and pulsing and golden. The clouds were beautiful animals descending from the skies. MacArthur could reach out and touch them. He could fly! He could fly—fly like the animals in the clouds. What was happening? This was not real. His intellect struggled to overcome his senses, but he was no longer sure of anything. Something was wrong with his body—with his mind. He was hallucinating. It was too real, too vivid. Golden horses! Golden horses, heavy chested with silky manes streaming, were running over the prairie. Beautiful. So beautiful. He could smell them.

MacArthur was afraid to move. His very being eclipsed his corporeal form, as if he would burst his skin like an overinflated balloon. The spinach stuff! He stopped chewing. He dimly deduced that the dwellers' stimulant was causing him to hallucinate. He spit it out just as his arms and legs seemed to disappear; he fell forward unimpeded, like a falling tree, squarely on his face. Helpless, mouth open and drooling into the tundra, he watched magical horses gallop across the plains just paces in front of him, thundering hoofs vibrating the ground. What magnificence! Euphoric, he managed to roll over on his back and stare at the sky. Everything was beautiful.

"The thickweed has taken over!" Brappa exclaimed.

The stampeding herds were clear, and a veering wind kept the invisible musk cloud at bay. Braan looked back at the other long-legs, Giant-one and One-arm, stumbling drunkenly over the prairie grasses in the far distance.

"He has spit it out. He will recover," he announced. "Let us skin the buffalo."

Brave-crazy-one lay spread-eagled, eyes glazed. Braan picked up the discarded wad of thickweed pulp, broke it apart, and placed it in his leather pouch. The hunters pulled out knives, and each headed for a downed animal.

Braan was not long at his task when he noticed the stricken long-legs staggering toward him, head in his hands. His comrades were trying to help him, but Brave-crazy-one rejected their assistance.

"The long-legs recovers," Brappa screeched.

"Its head will surely ache," Braan warbled.

Buccari adjusted her position so that the light from the extravagant campfire fell more directly on the dweller message. She half listened to the raucous banter, feeling peculiarly light-hearted. They were starting a new life, their new settlement was born. And they had just finished their first year on the planet. Not an Earth year—a full Genellan year: four hundred days, each day twenty-six hours long.

"I saw horses. Golden horses!" MacArthur declared.

"You're crazy, Mac," Fenstermacher said. "You were drunk as a dog."

"Leave him alone, Winfried," Dawson said. "Look what he did for us. What a feast."

"Dawson's right for the first time in her life, Fenstermacher," Wilson said. "Stop picking on Mac and be thankful you've survived a year on this planet. I don't know how we managed to put up with you."

"Yeah, Winnie," Lee said. "Happy anniversary to us all."

Cliff dwellers and humans sat around the evening fire. The midsummer sun had reluctantly settled behind the soaring peaks, leaving clear skies layered in vivid orange and deepest blue above the stark sawtooth silhouette. The meal was over, but the campfire burned brightly, a celebration of survival.

MacArthur's provision of buffalo steaks and hides had changed the dubious nature of the occasion into a festive and social mood. The campers reveled in the telling and retelling of MacArthur's adventure, embellishments growing with each new version. MacArthur regaled the listeners, humans and cliff dwellers, with outrageous histrionics and exaggerated sign language. The marine danced around the fire, pulling Tonto along behind him. The young hunter parodied the dancing human, and soon all the hunters were jumping to their feet and dancing a pagan conga, whistling and screeching in a snaking line behind MacArthur, while the humans pounded out a rhythmic chant, clapping and laughing.

The dwellers had taken to joining the humans at their evening campfire. The taller guilders had grown comfortable with the humans, having found living with them more tolerable than living in the woods with their hunter cousins. A tent adjacent to the campfire had been provided for the visiting workers, while the hunters remained content inhabiting the rocks on the wooded peninsula, close to the fish.

Dancing shadows cast by the flickering firelight struck the newly risen stone walls and foundation of the main lodge looming above the fire pit, sheltering the flames from steady northerlies. With the help and guidance of dweller stone carvers, construction of the lodge had moved rapidly, and its stone walls were nearing completion.

The stone carvers were not the only ones to make a difference in the new community. With the frosts behind them, and despite some insect pests, the crops planted from seed flourished. The gardeners were intrigued with the variety and impressed with the robust qualities of the fruit trees and vegetable plants. When Buccari presented them with a sampling of the seeds, they behaved as if they had been given precious gems, falling to their knees in effusive gratitude.

In addition to helping with the crops, the gardeners spent time with Lee, gleaning and gathering medicinal roots, tanning agents, and herbs. The gardeners had much earlier shown Lee a dark, pulpy plant, giving her an emphatic caution to its use—a medicinal narcotic. Using Lizard's writing skills as the communication vehicle, the gardeners described the weed's primary medical benefit—it was a potent but potentially lethal painkiller. MacArthur's exploits had revealed yet another use for the thick, blackish leaves.

The dancing MacArthur fell to the ground exhausted, and chirping hunters piled on top of him. Tonto stood on the marine's chest and whistled sharply, his whistle soaring into the ultrasonic realm as MacArthur suddenly sat up and lifted the dweller high in the air. The other hunters tumbled backward as the laughing MacArthur regained his feet, hugging Tonto close to his chest. He placed the hunter on the ground and bowed low. The hunters, all of them, bowed in return.

MacArthur flopped on a log, and the other dancers stumbled and hopped back to their seats, tweeting and chirping.

"You didn't see them?" MacArthur asked Chastain and

Tatum for the twentieth time since awakening from the thickweed stupor. "They were beautiful. I could smell them!"

"We were too far away, Mac," Tatum answered. "I thought you were dead. And the stink was too much. We both kept passing out. I don't know how you were able to walk so far and stay conscious. We thought you were dead for sure."

"Beautiful," MacArthur said softly. "Horses. I smelled them."

"Well, at least now we know how to get close to the buffalo," Chastain said. "That locoweed grows along the river. I picked some."

"Careful with that stuff," MacArthur chided. "My head still hurts."

"Yes, be careful," Lee pleaded. "We need to experiment with it first. It's obviously a mind-altering substance, possibly habit-forming. It may have permanent effects."

"MacArthur's mind don't need any more altering," Tatum offered. "He already comes up with enough crazy ideas. You should have seen him staggering after those buffalo!"

"Don't get him started again!" Shannon shouted, and everyone laughed.

"Why don't you ask Lizard about the horses, Mac?" Buccari asked. She and the guilder had been sitting on adjacent flat rocks, industriously scrawling messages to each other in the flickering firelight. "I could use some help, and since Hudson's still enjoying the sunny south, it looks like you're elected."

"I don't know how much help I'll be." MacArthur slid next to her and grabbed a writing implement and a clean parchment. She watched as he deftly made the interrogative signs and added a series of action icons describing the hunting activity. Lizard watched.

MacArthur's skills had progressed markedly, almost on par with Hudson's but still short of Buccari's. The mood around the campfire became quiet and peaceful, with everyone patiently waiting for MacArthur's written query. Dawson hummed as she rocked Adam, the fire crackled and popped, and the modest noises satisfied everyone's need for society.

Buccari moved out of MacArthur's way and turned her back to the fire so she could more easily puzzle out the long message Lizard had just prepared for her. Two hunters had flown in from the dweller colony late in the day, bringing instructions for Captain. The cliff dwellers had spent almost an hour among themselves prior to the evening's feast, and Lizard was communicating the essence of that meeting to her now. Captain sat stoically nearby, alertly watching every move.

Buccari broke the serenity.

"The dwellers all leave tomorrow," she said, getting everyone's attention and eliciting groans of disappointment.

"All of them? Even the stone carvers and gardeners?" Lee asked. "Why?"

"First, the bear people will be back soon," Buccari said. The dwellers disappeared into the forests at the first sign of a konish airplane. "Secondly, and more importantly, the hunters must return for a salt mission. The hunters will not leave the guilders here unprotected."

MacArthur looked up from the drawings. "A salt mission, eh?"

"We'll miss our friends," Lee said.

"But it will be good to see Mr. Hudson and Chief Wilson again," Dawson said. "I bet they'll have a million sea stories."

"After two weeks with the bugs," Shannon put in, "they'll be glad to get back."

"I don't know," Buccari said. "The way Hudson went on about how warm it was there, neither one may ever come back."

"Finished," MacArthur announced, handing Lizard his message. The cliff dweller scanned it before starting his reply, and as usual, the guilder was quick. He handed his reply to MacArthur. On the parchment was a clean and precise line drawing of a muscular, short-legged horse, its mane and tail flowing.

"That's it!" MacArthur shouted. "Look at this! This is what I saw!" He held the drawing up for the others to see, then abruptly sat down and began adding to the message. Buccari watched over his shoulder and quickly grasped MacArthur's intention.

"They certainly must have thought of it before," she said. "There must be a reason why they haven't used the horses to carry salt bags."

"They aren't strong enough to control a horse," MacArthur said, handing Lizard his response.

Lizard looked at the sequence of icons thoughtfully. He communicated with Captain for several minutes, and the hunter became very excited—unusual for the stolid warrior.

"What's his problem?" Fenstermacher yawned.

"We're going to catch us some horses," MacArthur said.

THIRTY-FOUR

DISCOVERIES

Two abats banked over the settlement. Standing under the big solitary hardwood tree next to the tombstones, Buccari watched the aircraft. She turned and walked up the hill, away from the cove. This arrival was special: Hudson and Wilson were returning. She dispatched O'Toole and Petit up the steep trail to the landing area to greet the two men and escort their alien visitors. Two hours later all had returned to camp.

"Welcome back, Chief!" Goldberg cried, rushing to hug the portly man.

"You're still ugly, Chief!" Fenstermacher shouted.

"Ohh!" Wilson groaned. "Now I know why I liked being away so much."

The returning men were surrounded. The visiting kones waited patiently, content to let the greetings run their course. Buccari, acknowledging her duty, walked around the knot of people and up to the towering kones, bowing. Et Silmarn removed his helmet and graciously returned the gesture.

"Welcome back . . . to our settlement," Buccari said slowly.

"Thang yew, Sharl," Et Silmarn responded passably. "Yew have-ah done much." His prodigious arm lifted and swept over the construction, sausagelike fingers pointing at the main lodge. Stone walls and chimneys were capped by a sturdy rafter frame for a high-pitched roof. A corner section and a long run of the log palisade were in place, and a plot of vegetables flourished in dark green abundance. Chips of wood lay thick underfoot, and the odors of resin and sawdust permeated the air. The humans had made their mark.

"We must prepare, Et Silmarn," she replied. "Winter is unforgiving."

Et Silmarn looked to Kateos for help. The female translated quickly.

"Yes! B-berry unfork-ah . . . even. Winner tooo cold-ah! It b-berry cold now!" The bulky alien clasped his own bulky shoulders, a universal gesture.

Buccari nodded, smiling inwardly, for it was a warm day. She turned to Hudson. "Welcome back—yet again, Nash. You must be used to the trip," she said.

"The lodge looks terrific!" Hudson exclaimed.

"O'Toole and Fenstermacher are first-rate carpenters, and MacArthur's friends have been a big help," Buccari replied cryptically, referring to the cliff dwellers. She noticed Kateos's questioning expression.

Hudson quickly continued. "The trip's a grind, but they let me fly. It's a big, wild planet, Sharl. It's beautiful . . ." He paused, his expression speaking for itself.

"I envy you," Buccari said. "You'll have to take me up for a view."

"You bet. The kones want us all to fly south. They're friendly, Sharl," he continued, "and Kateos will be speaking Legion better than you or me pretty soon. She's programming a voice recognition system that translates in real time. It doesn't work too well yet, but wait a few weeks." The konish female's face dropped demurely.

"She's an expert," Hudson continued. "She asks questions about tenses, grammar, nouns, verbs, sentence structure—everything. It was good to have Chief Wilson along just to give her a new subject to study and give me a break from all the questions."

"I'll bet he taught her some choice words!" Fenstermacher joked.

"Watch it, Fensterman!" Wilson shouted. "Or I'll tell the lieutenant not to let you go south." He turned to Buccari. "Oh, man, Lieutenant, it's wonderful! Rains a bit, but the place is beautiful—turquoise-blue ocean with wide, sandy beaches. And islands with lagoons. Trees with fruit—we brought some back for the mess. To be honest, I'm looking forward to going back."

Buccari looked at the sun-burnished, unworried face, the clear hazel eyes beseeching permission to return with the kones, a powerful testimony to the allure of the south.

"We missed you, Chief," she said. "Go check out the lodge.

Help Tookmanian decide how to lay out the galley—er, the kitchen."

Wilson's face flickered with disappointment as he moved away, taking the bulk of the chattering crew with him. Assisted by Chastain, the kones migrated to their campsite and set up their huge tents, leaving Shannon, Hudson, and Buccari standing alone.

"Hey, Sharl," Hudson said quietly. "Kateos started hitting me up for skinny on the drives. She and those two new guys really worked me over."

"What did you tell them?" she asked.

"Nothing worth knowing," Hudson snorted. "Give me a little credit. And watch out, they're recording everything. I mean, they're friendly, but they're damn serious about it."

She pondered the implications of Hudson's information.

"Gunner sure wants to go back," Shannon said. "Must be nice there."

"It really is," Hudson said softly. "Chief Wilson has found a home. I practically had to tie him down to get him in the abat. You should see him walking bare-assed naked down those beaches, bald head sunburned and his gut hanging out. You know, Sharl, before we got out of the 'vette, Virgil Rhodes said Wilson would die on a tropical island. Gunner took him seriously. I think he's already picked out the island."

"Well, I'm not ready for him to die yet," Buccari said impatiently. "We need all hands working—maybe even you, Nash. Winter will be here before we know it, and I'm—*we're* going to be ready."

"Why not move everyone south?" Hudson asked. "Like the kones want."

Buccari remained silent. She looked past the camp, surveying the verdant valley with its clear lake and frothy waterfalls.

"Welcome back, Nash," she said. "Sarge, take Mr. Hudson down and show him what the boys have done." She grabbed Hudson's arm and gently pushed him down the path. Shannon led the way, and the two men headed for the new construction. Buccari followed for a few steps and then stopped. She stared again at the magnificent scenery as if for the first time. Nagging doubts hectored her.

Hudson's unanswered question had struck a nerve. She thought of Commander Quinn's original reluctance to leave the plateau in favor of the valley before the first killing winter. Would they really have been better off in the valley? Or would they have just lasted a little longer without the cliff dwellers close enough to save them? Was this another verse of the same song? Should she order everyone south? Or should they persevere, continuing what they had started? Perhaps the coldness of the north was their best protection. Going south would only increase contact with the Konish government, and increased contact would inevitably cause problems. Of that, somehow, she was positive.

Decisions! Decisions! The frustration of leadership—the price of leadership. But Buccari had made up her mind. They would face winter in the valley, and they would be ready for the cold and deprivation. Maybe they would move to the warm and sunny south the next summer—maybe. Yet somehow the thought did not appeal to her; somehow it was important to stay near the cliff dwellers; somehow it was important to have them as an ally. Perhaps suffering through another winter would change her mind.

She walked over to the kones. Kateos brightened at her approach.

"The war on Kon continues, Sharl," she reported. "We cannot-ah tell anything new, but we are worried—worried about ourselves. No one knows what-ah to happen. We have not heard-ah what became of Et Avian, not-ah even if he live or died. Et Silmarn is, uh . . . concerned. He is like brother to Et Avian." Her loquaciousness was unfettered with her increasing command of the human language.

Buccari pushed; perhaps there was something to be gained. "What is the war about, Kateos? What do they fight over?"

"Power. They fight-ah for power. As always." Kateos removed her helmet and leaned onto her forelimbs, putting her eyes at the same level as the eyes of the sitting human.

"Are many kones dying?" Buccari asked.

Kateos snuffled and nodded her head. "The reports are, uh . . . not clear, b-but it-ah appear that-ah many kones have died—millions."

"Millions!" Buccari exclaimed. "Is there no concern for loss of life?"

"Yess. Yess, but-ah only as . . . as one values fuel in rocket or grain in silo. Our rulers not-ah concern for the masses. Unskilled kones—we call them *trods*—are numbers, statistics—po . . . tential soldiers or laborers or workers," Kateos answered, a metallic note in her deep voice. "Huhsawn, ah . . . Hudd-sawn has told-ah me much about your families and about freedom. Our evil system does not-ah permit these ideas."

"My world has many standards and many problems," Buccari said.

"B-but look at-ah you!" Kateos said. "You—a tiny female—are officer and leader! Leader of warriors. And Huh—Hudd-sawn says that-ah you are space pilot. That can never, never happen among konish female."

"Perhaps I am not a good example."

"Good example or not-ah, you have reached status of which konish females cannot even dream," Kateos said with a forlorn tone. "And your race has traveled across space—a, uh . . . miraculous, yes?—a miraculous thing to travel the stars."

Buccari's head jerked upward at the unintended confession. "You mean your race does not travel outside of your own—er, to other stars?"

Kateos looked confused. "Ah, no . . . I should-ah not talk abou' it-ah. It-ah is great mystery with my people. Kon has been attack-ah from space. My government-ah feels threat-ah by attacks from space. We want-ah to know how you fly between stars. We be asking you about—"

"We did not attack you," Buccari said, her mind racing: *The kones were not the Killers of Shaula.* "You attacked us. We came in peace."

"We not-ah know that-ah. Kon has been attacked before," Kateos rumbled, looking about nervously. "Many kones killed. We assume you come to attack us again and you tricking us."

"We have never been here," Buccari said. "My people did not attack yours."

"It was m-many years ago," Kateos stuttered. "P-perhaps your generals keep it-ah hidden for their own benefit."

"How many years, Kateos?"

"Over four hundred-ah years. Kone years," Kateos answered softly.

Five hundred Earth years! Five hundred years earlier humans had not even reached Mars, the hyperlight anomaly still a century from being discovered.

"Kateos, how long have kones been traveling to Genellan?"

"Many years, over nine hundred kone years," Kateos replied.

Buccari gulped. Definitely advanced—the kones had been flying in space for over twice the time humans had, *but they had failed to break the hyperlight barrier.* She was beginning to understand the game. She changed the subject.

"Why do you call yourselves evil? Your race has accomplished much," Buccari asked. "Your system works well. You are intelligent. I perceive you to be gentle and good. An evil system would be incapable of producing such beings."

Kateos thought for several seconds. "In many ways our culture, our system, works well. Very well," she remarked. "You have met-ah only scientists and technicians. Most science is the art-ah and, uh . . . uh, application of gentle logic. Our social system controls personality. It controls ours, uh . . . dispositions and our in-tellects. We are b-bred-ah to the task. If we gentle and good, it is b-because it makes us better at our jobs. We are b-bred-ah for job, with traits that-ah you describe."

"Bred to be scientists! How?"

Kateos sat back on her haunches and again pondered an answer. "It is old-ah system," she began. "Many generations have been . . . trained—yes? Of course, it begins with childs. All childs of common parent taken—sometime by force—at b-birth. Mothers and fathers never see childs. Only nobility allow the raising of childs."

"How can that be? Where do your childs, er—children go?"

"Ah, yes, it is children. First-ah go to government nurseries and then to schools. The schools—'training centers' is better translation—where they are sorted and trained and, if they, uh . . . genetically correct, molded into skill units. Skill units become scientists, technicians, officers, administrators, artisans, or farmers. The rest—most—assigned to unskilled labor: *trods*. *Trods* sorted by size and emotion and assigned—when very young—to become soldier, worker, field hand, or common laborer. *Trods* not gentle—they not raised to be gentle—although most *trods* be good-ah and well meaning."

"Everywhere? On your whole planet?" Buccari asked.

"Oh, yes! It-ah b-be for whole planet. The system work-ah too well. No one think of changing it-ah. Our farmers good farmers, our workers good workers, our universities . . . filled with hardworking students. Our soldiers be brave and aggressive—if not smart-ah. Unfortunately . . . uh, ambition and power be usual traits of our leaders, and strength be first important than smartness."

"It sounds orderly," Buccari said, amazed.

Kateos shook her head slowly. "Orderly? Yes." She dropped her gaze. "Sadness! It-ah is a sad life. I had not thought of r-reason before, but seeing your babies makes it-ah clear to me. We sad because there are no childs—children . . . no families."

"Why? Why no families?" Buccari asked.

"Konish solution to population problem. Long ago there many, many kones on planet. Too many. Not enough food."

"Your governments restricted breeding?"

"Only by requiring marrying. Only able to marry one time. It-ah crime to have children if not-ah married. Only married couples permit-ah to have children and must-ah be qualified by government-ah. That-ah how they control population. I lucky be married to Scientist Dowornobb. He intelligent and kind, and he make happy to me. We sure to have license to make children, especially since so many kones die in war."

"I am glad for you, Kateos," Buccari said, noting the konish female's sudden radiance. The radiance turned subtly to determination.

"I hold my baby someday," Kateos rumbled. "That-ah would make happy to me."

Buccari looked up to see Et Silmarn and two of the konish scientists crawling their way. Kateos straightened, standing tall while remaining on all fours.

"Sharl, I introduce Scientist H'Aare and Scientist Mirrtis to you," Kateos said. "They experts in space drives."

Buccari's internal alarms went off. The kones did not have the secrets of hyperlight. She guessed what was coming.

"We would-ah like to know how your ships travel between stars," Kateos continued. "We would also be able to fly between stars. We hope you help us."

The scientists began asking questions for Kateos to translate.

"Scientist H'Aare wants to know if your propulsion—" Kateos started.

"Kateos, Et Silmarn! These are difficult questions," Buccari begged.

"Yes, Sharl, but scientists will work-ah with you for as long as it-ah takes. Perhaps you come with us to Ocean Station, where—"

"Please, Mistress Kateos," Buccari said slowly, carefully. "Your interest is understandable, and when it is appropriate to do so, we will discuss these matters. Please understand that none of us is expert in the fields you are inquiring about." She realized that if it came down to negotiating permission for the humans to remain on this planet, any information provided freely would be unavailable as a future bargaining chip. Perhaps, just perhaps, the hyperlight theories would be their passport. Buccari was not proud of her disingenuous replies. Both she and Hudson were extremely knowledgeable about the hyperlight theories and applied algorithms, but information represented power, and they needed to marshal what little power was available to them.

Kateos spoke softly to Et Silmarn. The noblekone nodded his head.

"Sharl," he roared. "We thang you for what you have done. If you can help-ah us more, we thang you more . . . er, we help-ah you more."

"I understand," Buccari said.

Three days later Et Silmarn banked the aircraft on course and returned his view forward. Hudson was in the back with Scientists H'Aare and Mirrtis. Dowornobb and Kateos were crowded into the cockpit with the connecting hatch secured.

"The female Gol'berg-ah gave you information?" the noblekone asked.

"Yes. It was technical. I understood little," Kateos remarked sadly. "The female claims to know about interstellar drives. She is a technician of propulsion."

"They allow females to do technical functions?" the copilot asked.

"Yes!" Kateos answered too quickly and too loudly. The male kones on the crowded flight deck turned to stare at her. Involuntarily, she dropped her eyes.

"Sharl is lying?" Dowornobb asked. "I thought we could trust her."

"Sharl is smart," Et Silmarn answered. "She is protecting what little she has. After what she has done for us, I do not hold it against her. I still trust her."

"What about Gol'berg-ah?" Kateos asked. "Her information is valuable, though I do not respect her. She tells us these things because she is spiteful and full of hate for Sharl. I do not understand why she is disloyal."

Et Silmarn sighed heavily. "It is not for us to understand the aliens. On our next visit we will discreetly record what the female Gol'berg-ah has to say, and we will suggest that she and maybe some others accompany us to Ocean Station, although I doubt Sharl will permit that to happen. I do not like to work behind Sharl's back, but Et Avian's primary mission was to un-cover those very secrets."

"The humans are uncomfortable in our presence," the co-pilot said.

"It would be the same for us if the roles were reversed," Kateos replied. "They are frightened of the power we hold over them."

"They have seen nothing yet," Et Silmarn said.

The alien airplane flying along the river valley muttered into the distance. MacArthur, sucking on thickweed, waved at Tonto and Bottlenose, signaling them to come no closer. The fluttering of their wings would spook the trapped animals. Satisfied that his brain was clear, MacArthur extracted the masticated weed from his mouth and placed the lump of chewed greens in a pouch hanging from his neck. He looked to each side. Chastain and Petit skirted the left edge of the ravine, while Shannon and O'Toole took positions on the right, each marine carrying a lariat made of parachute shroud. Shaking out the coils of his rope and slinging aside his leather poncho, MacArthur stalked the terrified horses. Three golden beasts had been funneled into the narrow wash, their escape prevented by boulders and branches laboriously transported to the gully. Effort had borne fruit; the trap had worked.

MacArthur swung the lariat easily, allowing the noose to expand. He nodded to O'Toole, who also began swinging his noose overhead, just as MacArthur had trained him. Only two would throw their ropes; any more would just get in the way.

"Go for the smallest one," MacArthur cautioned, his voice calm. "Throw for the neck. I'll go for the legs. Make it count!"

O'Toole crept along the edge of the wash, approaching the skittish animals. MacArthur, in the wash, stayed close to the bank, giving the animals room.

The largest animal, a stallion, took chopping steps directly at MacArthur and snorted, its bulging brown eyes surrounded with frightened white. The animal's streaming golden mane rippled and waved with abrupt motion, its long tail held high and flowing. Barrel-chested, mule-eared, blunt-nosed, heavy-legged with large feet and knobby knees, the animals did not match MacArthur's boyhood memory of his grandfather's Calgary ranch horses, but they were definitely horses. The sounds and smells were pure horse, and they were beautiful, powerful animals.

MacArthur flattened against the rock wall of the ravine. The stallion bolted past, trumpeting a loud, rasping whinny. The mares, confused and frightened, reared and twisted, leaping to follow the stallion's lead.

"Now!" MacArthur shouted. He stepped in toward the last animal and made a well-timed throw, looping one foreleg and tangling the other. He dug his feet into the ground and wrapped the lariat around his back and shoulders. Excited, O'Toole threw too hard, missing high. One mare thundered by and was free. The second frightened female took her first step and fouled in the snaking rope, jolting MacArthur from his feet. The marine sprawled in the dust and was dragged along for a stride and a half before the mare stumbled to the ground, the lasso intertwining her forelegs. MacArthur and the horse regained their footing simultaneously, and the golden horse leapt sideways and kicked, jerking hard to free its encumbered foot. MacArthur resumed his wide stance, grabbing the line and bracing himself for the inevitable muscle-wrenching tug, but he was too slow and too weak. His hands were burned viciously as the line spun through his grasping fingers. Feeling diminished resistance, the horse leapt to a gallop, and MacArthur—on his knees in pain—watched, powerless, thinking all was lost.

Not to be denied, Chastain jumped to MacArthur's side and made a dive for the trailing end of the lariat. And missed. But the horse's rapidly moving legs whipped the rope into a tangle ensnaring her own rear legs. Again the horse crashed to the ground. As the determined mare struggled to her feet, the quick-footed O'Toole dashed to the horse's head and slipped his noose over her neck. Chastain made another gallant effort to reach the bitter end of MacArthur's tangled line and was successful. The combined resistance from the two ropes threw the animal off balance, and the unfortunate horse tripped for a third time. MacArthur grabbed Chastain's dropped lariat and dashed forward, making a quick looping throw that settled over the golden neck.

"Sarge! Hold this line. Give me yours!" he shouted as Shannon joined the fray. The sergeant did as he was told, and the horse was held at three points. Struggling fiercely, the indomitable beast searched for leverage that could still make a difference. MacArthur darted forward and, risking injury from flying hooves, looped a fourth lariat around the animal's rear leg. The powerful animal, tangled and restrained from multiple directions, gave a last valiant struggle and fell solidly onto her side. Except for labored breathing and an occasional flailing leg, the mare lay still.

MacArthur, on his knees and gasping for air, handed the taut rope to Petit. As he released his grasp, the ache from his fingers and hands shot straight to his brain; he squatted on his haunches, head back, his throbbing hands held tightly in his lap. Petit pulled on the lariat.

"Damn, Mac! This rope's all bloody!" he shouted. "You okay?"

MacArthur looked at his lacerated palms and winced.

"Mac wouldn't have fun if he didn't bleed," O'Toole grunted, heaving on his rope.

"Slack up, Terry," MacArthur gasped. "You're cutting her wind."

Moving quickly, before his fingers locked up, MacArthur shook out a pair of hobbles and slipped them over the animal's trembling legs. He dropped another noose over the horse's head and slipped off his hide poncho, wrapping it around the mare's head. Then, breathing mightily, he lay exhausted on the ground, his weight against the magnificent animal's back.

"Let her up," he exhaled. "Be ready!"

THIRTY-FIVE

FERRY

The soft, full light of a late summer morning revealed a straggling group of humans—a foraging party—carrying empty sacks and crude buckets along the receded waters of the great river. Schmidt's thick thatch of flaxen hair gleamed like a white pearl, while their towering height clearly marked Tatum and Chastain. Fenstermacher, Goldberg with her baby, and Wilson rounded out the complement. The humans wore ragged jumpsuits, or at least remnants of jumpsuits; several had cut off the lower portion of the jumpsuit arms and legs. One or two had augmented their attire with hide ponchos, but all wore leather sandals laced up their calves.

The foraging party worked its way downstream along the gravel-strewn bank, leaving the roaring cataracts and sparkling mists behind. Once past MacArthur's valley, the great river settled to a more placid course. The main channel widened, and the current diminished; narrow river islets dotted the watercourse; and river otters and long-legged waterbirds abounded. In many respects it became a long, narrow lake, easily crossed with a dugout canoe. Human traffic over its span was necessary, primarily to gather furs and buffalo meat. The demands of this traffic precipitated another Fenstermacher innovation—a ferry.

The ungainly log raft floated between boulders in the eddying river waters. It was secured by four spring lines, its two big oars shipped and secured alongside; a smaller sweep oar—the tiller—hung down in the water at the stern. Fenstermacher and Chastain, wading in the gentle current, grabbed the lines and hauled the tall raft shoreward until it grounded. The group waded in to board, with Tatum taking the baby from Goldberg until the mother was safely pulled up.

"Tatum, you want the tiller?" Fenstermacher asked, standing in the water.

"Nah, I can row," Tatum said with confidence. His strong right arm had compensated for the missing left one, developing into a mass of ropy sinew greater than a large man's thigh.

"You big dumb guys are all alike," Fenstermacher snorted. "Beppo, keep an eye on Tatum. Make sure he pulls his weight. I'd hate to depend on Chief Cookie."

"*Ja*, you bet." Schmidt laughed, climbing aboard.

"You know, Sandy," Wilson said. "I bet that's one fart that would actually sink, if we drop him in the middle of the river."

"Particularly if we put some rocks in his shorts," Tatum added.

"That's mutiny, assholes!" the little man snarled. "Belay the chatter and attend your oars—smartly, I say."

Laughing heartily, Tatum walked to a stout oar and took his position. Wilson grabbed the other, and the two rowers kept the raft pointed into the current as Chastain and Fenstermacher cleared the lines.

"Lieutenant Buccari is coming," Schmidt said, pointing upriver.

Buccari, wearing a faded jumpsuit cut off at the knees, sprinted over the rocks. A pistol belt worn like a bandolier flopped as she ran, and her long, braided ponytail bounced behind her, flashing in the morning sun. Fenstermacher held the last line as the raft swung to the current.

Brappa circled on the weak thermal. Craag struggled to hold altitude, still striving to catch the poorly defined updraft that Brappa had somehow managed to exploit.

"Perhaps we should return to the riverbank, Craag-the-warrior," Brappa screeched, proud that he had gained an altitude advantage.

"It is early for thermals, young friend," Craag wheezed as he flapped mightily. The veteran was not going to admit defeat. The great river, deep green in the golden morning, flowed easily below them. The hunters were barely a third of the way across and were rapidly approaching the point where they could no longer glide to either shore.

Below and downstream, Brappa watched the long-legs climbing onto their platform of wood.

"We could descend to the river and float over with the long-legs," Brappa said, trying to give the older hunter a face-saving alternative. The updraft stiffened. Brappa detected a satisfying lift.

"No need, Brappa, son-of-Braan," Craag screamed, suddenly heaving past Brappa's altitude. "This updraft will boost us to heights adequate for the crossing."

Brappa acknowledged. In close formation, the hunters allowed themselves to be carried upriver by the gentle but persistent thermal. Then Brappa saw the eagles.

"Thanks, Fenstermacher," Buccari hailed. She splashed thigh deep in cold water and clambered easily up the wooden structure of the raft, getting a hand from Chastain. Fenstermacher followed her aboard, bringing the last line. He grabbed the tiller and yelled orders for everyone to haul together. Schmidt sat down on a stern post next to Chastain and helped make up the lines.

"You almost missed the boat, Lieutenant," Wilson said.

"Wouldn't be the first time, Chief," Buccari answered. "I want to watch them with the horses. Tookmanian said you were heading over to forage for thickweed."

"And to pick up some buffalo, too," Wilson huffed as he

pushed on his oar. "O'Toole says they got a new kill butchered and ready to go."

Buccari looked down at the splintery surface of the raft and noted bloodstains left behind by earlier cargoes. Also lying in the center of the raft was the newly constructed ramp for moving the horses onboard. Goldberg, with Honey cooing softly in her lap, sat on the fragrant fresh-hewn wood. Buccari made eye contact with the young mother and smiled. Goldberg reciprocated with a cold nod.

"How's Honey, Pepper?" Buccari persisted. The infant was recovering from a racking cough. Several days earlier the gardeners had prepared a sour-smelling herbal mash that Lee had force-fed to the baby. It had had a positive effect; the cough had diminished, and the baby had recovered a healthy tone.

"Better, thanks . . . sir," Goldberg replied with the warmth of a north wind.

Buccari glanced up and caught Tatum looking at her. He shrugged with sympathetic bewilderment. She walked forward and sat on the front edge of the raft, legs hanging over the blunt bow. The low morning sun reflected from the river, and fish rose to summer bugs flitting and skittering over the gentle current. Fenstermacher mumbled a soft cadence for the oarsmen and steered at an angle to the current, keeping the raft on a steady course for the opposite bank. With each coordinated swing of the oars, thole pins groaned in their leather pivots and the heavy raft surged forward, thrusting a crush of white water before it. Closing her eyes to the warm glare, Buccari lay on her back and allowed the slow, splashing tempo to melt her anxieties.

Presently the raft glided into a small cove, grounding against rocks still in cool morning shade, waking Buccari from her catnap. She sat up and stretched. The rocky riverbank was steep but not high, and Chastain, with mooring line in hand, jumped to dry ground. The sandy terrain leveled out and then climbed steeply to a grassy clearing above the river's highwater mark. Thick undergrowth and a lush stand of trees closed in the rear of the lea. Silhouetted against the trees, MacArthur sat on a large rock at the edge of the clearing. Two golden horses stood alertly behind him.

"Good morning, Lieutenant," MacArthur shouted. "You looked mighty comfortable out there." Field glasses dangled from his neck.

Buccari was impatient with Shannon, O'Toole, and Mac-

Arthur for the amount of time they had been spending with the horses. She did not appreciate their enduring absence from the camp. There was too much heavy work to do, and the horses could help. She wanted the horses transferred to the other bank.

"It must be something about this side of the river that makes everyone forget the work they're supposed to be doing," she answered.

"Ah, Lieutenant," MacArthur rebutted mildly. "We've been working hard over here, too. But you're right. We need the horses across the river."

That the horses were sufficiently docile to be transported over water was amazing in itself. The first mare captured had been nervous and frightened; none of the men could calm her enough to start training. She had refused to eat or drink, and she had thrashed and struggled so much that MacArthur had worried for her health almost to the point of setting her free. However, another horse—a stallion—was caught using the same tactics employed to capture the mare. When the newly captured horse was put in the paddock with the first animal, both animals calmed down, taking food and water from the humans as if they had always done so.

MacArthur dared to mount the mare. Surprisingly, the animal reacted mildly to the presence of a human being on its back. It bucked and pranced about a bit, but then it just stood there, accepting the human's right to the superior position. Within another week both horses were answering basic riding commands. The stable on the north side of the river was expanded, and two more horses were captured. MacArthur, Shannon, and O'Toole were like children with their first pets.

A shrill whistle sounded overhead. Buccari looked skyward. Two cliff dwellers, membranes folded to their backs, were descending in a panic. High in the deep blue heavens two great eagles soared lazily in the bright sunlight. But lower, a third eagle had folded its wings and was plummeting from the skies in pursuit of the hunters.

Buccari leapt to her feet. The diving eagle grew larger, its spreading talons swinging downward—right for them. Reflexively, she pushed Goldberg and Honey over the side and into the deep, cold water and dove in after them. Tatum, Wilson, and Schmidt followed in quick succession, splashing noisily into the relative security of the river, clinging close to the protective overhang of the raft. Only Fenstermacher remained on deck. The resolute raft captain seized a fending pole and wielded it like a lance.

The hunters extended their wings and pulled up from their headlong dives, with the eagle closing rapidly. Buccari brushed river water from her eyes and looked up at MacArthur. The marine was on his feet, assault rifle aimed skyward. The hunters leveled out above the raft and shot past MacArthur's position, gliding with a rush of wind into the narrow confines of the trees, an area too restricted for the eagle to follow. The eagle flared above Fenstermacher's head, spreading its wings to an unbelievable span, an embrace throwing a mantle of darkness over the shoreline. Its yellow eyes focused on Fenstermacher, glowing with atavistic hate but also with a glint of fear.

Buccari winced, waiting for the inevitable explosion from the rifle, but MacArthur stood steady, staring through his sights. He had but to pull the trigger and the eagle would be annihilated. The eagle was almost stationary; its massive wings beat powerfully, slowly lifting the great predator—an easy shot. Steadily it retreated. Buccari felt the skin crawl on her head; an overwhelming sense of relief flowed through her. She watched MacArthur blow air from his lungs and lower the weapon.

"Get out of here, baby," she whispered. And it was gone, the swishing of its wings diminishing to silence.

"I didn't hear anyone sound swim call!" Fenstermacher yelled, standing at the edge of the raft, glaring ferociously at the people treading water. He jumped back from a mouthful of river spit in his direction. Honey howled mightily.

"About time you got here, Fenstermacher!" MacArthur shouted, setting the rifle on the ground. "We got work to do. Get that raft secured and let's get the ramp up."

"Up yours, Mac!" the feisty boatswain's mate shouted. "I'm early, and you know it. And don't go yelling at me. I'm officially a hero. I chased that buzzard away while these fishies were flopping around in the water." He turned back and bent over the side. "Chief, I ain't never going to let you live this down."

Honey bawled as the dripping swimmers pulled themselves from the river. Chastain and Fenstermacher brought the raft broadside to the bank and secured it fore and aft. Buccari, soaking wet, started up the path winding toward MacArthur's position. Goldberg gradually soothed Honey to a hiccuping calm as the members of the foraging party sat on the river rocks, letting the dappling sunlight warm their wet bodies. Insults flew fast and furious, and soon everyone was laughing too hard to speak.

As Buccari arrived at MacArthur's vantage point, X.O. and Tonto hopped from the woods. The hunters craned their necks as they waddled from beneath the tree cover, searching the skies. Satisfied that the threat had disappeared, they hopped up on boulders and watched the humans with great interest. MacArthur gave them hand signs that meant "Death close" and pointed to the sky. The cliff dwellers chirped animatedly, and X.O. signed back "Death always close."

The hunters turned and bowed to Buccari. The little creatures treated MacArthur and Buccari differently from other humans, showing each of them peculiar forms of respect. To Buccari they were formal and deferential; whenever she moved or spoke, they took note and adjusted to her position as if she were a local sun and they were her planets. To MacArthur they demonstrated a marked camaraderie, and they invariably followed him whenever they were around. It was with MacArthur and, to a lesser degree, Buccari that they attempted to communicate. To all other humans they were remarkably indifferent.

"A bunch of clowns," MacArthur said, looking down on the dripping hilarity.

"Laughter's great," Buccari commented, removing her dripping pistol belt and hanging it on a convenient branch.

"I don't hear you laughing," he said.

She looked at him without humor. "I have other things on my mind, Corporal. Like getting you guys back on the other side to do some work."

"Okay, okay," he said. "Point's made! But we're the least of your worries. These horses are going to make a big difference."

Buccari felt his steady look, and her eyes were drawn to his. She lowered her gaze to the river.

"Hey, Chief! Move everyone down the bank," MacArthur shouted. "The fewer distractions, the better."

Wilson waved, and the foraging patrol made its way upriver.

Buccari turned from the river and once again found herself staring into MacArthur's gray eyes. Neither spoke. The spell was broken by the chirping of the dwellers; the alert creatures gawked curiously into the woods. Buccari detected the sounds of approaching animals. Soon Shannon and O'Toole hove into view, descending the steep path that dropped from the cliff tops. They led two horses loaded with butchered segments of buffalo into the small clearing. The meat, wrapped in skins, was unfastened and dumped on the grass. Tiny insects buzzed about the bloodied skins.

"We're waiting, Winfried," MacArthur sang out. "How're you doing?"

"Ready here!" Fenstermacher shouted back. He and Chastain brought the raft against the bank and positioned the sturdy ramp. The height and steepness of the bank made the incline of the gangplank negligible.

"Okay, Terry. Let's do it!" MacArthur grabbed the reins of one of the horses, leading it down the last section of steep path. O'Toole followed, leading a second horse, leaving Shannon to hold the other two. Buccari stood on the edge of the clearing and watched.

"Lieutenant?" Shannon asked. "Sir, would you watch the horses?"

"Sure, Sarge," she responded, walking over and taking the reins. Shannon bent down, grunted a parcel of buffalo meat over his shoulder, and trotted down the trail. The horses, sniffing and snorting, nervously accepted Buccari as their caretaker.

Loading proceeded without incident. The first two horses, eyes covered, were carefully led onto the raft. The sturdy craft accommodated their great weight, but Fenstermacher wisely interrupted the loading to reposition the raft out from the shore so that it would not be held aground by the increased draft. MacArthur crooned as he secured the horses to the raft, each with three lines. While MacArthur and Shannon were securing the horses, O'Toole and Chastain climbed back up the path and retrieved the butchered buffalo. With everything made fast, MacArthur looked up at Buccari.

"Lieutenant," he said, "would you mind staying with the horses? We'll send O'Toole off on the other side and get back for the second trip that much sooner."

"I could help with the oars," she replied. "O'Toole could watch the horses."

"Nah!" he replied. "The raft is sitting low. The more muscle, the better, and the horses are behaving. Let 'em graze. You okay with that?"

Buccari looked from MacArthur to the horses and back. "Hurry up!" she shouted.

MacArthur jumped into the water and helped Chastain stow

the ramp on the crowded raft. Shannon and O'Toole stood by
the nervous horses. The raft was fended away and propelled
toward the opposite shore, a cliff dweller perched on each forward corner—bizarre figureheads.

Alone with the horses, Buccari explored the small clearing,
which was suddenly quiet and peaceful. In the stillness of
morning she listened to the muted buzzing of insects and the
gentle gurgle of the river. In the distance Honey continued to
complain. The sun's rays cleared the wooded high ground
close behind her, the warmth a welcome change from the
chilly shade. She was still wet.

The horses grazed contentedly. Sunlight slanted down and
warmed her. She picked up the field glasses. The raft, a speck
in the distance, had reached the far bank, and the marines were
moving the horses ashore. Two down and two to go. She laid
the binoculars on MacArthur's gear, next to the assault rifle,
and leaned back in the grass. A cloud drifted overhead.
Buccari imagined it to be a rabbit. She yawned.

The pastoral quiet was shredded by a blood-curdling
scream—Goldberg's. Explosive reports of a rifle punctuated
the plaintive wail, and booming echoes reverberated along
the river valley, accompaniment to Goldberg's mournful
keening. Buccari instinctively realized what was happening.
She searched the skies. The dark, sweeping form of a great
eagle soared along the riverbank, the susurrant sound of
beating wings distinctly audible. Suspended from the raptor's talons was the tragic and unmistakable figure of a human baby. Its pitiful screams pierced Buccari's soul.

She dove for the rifle and rolled to a kneeling position. Pulling the weapon firmly to her shoulder, she released the safety
and selected full automatic. The eagle, baby writhing frantically in its talons, was slightly higher and abreast of Buccari's
position. Putting the sights on the eagle's neck, Buccari held
her breath, aimed with calculated deliberation, and squeezed
off a burst. The eagle's head blew sideways with the impact of
the heavy-caliber slugs, and the great bird tumbled about the
axis of its wings, losing its grip on the tiny victim. Both creatures flailed the air.

She dropped the rifle and sprinted down the winding path,
watching the infant splash into the slowly moving river.
Buccari dove into the cold current and swam hard. Nothing—
she saw nothing. She kicked strenuously to the surface, pulling
her head high out of the water; she scanned the surface for

signs—any sign! The eagle's carcass floated slowly downstream, and she stroked toward it.

Bubbles! Small bubbles only meters to her right. Buccari porpoised forward and stroked downward vigorously, staring with open eyes into the green water. Like sun rays streaming through cathedral windows, shafts of sunlight angled into the depths. Far below something glowed, faintly reflecting the prism-shattered light. A thin trail of bubbles danced and wiggled upward from its vicinity. Buccari crawled with desperate energy toward the fuzzy whiteness, stroking and frog-kicking, fighting the buoyant forces. At last she touched it—the yielding smoothness of skin.

Buccari grabbed hold of a limb—a leg—and pulled for the surface, lungs bursting but panic held in check by the exhilaration of reaching the child. An eternity lapsed. Panic dominated her senses just as her frantic hands clawed from the resisting liquid and into the warmer emptiness. She exploded from the river, spewing water from mouth and nose. Coughing and kicking convulsively, she held the child out of the water with both hands. Honey's eyes were rolled back in her head; angry bruises contrasted against fish-white skin; blood trickled from her nose. Buccari held the limp form close and tried to orient herself. Shouts attracted her attention. She glimpsed Tatum and Schmidt running along the bank. Farther upstream Wilson assisted the screaming mother.

Holding the baby's head above the water, Buccari rolled over and sidestroked shoreward with her free arm. Tatum, distraught, panting and gasping, met her neck deep in the water and relieved her of the limp child. He stumbled from the water, holding his baby high in the air. Buccari swam several more yards before she touched bottom, and then she struggled to drag her exhausted body from the frigid water. Still knee-deep, she collapsed, spent. She vomited.

On the bank, Tatum held Honey upside down by her leg. With his one arm he shook the child in spasmodic jerks. Water poured from the child's tiny mouth.

"Beppo! Slap her back!" he shouted. Schmidt followed orders, his face contorted with tragic concern. "Harder!" Tatum shouted, his voice shrill, the frustration of having only one arm written across his countenance. Nothing! Just the pitiful claps of a strong hand against the small frame of an infant.

"Hold her head up!" Tatum bellowed. Schmidt brought the small face upward, and Tatum covered it with his own. Des-

perately holding his strong lungs in check, he blew softly into
Honey's bloodied nose and mouth. On his third breath she
burped; her small hands jerked, and her eyes opened. She
coughed, regurgitated water, and coughed again. And then
she screamed, a strong scream, a mixed scream—a scream of
pain but more important, a scream of anger—a healthy scream
of anger. Tatum roared in ecstasy, holding the child to his
trembling breast.

"She's alive, Lieutenant!" He sat down in shallow water
next to Buccari, the bruised and battered child bellowing in his
lap. "You saved my baby's life!"

Buccari, still awash in the river, looked up and smiled at the
overwhelming affection shown by the tall marine. She reached
up to pat Tatum's knee, and he grabbed her hand, kissing it
and holding it to his tear-streaked cheek.

"The horses," she gasped. "Where are the horses?" She
raised her head and was relieved to see the horses standing
where they had been left, staring down from their vantage
point, grinding mouthfuls of grass. She had not wanted to dis-
appoint MacArthur.

THIRTY-SIX

SCARS

"You old fool! What more do you know of this matter?"
Jook thundered.

Et Kalass's facile mind searched through his alternatives and
their consequences. He decided to hold to his plan. It was the
closest to the truth.

"My concern for Et Avian overcame good judgment, Exalted One," the minister said. "I promised on his father's
deathbed that no harm would come to him."

Jook looked down from his throne, fuming darkly. "Ah! No
harm ever? A foolish promise, Minister. So, another case of

the nobility and their children. How tender!" He simpered sardonically.

Et Kalass dared to speak, "Et Avian's discoveries—"

"General Gorruk would have your head!" spit the emperor-general. "I should give it to him! Using boosters without authority—a gross assumption of power!"

Since the rout at Penc the war had gone badly. Gorruk was consumed with fending off vicious counterattacks. Missiles had resumed falling on northern territories.

"But Great and Powerful One—" Et Kalass started.

"Discoveries! You speak of discoveries," Jook preempted imperiously. "What do we know of the aliens? It is said that Et Avian has captured an alien alive."

"True, Your Greatness, though—"

"Bah! Why am I talking to you? Where is Avian?"

"In grave condition, Greatness. He faces multiple surgeries and extended rehabilitation."

"He has managed to survive an interplanetary acceleration. You are withholding something." Jook rose to his imposing height and glared down. "Bring Et Avian to me."

Et Kalass turned and scurried from the imperial chambers.

After three days Buccari's buttocks and thighs were chafed and bruised. And the obstinate beast had just given her a painful nip on the shoulder.

"You okay, Lieutenant?" MacArthur asked, his voice concerned but his face smug—his first spoken words to her in days. He galloped up and grabbed the balky mare's reins, leaping from his stallion. "You can't be turning your back on that horse."

Buccari rubbed the tender spot and concentrated on holding her temper. Coming on the salt mission had been her idea; MacArthur had not wanted her along, fearing for her safety, but she had persisted.

"I guess I missed that on the checklist," she responded.

"Beg your pardon, Lieutenant?" MacArthur asked.

"Nothing! Nothing. Just a little pilot humor. Give me a boost." She grabbed the reins and moved over to the port side of the four-legged creature. She straightened the leather blanket, tightening the knot in its girth strap. MacArthur bent down and grabbed her left boot and the back of her thigh. On three, he lifted and she jumped, swinging her right leg over the animal. She landed with a painful grunt. MacArthur turned and quickly swung up on his own mount, his shoulders gently shaking.

"Stop laughing, Corporal!" Buccari yelled, but her command disintegrated with a whimper.

"Aye, Lieutenant. Stop laughing, aye." He trotted off.

Buccari tried to ignore the trauma inflicted on her stern. She clicked her tongue and shook her reins. The horse bent its head and nibbled the grass at its feet.

"Move, stupid!" she yelled.

"You yelling at me, Lieutenant?" MacArthur shouted back at her.

"No," she shouted. "Not this time," she added under her breath.

"Giddap!" she barked, kicking her heels. The mare surged to a spine-jolting lope; she hung on, bouncing painfully, until her horse caught up and fell into trail, settling into a rolling walk. More passenger than pilot, Buccari relaxed and studied her surroundings. A covey of ptarmiganlike birds flushed from a weedy runnel sputtered into the air, scattering downwind and bringing Buccari's eyes up to the vistas around her. Above them, hunters—Tonto and Bottlenose—soared easily on buffeting thermals. A stately line of sunstruck squalls paraded across the dusky horizon, dragging thin sweeps of rain. Two-thirds of a rainbow magically appeared in the near distance and serenely faded into ephemeral memory. Scattered cumulus clouds drifted past, yet the skies overhead were so fresh and clear that the hunters were never hard to discern despite their altitude. And the hunters were not alone in the skies—giant eagles also wheeled in the clear air, keeping their distance and posing no threat. Visible to the southeast, musk-buffalo grazed with singular purpose, the great bulk of their number shielded from sight by rolling tundra. Their odor had been absent for more than a day, the prevailing winds an ally. Instead, the sweet, musty scent of late summer wildflowers assaulted Buccari's senses, the pink and blue blossoms contrasting sharply to the gray-green of the taiga.

Hunters screamed. Bottlenose glided rapidly ahead and out of sight beyond a low line of humpbacked downs. Tonto remained overhead, swerving in a nervous figure eight.

"We must be getting close," Shannon remarked.

Tonto screamed urgently and loudly. He hovered, flapping his wings.

"Let's keep moving. Something's up," MacArthur shouted,

chucking his reins to the side and heeling his horse into motion.

Tonto broke hover and glided out of sight behind the ridge. The riders crested high ground, and the rolling prairie dropped dramatically at their feet, leveling abruptly on the geometric flatness of the salt plains. The vista was dotted with activity. An arm of the musk-buffalo herd rumbled to the east, raising a gritty cloud of dust. Nightmare packs harried the herd flank, breaking out stragglers and calves, the kills marked by congregations of buzzards and eagles fighting for carrion. Buccari's horse trailed MacArthur's surefooted mount down the steep decline, and the others followed.

Three hours of trotting found them on the dry patches of crusty alkaline ground, the terrain making the going easy except for the acrid billows lifted by the horses' hooves. The riders spread out in a line abreast to avoid the dust. Sight lines across the salt flats were blurred with thermal distortion, but they could finally see the compact figures of cliff dwellers. Something was peculiar. The realization struck home—the cliff dwellers were fighting nightmares! Hundreds of the horrible beasts had encircled the small creatures.

Braan, leader-of-hunters, did not know what to do. Normally he would signal his warriors to jettison their bags and rise on the powerful thermals. Only this time the decision was not simple, because the long-legs were approaching—ironically, coming to help the hunters. The long-legs could not escape into the air.

Growler carcasses riddled with hunters' arrows littered the field. Sentries bravely darted among the kill, retrieving precious missiles. Hunters were injured, but only one so severely that he could not fly. That hunter, a sentry, must die if the expedition took to the air.

"Thy decision, Braan-our-leader?" Craag queried. A bleeding claw mark was on his neck. "The growlers circle closer."

Braan turned to the approaching horses and their long-leg riders. A good idea—using horses to lift the burden from the shoulders of his hunters—but now it seemed foolhardy.

"Jettison the salt bags and take flight!" Braan screamed. Craag loudly echoed the command. The hunters screamed in bedlam. Salt bags not already dropped were let go, and hunters flapped their membranes, leather wings cracking and snapping. The creatures desperately reached for free air, wingspans over-

lapping and conflicting. The cliff dwellers elevated from the
salty surface of the planet—except the injured novice, his hand
and forearm broken, his left wing shredded.

The hunter leader glided to the bleeding sentry and landed
with a dust-throwing skid. It was Braan's fateful job to mercifully terminate the young hunter rather than leave him to the
torture of the scavenger pack. Braan had helped many warriors
die. The novice stood bravely erect, eyes shining with black
glory, honored to die at Braan's hands. But then the sentry's
head jerked in alarm as he whistled a warning. Vicious growls
shuddered in the air, and Braan looked up to see growlers
prowling close—too close. There would not be time to dispatch the sentry, yet Braan could not desert the injured one.
Braan screamed and drew his sword, and the hunters stood
back to back, ready to do final battle. A mighty fanged beast
broke from the skulking siege and bounded forward, its tail a
whipping, whirring blur.

Brappa landed at Braan's left side, his bow singing. The
growler died in midleap, two arrows jutting from its skull.
Braan looked over his right shoulder and saw Craag nocking
another arrow.

"Flee!" Braan screamed at his cohorts. "It is my order! Fly
away! Craag, thou art in command. Who takes charge? Fly
now!"

Craag had no time to answer, but neither did the growlers
have time to attack.

Buccari lost control of her mount. The reins were useless;
the thick cords of its neck resisted all efforts to change direction. The mare plunged across the salt flats, her gallop a soothing change of pace—except for the breakneck speed. Buccari
grimly held on to the thick mane with both hands. She dared
to glimpse sideways. The other horses also dashed headlong,
riders powerless to sway or slow the beasts, though MacArthur
sat erect and had taken out his rifle. Buccari returned her view
forward to the nightmares. They were scattering, feral eyes
wide in fear. Her horse bunched its muscles and drove hard to
overtake the retreating predators, lunging into their midst.

Buccari redoubled her grip and tried to anticipate the steed's
terrific acceleration and swerves. With nimble strength the
golden animal drove panicky nightmares in tightening circles,
working in concert with other horses. When a collection of the
slavering beasts were made to collide back upon themselves,

rendering them directionless and confused, one of the horses would charge into the pack and trample them with unbridled fury. It was during one of those moments that O'Toole was thrown. Buccari watched him crash to the ground. The horses avoided the fallen man, driving the nightmares clear.

The hunters on the ground screamed in fright and huddled together. Horses rumbled past, thick legs crashing like earth-drumming pistons, trampling the bodies—living and dead—of the growlers. Braan, sword held impotently, watched as the golden animals, helpless and frightened long-legs clinging to their backs, towered on hind legs and crashed hooves down on crippled growlers, crushing life from the whimpering and howling devils. Flashing teeth grabbed and snatched at the cringing beasts, powerful hind legs delivered deathly blows, and growlers fell by the dozens. Scavengers scattered in rout, and the horses pivoted and pranced nervously, looking for more victims. It was over. The horses, one riderless, nerves high, tails twitching, danced sideways as they converged in a trot around the awestruck cliff dwellers.

Tentatively, like dry falling leaves, the troop of dwellers drifted down from the skies and formed up by the discarded salt bags. Craag comically recovered his demeanor, bowed in apology to Braan, and moved away to take charge. Brappa, leading the injured novice, followed Craag, leaving Braan—the diminutive hunter—standing erect, if uncertain, before the towering, prancing horses.

O'Toole limped in their direction; he smiled awkwardly and waved.

"Holy shit!" Shannon shouted. His thick silver hair was blown askew; perspiration rolled from his brow, and his eyes were wide in astonishment.

"What happened? What made them do that?" Buccari asked, heart pounding. The muscles in her forearms and thighs ached from exertion.

"They evidently don't care for nightmares, either," Mac-Arthur said. "I wonder why they let us control them or pretend to control them."

The horses settled down, and Buccari gingerly dismounted, joining O'Toole on the ground. Shannon and MacArthur did likewise, apprehensively watching their powerful mounts. The horses, breathing hard, dropped their heads, sniffing and snorting at the salt beneath their feet. Captain, small and frail, bravely if tentatively approached the tall humans and their taller horses. The horses eyed the small creature disdainfully, sniffing the air in its direction as the nervous hunter bowed politely if quickly. Buccari reciprocated, and MacArthur started rapidly gesticulating, flashing sign language to the cliff dweller. Braan answered with equal fervor.

"They're ready to go," MacArthur said. "They've been waiting for us."

Buccari knew the horses would be loaded with bags of salt, requiring the humans to hike to the river. MacArthur had made that clear when he was trying to dissuade her from coming. But after the beating her rear end had taken for the last four days, walking was a welcome alternative.

"How long will it take to get to the river?" she asked.

"Captain says five days, maybe six," MacArthur replied.

Jook stared with regal scorn as Et Avian, listing slightly with the weight of his cast, moved haltingly to the foot of the imperial throne. Et Kalass and an aide flanked the injured noblekone, assisting his movements. Et Avian, appearing feeble and infirm, made no effort to show obeisance but only raised his face to stare at the Supreme Leader.

"You requested my presence, Leader of Leaders," Et Avian said weakly.

"Almost eaten by a bear, eh?" Jook snarled. "The physicians say that you are lucky to be alive and that you may yet lose the use of your arm."

"The bear is dead, Great One," the noblekone parried. "For the bravery of the aliens."

"So says your report," Jook reflected. "They must be powerful. Well armed."

"If you have read the report, then you know that is not the case. They are of slight proportions, perhaps one-third the mass of a kone. Their weapons are modest chemical implements. They do not present a danger to our planet." The dialogue visibly sapped the noblekone.

"A most presumptuous conclusion. You have only seen a shipwrecked sample of this race. Is it so easy to perceive their nature?"

"Your skepticism is healthy, Great One, but mine has been mollified. The aliens sacrificed their lives to save mine. There

was no reason for their bravery other than an inherent sense of
goodness and compassion."

"Goodness and compassion. Goodness and compassion!
Dangerous attributes on which to base an alliance. What have
you learned of their technologies? That would be the brick and
mortar with which we could build." Jook paraded down the
wide steps and peered deeply into the invalid's unblinking
eyes.

"Your Greatness!" Et Kalass interceded. "Et Avian is not up
to this. I beg of you! Permit us to withdraw before we do him
further harm."

"I can tell you nothing of their technologies—as yet, my
leader," Et Avian whispered. "My science team is persisting in
this area. I have received reports, very sketchy reports, that
contact has continued. If the communication satellites were operational, we could have current information, including video."

"As you know, my noble scientist," Jook said, turning and
remounting the stairs, "we are at war. In wartime, information
is the first victim."

"I beg of you, Great One! We must give aid to this kone immediately. His mortal health is in jeopardy," Et Kalass be-
seeched.

"Very well, Minister," Jook replied. "But see that he does
not travel far."

Et Kalass grabbed Et Avian's shoulders, gently turned the
injured noblekone, and led him unsteadily away. Jook watched
them depart, settling his massive bulk. A burgundy-uniformed
officer appeared from behind the throne dais and crawled to
the reception area. The intelligence officer made obeisance to
the Supreme Leader.

"Do you understand your mission, Colonel Longo?" Jook
asked.

"My duty is to serve, Leader of Leaders," Longo fawned.

"Your duty, Colonel Longo, is to capture the aliens. They
represent a strategic objective of growing importance. We must
capture them and cultivate them as allies. And if we cannot do
that, then we must kill them. Do you understand?"

"Your orders are clear, Great One," Colonel Longo said.

"Depart," Jook ordered, "and do not fail."

Longo bowed low, pivoted sharply on all fours, and trotted
briskly from the imperial chamber. Jook sat silently, recognizing how tenuous his grasp on power was becoming. Gorruk's
army was no longer dependable, and the nobility-controlled

militia was more threat than comfort. The dissipated ruler leaned back on the throne lounge and allowed his anguish to swell within his breast.

Chief Scientist Samamkook and General Et Ralfkra met Et Kalass and Et Avian at the formal entry to the Public Safety Ministry. A gaggle of doctors and nurses attended Et Avian as he stumbled from the hovercar.

"Take him to my chambers," Et Kalass ordered, shaking his head woefully. The procession moved quickly to the lifts and up to the minister's suite of offices and rooms. The stricken noblekone was placed on the minister's own bed. The ancient Samamkook, trembling and feeble, was also shown to a lounge and ordered to recline—a great honor in the presence of nobility. Minister Et Kalass, a look of despair governing his features, stood silently over Et Avian, while General Et Ralfkra took charge and graciously directed the assisting multitudes to leave. Anxious staff members slowly filed out, and Et Ralfkra followed them through the anterooms, shutting and locking the security seals on the great doors. The militia general returned.

"A performance without rival," Et Ralfkra declared.

Et Avian swung his legs over the side of the bed. Standing erect, the noblekone unhooked the straps securing the massive body cast and ripped it from his body. He grimaced. A spiderweb of scars flowed over his shoulder and across his chest.

"Your report, General," he said, slipping on a mantle. "Are we ready?"

"Not yet," General Et Ralfkra replied. "It is close, but we need more time."

"Time! More time! When then?" Samamkook asked, his voice weak but his tone adamant. The old commoner, brittle and rheumy-eyed, shifted feebly in the chair.

"Easy! Easy, my old friend," Et Kalass cautioned. "It must be at the right time or it will be for naught. We—"

"If I am to be part of your great plan, then you had best accelerate your timetable," Samamkook interrupted. He laid his head down and sighed impolitely.

"There is no hurry, sir," Et Kalass replied with great respect in his voice. "For you will not die—not as long as you have a job to do."

"Thank you for your opinion, Lassie," Samamkook said. "But you have little to say in the matter."

Et Avian remained silent. He rested his hand on the old commoner's shoulder.

After four days of clear weather and hard hiking, the salt mission returned to the valley of the great river and were met at the top of the bridge valley by sentries prepared to assist them in the final uphill portion of their trek. The salt bearers were tired, but the horses had made a profound difference. Sixteen hunters, including the injured novice, had been relieved of their burdens by the golden animals. The unburdened hunters took shifts among the other salt carriers, preventing the crippling fatigue of the long hike back from the flats. The line of cliff dwellers headed down the valley trail to the bridge and the river crossing, leaving the humans behind.

Under a lowering overcast the horses were pointed south, paralleling the river valley. Ahead lay the valley of the smoldering pinnacles, and beyond that the ferry crossing to MacArthur's valley—a two-day ride—the final and shortest leg of their journey. Buccari was ready to climb back on the wide back of the golden horse.

"Whose idea was it to come on this trip, anyway?" she asked.

"Don't get me started—sir!" MacArthur bellowed over his shoulder. Buccari ducked and grimaced at O'Toole. It started to rain.

It rained all day and intermittently during the night, leaving the twin volcanoes shrouded in low overcast. The horses and their riders slogged along the undulating shoulder of the river valley and past the location where Chastain and MacArthur had first come to ground. The mists were thick, and the only sign of the volcanoes was a sulfurous odor. On the second day a chilly wind blew from the north, aggravating their discomfort, their rain-soaked skin damaged by constant rubbing and chafing against the horses' backs.

The riders plodded in single file, traversing steep terrain that merged with the low clouds. They moved across the sloping margins of a ridge that ran away into the mists. On one side lay the river valley; on the other, the downs of the prairies. MacArthur ranged slightly ahead, leaving O'Toole, Buccari, and Shannon to bring up the rear.

"Whose idea was it to come on this trip, anyway?" O'Toole

asked, turning around and directing his voice softly down the line of horses.

Buccari smiled painfully. "Don't get me started!" she said pompously.

Shannon's rumbling bass chimed in: "Don't get me started, either."

They laughed at MacArthur's expense—only hours to go before they reached the ferry crossing. The thought of returning to the warmth and comfort of their settlement was salve to their fatigue and injury.

Buccari, her rear bruised and sore, shifted uncomfortably and stared into the mists. There was little to see. The land fell away steeply toward the river on the right and gradually toward the northern plains on the left. Outcroppings of rock, gravestones in the fog, lifted from the tundra. Buccari's horse tensed; it neighed, a loud noise in the misty silence. All four horses were suddenly nervous, shaking their manes and flicking their tails.

"What is it, Mac?" Buccari asked. The corporal had halted.

"Wind's changing direction," Shannon said. "I can smell buffalo."

"Keep moving," MacArthur ordered, hauling on his reins. Shannon and O'Toole followed. Buccari was left in the rear, her horse balking until she gave it a hard kick. It moved skittishly, prancing sideways. She raised her head to yell for help—and detected movement in the rocks.

"We've got company!" Shannon bellowed.

The huge reptile sprang from the rocks, front legs high in the air, stiletto claws extended, a terrible hissing emanating from its saw-toothed maw. Buccari's horse reared and twisted to meet the attack, but the dragon was too quick. It impacted squarely on the horse's rump, one lightning claw flicking hotly against the side of Buccari's head. The stricken horse threw the dazed officer to the ground. She landed hard, rolling down the steep hill, limp and just clinging to consciousness.

Even before she stopped rolling she heard the staccato explosions and saw the muzzle flashes of automatic rifle fire. Holding her head, she looked up through thick mists made worse by her dizziness to see the flared-necked reptile drag the struggling horse to the ground, its great maw locked on its haunch. More bursts of automatic rifle fire, and the screeching mass of scales and teeth fell over. Its great tail slammed the ground twice, shuddered, and was still.

Hamstrung, her noble horse screamed horribly, struggling to stand on useless hind legs. Buccari watched in great sorrow as MacArthur walked through the shroud of fog to fire two rounds into its ear. She tried to stand, but her rubbery legs would not cooperate; the hillside spun, and she lay down to keep from passing out.

The silence was deafening—and short-lived. A bestial roar broke the calm, horrible and primordial, loud and resonant despite the fog. And then another. The echoes at last surrendered to wet and heavy stillness.

Buccari struggled to a sitting position and was relieved to see MacArthur bounding down the hill. She put her hands to her throbbing head and tried to focus on something—something big—that moved through the mists. It stopped and retreated, melding smoothly into the grayness. MacArthur skipped noisily down the steep, shingle-strewn grade, suddenly pulling up short. He saw it, too. He planted his legs and fired a burst into the fog. A hideous screech lifted the hair on her neck, and something sprinted along the scrabbly rock, its crashing footfalls lingering in the stillness.

"Hold still, Lieutenant!" MacArthur shouted, stalking backward.

Buccari felt warmth running down her cheek; she touched her face and then stared dumbly at the bloody fingers. MacArthur, his head pivoting constantly, knelt next to her.

"I'm bleeding," she said weakly. "I'm going to have a scar like you."

"You're lucky to have a face," MacArthur hissed. His clear eyes blazed into the fog, trying in vain to regain sight of the animal. "What the hell was that—can you walk?"

"Don't know," she said. She made an effort to stand, but her legs wobbled and she collapsed. MacArthur slung his rifle over his shoulder.

"Cover me!" he shouted up the hill. He bent down and picked her up, cradling her in his arms. Standing erect, he juggled her body several times to get it positioned and started hiking up the hill.

"Easy!" she said. "My head aches."

"I know all about headaches," MacArthur said.

She wanted to reply, but all discussion was ended by another primeval scream that flowed into a rumbling roar and ended with a reverberating growl. MacArthur staggered up the steep hill, occasionally stumbling to his knees, causing Buccari's head pain to surge and pound. He regained the summit and set Buccari down roughly. Shannon and O'Toole were on either side of the nervous horses, staring into the mists. O'Toole kept glancing sideways at the fallen reptile, muttering like a crazy man.

"I think I can get up now," she said.

"Hold still. Let the bleeding stop," MacArthur snapped. Shannon handed him a grimy cloth. MacArthur reduced it further, ripping it into strips and binding Buccari's wound. "Hold pressure on it," he ordered.

"Let's move," Shannon said. "The carcass should keep them from following us. We've used enough ammo."

"Roger that," MacArthur agreed. "Help me with the lieutenant."

MacArthur swung up on his horse. Buccari was lifted up behind him.

"Hang on," he directed. "And keep talking."

"I ... I'm okay," she mumbled. She reached around MacArthur's slim waist and clasped her hands together, pressing her good cheek to his wide back. She could feel the hard muscles in his body working as he twisted. The horse moved at a nervous trot. She groaned softly.

"Sorry, kiddo ... sir," MacArthur said tenderly.

A kilometer later they backed the pace down to a walk. The weather lifted to the shifting winds; visibility increased rapidly, and the river was revealed with shafts of sunlight breaking through the scattering overcast. The horses calmed, as did the riders.

"That was a goddamn dinosaur," Buccari said, taking a deep breath.

"No shit," MacArthur answered, looking over his shoulder.

Buccari blinked against the throbbing pain. She moved one arm from MacArthur's waist and tentatively tested the bandage, trying to gauge the length of the gash. It ran from her scalp, just over the ear, to the fat part of her cheekbone, almost to her nose.

"Adds character, Lieutenant," MacArthur said, as if reading her mind. "It'll take a lot more than that to ruin your looks."

"Thanks, Mac," she said, genuinely flattered. She returned her arm to his waist.

"And Lieutenant, I'm glad you came on this trip," he continued.

"Now I know you're lying!" she retorted. "I lost a horse."

"You didn't lose the horse. It could just have easily been any of us. That dragon was going to get any horse it wanted," he said. "No, I'm glad you came, because now you can see how important the horses are. The horses will make the difference between us living or dying on this planet. But I'm real sorry you had to get hurt."

"Me, too," she said. They continued on in silence for many minutes, starting a descent into the familiar narrow valley leading to the ferry landing.

"You're probably right about the horses, Mac," Buccari finally said.

"Of course I'm right," MacArthur responded, cocksure.

"Arrogant asshole!" she replied.

"Affectionate nicknames! Thank you very much." He reached back and gave her a gentle, lingering pat on her thigh.

"You stink," she said quietly. She looked at his hand but made no effort to move it away.

"So do you," he replied.

"No, I don't. I'm an officer and a lady."

"Well, one out of two ain't bad."

"What's that supposed to mean?" she asked.

"Nothing, nothing, er . . . just a little marine humor."

Buccari grabbed a handful of the marine's skin and pinched hard.

"*Aarrggh!*" he shouted loudly.

"You're lucky I don't have a knife."

THIRTY-SEVEN

AUTUMN

Hudson settled into the acceleration chair. The crew of the booster rocket worked efficiently, giving clear evidence that konish space travel was a routine event. A konish full-pressure suit and helmet had been modified for his use, but it was not elegantly done. It hung on him, and he was certain the impending g-forces would efficiently locate all spots where the material was gathered.

"The flight-ah will take-ah forty of your minutes, Hudsawn," Kateos said, strapping in next to him. "If you have difficulties, please tell me." Her proficiency with Legion was incredible. His own facility with the konish tongue was growing slowly but growing nevertheless. Kateos drove them to learn each other's language, and she was making progress with the voice recognition and translation computer programs.

Hudson was to spend the winter across the planet, at Goldmine Station. It was Kateos's idea, seconded immediately by Buccari. A common language was necessary. Without adequate communications an accord between the races would be unlikely. Hudson's role as emissary and translator was formalized.

The modest domicile was high on the cliffs—windy, cold, and near the dangers of carnivorous interlopers—but it was his. He was master. Brappa, son-of-Braan, glided onto the terrace of his new home. Gliss, beautiful and nubile, waited on the windswept rock, dark growlerskin pulled tightly around strong, capable shoulders. The sight of his wife caused Brappa's heart to soar with boundless spirit. Gliss opened her arms, and Brappa embraced her. Scandalous behavior, yet understood and forgiven: the fervor of youth.

"Husband," she said, "a meal is ready, and thy rooms art warm."

"Thine eyes art the only warmth I need," Brappa said, singing the famous words of love. "I have missed thee dearly. Now we live our lives as one, for I am home."

Glorious words. The salt vaults were filled, and the hunting forays were over. Home were the hunters, and happy were their wives and families. It had been a good year with but few hunters lost or injured. Many gave credit to the long-legs for the colony's good fortune.

Gliss was radiant; Brappa knew she wanted many children. The delighted pair turned to their entryway and halted, for sonic echoes lifted on the breezes. Familiar sounds—friendly noises—separated from the ambient background, and distinctive echo patterns grew louder.

Their time alone would have to wait. Brappa looked out over the chasm.

"They come," he said unnecessarily. The lovers faced the steamy emptiness. Two young cousins flapped happily to the terrace wall and took perch, and then Braan and Ki wheeled into view, landing with athletic prowess, followed by Craag and his mate, and then the venerable patriarch, Veera—grandsire to Gliss—lifted above the terrace wall, alighting with stately dignity. The terrace was quickly overflowing with family and well-wishers; lesser members of the clans perched on the walls and rocky cliffs.

"Thy manners, my son. Thou wouldst invite thy guests into thy home," Ki said, softly and formally. "'Tis impolite to keep friends on the terrace overlong."

"Our home is thine," said the nervous Gliss, using a timeless litany. "Please enter and sing." She turned and hurried inside, panic on her young and beautiful face. Brappa followed, leading the multitude into his humble three-room warren.

Food and drink were brought, and the singing was vibrant. What more festive than a homewarming and the celebration of the coming of winter combined? The celebrants and their gleeful noise overflowed the friendly confines. Neighbors stopped to partake in the cheer and goodwill. Singing spread over the cliff face, and it was a night for the ages.

Resplendent, the valley was touched with the magic wand of autumn. Forest pine, emerald fir, and blue spruce gave depth and contrast to brilliant tendrils of russet and gold. Dry, brittle leaves dusted with frost layered the forest floor, and on crisp mornings an earnest film of ice margined the lake, laminating the stony beaches with a frosty glaze. It was cold, but as the days shortened, the sun shone brighter.

Day's end. Dusk: a peaceful, chilly gloaming settled over the valley; stars twinkled in deep velvet. Standing at the threshold of her stone cabin, Buccari watched Dawson, her infant carried papoose fashion, walking across the common. The tall redhead smiled and waved enthusiastically. Buccari reciprocated.

A commotion came from the horse barn, the horses neighing and prancing; O'Toole was feeding them. Threads of smoke wafted into the twilight; the homey smell of wood fire bespoke the coming mealtime. A palisade of sturdy pine boles, strong enough to deter bears and buffalo dragons, ran the perimeter of the settlement, with a stout gate that opened to the lake. Two smaller doors provided alternative escape or entry routes. Guard posts, uniformly box-shaped, stood at four of the five corners of the fort, and Shannon, at Buccari's insistence, kept at least two manned at all times.

The harvest had been bountiful. A round stone structure stood next to the horse barn—a grain silo—filled with raw grain. Tookmanian had built an oven in which to bake biscuits and coarse breads, using yeast and small amounts of salt and honey provided by the cliff dwellers. Bread, wild tubers, herbs, berries, buffalo steaks, and the abundant fish of the lake provided a healthy diet.

Buccari studied her callused hands with pride. She was proud of herself and her crew. Most of them were warming themselves inside the sturdy lodge, where Wilson and his kitchen staff were moving across the rough-hewn floor preparing the evening meal; the ongoing watch was already eating. She debated a shower; the lodge had running water of sorts. The friendly spring on which they had centered the camp had been channeled through stone and leather aqueducts directly into the lodge, and a large beaten-metal pot of water hung suspended over a fire in a room off the kitchen. The hot water was used for washing—clothes and bodies. Fenstermacher had contrived plumbing that fed an adjustable mixture of icy spring water and hot pot water. The lines to take showers were long, and the warm water pot was always in need of replenishment. Buccari decided against the shower. She would clean up inside her own hut.

Buccari retreated into her abode, closing the thick door; leather hinges squeaked softly. The shutters were already pulled to, and she could feel the glow of the fire radiating and warming the single room. No more than six paces square with a floor of hewn wood, to Buccari the hovel was a castle. The fireplace, built with a wide-stepped hearth for corded wood, dominated the back wall. The door stood centered in the front, and shuttered windows penetrated the side walls. A low ceiling formed a loft in which she had made her bed. A stair built into the wall slanted steeply upward.

A dweller-made water pot warmed on the hearth. She tested the temperature and, satisfied, poured water into a smaller bowl resting on the squat wooden table. She stripped off layers of fur and hide and stood near the glow of the fire, scrubbing her tough skin with a coarse cloth, noting with fascination the fine dark hair covering her body—thick and curly in places. She dried off with a clean rag. The humidity was low, and her skin tightened in the dry air. Her fingers absentmindedly trailed across her cheek and too easily found the puckered line of scar tissue. She picked up a survival mirror and viewed the disfigurement. It could not be changed. Sighing, she pulled on an elkhide shift just as a knocking came at the door.

"Come in," she shouted, sitting on a stool and pulling on pelt-lined boots crafted by Tookmanian. The laconic weapons rating was teaching her how to work leather. The door opened, and flickering firelight revealed Goldberg; the fur-clad woman stood back from the entrance.

"Come in, Pepper. It's cold." Buccari stood. Though taller than the lieutenant, Goldberg seemed a child in Buccari's presence. "Sit next to the fire." Buccari motioned toward the fur-covered bench built into the stone hearth. Goldberg walked to the seat and sat down, eyes on the ground.

"Just washed up," Buccari said. "It's too much trouble to get warm water in the lodge, and besides, the guys all sit out by the fire and make fun . . . laughing and hooting."

Goldberg reluctantly smiled. "I know what you mean," she said. "You're lucky 'cause you're an officer. They actually behave around you. You should hear the crap that Nancy and I get, or Leslie even. Hell, they can be real dickheads, er—excuse me!"

Buccari chuckled. "That's okay. Pretty close to my sentiments, too."

Goldberg drew a deep breath and made a choking sound. She put her face in her hands and began sobbing. Buccari sat and watched, perplexed.

"I'm sorry, Lieutenant. I'm so sorry," Goldberg uttered at last, sniffing. "I've wanted to apologize for so long!"

"Sorry, Pepper?" Buccari asked softly. Anxiety welled within her breast.

Goldberg dared to look Buccari in the eye and blurted, "I told the kones about the hyperlight drives." Her crying exploded to a higher level of intensity, her body racked by sobs. "I'm sorry," she choked.

Buccari sat heavily, shocked and speechless. Why? she wondered. Goldberg sat and sobbed. Buccari's emotions organized themselves, and anger dominated.

"I don't understand, Pepper. What did you tell them? Why?" she demanded, her voice rising in pitch and volume. She stood, fists clenched, and moved toward the wretched female. She wanted to strike her. She stopped and turned away, chewing on her knuckle. Goldberg's narrow shoulders sagged, and she bawled great tears.

"I—I wanted to hurt you," Goldberg gasped finally. "I was jealous. You're never taken for granted or pushed around like the rest of us. You don't have to clean fish or—or do other things. You aren't treated—"

"Enough!" Buccari said, steel in her tone. "I don't need that. Not now. We can talk later. It's important, but later, okay? What did you tell them?"

"I was so wrong. You saved my baby's life. I'm sorry."

"Enough. Pepper, what did you tell them?"

Goldberg straightened. She swallowed and glanced sideways.

"Grid generators and power ratios," she said, gaining composure. "I never understood the matrix relationships, but I explained—"

"Did you talk about hyperlight algorithms? The Perkins equations?"

"I don't understand them. They never taught us that level of math."

Buccari sighed with relief and pulled the stool closer to the fire. Relentlessly, she interrogated the technician. After an hour of punishing questions Buccari determined that Goldberg was exhausted and incapable of providing new information. Buccari moved toward the door.

"We may be okay," she said. "Power ratios and grid relationships are important, but they won't get far without the equations. Did you tell them who else knows? Did you mention Hudson or Wilson or Mendoza? To whom did you talk?"

"I told them you knew a lot more than you've been telling them."

"Who, Pepper? Who did you talk to?"

"Kateos and Dowornobb. Those other two guys, too. The new ones."

"Mirrtis and H'Aare?"

"Yeah, whatever their names are. I haven't talked to them since you rescued Honey. Honest! I've avoided them. Please forgive me. I'm sorry!"

Buccari grew implacably somber, pacing the confined floor. She turned on Goldberg abruptly. "I deeply wish that you hadn't done it, Pepper. It's serious, Pepper. I don't know if I can explain to you how serious it is. It's deathly serious. What you did is justifiably punishable by death—disobeying a direct order and providing classified information to a potential enemy. No, to a *known* enemy! Men—men *and* women—have died, have been executed for much, much less."

Goldberg whimpered miserably and dropped her head. Buccari collected her thoughts. She weighed the obligations and responsibilities of her rank and position and looked down at the dejected female.

"What's done is done, Pepper. It can't be reversed. You did the right thing to tell me, and I'll not punish you. Under the circumstances that wouldn't make sense. We have other problems to deal with, and your help is needed if we're to survive. I need your help, Pepper. I desperately need your help. Do you understand me?"

Goldberg nodded sharply.

"Good night, Pepper," Buccari said.

Goldberg stood. "What's next?" she asked. "With the kones, I mean."

"Let me think about it," Buccari replied. "There's no hurry, is there? Winter's almost here. We won't see a kone for five months, maybe longer. For now, just forget about it. It'll be our secret." She forced a smile and opened the door. Goldberg quickly exited, head down.

Buccari shut the door and slumped next to the fire, staring into the flames, a burgeoning sense of depression and helplessness displacing her former contentment. Her deep thoughts masked the passage of time. As the fire mellowed to a soft glow, the temperature inside the hut dropped. Buccari felt the coolness and stirred to throw a log on the fire. She pulled a silky rockdog fur over her shoulders and yawned. A soft knocking brought her reluctantly alert.

She moved to the door and opened it. MacArthur. His exploration expedition had returned. The handsome marine, his skin burnished, hair and beard streaked by the sun, stood at her threshold, smiling shyly. His gray eyes, made all the brighter by his tan, reflected the glow of her hearth. His smile dissolved. She saw her own concern mirrored in his sharp features.

"Missed you at evening meal, Lieutenant," MacArthur said tentatively. An aroma of cooked meat drifted in with him. "Gunner thought you might want a piece of mountain goat. Told me to bring it over."

She tried to respond, but her voice failed. She dropped her eyes.

"Wait until you see the rack from this monster," MacArthur continued nervously. "Horns as thick as my thigh. We found a big herd up at the head of the valley. There's a glacier and a lake, higher up. Tatum and me found a cave, too. Big cave. It'll make a good hunting camp. We can store meat there, with ice, during the summer."

Her stomach grumbled, and she looked up, embarrassed. They both laughed.

"Come on in, Mac," she said, standing away from the door. "Glad you guys are back. Tell me about the scouting mission. Mountain goats, eh?"

"Yes, sir, and we saw what looked like a big cat, too. We got us a big, wild valley. Goes way up . . . way up . . ." MacArthur said, staring too long into her eyes. She looked away. "Everything okay, Lieutenant?"

"Checking good, Corporal," she said, forcing a smile but avoiding his gaze. "I'm starved. What's it taste like—the meat?"

"Won't lie to you, sir," MacArthur deadpanned. "Like what you think Fenstermacher would taste like, only tougher. Tookmanian wants to use it for shoe leather." He moved past her and set his burden down, pulling back its cloth covering with a small flourish and a bow.

She picked up a chunk with her fingers and took a bite of

the tough, grainy meat. It was delicious and still warm. She looked up and smiled, but as she put her finger in her mouth to lick off the grease she started to cry—deep, shoulder-heaving sobs. She could not help herself. Ashamed of her weakness, she turned her face to hide behind her hair.

Minutes went by, the quiet of the hut marked only by the crackling fire and her racking sobs. She heard MacArthur move closer, and then his hands gently pushed her hair aside. His callused fingers trailed delicately along her neck. She tried to turn farther away, but the marine grabbed her chin firmly. His other hand cupped the side of her face. She closed her eyes, squeezing hot tears from them. They ran down her cheeks, growing cold.

"Lieutenant, what's wrong?" MacArthur whispered.

She blinked at the tears, tasting the salt on her lips. Again, she tried to twist away, but MacArthur refused to let go. With his hands cupped around her jaw and neck, he raised her face. Wiping her nose with the back of her hand, she opened her eyes. MacArthur's bright eyes were tragically saddened, welling with empathy.

Surrendering, she stepped close, putting her head and hands on his chest. One of MacArthur's hands moved gently to the back of her head, and the ebony fur slipped from her shoulders. MacArthur deftly caught it and brought its musky silkiness around both of them. At the same time he slipped his arms beneath its warmth and around the small of her back, pulling her into a tender embrace. She shuddered, dropped her hands, and lifted her chin.

"Corporal MacArthur," she said as firmly as she could.

"Yes, sir, Lieutenant," he answered huskily.

"Tonight," she whispered, "please. Don't call me lieutenant."

"Aye, sir," he said, bending and kissing her gently on the lips.

She responded passionately, desperately. His hands moved with possessive strength, fueling her emotional spiral. Her fur slipped again, and this time it fell to the floor. She shivered, but not from the cold. Tears continued to pour down her cheeks, wetting both their faces and seasoning their kisses with salty intensity.

MacArthur slowly, reluctantly, pulled his lips from hers.

"What's wrong . . . Sharl?" MacArthur begged, holding her at arms' length.

"Nothing, Mac. Nothing. It's my problem."

"Sharl, let me help you."

"You are, Mac. More than you can ever know. Hold me . . . kiss me."

SECTION FOUR

DENOUEMENT

THIRTY-EIGHT

SECOND WINTER

Hudson awoke feeling rested. He threw back his sleeping bag and rolled from his tent. A thin layer of snow covered the ground, and a gusty breeze brushed the powdery layers in short bursts. Hudson was chilly, but he was also naked. Turning his back on the transparent wall, he returned to his tent and grabbed his konish jumpsuit. Tailored to his human body, the rubbery material was thick and warm—too warm. He would have preferred a pair of trousers and a short-sleeved shirt, but living in a hothouse was better than living out in the snow.

Dowornobb arrived with breakfast. Whatever it was, at least it was not fish. Hudson had finally demanded a respite from the monotonous diet, and it was humorous to the kones, because the kones thought he liked fish.

Dowornobb sat silently, a somber expression on his normally animated features.

"You worry, Master Dowornobb?" Hudson asked in functional konish.

"I wait for Mistress Kateos before telling you, Master Hudson," Dowornobb replied. "A rocket from Kon reached orbit last night—a military rocket."

Hudson looked up, fork suspended in midflight. Kateos arrived with food for herself and Dowornobb. She sat. Neither kone touched their meal.

"They not friendly to my people? They wish us harm?" Hudson asked.

"We do not know what they are going to do. Perhaps they wish you harm," Dowornobb continued, "and perhaps not. You should stay hidden until we understand their—"

"No," Kateos said in sibilant, gravelly Legion. "They know

371

you here. They know." She pointed into the sky, her expression somber. "They asked-ah to see you."

Hudson's healthy appetite faded. His attention was captured by an escalating rumble. The ground vibrated.

"They come," Kateos said. "Their landing happens now."

Hudson looked up through the dome to see a white-hot column of flame—a tongue of energy evaporating the clouds, cleaving a wide ovate tunnel through which could be seen blue morning skies. Ground vibration increased as the black cylinder smoothly slowed its vertical descent. It hovered over the rocket pads and settled almost imperceptibly onto its gantry dock. Firmly planted, the powerful engines abruptly shut down, leaving sudden and disconcerting silence.

"We must-ah leave you now," Kateos said.

Dowornobb and Kateos hastened through the maze of passageways linking the domes, joining Et Silmarn at the air lock. Indicator lights revealed the air lock to be in the final stages of pressurization.

"Any news?" Dowornobb asked. "Have they brought supplies?"

"It is not a freighter," Et Silmarn snapped. "It is a warship—a heavy lift interceptor. I doubt they bring anything but trouble."

The air lock hissed open. The arrivals lumbered forward. All wore military uniforms, and many were armed. One individual grew disconcertingly familiar.

"Longo!" Dowornobb blurted much too loudly.

"Colonel Longo, if you please," the leader of the detachment said flatly. "Realize with whom you are dealing." Longo wore the dark burgundy of the security apparatus.

"You are a spy!" Kateos said spontaneously.

Longo fixed her with a glance of steel, his diplomatic veneer momentarily transparent. He turned rudely away.

"I am aware of what has happened on Genellan," Longo said, addressing himself to Et Silmarn. "I am here to continue the investigation." He peered around as if looking for something in particular. "It has been reported that you are holding one of the ... aliens. I wish to see it."

"They call themselves humans," Et Silmarn replied, "and one is here as our guest, most excellent Colonel." The noblekone's distaste was thinly suppressed. "The humans have demonstrated their peaceful intent."

Longo stared sternly and smiled. "Of course—Your Excellency. But as the official representative of our government I must verify that ... peaceful intent. A formality, of course. Where is this pacific creature? Why is it not here?"

"It only suffers our environment, most excellent Colonel," Et Silmarn replied. "Elevated pressures cause gases to be dissolved in its bloodstream, and it takes many hours and a slow decompression to relieve. Also, the human considers the temperature in our domes unbearably warm. It possesses a strange, er ... a fragile physiology—except for its tolerance to cold."

"Are you telling me that I must go outside—in the winter—to meet with this creature?" the astounded Longo replied.

"No. It is cold outside, even for the human," Et Silmarn told him. "The human—he is named Huhsawn—lives in our agricultural dome."

Dowornobb detected a faint whiff of fear emanating from the colonel.

"Of course," the noblekone continued impassively, "we have extensive video and photographs documenting the aliens. If you would avoid confrontation, you could review our research materials instead, most excellent Colonel."

Longo did not react to the insult. "Your suggestions have merit, Your Excellency."

In the final analysis General Gorruk's greatest military achievement was his retreat. It was masterfully executed, but then, he had no alternative. His supply lines were severed. It was but a matter of time before his armies were isolated and destroyed.

His plan centered on demonstrating a massive offensive, preparations for which enabled him to position thousands of airfreighters and railcars. Retreat was not imagined as an option, and so the combatants prepared for the ultimate confrontation of the war—an apocalyptic battle. Millions of konish soldiers moved across the blackened battlefields, girding themselves for death. The northern soldiers had no choice; running and fighting had the same result—death. Resigned to the more merciful death of combat, the northern armies marched with desperate resolve.

Gorruk goaded his legions to frontally engage in another attack frenzy. While the southern defenders hunkered down and decimated the oncoming northerners, Gorruk began loading soldiers and arms onto freighters and railcars, using expendable infantry to defend terminals and landing strips—mostly against his own forces as they panicked and broke. Ultimately only a third of his expeditionary forces were killed or captured—fewer than two million kones. That he escaped at all, much less with his army intact, served as a great testimony and tribute to his military genius.

Testimony to his character was less flattering. Thwarted from victory against the southern armies, Gorruk turned to new targets—his own government. Twenty-six main attack missiles hit the Imperial Palace and the ministry buildings within seconds of each other. The structures and their vicinities were vaporized, along with Emperor-General Jook the First and the Imperial Body Guard. Gorruk arrived in the sundered city at the head of a column of crack troops carefully held in reserve from the ravages of war.

Not a single member of the nobility was caught in Gorruk's blitz; all had conveniently departed the city. When informed of this, Gorruk became infuriated, ordering intelligence officers put to death. Yet despite obvious danger, noblekones returned to their duties, the exception being the militia high command and the ministry functionaries. Gorruk did not understand this happenstance, nor did he endeavor to disrupt it, for he realized that no government could function without the economic underpinnings that were largely managed by the nobility. Reluctantly accepting their critical value to his short-term success, Emperor-General Gorruk the First went about establishing a new government on the northern outskirts of the capital, safely behind the ramparts of his main military headquarters. Construction crews began work on a palace to rival all palaces, a bunker to rival all bunkers.

He would deal with the nobility at a more convenient time. The government was his, and now he would govern.

Hudson watched Longo and his soldiers leave the agricultural dome.

"Colonel Longo was polite," Hudson said, relieved to have the confrontation behind him. The meeting had been short, the temperature in the dome uncomfortably cool for the kones. And anticlimactic—Hudson had agonized through the long hours prior. Et Silmarn, Kateos, and Dowornobb said nothing until Longo and his subalterns had departed the dome.

"Be not-ah deceived, Hudsawn," Kateos said in Legion. "Colonel Longo is a senior security officer, a trained liar. You must-ah be careful."

"But Mistress Kateos, my people must deal with your government sometime," Hudson remarked. "There are so few of us. Why would your government not let us settle on Genellan? We could not exist on Kon. What other option is there?"

"There is at-ah least-ah one other option, Huhsawn," Et Silmarn said, speaking the human's tongue. "It-ah is not-ah a good one."

Longo dismissed his soldiers. He cantered into the austere quarters reserved for visiting dignitaries and looked out the window. Blue shadows raced over snow-covered ground, the overcast shattered by the sun and wind. Longo shivered and turned his back. His distaste at being on the forsaken planet was deep.

"A miserable place," he said aloud, but he was not really in an ill mood. The meeting with the alien—the human—had gone well. Longo was impressed with the alien's ability to speak the konish tongue. The buzzer on his entry sounded.

"Enter," he said.

A messenger stood at attention on all fours. "Colonel Longo! We have received word General Gorruk has taken control of the government. Jook the First is dead."

Longo's mouth dropped open, and then his gape turned into an opportunistic grin. General Gorruk was a formidable kone yet a known entity. Longo's smile broadened. Emperor-General Gorruk would, of course, be interested in his mission. The security officer drafted a message reaffirming his loyalties and summarizing his activities.

"Send this through your most secure means. And retransmit the latest summaries of our interrogations—and the videos. Include the videos," Longo commanded.

Gorruk's response arrived four hours later:

TO: SECURITY COL. LONGO
FM: EMPEROR-GENERAL

CLASS ONE SECURITY/COL. LONGO'S EYES ONLY

AM AWARE OF YOUR ACTIVITIES. ALIENS REPRESENT THREAT. LO-
CATE AND ELIMINATE USING ALL MEANS AT YOUR DISPOSAL. RE-
PORT STATUS DAILY. IF ADDITIONAL RESOURCES REQUIRED, SO
STATE.

GORRUK

Longo stared at the short message. An idea sifted into his
consciousness. It was risky, but he would dare to send a
countersuggestion. The intelligence officer sat down at a keyboard and drafted a reply:

TO: EMPEROR-GENERAL GORRUK, SUPREME LEADER
FM: SECURITY COL. LONGO

CLASS ONE SECURITY/GENERAL GORRUK'S EYES ONLY

NO ADDITIONAL RESOURCES ARE REQUIRED.

UNLESS YOU DIRECT OTHERWISE, MY PLAN AS FOLLOWS. WILL
PRESERVE LIFE OF THE ONE ALIEN IN MY CONTROL. WILL USE TO
ASSIST IN GETTING CLOSE TO REMAINING ALIENS. IT IS WINTER
AND TOO COLD FOR OPERATIONS WHERE ALIENS ARE LOCATED.
IN LOCAL SPRING (KON DATE: 13M26) AN EXPEDITION TO THE
ALIEN ENCAMPMENT WILL BE MOUNTED. ALIENS WILL BE LIQUI-
DATED OR CAPTURED AS YOU DIRECT.

LONGO COL. SECURITY

Longo coded the message into the burst transmitters and,
with burgeoning trepidation, punched the transmit button.
Gorruk's response arrived two hours later:

TO: SECURITY COL. LONGO
FM: EMPEROR-GENERAL

CLASS ONE SECURITY/COL. LONGO'S EYES ONLY

KILL THE ALIENS. HOW YOU ACCOMPLISH THAT TASK IS UP TO
YOU. DO NOT FAIL.

GORRUK

* * *

"Is winter never going to end?" Buccari sniffed. She stood shivering in front of the fireplace. Her feet were wet, and her toes were frostbitten—again.

"It's almost over," MacArthur whispered, teeth chattering. They had bravely attempted a patrol of the perimeter. The biting cold had turned them back before they reached the palisade wall. "I don't give it another month. It was balmy outside."

Buccari looked at his windburned features and laughed softly. As Buccari and MacArthur talked, Tookmanian made a rare appearance outside the labor room to add wood to the galley fire. To no one's surprise, the tall saturnine man had taken charge of the birthing. A tarpaulin hung across the entrance to the water room, isolating it and converting it into a labor room for Lee. The dried wood crackled and popped as it ignited, and a gust of wind rattled across the roof. Tookmanian disappeared behind the curtain.

"How's Les doing, Nance?" Buccari inquired.

Dawson lay drowsing next to the fire. She and Goldberg had alternated waking hours through the night. The pregnant female's water had broken in the early morning hours, and Lee had been in painful labor ever since.

"Don't know, Lieutenant." Dawson yawned. "She's asleep, but I don't know if that's a good sign or not. At least it keeps Winnie quiet."

Fenstermacher lay bundled in a corner, sound asleep. Sleep had been hard to come by, and most of the men were upstairs in the loft trying to recover from the long night. Mendoza and Schmidt sat at the table, helping Tatum and Shannon take care of the babies. Miraculously, both infants napped. During the previous night and day they had efficiently taken shifts whining and screaming. The confined space of the lodge had never seemed smaller or more crowded.

The silence ended. Everyone's attention was collected by a gulping, gasping groan followed by loud grunts. Fenstermacher leapt awake and dove through the slitted opening. Dawson, moving more slowly, followed. Agonizing minutes crawled by.

"Okay! Okay!" came Tookmanian's deep voice. Lee yelled and gagged.

"Don't hold back, Leslie," Dawson spoke. "Go ahead and scream."

"Okay, Momma. Push!" Tookmanian growled. "Okay! Okay! Okay! Okay!"

"Come on, Les," Goldberg encouraged. "You can do it!"

Lee screamed—a deep, throaty roar never expected from the shy medic. Outside the curtain the crew stared with grieved wonder, unable to shut out reality by simply closing their eyes. It was a prison. Deathly cold beyond the stone walls of the lodge, it was too cold to leave; they were trapped! They shared! If not the pain, all hands shared the uncertainty and the stark terror of the suffering mother's plight. They were joined in tribulation, and they prayed—prayed with all their might to whatever greater power they could invoke.

"Oka-a-a-y-y-y!" Tookmanian announced, a statement of triumph.

Courage and hope welled. The inmates bravely made eye contact with their fellows. The newborn baby's lusty cry was a clarion call for life, and collectively held breaths were expelled, forced out by joyous cheers. The older infants added to the bedlam with frightened cries.

Dawson appeared, finger to her lips. "Shhhh! It's a girl! Shhh!" she admonished, but she was smiling as she disappeared into the water room.

Buccari looked about. The realization that she was the only woman not involved in the birthing caused discomfiture, and she did not know why. She did not have time to ponder her concern. Dawson, leather apron bloodied, burst from the curtain with two pots. "Fill up the water pot with snow and get it boiling. Quick! We need more hot water!" she brusquely ordered to no one and to everyone. Mendoza and Schmidt hurried to obey.

"Is everything all right?" Tatum asked.

"She's hemorrhaging," Dawson muttered as she went behind the curtain.

In her hurry Dawson left the curtain partially open, exposing a forceful firelit tableau. Tookmanian, an expression of stoic resolve set firmly on his craggy features, bent over the exposed body of the mother, tense arms bloody to the elbow. A frightened Goldberg stood at the head of the bed, the raw newborn in her arms displayed for the mother to see. Dawson, wild hair tangled and bedraggled, stood erect, holding clean rags at the ready, bravely awaiting her next assignment. Fenstermacher, his back to the opening, knelt on the wooden floor.

"Oh, Leslie. We have a baby, Leslie. We have a baby," Fenstermacher sobbed. The little man put his cheek next to Lee's and held her hands. "I love you, Leslie. Oh, Les, I love you so much. Don't leave me."

THIRTY-NINE

RETURN OF THE FLEET

Admiral Runacres deployed his motherships in staggered columns, line ahead, with *Tasmania* in the vanguard at two tactical spans and *Eire*, carrying his flag, next in line. All active signal emissions, except for directional laser communicators, were suppressed. All passive detection systems indicated that their hyperlight arrival was undetected.

R-K Two, the home planet of the belligerent aliens, spun in its orbit on the far side of the system, and Rex-Kaliph, the blazing yellow sun-star, masked the fleet's approach to R-K Three. Runacres ordered a flight of three corvettes to probe the system's defenses and explore the suspected alpha-zed planet.

After a three-day transit *Peregrine One* descended into a survey orbit. Two more corvettes stood off from the planet, acting as pickets and communication links for directed laser transmissions. Crowded in the corvette's science laboratory, Quinn's survey team intently scanned the planet with every passive means available. After ten orbits they had detected no radar or communication signals, alien or friendly.

"It looks cold down there," Carmichael, the corvette pilot, said over the science circuit.

"It sure is, Commander," said Godonov, Quinn's geological assistant. "The planet has an eccentric orbit. Practically the entire planet is experiencing winter conditions right now. It's very cold. The good news is that spring should be breaking soon."

"Tell Commander Quinn to find something soon," Carmichael replied. "We're a sitting duck."

"You'll be the first to know, Jake," Quinn interjected.

"I better be," Carmichael replied. "Good luck, Cassy."

"Thanks," Quinn signed off and pushed over to the master

379

console, rechecking the emission scans. "Damn!" she said softly.

"Something wrong, sir?" Godonov asked.

"No, Nestor. It's just I wish something—anything—would show up. There's nothing here!" Exasperation was manifest in Quinn's voice. Her frustration generated a contagious despair.

"Come on, sir," Godonov replied. "It's the most encouraging planet the Legion has ever seen—alpha-zed beyond doubt."

Quinn said nothing.

"We'll find them, Commander," Godonov said. "We've overflown only thirty percent of the planet. The IR target backlog is still building."

"Nothing but volcanoes and lots of those," Quinn sighed.

An alarm sounded. The officers jerked, gyrating in null gravity.

"We're being lit up!" Carmichael's tense voice came over the command circuit. "I have solid radar tones and repeatable signals. We're being localized!"

Quinn moved to the master console and verified the emissions readout.

"Roger, contact," she said over the science circuit. "Our systems are picking up the pulses. We're definitely being painted. It appears to be standard search radar and not target acquisition. Source position is coming out now."

"Huhsawn, we think-ah your ship-ahs come back-ah," Dowornobb said.

Hudson had to concentrate on what Dowornobb was saying before he allowed the meaning to sink in. He had reconciled himself to never being rescued.

"What are you saying, Master Dowornobb?" he replied in konish.

"Your people are back, Master Huhsawn," Dowornobb said, grateful to speak his own language. "We have detected an object in orbit. Not a konish ship."

"Not a konish ship?" Hudson gasped. "Does Colonel Longo know?"

"I know not, though it can only be a matter of time. He has soldiers stationed in the control areas. Mistress Kateos is checking."

"I could try talking to them on the radio," Hudson said excitedly. The realization drove home. His scalp crawled. The fleet was back!

Hudson noticed Dowornobb flinch and subtly adjust his posture.

"Yes, you could," came a powerful voice—Longo's. Bareheaded but wearing a burgundy Genellan suit, the officer cantered into Hudson's camp. Four soldiers armed with blasters and wearing full combat suits trailed behind. "But I would rather you did not."

Hudson tried to think. Why not? he wondered. It was the nightmare he had been warned of. He swallowed and stared Longo in the eye.

"Good afternoon, most excellent Colonel," he said. "Of course, as your guest I would be at your pleasure to communicate with the, eh . . ." He could not come up with the correct konish word. "With the, eh . . . not known . . . spaceship."

"Your cooperation is appreciated, Master Huhsawn," Longo replied, inadequately civil. "The, eh . . . *unidentified* spaceship will be contacted at the appropriate time. We will certainly call you to assist us. For now I request that you remain in our dome. I leave soldiers to keep you company. I am sure you understand my meaning." He turned and departed without waiting for a reply. The soldiers deployed to the entrances.

Kateos and Et Silmarn had quietly followed Longo into the agricultural dome. Kateos bowed her head and lowered her eyes, as was expected. When Longo was comfortably by their position, she cast an overtly obscene gesture at his receding form, much to the surprise and poorly concealed delight of Et Silmarn.

"My mate!" Dowornobb begged, looking nervously at the sentries. "Do not antagonize authority. Your disrespect will be reported."

"I apologize, my mate," Kateos said. "Of course you are correct. I will harness my feelings." She checked that Longo's sentries were out of hearing.

"I am happy for you, Hudsawn," she said. "They will rescue you."

"I wish I were as confident." Hudson walked over to the dome and stared out at the wintry view. "Colonel Longo may have other ideas."

"Wha' do-ah weee do-ah nex'?" Et Silmarn asked.

"One of us needs to get to a transmitter," Hudson said.

COMINT alarms sounded. Something had been intercepted, something that qualified as intelligent communication. Quinn jerked awake at her station and watched Godonov move to the monitoring system and disable the alarm. He cleared the system and began interrogation. Quinn's intuition screamed. She floated over to watch. She was frightened.

Godonov turned toward her so quickly that they collided.

"Contact!" he yelled. He returned to the console. "What tha—? It's just a series of pulses. I wonder what the computer thinks it is. I need to pull the logic analysis." He paused for several seconds, staring at the output. "Would you look . . . It's Morse code!"

"What does it say?" Quinn asked, her stomach fluttering.

"I'm running it through a conversion. I can't read ditty code."

He punched his keyboard, and the screen changed to a textual format. Quinn was afraid to look. She closed her eyes and prayed. An eternity passed.

"What does it say, Nes? What does it say?" she cried.

Godonov hit keys. The decoded message raced across his console:

EXERCISE EXTREME CAUTION—REMAIN PASSIVE—YOU ARE STANDING INTO DANGER—SEVENTEEN SOULS *HARRIER ONE* CREW ALIVE—CHECK LATITUDE FOUR THREE DASH FIVE FOUR NORTH AND INTERSECTION OF BIG NORTH SOUTH RIVER—HUDSON TLSF AR

"Nash!" Quinn whispered.

"Commander?" Godonov queried.

"Nashua Hudson. My husband's second officer. Anything else?" she asked briskly. She moved to her console; her fingers trembled.

"That's all. It was repeated a dozen times and then nothing."

"Patch the message to Commander Carmichael. Have him maneuver to optimize coverage of the reported latitude and tell him to drop to low orbit. Get the rest of the survey team up here." Quinn felt bitter panic welling within.

Dowornobb finished running the program that generated the peculiar sequence of dots and dashes. He had expected Longo's soldiers to be guarding all radio access, but it had been ridiculously easy to transmit the radio message by using the station's computer network. He strolled nonchalantly from the planet's surveillance center.

Colonel Longo and a squad of soldiers loped down the corridor. Dowornobb swallowed and kept walking. It made no sense to run; there was no escape. He made an effort to pass in the wide hall, but one of Longo's flunkies stepped in front of him, pushing him against the windowed wall. The thick glass vibrated with the force of the impact.

"Scientist!" Longo said, his voice venomous. "What were you doing?"

"Huh ... I was, eh ... I was—" Dowornobb struggled to invent an alibi.

"He was reestablishing a datalink to our photo satellites—on my orders," Et Silmarn shouted from behind the soldiers. "I am updating our research. We have many scientific projects under way, as I am sure you know ... most excellent Colonel." The noblekone elbowed his way through the crowded corridor. Kateos meekly followed him through the soldiers.

Longo gestured impatiently. A soldier stood to attention.

"Sir, the transmissions are not satellite commands," the soldier barked.

"Ah ... because the link was malfunctioning," Dowornobb stammered, trying desperately to support the noblekone's tenuous excuse. "I ran a narrow portion of a subroutine used to reset parameters within our internal program. The program is not related to actual satellite mechanics, so it is unlikely your technicians would be familiar with the program calls." He continued with a tirade of technical jargon until Longo held up his hand. Longo stared at his technician.

"Well?" he demanded.

"Sir, I am only a communications technician. The scientist speaks of matters that I cannot comment upon. What I understand seems reasonable."

Longo abruptly dismissed the technician. He turned to Et Silmarn. "I will not dispute this thin rationalization, Your Excellency, but it was specifically ordered that no one was to use the radios. I am annoyed that you have seen fit to avoid cooperation. To illustrate my irritation, I am placing Scientist Dowornobb under official arrest. He will be confined until I decide what to do about this."

Kateos burst forth, "But you have no right. He has done noth—"

"Arrest the female, also. I have had enough of her bad manners." Longo turned his back on the unfortunate kones. "Take them away."

"Excellent Colonel," Et Silmarn said, his emotions held in check with obvious effort. "I remind you that those two scientists have the most experience in dealing with the aliens. You have need of their services."

"You are too modest, Et Silmarn," Longo replied. "I have the translation computer. I have you. You are obviously intelligent enough to understand the consequences, whereas your impetuous comrades do not. And you forget—the alien! The alien speaks our tongue extremely well. So you see, I have absolutely no need for those ill-mannered intellectuals. I may suggest ... Your Excellency, if you wish them to remain— shall we say—in good health, it would be prudent for you to cooperate with official policies. Do you understand, Your Excellency? Now take them away."

The soldiers moved. Dowornobb was shoved to the floor and kicked.

"Unspeakable savages!" Kateos screamed, and rushed toward her mate. A soldier pushed her roughly to the ground.

"No, Kateos! *Nooo!*" Dowornobb bellowed, twisting to help his mate, but the appalling crunch of a thudding truncheon on his skull obliterated his consciousness.

"Exalted One, Colonel Longo reports the presence of unidentified spacecraft in orbit around Genellan," said one of Gorruk's subalterns.

"What?" Emperor-General Gorruk snapped, looking up from his meal.

"Colonel Longo reports with certainty that the aliens have returned." The underling dropped his chin to the floor.

Gorruk jumped erect. "The alien fleet has returned! How many ships?"

"Colonel Longo confirms three ships in the vicinity of Genellan, Exalted One. He categorizes the ships as escort vehicles and not interstellar vessels. He has not located the enemy fleet yet, but he has provided us with most likely sector information. Colonel Longo has launched two reconnaissance probes and expects to provide vectors for planetary defense interceptors within the next moon cycle. He recommends that the first interceptor wave be launched immediately."

The alien invasion fleet had returned! Gorruk had no choice but to convene the global defense organization. The defense of the planet was governed by treaty, although as leader of the largest konish military power and as a general officer in the

Planetary Defense Command, he could initiate defensive activity. Sustaining the attacks would require the authorization of the Planetary Defense Senior Command, a neutral staff appointed and approved by all governments on the planet. The thought of having to deal with the international body gave him indigestion, but they were unlikely to obstruct his efforts. The racial memories of the first invasion weighed heavily on all kones.

"Alert Planetary Defense!" Gorruk ordered. "Longo's recommendations are sound. Launch the first wave on my authority. Direct Longo to attack the orbiting ships."

"Colonel Longo has a recommendation, Exalted One."

"Now what?" Gorruk asked, displaying impatient fury. "What is it?"

"Colonel Longo states that it will take two moon cycles before our interceptors close within combat range. He proposes a coordinated attack on the orbiting ships at that time. To attack sooner would alert their fleet to our intentions."

Gorruk pondered the suggestion and acknowledged its merits.

"Send my concurrence to Colonel Longo."

"Peregrine has located the likely site of *Harrier*'s crew," the corvette group leader reported. "Commander Quinn has a good photo on what appears to be a man-made site, although clouds and snow cover make it difficult to resolve. We're queuing up high magnification now."

As the group leader spoke, the image on the screen changed to reveal an optical stereo close-up of the planet's surface. The wide expanse of a snow-covered lake was stitched by linear trails, apparently footprints. The trails converged at the gate of a stockade. The stockade presented itself as an attention magnet, straight lines forming an irregular pentagon. The dark rectangles of building structures, with IR chimney signatures, testified that it was an inhabited encampment.

"What makes us positive those are our people?" Runacres asked.

"We're not positive, Admiral," a staff intelligence officer answered. "Maximum magnification reveals bipedal creatures, but they're wearing bulky clothes—furs. Our assessment is based primarily on the settlement's proximity to the position given in Ensign Hudson's message. And, uh . . . we have found no other candidates, Admiral."

"How close to the domed station is it?" Wells asked.

"Not even on the same continent, Captain, although there is a preliminary report of another, smaller fixed-base facility on the same continent as our people," the group leader answered. "Let me put the situation plot back up."

The projected image changed to an abstract holographic depiction of the planet. The image was rotated, revealing the sites under discussion.

"The newly discovered site is located here, near the ocean outlet of the same large river that flows next to the suspected *Harrier* site. We're bringing up photos, although they are quite oblique." The images changed, revealing a long-distance and coarse-grained depiction. "Strangely, IR gives us no imaging. We think the facility may be cold iron. *Peregrine* has scheduled an overflight within the hour."

"Go back to the *Harrier* site," Runacres ordered.

The recce photo reappeared, and the group leader clicked in to maximum magnification. He positioned the laser pointer on the screen.

"Horses," he said. "Or something that looks like a horse."

"Horses!" Runacres exclaimed. "Domesticated animals would indicate an indigenous species, don't you think? Has there been time to domesticate wild animals?"

"I can't answer that, Admiral," the intelligence officer replied. "No one around here knows much about horses. Although if there were an indigenous village-building population on the planet, statistically we should have discovered them much sooner. There would likely be many more sites, and those would likely be nearer the equator."

"Any more news on the satellites?" Merriwether asked.

"Sensors have detected seven satellites, Captain," the intelligence officer said. "Five appear to be downward-looking birds. The other two have intermittently tracked our units with surveillance radars, and one of them has been actively communicating. We estimate it to be a manned, er . . . so to speak—an alien ship with a crew onboard."

"It would appear our arrival is no longer a secret," Merriwether said. A funereal silence settled over the briefing room.

"Commander Quinn has requested permission to drop in," the group leader said, breaking the spell. "She wants to put a lander on site. The area across the river has been terrain-mapped and qualified. The weather isn't cooperating, however.

A heavy cloud layer has moved in, and surface winds are gale force and higher."

"Denied," Runacres replied. "I want more information and better conditions."

Wells's communicator sounded an override alert. The operations officer listened carefully and acknowledged.

"Admiral, we have detected multiple up-Doppler radars in search mode," Wells announced. "Something's headed our way."

Runacres snapped to his feet. "Franklin, general quarters. Direct *Tasmania* to go active," he ordered. "Group leader, intercept and destroy all contacts."

"Standard warning messages, Admiral?" the corvette commander asked.

"Intercept and destroy, Captain."

"Colonel Longo," the technician reported. "Telemetry has terminated. Analysis suggests our probes were destroyed. Enemy radar emissions have also terminated."

Longo cared not. He had located the enemy fleet. At least six and as many as eight large interstellar vessels had been imaged. The position fix was firm, and the PDF interceptors were accelerating toward datum, without the need to employ search radars.

He looked up at the scientists kneeling before him.

"We must terminate our interview," Longo ordered. "Your loyalty will be rewarded, and your services will be requested in the future."

Scientists Mirrtis and H'Aare bowed obsequiously and departed. Longo watched them crawl away, realizing that despite Emperor-General Gorruk's instructions, he would not kill all the aliens. An avenue to power was opening.

FORTY

SPRING AGAIN

Lee's infant was named Hope, and Hope grew fat and healthy. Lee did not die. She clung to life, but a profound weakness hung over her, just as winter held sway over the valley—deep and cold. Fenstermacher doted on her, staying at her side to the exclusion of his other duties, and Buccari overlooked his dereliction in favor of his dedication, for the shy and unassuming Lee was everyone's friend; all hands anguished for her recovery. Lee's invalid condition punctuated the universal feeling of helplessness that grew with every continuing day of endless winter. Spring—would it ever return?

A tired mantle of snow layered the ground in crusty, porous drifts, yet the harsh absolutes of winter had softened; inquisitive rodents, energetic birds, and darting insects made tentative appearances. Nothing green yet, but the nude tree limbs swelled imperceptibly and hints of bud color shaded the extremities of branches. The warm breath of spring descended lightly on the dirty mirror of winter.

Late on a bleak overcast morning the new season arrived with a discordant symphony on the great river. Great chunks of ice shattered and twisted; the irrepressible liquid force of the river crushed its own brittle armor, causing the ground to tremble and the air to vibrate. The awestruck humans assumed that another quake had rattled the land; there had been many since their arrival, but these sounds were peculiar—drawn out, animate. The earthlings stared in wonder as the moaning and crunching continued unabated.

"The river!" MacArthur shouted, a distant memory of Canadian springs returning. "The river! The river ice is breaking up. Winter's over!"

And then it started raining.

* * *

Hudson wondered what was happening. The guards were restive. Operational activity over the past day had increased; military landing modules had made numerous trips to the army transport in orbit. Something was happening or about to happen.

The guards shifted nervously. Hudson turned to see Et Silmarn in the company of soldiers coming down the rows of vegetables. The noblekone carried a familiar-looking bundle. Hudson bowed politely. The noblekone held out Hudson's konish full-pressure suit, the suit used for the suborbital flight to Goldmine.

"Master Huhsawn. It-ah time to return to your people! Put-ah on your space suit-ah," Et Silmarn ordered. Hudson could hear the kone's helmet radio transmitting. Longo must be monitoring the conversations, using Kateos's translation programs.

Hudson's anxiety swelled. Were they going to let him go? Or were they using him as bait?

"It will take a few moments," he said, using the konish language.

"Colonel Longo has-ah order you to get quick ready," Et Silmarn replied, sticking to Legion. "You have-ah time to dress with your warmest clothing. We leave now."

"Your command of my tongue is excellent," Hudson said in konish, talking as he put his things in order, buying time. "I am proud of your progress. Is there any reason why you are speaking my tongue? Are you testing Kateos's translation computer?"

Et Silmarn smiled uncomfortably. "Thank-ah you for compliment. You are most kind-ah, and logic is correct-ah. No more questions. Please to hurry."

"Cassy," Carmichael announced over *Peregrine One*'s command circuit. "Fleet acknowledges your recommendations, and flag operations has cleared us for a landing. Commencing return to low orbit. We'll launch a survey team as soon as we are in position to deorbit the lander."

"Roger, Jake," she replied. "Finally!" she added under her breath.

"Holy torpedo, look at the size of that thing!" Godonov stammered. He stared through the optical telescope, his hands deftly working the controls.

"What is it, Nes?" Quinn asked.

"That manned alien platform we've been tracking—the big one. It must be an interplanetary ship," Godonov said. "It's maneuvering in low orbit. We'd better tell Commander Carmichael. Here—take a look! You won't believe it."

Quinn stared into the instrumented viewing reticle. Godonov's assessment was correct; she double-checked the magnification settings. The satellite—the spaceship—was a thousand meters in length! The telescope's motion-detection indicator started flashing. Quinn increased the magnification to maximum in time to see objects separate from the larger craft. Engines bloomed in retro-burn, and the two craft dropped from sight.

"Tell Commander Carmichael the alien ship just deployed and retrofired two objects, probably landing modules. Something tells me they're looking for the same thing we are."

After days of rain only a few dirty pockets of snow remained. Rivulets of silty water poured from the mountains; streams swelled with impatient force, and the great river, usually not loud enough to be heard from the settlement, thundered and crashed. Sunlight weaved through scattered clouds, highlighting the proliferating buds and blossoms. Grasses poked fine needles through the humus, metamorphosing the dull and dirty ground into glorious shades of emerald. Fragrant wildflowers bravely spread their petals in random abundance.

Lee, wrapped in furs, reclined in the intermittent sunlight, enviously watching the bustling settlement. Baby Hope slept soundly at her mother's breast. Fenstermacher stood on the threshold of the stone hut, leaning against the open door frame.

"You sure you're comfortable?" he asked. "I can get more furs."

"I'm fine, Winnie," Lee replied, her voice regaining much of its strength. "I need to get back on my feet. There's work to be done. It's time to start planting."

"Buccari gave me orders to take care of you and to keep you on your back," Fenstermacher announced. "And I intend to follow those orders—for the rest of my life."

"What? To take care of me or keep me on my back? I don't think that's what the lieutenant had in mind."

Fenstermacher looked at his feet with a silly grin on his face.

"Go fishing," Lee suggested. "Here comes Nancy to keep

me company. Get out of here. Beat it." Dawson, carrying her baby, dodged across the muddy ground.

"I can take a hint," Fenstermacher said, grabbing his fishing gear off the wall. He was pleased to be at liberty. Leslie was finally well and growing stronger. He never wanted to worry that much again. He was a proud father, a happy man, and he was particularly delighted to be going fishing.

Shouts grabbed his attention. A hundred paces downhill, moving away from the cove, was a huge bear, its hide moldy and ragged. It trundled along, still logy from hibernation, looking over its mane-covered shoulder. Chastain and O'Toole chased after it, jumping up and down and shouting, while Shannon stood, an assault rifle poised at his shoulder.

The bear became irritated at its human hounds. Deciding the two-legged creatures had become too brazen, the truculent ursine wheeled on its pursuers and feigned a charge. O'Toole and Chastain turned to run, collided with each other, and fell in a tumbling heap. They struggled to regain footing on the muddy ground, their feet slipping and sliding in a panicky flurry. Shannon sprinted forward, shouting. He fired a precious round into the air and then took deadly aim. The cranky bear recoiled at the explosive report and galloped for the woods.

Fenstermacher broke the silence, hooting at the bear chasers, while Chastain and O'Toole knocked mud from their clothes. Hearing his laughter, they looked up, chagrined.

"You should've seen the looks on your faces!" Fenstermacher shouted. "You guys need new skivvies. That's why the ground got slippery. What a story for the campfire."

"Ah, come on, Winnie," Chastain pleaded.

"I don't see you chasing bears, Fenstermacher," O'Toole challenged.

"I ain't that horny," Fenstermacher retorted, "or that stupid!"

"Easy there, friend," Shannon counseled, ambling in Fenstermacher's direction, a disarming smile on his face. "These gentlemen were only following my orders. You wouldn't want to embarrass them for that, would you?"

"Shit, yeah! Damn straight! What a legend this will be! You guys'll be famous by the time I'm—gerk!" Fenstermacher was throttled by Shannon's thick forearm around his throat. He felt his feet lifting off the ground. He dropped his fishing equipment, using both hands to combat the iron grip.

"Now run that by me again, Winnie, old friend," Shannon

said calmly. "Tell me how brave you think these upstanding men are." He eased the pressure.

"Brave—my ass!" the incorrigible Fenstermacher gagged. "Couple of—clowns!"

Shaking his head, Shannon handed Fenstermacher bodily to Chastain. Chastain grabbed him with meaty hands as if he were a sack of flour.

"He's yours, men," Shannon said. "Use your worst judgment."

Chastain, smiling, turned toward the lake but stopped suddenly. His smile evaporated. He glanced upward. "What's that?"

Chastain's grip loosened, dropping Fenstermacher to the ground.

"What's what, Jocko?" Shannon asked, slinging the assault rifle.

"That noise . . ." But everyone was hearing it now—feeling it. The low-pitched ambient rumbling had graduated to full-throated thunder.

"There! Over there!" Fenstermacher shouted, pointing into the sky. Everyone turned to where he was pointing, staring into the overcast.

A glowing, white-hot blade of flame stabbed through the ragged layer of gray clouds. The screaming exhaust smoothly descended until its source was visible—the black cylinder of an alien landing module. And then a second one! Two black cylinders on hot plumes of fire broke through the clouds. Clear of the overcast, the alien vessels slid slowly across the northern sky, descending smoothly into the valley. A bedlam of rocket exhaust, already at crescendo, increased to an exploding hell. The humans grabbed their ears and ducked, rational thought eclipsed by the single reflex of fright.

The alien engines of hellfire and tumult terminated lateral movement and hovered over the shore of the wooded lake. With startling abruptness they settled into the trees. Humans daring to look into hell watched the columns of flaming exhaust explode into the forest and shoot sideways, their obscene power supporting the landing modules ever lower, lower, until they were obscured by billowing smoke. The explosive chaos ceased.

The silence was worse. Nerve endings deadened by sensory onslaught were triggered into paroxysmic action. Ringing ears and glare-shocked eyes sent belated pulses of energy to the brain. Muscles reacted randomly, and stomachs, bladders, and bowels rejected the tenuous control of the nervous system. Human thought groped for references, but all logic dictated panic; men and women screamed.

The first recognizable sensation was the blast of heat rolling over the settlement, followed by the fragrance of burning wood. Sensations! Links to sanity; the hypnosis of terror was broken. Fenstermacher staggered to his feet and looked about. Shannon, eyes slit with ferocious intensity, had unslung his rifle and was poised to shoot. Chastain, great brown eyes surrounded with white, was crouched low, ready to spring. Shannon was shouting, but Fenstermacher was unable to distinguish any words, only an infernal buzzing. O'Toole stumbled in circles, wide-eyed and witless. Shannon grabbed the marine by the elbow and slapped him. Confusion reigned. Fenstermacher realized that Shannon was shouting at him. Concentrating with all his might, he could hear the sergeant's voice, a tinny whisper under a waterfall of ambient noise. It increased in volume and fullness.

"—get back to the stockade!" Shannon shouted.

Fenstermacher dumbly nodded, grateful to hear again. He turned toward the stockade and stumbled uphill. He halted as Buccari sprinted toward them.

"W-what are we going to do?" Shannon asked her.

"Let me think!" she shouted. She held her hand over an ear.

The acrid smell of burning wood assaulted Fenstermacher's senses. Vivid tongues of orange flame danced above the treetops, and black billows tumbled into the sky. Wilson and MacArthur came running along the shore to join the collection of haggard humans on the cove beach.

"Sarge!" Buccari shouted. "Collect the women and children and get out of here. Take the horses and get moving into the woods."

"Mac," she went on, shouting more loudly than necessary. "I want you to round up everyone else and report back here—with weapons! When Shannon's clear, I want you and Chastain to come down the shore until you can see me or Chief Wilson. Wait for signals. Stay spread out and don't get closer than three hundred meters unless I call you in. If you can't see us, don't do anything stupid. Fall back and try to stay alive."

"Aye, aye, Lieutenant," MacArthur replied firmly, but his eyes showed concern—concern for Buccari. She waved him away and turned to Wilson.

"Gunner, you and I are the reception committee! Let's go."

"A dream come true," Wilson muttered, jaw tight.

The clutch of frightened humans broke apart. Fenstermacher sprinted for the palisade gate, his fishing gear lying in the mud.

The spring thermals were weak. It had taken Brappa and Kibba two days to make the downwind trip. Full-fledged warriors, the proud young hunters had been selected to make the first contact of the year with the long-legs—a great honor. They were still far away when the engines of terror broke through the clouds. Brappa screamed warning signals and accelerated his glide. With a freshening wind carrying them southward, the cliff dwellers lifted high on firming updrafts. The scar gouged out of the forest by the alien vehicles was a carbonized gash on the shores of the lake. Everything within bowshot of the sinister black cylinders was cauterized into ash.

Two long-legs stood on the verge of the destruction; Brappa recognized Short-one-who-leads and One-who-cooks. Two more long-legs, Brave-crazy-one and Giant-one, ran along the lakeshore toward the landing site. All carried weapons. Brappa returned his scrutiny to the alien ships. An open entrance was visible in each vessel, and uniformed aliens—bear people carrying weapons—were descending to the ground.

"Bear people! The long-legs are in peril," Braan whistled. "Stalwart Kibba, return and inform Braan-our-leader of what we have seen. We will have war!"

Kibba screamed and climbed for altitude, the weariness in his wings eclipsed by his mission. Brappa soared over the troubled valley.

Buccari and Wilson rounded the charred trees. A thick smell of ash and smoldering wood permeated the smoky air, and the ground was fused into crusty blackness. The alien vessels loomed high, easily the height of a lunar yard booster. Their massive engines had excavated prodigious craters over which the heavy craft were suspended, supported by articulating buttresses. Buccari looked back along the beach and saw MacArthur and Chastain far in the distance. She turned to the konish landers. Three aliens dressed in burgundy suits approached, crawling on all fours.

"Stay here, Gunner," Buccari ordered. "Keep MacArthur in sight. Take this." She handed Wilson her pistol and left the lakeshore. Heat from the hot cinders crept around the soles of her sandals.

Forty paces from the approaching aliens she halted and held her ground. She searched for Hudson to no avail, but she saw Et Silmarn; his distinctive light gray suit stood erect in a hunched cluster of black-uniformed armed kones. She counted twenty aliens.

The party of wide-bodied, burgundy-uniformed kones crawled up and stopped. The leader lifted gauntleted hands from the ground and stood erect, towering disconcertingly. The giant looked beyond her. It removed its helmet and nodded. Buccari nodded curtly. The other kones kept their helmets on. One of them, carrying a blaster, removed a black box from a commodious uniform pouch and placed it on the ground.

The leader spoke loudly in his own language. After a short delay the disembodied translation came from the electronics box: "I greet you."

Disgusted, Buccari looked down at the box as if it were dog offal. She did not need a talking box. Where was Kateos? Where was Hudson?

"Et Silmarn!" Buccari yelled past the kones. "Where is Hudson?"

The soldiers guarding the noblekone rose on their hind legs and adjusted their positions, blocking the noblekone from her sight.

"Talk to me," said the uniformed kone, the monotonous, mechanical translation giving no hint of emotion or inflection. "Speak slowly."

Buccari squared her shoulders and stared up at the hulking monster. "You have one of my people," she said firmly. "Where is Hudson?"

The kone listened as the box translated. Buccari was frustrated and angry, her fears completely forgotten. The shock of the tumultuous landing had passed, and her fury boiled at the thought of what had happened. There was no reason for them to land this close. Just a few meters closer and her people would have been crippled or killed.

"Yes, we have Huhsawn," the box replied. "He—"

"Where is he?" Buccari demanded, shouting over the kone's words. "If you have him with you, then bring him here! Now!" The translator computer garbled noises.

The kone spoke again, slowly and with more volume: "Please wait for me to finish speak—"

Buccari's jaw jutted out. She gave the alien an iron glance, stomped over to the electronics box, and kicked it tumbling backward. Her sandaled toes hurt like hell.

"Hudson!" she shouted with bald rage. *"Huhsawn!"*

The giant retreated a half step. A subaltern apprehensively sidled to the box and picked it up, checking for damage. It was apparently inoperative. The aliens talked among themselves. One departed, dogtrotting across the cinders. The alien in charge peered down at Buccari with a curious look on his face. She could smell his fear.

The incongruity of size was comical. Buccari felt like a rabid mouse. There was no reason for the huge alien to fear her and there was every reason for her to be standing in stark terror, but her anger was controlling the confrontation. Could she control her anger? She observed Et Silmarn and a smaller figure—Hudson!—coming her way, escorted by four black uniforms.

She watched them approach, feeling her intensity dampen. The compact formation stopped short of her position, and the subaltern moved briskly forward with another voice translator identical to the first one. He connected a coiled lead from the leader's helmet to the box and stood at his side, holding the box and watching Buccari carefully. The leader of the aliens put on his helmet.

Hudson's mouth was twisted into a worried smile. Buccari waved, and he hesitantly waved back or, more accurately, pointed skyward with a jabbing finger. Hudson's appearance mollified her anger. She was cooler, more objective, and surprised at her audacity. Boldness was working to her advantage.

"Why did you land so close?" she asked, retaining the initiative. "We have had injuries." She heard the metallic voice of the computer remanufacture her words. The alien leader listened carefully and spoke several sentences.

"We apologize," the box announced. The alien spoke in short phrases. "We wanted to come down . . . on this side of the river. Once our landers were committed to land . . . we could not alter their trajectories . . . I am told that you and Huhsawn . . . are both ship pilots, so you must understand our plight . . . I am sorry . . . It must have been loud."

His excuse was plausible. An orbital descent on a planet this dense would be a fuel-critical maneuver, particularly for the nonaerodynamic vertical-thrust machines flown by the aliens. She was not happy about it, but she would concede the issue.

She reminded herself that it was futile to fight the kones, that cooperation would be their best chance for survival. She struggled against mutinous instincts.

"Why are Hudson and Et Silmarn being guarded?" she asked, speaking slowly. "Is Hudson not free to rejoin his kind? Where is Kateos?"

"You are the one called Sharl," the box answered. "The research files . . . say good things about you . . . Is it true you are . . . a female of your species?"

"I am the senior officer," she replied, anger welling. With effort she contained herself. "Yes! I am Sharl. Allow me to speak with Hudson."

"Huhsawn will be brought forward," the box said. "Forgive the delay . . . but we desire to test this . . . translation computer without prejudice of knowledgeable assistance . . . It works well, yes?"

"Given a chance," she responded sheepishly, her toes still smarting.

The kone stared impassively. She could no longer smell its fear.

"I am Colonel Longo. As official representative . . . of the governments of Kon and of the Northern Hegemony . . . I have been ordered to establish contact with your race . . . and to define the preliminary conditions for relationships."

Relationships! That sounded encouraging.

"I am Lieutenant Sharl Buccari," she responded formally, "of the Tellurian Legion Space Force. It is our wish to cooperate fully with your government."

"Very well, Lieutenant Sharl." The kone turned away and talked to his subordinates; the sound was not processed by the computer. One subordinate loped over to Hudson's guards and returned with Hudson in tow. Her cooperation was being rewarded.

"Hello, Nash!" she shouted as soon as he was in easy voice range.

"The fleet's back, Sharl," Hudson responded, but the kone held up his hand and said something loud and curt. Hudson obviously understood.

The fleet was back! Thunderstruck, she barely heard Longo's admonition.

"Again," Longo said. "I must ask that you speak one at a time and slowly . . . so the translator can operate effectively . . . for my benefit." He looked at both of them. "Allow me to continue ... Master Huhsawn, Lieutenant Sharl has expressed her desire ... to fully cooperate with my government. That is also your desire. Yes?"

Hudson shot back an answer in the alien tongue even as the box was asking the question. "Excellent Colonel," the box translated Hudson's words. "What is it that you wish us to do?"

Colonel Longo stared angrily at Hudson. He turned to Buccari.

"This location is not conducive to establishing relationship ... that my government wishes to have with your race. Cold and remote ... I have been ordered to relocate all humans to Goldmine Station ... where it will be much easier to communicate ... Your race is hardy, but you will be more comfortable in a southern climate ... and we have a domed facility that you may use ... Huhsawn will attest to the comforts of our base."

Buccari tried to think. The fleet was back! The fleet was back! That thought pounded through her consciousness. She forced herself back to reality. She had to deal with the present—dreams would come later. She listened as Longo repeated himself. She knew the kones would ask them to relocate. It made sense from the kones' point of view. She looked at Hudson, trying to gauge his expression. There was much unsaid.

"When and how do we accomplish this relocation?" she asked, trepidation growing strong within her breast. The fleet was back. Everything was different.

"There are nineteen humans, is that not correct?"

"Yes, nineteen, er—no! Twenty," she replied. She looked at Hudson. "Lee had a baby girl." Longo tilted his head curiously.

"Now! This day. We act on this day," the kone continued. "I have the means to lift your group ... I have but to bring down another module ... Of course, that will mean another very loud arrival ... All can avoid danger by moving into the landers already on the ground ... They are soundproof."

The computer cranked out Longo's words like assembly-line cookies, with no inflection or accent, no tone, no emotion, but the words were sinister—the spider talking to the fly. Buccari looked down at her ash-blackened feet and contemplated a simpler life. She desperately missed flying spaceships. Cheating death on a day-to-day basis as the pilot of a complex and powerful spacecraft was so much simpler than facing death even once with one's feet planted firmly on the ground. Pain and death came slowly on the ground. She shook herself from her confused trance.

"Colonel Longo," she said, her voice firm. "We will comply with your recommendation."

Longo put his hands together and turned away, a look of satisfaction on his face. Buccari continued talking before he could give orders.

"However," she said, a corner of her brain frantically formulating a plan, "your landing was of such violence . . . that most of my people have fled. It will take several hours, if not days . . . to retrieve them. Is it possible to schedule another meeting at first light tomorrow morning? I will have everyone assembled at that time . . . or at least be able to give you a better estimate of exactly when we will be ready."

Longo deliberated Buccari's request.

Hudson spoke up quickly in konish.

"Most excellent Colonel," the box translated his words into Legion. "Et Silmarn will be of assistance in providing assurance to our people. He is well known and trusted. Would you not allow him to come with us?"

Buccari nodded at Hudson's words. They had reseized the initiative.

Quinn felt the lander slip its moorings and accelerate laterally. She clutched her data pad, tightened her restraints, and suppressed her fears. The EPL was floating free in orbit, drifting alongside the greater bulk of the corvette. She shared the passenger compartment with Godonov and two marines. It would not be long now.

"Lander's clear," reported the EPL pilot.

"Roger," Carmichael answered. "Reentry window in ten minutes. Let's look sharp. We may not have too many chances to get on the ground. You're cleared for retro-burn."

"Aye, Skipper," the pilot replied. "Checking good."

"Commander Quinn," Carmichael transmitted, "your pilot's got orders to return to the ship within five orbits. If you need more time, give me some warning. We're on a short leash. Good luck with your search."

"I understand, Commander," she replied. "And thanks."

* * *

"I urge-ah caution," Et Silmarn said as they marched over the cinders. "Colonel Longo wishes your people to walk-ah onto his lander. Letting Huhsawn and me go is . . . gamble. Longo think it-ah make him look-ah honest. Is good gamble. Where I go without-ah compressor fuel?"

Buccari glanced over her shoulder. Longo stood watching them.

"Where's the fleet, Nash?" she asked. "In orbit? How many ships?"

"Can't be sure, Sharl," he replied. "Kateos says at least one corvette is in orbit. I tried to get a message out, but there's no way of knowing if it was received."

They marched over the devastated ground. Her exultation at the fleet's return had dampened; the realities of their predicament were overwhelming.

"Can't trust Longo," Buccari said. She set her jaw and stared straight ahead. The fleet's return had changed the equation. Rescue was a possibility.

"Longo is up to something, Sharl," Hudson said. "He threw Dowornobb and Kateos in the brig and tried to prevent me from communicating. His sincerity needs a lot of work."

"Colonel Longo speak-ah for my government-ah," Et Silmarn said. "To my government-ah you are threat-ah. You will be attacked."

"We didn't attack your planet!" Hudson almost shouted.

"But-ah can you prove it-ah?" Et Silmarn asked.

"No, of course not," Buccari answered. "Not without time and the ability to communicate with our ships."

"Not-ah matter," Et Silmarn said. "The governments of my planet-ah will not-ah wait-ah. They have taken vows to destroy all attackers."

As they crossed the blackened land, Buccari juggled the implications of the noblekone's warning. They rendezvoused with Wilson on the blasted and littered beach and moved faster, their withdrawal obscured by forest. MacArthur and Chastain were farther down the beach. Buccari started jogging, collecting the marines on the run. Passing MacArthur, she was startled by the cracking wings of a cliff dweller taking flight from a nearby tree.

"Tonto," MacArthur said, shaking Hudson's hand. "He's worried, too."

"The fleet's back, Mac," Buccari said, and her eyes welled with tears. No one noticed.

FORTY-ONE

CONFRONTATION

Runacres stared at the quiescent status panels. Fleet radars were suppressed, and passive detectors revealed no alien signals—no radars, no lasers, no directed electromagnetic transmissions on any wavelength. Nothing for weeks now. Runacres was anxious to get the lander down on the planet. Once he had his people back, then he could think about other options, such as how hard to fight for the chance of winning a planet. How badly did the people of Earth need a new home? How desperately?

"Admiral, *Peregrine* has activity on visual sensors," the tactical officer reported. "They have confirmed objects eclipsing stars."

"Identification? Any trajectory estimate?" Runacres asked.

"No, sir. Attempting to develop parallax triangulation."

"Has *Peregrine* launched her EPL?"

"Apple's out of the bay. Approaching envelope. Retro-burn imminent."

"Keep me informed," Runacres ordered.

"Aye, aye, Admiral."

Runacres stared at the blank situation plots. He could ill afford to wait. His best strategy was to engage early, picking off attackers at long range.

"*Tasmania*, go active. Link to fleet tactical," Runacres ordered.

"Aye, aye, Admiral," Wells replied. "*Tasmania* to go active immediately! Patch data to central operations. *Tasmania*, go active, now!"

Tasmania's search radars exploded into search mode. Electromagnetic pulses radiated omnidirectionally, reaching out for solid surfaces from which to rebound. The main situation plot glowed subtly, shifting through muted tones of magenta and blue as it tuned to the datalink.

Suddenly returning signals were processed; pinpricks of light appeared—radar contacts. Many contacts! Battle computers assessed and designated targets, immediately locating and classifying motherships and corvettes. A planet symbol illuminated, revealing the relative position of R-K Three, and two of the three picket corvettes stood out from the mass of bogies, registering friendly identification codes. The third corvette, *Peregrine One*, rounded the planet on its orbital track as Runacres watched.

But the computer also generated multiple threat warnings, and target acquisition radars automatically powered up into standby—precomputing firing solutions. There were many, many targets, the nearest only three to four days away from engagement range, given present vectors.

"Good God!" an unidentified voice gasped on the main battle net. Hundreds—thousands—of targets presented themselves on the large status screen—whole constellations of attacking interceptors and rockets and, no doubt, decoys.

"Enough praying. Defensive condition one. Set modified general quarters," Runacres ordered calmly. "Signal battle formation one one delta. Clear all ships to go active. Let's start dividing these bogies up, shall we?"

"All ships going active," the tactical officer echoed. Alarm Klaxons erupted into a discordant, nerve-grating wail.

"Abort the landing. Order *Peregrine One* to recover her EPL," Runacres commanded. "Group leader, recall all corvettes. Launch the corvette screen to the attack axis."

A raw sun climbed above the river bluffs. Longo looked out the open hatch of his landing vehicle. There was no sign of the humans. He was furious! Everything was going wrong. And the orbiting alien vessels had suddenly departed—escaped. He had waited too long. Gorruk would be furious. Longo's primary objective—capturing and killing the aliens on Genellan—had become that much more important. The intelligence officer shivered in the damp morning air; he increased the temperature on his suit controls.

"Colonel Longo!" a sentry shouted. "Aliens approach."

Longo exhaled with relief. He returned to the opened hatch and stepped through it, recoiling at the cloying smell of wet ash, pervasive even through helmet filters. In the distance, across the wide expanse of dew-dampened cinders, two humans approached. Halfway across the clearing one stopped and waited, while the other kept coming. Both aliens were tall and human. The female, Sharl, had not come back, nor had Et Silmarn. The absence of Et Silmarn did not bother the colonel overly much; the requirement to replenish fuel in his breathing unit was the equivalent of a death sentence. Longo recognized Hudson.

"Respects, Master Huhsawn!" he shouted, masking his distaste for the frail alien.

"Greetings, most excellent Colonel," Hudson replied.

"What news? Lieutenant Sharl is not with you."

"Lieutenant Sharl apologizes, but she is injured," Hudson said. "She sprained her ankle trying to find our people. It is not serious and will take but a few days to mend."

"A few days! Unfortunate. Can we help to convey her back to the modules?"

"That is the least of our problems," the human said. "It has not gone well, most excellent Colonel. Half our number are as yet unaccounted for."

"What are you saying, Huhsawn?"

"We are anxious to obey your recommendations. It is cold here. Lieutenant Buccar—er ... Lieutenant Sharl suggests you return to the orbiting ship instead of waiting in the cold. In two or three days we will be ready. If you equip us with a transmitter, we could give you status updates. Et Silmarn has experience with your radios and has volunteered to remain with us for that purpose. Of course he would need another breather canister."

They stall, Longo thought. He stared silently at the puny alien.

"Unfortunate," he growled finally, barely controlling his fury. "It is not a trivial matter to return to orbit—fuel considerations and other things. Why not bring those that have been recovered to the landers?" Perhaps Gol'berg would be in that group.

"But we need every available person to help search," Hudson rejoined.

"We wait one more day, Huhsawn. Inform Et Silmarn that I wish him to return," Longo snarled. "Immediately." All pretense of diplomacy evaporated.

Hudson bowed slightly, turned, and walked slowly away.

* * *

The next morning arrived clear and cold. Behind the walls of the settlement MacArthur inhaled the crisp air. It was going to be a beautiful day and warm. He grimaced at the thought. It was going to get damned warm, but not from the sun! He had been surprised and impressed by Buccari's orders to set up the ambush. He never dreamed she would fire the first shots, but their survival hinged on taking the initiative away from the better-armed aliens. There was no turning back.

The marine, standing alone in front of the lodge, kept an intent eye on Tonto. The cliff dweller perched in the highest tree on the peninsula, with a clear view of all approaches to the settlement.

Tonto screeched. Kones were on the beach and headed toward the settlement! MacArthur whistled an acknowledgment. He jogged to the guard tower closest to the kones' point of approach. Petit and Chastain peeked down at him.

"One more time. When I start shooting, you guys take two shots each! To kill!" he said emphatically. "Two well-aimed single shots. No bursts. Shoot quick and get the hell out of here! Go straight for the back gate. No heroes! You got me?" Both men nodded, and MacArthur turned away.

"Mac!" Chastain shouted. MacArthur stopped abruptly and looked back.

"No heroes, Mac," Chastain pleaded.

MacArthur tightened his lips but said nothing. He sprinted toward the guard tower farther up the hill. O'Toole and Gordon watched him approach. MacArthur gave them the same instructions and then dashed back to the lodge. He stomped up the tall wooden stairs, crossed the porch, and went through the doors.

It was cold inside the dark lodge; no fires had burned in its fireplaces for three nights. He scaled the ladder to the loft. It was brighter there; three rifle ports penetrated the logs, and the sun's rays angled sharply through the freshly hewn openings. Buccari, Hudson, and Shannon waited for him, their somber features illuminated by the brilliant patches of sunlight. Their attic perch afforded a clear field of fire over the palisade. Buccari poked a carbine through a port.

"Bugs are on the way, Lieutenant," MacArthur reported. He looked through one of the ports. The tops of the alien landers reflected dully in the distance. The air was sharp and clear, and a fresh breeze was rising—a beautiful day. Tonto screamed and flapped from the tree, catching a thermal and soaring upward.

"They're in the woods," MacArthur said. "Time to go to work."

"Sharl! I'm going down to the gate with MacArthur," Hudson said.

"Yeah, the best pistol shot in the world couldn't hit anything from here," Shannon agreed.

"Okay. Be careful," Buccari said, keeping her face to the rifle port.

"You be careful, too, Lieutenant," MacArthur said. "Once they start hitting this tinderbox with lasers, you'll wish you had changed places with us. Don't wait around."

Buccari turned her head and smiled bravely, without joy but with obvious emotion.

MacArthur took a deep breath and headed for the ladder, with Hudson following. The men descended, dashed outside, and sprinted across the common toward the main gate, each carrying his heavy-caliber pistol in front of him. They positioned themselves behind the partially open gate doors and sighted through the hinge openings—and waited. With short-range pistols, it was up to them to take the first shots.

After they fired, they would start the retreat, leading everyone through the rear sally gate to a rendezvous in the thick woods a kilometer in the hills, where Et Silmarn and the heavily burdened horses were waiting. Tatum and Wilson had taken everyone else into the mountains to one of Tatum's hunting camps, a cave at the top of the valley. Buccari's objective was to delay the kones long enough to get the slower-moving women and children clear of danger.

An eternity passed. Suddenly Tonto screamed. MacArthur peeked through the hinge opening and observed movement in the underbrush. He froze. Konish soldiers, giants deployed at wide intervals, appeared at the edge of the clearing—a mountain range of aliens. Broad, hulking forms broke from the spring foliage and advanced before the stockade, laser blasters and short-barreled cannon at the ready, burgundy-uniformed officers following in their wake.

Once clear of the trees, the line of behemoths halted, and three scouts crawled cautiously across the expanse of open ground toward the main gate, sweeping the area with IR detectors. Their commander moved forward until he was even with the front rank. He pointed uphill, and three giant soldiers trotted out to the flank, while the rest of the titans slowly converged on the gate. MacArthur worried that the kones would outflank the ambush. Fifty paces short of the stockade a scout shouted an alarm and halted, pointing his heat detector at the gate. The others brought weapons to bear. The phalanx of kones, already down on all fours, dropped their ponderous bodies to the ground.

"On three," MacArthur whispered. "One . . . two . . . three!"

Hudson fired through the narrow crack of the gate hinge while MacArthur stepped into the gate opening, crouching low and firing three times. They were so close. A konish scout twitched in his sights as his bullets impacted.

Laser blasters belched singing pulses through the gate, spewing like incandescent water hoses toward MacArthur's crouching form. Blue lightning beams reverberated across the short distance and exploded against the wooden structure. Konish infantry cannon firing in machine-gun bursts joined the barrage, their explosive shells thumping into the wood and detonating, but MacArthur was already clear, rolling away from the exposed door. The blasts from the lasers and cannons did not hit Hudson, but the explosive force of their discharge against the doors caused both gates to burst into flame and swing violently. The palisade gate became a flaming flyswatter, crushing Hudson against the wall of the fort and enveloping him in a blossoming conflagration.

Sprinting across the open field, MacArthur realized there was no hope for the officer. Over the bedlam of konish fire he heard humans firing—the loud, cracking explosions of assault rifles and the higher-pitched snaps from Lieutenant Buccari's carbine. He counted at least five carbine reports alone—too many shots! They were still firing from the lodge as answering laser pulses and cannon rounds sang overhead. MacArthur could see the effect of the konish barrage raking and exploding against the wood and stone of the main lodge. He glanced over his shoulder. The guard towers were gone! The stockade walls that had supported them were engulfed in a licking yellow inferno, but four marines were on the ground sprinting his way. As he passed the lodge, the roof exploded in flames, laser beams and artillery shell explosions fueling the fire like so many bellows gusts. Burning chunks of wood sailed through the air, sizzling and clattering to the ground. He stopped, frozen with grief.

Chastain dashed up and yanked MacArthur's arm, forcibly pulling him into a run. MacArthur ran dumbly for twenty more strides and then stopped to look back at the lodge, his stomach knotted and his head spinning. A shutter in the rock wall burst open. Ugly black smoke billowed forth, and two fast-moving figures clambered through the opening and hit the ground running. Adrenaline flushed MacArthur's body. His entire being soared with exhilaration. He turned and sprinted along with the others until they made the rear gate. All made it, except for Ensign Hudson.

Longo gained the stockade in time to see humans running out the rear gate. His soldiers fired at their backs, but the power packs had been drained by the assault barrage. None of the infantry cannon hit the mark.

Longo cantered through tumbling smoke, past the burning gates, and into the compound. He surveyed the gutted lodge, noting with satisfaction that nothing could survive the roaring flames consuming its structure. A subaltern trotted up to him.

"Four of our soldiers are dead or dying, Colonel. Six are wounded—two seriously," the subaltern reported. "All blaster units need to be recharged. We are vulnerable."

"At least it is warm for a change, is it not?" Longo asked. The aliens were turning out to be considerable adversaries. He had badly underestimated them.

"Yes, Colonel." The settlement roared with the flames of destruction.

"Did we do any damage?"

"Yes, Colonel," the subaltern reported. "One is gravely injured at the gate. It will probably die. The one called Huhsawn."

Colonel Longo smiled. "Ah! A small victory," he said, "but a victory nevertheless. Have the blaster soldiers form up and return to the landers. Recharge the blaster packs and bring them back as soon as you can. Order reinforcements down—armed with cannon and small bore. We have enough blasters. Take the alien back to the lander and see what can be done to keep it alive. A hostage may prove useful."

Brappa sailed overhead, lifted by hot updrafts. He slipped against the press of the thermals and surveyed the activity. The battle had been brief, but every settlement building was in flames. A column of loping bear people hurried along the beach in the direction of their ships. A clutch of wounded soldiers straggled more slowly. Bear people still in the settlement had taken positions along the palisade's remaining back wall.

Two huge soldiers had slipped through the sally gate and were tentatively crossing the stretch of cleared land.

Brappa lifted his gaze uphill. The long-legs had arrived at their rendezvous point and were retreating in good order. Brappa could see the heavily laden horses and the broad figure of a bear person. Brappa wondered at the wisdom of accepting the bear person into their ranks and of taking the horses. All would be easy to track.

Long-leg death sticks cracked. Brappa observed puffs of smoke at the edge of the forest. One of the bear people went down, and a blend of thunderous explosions sounded as the bear people unleashed a volley of return fire. Trees disintegrated in crackling flames and explosions, but Brappa caught sight of two long-legs sprinting and dodging through the incinerated boughs. He was not surprised to recognize Brave-crazy-one and Short-one-who-leads.

Tatum helplessly observed the black pall of smoke above the settlement. Intervening ridges blocked his view, and he could only guess at the magnitude of destruction. Tatum slid down from the steep ridge of the glacial moraine and returned to the cave. A single large entrance and two narrow clefts provided access to its multiple chambers.

Tatum climbed over the boulders obscuring the wide, waist-high main entrance. A rivulet of glacier melt ran nearby. The nearest arm of the imposing blue-green glacier was only three hundred meters away, an icy chill testifying to its proximity. The glacier's physical splendor was reflected on the surface of the moraine lake, whose silty emerald waters meandered beneath and past the boulder-shrouded cave entrance, narrowing and draining into the lake valley below. The cascades of the upper falls were just below the hunting camp, and the noise of the falling water thundered in the background.

"What did you see, Sandy?" Dawson asked. Worry pinched her features. "Is it still burning?" She moved back from the cave entrance.

"Still burning," Tatum fretted. "Been over four hours." After a few paces the ceiling lifted high enough to where even he could stand erect, but he sat down heavily next to Goldberg and took Honey into his lap. Everyone stayed close for warmth. Tatum would not let them start a fire until darkness could obscure the smoke.

"What should we do?" Fenstermacher asked. Lee and her infant lay next to him, both covered in furs and fast asleep.

"Sit and wait," Tatum replied. "We're on our own."

"What happens if the bugs win?" Fenstermacher asked.

"No way!" Tatum shot back. "We'll tear them to pieces."

"How can you say that?" Fenstermacher asked. "The big uglies have the firepower. Wonder why Buccari decided to fight."

"Because the fleet's back, and judging from what happened, it's a good thing she did," Wilson said. "As long as we're not captured, we can still be rescued."

"How long?" Dawson said. "How much longer can we hold out?"

"This is our planet," the taciturn Tookmanian suddenly interjected. "The kones don't know it, but it's ours. It's—it's our moral right."

"Moral right, Tooks?" Fenstermacher huffed. "Stick to your sewing!"

"Morality has nothing to do with it," Wilson said. "It's called survival."

"In the long run they are the same," Tookmanian replied, staring blankly at the opposite wall. Silence fell over the haggard survivors.

Buccari worked the soreness from her back and the burning ache from her old injury; it felt as if she had sand in her shoulder socket. Her hair was singed and brittle from laser strikes; her cheek had blistered. But most of all, she mourned Hudson.

"Tonto says we took out maybe six or seven of them," MacArthur said. "That leaves only fifteen or sixteen. That's a pretty good day."

"So much for the element of surprise," Buccari said. "The rest will be a lot harder to hit." She looked around at the cold, tired faces. The silvery moon was three-quarters full, giving everyone a sinister and shadowy visage. She puzzled over their next step.

"Ammo status?" Shannon demanded.

"Two hundred eight rounds standard—thirty pistol," O'Toole answered.

"Phew!" MacArthur replied. "Get ready to fix bayonets."

"Can't we steal some of their weapons?" O'Toole asked.

"We need another breather canister for Et Silmarn," Buccari

said. She looked at the big kone. Et Silmarn stirred, pushing
off the furs.

"It-ah . . . makes sense . . . for me-e-e to go back-ah," he
said. "It too cold, Sharl. My fuel is gone in five days or less.
I am burden to-ah you." He stood on his four limbs and stared
at the humans, the moon's reflection on his helmet visor making it brightly opaque. "Even if could-ah get-ah more fuel
tanks, it-ah would-ah only be matter of time. I am dead-ah either way." He turned and ambled slowly downhill.

"Et Silmarn," Buccari said firmly. The scientist turned. "We
will be rescued. When my people come, we will take you with
us. We can make fuel for your breathing unit."

"But-ah will they come in time?" the kone asked.

"More fuel," Buccari said grimly. "We'll get more fuel."
She turned to face Shannon. "Sarge! The night's ours. It's too
cold for the kones, but they'll have posted sentries. We're going back to the lake and liberate as many fuel tanks and weapons from those sentries as we can."

The marines rumbled their approval.

"Yes, sir," Shannon replied, squinting up at the gibbous
moon.

"Yes, sir," MacArthur said. He had been sitting quietly. "But
with all due respect, Lieutenant . . ." He looked at Buccari, his
eyes shrouded in the blackness of moon shadows. "With all
due respect, I think, er . . . I recommend you hand off that carbine to one of the men, er . . . one of the marines, and that you
lead our konish friend here and the horses up to the hunting
camp. Someone has to get that stuff where it can do some
good, and it makes more sense to have the marines—not the
generals—doing the fighting." He said the last sentence rapidly, as if afraid she would interrupt.

Buccari stifled a rush of anger. That certainly had not been
her plan, but it made sense. There were not enough weapons
to go around, and the supplies had to reach the rest of the
crew. MacArthur had a point. And besides, he had promoted
her to general.

"Okay, Sarge, I hate to admit it, but Mac's right. You're in
charge," she said. "Good luck, good hunting, and bring everyone back with you." She turned to the kone. "Et Silmarn, you
do not have a good choice. Sergeant Shannon will try to get
more fuel. If he is not successful, then you must decide where
you wish to die."

The noblekone looked up and said, "You are right-ah. I am

dead-ah either way-ah. I die free. Lead-ah and-ah I will follow,
Sharl."

Buccari glanced at the marines one last time, stopping at
MacArthur. "We owe them for Nash Hudson and for Bosun
Jones," she said grimly. "And for Commander Quinn and
Virgil Rhodes. We owe them."

She collected the horses and started walking. Et Silmarn followed.

They hiked all night. Gunfire broke the distant stillness on
two occasions, yet Buccari was encouraged because each in-
stance was short-lived. The noblekone and the earthwoman
kept walking. And kept climbing.

The unlikely duo and their horses hiked throughout the next
morning, their view of the ruined settlement eventually hidden
by trees and intervening terrain. The sun slipped from its zenith as they reached a tree-dotted ridge near the far end of the
valley, the lip of an exposed, talus-strewn bowl. Once they
were past the small stand of yellow-barked firs, the bowl rose
steeply to the final wall of the valley, from which plummeted
two separate billowing cascades. Those crashing waters joined
in a crystalline tarn nestled deeply within the sun-drenched
bowl. The confluence of waters smoothly overflowed the
granite-cradled pool and continued through a channel of riven
rocks, journeying onward and downward to the lake in the distant valley and beyond. Buccari and Et Silmarn's path lay
across the bowl, opposite the water, where a rock-tumbled cleft
angled across the bowl and breached the barren face of the
escarpment—a challenge for the horses.

"We'll wait until dusk," Buccari said, wiping her brow. It
would required two hours of hard hiking to cross the open
stretch of mountainside. Taking the golden horses across the
traverse in daylight could expose them to the searching eyes of
the aliens.

"You are capable of great-ah effort," Et Silmarn said. The
noblekone had kept up, but the increasing elevation was taking
its toll.

"Fear pushes hard," she replied. "It's easier to work than to
worry."

"Ah, yes . . . fear. Slow death. It-ah is difficult to face death
slowly," the noblekone wheezed. He sat down on a slab of
sunlit granite. "Too much time to . . . consider the, ah . . .
meaning of living. I am afraid and also very tired."

"You are brave," Buccari said. "Do not talk. Rest now."

"And you, too, are brave," the noblekone replied. "I am not-ah so brave. I am afraid to sleep-ah, for I may never open my eyes. It-ah is so cold."

"We'll get more fuel," Buccari answered. "Sleep. Go to sleep. It will be better when you wake up." She pulled supplies from the horses' backs and grabbed several fur hides. She covered the reclining kone with animal skins, wondering how he could be comfortable lying in the sun under layers of fur. The mountain air was brisk, but the exertions of the climb had caused her to perspire freely.

"Ah!" he groaned. "At last-ah warmth. Thang you, Sharl. Thang you."

"Go to sleep." Within seconds she could tell from the kone's breathing that he had given in to his fatigue. It had been many stressful hours since either one of them had slept. After hobbling the horses, she threw down another thick fur, but in the shade. She rolled herself in it and instantly submerged into the deepest of slumbers.

Direct sunlight assaulted her eyes. Wet with perspiration, she blinked awake, wondering how long she had been asleep. The sun had traveled across a wide arc—she estimated three hours. It seemed like three minutes. She wobbled to her legs and looked at the slumbering kone. Her head ached, and her mouth tasted foul. She struggled to focus her eyes and was startled by a cliff dweller—Tonto—sitting alertly on a rock next to Et Silmarn's head. The hunter, bow in hand, an arrow nocked, was focused on the sleeping kone. Tonto turned and, seeing Buccari awake, hopped away from the kone, stowing his bow and returning the short arrow to its quiver.

Buccari checked the horses grazing across a patch of wild-flowers and grasses growing in the shelter of the spindly grove. She moved her trail-battered body close to Tonto. Alert and unafraid, the hunter looked at her. She noticed the scars on his forearms, the vestiges of his broken arm. The day of the earthquake on the plateau lake seemed so long ago. They owed so much to the strange little creatures.

She signed: "Greetings, warrior." Tonto returned the saluta-tion. Buccari pointed to his bow and to the kone and signed: "Why guard?"

Tonto looked at the alien and signed back: "Danger. They kill."

Buccari nodded. She pointed to the cliff dweller and then to herself. "We also kill," she signed. "We friends," and "Bear person is friend."

The cliff dweller looked over at the sleeping kone again. "Not friend. Bear people kill your people," Tonto signed ambiguously.

"What?" Buccari gasped aloud. "What happened?" she shouted. Et Silmarn stirred. Buccari signed frantically, trying to find out what had happened to the marines. The cliff dweller recoiled at her hysteria, his sign language confused.

"Take it easy on the little guy," MacArthur said.

Buccari whirled at the sound of his voice. She turned to see all six marines hiking over the tree-lined ridge, carrying strange weapons and two large breathing-unit tanks. Et Silmarn was immediately on his hinds, his sleep-swollen eyes, wide and unblinking, fixated on the metal tanks full of precious fuel. His death would come more slowly.

"Are—is everyone all right?" Buccari asked. Shannon lagged far behind, and Chastain was helping Gordon.

"Sarge hurt his back, and Gordon got burned pretty good on one shoulder," MacArthur reported. His voice was energetic, but he was clearly exhausted. "We iced two bugs, and it only cost us eight rounds. That's a good ratio."

"And we got these bazookas and eighty rounds in trade," Petit shouted. "Helluva deal!"

"Shoot!" O'Toole joined in. "We've taken out almost half of them in one day. This is going to be a piece of cake. A friggin' piece of cake!"

Tonto whistled sharply, then hopped across the campsite and climbed the low rise overlooking the valley. They heard a noise, a sickeningly familiar rumble. The rumble turned into raging thunder, dragging their gazes high into the dark blue skies. Two brilliant white-hot sparks fell from above, growing ever larger and emitting ever louder and more violent noises. The arc-light flames appeared to descend directly on their heads, but as the infernos neared the surface of the planet, gradually slowing their descent, it became obvious that the two newly arrived landers were settling on the lakeshore, within kilometers of the first konish landers. The awestruck onlookers covered their ears and watched as still more trees exploded into flames and shock-induced ripples fanned across the distant waters of the valley lake.

The corrosive sounds of the lander retros died suddenly, and the anguished refugees removed hands from ears as if they were one being. The silence was deafening. Oily black smoke poured upward from the expanded ring of destruction and was lifted and rapidly dispersed by a steady breeze from the northwest. Pebbles and small rocks, shaken from their precarious resting places, tumbled from the mountain behind them.

"A frigging piece of cake," O'Toole moaned.

"Hell! Reinforcements! They got reinforcements!" Petit cried.

"What're we going to do?" Gordon whined, holding his shoulder. The surface of his leather poncho was blackened and shot with ragged holes. He was lucky to be alive.

MacArthur turned abruptly. "So what? So frigging what? What's a few more? There'll never be enough of them." He swept his arm across the verdant valley. "This is only one small valley. We'll hide. We'll fight! We'll use bows and arrows! Spears!" He looked at Buccari, pewter-gray eyes shining like headlights from deep within a drawn, soot-blackened face.

Buccari looked back at the determined marine, and her own spirits surged. "Mac's right," she said. "And don't forget—the fleet's up there. If nothing else, these clowns will draw attention our way. I'm counting on getting rescued, but if we can't be rescued, then by God, we'll fight!"

"Lieutenant," Shannon said quietly as he limped from the group, his back contorted, "I'm with you all the way, but if you don't mind, I'm going to lay this old body down. I recommend everyone rest up as much as possible, 'cause we'll be needing it."

FORTY-TWO

CONFLICT

Runacres, in full battle armor, scanned a simulation of the fleet defenses, gaming his alternatives. He glanced at the main

situation plot as the last corvette to reach station glided into
position. A signal illuminated on his panel.

"Yes, group leader?" Runacres responded, clearing his
screen.

"Screen commander reports all corvettes on station, Admiral," the corvette commander announced. "Countermeasures
plan Beta Two implemented. Enemy engagements imminent."

"Very well," Runacres said stonily, cinching his harness.
"All units cleared to fire, Franklin."

"Aye, Admiral. Weapons free," Wells replied. The operations officer punched an interlock release, and ominous warning lights flashed on the weapons display.

"All 'vettes report maximum readiness," the group leader
said. "No exceptions."

"Very well," Runacres snapped, switching circuits to screen
tactical. Transmission levels were high, but radio discipline
was sound; terse position and target commands flashed from
ship to ship. Runacres watched and listened with grim pride as
the disposition of picket units changed dynamically, flowing
subtly to counteract the movement of the approaching foe.

The spearhead of the attack dove directly for the heart of the
corvette screen. The initial engagement was like the first drop
of rain hitting a metal roof. *Eagle One*, the flagship's lead corvette, called "weapons away," and the tactical status board depicted a spread of kinetic energy weapons being fired at the
leading alien units. A kill was indicated. Runacres heard dim
cheers echoing beyond the Legion transmitters, but exultation
was brief; the onslaught—the downpour—pounded on their
metal roof. Fierce engagements cluttered the radio as confusion
and anxiety replaced order and control.

Directed energy weapons sparkled in the immensity of
space; laser pulses arced at the speed of light to collide with
oncoming warheads; missiles exploded in tremendous fireballs;
yet the explosions and laser blasts were but faint blooms and
razor-thin coruscations in the overwhelming vastness of the
lightless vacuum. The widely dispersed corvettes, arrayed in a
three-dimensional stack, slashed and parried, striving desperately to keep the flood of targets from passing, but the stream
of enemy rockets approached too rapidly and across too wide
a front. Runacres watched with approval as the screen commander initiated a large sag vector, but the defenses could not
handle the rate of engagement or the enemy's speed advantage.

It was over quickly; the enemy swept through the screen at time-distorting speeds.

"Attack has penetrated defenses. Thirty enemy destroyed," the tactical officer reported. "Screen units in pursuit. Now thirty-three enemy destroyed. Now thirty-four."

Electronic icons representing more than sixty surviving enemy attackers streaked across the main situation display. Targeting computers designated each blip with codes: symbols for range and arrival times, velocity and size, probable destination target, and defensive responsibilities. *Tasmania*, the lead ship in the column, was being tagged heavily as a primary target. *Eire*, the second ship in the column, the flagship, was also lighting up.

"*Tasmania*'s on the bull's eye," Runacres said. "Order her back to half interval. Direct *Baffin* and *Novaya* to hammerhead the column. Close up the gaps."

"Aye, aye, Admiral," Wells replied, keying his console.

"Forty-two enemy destroyed, Admiral," the tactical officer reported. "Screen units have closed to main battery range and are disengaging."

"*Tasmania*'s opening fire, Admiral," Wells said.

Motherships having clear fields of fire engaged the enemy interceptors with main energy batteries, their ordnance employment indicators flashing cheerfully on the status panels, but radio transmissions on the tactical circuits were deadly serious. Fifty-eight alien interceptors made it through the corvette screen. All but one were destroyed before reaching lethal weapons range.

Tasmania, at the point of the formation, was engaged by the highest density of incoming missiles. Her defensive systems had been saturated. One last enemy drone, mindless and with an intense singularity of purpose, breached the vicious gauntlet of fusion beams and kinetic needles—a meteor streaking malevolently close aboard *Tasmania*, where it finally dropped from radar. Tactical plot signaled enemy ordnance detonation.

Runacres stared belligerently at the status panels. With the explosive destruction of the last drone, all enemy missiles and decoys had been accounted for—the first wave of attacks was over.

"Sir, *Tasmania* has taken a hit," the tactical officer said. "Damage control reports are coming in. Radiation levels have been contained within radtox critical, but she's been hurt.

Overpressure shields were penetrated, and hyperlight generators are seriously damaged. She's drifting."

"Captain Wells, bring *Tasmania* down the line when able," Runacres ordered. "Keep her in the grid and maintain HLA links. Order *Eire* to take the guide."

The Planetary Defense Council convened, decreeing all global disputes suspended.

"Our first wave has engaged the enemy fleet," said the Planetary Defense Command briefer, a senior officer with a pronounced southern hemisphere accent.

A rumble of excitement arose from the audience representing the thirty-three nations of Kon. Emperor-General Gorruk and the ten northern hemispheric governors, all under Gorruk's imperial hegemony, reclined in prominent front-row lounges to the left of the center aisle, their staffs and retinues filling in behind. Chief Scientist Samamkook, silent and brooding, sat behind Gorruk. On the right side of the briefing center sat the southern hemispheric leaders. The southerners had squabbled over seniority and protocol, causing Gorruk to grind his teeth in frustration. How could his armies have been defeated by such rabble? The presence of Marshal Et Barbluis, his battlefield nemesis, as a member of the southern delegation particularly rankled.

The Planetary Defense Command senior staff, including Gorruk's appointed legation, occupied seats around a semicircular table beneath the briefer's podium. Heavily armed PDF troopers guarded the entrances and exits to the auditorium. Gorruk chafed at the necessity of submitting to the decisions of the Defense Council, yet he took solace in having controlled the meeting site selection. The Planetary Defense Council was convened in Gorruk's new command bunker, a magnificent edifice. Gorruk's reign was still young, but he had thrown every resource available into completing his seat of government, and befitting its military character, the buildings were heavily fortified and secure. Gorruk laughed at the presence of Planetary Defense troopers. Ten thousand of his battle-hardened soldiers were mere seconds away. There could have been ten times that number, but Gorruk had been forced to deploy the bulk of his remaining forces to maintain control over the dispersed militia troops.

Of course, the members of the southern delegations and the Defense Council had objected to the venue, but Gorruk had exercised his prerogative as leader of the largest populations and as a general officer in the PDF. The council had no legal alternative. The need for common defense outweighed the fear and distrust all of Kon held for the leader of the northern hemisphere.

Gorruk returned his attention to the briefing. Displayed on the immense luminous wall screen behind the briefer was a planform depiction of the planetary system. The scale was set to optimize the orbits of Kon and Genellan, both planets represented by points of white light. The planets, orbitally opposed, were separated by the full width of the display. The sun-star in the display's center was a three-dimensional orange globe.

"One missile penetrated the enemy defenses," the briefer continued. "We have no damage reports yet, but it appears that at a minimum we have disrupted their picket screen." The briefer pushed buttons on the podium, and the display zoomed rapidly into the region of conflict, giving the viewer a sensation of tremendous acceleration. Planets and stars disappeared, and a schematic representation of the alien fleet filled the screen.

"Composite radar returns received from our attacking missiles reveal the disposition of the alien fleet at the time of attack. Eight interstellar vessels are confirmed and at least thirty smaller ships—pickets or scouts. Updates from the second and third waves are beginning to arrive. As you can see, their picket screen has lost its organization. It will cost them fuel and time to regain position. Each subsequent attack will further degrade these defenses."

The wall presentation zoomed away from the alien fleet to reveal multiple brilliant red arrows. Relative to the great distances of the planetary system, the arrows were near the battle zone.

"Second wave—twenty piloted interceptors and eighty drone missiles—will engage by this time tomorrow. Third and fourth waves, the same mix, will arrive simultaneously less than four hours later. Preparations for additional attacks, if necessary, are under way." The audience stirred as the briefer paused to review his notes.

Unbidden, Emperor-General Gorruk stood and turned to face the assembly. "We will saturate their defenses and overwhelm the alien fleet," he announced loudly. "The invaders will be destroyed or repelled, and once again we will have satisfied

our vows." The audience turned to stare, and a low shoveling
of impudent hissing could be heard emitting from the southerners.

"Thank you, most excellent Emperor-General," said Defense
Commanding General Talsali, quelling the disturbance with his
gavel. "Perhaps it would be prudent to advise caution until the
outcome of the battle is better defined." General Talsali, a non-
aligned northerner, was the officer in command of the Planetary Defense Command. He was quite senior, having survived
several regimes, but his voice was clear, his tone giving no indication of emotion or judgment. General Talsali was renowned for his diplomacy, a necessary survival skill.

Gorruk glowered at the Planetary Defense commander,
searching for a hint of sarcasm or disrespect, any excuse to initiate a rebuke, but none was apparent. Gorruk reclined in his
lounge, and Talsali recognized a member of a southern delegation. The delegate rose to his hinds and turned in Gorruk's
direction.

"Emperor-General Gorruk," said the southern official, a wiz-
ened noblekone. "We find it disturbing that aliens have been in
our system all this time and only your government has been
aware of that fact."

Gorruk had been forced to confirm the presence of aliens on
Genellan in the face of persistent and pointed inquiries by the
Planetary Defense Command, no doubt the work of the elusive
Et Avian and Et Kalass. Exasperated, Gorruk bolted back to
his hinds and faced his accuser.

"You speak from ignorance!" he responded. "I answer not
for what transpired under my predecessor. The presence of
aliens was only recently made known to me, and I assure you,
had I known sooner, I would have done everything in my
power to eliminate them—sooner."

"That is not my point, most excellent General," the southern
official replied, ignoring the insult. "Should we not make an
effort to communicate?"

"As I have reported," Gorruk snapped, "it has been attempted, and the aliens reacted aggressively. One of our most
capable scientists was killed while in their hands," he said
sternly. "They are hostile." The delegates looked at each other,
some skeptically, but most shook their heads in fearful condo-
lence. Xenophobia ran deep.

"The fact remains," Gorruk continued, "another fleet of
alien interstellar ships has penetrated deep within our system.

What other explanation for their persistence than aggression? Remember our vows. We have sworn to repel invaders from space." The vast majority of delegates nodded and rumbled their acknowledgment. The vows were sacred rituals of their history. Gorruk sensed the groundswell of support. "The mission is clear. We must destroy the perfidious enemy! You will appreciate my vigilance and decisiveness before this is over!"

The crowd rumbled in support of Gorruk's position. The inquisitor sat down and turned to discuss the issue with his neighbors.

"Your vigilance and decisiveness are beyond reproach, Emperor-General," Talsali interjected, turning to the audience. "The obligations of the vows are compelling. We must not let our planet be attacked again. Aliens have arrived in our system, and their intentions must be assumed hostile. We press the attack."

The second wave of interceptors bore down on the ragged screen. Two divisions of corvettes had been assigned new coordinates to compensate for the weakening of the battle defenses caused by *Tasmania*'s engineering casualty. Carmichael piloted *Peregrine One* in a mad, fuel-consuming dash to its new assignment.

"On station, Commander," his copilot announced. "Retro checklist complete. Weapons are up, and all stations are ready. Fuel state twenty-two point three!"

"Roger, report in to screen commander." Carmichael set the tactical displays at maximum range and noted the advancing progress of the first few enemy missiles. Fuel was now his biggest concern. Fortunately, the first wave of enemy missiles had all been target-locked—the missiles had not maneuvered—and fire-control solutions required little expenditure of fuel. *Peregrine One* had taken out two missiles. Regardless, Carmichael would have to conserve fuel. He hit the maneuvering alarm and punched the ignition control button for retrograde burn. The "backward" flying corvette firmly accelerated to zero velocity relative to the screen's moving-reference datum.

"*Eire* has taken the point. Coordinates are updating," the second officer announced. "*Tasmania*'s still drifting to sector two, and her drift rate has increased. They've been unable to get her to link."

"Can she return fire?" Carmichael asked.

"Only partially," the second officer responded. "Two of her

primary batteries are disabled, and she can't maneuver. She has coverage gaps, and she's masking defensive fire from the motherships in that sector."

"Bad news—" the copilot started to say.

"*Osprey*'s engaging!" the second officer interrupted, his voice pitching higher. "She's reporting maneuvering targets!"

"Picnic's over, kids," Carmichael said quietly.

Merriwether stared at the flagship's tactical display. Her stomach churned bitterly. She watched *Tasmania* drift inexorably out of the grid.

"We are at station limits, Captain," advised the officer of the deck, his voice hinting at anxiety.

"Maintain station on *Tasmania*," Merriwether said calmly. "Establish and hold grid link. We are the guide. Admiral Runacres will keep everyone together. Order all nonoperational crew to their lifeboat stations and notify weapons they are cleared to fire."

"Aye, sir," said the officer of the deck, turning to his console.

"What is Merriwether doing?" Runacres demanded, peering down at the flagship's command bridge. "She's taking *Eire* off the guide bearing!"

"Captain Merriwether is keeping *Tasmania* in grid contact," Wells reported. "*Eire* still shows a partial link."

"She can't do it alone. Direct *Baffin* and *Novaya* to support *Eire*'s movements," Runacres ordered angrily. "Swing TDF a half span to sector two."

Merriwether was going to have some explaining to do. She was causing the fleet defensive positions to collapse to one side. The enemy could exploit the maneuver and concentrate its attack. Runacres scanned the situation plot and noted with grim satisfaction his motherships moving smartly along the new defensive axis defined by *Tasmania*'s excursion. It would take two hours to complete the realignment. Too late to make a difference in the fleet defenses, but it was the right thing to do. It was the only thing to do.

"Engaging alien screens, flight leader," the konish copilot said.

"Yes," replied the interceptor pilot and division flight leader. The noblekone pilot scanned his tactical display, checking

the disposition of his attack squadron. The other interceptors
were in position. His mission was to trail two flights of drone
interceptors through the picket screen. While the first flight
disrupted the screen defenses, his flight was to follow the subsequent brace of drones through the gap.

Everything was proceeding according to plan. His tactical
display depicted engagements in progress. The alien energy
beams were powerful; two of the leading drone warheads had
already been destroyed. He wiggled his broad shoulders and
stretched his neck, trying to loosen the tightness. He scanned
the limitless blackness of space before him, the enemy ships
invisible in the distance.

Brilliant light ahead! A flowering incandescence provided a
reference point in the infinite distances, and his rocket streaked
by white and pink wisps of brightness as if they had never
been there. A missile ahead of them had exploded, probably hit
by an alien picket's beam of destruction. His interceptor flight
was in the battle zone.

"Enemy ship closing from sector three," the copilot calmly
reported.

The pilot checked the tactical display and saw the symbol
for an alien approaching. Another enemy symbol popped onto
the range screen—this one directly "overhead"—also closing
on his track. But neither of the enemy ships carried enough
speed; their vectors were inadequate to intercept. The konish
ships were through the screen! The flight leader shifted his attention to the radar returns of the distant starships.

Carmichael cursed. "We can't catch them!" He watched in
vain as the enemy flight eluded them, moving too fast for an
intercept from his position. Another flight of enemy missiles
appeared on the screen, and Carmichael horsed *Peregrine One*
to a new vector, accelerating abruptly, using precious fuel. He
would not allow another flight to penetrate his sector.
"Downlink the enemy positions back to fleet ops and pass the
alert. That first group looks like trouble."

"Aye, aye, Commander," the second officer shouted.

"Our fuel situation stinks, Commander," the copilot interjected.

"I know! I know!" Carmichael retorted in exasperation.
"We'll make a pass at these targets, and then we have no
choice but to bingo. Set up a lead pursuit. You got the ship."

Carmichael pushed back from the controls, flexing his

hands, and the copilot took over. They had knocked out two more enemy missiles, one of which had been piloted, but how much longer could they keep it up? The screen ships were scattered over a wide area, most in pursuit, some destroyed or disabled by action, and some—like *Peregrine One*—too low on fuel to pursue at high power. How much longer would they be able to keep up their end of the defensive load? The motherships could not handle everything.

Tasmania drifted helplessly, spewing lifeboats into the darkness. Only skeleton crews manned battle stations. The lifeboats, infinitesimal motes, each with a cargo of frightened human beings, floated away on preassigned vectors, their tiny strobes flickering nervously against the never-ending blackness of deep space.

Belligerent konish spaceships maneuvered to attack, and *Tasmania* was again their focus. *Tasmania*'s skipper noted with helpless resignation the flagship maneuvering from the battle axis to support his ship's precarious situation. He could ill afford to dwell on those thoughts: a flight of two alien interceptors approached his weapons perimeter, another flight of four followed closely behind, and four more were behind those. They were coming to destroy his ship.

"Main batteries are recharged. Weapons has good lock, Captain," his officer of the deck shouted. "All targets are acquired."

"Very well," the captain replied. "Commence firing at range limit."

The first two alien missiles disintegrated just after entering *Tasmania*'s firing range, the mothership's lethal directed energy batteries lashing out with massive power and accuracy. The next flight of four missiles poured through the same gap. The aliens had deduced that the Legion lasers needed charging time, and the safest place to attack was through the "craters" made by previous discharges.

A second pair of *Tasmania*'s energy batteries deflected hard over to cover the vulnerable sector, locking on the approaching flight. The battery director confirmed acquisition and target lock. She depressed the trigger button, and the great engine of power embedded in the operations core of the mothership hummed its deadly tune. The firing aperture flicked open, and the glassy eyeball of destruction flared for a full tenth of a second, darting the pulse of pure energy instantaneously across the great gulf of space. Nearly instantaneously!

In that fraction of time three of the interceptors jinked outward, leaving the lead ship to maintain its course. The lead ship was vaporized as the huge, hot beam raced through its molecules. The surviving ships weaved and darted along vermicular paths, but their tracks were unerringly defined by their common objective—the *Tasmania*.

Tasmania unleashed another laser blast of energy, and only two interceptors remained.

"*Tasmania*'s fire control has been overwhelmed, Captain Merriwether!" *Eire*'s weapons control officer reported. "She's receiving fire!"

The flagship was also fully engaged, and the big ship's energy batteries, located twenty-eight levels below the bridge, were firing beyond rated capacity. Seven enemy missiles had been annihilated. More were inbound. Merriwether switched her helmet circuit to pick up the bridge-to-bridge communications. She listened to the excited intership gabble. *Tasmania* reported two more hits to her operations core.

"Can you help her?" Merriwether demanded over the command circuit.

"It'll be a tough shot, Captain. The enemy's between us and *Tasmania*. We may hit our own ships or the lifeboats."

"If you get a good shot, take it!" Merriwether ordered.

"Aye, Captain."

Within seconds the weapons control officer came back up. "Sir, *Tasmania*'s clean, but she'll need another new coat of paint. We picked the last two bogeys right off her back."

Merriwether acknowledged and switched her attention to her own ship. Three interceptors were closing on widely separated tracks. One of them disappeared from the screen—a kill. Moments later a second one was destroyed. The third enemy ship pressed closer and closer through the most active quadrant, taking advantage of the recharging batteries. Merriwether wondered if her weapons people had spent too much time worrying about *Tasmania*. The bogey streaked within lethal firing range. The collision alarm sounded, and Merriwether felt the hollow crunch of explosive impact somewhere deep within her ship. The enemy interceptor had thrust its knife.

The konish pilot swept past the looming shape of the alien ship, maneuvering desperately to avoid the sure death of energy beams. With grim satisfaction, he watched his laser ripple across the thin metal skin of the starship. His missiles had already struck home. Every second of survival this close to the enemy was a victory, his radar images flashing back to Kon, sending vital intelligence data to Defense Command. The information would increase the success of subsequent intercepts, and his death would not be in vain, for he knew he would surely die.

The alien energy beam struck with merciful instantaneity, and the pilot's atoms joined those of his ship and became one with the universe.

"Damage control, I need reports, now!" Merriwether demanded. The second wave had been destroyed.

"All operations stations are functioning," the officer of the deck reported. "We took missile hits in the core, Level 10, frame 123, above the 'vette bays. Overpressure shield is intact, but battle armor in bay number one is penetrated. Damage control reports numerous residual fires. Habitability ring was holed by laser blasts in two places. Preliminary casualty report is four dead, ten injured, and eight missing—probably overboard."

Merriwether second-guessed herself—she should have launched lifeboats.

"The fleet? How's the fleet?" she asked her operations officer.

"Three corvettes lost, Captain," the operations officer responded. "Including *Eagle One*."

"How's *Tasmania*?" Merriwether asked, shaking her head. *Eagle One* was hers.

"She's in bad shape, but she's asking us if we need any help."

Merriwether smiled grimly.

"*Peregrine One* is requesting a tug assist for a no-fuel approach, Captain," the officer of the deck reported. "She's completely out of fuel, and *Tasmania* can't take her aboard."

"Bring her in. Can she make it on her own?"

"Negative," the officer of the deck said. "She's bone dry and coasting. We have tugs collecting lifeboats in position to intercept."

"Have one of the tugs bring her in," Merriwether ordered.

The officers of the Planetary Defense Senior Command filed into the amphitheater and took their usual seats at the semicir-

cular table beneath the briefing stage. Gorruk was irritated by
the briefing delay. He was too busy to be sitting idle, waiting
for others to be on time; the responsibilities of running half the
world were pressing. And rumors of strange militia movements
were filtering in. Gorruk sat and fumed, his gaze wandering
about the auditorium.

His scan stopped suddenly. Chief Scientist Samamkook was
fraternizing with newly arrived noblekones, immersed in deep
discussions, on the *other* side of the center aisle—the enemy
side. Gorruk's anger flowered explosively. General Talsali addressed the room, but Gorruk was not listening. Why would
Samamkook be consorting with southerners? Gorruk studied
the noblekones in Samamkook's company. They were familiar,
but Gorruk could not place them. The cluster of noblekones
and Samamkook turned to stare directly at him, their eyes unwavering.

"General Gorruk!" Talsali said loudly, clutching at Gorruk's
attention.

Gorruk levered his steely glance from Samamkook and
turned to face the podium. "Excuse me, General. Were you addressing yourself to me?"

"Yes, most excellent General," Talsali replied sternly, in a
decidedly undiplomatic tone. "We have received a petition to
suspend the intercepts. It has been presented to and approved
by all legal authorities of the southern hemisphere. I have been
asked to seek concurrence of the northern governments."

"Suspend the intercepts? Absurd! We are under attack!"

An angry murmur swelled.

"What are the results of our second wave?" he demanded.

"The intercepts go well, most excellent Emperor-General,"
Talsali replied, polite in form only. "Our preliminary assessment is that two alien starships have been disabled, one of
them severely. Their defensive screen has broken down, and
the screening ships have suffered losses. Our next two waves
are in position to severely damage the enemy fleet. Perhaps to
destroy it."

"And you want to stop?" Gorruk was dumbfounded.

"It is not solely my decision, most excellent General," the
defense commander responded. "New information has become
available indicating the aliens have come in peace. I seek permission to suspend our attacks while this evidence is presented
and corroborated."

Gorruk shot Samamkook a glance. The old kone crawled toward the podium.

"Who presents this evidence?" Gorruk demanded.

"It is your own science adviser, most excellent General, the renowned astronomer Chief Scientist Samamkook," Talsali said, his voice seeded with sweet irony.

Gorruk stood erect. "Madness! Scientist Samamkook! Return to your seat! The governments of the northern hemisphere do not support this insanity. I demand that the interception of the alien fleet continue with full fury and commitment."

Samamkook labored up the ramp to the briefer's stage. Gorruk's face turned black with rage, and the tendons in his monstrous neck pulled the skin tight. Talsali prudently took several retreating steps, falling back on all fours. Two of Gorruk's generals galloped toward the exits. Planetary Defense troopers hesitated but let them through.

"You have forgotten where you are!" Gorruk screamed, spittle flying from his gaping mouth. "This is my realm! You are here at my pleasure!"

"Not your realm, General," Samamkook said, his brittle old voice amplified by the sound system. He stood erect at the briefer's lectern, stretching his twisted and withered form into a regal posture. "You stole it from a thief. We recover it in the name of the ancient rightful rulers." The audience gasped.

Gorruk could not believe his senses.

"What authority—by what power do you make this pronouncement, Scientist?" Gorruk inquired with a wolfish snarl. A commotion could be heard in the hallway—no doubt his soldiers. He would soon put an end to this ancient upstart.

"As steward for the Regent of Ollant!" the tottering scientist announced. "As steward for the Regent of House Ollant, I command that our attacking forces be recalled immediately. I speak for all northern kones, noble and common. The aliens are not our enemy. Our enemy is here, in our midst! Gorruk be damned!"

Gorruk looked up, astounded. The old kone had gone insane.

"You old fool!" Gorruk growled, regaining his composure. Imperial army soldiers and their officers appeared at the entryway. The PDF troopers fell back. Gorruk turned to face Talsali. "This is a joke. Order your troopers to eject the senile old fool from the briefing room. The attacks will continue! The aliens must be destroyed! If you cannot do your duty, I will have it done for you, General Talsali."

"I am afraid it is not that simple, General," came a familiar voice. Gorruk turned to confront the intruder. It was Et Kalass, throwing back the hood of his white robe as he made his way to the front of the room. General Et Barbluis and other noblekones followed in his wake.

"General Gorruk," Et Kalass announced with nervous gravity. "You have been deposed. In the name of the—"

"Deposed?" Gorruk snarled. "You are all dead!" He turned to his generals and barked orders, but a low, thunderous rumbling far in the distance—artillery fire—captured his attention. He stood straighter and sniffed the air.

"General Gorruk!" Et Kalass shouted, his voice shaking. "It is useless to resist! Your army cannot help you. For once in your life, resist combat! Do not cause more death."

Gorruk's generals, roaring orders, rushed for the exits.

"I will see you die at my own hands," Gorruk menaced, advancing on the noblekones. Et Kalass bravely held his ground, but his fear smell added strongly to the growing symphony of odors.

Detonations shook the structure's foundation. Armored windows high overhead vibrated like timpani; air pressure in the bunker fluctuated violently with the passing shock waves. Gorruk stared upward. Another explosion, massive and perilously close aboard, reverberated through the building, shattering windows and knocking kones to the ground. Gorruk recovered his balance, shot a glare at the noblekone, and trotted toward the exit. Revenge could wait.

A loud commotion stirred at the main entrance, and the assembled kones turned as one to see what was upon them. Smaller explosions sounded, and the singing ring of laser blasters resounded in the near distance. The odor of burned air wafted into the auditorium, and council members started flowing to the exits; a tight panic ensued. On one side of the building a dozen imperial soldiers, their faces blackened and bloodied, retreated inward, blocking the side exits. Gorruk pushed his way through the crowd, but as he reached the main entryway, the thick inner doors burst open and militia soldiers poured onto the floor, laser blasters and small arms ready to fire. A squad of Gorruk's soldiers rushed bravely forward and was annihilated. Other soldiers threw down their weapons and lay prone, arms empty and extended.

Gorruk did not flinch. He rose on his hinds and faced the enemy, his face flushed with anger and contempt. Et Avian, dressed in combat uniform and surrounded by elite militia guards waving their weapons, stepped through the press of soldiers and halted before Gorruk. At least twenty laser blasters focused on the ruler's hulking form.

"General Gorruk! Do you submit?" Et Avian demanded, his voice strained with emotion. Endless explosions continued in the distance. The very ground heaved.

Hundreds of angry red barbs, symbols for enemy ships, hurtled toward the blue and white icons representing his fleet. The pilots of the alien vessels were heedless of their own safety, totally committed to destroying the human fleet. The corvette screen was nonexistent; eight of the valiant craft had been destroyed, and the others were low on fuel and scattered across the vastness of space. *Eire* was operational, but *Tasmania* was reduced to space garbage and was jettisoning the balance of its crew. Lifeboat beacons dotted the tactical plot. The next engagement was less than an hour away.

"Captain Wells, bring the fleet to grid stations!" Runacres commanded, wrenching his eyes from the tactical display. "Prepare for hyperlight entry. On my command!"

"But Admiral, *Tasmania*'s link is down. Her lifeboats!" Wells remonstrated.

"Admiral, the corvettes!" the group leader exclaimed.

"Obey the order, Franklin," Runacres said sternly.

"Aye, aye, Admiral," Wells said. The operations officer initiated a command sequence on his control console. Warning Klaxons resounded throughout the fleet. Runacres pushed off from his command chair and floated to the end of his station tethers. He pounded gloved hands together in frustration. More deaths on his hands. Meaningless deaths.

He looked up to see Cassy Quinn standing quietly at the back of the flag bridge and vaguely remembered that *Peregrine One* had diverted to *Eire*. She was staring at him. Runacres signaled for her to approach. Quinn pushed off from the bulkhead and glided to his command station.

"We're leaving, Commander. I'm sorry."

"You did everything possible, Admiral," Quinn replied. "You have nothing to be sorry—" The brave officer choked in her welling grief.

"Admiral! Admiral!" the tactical officer shouted. "We have

established radio contact with the aliens! They are speaking
Legion, Admiral! Very good Legion."

"Wha-a—?" Runacres turned from Quinn.

"We have radio contact! From a broadcast source on R-K
Three. Transmission delay is five seconds," the tactical officer
shouted. "They want to talk to our leader—to you, sir! Linking
to command frequency."

"Notify ship captains to monitor," Runacres ordered. He
tried to analyze the confusing facts. Why would they be trying
to talk now? Their attacking forces had routed his fleet. It had
to be a trick!

"Patch in Commander Quinn," he ordered, turning to face
the planet survey officer. "I may need your help, Cassy."

"I'm ready, sir," she replied, her eyes welling with tears.

"Keep everyone alert and ready to jump, Franklin,"
Runacres commanded the operations officer. "Order out all
tugs and recover the lifeboats still in the grid. How much time
until the next engagement?"

"Five minutes before the corvettes are engaged, Admiral,"
Wooden reported. "All are low on fuel and ordnance. They're
hung out to dry—"

"All motherships except *Tasmania* can jump on command,"
Wells interjected.

"Very well," Runacres answered thickly. "Let's hear what
our . . . hosts have to say." He looked over to Quinn, and she
nodded back, her jaw firm. He selected the command frequency, and a deep, rumbling accent could be heard speaking.

". . . urgent that-ah I talk-ah your leader. Please connect-ah
me with your commanding general." Silence cut with static.

Runacres looked around the flag bridge and inhaled deeply.
"Fleet Admiral Runacres of the Tellurian Legion Space Force,"
he broadcast. "Identify yourself and by whose authority you
speak." The circuit was silent for long seconds as the radio signals flew across the wide distances.

"Fleee Ad-ah . . . miral Run . . . aakerrs," the voice returned
hesitantly. "I am Scientist Kateos, speaking for Et Avian,
Prince of Ollant, and-ah the konish people." More silence, as
if the speaker were intimidated by its own responsibility.

"We have come in peace," Runacres said, initiating the conversation. "Why have you made unprovoked attacks on us?
Over." Seconds dragged by.

"The answer to your question is not-ah simple. It-ah take
time to explain, and-ah the explanation can be saved for a

more better time," Kateos replied, her voice firmer. "We have stopped our attack. Do not-ah continue your attack on us. Please respond-ah."

"We have not attacked you. We are defending ourselves. Over."

"Over? Ah, yes. That means it-ah is my turn to speak. It-ah is sometime difficult to tell the difference between attacking and defending, Ad-ah . . . miral. I ask that-ah you demonstrate your peaceful intent-ah by halting forward progress. Not-ah all of my people are convinced you come in peace. Cooperation will serve to illustrate your peaceful intent. Please respond-ah, ah . . . over."

All the people on the bridge looked at each other with amazement.

"We will cooperate, but you must have your ships turn back immediately or we will be forced to open fire. Over," Runacres replied.

"The recall command has been sent-ah to the interceptors. You will see them terminating attack momentarily," Kateos replied. ". . . Over."

Runacres looked at Wells, certain that it was a trick—a trick to hold the fleet in subspace long enough for their interceptors to close.

"Tracks show a slight deflection, Admiral," the harried operations officer responded. The tactical officer nodded her head in agreement.

Runacres looked at the situation plot.

"Course changes are increasing rapidly, Admiral. They are reducing forward speed and swinging away!" the tactical officer reported.

Runacres watched hypnotically. He could see the course changes, evident even on the larger situation plot. He forced out a lungful of hot and metallic-tasting air.

"How do we know this is not a trick, and how did you learn our language?" he asked. "Over." More time than usual passed.

"We do not-ah deserve your trust-ah, Ad-ah . . . miral," Kateos finally said. "I hope that-ah we will demonstrate a more peaceful behavior in the future . . . so that-ah you will grow to trust-ah us. You are wise to be cautious. The leadership of my planet is experiencing grave challenge. It-ah is our intention to conduct-ah diplomatic communications with you as soon as we stabilize our government-ah. It-ah will take many days. I have been told to inform you that-ah you should not-ah perceive our apparent confusion as a weakness. More interceptors are being prepared. That-ah is what I was told to tell you."

"As far as learning your language," the alien's voice said enthusiastically, "I have had-ah excellent teachers, Nashooa Hudsawn and Sharl B-Bru ... B-Buu ... shar ... B-Bruusharry. It is difficult for us to say. Lieutenant Sharl is the leader of humans on this planet ... Over."

Runacres recognized the names of the corvette officers and looked worriedly at Cassy Quinn. Buccari in command meant in all likelihood that Jack Quinn was dead. The distraught officer stared at her feet, a constellation of teardrops floating about her face. Suddenly she straightened and shattered the floating water globules with the back of her hand. She looked at Runacres and smiled bravely.

"Those names are important to us," Runacres continued. "We are anxious to recover our missing crew. What can you tell us of their condition? Are they safe? Over."

"Their condition is unknown, although we have reason to be concerned-ah." The alien's voice became serious. "A military party is attempting to capture them. That party is led by an officer swearing allegiance to the same leaders that-ah conducted the attacks against-ah your fleet. It-ah is likely they are in danger. Over."

"What can be done to help them? Over."

"Very little," Kateos responded. "We are sending numerous messages to the soldiers, but they refuse to acknowledge receipt of orders."

Runacres stared at the situation plot. The enemy tracks were clearly reversing.

"Scientist Kateos, please notify your government of our gratitude for halting hostilities. I look forward to establishing peaceful relations with your race. But I would also ask your government to permit us to send ships to the third planet so that I may provide assistance to our people. You have indicated they may be in danger. I cannot sit here and not help them. Over."

Static-filled seconds crept by.

"I will relay these concerns to my government-ah," Kateos finally replied. "However, I cannot authorize the request. Please wait. Over."

"We wait for your next transmission. Please hurry. And thank you." Runacres turned to look at his bridge crew.

"Group leader, get all corvettes back on board! Let's get this fleet in shape. We have time to get everyone in the grid. And I want three corvettes ready to go back to that planet. Commander Quinn, you're in charge of the landing party."

FORTY-THREE

FINAL BATTLE

MacArthur leaned against the lee of a tree trunk, seeking relief from the chilly wind. It had been an arduous hike back down to the valley floor. A layer of clouds scudded overhead, and desultory raindrops, heavy and frigid, plopped on the ground as gray-shrouded dusk descended on the valley. Most of the humans lay on the ground, wrapped in their ponchos, trying to sleep. Their number had been augmented by Tatum, Mendoza, and Schmidt, offsetting the absence of the injured Gordon, who had been left behind at the high camp. Fenstermacher had wanted to join the fighters, but Buccari ordered him to stay behind with Wilson and Tookmanian to take care of the women and children. Buccari had also ordered Et Silmarn to remain behind. The konish scientist was their last best hope of establishing friendly relations; he could explain to konish authorities why earthlings were attacking and killing kones.

"Why can't we just hole up?" Petit whined. "They'll never find us."

MacArthur wanted to shout, but Shannon beat him to it. "Shut up, Petit!" The sergeant was obviously still in pain.

"Easy, Sarge," Buccari sighed. She walked over to Petit. "Petit, if you want to go back, go. I won't ask you to join us if you're afraid."

The powerfully built man looked at the ground and shuffled his feet.

"We're committed," she continued, eyes flashing in the dim light. "We're almost out of ammo. Now's the time to capture weapons—to take charge of the situation. Now's the time to do what Tatum and Sergeant Shannon wanted to do all along. Et Silmarn says these are the only soldiers on the planet. It will take them months to get reinforcements. You've seen these guys in action. We can take them down, and if we capture the landers, we get our hands on more weapons and on a radio. Do you understand? We can defend ourselves, and we can call in the fleet. We may never get another chance."

Petit nodded. "Yeah, Lieutenant. I'm sorry, sir," he mumbled.

Buccari slapped his shoulder and gave him an encouraging smile, her scarred face disturbingly powerful in the murky light.

MacArthur moved away from the somber cluster. He trudged up the heavily wooded rise shielding their campsite from the aliens. Tatum stood watch at the crest. MacArthur crawled on the wet ground until he lay by Tatum's side, and the two marines peered through the damp dusk, looking down on the four evenly dispersed landers.

"How's it going, Sandy?" MacArthur asked.

"Just frigging wonderful, Mac," Tatum sniffed. Drops of rainwater fell from his cap brim. "Beats baby-sitting. I was beginning to think Lieutenant Buccari didn't trust me." He rolled onto an elbow and spit.

"She trusts you, Sandy. She wanted you here. She told me so herself."

Tatum looked over at MacArthur. "No kidding? She said that?"

"As sure as I am lying here in the mud," MacArthur replied.

"She's something else, ain't she?"

MacArthur nodded.

Soft whistles floated into his awareness. MacArthur responded with two chirps, and Tonto hopped from the wet darkness. Tonto was not alone; six other hunters, including Captain and X.O., followed him up the valley slope. MacArthur's spirits rose; they had reinforcements, too!

"Colonel, we have received orders from Planetary Defense Command to recover the landers and return to Kon. We are specifically directed to break contact with the aliens." The subordinate, on all four legs, stood at rigid attention.

Longo sat in his acceleration chair in the relative warmth of the landing module. Emperor-General Gorruk's removal from power was disturbing, but one objective continued to dominate his reasoning: the secret of the alien's interstellar power drives. If he could but gain that knowledge, his grasp on power would be secure. But how?

"We do not take orders from Planetary Defense," he snapped. "Status on security?"

"Colonel, overlapping security perimeters have been set up. Sensors have detected only indigenous animal life. Reconnaissance drones will launch as soon as the ceiling lifts, as you ordered."

"Very well," Longo replied. "No more games."

The winds had slackened. A shiftless moon peeked through sodden clouds and then disappeared, leaving the night even darker, and from the blackness a miserable drizzle fell. Humans and hunters, cold and wet, huddled together.

"They got night vision cameras and IR detectors everywhere," MacArthur reported. "We saw ten bugs outside the modules, but they're too far inside the sensor perimeter. We might be able to pick them off in daylight, but it's a tough shot at night."

"We really scared them," Tatum added.

"Is there any way we can take out the damn sensors?" Buccari asked.

"I've got some ideas—" MacArthur started to say.

Tonto, standing watch on the ridge, whistled softly.

"Listen," Tatum whispered urgently.

In the distance an angry high-pitched engine erupted into life.

"We've found them, Colonel," the subordinate reported. "They are near—within mortar range. Mortar crews are prepared."

Longo had not expected success so quickly. He turned up the temperature on his Genellan suit and moved quickly through the air lock hatch into the frigid darkness. The drones were controlled from the reconnaissance module housed in the last of the four landers in the line. Walking across the soggy ash, Longo noted shadowy figures standing guard at the foot of

the landers. Two separate groups of soldiers, standing clear
of the landers, huddled about their equipment, a silver-green
luminescence from their electronic systems outlining their
forms. Other soldiers remained inside the modules, out of the
elements but on alert in case any movement was detected
within the perimeter. After hiking the full length of the secure
area, Longo and his retinue boarded the reconnaissance module
and moved into its cramped lab. Technicians came to attention.

"Carry on!" Longo ordered brusquely. "Where are they?"

Longo looked at the video with morbid satisfaction. The
aliens showed as a cluster of fuzzy, light-gray hot spots nestled
within dark, cold, vertically viewed vegetation. Occasionally
an extended arm or leg could be clearly perceived as the
hunted creatures milled about beneath the drone's camera.

"Do the mortar teams have telemetry?" he asked.

"Yes, most excellent Colonel!" the senior technician gushed.

"What are you waiting for?" Longo shouted. The images
were dispersing.

"Y-y-your . . . your order to fire, most excel—" the subordinate said.

"*Fire!*" Longo screamed. "*Fire!* You idiot!"

The subordinate blurted commands into his radio, and a pair
of hollow thumps sounded immediately. Mortar rounds sped
into the night.

The angry engine hovered high over their heads, invisible in
the night sky. Buccari squinted into the falling mists but to no
avail.

"Move out, *now!*" Shannon shouted. He scrambled up the
rise to see what was happening, and Buccari followed.

"Spread out and take cover uphill!" the sergeant yelled. She
saw MacArthur running at the cliff dwellers, herding them,
giving them panicky signals to move away from the area. They
needed little inducement.

"What's the deal, Sarge?" Buccari asked. "Can't we shoot it
down?"

"Hell, can you see it?" Shannon said, craning his neck to
peer into the night. "Sounds like two of them. You better get
moving, sir. Now!"

Burping gouts of fire erupted from the vicinity of the alien
landers.

"Oh, no!" Shannon exclaimed. "Everybody down! *Incoming!*" he bellowed into the night.

The sergeant grabbed Buccari and threw her violently to the soggy ground, crushing her body with his own. Buccari's wind was knocked from her lungs, and her face was pushed into the muddy humus. She gasped for air. Suddenly the night was filled with shrill, screaming whistles. Explosions thundered into the ground, and Buccari felt Shannon's body jolt violently. The sergeant groaned softly and then was quiet.

"Damn, you're heavy, Sarge," Buccari grunted, struggling to breathe. No answer. No movement. She heard the drone buzzing overhead and then more demonic whistles. The ground heaved violently, and Shannon's body twitched spasmodically as the blasts rolled over them, and then she felt his blood, warm and wet. Frantic, she wriggled out from under the grotesquely limp body and staggered to her feet.

"Oh, Sarge! No, Sarge!" Buccari, still on her knees, wept. Shannon was dead, his back ripped open by shards of hot metal.

She looked around, dazed, her ears ringing with concussion. The irritating noise of the drone pushed its way into her consciousness, and anger welled within her. The drone seemed closer. She looked up, and there it was—a hard black form, a darker hole in the dark skies, hovering off to the side. She grabbed Shannon's assault rifle and snapped it to her shoulder. Exhaling, she aimed and fired a burst, pulling the sights across the target.

"Save the ammo!" MacArthur shouted, suddenly appearing from the dark. "Wait till daylight." He ran up to her, tripping over Shannon's form. "Get out of here," he said, kneeling to check Shannon's throat for a pulse. "*Move*, Lieutenant!" he shouted, grabbing the dead man's ammo belt and field glasses.

Buccari ran. Two more white flashes illuminated the bottoms of the clouds. Buccari and MacArthur dove behind a litter of fallen trees as whistling mortar shells *car-rumphed* into the wet ground, vomiting trees and dirt into the air. Hot shrapnel whistled and pinged through the forest, clipping tree branches and leaves, an expanding buzz saw laid on its side! Ear-shattering impacts walked up the valley slope and spread apart, chasing the retreating humans. Buccari and MacArthur jumped to their feet and dashed across the hillside, climbing ever higher as debris fell around them. Explosions lit up the night. The mortars started firing independently, and rounds fell continuously. After a hundred meters MacArthur reversed their traverse and headed back toward the others, continuing to climb. An eternity passed. The mortar fire stopped, but the infernal buzzing of the reconnaissance drone hung in the darkness above.

"We're out of range," MacArthur gasped.

Buccari struggled to get her wind. She heard crashing and stumbling ahead. MacArthur whistled softly.

"That you, Mac?" Chastain's voice shouted back from the shadows.

"Yeah, Jocko. And the lieutenant. Who's with you?"

"Mendoza and Schmidt," Chastain replied. "Schmidt's injured."

They caught up. Chastain and Mendoza were assisting Schmidt, though Schmidt was trying to shake them off. Blood trickled from Schmidt's ears, and Mendoza's cheek was ripped, a flap of skin dangling free. Schmidt had lost his rifle.

"Who else've you seen, Jocko?" Buccari asked. "Anyone else get hurt?"

"Petit," Mendoza said. "Caught a round in his lap. Nothing left."

Buccari saw shadows tramping upward through the thinning forest of pines and firs. MacArthur shouted names, and one by one everyone answered, sometimes needing voice relays to communicate over the distances. Everyone but Petit and Shannon. Buccari passed orders to climb to the tree line. There they would rendezvous and decide on their next move. They climbed silently, gradually walking into a foggy overcast. The snarling engines of the drones fell behind, the cloud ceiling too thick for its detection systems.

"What have I got us into?" Buccari sighed. "Shannon's dead . . . and Petit."

"So they earned their paychecks!" MacArthur shot back. "Can it, Lieutenant! Shannon knew what he was doing. Your plan was good. We didn't know about their air force."

"A big screwup," she spit.

"Nothing's changed," MacArthur said. "We have an air force, too." Tonto and X.O. hopped out of the night. Captain followed but signaled bad news: bear people were pursuing.

"You mean the cliff dwellers?" she asked.

MacArthur lifted his pistol. He pulled the slide back, chambering a round. "Air-to-air combat," he said. "Just have to find the right time and place."

* * *

The clouds departed with the night. Morning arrived calm and bright. Longo's soldiers marched at a steady, four-legged lope up the slope of the valley, much faster than a human could walk. The mortar team followed more slowly. The overcast had made it impossible to keep the aliens in contact, and Longo had held his position on the valley flank until daybreak. With clear skies, one of the drones immediately regained contact, clearly marking the location of the aliens and eliminating the danger of another ambush.

"They are moving along the top of the ridge, Colonel," the subordinate reported. Longo grunted and kept hiking. And thinking. The drone had detected seventeen infrared signatures. Nine of the signatures were distinctly larger and much warmer than the other eight. His technicians indicated that the larger signatures were the aliens, of which only seven were left; they had passed one insect-covered body and the remains of another. What were the eight smaller IR signatures?

"We have adequate light for video, Colonel," the drone technician reported. "The smaller IR signatures have been identified as small two-legged animals."

"Pets?" Longo remarked. "I was not aware of two-legged animals on this planet."

"Mountain fliers, most excellent Colonel," the technician offered. "Five disappeared in the night. Only three remain."

"Mountain fliers, eh?" Longo mused. He pondered their presence and discounted them. "Which of the aliens have you identified?"

"The female that leads them and seven of the soldiers," the technician answered.

The drones were tracking the warriors—the soldiers and their puny female leader. The other females, including Gol'berg, were somewhere else. Where? The reconnaissance drones with their cameras and heat detectors would find them, too, eventually—after the warriors were eliminated. Without soldiers to protect them, they would be that much easier to capture alive.

The sun stretched to its zenith, and Buccari stared anxiously at the cloudless skies. The barrel-shaped drone throbbed and hummed its irritating tune far above their heads, out of rifle range. It was newly arrived with a fresh load of fuel and charged batteries after relieving the first drone that had been monitoring them. The humans lay scattered about the rocks, some sleeping, some chewing on their last rations of dried meat and fish. They had climbed high above the shoulders of the valley and were perched on the flank of a rocky tor, its peak topped by twin pinnacles.

Even in her fatigue and fear Buccari marveled at the immensity of the land. To the west the valley lake radiated a luminescent blue light of its own. Beyond the valley and ranging to the north and south were the snowcapped mountains, uprisings of granite that defied description and gravity, and to the north and east could be seen the great herds of musk-buffalo, largely returned from their winter pastures to the southeast. Directly behind her, to the east, the terrain plummeted sharply into a series of mountain defiles, steep-sided, barren, with sheer cliffs and knife-edge ridges.

"I'll be damned! Where are the thermals?" an exasperated MacArthur exclaimed. "They'll find us before we can take out the drone."

"Shouldn't we head for the woods?" Tatum asked.

"We have to take out the drones, Sandy," Buccari replied. "As long as they can track us from the air, we don't have a chance." The last scraggly stands of yellow-barked firs were far down the ridge.

"How far behind us are they?" O'Toole asked.

Tonto lay on a grassy spot between boulders, his thin chest heaving. The hunter had returned from a scouting mission, his heart nearly bursting.

"Tonto says close," Buccari said. She watched MacArthur stride over to where Captain and X.O. perched on craggy rocks.

"A great honor," Braan chirped, awed by his responsibility. He tugged on the holster, ensuring that it rode snugly and did not interfere with the motion of his sinewy arms. The weapon's heft was worrisome, but Braan had carried far greater loads aloft.

"If any hunter is to have such honor 'tis thee, Braan-our-leader," Craag responded. Craag basked in his leader's glory. The weapon was beautiful, giving the user great pride. The weapon was powerful, giving its wielder great strength. Deadly strength.

"Brave-crazy-one approaches," Craag reported. "He is most anxious."

Both hunters turned to formally acknowledge Brave-crazy-one, their fellow warrior. At that moment a fresh breeze swirled between them, and the hunters unfurled their membranes in anxious anticipation. Brave-crazy-one turned at the gust of wind and pumped his arms. The long-legs next stepped up to Braan and grabbed the cliff dweller by the shoulders. Brave-crazy-one pulled the pistol from the holster and made one last check of the chambering mechanism. Replacing the pistol, Brave-crazy-one took a step backward and bowed low. Braan returned the bow and turned to face Craag. The hunters screamed the death song. Wings cracking, they leapt from their perches and glided down the slope of the hill, their mission begun.

Braan screeched a turning signal, and the hunters banked gently to the east, seeking vertical movement in the air around them. Thermal activity was weak but increasing. A steady updraft climbed the flanks of the ridges, and Braan followed that path of least resistance, making vertical progress, but slowly. He dug at the air with his wings, and Craag followed. A strong thermal swept under them, and the hunters held their wings rigid, riding invisible billows ever higher. Gradually they eased above the whining machine's altitude but remained separated laterally by many spans. Braan peeled away from the thermal and set his wings for optimum glide, making straight for the target. The weapon was heavy, and Braan could feel his descent increasing rapidly. The leader of the hunters screamed and wheeled away, searching for another boost.

"Crap! There they are!" Tatum shouted. Aliens galloped over a rolling, grassy hump far down the ridge, appearing huge even at a great distance. "They can really move!"

"We're too late," Buccari said. "Head for the woods."

"On your feet!" MacArthur shouted.

"Move out!" Buccari ordered. "Head for the tree line. Don't bunch up. If we get separated, head for the high camp. Make sure you aren't followed."

"Move out! On the double!" MacArthur shouted.

"Let's go! Scatter and hide!" Buccari yelled. They sprinted from the rocks, Chastain and Mendoza leading the rush.

Chastain stopped abruptly, sliding in the loose rock.

"Oh, no!" Mendoza yelled. "More of them!"

Coming from the most direct route to the tree line were six konish soldiers, spreading out at the base of the elevation, cutting them off!

One of the aliens, forging ahead of the others, pointed his laser blaster at the clustered humans, and a flash of blue-green light zipped by, noiseless. Mendoza screamed, holding his face. "Aarrrgghhh! I can't see!" he bellowed.

"Everybody back!" Buccari shouted. They retreated, scrambling for cover—except MacArthur. The corporal fell forward, his assault rifle pointed down the hill. A single shot exploded from his weapon, and the lead kone dropped like a sack of sand. The alien soldiers stopped and ducked behind scattered rocks.

"They are trapped, most excellent Colonel," the subordinate gushed. "We have them pinned down. There is a precipitous cliff beyond."

"They have the high ground," Longo said, surveying the terrain. "The lasers have insufficient range. How soon before the mortars arrive?"

"In less than an hour, most excellent Colonel."

"Bring the translation computer forward," Longo commanded. "Perhaps they will consider surrendering."

"How's Mendoza?" Buccari asked, tightly gripping the carbine.

"He can still see out of his right eye, but his left eye is in bad shape," O'Toole responded. He squatted with Buccari and MacArthur. Large boulders protected them from sporadic alien rifle and cannon fire.

"What're they doing?" O'Toole asked. The firing had stopped. Buccari and MacArthur peeked around lichen-covered rocks. Two konish soldiers marched across the open ground and came to a stop. One wore the burgundy uniform of an officer.

"It's Longo. He wants to talk," she said. "They have the translator."

"You think it's a trick?" MacArthur asked.

"Only one way to find out." She jumped up and started walking down the rock-studded slope, leaving her weapon behind.

"Coming with you, Sharl!" MacArthur shouted, and ran after her. ". . . sir."

Braan and Craag soared high above the offensive machine. Brave-crazy-one had cautioned him against approaching too

closely, saying there was grave unseen danger. The hunters circled warily downward, their target directly beneath them. It
was very loud.

"You have no escape," Longo rumbled through the translation computer. He towered over the humans. "Continued resistance is futile. Surrender and you will not be harmed."

"How can we be assured of that, Colonel Longo?" Buccari
asked.

MacArthur scanned the disposition of soldiers. The drone
whined overhead.

"You have no choice," the box said.

"Why must we surrender?" Buccari asked. "Can we not remain here in peace?"

"That has already been explained," the box said. Longo
shifted impatiently. "If you do not lay down your weapons and
come with us . . . then I will have to track you down and deal
with you . . . more forcefully."

"There must be some other option," Buccari said.

Longo paused, carefully considering his words. "I am sure
you would not want more harm to come to Master Huhsawn,"
the box finally said.

"Hudson!" Buccari blurted. "No! Is he alive?"

"He's dead, Sharl!" MacArthur shouted. "He's playing with
your mind!"

"I assure you," the box said, "Master Huhsawn is alive—if
just barely."

"Sharl—Lieutenant! He's dead," MacArthur said. "And
even if he isn't, he might as well be. We got other people to
worry about."

"I—I understand. Allow me to return to my people and discuss the matter," Buccari answered with obvious difficulty.

"Of course, but realize that if you choose to run . . . I will
track you down like an animal." Longo pointed at the drone,
his expression universally sinister.

The muted bark of a pistol sounded directly over their
heads, and the engine noises halted. MacArthur glanced skyward to see the drone plummeting from the sky, its counter-
rotating blades whirling silently. A hunter—Captain—fell
alongside the drone, flailing his wings, struggling to regain
control. He recovered, his wings beating heavily but without
altitude gain. The drone accelerated straight down, crashing
into the ground with a hollow noise, and then the fuel ex-

ploded with a magnificent ball of yellow and red flames. The dweller glided swiftly out of sight behind an outcropping of rock.

"Excuse us, Colonel," Buccari said with exaggerated dignity. She turned and walked away. MacArthur followed at her heels, skipping backward and watching for an attack.

Buccari ordered them to retreat high into the rocks until they were only a few dozen yards below the twin pinnacles at the peak. Alien rifles and laser blasters fired sporadically, providing cover for konish soldiers as they scurried to more advanced positions. The humans suffered burns, but the kones paid dearly. O'Toole and Tatum each picked off two soldiers, halting the forward movement of the aliens.

Using Chastain's great strength, the humans positioned boulders, toppling them over onto other rocks to make impenetrable covered fortifications. Those bunkers commanded excellent fields of fire; the kones would suffer for a direct assault. The biggest question was ammunition. And after ammo was time.

"Why aren't they attacking?" Chastain grunted. The big man, with help from MacArthur and Schmidt, heaved a particularly large rock over a small drop. It fell into place with a grinding crunch.

"Don't know," MacArthur huffed, jumping down and inspecting the handiwork. "Okay, Beppo, this one's yours."

Schmidt, blond beard dirty and caked with blood, moved into position, sticking the barrel of a captured weapon through the triangular opening made by the stacked rocks. Everyone was in position.

"They're setting up the mortar," Buccari said. She stood motionless on a prominent crag, staring down the slope through field glasses, an inviting target. The cliff dwellers stood close by, giving balance to Buccari's solitary form, statues on rocky pedestals set against a metallic blue sky. An occasional alien bullet *ping*ed off the rocks.

"Uh oh," O'Toole said. "That mortar will beat us to pieces."

"Lieutenant!" MacArthur barked. "With all due respect, get your ass behind a rock."

Buccari pulled the glasses from her eyes and hopped down. "The other drone is coming!" she declared. "That's what they're waiting for."

MacArthur could hear its engine whining in the distance.

Captain whistled and looked at MacArthur. MacArthur nodded and pointed into the sky. All three cliff dwellers launched into the air, their wings cracking as one. As before, they glided downward and to the east, gaining speed and seeking currents to lift them. They quickly left the range of vision.

"Everybody down!" MacArthur shouted. "In your bunkers!"

He slid into his rock emplacement, assault rifle in hand. He watched Buccari as she did the same, only a few paces away.

"Some leader I turned out to be," Buccari snarled.

"Cut the crap," MacArthur replied. His mouth snapped shut. The unmistakable sound of a double sonic boom rumbled across the valley. His eyes jerked up into the sky.

"A lander!" Buccari shouted. "That was ours!"

A thin cheer rose from the rocks. Joy was short-lived; the mortar *harrump*ed into activity, a screaming whistle followed, and the first of many explosions showered rock and dirt over their heads. The mortar rounds landed with accuracy, exploding around the dug-in humans. Granite rocks shielded them from the direct effects of the blasts, but the rocks also provided a multitude of hard surfaces. Shrapnel careened from all directions; ricochets screamed and pinged crazily.

MacArthur heard Buccari cry out. He was immediately at her side.

"Where're you hit, Sharl?" he asked, near panic. Buccari's head was back, mouth gaping, struggling to breathe.

"I'm ... I'm okay, Mac," she gasped, sucking air. "Get back."

"You're hit!"

"I'm fine, Mac," she wheezed. "I slipped and knocked my wind out." She flexed her left arm and wiggled her fingers.

MacArthur gently pulled her away from the rocks and saw blood trickling down the granite boulder. Frightened, he peeled the shredded, red-sodden jumpsuit from her shoulders. Another round exploded nearby, and another. He ducked low, clasping Buccari in his arms as killing shards buzzed about their shelter.

A brief lull ensued. A smattering of return fire from the dug-in humans filled the void. MacArthur shifted his position and carefully examined the lieutenant's injuries.

"You're lucky," he said, exhaling with relief. "The bleeding is already stopped, and I can see metal. The fragments were spent when they hit you. Bite on this!" He handed her his knife scabbard. "I'm going to dig them out."

MacArthur was quick. Warm splinters of shrapnel dropped

to the ground, clinking wetly on the rocks. He wrapped hide
and strips of bloody material tightly around her torso.

"That's all I can do," he said. He made her put on his coat.

"Thanks, Doc," Buccari breathed heavily as the pain receded. "Will . . . will I still be able to play the accordion?" She
sat upright and leaned gingerly against the rocks. A mortar
round thudded to the ground close by, and more shrapnel
screamed around them. She ducked into his arms, moaning in
pain and fear. MacArthur hugged her passionately.

Mortar fire stopped, and he pushed her away, not looking at
her face. He tried to hide his tears.

"What's wrong, Mac?" she asked. "We're going to get out
of this; I know we are. The fleet's coming. You heard the lander."

He smiled sadly. "It's funny, Sharl. That's what's bothering
me."

"What? Why?" She stumbled, wincing.

MacArthur moved to his knees.

"Sharl," he said, holding her hand. "We belong to different
worlds. The fleet's back. You can—you'll *have* to return to
your world. You're an officer. I'm a grunt."

"Bullshit, Mac!" she responded, green eyes flaring. "This is
our world! Yours and mine. It's a new world, and we'll write
our own rules—our own philosophies."

MacArthur looked at the bloodshot eyes staring out from her
scarred and blackened face. He stroked her tangled, singed
hair. "We better worry about one problem at a time. That
shoulder's going to make it hard for you if we have to climb
down the back side."

"Don't worry about me . . . Corporal."

MacArthur smiled, but the smile evaporated with the realization that the mortar fire had not just paused, it had ceased. He
jumped to his feet and peeked above the rocks. "Sandy! Terry!
Anything happening on your side?" he shouted.

"All clear here!" Tatum shouted. "The bugs are still butts up
in the rocks."

"Look!" Buccari shouted, coming up to join him. "The
drone!"

"Colonel!" the subordinate shouted. "The drone! Birds are
attacking."

"Not birds," Longo snarled. He scanned the skies with binoculars. "Birds do not carry weapons. Command the drone

back to us and lower its altitude. Order the soldiers to blast those creatures!"

Longo watched anxiously as the mountain flier closed inexorably on the descending machine. He could not afford to lose his last drone.

"Make it go faster!" Longo shouted. "Faster!"

"It is already at maximum speed, Colonel," the subordinate said. Both officers watched the drone technician anxiously, praying for the soldier to perform a miracle.

Ironically, if the bear people had made the drone climb, the hunter would have been frustrated. As long as they continued to lower its altitude, it was possible for Braan to continue pursuit. The hunter dove at the noisy craft, closing on his objective, planning his moves. Gaining speed by pulling in his wings, the hunter accelerated and swooped below the helicopter, passing it by. Braan curved his membranes and started an arcing movement, giving him an upward ballistic trajectory. Pulling in his wings, the creature carved a graceful parabolic path, all the while spinning his body to face the approaching drone. With gravity killing his vertical momentum, Braan pulled the pistol from the holster and, holding it with both clawed hands at arm's length, sighted down the barrel at the onrushing machine.

Braan, the leader-of-hunters, fired one shot at point-blank range before the drone crashed into his body.

"It hit him!" MacArthur shouted, binoculars pressed to his eyes. The drone halted in midair, pieces of metal peeling away, the plane of its rotor blades tilting. Captain's limp form was dashed aside, tumbling from the skies. MacArthur focused on the falling creature, but he could still see the drone veering crazily. The drone wobbled, seeking to stabilize itself, and then rolled with a jerk over onto its back. MacArthur thought the spinning blades would strike the hunter, but Captain had fallen clear.

"Come on, Captain! Fly!" MacArthur exhorted. "Come on!"

One of the creature's wings slipped open, and Captain rolled in midair. The hunter's line of fall was deflected, but it remained precipitous.

"You can do it!" MacArthur was yelling. "Fly, you little bastard! Fly!"

The hunter's wings stiffened. The plummet turned into a

swoop, and Captain sailed unsteadily over the ground, wobbling through the ranks of the konish soldiers. The drone exploded beautifully in the background. The humans cheered. MacArthur screamed in joy.

But not for long. The scattering soldiers, recovering from the drone's crash, shifted their attention to the flying creature. Soldiers scurried to position, raising laser blasters and rifles. Captain struggled to the east, following the rolling terrain leading to the cliffs beyond. As he cleared the last konish soldier, the blasters opened fire. The hunter dipped and climbed, swerved and turned, covering more than half the open ground to the cliffs, but he was losing speed, the evasive maneuvers eroding his velocity. When he was almost to the cliff's edge, a blaster beam spun him around. Captain collapsed into a curled ball and fell with a sickening slide into the rocky ground beyond the grassy swell of the ridge. He had almost made it.

High overhead the orbiting hunters screamed fiercely.

"He's still moving!" MacArthur shouted, standing and staring through the field glasses. "Cover me!" Dropping binoculars and rifle, he sprinted down the rocky terrain. Captain had crashed short of the cliff's edge, but the cliff dweller had made it over the rise of the ridge; the konish soldiers could not see the fallen hunter from their positions. If MacArthur could reach the boulders at the foot of the high ground, he could make it out to the downed hunter; the curve of the ridge would protect him. He bounded down the hill.

MacArthur heard a laser beam sing by his head and realized his beard was on fire. He dove behind rocks, slapping at his burning hair, feeling layers of skin slip from his cheek. The smell was nauseating. He heard loud noises and looked back. Chastain and Buccari were following him down the slope, jumping from rock to rock and providing furious covering fire. The lasers stopped, but konish infantry cannon erupted, and explosions rippled all around him.

MacArthur rolled across an opening in the rocks and hit the flat grassy crown of the ridge on his feet, running downhill, trying to put the rolling hump of the ridge between him and the aliens. Another laser beam sang past his neck, and then he was below their line of sight. A hundred meters distant, Captain staggered toward him, limping severely, wings dragging on the ground. The cliff's edge fell away to MacArthur's right—a vertical drop. MacArthur closed the distance to the hunter in sprinter's time, ignoring the dizzy precipice.

Captain still held the pistol in his hands. MacArthur grabbed the weapon, stuck it in his belt, and picked the cliff dweller up in his arms like a child. The battered creature's eyes were tightly shut. He chirped softly, plaintively, and was silent. MacArthur turned to start his way back to the rocks and saw konish soldiers charging over the ridge, pouring laser and cannon fire into the rocks where Buccari and Chastain were hiding. MacArthur, hugging the hunter close to his chest, fell to his knees behind a low wall of boulders and watched two of the kones fall to return fire. Ammo's gotta be about gone, he thought, panic setting in.

Soldiers detached from the main body and made for MacArthur's position. Still hugging the dweller, MacArthur pulled the pistol, raised himself to his knees, and fired two shots at the lead kone. The alien's helmet shattered as the giant fell backward, and his mates moved to take cover. MacArthur took aim at another soldier and pulled the trigger; one round exploded from the pistol barrel and then—*click, click, click!* The marine looked around in desperation. He had no choice. He put his head down and jumped to his feet, not feeling the weight of his burden. Protective cover was only a stone's throw away.

Four strides into his sprint, he was hit. And hit again! An electric, numbing jolt ran up his spine. Agony! He pushed his legs to move, but they refused to obey. Explosions! Explosions lasted forever, and he drifted into merciful unconsciousness.

Buccari felt searing pain deep in her shoulder. Every time she fired the assault rifle, it pounded her torn muscles. She wiped perspiration from her eyes and fumbled with her ammo belt. There was only one clip left. Chastain, from his position below her, jumped around a boulder and fired his rifle. A salvo of answering laser beams rang through the air. Bullets splattered the rocks, exploding their surfaces into shards and chips of granite. Chastain slumped behind the boulders and looked up at her, his face red and blistered, his beard smoking. He was crying.

So was she. Buccari felt the grip of panic. Her hair was singed short, and blisters were rising on her cheeks. In the open, on the ridge beyond the rocks, MacArthur lay sprawled on his back, not moving. Captain lay next to him, wings draped over the human's still form.

"He's down, Jocko!" Buccari shouted. "We can't save him! We can't!"

Chastain said nothing, his shoulders shaking. Cannon shells exploded in rolling waves around them, showering them with rock splinters. Laser beams cooked the air. Chastain leapt to the side and fired his assault rifle, the quick burst emptying his magazine; the metal clip rang on the ground. He jerked behind cover and resolutely shoved in another ammo clip. Buccari knew it was his last. More cannon shells thudded among the rocks, and shrapnel tap-danced over the mountain granite.

"I don't want to leave him, either, Jocko!" she shouted in despair. "He wouldn't want us to die, Jocko. Not when we can get away."

Gunfire erupted from higher up. She broke her stare from the attackers and looked up to see Tatum making his way through the boulders along the back side of the ridge. She figured he was starting the escape. With one arm he needed a head start. If Tatum could make it, then she could, too. She turned back to the aliens and steeled herself to take another shot. She heard her name being called. Tatum was yelling at her! She turned back to him. He was cupping his hand and bellowing, but the noise of the battle was too loud. A lull struck, and she could hear some of his words.

"Hang on ... cliff dwellers ..." he shouted.

Cliff dwellers? Tonto and X.O.? What could they do? She looked down at Chastain. His rifle pointed at the ground. He was staring into the sky. She followed his gaze. Cliff dwellers! Hunters! Hundreds of them—thousands! Like a thin layer of smoke from the west, still far away. A shrill whistling drifted on the wind. The konish soldiers stopped firing, all staring at the oncoming horde.

"Keep firing!" Buccari screamed. She stepped around the rock and took aim at a konish soldier. The assault rifle kicked her shoulder, and the soldier collapsed. The others followed her lead, and the confused kones tried to direct their attention in both directions. Laser blasters, their power diminishing, raked the rocky mountain while cannon shells exploded without interruption.

"Colonel Longo!" the subordinate shouted, nervously looking at the black cloud spreading across the sky. "Power cells are running down. Should we not consider withdrawing?"

Longo stared at the leading elements of the mountain fliers.

The first arrows struck, and Longo realized the situation had swung badly out of control. A torrent of short, metal-barbed shafts rippled across the grassy ridge—a thin, swift downpour of pain. Longo looked at his thigh; a black-fletched arrow protruded from his haunch. Pain coursed through his leg.

"Blasters!" Longo screamed. "Shoot the fliers! *Shoot them!*"

Kones swung their weapons to the new enemy. None of the soldiers had been killed, but most had received painful wounds; several had been incapacitated by multiple wounds. With the fear of death expanding in their souls, the konish soldiers swept their fading beams through the massed flying creatures, raking dozens of them from the sky, praying their power cells would last. Another wave of arrows splattered across the konish lines. Four kones went to their knees, still trying to fire their weapons, knowing they were dying.

And another wave. Longo counted six arrows in his body; the one in his neck prevented him from issuing orders. He, too, was dying. More hunters fell from the sky, small bodies burned and broken, many with arrows still nocked in their bows. More kones succumbed. More arrows, more arrows—more arrows.

The kones lay dead, mountainous carcasses bristling with black shafts. Sprinkled around the bulky bodies of the kones were dozens of small wasted forms, the twisted and charred bodies of dead hunters. A horde of living hunters—sorrowful victors—descended from the skies and formed orderly groups.

Buccari ran down the hill toward MacArthur's limp form. Chastain beat her there, along with X.O. and Tonto. Chastain threw his jacket over MacArthur's torso. The hulking marine looked up and moved to stop her.

"No, Lieutenant. It's real bad," Chastain sobbed, tears rolling down his blistered and blackened face. "Mac's not going to make it."

"He's alive?" Buccari asked.

Chastain nodded, holding her tightly by the shoulders.

She shook loose and staggered the short distance to where MacArthur sprawled, his legs angled grotesquely. The body of the dead hunter embraced the marine, both forms covered by Chastain's jacket. Captain's black eyes stared vacantly into the blue sky. As Buccari stumbled up to the fallen warriors, X.O. moved to close the fallen hunter's eyes, all the while whistling a shrill, mournful wail. Tonto stood close, visibly trembling but also whistling mournfully.

MacArthur's chest heaved in shallow, pained breaths. She knelt down, putting his face in shadow. He blinked, his eyes focused, and he turned his head to her. His hand lifted from the ground.

"Hold ..." he gasped. "Sharl ... hold my hand." Tears rolled across his tortured face. Buccari took the strong, callused hand in hers and held it to her cheek.

"Let me ... touch you ..." he whispered. She relaxed her grip and felt his fingers glide over her face, lingering on the line of her scar.

"Mac," she sobbed. "Mac, I ..."

"In truth, you're beautiful, Shar—" His hand tightened around her wrist, and the light in his gray eyes faded out.

FORTY-FOUR

CITIZENS

Cassiopeia Quinn stood on the new planet, more resolved than bereaved. She had work to do—hard work—on a new planet, a planet with limitless potential, something she had dreamed of, something she had trained for. But she had forgotten about gravity. Her heart struggled to force blood to her extremities; her legs felt leaden, her head ached, and she was cold. Patience, she told herself. It had been only two weeks since they had landed.

"You okay, Commander?" Godonov asked. They had finished checking the lake station survey instruments. "You're pale."

"I'm okay, Nes," she replied. "Just tired."

"You should take some time off and relax," he said. "You've been working too hard. Enjoy the scenery." He waved his hand at the hanging glaciers and snowcapped mountains. Bronze-tufted ducks, alarmed at their presence, ran along the water's surface and glided across the smooth surface of the lake. A large fish rolled its belly at them.

"You're right, but I'm too excited to relax," Quinn answered.

The Legion scientists walked along the lakeshore and rounded the forested point of the protected cove, receiving welcome shelter from the cool lake breeze. The settlement clearing spread before them. Kateos and Dowornobb, helmets off, reclined on sun-washed grass above the sandy beach. Dowornobb waved.

"Good-ah news!" he shouted. "Master Huhsawn has regained-ah consciousness. We just-ah receive radio transmission from your fleet-ah. The doctors say that-ah he will-ah live."

An oppressive weight lifted from Quinn's shoulders. Nashua Hudson's survival had defied logic and reason. His flesh cooked and his bones crushed, the ensign had been evacuated on the first EPL off the planet and immediately had been taken at full military thrust to the medical facility aboard *Tierra del Fuego*. The accelerations and stresses of planetary escape worked against success; Hudson died en route and was revived—twice. Fleet doctors and equipment could perform near miracles on a living being but could do little for a dead one. Hudson's infirm body and nearly orphaned soul made it back to the fleet and were welded together. Healing would take much longer.

"Wonderful," Quinn said, a catch in her throat. "That means so much."

"To us, too, Commander," Kateos said, standing. "Hud-sawn is our good friend. We walk with you." Dowornobb stashed the remains of their picnic in his suit pouches.

They walked in silence past the circle of ash and charcoal that marked the perimeter of the settlement ruins. The palisade gate frame still stood, as did the blackened stone foundations of most of the buildings. Guilders working on the new construction moved nervously from the paths of the kones.

"Ah, there are Citizens Dawson and Gol'berg with their babies," Kateos announced, brown eyes widening. "Come, my mate, and let us say hello. I want to hold a baby."

"Again!" Dowornobb smiled at his mate's tender enthusiasm. The kones trotted away.

"Excuse me, Commander," Godonov said, "I should get started across the river if I'm going to catch the next apple. Fenstermacher has a ferry leaving in a half hour."

"All right, Nes," she answered. "I'll be back on *Eire* in three days."

She found herself standing alone. Reconstruction banged

and clattered about her; rock walls were being cleaned and re-assembled. The lodge roof had been framed with new timbers. Winter was near; the survivors of *Harrier One* worked fever-ishly to restore the settlement.

Quinn self-consciously forced herself not to stare at the bare-chested men working the timber and rock. She was no prude, but she still was uncomfortable with their hairy bur-nished bodies. Laser Corporal Tatum smiled at her as he hur-ried by with a tree trunk held firmly by one herculean arm over his sinewy shoulder. The man's head was covered with reddish-blond hair pulled into a ponytail that approached his waist; his wide mustaches flowed into a thick beard, and his chest and back were pelted with a wiry rust-colored gauze. His face was florid, the skin peeling and peppered with freck-les. Quinn had to remind herself that the kones and cliff dwel-lers were the aliens.

In the middle of the ruins, next to a large campfire, stood three konish tents. Et Silmarn, without his helmet, stood close to the fire, watching the activity. She walked up to the noblekone, anxious to share the fire's warmth.

"Governor Et Silmarn," Quinn said in halting konish. "I use your fire."

"Good-ah day, Commander Quinn," Et Silmarn replied in Legion. "You speak-ah my language better with-ah each day. We soon not-ah need Mistress Kateos's translator. Please join me. It is cold-ah. How do they work-ah with bare skin?"

"Work keeps them warm," Quinn said, although she won-dered about the same thing.

"It-ah goes well," Et Silmarn said. "Perhaps Sharl is cor-rect-ah to rebuild-ah. I should not-ah have demand—is *demand* right word?" Quinn nodded. "Should not-ah have demand-ah Sharl move all humans to Ocean Station for win-ter."

"You are not still angry with Sharl?" Quinn asked.

"No," the noblekone said. "Only, uh . . . hurt-ah feeling. Sharl said-ah Longo wanted humans to move south. It was insult-ah. I am not-ah Longo."

"She meant no insult, Et Silmarn."

"This I know. Sharl has pain in heart-ah."

Quinn nodded sympathetically and then remembered her du-ties.

"Admiral Runacres is scheduled to arrive tomorrow," she said, switching to Legion and reaching into her haversack.

"After the services are over he would like to have a meeting with you, and he proposes the following agend—"

"Commander," Et Silmarn said. "When Et Avian—uh, King Ollant appoint me governor, he make-ah it-ah clear that-ah all discussions with humans must-ah involve Citizen Sharl. We should-ah find-ah her, yes?"

Buccari spent hours hiking in solitude. Often she climbed to the top of the valley and walked in the fields of wildflowers mottling the grassy, humpbacked ridges. Hunters were always with her, sometimes soaring far above, sometimes hopping along behind. Always with her, always armed and vigilant, and she was glad for their silent company.

A familiar double sonic boom sounded far overhead. Buccari searched the deep, cloudless blue skies and presently saw the EPL gliding across the landscape on final for a landing beyond the river. Her forearms tightened involuntarily; her fingers curled as if grasping heavy flight controls and power quadrant. She watched the EPL, so small in the distance, enter its landing transition, flames belching in vivid colors. Smoke and debris momentarily hid the craft from her view. Her stomach sagged with the sensation of deceleration, and she vicariously sought the comforting contact of touchdown. Engine noises racing across the wide river valley and the intervening distances finally reached her ears. She looked down at her feet and the solid ground beneath them.

She exhaled and turned back toward the path. She had official responsibilities now, but she laughed as she realized that Runacres—Fleet Admiral Runacres—would have to ask her permission to step foot on the planet. Her new status had become a private joke between them, but the admiral had also offered her a corvette command. That she took seriously. She walked faster.

The chaplain finished the memorial service, and Admiral Runacres looked up from his prayer. Honeybees buzzed in the warm stillness, and a gentle breeze, cool and welcome, came off the lake, stirring the waters of the cove and refreshing the gathered mourners. They were assembled beneath the spreading tree that stood alone in the clearing before the blackened walls of the stockade. Runacres signaled the honor guard, and seven Legion marines sweating in full battle rig fired volleys over the graves of the fallen. The ceremony was over. There was no bugler, but the crying babies, frightened by the rifle reports, made their own accommodation.

Deep in somber conversation, Buccari and the towering Et Silmarn marched away from the ceremony and the rock cairns. The cairns were grave markers for Scientist Lollee, Lander Boatswain First Class Jones, Sergeant-Major Shannon, and Private Petit. The surviving crew, except for Nash Hudson, who was in a hospital bed aboard *Tierra del Fuego*, broke from their loose formation: Gunner Wilson, Terry O'Toole, Nancy Dawson, Jocko Chastain, Sandy Tatum, Billy Gordon, Winfried Fenstermacher, Pepper Goldberg, Tooks Tookmanian, Toby Mendoza, and Beppo Schmidt. The survivors wore new uniforms, but beards and ponytails more than offset the martial ambience. Leslie Lee, the only crew member not in the ranks, sat on a tree-shaded blanket, taking care of the complaining infants. The formalities over, she let the toddlers move off the blanket and stood to follow their movements, gently rocking her own sleeping baby. Dawson and Goldberg walked to the blanket. Dawson, disconsolate, sobbed on Goldberg's shoulder.

The other dead were not forgotten, their resting places just farther away. Commander Quinn, Warrant Officer Rhodes, and Private Rennault lay in peace, buried on the plateau, so long ago and far away; Corporal MacArthur and the cliff dweller known as Captain, along with sixty-three hunters and thirty-eight konish soldiers, were buried under the wildflowers below the pinnacles high on the valley shoulder—the fallen heroes of battle. Certainly not forgotten.

"Touching," Merriwether said. "They have gone through a great deal."

"Yes, they have," Runacres replied, walking down the gentle slope toward the lakeshore. "And no doubt they have much more to face."

"How soon is your meeting with Et Avian?" Wells asked.

"It's scheduled for two months from today. It's actually with the Planetary Defense Council," Runacres answered. "That's what Buccari and Et Silmarn are discussing right now, whether that's too soon."

Runacres told himself to wait patiently. He sat down on the grassy slope and looked over to where Buccari and Et Silmarn were conspiring. Merriwether and Wells followed his lead, with Captain Wells displaying exaggerated chivalry to the flagship's commanding officer. Merriwether giggled like an adolescent, causing both men to grin stupidly. It was a beautiful day.

"How many people will be allowed to settle on the planet?" Merriwether asked.

"I can't get a straight answer," Runacres said. He had petitioned to immediately transport more humans to the surface of Genellan and to establish a schedule for future immigration. There was no shortage of volunteers within the fleet, and he knew what the response would be when he returned to Earth; there would be riots. Graft and corruption would reach new heights for the rich and powerful who desired to emigrate, for surely only the rich and powerful would have access. But that was not his concern. He discovered planets; he did not govern them. In that respect he felt sorry for Buccari.

"Rumor says that Et Silmarn doesn't like your schedule," Wells said.

"Actually, I think it's Buccari that's objecting," Runacres laughed. "And I'm proud of her for that. I look forward to getting her back in harness."

"Has she really agreed to return to duty?" Wells asked.

"She'll be back," Runacres said. "She's too good a pilot to grow roots."

"Admiral, have you thought about it?" Merriwether asked. "Growing roots?"

"Thought about it, Sarah? Yes," Runacres said. "But no, not yet. I'm too old to be a Boy Scout. I'll give this paradise a few more years. Besides, humanity's biggest problem may still be ahead."

"How so, sir?" Wells asked.

"You haven't forgotten Shaula, have you?" Runacres asked. "There's an old and belligerent race out there. It attacked us twenty-five years ago, and it probably attacked this system over five hundred years ago."

"You think it's the same race?" Merriwether asked.

"Who knows?" Runacres replied. "Regardless, there's a great danger out there. I have a feeling we'll face it again in our lifetimes."

He listened to the happy noises of the children and envied their bliss. He ran their names over in his mind. They were famous. The oldest, Honey, ran along the beach cove, splashing the lake waters; little Adam followed, waddling in her footsteps; the youngest baby—Hope—still in her mother's arms, was just awakening.

EPILOGUE

Buccari breathed deeply. Beach smells redolent of wet sand and seaweed—the odors of ocean tides—rose to meet her. Her senses responded to a symphony of stimuli. She touched warm ocean waters with bare toes and, listening carefully, heard plaintive sounds drifting inshore, inshore through the fog. The sweet sounds of Trident's horn, soft and temporal, lingered only for seconds before trailing into the background, a mysterious sound. Genellan had many mysteries.

She stared seaward, into the thick bank of fog standing offshore, a curtain of inscrutable gray cotton obscuring the infinite distances to the open horizons, but she knew a horizon was out there somewhere. Overhead the morning skies bespoke the coming of another balmy day, and at her feet the surf frothed softly, a comfortable metronomic hissing sound—water gliding over sand. The breeze freshened; she could not feel the wind, but she could see it. The fog bank receded perceptibly, and clusters of tiny ripples marred the mirror-smooth surface of the low swells and gentle waves. Cat's-paws, the ripples were called, and she understood why.

The breeze wandered ashore, blowing her dark hair, fine and lustrous, across her face. She reached up innocently and brushed it aside, touching the long scar on her cheek. Her fingers lingered, as they often did—the scar a bittersweet memory. She slowly dropped her hands, and they fell naturally, with fingers spread around gravid belly. She felt the burgeoning existence, a reminder of the past and an element of the future. A wonderment.

Difficult for her to comprehend, this biological activity in her womb. Her mind was facile and her intellect expansive; rarely did processes or systems cause her confusion. Reason was her ally, and logic was a well and often-used tool. Yet somehow, in some way, this was different, and the limits of her intelligence were tasked. This was so very different; her body was performing on its own, and it was creating something— something from almost nothing. A miracle—it was a miracle, the miracle of life, and a new beginning, exquisitely profound.

Fine white sand squeaked behind her, and she turned to see the great mass of Kateos plodding across the strand. Buccari moved back from the warm ocean, sensitive to the kone's fears and perceptions. The human raised her hand in greeting, and the kone, rising onto her hinds, replied in kind. Kateos removed her helmet.

"The fog-ah is lifting," the kone said. "Soon you will see them."

"The whales? Does the noise come from the whales?" Buccari asked. The horn again—a high-pitched moaning close inshore, and distinct clicking sounds, the loudest she had heard yet.

"Yes, they are come back. That is their call," Kateos replied, taking a nervous step away from the water's edge. "That-ah one is very close to shore. Look, the fog goes."

The friends stood on the shore and watched as freshening breezes lifted and parted the veil of fog until only scattered clouds remained. The horizon expanded to the full limits of Buccari's elevation, and she observed the churning caused by giant ocean creatures. Great mammals surfaced constantly, and puffs of vaporous steam hissed from their blowholes. Colossal rounded backs, barnacle-encrusted, smoothly cleaved the ocean surface, and languid flukes gracefully arched into the sky.

"They come here to bear their young, just as you have. Your beautiful baby will be born here, too," Kateos said, rapture in her voice.

"Yes, it will be born by the sea," the human replied. "And then I must return to MacArthur's valley. Just as the whales return to the deep oceans."

They stared in silence, watching the endless movement of nature.

"Will you return to space, Sharl?" the kone asked enviously, dropping back on all fours so that she could stand face-to-face with her human friend.

Buccari looked Kateos squarely and deeply in her kindly face.

"The deeper oceans of space . . . Maybe, my good friend. Maybe."

ABOUT THE AUTHOR

Scott G. Gier was born in Aiea, Hawaii, in 1948. He received his undergraduate degree from the U.S. Naval Academy at Annapolis and his MBA from Santa Clara University, Santa Clara, California. He served in the United States Navy for six years and now works with a software company in Arizona.

He has been married for twenty-six years and is the proud father of two children; his interests include backpacking, bird-watching, contemplation, and worry.

He says of himself: "Still haven't grown up (just old)."

DEL REY DISCOVERY

Experience the wonder of discovery
with Del Rey's newest authors!

TURN THE PAGE FOR AN EXCERPT
FROM THE NEXT
DEL REY DISCOVERY:

Commencement
by Roby James

I want to write it as it happened—the processes and the progresses that brought me to where I am, the ways I changed and the ways I stayed the same. I want to tell it as if it were a story, even though of all the things I thought my life would be, *story* is not a word I would have chosen. And yet, Jasin Lebec once told me we all write stories with our lives. It's just that we're not aware that's what we're doing, so we never read them as a whole creation. I promise to read this when I've done writing it. It will help build the foundation I can go on from.

I didn't even begin the journal until after we arrived at Stronghome, and life keeps moving forward, even as I write about the things that have happened—are happening— happened before I got to this world. So I may never catch up with where I am. Somehow that's almost fitting.

The first thing I remember is hearing the fire. The crackle seemed to penetrate the darkness in my mind, and then on my closed eyelids I saw the pattern of moving light. I felt the pain simultaneously. It had been years since I'd felt anything more than a minor cramp, and for a moment or two the shock of the pain's intensity made it impossible for me to think clearly.

I fought to master the gather and take a deep breath, and as I felt I could, the reflexes snapped into place and the pain began to lessen. The capacity for logical thought returned slowly. When I had gathered enough to hold the pain back into a dull, aching throb, I concentrated my awareness behind my breastbone and spread it outward, gathering more as I did so. My assessment showed that I had one cracked and two broken ribs, a dislocated shoulder, a broken arm, assorted abrasions, contusions, scrapes, and a badly gashed ankle. I was bleeding from numerous cuts in addition to the ankle, but those didn't worry me. Without trying to open my eyes yet, I began instantly to seal off the bleeders in the ankle. The protective edge of my gathering had now shut down all the pain receptors from the injured areas, allowing me the luxury of comfort as I slowly knit the cells on both sides of the ankle cut—first deep inside, then closer and closer to the surface.

As soon as that was nearly healed, I went to work on the ribs, carefully joining cell to cell, almost unconsciously blessing my luck that there were no bone spurs at any of the breaks. I got the shoulder and the arm repaired next, and was tiring fast when I heard the voices approaching.

"There's the fireball!"

"Over here, look over here!"

Footsteps came closer and then, "It's a woman, and she's alive!" It was very near and filled with amazement, but, for the moment, I didn't want to pay attention to it. I was marshalling my strength to prepare to open my eyes. I couldn't remember having been in anything that could have crashed, not floater, nor groundcar, nor lander. The last thing I could remember was running up the long flight of steps to the entrance of Government House, on my way to Mortel John, Kray, and Coney, who stood at the top of the steps, waiting for me. And now the surface under my heels, hips, and shoulders was rough, uneven, softly padded with some kind of what felt like vegetation. Clearly, I was no longer in the paved environs of Government House.

"Don't try to move her. Get Dogul, and hurry!"

The crackling sounds of the fire almost drowned out the words. I risked opening my eyes. It was dark out, and the light I had seen through my eyelids came from a huge fireball, several meters away to my left. Whatever I had crashed in would soon be only cinders and ash. Several people ran through my line of sight, between me and the flames, dark shadows on the face of the inferno. I hadn't yet tried to move my head, because it would take more energy, and I was stretched too thin between repairing the injuries and holding back the pain.

The fireball flared up suddenly, and then seemed to subside, leaving a softer, darker night. I realized that, incomprehensibly, some of the people were carrying torches, and then, gathering a little more and turning my head slightly, I saw that there were trees in my field of vision, too—huge, old, thick-boled trees that towered up into the darkness.

This wasn't a world I knew. This had to be a natural area, but one that was unbelievably ancient, and the cities had to be some distance away. I ran quickly through a catalog of the worlds on which I had been, and I didn't know any with natural areas as old as this one was.

"Here, Dogul, she's over here."

I pulled in my senses to face this person called Dogul—and again I was surprised, as the torchlight revealed a woman of great age, but not age as it came in the Com, with dignity, ease, and grace. This was an aging of wrinkles on leatherlike skin, eyes meshed in a net of deep lines between a headbanded cowl and veil and a chin band.

"Are you aware?" she asked. Her voice was raspy, brisk, not unkind, but not deeply concerned. I nodded, just perceptibly, unwilling to risk speaking just yet. "I'm surprised—" she started to say, then broke off in mid-speech. "The torch," she said instead.

Bright light suddenly intruded on me, and I had to close my eyes. So much of my energy was gone now that I did not even want to try irising my pupils down faster than normal.

I heard Dogul say, "Get a litter. Bring it here as soon as you can. You, Vulin, get up to the Stonehouse and tell the Meltress—not the Melster, mind you—the Meltress that I beg an audience. Go!"

She bent over me again, and I felt her hands gently exploring my body and my limbs. The torchlight dimmed a little, and I opened my eyes again, blinking a few times. Dogul's exploration had reached my ankle. I heard a sudden intake of breath, and she straightened for a moment, then leaned close to my face.

"Listen to me," she said in a low voice. "It is dangerous to practice Samish arts here. You may not know, but this is Honish land. If you value your life, do no more, and be thankful one such as I found you."

She straightened and turned away before I could react, but that was probably just as well, because I had absolutely no idea what she was talking about. I understood most of the words she'd spoken, but the sense of her warning eluded me. Because I was exhausted in addition to valuing my life, I stopped any further attempt to gather, ceased repairing my cuts and bruises, and used my remaining strength to keep the pain receptors closed. In my mind I catalogued the planets I'd been to in my slightly more than twenty standard years. I needed a logical train of thought to believe I was still in control, and I fastened onto needing to know where I was. There was Steressor, where I had been born and certified as a talent; Werd, where I had been trained, tested, and graded as the first Class A of my generation; Koldor, where the higher-level Com training was undertaken and completed; and Orokell, seat of the Com. Those were the civilized worlds, not one of which had a natural area with trees in it that looked to be hundreds of years old, and not one of which supported wrinkled women in archaic headgear. Then there was the nameless test world where I had done my Tenday, but I knew it to be all desert, not forested, not peopled with anachronisms.

Where *was* I? How had I gotten here? How could the Com have misplaced a just-graduated Class-A talent? I was too valuable for this.

Trying to think logically—and the growing stress of not reaching a conclusion—drained me even further. Some of the control over my pain slipped, and I began to ache. A soft groan escaped me involuntarily, and Dogul leaned back over me. "Better to be silent," she said.

If I had not been in pain and exhausted, I would probably have laughed. There was something so ludicrous about the strangeness of all this, something bizarre, out of mesh with all objective reality. I even irrationally supposed that I could be dreaming some kind of Arthurian legend.

"Here comes the litter, Dogul."

"Slide it down here beside her. I want to move her as little as possible."

I felt a genuine stab of fear at the idea of being moved. Somehow in my bewilderment, reality had crystallized around the firmness and solidity of the ground beneath me, as once in classes it had centered on my prowess in training. I was too tired to fight both pain and fear.

Several pairs of hands moved me quickly, a little roughly, onto the litter. All my control, exerted hard, didn't keep enough of the pain at bay, and I cried out against my will for the first time since childhood. I felt abruptly shamed by it. A Class-A talent should never have been taken unaware by a thing like simple pain.

As the litter lifted and Dogul threw a rough cloth over me, exhaustion took over, all the rest of my control slipped, and the world grayed out. I was not really unconscious, just withdrawn and subdued, protected, away from the confusion. Nothing from the outside disturbed me for an indeterminate time, and then the light brightened, and a soft, low-pitched woman's voice intruded. "What is all this about, Dogul?"

I brought myself back to some measure of awareness. The litter had halted, but had not been set down. A torch was closer. As I heard Dogul say, "Meltress, please come and see," I opened my eyes. Dogul was bowing to a thin woman of unknown age, wearing a fine but shapeless robe and a much more delicate version of the cowl and veil. She looked at me for a long moment, then looked at Dogul, and seemed to be calculating something.

At last she asked, "She came with the great fireburn we saw from the walls?"

"She was with it when we found her, Lady Meltress," Dogul answered. "I thought you would want to see. The stars have truly blessed you."

The thin woman looked back at me again, and the corners of her lips lifted in what I was hard put to call a smile. "You have done well, Dogul," she said. "You will be rewarded. See that her hurts are attended." Then she was gone from my field of vision.

When Dogul bent over me again, she was smiling. "Now we'll take you to rest, pretty one," she said with satisfaction. I let myself drift back into the grayness. Until I rested, I would be good for nothing. My reserves were low, and I had to deep. I fell asleep and had deeped before the litter stopped moving.

I awoke suddenly, as always emerging from deeping into sleeping first, then fully aware in an instant. The remembered pain kept me from moving quickly, but as I turned my head, I saw a young woman in a clean but worn robe rise from a stool and go to the door. The door was made of wood, banded with some sort of hammered metal. The walls around the low bed in which I lay were of mortared stone.

The young woman slipped out the door, leaving behind some sort of rough cloth she'd been sewing. I knew what hand sewing was, in a historical sense, but I'd never before seen anyone *do* it. Suddenly, there was a logic to the trees, the wrinkles, the clothes, the room, and the sewing. "This is a wilderworld!" I said aloud. What in the name of sentience was I doing on a wilderworld? They were proscribed. And if I had crashed here, would anyone know I was here? Could anyone come and get me from a wilderworld even if they knew it?

The latter thought I quelled quickly as I sat up, damping away the remaining aches and pains. I was the Class A. The Com would move whole worlds to get me back.

I wanted to get up, but first I had to test my injuries. I had been able to heal nothing fully before I ran out of time and energy. Under the coarse, loose shift I'd been dressed in, my ribs had been tightly bandaged—the cracked one I had not been able to repair at all had obviously been diagnosed. So my breathing was a little restricted. My bad arm was discolored from elbow to shoulder, but I had gotten the break knitted and the shoulder back in place well enough so that most of the surrounding muscles were not badly damaged. The various cuts, scrapes, and abrasions had some sort of salve on them. Nothing was serious—I had taken care of the worst ones myself.

The door opened, and Dogul came in, followed by the young woman, who was carrying a tray with a bowl and a mug on it.

"How do you feel?" Dogul asked.

"All right," I said cautiously. "Where am I?"

The young woman put the tray down on my knees. The bowl contained what looked like a thick vegetable broth; the mug, a thick, yellowish, milky liquid. Dogul answered, "You are in the Stonehouse of the Melster Lewannee and his Meltress. They have kindly agreed to see to your healing."

"I can see to my own healing," I said. "Where is this stone house?"

Dogul gestured sharply to the young woman to leave the room, and she did so, closing the heavy door behind her. When it had closed, the old woman demanded, her face twisted with anger, "Are you mad to speak that way in front of a serving-maid? If it becomes known that you are Samish, you will be put to the ax, and then where will our plans be? We need only two more days, the Meltress and me!"

Common sense told me that I would learn more if I didn't alienate her, and logic said that I needed to learn. What she had said had little meaning for me. "Samish" was a word I had heard before, but didn't understand. "Our plans" meant nothing. "The ax" also meant little, but it sounded ominous in context. One of the things Mortel John had labored long and hard to teach me was diplomacy. I decided to see if I could practice it.

"I'm sorry if I spoke without thinking," I said, trying to

sound sincere, "but I'm very confused about how I got here and what's going to happen to me."

Dogul accepted the apology and gestured to me to eat. I needed strength, so I did, even though the soup was unappetizingly coarse and the ivory liquid was warm and overrich. While I ate, Dogul told me that she was keeper of the servingmaids for the Lady Meltress Lewannee. "Now what is your name, and where do you come from?" she asked.

I thought quickly about status and advantages, and then I said, "I am the Lady Ronica McBride, and I come from a big house very far away. It's called Government House."

Dogul's eyes grew wide enough to add to her wrinkles, then narrowed down, and she stared at me for a time. I finished eating and waited her out. Then she made a sound I could only interpret as disgust, and twisted the side of her mouth down. "It'll do you no good to put on airs now," she said. "You're not with the stars, and you're only a filthy Sammat. We'll call you Ronca—that's a good enough name for a servingmaid."

Anger and pride rose up in me at once. How dare she! "I am no one's servingmaid!" I said hotly.

She as good as sneered. "You'll be that, or you'll be dead," she said. "My Lady Meltress owes a debt that she's going to use you to pay. That's what you're worth to us, and what happens to you after we've sold you is no concern of mine."

She was smug and standing above me, and I was angry. In a second, I had gathered and tried to sting her, to hurt her and make her regret her words.

Nothing happened.

The gathering occurred normally, instantaneously, but the sting was not there. I could not project. It was as if I had not even made the attempt. I was shocked into complete silence, my mouth open, my skin suddenly cold. It was horrible.

Dogul stared at me.

I took a shuddering breath, fought for calm, and reached inside me to look for the sting where it had always been, no longer concerned with anger or hurting. The reflexes were there, the paths along which I gathered were there, but the sting was totally absent. It was as if that part of me had been amputated. Something seemed to break inside me, and I hurled the tray away from me and swung my legs over the side of the bed, crying, "Bring me a mirror! Bring me a mirror now!" When she didn't move for a moment, I shouted, "What are you waiting for? Hurry! A mirror!"

Dogul debated only for a second. Perhaps, it occurred to me much later, I had no value to her if I was raving. She went to the door and gave an order to have a mirror brought.

I gathered to exert control on my diaphragm muscles and my pounding heart, for in a few minutes, I would have been over-oxygenated. But I couldn't stop the trembling.

The ability to project is the sign of Class-A talent. Mortel John—one of the overwhelming majority of people who did not have that ability, but perhaps the only one who could train it—called it "stinging." Gathering is the Class-C sign. We generally believe that everyone has it to some degree, in muscular strength, in the immune system, in physical ability, in what was once called biofeedback. But those with higher-level, more easily controllable gathering abilities are very rare—perhaps one or two to a world. Pathfinding is the sign of a Class B, and it is rarer still—perhaps one true talent to a few dozen worlds. Pathfinding takes the ability to gather and applies it to things, to get them to open themselves, to show how they operate, to allow their usage in other than "normal" ways. One true Class B can operate a star cruiser entirely alone, using the cruiser itself as crew.

As the Class A, I possessed all of the signs—gathering, pathfinding, and stinging. I had been told that at the age of two I had been in control of a pack of children, some as old as ten, and that that was the way the government of Steressor had identified me for testing. My kind of talent was so rare that more than one Class A in a generation was considered unheard of—I was, Jasin Lebec told me, the only Class A to be identified as stable in two generations. Therefore, I was of the highest possible value to the Com, the confederation of MIs, and all civilized worlds.

The Drenalion, the Com's army, came and took me away from what I can only assume were relieved parents—a young Class A is a tyrant by nature. My parents, I had been told, were colonists in the Steressor city of North Gate, and I had had a normal brother and sister of whom I had no memory. The Drenalion brought me to the school for extraordinary talents on Werd.

There, Mortel John was my teacher for the next eighteen years—mine, Coney's, and Kray's. We were the three talents, all of an age, given into his keeping. Coney was several months younger than I, thin and blond and overly wise, as early as age four—and especially after age fourteen, when he was my friend. Kray was several months older, wiry and taller even before we hit puberty. We were together all through my memories, the three of us and Mortel John, my only family.

I mistreated them all at first, according to Mortel John. I was wild with the power of uncontrolled ability, a despot at four, an unrulable, selfish baby. I have been told about the first time I didn't get my own way, not what I demanded—it certainly doesn't matter now, and it was probably insignificant then. Only a rare child, like Coney was, takes a stand on anything of significance. Mortel John said no to me, and I tried to compel him by projecting to make him give me what I wanted. Then he set his full strength against me and resisted. I could not have been more than a baby, and he refused to bend, holding out against the potent force of my stinging. His reserves were much greater than mine then, and he told me long afterward that he had also taken a very rare drug to make him even less vulnerable. He stood against me, stolid and unyielding, until I was exhausted from battering on the rock of his will. I threw a tantrum, and when it was done, he carried me to my room. The next day, he began training me in earnest. After that humiliating loss, I never stung him again. But from that day until the one when I awoke in the strange bed in the tiny room on this wilderworld, I had never been without my Class-A sign, my weapon, my sting. When I reached for the sting to touch Dogul, and it was gone, I couldn't be sure that I was myself any longer.

The door opened and hands thrust a polished metal circle at Dogul. In a moment, I was holding it. The face that looked back at me in desperate confusion was indeed my own. My wide blue-green eyes looked as they had when I last remembered seeing them, under the gold helmet of a graduating Class-A talent. My face was unscarred by the crash, its shape the same, my long, light brown hair tangled, but framing it as it always had. I studied it minutely. It was a little different, but not in any way I could identify. Perhaps the absence of the sting was a result of the crash. Perhaps it would come back to me when my full strength returned. I decided that it would; of course it would. It had to.

I hadn't realized how hard I was gripping the mirror until I became aware of the ache in my hands. I sent a wave of artificial relaxation down my arms and dropped the mirror on the blanket beside the spilled tray. Dogul had been watching me closely, and I suppose she didn't want to risk another outburst, so when I asked her, "Dogul, do you know how I got here?" she answered at once.

"The stars brought you. I accepted you to fill my Lady Meltress's need."

I tried again. "The fireball that was burning beside me. Do you know what caused it?"

"The stars," she repeated. "It was a piece of the stars, and it brought you to earth." Still watching me to make certain that I did not explode again, she called in the young servingwoman to clean up the tray and the mirror, and then both of them left me alone.

I sat still on the bed for several minutes, not really thinking about anything in particular. Then I got slowly to my feet. The shapeless shift I was wearing was much too big for me, and I was barefoot. There was no hint of anything I had been wearing when I'd crashed on this world, and I had no memory of what it might have been. I moved strength down to my still injured ankle, even though I really hadn't had time to process the food I'd eaten. Then I limped the few paces across the room to the window.

I was about twenty meters off the ground, in a tower behind stone battlements, and the prospect from the window was of a yard within the guarded wall, some fields outside, a stretch of open land, and then the forest, stretching for miles. Truly, a wilderworld.

I hobbled to the door of the chamber and pulled on it. It was locked from the outside. Balancing myself carefully on my good foot, I hesitated briefly in apprehension, then rested my fingertips against the lock mechanism. I gathered and sought to pathfind the lock. The reflex behaved exactly as it always had, and the lock told me, through my fingertips, how it worked. I gathered again, turned the mechanism, and unlocked the door.

The gathering tired me more than I was used to, and I didn't feel strong enough to go wandering yet. So I relocked the door without opening it and went back to the lumpy, straw-filled bed. If you let your jailers know that you can get out, they will only make it more difficult for you.